Paul Adam is a journalist and the author of several critically acclaimed novels including *Genesis II* and *Flashpoint*, and most recently *Enemy Within*. He lives in Sheffield, the city of his birth.

By the same author

PAUL ADAMS OMNIBUS

Unholy Trinity
Shadow Chasers

PAUL ADAMS

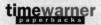

A *Time Warner* Paperback

This omnibus edition first published in Great Britain by
Time Warner Paperbacks in 2006

Copyright © Paul Adam 2005

First published separately:
Unholy Trinity first published in Great Britain by Little, Brown in 1999
Copyright © Paul Adam 1999

Shadow Chasers first published in Great Britain by Little, Brown in 2000
Copyright © Paul Adam 2000

A CIP catalogue record for this book
is available from the British Library.

ISBN-13: 978-0-7515-3786-4
ISBN-10: 0-7515-3786-1

Printed and bound in Great Britain by
Clays Ltd, St Ives plc

Time Warner Paperbacks
An imprint of
Time Warner Book Group UK
Brettenham House
Lancaster Place
London WC2E 7EN

www.twbg.co.uk

Unholy Trinity

PART ONE

PROLOGUE

Milan, April 1945

It was all over. Domenico Salvitti was certain of it. He could see nothing before him now save capture, a show trial and the hangman's noose. He was surprised how calm he felt, how strangely serene in the face of inevitable defeat. Was it resignation, he wondered, or simply relief that the end was in sight?

'Your meal, *Eccellenza.*'

Salvitti placed the tray of grapes and milk on the desk and stepped back, waiting for the Duce to dismiss him. But Mussolini barely glanced at the food. He stared up at his aide-de-camp, looking right through him as if he weren't there. Salvitti stood rigidly to attention, his gaze fixed on the ornate wooden carvings on the wall of the office, but in the silence that followed he found his eyes being drawn irresistibly to the face behind the desk.

The Duce had changed. His once plump features were pale and haggard now. His eyes, bloodshot from lack of sleep, seemed haunted with memories of what had been and a chill foreboding of what was to come. His health, always a problem, had deteriorated markedly over the past few weeks. He was a physical wreck, his pain-racked body a frail, fading vestige of the tyrant who had mesmerised and inspired a nation.

Yet if his body was close to collapse, his mind was more fragile still. He'd lost the ability, or the will, to make a decision. Sitting there behind the polished walnut desk, he was distracted, listless; fiddling with papers, trivial intelligence reports and irrelevant gossip which even now arrived hourly from the outposts of his ever-shrinking kingdom. He'd vacillated throughout the war, throughout his career, to avoid having to confront the important issues. But now, in these final days, it seemed a fatal, unforgivable weakness.

'What did you say?' he asked abruptly, as if only just aware that Salvitti had spoken.

'I brought the food you asked for, *Eccellenza*.'

Mussolini looked down at the tray without interest. He'd reverted to his old habit of eating nothing but grapes and milk, sometimes six or seven litres a day, despite the havoc it wreaked on his stomach. He plucked off a grape and toyed with it in his fingers, his thoughts elsewhere.

'Will there be anything else, *Eccellenza*?' Salvitti said.

Again, the Duce appeared not to hear him. Rising from his chair, he walked to the window and looked out briefly before turning back to face his aide.

'You have been with me a long time, *Seniore*,' he said.

'Yes, *Eccellenza*.' Salvitti straightened a little at the use of his old militia rank. He was a major now in the Republican National Guard, but still at heart a Blackshirt. He felt a faint stirring of pride in his belly, remembering the soldier he'd been, remembering the times when triumph, not defeat, had been his companion in arms. He still wore the skull-and-crossed-rapiers badge of the Duce's personal bodyguard; the

4

medal ribbons from Ethiopia and North Africa were a patchwork of colour on his left breast; and at his belt he carried a dagger inscribed in Mussolini's own handwriting: '*Ai Moschettieri silenziosi, fedeli* – to the silent, faithful Musketeers.'

'There are few of us left, *Seniore*. I have been deserted by all except my most trusted comrades. What shall I do? What can I do?' Mussolini muttered over and over, pacing restlessly across the floor behind the desk.

Salvitti didn't reply. He wasn't even sure he was expected to. The Duce seemed to be talking to himself, throwing out rhetorical questions in the hope that if he repeated them often enough the answers would somehow come to him.

Salvitti had no illusions about their chances of survival. He'd brought in the latest radio messages not half an hour ago. They lay untouched in a neat pile on the desk. Mussolini had either forgotten about them or, more likely, chosen to ignore them for fear of what they contained.

They made sobering reading. The Germans were in full retreat everywhere, fighting a bloody rearguard battle against the Red Army in the streets of Berlin, struggling to cross back over the Alps before they were swept up in the Allied liberation of Italy. Genoa had been taken by the partisans and Fiume by Tito. Mantua and Brescia had fallen to the Americans who were advancing at breakneck speed along the Bergamo road. They would be in Milan in days, perhaps less than twenty-four hours.

Salvitti knew they had only one course of action left open to them. Surrender to the partisans or the Allies was out of the question, it could lead only to certain execution, whilst fighting on to the end, though glorious, would be nothing but a futile gesture. They had to get out immediately and hope for sanctuary in Switzerland. The Duce must know that, yet he was dithering, paralysed by indecision. It was almost as if he were waiting for something before he acted.

'We have come this far,' Mussolini was saying. 'I will never surrender. Never. I have the men. There are thirty thousand loyal soldiers waiting for me in the Valtellina. We will make our final stand there and die with honour. Better to live one day as a lion than a thousand years as a sheep.'

Salvitti stared at him, wondering if he had taken leave of his senses. This was not the first time the Duce had talked of a last stand in the mountains, but surely he knew by now that it was a fantasy? They'd be lucky to raise three hundred men, let alone thirty thousand. Yet self-delusion was the key ingredient of Mussolini's character, carefully fostered by the sycophants and flatterers with whom he'd surrounded himself for years. There was no one who dared to tell him the truth.

The Duce came to a halt behind his chair and fixed Salvitti with the wide-eyed glare he used for intimidating opponents. A trace of his old vigour had returned, a tiny spark of hope seemed to have been rekindled in the ashes of his spirit.

'Are you with me, *Seniore*?' he asked.

Salvitti hesitated. His loyalty had always been unquestioning, but he wondered now whether it was his duty to snuff out this nonsense about the Valtellina. For Mussolini's sake, and for the sake of all those who were left.

'*Eccellenza* . . .' he began, searching for the right

words. But the sentence was never completed for at that moment the door of the office flew open and Luigi Gatti, the Duce's personal secretary, ran in.

'They're here, *Eccellenza*,' he said breathlessly. 'They've arrived.'

Salvitti's stomach lurched violently as the shock wave of nausea overwhelmed him. Gatti could only mean the Americans, or the partisans. Salvitti reached for the pistol at his side. But before he could snap open the leather holster, a group of four men came into the office behind Gatti and he realised his mistake. The men were unarmed civilians, their leader a Roman Catholic priest. Salvitti's fear turned to sudden concern. Was this what the Duce had been waiting for? Was he more sick than anyone knew and had sent for a priest to hear his final confession?

'*Eccellenza* . . .'

'Thank you, Major. That will be all.'

Gatti had his hand on Salvitti's arm and was guiding him smoothly towards the door. Salvitti glanced at the priest and his three companions as he passed, but he hardly had time to register their faces before he was out in the corridor, the door to the office closed firmly behind him. There was something familiar about the priest, yet Salvitti was sure they'd never met, and the other men, though they wore overcoats and hats, didn't look like civilians to him. They looked like soldiers.

Salvitti went back down the corridor to his own office. Looking out of the first-floor windows into the courtyard of the Palazzo Monforte, he saw a canvas-backed Fiat lorry being unloaded by Blackshirts. They were transferring heavy wooden boxes to two other lorries parked near the exit. A fourth truck, with German markings on its sides, came through the archway into the courtyard. An SS lieutenant and a squad of SS soldiers jumped out and ran into the building.

Something was happening. Salvitti didn't know what. But he resented being kept in the dark. He resented the secrecy, the arrogant way Gatti had ushered him out of the Duce's office and, increasingly, he resented Mussolini's own short-sighted intransigence which had brought them to the brink of disaster.

Salvitti's loyalty was waning; Mussolini had forfeited the right to it. In the face of the chaos, the uncertainty around him, Salvitti began to realise that if he did not look after his own interests, no one else was going to. Standing there at the window, watching the people coming and going across the courtyard, he started to plan his escape.

They moved out of Milan in the early evening, heading north for Como. Before they left, Mussolini called Salvitti into his office and entrusted to him a leather pouch containing his personal papers. The Duce was in good spirits, more optimistic than he'd been for several days. He had a machine-gun slung over one shoulder, though it was doubtful he knew how to use it, and a camera in his hand which he gave to his aide.

'You will take a picture, *Seniore*. To mark our departure.'

Salvitti followed Mussolini down the steps to the courtyard where a convoy of lorries and cars and their SS escort was waiting. The other leaders of the Fascist Republic of Salò, among them Bombacci, Pavolini, Graziani and Mezzasoma, were already assembled in a group. Mussolini took his place in the centre of them and assumed the heroic pose he'd favoured in earlier times when newspaper photographers and reporters were assigned to record his every twitch for posterity.

There were no journalists around now: those with any sense were keeping well away from the Palazzo Monforte, nervously calculating how to defend their spineless support for Fascism to the vengeful partisans who would soon control the city. Salvitti found the whole exercise absurd – posing for photographs with the American Fifth Army only hours away. But he followed the Duce's instructions, promising himself that they were the last orders he would have to obey.

The whole farcical performance over, Mussolini strutted away from the camera, announcing melodramatically: 'To the Valtellina.'

They departed minutes later in a long line of cars and lorries, Luigi Gatti sitting on the bonnet of the leading vehicle with a machine-gun across his bony knees. Salvitti was in the middle of the convoy, driving one of the trucks he'd seen being loaded in the courtyard of the *Prefettura*. Behind him came cars containing the lesser lights of the Fascist Republic, two lorry-loads of SS men and an Alfa Romeo containing a Blackshirt driver and, discreetly hidden in the back, Mussolini's mistress, Claretta Petacci.

It was ten o'clock by the time they reached the *Prefettura* in Como. Mussolini installed himself in the Prefect's office and held a subdued conference with his remaining ministers. There was an air of panic about the place. The telephone lines were still up and every few minutes a messenger came running along the corridor with more bad news. The Allies were drawing inexorably closer. Salvitti was on edge, his guts in the almost continuous clutch of a debilitating fear. The calmness he'd felt in Milan had gone now they were on the move. The Americans and the British terrified him. They were battle-scarred troops, hardened by the slaughter on the beachheads of Salerno and Anzio, the carnage at Cassino and on the Gustav, Trasimene and Gothic lines. They would show no mercy to the Duce or anyone caught with him. Equally worrying were the partisans. Milan was now in their hands and Lecco too, only twenty-five kilometres away on the eastern leg of Lake Como. The net was closing in on them rapidly, yet still they delayed. Salvitti's nerves were screaming.

Finally, in the early hours of the morning, they left Como to head up the western shore of the lake. This time, Salvitti made sure he was at the very back of the convoy.

Fifty kilometres north of Como, just outside the village of Musso, they were stopped by partisans of the 52nd Garibaldi Brigade. A barrier of boulders and fallen trees had been erected across the lakeshore road. There was no way round it. There was water on one side, a steep rock escarpment on the other. The partisans were rough mountain men, communists wearing leather jackets and red neckerchiefs. Poorly armed with shotguns and a few standard-issue army Carcano rifles which were half a century old, they were no match for the SS detachment in the convoy. But the Germans had no stomach for a fight. They wanted only to get home as quickly as possible.

Lieutenant Birzer, the SS commander, walked forward to talk to the partisans behind the barricade. When he returned to the convoy, he went straight to Mussolini's car to tell the Duce that the Germans would be allowed through, but no Italians.

Mussolini's shoulders slumped. 'So,' he said softly. 'This is it.'

'There is still a chance to save yourself, sir,' the lieutenant said. 'Put on one of our overcoats and a helmet. We will try to smuggle you through with us.'

The Duce shook his head. He knew it was hopeless. Fatigue and resignation had drained the strength from his ailing body. But Birzer persisted.

'You must, sir. I insist.'

Mussolini shrugged wearily and submitted. He allowed the lieutenant to dress him in an SS corporal's greatcoat and steel helmet, then clambered up into the back of one of the German lorries. He was so weak he had to be helped forward to a seat behind the driver's cab where he sagged down in a heap and closed his eyes.

The roadblock was cleared and the Germans passed through unhindered. But the reprieve was shortlived, for two kilometres further up the lake, at Dongo, the lorries were stopped again in the village square and searched by more partisans. They found nothing suspicious in the first truck, but in the second the political commissar of the brigade stopped by the hunched body in the front corner and studied it carefully. The soldier appeared to be either drunk or asleep, his helmet pulled down over his eyes.

The commissar shook him by the shoulder. 'Let me see your face,' he said in Italian.

11

The soldier lifted his head so the light caught his pallid skin and unshaven jowls. He put up no resistance as his helmet was removed to reveal the familiar shaven pate underneath.

The commissar looked at him for a long moment. 'Duce,' he said without emotion. 'We have been waiting for you.'

Salvitti wasn't in the convoy when it was halted at Musso. He'd left it an hour earlier as they snaked along the narrow road beside the lake. It was just before dawn, the first rays of the sun beginning to brush the surface of the water, when he'd allowed a gap to open up between him and the car in front. Gradually the gap had widened until, in places on the twisting road, he'd lost sight of the rest of the convoy altogether.

He let himself fall further behind, marking off the villages as they passed through them. Then, just after Argegno, he braked heavily to allow the other vehicles to disappear round a corner, and veered off up a side road. He knew no one would come back to look for him. They were too scared, in too much of a hurry to outrun the advancing Allies, to bother about one man and a truck.

Salvitti stayed on the side road for a short distance before turning off up a rough, unpaved track. In the distance, their peaks silhouetted against the lightening sky, he could see the ridge of mountains that marked the frontier with Switzerland.

The partisans held Mussolini and his mistress – captured at Musso with the other Fascist leaders – in a remote farmhouse high above Lake Como. The Duce seemed ill. His eyes were yellowish and dead and, with his hollow cheeks and grey stubble, he looked like a man of eighty. Claretta attempted to console him but he just moped gloomily by the window of their bedroom, refusing to talk.

It was late in the day when they heard the sound of footsteps on the stairs, someone running up in a hurry. The bedroom door flew open and a tall man in his thirties burst in. He was wearing a brown mackintosh and a scarf in the national colours of red, white and green.

'Quickly,' he said abruptly. 'We're leaving.'

Mussolini and Claretta looked at him blankly, still taking in his words.

'For God's sake, I've come to rescue you,' the man said, his impatience turning to irritation.

'Who are you?' Claretta asked.

'Get your things together. Come on, we have to hurry.'

He took their arms and all but forced them out of the bedroom. Claretta and Mussolini struggled into their coats as the man pulled open the farmhouse door and dragged them out on to the path. There was no sign of the partisans.

They slithered awkwardly down the wet track, splashing mud over their shoes and ankles. Claretta removed her high heels to find a firmer footing on the precarious slope. The man in the mackintosh held their arms, urging them to go faster.

In the central piazza of Bonzanigo di Mezzegra they paused to let Claretta put her shoes back on. Her stockings were torn to shreds and soaked through. A couple of village women washing clothes in the stone trough at one end of the square glanced up at them curiously as they hurried past. There was a small black Fiat parked at the bottom of a flight of steps just below the piazza, the driver waiting inside with the engine running. The man in the mackintosh opened the rear door.

'Where are we going?' Claretta asked. The Duce seemed in a daze, happy to do as he was told, but she wanted more information.

'Please, get in. Every minute is vital. The Americans are everywhere, trying to locate you.'

He pushed them inside and slammed the door. The car was already moving off down the hill as he opened the front passenger door and jumped in.

They'd gone only a short distance down the corkscrew road when they reached the neighbouring hamlet of Giulino di Mezzegra. The man in the mackintosh signalled to the driver who stopped outside the gates of a large house.

'What's going on?' Claretta demanded.

'Get out, please.'

'Why, what's happening?'

'We have to wait here until we check the road to Azzano.'

He helped them out and escorted them through the gates. On one of the stone gateposts was a faded number 14 and the words Villa Belmonte.

They walked down the side of the villa, which appeared to be closed up and deserted, the paint peeling off the wooden shutters. The garden was wild and overgrown. Vines and unruly tresses of bougain-villaea hung from rusty iron balconies. Branches of trees clawed at their hair as they ducked to pass beneath

14

them. At the back of the house the vegetation suddenly parted to reveal a glorious vista of Lake Como and the red roofs of Bellagio.

'This will do,' the man in the mackintosh said.

Claretta turned and noticed for the first time that he was carrying a machine-gun.

'Who are you?' she asked again.

'My name is Colonel Valerio.'

As soon as they heard the *nom de guerre* they knew he was a partisan. Mussolini went ashen. Claretta felt her legs give way beneath her and she clutched at the garden wall to hold herself upright.

'I have come from the Committee for National Liberation in Milan. I have orders to execute you.'

Claretta cried out involuntarily. She began to plead with him, getting more and more hysterical. But Mussolini silenced her with a curt gesture.

'Enough!'

He took her hand in his and held her eyes for a moment. She was weeping.

'No, no, please.'

'*Addio*, Clara,' the Duce said.

He straightened his shoulders and turned to face Valerio. The colonel met his gaze implacably, then lifted his machine-gun and squeezed the trigger.

'*Merda!* Not again.'

Domenico Salvitti gunned the engine of the truck, forcing it over the lip of the incline before jamming on the handbrake and jumping down from the cab. Steam was pouring out from beneath the bonnet in a dense white cloud. Salvitti ducked under it and struggled to find the catch above the boiling radiator grill. The bonnet clicked open. He averted his face as more burning vapour hissed out, then propped the bonnet open and stepped back, letting the steam disperse.

He was making slow progress. Three times already the lorry had overheated. There was a leak somewhere in the cooling system but Salvitti didn't have the tools to fix it. He kept filling up the radiator with water and praying it would last long enough to get him nearer the frontier, but every couple of kilometres it blew again.

He took an oily cloth to protect his fingers and gingerly unscrewed the radiator cap. The last remaining water and steam spluttered out. Salvitti retreated to a boulder overlooking the valley far below and sat down, waiting for the system to cool enough for him to replace the water from the jerry can in the cab. He wished he had some cigarettes, but he'd smoked the last of his *Nazionali* hours earlier.

He needed something to calm his nerves. He didn't know where he was. The frontier might be five, ten kilometres away, maybe further, he wasn't sure. He knew there'd be partisans in the mountains and *Guardia di Finanza* border guards. The more he delayed, the greater his chances of being caught. He pondered whether he should abandon the truck and continue on foot. It might be quicker, especially as he had no pressing reason for staying with the vehicle.

He glanced up sharply, suddenly wondering what was in the back of the lorry. Until now he hadn't thought to look, he'd been so preoccupied with his escape. He stood up and went round to the rear, untying the ropes securing the canvas flaps and letting the wooden tailboard drop down. Then he rolled the flaps out of the way and clambered inside.

ONE

Rome, present day

There were times – nearly every morning, in fact – when Elena Fiorini wished that she didn't have to see the dawn when she got out of bed. That, just once on a weekday, she could stay beneath the sheets until the full light of day made sleep impossible.

She couldn't imagine such a luxury. You got used to the permanent feeling of exhaustion, the sore eyes and thick head, but that didn't mean they became any more bearable. It was still an effort, still an act of masochistic self-discipline, to drag herself out from the covers when her body and mind were begging to be left in peace.

She slipped on a thin cotton robe and padded through into the kitchen. The ceramic floor tiles were cool on the soles of her bare feet. She put coffee and water into the stainless-steel espresso pot and stood it on the stove to boil. Out of the window, the city too was emerging reluctantly from the night. The sunrise, whatever tourists and romantics liked to think, was rarely a poetic orange. It was grey, sometimes muddy, nearly always a disappointment as the sun struggled to break through the haze of smog and traffic fumes. Elena opened the kitchen window. There was already something sluggish about the air. She was starting to

17

feel the weight of the summer heat that in a few hours
would be insufferable.

She went into her study and contemplated the mess
on the top of the desk: the sprawl of legal papers, statements, affidavits, briefs; the plate daubed with the oily
remains of the previous evening's *insalata mista* and the
glass and empty bottle of Valpolicella that reminded
her she was drinking too much. She pulled a face and
extricated the papers from the clutter, sorting them
quickly into piles and squeezing them into the worn
leather briefcase by the chair. It must have weighed ten
kilos, maybe more. Elena sometimes thought the only
exercise she got these days was lifting that briefcase.

The smell of coffee took her back to the kitchen, then,
espresso in hand, she went into the tiny bathroom
where she washed and applied her make-up. Her work
clothes were already laid out on the bed in the guest
bedroom which, since she never had any guests, she'd
turned into a dressing room: white blouse, sober dark
skirt and jacket, the loathsome, almost compulsory,
uniform of her profession. She always made sure she
selected them before she went to bed, a piece of efficient
organisation marred only by the fact that she usually
changed her mind in the morning and decided to wear
something completely different.

She slipped the skirt on and examined herself in the
full-length mirror on the wall, trying to decide if it
made her hips look too big. She'd never been skinny,
at least not since she was a teenager, but she worried
about her weight, convinced she was slowly turning
into a typical Italian *mamma* without the excuse of
having had children first. This was when she missed
her husband most – probably the only time she missed

him – when she needed reassurance about her figure. Confirmation that, though she might be thirty-five and feeling it, she was not also an unattractive blob of cellulite. She needed a man to tell her she looked nice, to give an opinion on which clothes she should wear – not that she had ever taken much notice of Franco's views if they didn't correspond to her own. He had been there to approve her choice, to bolster her self-esteem, not to tell her what to do.

The skirt, she decided, was acceptable this morning. But the blouse had to go. She selected another one and put it on, adding a turquoise silk scarf and silver clasp at the neck as a statement of individuality. She would remove them if she had to appear in court, in case the judge was blinded by her outrageous flamboyance.

She felt something rubbing up against her leg and looked down. It was Livia, the plump, self-satisfied cat that shared the apartment with her but only occasionally deigned to acknowledge her landlady's presence. Elena didn't pick her up. She didn't want grey cat hairs on her skirt, partly because they were unsightly, partly because she didn't like anyone in the office – except a few close friends – to know she had a cat. She hated the stereotype of the woman living alone with a cat. The insulting connotations of loneliness and frustrated desire for offspring, neither of which was true in her case. She hadn't really wanted the creature – it had been forced on her by an aunt desperate to get rid of an unplanned litter – but she'd grown quite fond of it. It was sleek and well-groomed, in contrast to the mangy felines outside in the city; the bony, hard-eyed cats foraging for food in rubbish heaps or hissing at tour groups in the Roman Forum.

Elena picked up her bulging briefcase, wincing as it banged against her knee, and went to the front door. Livia strolled after her and watched as she left, showing no inclination to follow. Livia never went out of the flat. Elena sometimes wondered if that was cruel, but cats weren't people. If they were warm and well-fed, they didn't need or desire adventure. That was all Elena wanted too: a quiet, unexciting existence. She was far too tired for adventure.

Andy Chapman lay back on the pillows and watched Gabriella come in from the shower. She stood at the foot of the bed and peeled off her towel, bending over slightly to dry herself.

Sunlight broke in through the slats in the shutters, playing over her lithe body as she moved. She lifted her head and looked at him, not at all self-conscious about her nakedness.

'Enjoying yourself?'

He smiled lazily. 'Beats breakfast television any day.'

'Am I supposed to take that as a compliment?'

She turned to face him, rubbing the towel over her breasts. She liked being watched. Why else did she come back into the bedroom to dry herself?

'Come over here,' Chapman said, 'and I'll pay you the ultimate compliment.'

Gabriella gave him a look of mock, wide-eyed amazement. 'What, again?'

'We've got time.'

'I have a train to catch.'

'We don't need long.'

'Speak for yourself, *carino*,' she said and Chapman laughed.

She put on her pants and bra, smiling at him provocatively. He kept his eyes on her, thinking how sometimes it was more erotic watching a woman putting her clothes on than taking them off. She slipped the cool, sleeveless dress over her head and let it drop slowly down over her body, smoothing out the creases with the palms of her hands. Then she ran a comb quickly through her hair and checked her appearance in the mirror.

'How do I look?'

'You know how you look,' Chapman said.

'Sometimes it would be nice if you told me.'

'You look like a million lire.'

She picked up a pillow and threw it at him. He caught it in front of his face. He could smell her scent on the pillowcase.

'Did you make coffee?' he asked.

'It's in the kitchen.'

'Bring me a cup before you go.'

'Do I have to do everything for you?'

Chapman grinned. 'Well, not quite everything. Or had you forgotten?'

She went out and returned with the espresso in a tiny china cup. She put it on the bedside table and leaned over to kiss him briefly. Chapman reached for her, but she was too quick. She backed away from the bed and picked up her handbag and overnight case.

'*Ci vediamo*, I'll see you,' she said casually.

'Next week?'

She paused, turning. 'That depends on my husband.'

Chapman nodded and watched her leave. For a moment, he'd almost forgotten she was married to someone else.

* * *

21

He walked to work through the narrow streets and *vicoli* – the tiny alleys – of Trastevere, the ancient medieval quarter on the west bank of the Tiber where he rented his apartment. He had a car, parked hazardously in a nearby piazza, but he would never have dreamt of using it to get to his office. An hour in a poisonous Roman traffic jam was not his idea of a good start to the day.

In Imperial times, Trastevere had been the docklands of Rome, the riverbank lined with warehouses and quays where ships bringing grain and olive oil and spices and a thousand other commodities were unloaded. It was a ghetto for foreigners and immigrants, a warren of courtyards and tiny houses, drinking dens and brothels where the sailors went for long nights of debauchery with girls from Syria and the Levant. There were still foreigners in the quarter – long-term residents, itinerants passing through or the coachloads of tourists who came here at night to eat in expensive restaurants and have their handbags snatched by youths on scooters.

Chapman liked the character of the area. The vine-clad walls and cobbled streets, the crowded squares and cool, deserted churches. Like the rest of the city, it was choked with cars, its inhabitants slowly suffocating beneath a cloud of carbon monoxide, but he'd grown accustomed to its alluring air of Bohemianism, the tawdry dilapidation of its buildings, and wouldn't have wanted to live anywhere else. It had its drawbacks, of course. The noise, the tourists, the thieves and drug dealers who loitered in the squares, not to mention the flashy young bankers and brokers who'd moved in during the eighties and who were little different from the criminals except that their particular forms of robbery and extortion were legal.

He crossed the Tiber on the Ponte Sisto before plunging into the maze of shady streets around the Campo de' Fiori, dodging the traffic on the Corso Vittorio Emanuele to walk up past the Pantheon and the Parliament building at Montecitorio. In Piazza San Silvestro he gulped down another espresso in a bar before going round the corner to the *Stampa Estera*, the foreign press club which served as his office.

He went upstairs to his desk and checked the news wires to see what was happening. Then he opened his mail and settled down to read through the Italian papers, seeing which stories might interest London, which pieces he could lift and rewrite or follow up. Let the Italian journalists do the work for him, the agencies and the earnest young men at Associated Press.

He'd been there half an hour or less when the telephone rang. He picked it up.

'*Pronto.*'

'Andy, it's Enzo,' the voice on the line said in Italian. 'You busy?'

'Not particularly. Why?'

'The Red Priest is dead. I'll pick you up in five minutes.'

TWO

'What happened?' Chapman asked as they paused at the traffic lights at the top of Via del Tritone.

Enzo Mattei shrugged noncommittally. 'I don't know. They didn't say.'

Chapman knew better than to ask who 'they' were. Enzo had contacts in every stratum of the criminal justice system. He'd never reveal who'd called him.

'Accident? Natural causes?'

'Doesn't sound like it. There's a scene-of-crime team there from the *Questura*.'

Chapman nodded and glanced sideways at his friend. Enzo was excited, he could tell. There was something in his manner that gave it away. The alert, slightly hunched position over the steering wheel, the impatience in his eyes as he waited for the lights to change. He must have covered hundreds of murders in his time, yet he still found something exhilarating in the prospect of another one. The Red Priest was different, of course, but Chapman was nevertheless disturbed. There was something unhealthy about a fascination with violent death.

They sped away up the Via Barberini and across the junction with the Via XX Settembre, overtaking a bus near the Piazza della Repubblica in a display of driving

24

reckless even by Roman standards. Chapman closed his eyes, trying to work out where they were going by the use of his other senses alone. They kept straight ahead so he guessed they were heading towards Termini, the central railway station, a conjecture which was confirmed when he heard the faint echo of the *Ferrovie dello Stato* public address system announcing a platform change.

They turned right, then almost immediately left, slowing down. Chapman opened his eyes and saw the police cars double parked in front of them. Enzo pulled up on to the pavement and left the car there illegally, right under the nose of a uniformed cop. The officer didn't turn a hair. It was beneath his dignity to notice a simple traffic violation – the province of the *Vigili Urbani*, not the police – and besides, from the nod he gave Enzo he clearly knew who he was. Enzo was acquainted with most of the officers in the city; probably half of them were on his payroll, or looking to be.

'Come on,' he said, walking briskly up the street to where the police had taped off an area outside a scruffy four-storey building.

It was a seedy district, like most neighbourhoods adjacent to big-city railway stations. Cheap hotels and *pensioni* vied with gimcrack tenements for the most unprepossessing frontage. Piles of rubbish lay festering in the gutter outside shabby apartment blocks whose occupants – many of them immigrants, all of them poor – were crammed in, two or three families to a floor, sharing kitchens, bathrooms and the communal stench of sewage and refuse.

A plastic body bag was being carried out to a waiting

ambulance, witnessed by a motley collection of neighbours, passers-by and bored cops.

'Damn,' Enzo said. 'They might have waited for us.' He always liked to get a glimpse of the corpse if he could. It gave you a better feel for the case.

He ducked under the tape. A uniformed *poliziotto* turned to block his path, then stopped, recognising him. He waved Enzo through, but took a closer look at Chapman.

'It's okay, he's with me.'

Chapman followed Enzo under a stone archway and into a dingy courtyard. Above them, the sky was almost obscured by the tiers of washing hanging out to dry. There was a smell of fried onions and exotic spices, more African than Italian.

A broad flight of stairs disappeared upwards into the bowels of the building. In one of the shadowy corners at the bottom, Chapman noticed a discarded hypodermic syringe. There was a lift shaft in the middle of the stairwell, caged in with steel mesh, but the lift itself was on one of the floors above. Enzo pressed the button. Nothing happened.

'The bastards have wedged the doors open. We'll have to walk.'

Chapman grinned at him. Enzo hated exercise, unless it was the kind you could do in a car, or from an armchair watching television. Anything more strenuous was for trained athletes only.

They plodded their way upwards, pausing on each landing for Enzo to get his breath back while pretending to examine the name cards outside the apartments. When they reached the second floor they could hear the activity above them. Footsteps echoed on the stone floor, then the lift cables started to whir as someone descended.

The door to an apartment on the third floor was open. Enzo and Chapman walked in unhindered and paused in the hallway. The internal doors were all propped open and men in spotless white coveralls were drifting in and out of the rooms with bags, brushes, fingerprinting dust, all the arcane tools of the forensic scientist's trade. None of them gave the two men a second glance.

It was a dark flat, plainly furnished, with polished wooden floors strewn with a few threadbare rugs. It wasn't particularly large, but it had an air of spaciousness because of the lack of clutter. There was no furniture at all in the hall and, from what Chapman could see through the doorways, very little more elsewhere. The bedroom contained an ancient mahogany bedstead, a simple wooden cross on the wall above it, and that seemed to be all. It was as bare and functional as a monk's cell.

They walked down the hall into the main living room where a group of men in crumpled suits – detectives from the *Questura*, police headquarters – were talking to one of the scene-of-crime officers. Enzo let his eyes wander around the room, keeping out of the way, but noting anything of interest. A wooden chair was tipped over on to its side in the middle and there was a stain on the rug nearby which looked like blood. Enzo took out a pad of paper and scribbled on it.

One of the detectives – sporting a grey suit and vivid yellow tie – looked round and noticed them. He nodded at Enzo and continued his conversation with his colleagues. Chapman found it slightly unbelievable, the casual way they were allowed to stroll into the scene of a murder without anyone stopping them. It was completely outside his experience of crime reporting in the UK. Enzo was careful not to interfere with anything but, nevertheless, the liberties he was granted were extraordinary, reflecting both his closeness to the police and, Chapman guessed, the depths of his newspaper's coffers when it came to tip-off fees and retainers for the right people on the force.

The detective in the yellow tie came over and Enzo asked him what had happened.

'We don't know yet.'

'Cause of death?'

'Same.'

'Come on, Guido.'

'It's true. We won't know until after the autopsy.'

'When was he killed?'

'Last night, the doctor thought. Maybe the early hours.'

'Who found the body?'

'A nun. One of the sisters who . . .' He broke off suddenly, his expression changing, exhibiting a mixture of guilt and apprehension. Like a small boy caught doing something he knows is wrong.

Chapman turned round and saw a woman standing just inside the doorway. There was a tall, hard-looking man beside her in the uniform of the *Polizia Giudiziaria*, the Judicial Police who served the magistracy, but Chapman knew it was the woman who had silenced the detective. She was of medium height, her dark brown hair – cut just above shoulder level – combed back above striking green eyes, and her figure full enough to be curvaceous without being plump. She exuded a quiet, but noticeable, air of authority.

She looked at Enzo, her brow furrowing. 'Who let *you* in?' she said wearily, as if this had happened to her before.

Enzo put his notepad away and shifted awkwardly. 'I was just leaving, dottoressa.'

'I know you were.'

Elena was irritated rather than angry. She didn't like breaches of procedure, not because she had a mania for rules, but because it was bad practice. It made for sloppy police work and that impeded her own duties.

'But as I *am* here, perhaps you'd like to make a comment for the record?' Enzo said, pushing his luck.

Her cool eyes settled on him. 'If I have any comment to make, I will issue it through the usual channels later.'

'Of course.'

She was glaring at Guido now. 'You know the rules about press coverage, detective.'

Guido looked down, mumbling something indistinct. Chapman edged away, getting out of the firing line. But Elena didn't pursue it further. She'd made her point.

'*Buon giorno*, Signor Mattei,' she said to Enzo. 'I don't expect to see you this close to a crime scene again.'

He held up his hand placatingly. 'I'll see it doesn't happen again, dottoressa.'

She rolled her eyes. 'Get out.'

She moved aside to let him exit, watching to ensure he left the apartment before she turned back to the detectives. They'd straightened themselves up and were trying to look alert, professional. Chapman, over in front of the window attempting to blend in inconspicuously, felt almost sorry for them.

'Now, what have we got?' Elena said.

There was a silence. Then Guido replied sullenly: 'We had a call about an hour ago.'

He'd lost face, being reprimanded in front of his colleagues. Elena didn't care. She was used to a certain amount of hostility, of veiled disrespect. Cops didn't like deferring to a woman, even if she was a magistrate. She knew they vilified her behind her back, resented her power. It was the lot of her sex that qualities which in a man were seen as strength, in a woman were viewed as overbearing bossiness.

'A call from whom?'

'A nun. Sister Anna Maria. She helped Father Vivaldi with his work. She came upstairs this morning. The door to his apartment was ajar. She came in and found him lying on the floor, dead, over there by the chair.'

Elena gave the room a cursory examination. She'd get the police and forensic reports later. All she needed now was a general picture.

'What's the preliminary assessment of how he died?'

Guido shrugged. 'He was in a bad way. He was stark naked and he'd been severely beaten. There were marks of torture on his body. Cigarette burns, they looked like.'

Elena winced. This was a priest, a devout man of God, they were talking about. Who would do that to a priest?

'This nun, has she made a full . . .' Elena stopped. She'd suddenly become aware of the man by the window. Detached from the other detectives, he was listening intently to the conversation without being part of it. She'd noticed him earlier, but only now realised she didn't know who he was.

'Who's that?' she said to Guido. 'Is he from the *Questura*?'

'He came with Mattei.'

Elena's mouth tightened, her eyes narrowing furiously. 'You're a journalist?'

Chapman held her gaze without flinching, a look of innocent bemusement on his face. 'Yes, I thought you knew.'

'What's your name?'

Chapman told her.

'You're a colleague of Enzo Mattei's? I told him to leave so how come you're still here?'

'You didn't say anything to me.'

'Don't play games,' Elena snapped. 'Your papers.'

She held out her hand. Chapman produced all the documentation he carried with him: his press accreditation, his *permesso di soggiorno*, residence permit, all the bits of paper required by the Italian state to prove he existed.

She studied them carefully. 'You're British?'

Chapman didn't reply.

'I asked you a question.'

'Yes, I believe that's what it says.'

There was an air of lazy insolence about him that infuriated Elena – his laid-back manner, the half-amused expression on his face.

'Well, Signor . . . Chapman,' she said icily, 'I don't know what you're accustomed to doing in your own country, but in Italy we don't tolerate reporters interfering with the scene of a crime.'

'I didn't interfere with anything.'

31

'Or eavesdropping on privileged conversations between the police and a magistrate. I have your name. I will have to consider what further action, if any, to take against you.'

She knew she sounded pompous, petulant, but he'd got under her skin.

'As you wish, dottoressa,' he said politely.

He sauntered slowly out of the room. Elena watched him, pursing her lips. She'd take no further action against him, of course, and he knew it. That annoyed her even more.

Enzo was waiting for him downstairs in the courtyard.

'You pick up anything of interest?'

'Not much. They kicked me out too soon.'

'Let's get a drink.'

They crossed the street to a bar and Enzo ordered a *caffè corretto*, espresso with a shot of gut-rotting *grappa* in it. Chapman had mineral water; he'd had enough coffee already that day.

'How do you drink that stuff at this time of the morning?' he asked Enzo as the barman slapped the cup down on the counter in front of him.

'You should try it. Gives the system a shock. Caffeine and alcohol, gets the brain working.' He took a sip of the coffee and ran his tongue over his lips. 'So what did you hear?'

Chapman told him what the detective had said about the priest's naked body, the marks of torture.

'Jesus!' Enzo exclaimed. 'That's nasty.'

He was genuinely shocked, a rare occurrence considering the ghastly things he saw every day in the course of his job. It wasn't that the details were particularly gory – not by Italian underworld standards anyway – it was the identity of the victim that made them so horrific.

Enzo was usually scathing about the clergy but, like most other Romans – even the terminally cynical – he had a profound respect for Father Antonio Vivaldi. *Il Prete Rosso*, the Red Priest, ran, or rather had run, a charity for the homeless and dispossessed, the street people who spent their nights and days slumped against the walls of the station, begging, rummaging through rubbish bins for something to eat, drinking cheap spirits to numb the pain of their lives. Father Vivaldi and his team of nuns provided a soup kitchen for these derelicts, dispensing food at lunchtime and in the evenings for anyone who needed it. In addition, *Compassione*, the name of his charity, ran a drug rehabilitation programme in the inner city and provided beds in a hostel down near the Tiber.

The Italian press – which loved to give nicknames – had christened him *Il Prete Rosso* after the Venetian composer and priest who bore the same name, except Vivaldi the musician owed the nickname to the colour of his hair while Vivaldi the latter-day priest owed it to the colour of his politics. He'd been a socialist of the old-fashioned variety. Not a compromised, card-carrying member of the former *Partito Socialista Italiano*, whose leaders and deputies he'd despised as self-serving opportunists intent, like all politicians, only on lining their own pockets, but a true socialist who believed in equality and justice and Christian compassion.

An outspoken critic of the Vatican's wealth and

money-making activities – which he equated, controversially, with the moneylenders in the temple – he had lived a life of spiritual and temporal simplicity. He railed frequently against the pomp and extravagance of the organised Catholic Church and what he referred to as the 'pampered prelates' in the Roman Curia. Such comments did not endear him to the Holy See which had attempted to discipline him on numerous occasions with no effect. Vivaldi simply ignored them and got on with his work, confident that both wider Church opinion, and the Italian public – who relished a stroppy priest – supported what he stood for. His death, particularly its violent nature, would stun, and sadden, the whole city.

Enzo stirred his coffee continuously, more to give his fingers something to do than because it needed stirring. He was a restless character, always fidgeting, always looking for the next distraction to burn off some of his surplus energy.

'They say anything else?'

Chapman shook his head. 'The woman noticed me standing there before I could pick up any more details.'

'She give you a hard time?'

'Not really. I think I'd be in a police cell, or hospital, now if she'd chosen to give me a hard time.'

Enzo smiled. 'She's tough.'

'Who is she?'

'Elena Fiorini. From the *pubblico ministero*.'

'She's attractive.'

'Not for you, my friend.'

'She wasn't wearing a wedding ring.'

'You noticed *that*?' There was a hint of incredulity in Enzo's voice. 'While she was giving you a bollocking and kicking you out on your arse?'

'You know me, I like 'em hard and domineering.'

Enzo grinned. 'A few people have got their hands burnt on that one. And not just their hands.'

'Yeah?'

'She's a ballbreaker. The police dread her being assigned to a case.'

'She bad to work with?'

'Just thorough. Makes them do their jobs properly. They hate that.'

Enzo downed the last of his coffee. 'You finished? Let's go and sniff around the neighbourhood. See what we can dig up before the cops queer our pitch.'

The nun was composed, but showing noticeable signs of distress. She was sitting very upright on a wooden chair in the *Compassione* office on the ground floor of the apartment building. Her legs were pressed together, her hands in her lap, the fingers tightly clenched. Elena came in, accompanied by Gianni Agostini, the judicial police officer who'd been upstairs with her. She was amused to see Agostini touch his testicles discreetly, a superstitious ritual among Italian men when confronted with a nun. Elena dismissed the policewoman who'd been sitting with the nun and pulled out a chair for herself.

'Sister Anna Maria? My name is Elena Fiorini. I'm from the public prosecutor's office. This is Inspector Agostini. I have to ask you a few questions. I hope they won't be too painful for you. Are you up to it?'

'Yes,' Sister Anna Maria said hoarsely. She cleared her throat. 'Yes, I'll be all right.'

'We can do this later, if you wish.'

'I'd rather get it over with now.'

'Very well. I'm aware it must have been a shock for you, Sister. Perhaps you would go through everything that happened this morning.'

The nun took a deep breath and began to speak in a quiet, almost overly calm voice, as if she were desperately trying to contain her emotions.

She'd arrived at the *Compassione* office shortly before eight o'clock. She was always the first to get there. A lay secretary came in later to do the books and the general administration, but Sister Anna Maria had responsibility for opening the office and the kitchen where they prepared the food for the needy.

'The first thing I do is make Father Vivaldi's breakfast. Just a *caffè latte* and some bread and jam. I pick the rolls up at the bakery on my way in. Father Vivaldi usually comes downstairs from his apartment at eight o'clock, but this morning . . .' She paused. 'This morning he didn't.'

'Had that ever happened before?' Elena asked.

'No, not that I can remember. He was always most punctual. I waited for him for twenty minutes, then went upstairs. I wondered if for some reason he'd gone away and left a note on his door for me.'

'Did he go away much?'

'Every now and again. He had family in the Abruzzi. But he always told me beforehand if he was going to visit them.'

'Are they his next of kin?'

'I believe so. He had a sister in Paganica, near L'Aquila.'

Elena glanced at Agostini who was taking notes on his knee. He nodded at her.

'I'll take care of it.'

'Go on, Sister,' Elena said. She studied the nun. She was young, probably in her late twenties, with a pale complexion and gold-rimmed spectacles. She wore a grey dress and a white head-dress which covered her hair but not her neck. She was plain, but not unattractive. Elena wondered, as she always did when she encountered a nun, what had led her to take the veil.

'When I got upstairs, I saw that the door to his apartment was ajar. I knocked on it, and called his name, but there was no reply. I didn't know what to do. I wondered whether someone had broken in during the night. This isn't a very nice area and, well, there are one or two people around here who are not very law-abiding.'

She gave them a brief, apologetic glance for her lack of Christian charity and continued: 'I pushed open the door and went in. His bedroom door was open so I could see he wasn't still in bed. Then I went through to the living room and . . .' She swallowed hard. '. . . And he was there . . . on the floor.'

Sister Anna Maria's mouth began to tremble. She twisted her fingers together in her lap and bit her lip, but the tears were already streaming down her face.

'I'm sorry, it's just that . . .'

'We'll take a short break,' Elena said. She stood up and turned away to allow the nun time to recover herself. Gianni Agostini came out of the office with her and they waited in the cramped dining area next to the kitchen. Stained wooden trestle tables and wooden benches were set out in rows across the room which had a distinctive canteen odour about it. Garlic and cooking oil and stale food.

'It can't have been easy for her, finding the body,' Agostini said.

'I know. This is going to be a messy one, Gianni.' She didn't mean just the interview with Sister Anna Maria. She meant the whole case.

Voices were raised suddenly out in the courtyard. There were heavy footsteps on the stone flags and three more nuns burst in through the door, pursued by an irate police officer.

'I told you,' he was shouting, 'you can't come in.'

The leading nun spied Agostini's uniform and came marching over. 'Are you in charge?'

She was a stout, formidable matron in her fifties, her coarse grey hair – like a clump of wire wool – scraped back and fastened above her neck with a metal clasp. Her face was plump and rosy, though anything but benign. There was a toughness under the soft flesh, an unwillingness to compromise, that reminded Elena of her convent school Mother Superior.

'Can I help you, Sister?' Agostini said smoothly.

'What's going on?' the nun demanded. 'Why have we been denied entry to our own premises? What's all this nonsense about Father Vivaldi? It can't be true.'

'I'm afraid it is true. Father Vivaldi was found dead this morning.'

The nun gaped at him. She took a step backwards and sank down on to one of the wooden benches. The other two nuns, both younger, clutched at each other, their faces set in the rictus of shock.

'Father Vivaldi's apartment and the office of his charity are sealed until we have completed our work,' Agostini said.

The nuns didn't appear to hear him. They were

looking at each other now. The two younger sisters sat down heavily. There were tears in their eyes.

'No, it can't be. Not Father Vivaldi,' one of them said, looking pleadingly at Elena and Agostini as if hoping they might change their minds and tell them it had all been a mistake.

Elena sensed a movement behind her. Sister Anna Maria came out into the dining area. She went to the two nuns and embraced them, all three weeping. Elena turned to the grey-haired nun.

'Sister Anna Maria found the body. She will need your help in the coming days.'

The nun nodded, still absorbing the news. Questions formed on her lips, but the words wouldn't come out. Elena answered without needing to be asked.

'We don't know why. We don't know very much at the moment. I'm sorry I can't help you more.'

The nun glanced at her companions, then back at Elena. 'The soup kitchen. We must provide something. The people round here depend on us.'

She seemed cool, untouched by what had happened, but Elena knew what she was doing. Nuns were accustomed to dealing with bereavement. They knew that, in grief, it was important to find some routine activity to divert the mind.

'Father Vivaldi would have wanted us to continue,' the grey-haired sister said.

Elena gave the request some thought before nodding. 'The office must stay closed, but I don't see any harm in opening the kitchen.'

The nun stood up. 'Sisters,' she said, 'we have work to do.'

Sister Anna Maria exchanged a few comforting words

39

with her friends, then went back into the office. She wiped her eyes with a handkerchief and crossed her hands in her lap again.

'I'm ready to continue now.'

Elena sat down opposite her and Agostini took out his notebook.

'After you found Father Vivaldi's body,' Elena said, 'what did you do?'

'Do?' The nun shifted uncomfortably in her seat.

'Yes. Did you touch anything? Did you take a closer look?'

'Oh.' Sister Anna Maria seemed relieved. 'No. I didn't go near the body.'

'But you knew he was dead?'

She bit her lip and nodded. 'I've seen bodies before. I knew he was beyond help.'

'Which telephone did you use to call the police?'

'The one on Father Vivaldi's desk.'

Elena pictured the layout of the room. The desk was by the window. She recalled its chipped legs, the scratched wooden surface uncluttered by papers or books. Sister Anna Maria would have had to step round the body to get to the telephone.

'You didn't disturb anything on your way to the desk?'

'No, I was very careful.'

'When did you last see him alive?'

'Yesterday evening. About eight o'clock. We provide an evening meal at six, then clear up.'

'Who locks up the kitchen?'

'That depends. Sometimes I do, sometimes Sister Graziella. Father Vivaldi often did it himself if he was working in the office. There are two sets of keys.'

'What did Father Vivaldi usually do after you left?'

'I believe he went up to his apartment and read or studied.'

'Did he do that yesterday?'

'I don't know.'

'Did he have visitors in the evenings?'

'I'm sorry, I can't help you. He was a very private man.'

'He lived alone?'

'Yes.'

'No domestic help?'

'A cleaner came in twice a week. We did his laundry for him – there's a washing machine at the back of the kitchen. His meals he took in the dining room with the street people. He led a simple, quiet life.'

Elena said nothing for a time. She could hear the clang of pans and utensils outside in the kitchen. The first aromas of onion and herbs crept in under the door.

'May I go now?' Sister Anna Maria asked. 'I'm needed.'

'How long had you worked with Father Vivaldi?'

'Less than eighteen months.'

'Were you close to him?'

The nun frowned, a little affronted by the question. 'I don't understand. What do you mean?'

'I mean, were you aware of any worries he had? Or fears.'

'Oh no, he would never have spoken to us of things like that.'

'So you don't know if he had enemies?'

'Father Vivaldi?' From her expression it was clear she thought the question ridiculous. 'He was a good man. A saintly man. He inspired love and devotion in everyone who met him. He had no enemies.'

'Thank you, Sister. We may need to speak to you again.'

The nun stood up and left the office. Elena wished that what she'd said about the priest would turn out to be right. That, for once, it was possible to find someone without enemies. But she was more worldly than a nun, her view of human nature more jaundiced. She knew that sometimes it was easier to hate someone for their virtues than for their vices.

Chapman had never encountered anyone who enjoyed talking to people as much as Enzo Mattei. Even by Italian standards he was exceptionally garrulous. His job gave him the excuse for asking questions, but that wasn't the only reason he did it; he simply had a genuine interest in the affairs of others. He'd been blessed with an innate sense of how to extract information from people and relished every opportunity to exercise his gift. He seemed to know instinctively who needed to be flattered, who needed to be cajoled, threatened or bribed. It was an enviable skill in a journalist.

They were across the street from the Red Priest's apartment block, knocking on doors in a similar scruffy four-storey building. They'd already been round all the neighbouring bars and shops, keeping ahead of the police who were doing the same thing, only more slowly and with none of Enzo's boundless enthusiasm.

Enzo collected facts and opinions like a prospector panning for gold, sieving through vast quantities of worthless ore in the hope of finding a tiny gleaming nugget that he could use. Chapman was bored – he knew the death of Vivaldi, however significant a story in Italy, would be of little interest to the English reader – but tagged along because he liked watching his friend work and, anyway, was too lazy to make his own way back to his office.

Enzo hammered on the door of a flat on the second floor. After a long wait, the latch clicked open and a woman's dark face peeked nervously out through a tiny crack. She looked like an Arab, her hair concealed under a black shawl. Enzo explained who he was and what he wanted. The woman stared at him, her eyes wary. She jabbered something at him in a foreign language and hurriedly closed the door.

'You get that?' Enzo asked facetiously.

'Only the gist. I think it was the same as the woman downstairs.'

'You think they're trying to tell us something?' He crossed the landing and rang another doorbell.

'Come on, Enzo, let's go. No one in this building speaks a word of Italian.'

'Just a couple more doors.'

Chapman sighed and leaned on the wall. Enzo was nothing if not persistent. They'd met several years earlier at the *Questura* in Via San Vitale. Then, as now, Enzo had been the crime correspondent for one of the big Rome dailies. A group of journalists had been waiting in an ante-room when a suspect in a murder case was brought in and taken through to an adjoining room to be questioned. Enzo immediately produced a stethoscope from his pocket, placed it on the door and relayed the details of the interrogation to his open-mouthed colleagues. That was his style.

He had no respect for official channels or orthodox methods. He did things his way.

The door opened on a chain. Another woman's face peered out at them. Only this time it looked Italian.

Enzo smiled at her and turned on his charm. '*Buon giorno*. Signora Guarino?' He'd got the name from the slip of card by the doorbell.

'Yes.'

He told her who he was, then he apologised for disturbing her and spun her some yarn about how a local shopkeeper had told him she was the best person to speak to if he wanted information about the neighbourhood.

The woman showed a flicker of interest. 'Really?'

'Could you spare us a few minutes of your time to discuss the tragic event across the road?'

'Reporters, you say?'

'Yes, signora.'

She unlatched the chain and opened the door. 'Come in.'

She led them through into the living room. It had an air of faded elegance. Furnished in a tasteful but dated style – like a fashion plate from a fifties magazine – it looked as if she'd bought everything forty years ago and changed nothing since. There were ornate mirrors on all the walls, armchairs and a sofa a little too decorative to be truly comfortable and lots of spindly tables covered in silver-framed photographs and other family mementoes. Something about the woman, and the predominance of photographs of a middle-aged man, made Chapman sure she was a widow.

'Who was it told you to come here? Signor Ramoni at the *alimentari*, I suppose.'

'Yes, that's right,' Enzo said without hesitation.

'I've lived here since I was first married. I know everyone. Except the foreigners, of course,' she added disdainfully. 'You wouldn't know it now, but this used to be quite a nice area. You used to be able to walk around in safety, at night as well as during the day. Now, well, it's North Africa, isn't it?'

Chapman caught Enzo's eye. He loved racist bigots. They liked to talk and didn't care what they said. The problem, usually, was shutting them up.

'My husband worked for the *fs* for thirty-seven years, you know. Worked hard as well. Not like the layabouts they employ on the railways today. Thirty years ago a lady could walk through Termini completely unmolested. Now you can't go two metres without being accosted by vagrants. Can I offer you something to drink, by the way?'

'No, thank you,' Enzo said. 'Did you know Father Vivaldi at all?'

'Oh yes. Is it true what they're saying? That he was murdered last night?'

Enzo nodded. Signora Guarino's eyes gleamed with undisguised curiosity. She was in her sixties, smartly dressed in a dark blue and white dress with a silver brooch above her left breast – the sort of woman who would always have her hair neatly permed and would die before she ventured out without make-up on.

'What happened?' she asked. 'Have they caught the person who did it?'

'Not yet. Did you know him well?'

She hesitated, reluctant to commit herself. Chapman guessed she probably said good morning to him in the street and that was it, but she didn't want to admit it

45

because of the kudos attached to an acquaintanceship with a celebrated murder victim.

'Well, he wasn't a close friend,' she said finally. 'He was a good man. He meant well but, personally, I blame him for much of the way the neighbourhood has deteriorated.'

'Why's that?' Enzo inquired.

'All those dreadful people he feeds. Those dirty tramps and drop-outs who hang around the streets begging for money. I mean, I'm not against charity, doing one's Christian duty by the poor, but most of them are young and able-bodied. They could get jobs, couldn't they? They could work, but they can't be bothered. Father Vivaldi encouraged that kind of fecklessness by giving them free meals.'

'Did you notice anything yesterday evening, or during the night?'

'I never go out at night. Those thieves and drunks are out there at night. They frighten me. They loiter about, injecting themselves with drugs, fornicating in the courtyards – oh yes, I've seen them. They leave their syringes on the street for children to pick up. It's a disgrace. The police should ask *them* what happened to Father Vivaldi. There's one I see all the time. He sleeps over there under the arch. A dirty fellow with long hair and a missing ear.'

'You're suggesting he had something to do with Father Vivaldi's death?'

'I don't know. But these people are never grateful to those who help them. Who knows, they probably killed the poor Father for the money in his pocket. To buy drugs or drink.'

Her mouth was a thin slit of disapproval. She was

getting things off her chest which had long rankled. Chapman had some sympathy for her. The area was undoubtedly seedy and the vagrants and immigrants *were* alien and threatening to a woman like her.

'Did Father Vivaldi have problems with any of the people he helped?' Enzo said.

Signora Guarino shrugged. The light from the window touched her face, throwing into relief the deep wrinkles beneath the powder around her eyes and mouth.

'I wouldn't be surprised,' she said. 'They're wasters. They're aggressive, probably dangerous. They live off charity yet people like that always want more. They despise decent, civilised people like us but they're happy to take our money to support their antisocial habits.'

'Some of them are genuinely destitute,' Chapman said. 'If Father Vivaldi hadn't helped them, many of them would be dead by now.'

Signora Guarino gave him a pitying look, as if to indicate he was a gullible simpleton for believing such liberal propaganda.

'Yes, well,' she said curtly, not condescending to enter into a discussion on the matter. But she couldn't resist adding: 'I don't suppose you live around here, do you? I have to put up with it, you don't.'

Enzo stood up. 'Thank you, signora. You've been most helpful.'

She flashed him a gracious smile. 'I'm glad to be of assistance. It's time the press highlighted the shocking things that go on here. What has this city come to when a man of the cloth can be murdered in his own home? It must have been terrible for that poor young fellow who found the body. I really feel for him.'

Chapman, already heading for the door, almost missed it, but Enzo picked up on it immediately.

'Which young fellow do you mean, signora?'

Signora Guarino looked puzzled. 'The one who came first thing this morning. A young man in a dark suit.'

Chapman drifted casually back across the living room, trying not to look interested. Enzo was standing with his back to the window so it was hard to see his expression, but his posture was alert, his head pushed forwards a little like a snake about to strike.

'You don't mean one of the plain-clothes police officers?'

'No, this was before the police arrived. I saw him at the window of Father Vivaldi's apartment.'

She took a couple of paces to her own window and pointed at the building diagonally across the street.

'It's that one there. I used to see Father Vivaldi sitting at his desk working.'

'What time was this, signora?'

'I don't know. Half past eight, maybe. He parked just up the street. I happened to notice because it was a very smart, shiny car. One of those dark blue ones that all the government ministers drive around in. I don't know the make.'

'You think it was a government car?'

'Oh no, it wasn't government,' Signora Guarino said firmly. 'It had SCV licence plates.'

Enzo's head jolted up violently, his eyes flicking across to find Chapman's. SCV. *Stato della Città del Vaticano*: the registration mark for the Vatican City.

THREE

The swaying towers of files on Elena's desk seemed to grow every time she set foot in her office, so much so that she was convinced they weren't simply paper and cardboard but some living organism that reproduced itself overnight. They tottered precariously around the edges of the desk like jerry-built walls, constantly in danger of tumbling down on to the floor which was practically invisible beneath yet more stacks of documents.

She picked her way through the obstacle course and squeezed into her swivel chair, manoeuvring her legs round into the narrow space under the desk which, so far, had escaped the relentless colonisation of the paperwork. How much longer it could hold out was a question she rarely had time to ask herself. She was so swamped with work, so desperately overstretched, that the chaos in the office seemed just a small, trivial symptom of the endemic disease that paralysed the whole criminal justice system.

The sheer volume of cases was choking the life out of the *pubblico ministero* and the courts. The average time it took to get from initial proceedings to completion of all appeals was now ten years. It seemed to Elena that, no matter what she did, it made not the slightest impression on the backlog of investigations and trials. The system was always on the brink of collapse, the magistrates like doctors struggling to keep a patient alive on a life-support machine that threatened to pack in altogether at any moment.

'What the hell is all this?'

She'd just noticed a new growth of files which had sprouted out of the surface of her desk since that morning.

Her colleague, Francesca Lauri, speaking on the telephone at the desk opposite, held up a hand. 'Just a second . . .' She finished her conversation and replaced the receiver. 'Vespignani brought them in while you were out. I've got a pile too.'

'Shit! Why us?'

'You know how it is,' Francesca said acidly. 'We spend all day polishing our nails and phoning our hairdressers. We must have time for another couple of dozen cases.'

'Where've they come from?'

'Mariani's off sick again. They're sharing his cases out amongst the rest of us.'

Elena gritted her teeth. 'As if we haven't got enough on our plates already. What's wrong with him? Yeah, okay, I know.'

She sighed. Armando Mariani was the living embodiment of their greatest fear. A magistrate who'd cracked up under the strain. Periodic absences for treatment for stress and exhaustion had become more and more prolonged, his time at work in between illnesses so short now that he was virtually on permanent sick leave.

'Vespignani says he's not coming back.'

'What, ever?' Francesca nodded. '*Dio*. Poor guy. I suppose it was expected.'

'His health's shot to pieces. He'll be on pills for the rest of his life, they say.'

'Christ! How old is he? Thirty-one, thirty-two?'

'No more.'

Elena grimaced. It could have happened to any of them. Could still happen. The line between coping – and none of them did any more than cope – and breakdown was wafer thin. They were ludicrously understaffed for the amount of work they had to handle.

She picked up her phone and rang the mortuary where the post-mortem on Antonio Vivaldi was being carried out. She spoke to the forensic pathologist and pushed him for an early report. 'I'll send someone over for it. I want it by this afternoon,' she said, dismissing the pathologist's protestations about pressure of work and time. 'This afternoon, dottore,' she repeated, putting the phone down.

She went out into the adjoining office where her clerk, Alberto Baffi, and two secretaries were crammed into a space about the size of a small boxroom – which, in fact, was what the office had originally been. The contagious growth of paperwork had spread in here too so that Elena had to peer over a formidable rampart of files in order to see Alberto's pinched face and balding head. He was writing laboriously in longhand on a pad of lined paper. There was a computer next to him – as there was in all the offices – but he avoided using it if he could. The monitor was partially buried under cardboard folders and the keyboard turned into a convenient, if uneven, stand for his coffee cup and saucer.

'Any messages for me?' Elena inquired.

Baffi flicked through a pile of yellow notelets next to the telephone. 'I took care of that one. That one too. That was irrelevant. Wrong office. Rubbish. Rubbish. Interesting, but still rubbish . . .' He pushed the scraps of paper to one side. 'Rossi called about the forgery case. I fobbed him off. He didn't believe me. You'll need this.' He handed her one of the messages. 'You won't need this. Or this. Defence attorney in the Falcone case called. I said you were out all day. More rubbish. Ditto. Oh, and Dottore Vespignani' – he pronounced the deputy chief prosecutor's name with undisguised contempt – 'wants to see you the minute you get in. So that can go in the bin.' He screwed up the note and tossed it over his shoulder, a purely symbolic gesture as the waste-paper bin was on the other side of the office.

'And your husband phoned,' he added casually. 'He didn't leave a message.'

Elena nodded, keeping her expression neutral. Franco had taken to calling recently, but so far she'd managed to avoid speaking to him.

'Thanks, Alberto.'

Baffi was a difficult, prickly character, but fiercely loyal to her. Elena didn't know how she would survive without him.

'Could you fix up a courier to go over to the mortuary and collect an autopsy report on Antonio Vivaldi?'

'Already?' He gave her a sceptical look. It usually took days for the post-mortem paperwork to arrive at the *Procura*.

'It'll be there. I've spoken to the pathologist.'

'Elena!'

Francesca was calling from their office. Elena stepped into the doorway. Francesca was holding up the telephone.

'*Questura*. Are you handling an armed robbery? Hold-up in a bar in Trastevere?'

'Not me.'

'It's on your desk,' Baffi interjected. 'In the files from Dottore Mariani.'

Elena pulled a face. 'I'll call them back,' she said to Francesca. Then to her clerk: 'Anything else I should know about those files?'

Baffi shrugged evasively. 'I didn't check them all.'

'Alberto.' She knew there was something he wasn't telling her.

He cleared his throat and looked away. 'You've got the Geminazza case.'

'Fuck!' Elena said to herself. That bastard Vespignani. The State versus Enrico Geminazza was one of those poisoned-chalice cases that no one in the office wanted to handle. It was a financial fraud prosecution which had been investigated by both the *Questura* and the *Guardia di Finanza*, the Revenue Guards, a nightmare situation at the best of times as it was complicated by rivalry and non-cooperation between the two different police forces. But it was primarily the complexity of it that made it difficult to deal with. It involved a lot of figures, several different foreign currencies, fiduciary accounts and offshore tax havens which were virtually incomprehensible to anyone but an accountant, or a crook, and Geminazza was both.

It would drag on for years, probably never get to trial and, if it did, no one in the court, including the judge and prosecutor, would understand what it was all about so it would probably end in an acquittal.

The file had been passed around the office for months, ending up on Mariani's desk because he was off sick at the time and couldn't complain. And now it had been slipped deviously into Elena's in-tray.

'I tried to reject it,' Baffi said apologetically. For once, the protective wall he'd constructed around Elena had been breached. 'But the deputy chief insisted you took it.'

'I know, Alberto. It's not your fault. Thank you for trying.'

Elena marched back to her desk, seething.

'That is just great. Just fucking great,' she said to Francesca, who grinned at her.

'It's not funny. Do I look like a mug or something? Why does every piece of crap in this office gravitate towards me?'

She knocked a pile of files angrily off her desk and sat down.

'Speaking of crap,' Francesca murmured under her breath.

'Good morning, Elena.'

Luigi Vespignani was leaning on the door-frame between the two offices, a supercilious smile on his pudgy lips. He was short and dumpy with a sagging belly and puffy cheeks which made him look as if he'd been overfilled with an air pump. He wore expensive clothes, from the finest, most exclusive tailor in the city, but no amount of cloth or craft could hide the deputy chief prosecutor's insignificant height and rather more significant girth. Francesca described him as the sort of ridiculous little man who ought be dangling as a mascot in the back window of a Fiat Cinquecento.

'Having a bad morning?' he sneered.

I wasn't until *you* showed up, Elena almost retorted. But she got a hold on her temper. He enjoyed riling the women in the *Procura*. She wasn't going to allow him the pleasure of a victory.

'I'm fine, Luigi,' she said.

'You got the files from Mariani?'

'Yes, thanks. It was good of you to share them with us. There were a couple of square centimetres of empty space on my desk that needed filling.'

His mouth twitched humourlessly. 'I'd hate you to find yourself with some free time and nothing to do.'

'I'll bear that in mind when I'm still here at ten o'clock tonight.'

'I wanted to see you. Didn't you get my message?'

'I haven't checked yet. I've only just got back.'

'That's what I wanted to talk to you about.'

He smoothed his fingers over his beard. He kept his hair a little long and had grown the beard and an upturned moustache because he thought they made him appear rather dashing – like a Gascon musketeer. Elena could never look at him without longing to reach for a razor.

'The Chief is holding a press conference this afternoon. He'll need you there.'

'Are you talking about the Vivaldi case?'

'Of course.'

'A press conference? What for?'

'He's been inundated with calls. There's going to be a lot of speculation about the case. It's best to get the facts out into the open as soon as possible.'

'I don't have anything to tell the press yet.'

'We'll give them what we've got.'

'Look, I'm snowed under here. I've got better things to do than talk to reporters.'

'Three o'clock, Elena. You brief me and the Chief just before we go in.'

Vespignani pushed himself off the door-frame and waddled out. Elena swore under her breath and glanced across at Francesca who was staring dreamily at the spot the deputy chief prosecutor had just occupied, her chin cupped in her hand like some lovelorn adolescent.

'Isn't he adorable?' she said in a husky Mae West voice. 'Don't you just want to tear his trousers off and shag him stupid?'

Elena laughed. Thank God for Francesca.

Chapman helped himself to a slice of peppered salami and a couple of *olive piccanti*, chewing on them thoughtfully as he looked around the crowded *birreria*. Enzo was across the table, a finger stuck in one ear, his mobile phone pressed to the other, talking to his newsdesk. Chapman took a sip of his beer and leaned back in his chair, letting the draught from the overhead fan cool the top of his head. It was stiflingly hot. The windows of the *birreria* were all open, but it seemed to make little difference to the leaden atmosphere in the room. Chapman could feel the beads of sweat on his forehead, the spreading damp under his arms and in his crotch.

Enzo put his phone away in the pocket of his jacket and picked up a piece of salami, folding it neatly into quarters and popping it into his mouth.

'You should try these olives,' Chapman said.

'Good?'

'Sear your throat.'

The marinade the olives had been soaked in was afire with pepper and crushed chillies. They went down particularly well in the Roman summer, as if burning your insides made the temperature outside somehow more bearable.

'You haven't left me many.'

'You shouldn't spend so long on the phone.'

'Do you want to call in?'

Chapman shook his head. 'Not from a noisy *birreria*. I like London to think I'm so busy I don't have time for lunch. Anything happening I should know about?'

'Not unless a row over state pensions and a multiple pile-up at Modena are front-page news in England.'

'You want another beer?'

'Yeah, okay. What did you order?'

'Pasta of the day. *Penne all'arrabbiata.*'

'Christ, Andy, I'll have a charred mouth by the time we've finished here.'

Chapman grinned and put out an arm to stop a passing waiter. He ordered two more beers.

'So,' Enzo said, undoing his tie and the top button of his shirt, 'have you figured out yet what the Vatican was doing there?'

'I've given it some concentrated thought.'

'And?'

'I haven't a clue.'

'That's no help.'

'They probably sent someone to make sure he was dead. They'll be glad to get rid of him, after all.'

'You're suggesting the Vatican had something to do

57

with his death?' Enzo warmed to the idea. It appealed to his weakness for conspiracy theories.

'It would make a good story, wouldn't it? The Pope taking out a contract on a rebellious priest. Sending over some frocked hitman to rub him out.'

'I like it,' Enzo said. 'Maybe an aging cardinal doing his last service for the Church. Strangling Vivaldi with his rosary, or poisoning the communion wine.'

'Too bad it doesn't fit the facts.'

'That's never stopped me before.'

Chapman smiled. 'Of course, we could always ring the Vatican press office and ask them who it was and what he was doing there.'

'How many years have you been here, Andy? You think the Vatican press office will tell us anything? Do you think they *know* anything? There's so much intrigue behind the Leonine walls, I doubt if God himself knows what goes on there.'

'So what do you suggest?'

Enzo paused while a waiter brought the beers and two plates of steaming pasta. He dipped a fork into the fiery sauce and tasted it, nodding his approval.

'First rule of journalism in Italy, maybe anywhere,' he said. 'If you don't know something, let someone else find it out for you.'

'And what exactly does that mean here?'

Enzo took a mouthful of pasta. 'You'll see.'

'Would you like to explain to us what an official of the Vatican was doing at the scene of the murder *before* the police?'

The question was so unexpected that for a moment the whole room fell silent. Then there was a collective shuffling of notebooks, of bottoms on seats as the journalists leaned forwards as one, smelling the scent of blood.

Elena felt her stomach, already queasy at this ordeal by media, plummet to somewhere in the region of her ankles. She hated press conferences, hated the television cameras, the photographers' flashbulbs. Many of her colleagues – Vespignani in particular – relished the exposure, but she was too self-conscious, too uncomfortable in the limelight to enjoy the occasions. She could perform in a courtroom, where she had command of her brief and a limited audience, but these unscripted skirmishes with the press unnerved her. There was too much scope for losing control of the situation, for an all too public humiliation.

It had started well. The chief prosecutor, Alessandro Corona, had made a brief statement, then thrown the conference open to the floor. Most of the questions had been straightforward, inquiries relating to the scene or forensic matters which Elena could avoid with an 'it's too early to say' or a 'we won't know until the reports come back from the lab'. She'd actually received the autopsy report before she went in to brief Corona and Vespignani, but she'd had no time to study it so she'd kept the fact to herself. She had no intention of letting a bunch of journalists know what was in it.

The proceedings had run smoothly for fifteen minutes and Corona had been on the point of ending the conference when, suddenly, Enzo Mattei dropped his bombshell.

The chief prosecutor stiffened visibly at the question and turned to Elena. 'Perhaps you would care to answer that one.'

Elena was furious – with Corona, with Vespignani who she knew had pressed for the conference to get himself on the evening news, but most of all with herself for allowing them to pressure her into attending when she knew so little about the case and couldn't conceal her ignorance.

'I'm sorry, could you repeat the question?' she said. It wouldn't make any difference, she still couldn't answer it, but it gave her a moment's respite.

She could see Mattei a couple of rows back, next to the irritating Englishman she'd thrown out of Vivaldi's apartment. They were getting their revenge now.

'Yes, dottoressa,' Enzo said. 'We have it on good authority that someone from the Holy See was in the Red Priest's apartment first thing this morning. And that he left before the police arrived. Would you like to comment on that?'

Elena took a deep breath, following her instincts to repel an awkward question with one of her own. She was conscious that every eye, every lens in the room was on her.

'What "good authority" are you referring to? Who told you someone from the Vatican was there?'

'You wouldn't expect me to name my source, dottoressa. Are you aware of any Vatican involvement in this murder?'

Enzo was overstating his case, but it was always a good way to get a reaction.

Elena evaded the question. 'I'm afraid I'm not pre-pared to answer that. If you or anyone else have infor-mation pertinent to this inquiry, you should make a formal statement. This is neither the time, nor the place to discuss unsubstantiated allegations.'

'Had the scene of the crime been interfered with in any way?' Enzo countered. 'Have you been in touch with the Vatican at all? Was Father Vivaldi's death related to his well-known, and very public, rows with the Curia?'

'Thank you, ladies and gentlemen.'

Elena gathered together her papers, aware that she was breaching departmental etiquette by terminating the proceedings herself. But she wasn't going to sit there taking all the flak while her two superiors looked on doing nothing to protect her.

She walked out of the conference room with as much dignity as she could muster and waited in the ante-chamber outside for Corona and Vespignani to join her. The deputy chief prosecutor came through the door first. Elena knew he was enjoying her discomfiture.

'That looked bad,' he said. 'Very bad. It looked as if we were running away. You shouldn't have done that.'

'What we shouldn't have done,' Elena said fiercely, 'is hold a press conference on a difficult case when we don't know what the hell happened.'

'Do you know anything about those allegations?'

'No.'

'Then find out.'

'Don't tell me how to do my job.'

'I'll tell you whenever I like, and you'll listen to me.'

'Luigi!'

Corona gave a warning shake of his head, then looked at Elena. He was tall and quietly spoken. He could be aloof and distant, but he always backed up his staff to the hilt. Elena had a lot of respect for him.

'I assigned this case to you particularly, Elena. You know what has to be done. Don't let me down.'

He strode away down the corridor. Vespignani lingered long enough to hiss, 'No more screw-ups, all right?' before scuttling after the chief. His black suit and short legs made him look like an overweight cockroach.

Elena guessed what had happened. That Vespignani had wanted this case for its high profile, but Corona had vetoed his request and given it to her instead. From now on, the deputy chief prosecutor would be looking over her shoulder, waiting for her to make a mistake.

She went to the ladies' toilets, the only place in the building where there was any privacy, and sat in one of the cubicles resisting the urge to cry. She was more upset by Vespignani than the press conference, but she hated herself for letting it get to her. She was tougher than that.

After a few minutes she went back to her office. Baffi approached her as she walked in, then saw her face and retreated. She picked up the telephone and called the headquarters of the *Polizia Giudiziaria*.

'Gianni,' she said when Agostini came on the line. 'The nun we talked to this morning, Sister Anna Maria. I want her brought in to the *Procura* immediately.'

FOUR

Sister Anna Maria looked up in bewilderment as Elena came into the interview room.

'What's happening? Why have I been brought here?'

Elena sat down next to Gianni Agostini and switched on the tape recorder on the table. She noted the time and date, the names of those present and informed the nun of her legal rights.

'Do you understand what I've just said?'

'I don't know why I've been . . .'

'Do you understand your rights, Sister?' Elena interrupted sharply.

Sister Anna Maria bit her lip and nodded. 'Yes, I understand.'

She was nervous, as were most people brought in to the *Procura* for questioning. Not sure what was going on, her initial indignation was gradually being overcome by the prick of a guilty conscience.

'Earlier this morning, Sister,' Elena said, 'you told us that you telephoned the police immediately after finding Father Vivaldi dead in his apartment. Is that correct?'

Sister Anna Maria nodded.

'For the tape, please.'

'Yes,' the nun said. 'That is correct.'

'Was that the only telephone call you made?'

Sister Anna Maria hesitated. Her eyes darted between Elena and Agostini. She knew what it was about now. Her sudden misgivings were clear in her face.

'Was that the only telephone call you made?' Elena repeated.

'I don't understand what this is all about.'

'It's a straightforward question, Sister. Did you telephone anyone other than the *Questura* after you found Father Vivaldi's body?'

The nun looked down. Her shoulders were hunched, her hands clasped together so tightly the veins were standing out from the pale skin.

'I should tell you,' Elena continued, 'that I have asked for the SIP records which will show how many calls were made from the apartment, at what time and to what numbers. It will make things easier for you if you tell us the truth now.'

Sister Anna Maria kept her eyes fixed on the table top, unable to look at Elena. 'I have done nothing wrong,' she said quietly.

'You telephoned the Vatican, didn't you?'

The nun was silent. Elena felt her anger start to simmer. Like any woman who'd been to a convent school, she had no illusions about nuns. She knew their capacity for deceit, for malice, for abusing their power was as great as anyone else's. On occasions, she could still feel intimidated by them, overawed by her childhood memories. But not now. She'd been lied to by a witness and was furious. That the witness was a religious only made the offence more reprehensible.

'If, as you say, you've done nothing wrong,' Elena said, 'why won't you answer my question?'

'I don't have to answer anything.'

'No, you don't. But I warn you, if you say nothing now and the phone records confirm that a call was made, I will charge you with obstructing a judicial investigation. That is a serious charge, Sister.'

Sister Anna Maria lifted her eyes. There was defiance there, but also trepidation. 'I am a nun. My first loyalty is to the Church.'

'Your first loyalty is to the truth. You telephoned the Vatican, didn't you?'

The nun looked away for a time. She gave a nod so slight it would have been easy to miss. Then her head swung back obstinately. 'But that is not an offence.'

'You lied to me this morning.'

'I didn't.'

'You said nothing about that call.'

'That isn't a lie.'

'You play with words, Sister. You know what I mean. And you know what you did. Is a sin by omission not still a sin?'

Sister Anna Maria flared indignantly. 'I think I'm rather better qualified to talk about sin than you.'

'So it would appear,' Elena replied drily.

The nun flushed. Elena followed up quickly, while Sister Anna Maria's resistance was undermined by shame.

'Why did you call them?'

'I did what any other nun would have done in my position.'

'Really? Is that part of your training then? Learning how to interfere with a murder investigation.'

The nun shot her a barbed glance. 'I needed advice. Have you any idea what it was like for me, finding

Father Vivaldi dead? You're probably used to it. You probably see bodies every day.' Her voice cracked then trembled as she went on, 'It's different for me. I knew him. I respected him. To find him there . . . in that condition . . . it was – it was horrible.'

She gave a little sob and bowed her head. Elena felt no sympathy for her. She knew she was being hard on the nun, but Sister Anna Maria had brought it on herself. There would be no breaks to allow her to compose herself this time.

'For advice?' Elena said. 'If it was advice you needed, they could have given it to you over the phone. Ring the police. That was the only advice you needed. Yet they sent someone over to the apartment, didn't they?' Elena leaned across the table, keeping her voice low and aggressive. 'Didn't they, Sister?'

Tears were trickling down the nun's cheeks. Elena glanced at Agostini. He was regarding the nun with concern. He gave Elena a look, as if to ask her to go easy. But she knew there was no gentle way to do it, not with an uncooperative witness.

'Who did you call?'

Sister Anna Maria shook her head, searching in the pocket of her dress for a handkerchief.

'Who was it?'

'This isn't fair,' the nun sniffed. 'You can't question me like this.'

'If you told me the truth I wouldn't have to.'

Elena waited. Sister Anna Maria remained silent.

'Sister.' Agostini was leaning forward, speaking softly. 'Answer the magistrate's questions. If you have nothing to hide, you have nothing to fear.'

Sister Anna Maria removed her glasses and dabbed

her cheeks with her handkerchief, taking no notice of the inspector. Elena gave her a few more moments then lost patience with her.

'I don't think you fully understand your position, Sister,' she said icily. 'I will ask you the question again. If you refuse to answer it, I will obtain an immediate order for your detention in the Regina Coeli prison.'

The nun's head jerked up. She stared at Elena through a film of tears. 'You can't do that. You wouldn't dare.'

'Wouldn't I? I have the powers, and I will not hesitate to use them. Have you ever been in the Regina Coeli? You know they don't segregate convicted prisoners and remand prisoners? Think of the people you'll share a cell with twenty hours a day.'

It was cruel, but Elena judged that it was necessary. There was a streak of stubbornness in the nun that had to be broken.

'Now, who did you call?'

Elena looked at her hard, her mouth taut with the bloody-minded determination that had made her a magistrate in the first place. The shock had stemmed Sister Anna Maria's tears. She knew Elena wasn't bluffing. She lowered her eyes painfully.

'Archbishop Tomassi,' she mumbled thickly.

Elena sat back in her chair. 'Thank you. And who is Archbishop Tomassi?'

'He is the secretary of the Sacred Congregation for the Doctrine of the Faith.'

The title meant nothing to Elena, but she understood when Agostini said: 'The Holy Office.'

'Ah, I see. The Inquisition.'

'It's not like that now,' Sister Anna Maria said

67

defensively. 'Things have changed. The Church is more tolerant.'

'Is it? Did Father Vivaldi find it more tolerant of his views?' The nun didn't reply so Elena continued: 'No, I'm sure that's not something you want to answer.'

She studied Sister Anna Maria. Her eyes were red and puffy, her cheeks still damp.

'Why him in particular? Why Archbishop Tomassi?'

It was a simple question, asked with no hidden agenda, but the nun shifted evasively in her seat as if it made her uncomfortable. It took Elena just a few seconds to guess the answer.

'Eighteen months. You said you'd been with Father Vivaldi for only eighteen months. You were put there to spy on him, weren't you? To keep an eye on him for your masters.'

'That's an outrageous allegation,' Sister Anna Maria spat out resentfully. But the reaction, for all its vehemence, was somehow unconvincing. Elena knew she'd guessed correctly.

'I doubt the archbishop came himself, so who did he send?'

'A young priest. I don't know his name.'

'Why?'

Sister Anna Maria took a deep breath. Her resistance had gone. She wanted only to clear her conscience now. 'He took away some of Father Vivaldi's things.'

'What do you mean?'

'His papers.'

Elena thought she must have misunderstood. 'His papers?'

'His files, his correspondence, his personal papers. The priest took them all.'

Elena sat back heavily, too stunned to respond for a time. Agostini's face revealed a similar, numbed astonishment.

Finally, Elena said: 'You're telling me this priest came to the apartment and searched it, with Father Vivaldi lying dead on the floor?'

Sister Anna Maria nodded. 'Yes, he cleared the desk.'

Elena resisted the urge to swear out loud. She didn't believe what she was hearing. The arrogance of the Vatican was breathtaking. To send someone to the scene of a murder, in what was technically a foreign country, and remove all the victim's personal papers; papers which might well be relevant to the criminal investigation. She found it nigh on impossible to comprehend. But as the initial shock subsided, she found herself boiling with anger.

'Do you know what was in the papers?'

'No. I wasn't privy to that part of Father Vivaldi's life.'

'How many were there?'

The nun shrugged. 'Quite a lot. He took them away in two plastic bin liners.'

'And where did he get the bin liners?'

'He brought them with him.'

'Did he say why he wanted the papers?'

'No. He just took them and told me to telephone the police, but to say nothing about his visit.' She was being more than cooperative now. Seeking absolution by blaming someone else for what she had done.

'Did he do anything else?'

'No.'

It wasn't just their arrogance that was astounding, Elena thought, but their stupidity. Did they think no one would notice the papers were gone, or notice the priest arriving and leaving with two bulging bin liners? She was troubled. The Roman Curia had many faults, but reckless stupidity was not generally considered one of them. She wondered what was going on.

'Is there anything else you haven't told me?'

Sister Anna Maria shook her head. 'Can I go now?'

'Not yet. I'll have a transcript made of this interview. I want you to sign it before you leave.'

'How long will that take? I have a great deal of work to do.'

Elena pushed back her chair and stood up, noting the time and switching off the tape recorder.

'You should have thought of that this morning.'

She opened the door. Sister Anna Maria was gazing up at her bleakly. She seemed drained by the interview. Her face, blotchy and swollen by tears, had the look of a lost child. Confused, upset, a little frightened. Elena wasn't proud of what she'd done in the interview, nor was she ashamed. The *pubblico ministero* wasn't a job for the squeamish.

She went out into the corridor. Agostini stepped out behind her and pulled the door to.

'What do you make of all that?' Elena asked.

'Incredible. What are we going to do?'

'I don't know.'

Agostini gave a sly smile. 'We could always raid the Vatican and haul this archbishop in for questioning.'

Elena grinned at him. 'If only.'

'He brought the bin liners *with* him?' Francesca was incredulous.

'So it would seem.'

'So it was premeditated? He came with the intention of removing evidence from the scene of a crime.'

'Yes.'

'Jesus.'

Francesca swung her legs out from under her desk and crossed them, tugging her skirt down to just above her knees. She bit a nail thoughtfully.

'Complicates things, doesn't it?' she said.

Elena nodded. 'Have you ever had any dealings with the Vatican?'

'No.'

'What's the procedure?'

'The same as for any other foreign state, I assume. Any judicial communication would have to go through the Foreign Office and the Italian Ambassador to the Holy See.'

'Mmm.' Elena pushed the files on her desk to the side and doodled idly on a pad of paper. 'I'd rather not make this official. Not unless I have to.'

'Elena, they removed evidence. How are you going to avoid making it official?'

'I could talk to the archbishop informally first. Discuss our positions.'

'He's a priest, what does he know about positions?' Francesca said with a lewd grin. 'Who is he anyway?'

'The secretary of the Holy Office. It's got some other name now but, as far as I can tell, it's the same thing. It still deals with questions of doctrine and morality, the denunciation of heretics, the discipline of priests. That kind of thing.'

'The hair shirt and scourging department. He sounds fun. Give him a call and see what he's doing tonight.'

'Can we keep this serious? I need to know a bit more about him. To know whom I'm dealing with.'

'You want to ring my aunt? She's very devout, goes to mass every day. She knows all sorts of people over there behind the walls.'

'You've kept her very quiet.'

'Yeah, well, you know, skeleton in the cupboard and all that. When she was young she wanted to be a nun. Fortunately, insanity doesn't run in the family.'

Francesca leaned down and picked up her handbag. She rummaged in it and pulled out her address book.

'You want the number?'

Elena called her. The aunt had met Archbishop Tomassi just once, at a function at the church of San Giovanni in Laterano, the Pope's seat as Bishop of Rome, but she knew a certain amount about him. A charming man, but shrewd, was her description of him. Intelligent, well-read, less sheltered than many priests in the Vatican City, he liked going to the opera and theatre and had a reputation as a fine pianist.

'How powerful is he?' Elena asked.

'As powerful as anyone in the Curia outside the Secretariat of State. The sacred congregations are all theoretically equal, but the Doctrine of the Faith is more equal than the others. He's a very influential man. A future cardinal for certain.'

Elena thanked her for her help and replaced the receiver.

'How does he sound?' Francesca inquired, looking up from her work.

'Cultured,' Elena replied.

'*Dio*. That's the last thing you want in a priest. Be nice to him. He's an official of a foreign power.'

'I'll be as diplomatic as I can.'

Elena looked up the number of the Vatican City main switchboard and dialled it. She asked to speak to Archbishop Tomassi.

'*Sacra Congregatio pro Doctrina Fidei,*' a man's voice said when she was connected.

Elena's mind changed gear, summoning up vague memories of school Latin and her university law studies. She was out of practice, but the translation came readily enough. Sacred Congregation for the Doctrine of the Faith. She hoped the rest of the conversation wouldn't have to be in Latin.

'Archbishop Tomassi, please,' she said.

'Who is calling?'

When he spoke in Italian, Elena noticed the man's foreign accent.

'My name is Elena Fiorini. I'm from the Rome public prosecutor's office.'

The line went quiet.

'Hello?' Elena said.

'I'll see if the archbishop is free.'

She was put on hold for a lengthy period before the man's voice came back on the line.

'What is it in connection with?'

'The death of Father Antonio Vivaldi,' Elena said.

'One moment, please.'

There was a click, another short delay, then a richer, more self-assured voice came on. 'Archbishop Tomassi. How may I help you?'

Elena told him who she was. 'I'm the magistrate in charge of the investigation into Father Vivaldi's murder.'

'Ah, so it is officially murder then?'

'I'm afraid so.'

'That is most unfortunate. Poor man. May I ask if you have made any progress in identifying his killers?'

'I'm not at liberty to divulge that. I wanted to ask you about Father Vivaldi's papers.'

After a pause, the archbishop said in a puzzled tone: 'His papers?'

'The ones that were taken from his apartment this morning.'

'And why would you think I knew anything about that?'

Elena felt her fingers tighten around the telephone. His manner annoyed her. It was hard to identify exactly why, but there was something condescending about it, as if he were doing her a favour by talking to her. He was also stalling, perhaps to gain more information, but it was a tactic she had no patience for.

'Because you sent someone over to get them, your grace,' she said, adding, to forestall any more pretence at ignorance: 'Sister Anna Maria told me she telephoned you after she found the body. Does it all come back to you now?'

Elena glanced across the office. Francesca was giving her a cautionary look. Elena nodded and made herself relax.

'Sister Anna Maria?' the archbishop said.

'The nun who worked with Father Vivaldi.'

'Yes, of course. Why should these papers interest you?'

'I was going to ask you the same question.'

'Father Vivaldi was a Roman Catholic priest. His papers are the property of the Church.'

'Not his private papers.'

'Sometimes it's impossible to distinguish between private and professional papers. We wouldn't want confidential material to fall into the wrong hands.'

'Are you implying the *pubblico ministero* might be the wrong hands?'

The archbishop gave a muted sigh of impatience. 'You're being oversensitive, dottoressa.'

'I don't think so,' Elena said, her resolution to be polite beginning to crack in the face of Tomassi's patronising opposition. 'You're aware it's a criminal offence to remove evidence from the scene of a crime?'

'Evidence? What evidence?'

'You know what I'm talking about, your grace. Anything relating to Father Vivaldi's personal life or his work may be relevant in establishing why he was killed.'

'These papers aren't relevant.'

'I'll be the judge of that. What exactly do they contain that you feel has to be kept from the Italian authorities?'

'I'm afraid I'm not at liberty to divulge that,' Tomassi said, smugly echoing Elena's own words.

She gritted her teeth. 'You had no right to take them. You are interfering in the investigation of a murder.'

'I'm not sure I like your tone,' the archbishop said curtly.

'I don't care whether you like it or not,' Elena replied, finally losing her cool. 'I want those papers returned immediately or I will be forced to take action to obtain them through more official channels.'

'You have no jurisdiction in Vatican City, dottoressa. The laws of Italy don't apply here.'

'What about the laws of morality? Do you think it right to impede the course of Italian justice?'

'I'm not doing that.'

'With respect, your grace, that's exactly what you're doing. I had hoped for your cooperation on this matter. It seems I may have to bring other pressures to bear on you now.'

'Oh yes, and what might they be?' the archbishop asked contemptuously.

'The press are already asking questions about the Vatican's involvement in this case.'

'I am not answerable to the press.'

'And public opinion? The opinion of law-abiding Italian Catholics? Are you answerable to them?'

'This is an internal matter,' Tomassi said. 'It concerns no one else.' But there was a trace of uncertainty in his voice for the first time.

'Father Vivaldi was murdered on Italian soil,' Elena said. 'It is a matter for the Italian authorities to investigate. I will not tolerate any obstruction.'

'You forget whom you're speaking to.' The archbishop's anger crackled down the line.

Elena paused. She didn't want her emotions to show. She wanted her response to be unruffled, professional.

'I will give you twenty-four hours to return the papers,' she said with cold precision. 'Then I will go public and issue a statement to the press outlining what you have done. If that doesn't persuade you, I will issue an *avviso di garanzia* informing you that you are under criminal investigation in the Republic of Italy.'

'This is outrageous. You cannot touch me,' he said venomously. 'I have diplomatic immunity.'

'In addition, I will make a formal request to the

Vatican Secretariat of State for your immunity to be lifted so that I can question you.'

'They will never agree to that.'

'You should understand that I will go as far as I need to get those papers back. I will not allow you to interfere with my duties. I suggest you think carefully about the consequences of your actions. Good day, your grace.'

Elena banged down the telephone and exhaled audibly. The fingers of her left hand were red from gripping the receiver.

Francesca was watching her, her mouth hanging open a little in disbelief. 'Now that's what I call diplomatic,' she said.

The archbishop balled his hands into fists and hammered them just once on to the surface of his carved wooden desk. He was livid, but he didn't believe in overt displays of anger. He allowed himself that one small gesture of frustration, then purged the fury from his system altogether. Emotions were something the mind could control, and he was a man who imposed a rigid self-discipline over his feelings. Anger had a purpose, but it was essentially atavistic, a throwback to man's more primitive ancestry. It was unseemly, and sometimes dangerous, in a man of reason. And Leonardo Tomassi, above all things, looked on himself as a man of reason.

He waited for the door to open and his secretary, Father Ivan Simčić, to enter the office.

'You were listening on the extension?'

Simčić nodded. 'She's bluffing.'

'Perhaps.'

77

'She wouldn't dare.'

'It's wise never to underestimate a magistrate. They have wide powers, and they are keen to assert their independence from the executive.'

'Do you intend to give back the papers?'

Tomassi drummed his fingers lightly on the edge of his desk, musing on his conversation with the public prosecutor. He would have preferred to be dealing with a man; someone whose mind and emotions he understood. Women were a puzzle to him. He had little experience of them, except for the menial servants and compliant nuns he encountered in the Vatican. Their moods, their weaknesses eluded him. He liked to know the nature of his adversaries before he decided on a course of action, but in this case he was fumbling in the dark.

Finally, he looked up at his secretary, his decision made. 'Telephone the Cardinal Secretary of State,' he said. 'Arrange an appointment for me to see him.'

'For when?'

'Tell him I'm on my way over now.'

Enzo received the ball wide on the left wing. He controlled it awkwardly with his right foot and barged his way past a defender. One of his sons came out to tackle him. Enzo feigned a swerve to his left, then went right, but Paolo anticipated the move, stopping the ball with his shins. Enzo got a lucky rebound off his knee and ploughed on, practically knocking the boy over and trampling on him. Ten yards from the goal-mouth, he lifted his head and blasted a shot high over the keeper's head.

Enzo threw up his arms in triumph and raced around

in a circle shouting, '*goooool*' in the manner of an over-excitable television commentator, as if he'd just scored the winner for Lazio against AC Milan. The kids on the makeshift pitch watched him with an air of long-suffering indulgence, unperturbed by the sight of a fat forty-three-year-old running around like a demented dog. Their fathers were just the same.

'It went over the bar,' Enzo's other son, Carlo, said phlegmatically when his father had completed his lap of honour and was bending over, hands on knees, whooping for breath.

'What?' Enzo gasped.

'It was over.'

'No way. Top left corner. Roberto Baggio couldn't have done better.'

'It doesn't count, Papa. It was three metres high at least,' Paolo said, joining in the dispute.

'You're joking? It was just over his head.'

Enzo looked around for support, but the players on his own side were drifting away, disassociating themselves from this family tiff.

'Andy, what do you think?' Enzo said, appealing to the only other adult in the game.

Chapman shrugged. 'It's hard to tell without proper goalposts.'

'Come on, it was in.'

'It was over, wasn't it, Andy?' Paolo said.

'I wasn't watching.'

'You're no use,' Enzo said in disgust.

'Goal-kick,' Carlo said, ignoring his father's protests and getting on with the game.

Enzo went into a sulk and marched back deep into his own half where Chapman was loitering in front of the goal with a glass of beer in his hand. He'd started off in goal, but the neighbourhood kids had sacked him after he'd let four past in as many minutes. He was now doing a feeble impersonation of a sweeper, occasionally kicking the ball upfield while trying not to spill his drink.

'You English,' Enzo snorted. 'You take nothing seriously. That's why you'll never win the World Cup again.'

Chapman grinned at him. 'You want some beer?'

'Put that down, you're embarrassing me in front of my kids.'

'What, you mean more than your football does?'

'Fuck off. That was a goal, wasn't it? You know it was. You saw the way I turned, the control, the devastating power of the shot, the sleek athleticism. Who did it remind you of?'

'Luciano Pavarotti?' Chapman ventured.

Enzo made a childish face. 'This is the last time I have you on my side. Go on, drink your beer. It's all you're fit for.'

They played on into the twilight until the youngsters gradually began to trickle away, called in to the surrounding flats by their parents. Carlo picked up the ball and they went in for dinner, Enzo still arguing with his sons about his disputed goal.

'My own flesh and blood,' he complained to his wife, Claudia, who rolled her eyes and told them to get washed with the patience of a woman accustomed to looking after three wayward children.

'Cleanest shot you ever saw.' Enzo was still chuntering on when they sat down at the table.

'What's he talking about?' Claudia asked Chapman.

'He put the ball into orbit and claimed it was a goal.'

'It *was* a goal,' Enzo spluttered indignantly.

'Only if the posts were on Alpha Centauri.'

'You see how he abuses our hospitality.'

'Just pour the wine, Enzo,' Claudia said.

It was a light meal; no heavy pasta to sit in the stomach overnight. Home-made *minestra in brodo* to start with, followed by veal escalopes, fried potatoes and a green salad, with fruit to finish.

Chapman enjoyed dining with the Matteis. Enzo was entertaining company and his young sons, when they could get a word in edgeways, were lively and talkative. Claudia was quieter than her husband – most people were – but this evening she seemed unusually subdued. Chapman attributed it to tiredness. She had a full-time job as a primary-school teacher as well as a home to run and Enzo was no help around the flat or in the kitchen. Once or twice, Chapman caught her looking at her husband with a puzzled, almost pained expression on her face. It was just a fleeting impression which he wondered about briefly then dismissed. Reading the nuances of a couple's marriage was a futile, often depressing, pastime and he tried not to do it.

But after they'd finished eating and the boys were watching television in the other room, Chapman was helping clear the table and carry the dirty dishes through into the kitchen when Claudia said casually: 'Two nights in a row, Andy. You must be a masochist.'

'Pardon?'

'Having dinner with Enzo.'

She was loading plates into the dishwasher, her back

half turned to him, but she looked round in time to catch the mystified glance he fired at Enzo.

'Oh, yes,' he said feebly. 'It's good of you to have me round. You know I love coming here.'

It was a weak recovery, but the best he could do. He rearranged the crockery on the kitchen table to avoid meeting her eye.

'You'll finish the wine with me, won't you?' Enzo said.

'Yes. I'll get my glass. I left it on the table.'

'I'll fix the coffee. Go and keep the boys company.'

Chapman went through into the living room. Carlo and Paolo were sprawled across a settee watching a game show of such mind-numbing fatuity it appeared to be aimed solely at the under-fives, in both age and IQ. That the contestants were all young women in varying stages of undress might possibly have accounted for the two boys' state of rapt concentration.

Chapman sat down in an armchair, letting the show wash over him, half listening for voices from the kitchen. But he heard nothing until Enzo came in behind him and put a tray of coffee down on the table.

'What's this rubbish?' he said.

He picked up the remote control and changed channels to howls of protest from his sons.

'Hey, I was watching that,' Chapman said.

'Far too intellectual for you. Anyway, I want the news on. Off to bed, you two. Go on, no arguments.'

They missed the opening headlines, but were in time to catch the report on Antonio Vivaldi's death. There was a clip from the press conference at the *Procura*, showing the prosecutors' reaction to Enzo's surprise question. Enzo chuckled as he watched their startled faces captured on film. Chapman looked at Elena Fiorini again, cool and composed at the beginning, mildly flustered as the question was passed to her for an answer, then back in control as she ended the conference. She'd handled it well, he thought. Better than the two stiffs sitting next to her, at any rate.

'It wasn't really fair what you did to her,' he said.

'What?' Enzo snorted. 'You going soft on magistrates now? They dish it out to others often enough. It's time they had a dose in return.'

'Did you get a comment from the Vatican?'

'No. You?'

Chapman shook his head. 'They'll have to comment now.'

He drained his glass of wine and started on his coffee while they finished watching the news bulletin. It was a long time before Claudia came in from the kitchen.

'I think I'll go to bed, if you don't mind,' she said. 'I'm tired. See you again soon, Andy.'

'Yes. Thanks for dinner.'

She gave a wan smile and left the room. Neither she nor Enzo looked at one another.

In the silence that followed, Chapman said: 'Maybe I should go.'

'No. I'm expecting something. It will interest you too. It should be here soon.'

They drank their coffee, talking desultorily. The atmosphere was strained. Chapman studied Enzo. He was staring blankly at the television, his thoughts elsewhere.

'What is it?'

'Uh?'

Chapman stood up and went to the living room door, looking out into the hall. The boys' bedroom door was closed and he could hear the sound of running water in the bathroom. He closed the door and sat back down.

'Did you tell Claudia you were with me yesterday evening?' he asked, keeping his voice low.

Enzo didn't turn his head. He gave no sign that he'd heard.

'Enzo?' Chapman was angry. 'Don't use me as a cover. I resent it. It makes me a party to the deception. I like Claudia. Don't make me lie to her.'

'Yes, yes, don't nag me.'

'Why do you do it? Claudia's so nice.'

'It's none of your business.'

'It damn well is when you use me to conceal what you're doing.'

'Look,' Enzo said tetchily, 'when you've been married fourteen years you'll understand. It's not serious.'

'It is to Claudia.'

'She doesn't know.'

'Of course she knows.'

Enzo rubbed his mouth with the back of his hand. He was getting angry now. An anger fuelled by guilt.

'You're one to talk. You're screwing some other man's wife.'

'That's different.'

'You think so?'

'I'm not committing adultery.'

'You're cuckolding her husband. Does that make you feel good?'

Chapman was silent. Enzo had a point. It was something Chapman didn't like to be reminded of.

'Okay,' he said wearily. 'Let's not fall out over it. But don't use me again, all right?'

Enzo nodded. 'I'll sort it out with Claudia. She'll understand.'

Chapman didn't contradict him. He knew women might forgive, but they never understood. Why should they?

The buzzer from the main door of the apartment block sounded out in the hall. Enzo got up quickly, relieved to find a distraction. He went out and spoke briefly into the entryphone, then went to the front door and opened it. Chapman heard the lift doors open on the landing, footsteps on the tiled floor, a few murmured words. Enzo came back in, clutching a plain brown envelope. He ripped it open and pulled out a couple of sheets of paper stapled together. They were covered in closely spaced type. He read through them, stiffening slightly as he neared the end, and handed the sheets to Chapman.

'What's this?'

'A copy of the autopsy report on the Red Priest.'

'*What?* How did you get that?'

'Read it.'

Chapman perused it carefully. It was clinical, matter-of-fact, full of unpleasant details that turned his stomach. Antonio Vivaldi, a fifty-four-year-old priest with a reputation for gentleness and compassion, had been stripped naked, gagged to stifle his screams and tortured in the most appalling fashion. The technical cause of death had been heart failure, but there was no question that it had been brought about by his violent treatment. His body was covered in burns and bruises caused by blows from some kind of blunt weapon.

'Jesus,' Chapman breathed.

'Sickening, isn't it?'

'Who would do that to a priest?'

'Look near the bottom of the second page,' Enzo said. 'The contents of his stomach.'

Chapman turned over the page and found the relevant paragraph. It listed the foodstuffs that had been found in Vivaldi's stomach and intestines, the remains of his partially digested dinner. One of the items was *olio di ricino*, castor oil.

The implications struck Chapman immediately. Back in the twenties, castor oil was known as 'Fascist medicine'. Mussolini's *squadristi* used to force people they didn't like – socialists, troublemakers, anyone who didn't agree with them – to drink it.

'You're saying Vivaldi was killed by neo-Fascists?'

'Looks like it.'

Chapman took a moment to absorb the information. 'Or someone who wants us to believe it was neo-Fascists,' he said.

Enzo pursed his lips sceptically. 'It's possible.'

'Don't you think they've made it a bit obvious?' Chapman knew that, in Italy, very little was as it seemed. The people were devious, instinctively wary of trusting anyone or anything. Hence their national pastime of seeing plots and conspirators everywhere.

But Enzo was prepared to take this one at face value. 'Subtlety isn't a Fascist characteristic,' he said. 'Arrogance and vanity are. I think they want people to know they killed him, a left-wing priest, a man of the people who loathed Fascists and all they stand for. It's a message, a gesture of strength. A challenge to the authorities. They're standing up and saying:

"We killed him. What are you going to do about it?"'

Enzo glanced at his watch and held out his hand for the autopsy report. 'Excuse me a minute. I have to call the newsdesk.'

FIVE

Elena read through the morning papers with a feeling of anger tempered by grim resignation. The leak of the autopsy results infuriated her, but she knew she would never find the culprit. It wasn't even worth trying. She felt no personal animosity towards Enzo Mattei; it was his job to get information before the authorities wanted to release it. But it was an irritating embarrassment for both her and the *pubblico ministero* that she could have done without.

Her phones had been ringing all morning. Reporters, television stations, news agencies, all wanting to know what progress was being made in the case. Baffi had fielded most of the calls, declining to put any press inquiries through, but Elena still felt the pressure, both externally and from within the office itself. Corona had sent a message saying he wanted to see her at eleven o'clock. It was an ominous sign.

She prepared herself as well as she could, ringing the *Questura* and the *Polizia Giudiziaria* for an update on their investigations, rereading the police and forensic reports, checking through the details of the post-mortem again before she gathered up her files and made the long walk down the corridor to the chief prosecutor's office.

She was shown in by a clerk. Corona was on the telephone but he gestured towards a chair. Elena sat down and put her files on the floor beside her. Corona's office was tidier than the others in the *Procura*, partly because it was bigger, partly because, due to his administrative functions, he had a smaller case-load than the other prosecutors so there were fewer files.

Elena looked around at the law books on the shelves, rehearsing in her mind what she was going to say to the chief. He caught her eye and raised his eyebrows apologetically, making an attempt to cut short his telephone conversation. But whoever was at the other end seemed determined to prolong it further.

Corona covered the mouthpiece with his hand. 'One moment.' Then into the phone: 'Yes, yes, of course. I will look into it straight away. Goodbye.'

He replaced the receiver and straightened the papers on his desk before lifting his head to look at her.

'Dottoressa, good morning. Thank you for coming to see me.'

He maintained an old-fashioned formality with his staff which made him seem colder than he really was.

'I wanted to speak to you about the Vivaldi case.' He produced a newspaper and turned it over so that Elena could see the screaming headline: 'Neo-Fascists linked to Red Priest killing.'

'You've seen this?'

Elena nodded.

'Do you have any idea where it came from?'

'It could have been several places. The morgue staff, the pathologist. The *Questura* and Judicial Police will both have received copies. Dozens of people may have seen the autopsy findings.'

PAUL ADAM

'And your office?'

Elena shook her head. 'Only my clerk and I saw it, to my knowledge. I trust Baffi implicitly. And I certainly didn't leak it.'

Corona screwed up his features as if he'd bitten into a lemon. Elena knew from experience that it was a prelude to his saying something unpleasant.

'This case is only a day old yet we seem to be making rather a lot of mistakes,' he said. 'A leak of a confidential document, a press conference at which a journalist appears to know more about what happened than we do. It's starting to make us look foolish.'

Corona never raised his voice. His views were always expressed in quiet, reasoned tones, like a bank manager talking to a valued customer who'd temporarily, and inadvertently, become overdrawn. But they wounded more than an outburst of pure rage because they played on the recipients' sense of loyalty, making them feel as if they'd personally let him down and had to make amends for their negligence. None of it was strictly Elena's fault, but she knew Corona blamed her. She was the magistrate in charge of the case. Any errors or omissions were her responsibility.

'I'll try to make sure it doesn't happen again,' she said.

The chief gave a murmur of approval and moved straight on to other matters. Reprimanding his staff was a painful duty and he never liked to linger on it.

'Where have we got to?'

Elena filled him in on the details of the case. He listened carefully, leaning forwards with his elbows on the desk. The tips of his fingers were pressed together in front of his face, his chin resting on his outstretched

90

thumbs. He was tall and gaunt, his thin hair drifting around untidily on top of his head. He had a lugubrious manner which made him seem rather dour, but he was not without a sense of humour. The staccato bark of his laugh, like a sudden burst of gunfire, could frequently be heard around the corridors of the *Procura*. But he was guarded, easier to admire than to like. He handled his staff, with their diverse personalities and egos, well. Like everyone else with power in the Italian legal system, he'd learnt the art of compromise.

'Do you believe in this neo-Fascist link?' he asked.

Elena avoided a direct answer, not wanting to commit herself without more hard evidence.

'I have instructed the police to follow it up. We'll see what they find.'

'Would they have a reason for killing Vivaldi?'

'That depends what you call a reason,' Elena replied. 'He was no friend of theirs, but then a lot of other people aren't either and they're not dead. There are plenty of thugs and sadists on the Right. Maybe they just wanted a prominent victim to torture and kill for kicks.'

Corona winced. They were both lawyers, trained to think in a logical, rational way. One of the truths they had to come to terms with in the *pubblico ministero* was that there were people out there in the real world who committed brutal crimes without any intelligible motive.

'Are there any forensic leads?'

'Nothing of real significance. There were some fingerprints on Vivaldi's desk which we have yet to identify. They might belong to his cleaner, or one of the nuns who helped him.' Elena paused. 'Or the priest who took away Vivaldi's personal papers.'

She thought she might get a reaction but, as always, Corona's face remained inscrutable.

'Ah, so that's what it's all about,' he said, almost to himself. 'The phone calls,' he explained. 'You seem to have upset our friends behind the Leonine walls. People have been ringing me all morning. Now I think I'm getting the whole picture.'

'Who's been ringing?' Elena asked, more sharply than she'd intended.

Corona lifted a calming hand. 'There will be no interference from any quarter in the conduct of your investigation. Have no fear of that. The Ministry has merely expressed an interest in the case.'

Elena's mouth tightened. The prosecutor's office was theoretically completely independent of the Ministry of Grace and Justice but she knew that in reality things weren't that simple. Pressures could be applied in other ways, debts called in, old friends pressed for favours.

Corona continued: 'They claim this isn't a strictly judicial matter, but a question of relations with a foreign state.'

'That's just sophistry,' Elena said. 'A crime has been committed and I will investigate it as I see fit.'

'And you have my full support. Tell me about these papers.'

She related the details of her interview with Sister Anna Maria. Corona's brow furrowed a little as he listened, but that was all the emotion he showed. At the end, he pursed his lips and said with unaccustomed passion: 'That is truly unbelievable. If I'd known that, my response to this morning's callers would have been quite different. You have spoken to the archbishop?'

Elena nodded and outlined the gist of her conversation with Tomassi. A wry smile touched the chief's mouth.

'You threatened him with an *avviso di garanzia*? That took some nerve. I doubt the eminent archbishop is used to being spoken to in quite that way.'

'He was being deliberately obstructive,' Elena said. 'I had no choice.'

'He certainly put you in a difficult position. Perhaps a *comunicazione giudiziaria* through the Foreign Office might have been a less contentious course to take.'

'And wait three months for a response? I wanted to act quickly, before the trail goes cold.'

'You think they're involved?'

'No. That's just press overreaction. A good story to sell papers. I think they're hiding the dirty linen, removing Vivaldi's papers in case there's something controversial in them, something they don't want aired in public. It's unlikely to have anything to do with his murder, but I need to see them, all the same.'

Corona leaned back in his chair and ran a finger over his lips pensively.

'I don't want you to take this as criticism, Elena. I assigned this case to you because you have a cool head under pressure. You don't play to the gallery. This investigation needs a low-key approach. Everything we do must be legal and necessary, done for a good reason, not for publicity or show.'

He paused, looking at her directly. 'The Vatican has many influential friends, and the magistracy many enemies – people who fear our independence. Be careful. Don't do anything impetuous. You have a career to think about.'

'I'm more concerned about justice,' Elena said.

'That is commendable. But without a job you won't be able to worry about justice.'

Elena stared at him. 'What are you saying?'

'The knives are out for you already, Elena. I will shield you from them as best I can, but you should be aware of it. Forewarned is forearmed. Keep me informed of your progress.'

He gave a thin smile to indicate that the meeting was over. Elena gathered together her files and stood up.

'I offer you this as friendly advice,' Corona said. 'Nothing more.'

'Thank you,' Elena said.

But as she walked to the door she couldn't help reflecting that sometimes there was only a thin dividing line between friendly advice and a threat.

The first thing Chapman noticed when they walked into the dining room was the overbearing heat. A thick blanket of warm air that wrapped itself around the body, clogging the nose and mouth so that you had to make a conscious effort to breathe through it. It was only then that the smell hit him. The more familiar odours he could identify immediately: onions and garlic and olive oil. It was the other smells, less obvious but equally pungent, which took him a moment to place. He realised it was the people in the room.

There were perhaps thirty of them. Men and women of different colours and ages, crammed next to one another on the wooden benches, all unique but all characterised by the distinctive features of the homeless. The men bearded or unshaven, faces and hands ingrained with dirt. The women blotchy and unhealthy-looking, lank greasy hair clinging to damp foreheads and necks. All of them clad in soiled and torn clothes, their tiny hoards of possessions clutched in plastic bags between their legs or on the benches next to them. The sour scent of unwashed bodies, of rancid sweat and dirty underwear, permeated the air.

Behind the counter that separated the dining room from the kitchen, three nuns were dishing out bowls of pasta with tomato sauce to a dwindling line of derelicts and tramps.

Chapman and Enzo watched from a distance, examining the faces bent over the tables.

'You see him?' Enzo said.

'I don't know. It's hard to tell, their hair's all so long.'

'Let's ask a few of them.'

Enzo approached the nearest table and leaned down. A grizzled old fellow with a shaggy beard and long matted hair was shovelling pasta greedily into his mouth, like a dog bolting its food. This concentrated, frenetic manner of eating was repeated across the room as if the down-and-outs thought the plates might be snatched away from them before they'd finished.

'Excuse me.'

The old tramp didn't look up. He grabbed a chunk of bread from the basket in the middle of the table and dipped it into his tomato sauce.

'Can I talk to you?'

The tramp grasped the edge of his plate and pulled

it closer to his chest, bending over so his face was only a few centimetres above it. He scooped more pasta up and crammed it into his mouth until his cheeks bulged like a hamster's.

'May I ask what you're doing?'

Chapman turned. One of the nuns, the oldest of the three, with greying hair and an expression of indomitable will on her face, was standing behind them.

'Do you have business here?' she asked curtly. 'Who are you?'

Enzo gave her his most ingratiating smile. 'Sister, I hope you don't mind. We just wanted to have a chat with some of these people.'

The nun ran her eyes over him suspiciously, then scrutinised Chapman with the same care. 'You're journalists, aren't you?'

'Yes,' Enzo admitted reluctantly.

'Leave now, please.'

'All we want to do is . . .'

'Now,' the nun said firmly. 'These people are very vulnerable. They don't want to talk to reporters. Particularly about Father Vivaldi.'

'This isn't about Father Vivaldi.'

'Really, you must think I'm stupid.'

'It's for a piece on the plight of the homeless. Perhaps we could interview you too, to discuss the work *Compassione* does to help these unfortunate people.'

'It's strange,' the nun said, 'that we've been here working amongst the poor for ten years and the press has shown almost no interest in what we do. Yet now Father Vivaldi is dead you suddenly want to write about it.'

'The publicity could be very good for you,' Enzo

said, faltering a little under the nun's stern gaze. 'Who knows how much it might help you.'

'You want to help us?' the nun asked, seeming to soften a little. 'You really mean that?'

'Of course.'

'Come here.'

She beckoned them after her, walking towards the exit. On the wall by the door was a padlocked metal collecting box with a slit in the top.

'This is how you can help us most. We rely entirely on donations for the running of the soup kitchen.'

Enzo hesitated, looking at Chapman. Then he shrugged and pulled out his wallet. He put a couple of ten-thousand-lire notes into the box.

'I hope that convinces you of our good intentions,' he said.

The nun turned to Chapman. He felt himself shrink under the implacable force of her stare. He took out his own wallet and added another twenty thousand lire to the box.

'Thank you, gentlemen,' the nun said. 'Will you leave now, please.'

Enzo gaped at her. 'What?'

'You've done your bit to help us and we're most grateful.'

'What about letting us talk to the street people?'

'Oh no, I can't allow that. That would be abusing their trust. They came here for food, not to be questioned by reporters. Good day, gentlemen.'

She herded them out through the door, not actually touching them but driving them before her by the sheer power of her personality. Enzo protested weakly, but his heart wasn't really in it. He knew when he'd been outmanoeuvred. The nun stood by the soup kitchen entrance and watched as they crossed the courtyard and went out through the archway on to the street.

'The cow,' Enzo said furiously, stopping in the narrow strip of shade along the front of the apartment building. 'The Mafia could learn something about extortion from her.'

Chapman leaned back on the wall and grinned at his friend, waiting for him to cool down.

'Forty thousand lire that cost us,' Enzo muttered through clenched teeth. 'And we didn't even get any lunch.'

'We did our bit for the homeless,' Chapman said provocatively.

'You think I care about the homeless?' Enzo took a few paces up the street, burning off some of his anger.

'When you've finished,' Chapman said mildly, 'let's get something to eat in the bar across the street.'

Enzo turned, grimacing. 'The food there will be terrible.'

'Maybe. But we'll be able to spot the tramps when they come out. She can't stop us questioning them in the street, can she?'

Enzo nodded. 'You know what pisses me off most? After twenty years of journalism in this city, I've finally found someone who can't be bribed. My faith in human nature has been destroyed.'

They ordered a couple of beers and two chicken salad *tramezzini*, then positioned themselves at the end of the bar nearest the street, from where they had a clear view of the entrance to the courtyard.

'At least the smell's better in here,' Enzo said. 'A few more minutes over there and I'd have passed out.'

Chapman took a bite of his sandwich. Mayonnaise oozed out and trickled down his chin. He wiped it away with a paper napkin.

'How's Claudia?' he asked.

Enzo shot him an irritated glance and looked down into his beer.

'Did you talk to her after I left?'

'This isn't a good subject, Andy.'

'I'm concerned. You're my friends.'

'We'll sort it out, okay? Talk about something else.'

They stood in silence and ate their sandwiches. Chapman sipped some of his beer. It was so quiet in the bar he could hear himself swallow.

Finally, Enzo said: 'I'm going to break it off. I'll tell Claudia tonight. Does that make you happy?'

'It's what makes *you* happy that counts.'

'I don't know what makes me happy. That's the problem.'

'Who is she?'

'No one. Just a girl.'

'How old?'

'I don't know. Twenty-four.' He glanced up. 'Yes, I know, I'm just another middle-aged fool. But I'm going to end it. I swear.'

Chapman gave a slight nod. He'd heard it before. She wasn't Enzo's first and certainly wouldn't be his last. He changed the subject to relieve his friend's discomfort.

'That was quite a splash you had this morning.'

'Wasn't it just,' Enzo said gleefully, relieved to be talking about something less contentious. His report on the death of Antonio Vivaldi had taken up most of the front page. It was a classic Italian tale of murder, religion and politics. The death on its own merited a fair amount of space. With the addition of a possible Vatican involvement in the killing, and then the circumstantial evidence of a neo-Fascist link, it was a journalist's dream. And Enzo, with characteristic flair and a touch of hyperbole, had milked it for more than it was worth. He had the ability to imply things without actually stating them baldly, a sort of code which allowed the reader to reach conclusions which Enzo, if it suited him, could deny having made himself. He didn't actually accuse either the Vatican or the neo-Fascists of involvement in the murder, but the facts of the case and the response of those two parties made them seem guilty – if you were of a cynical or suspicious nature, and all Italians were. The Vatican had refused to make any comment, so that automatically branded them as shifty and uncooperative. The various right-wing factions had issued denials but they were politicians so no one believed a word they said anyway. Enzo couldn't lose.

What he relished above all else though was scooping his rivals in the Italian press. That was cause for real satisfaction.

'Those pricks from *La Stampa* and the *Corriere* are floundering around like fish in a desert. They haven't a clue what to do,' he said uncharitably.

Chapman put down his sandwich and drank some of his beer. He was looking over Enzo's shoulder, keeping an eye on the building across the street.

'Not everyone had the benefit of the autopsy report,' he said.

'True, but then they don't know the right people to ask.'

'To bribe, you mean.'

Enzo chuckled. 'You check the Ansa wire before you came out?'

'No.'

'The Vatican's finally issued a statement.'

'Saying?'

'What you might expect. They're shocked by Father Vivaldi's death. He was a fine priest, a champion of the poor and weak, etc. etc. The usual bullshit.'

'Nothing about the official in Vivaldi's apartment?'

'He was there in what they call "an advisory capacity".'

'Which means?'

'God knows.'

'Who was he?'

'They don't say.'

'Any explanation as to why he was there before the police, and what he did?'

'Andy, this is a statement from the Vatican. You don't seriously expect it to tell you anything of importance, do you?'

'There's always a first time.'

Enzo gave a snort of amusement. 'You English are so wonderfully naive.'

Chapman straightened up and put down his beer. 'Here we are.'

Enzo twisted round to see what Chapman was looking at. A stooping old tramp in a stained green shirt and shredded trousers was coming out through the archway from the soup kitchen.

Chapman stuffed the last of his sandwich into his mouth and headed for the door.

They ran across the road and caught up with the tramp as he lingered in front of a shop window a few metres from the apartment building. He gazed up at them blankly with bloodshot, empty eyes.

'We're looking for a tramp with only one ear,' Enzo said. 'Do you know him?'

'Eh?'

Enzo repeated the question. The tramp muttered something over and over in thick Roman dialect and shuffled away on unsteady legs.

'What did he say?' Chapman asked.

'Nothing worth hearing. Leave him, we won't get any sense out of him.'

They walked back to the archway and waited for more vagrants to come out of the soup kitchen. Enzo was still clutching the remains of his *tramezzino*. He popped the last crust into his mouth and swallowed it.

'We'll be lucky to get much out of any of them,' he said. 'They're either too drunk, too insane or too bloody-minded to answer questions.'

'You make them sound like the Chamber of Deputies,' Chapman said.

Enzo grinned. 'That's rather unfair to tramps.'

'Let's try this one.'

Another of the street people was coming across the courtyard. They blocked his path and Enzo asked him the same question. He didn't appear to hear for he simply staggered around them and walked on, grumbling unintelligibly to himself.

'Is it the way I ask them?' Enzo said.

They moved to the side of the archway, watching a few more scruffy individuals come out. A woman turned in from the street and walked purposefully past them. Chapman caught a whiff of her scent. She had short, dark hair and big oval sunglasses covering her eyes. He watched her go into the stairwell of Father Vivaldi's apartment building and turn right, disappearing from sight into the vestibule which led to the *Compassione* office.

Enzo, meanwhile, had stopped another of the down-and-outs – this time a malodorous youth with a crippled foot and patchy beard – and was busy quizzing him.

'What?' the young man said belligerently.

'With one ear. Do you know his name?'

'Maybe.'

'What d'you mean, maybe? Do you know him or not?'

'You got any cigarettes?'

Enzo got the message. He took out a five-thousand-lire note and held it between his fingers. The tramp tried to snatch it but Enzo pulled it away out of reach.

'His name first.'

'Why d'you want to know? You cops?'

'No.'

'Gimme the money.'

'His name.'

'Beppe. Now gimme the money.'

Enzo let him take the note. 'Where can we find him?'

'Another.'

'What?'

The tramp was holding out his hand for more cash.

Enzo took a second five-thousand-lire note from his wallet. 'This is it. No more, okay?'

The tramp grabbed the note and stuffed it away in the pocket of his filthy trousers.

'Where is he?'

The tramp shrugged. 'Around.'

'Look, I gave you money,' Enzo said, starting to get riled.

'I gave you an answer. He doesn't have an address. He's just around. Here, Termini, along the railtracks. He could be anywhere. Now fuck off and leave me alone.'

Enzo reached out. 'Why, you little shit.'

'Enzo!' Chapman pulled him away. 'Let it go. Forget it.'

Enzo took a deep breath and nodded. The young vagrant curled his lip at them and limped off down the street on his deformed foot.

'The little bastard,' Enzo swore. 'This is becoming an expensive day.'

'I know,' Chapman said. 'Still, it restores your faith in human nature, doesn't it?'

'Let's get out of here. I've had enough of these people.'

'One moment.'

Chapman was watching the woman in the sunglasses come back across the courtyard. She was wearing a white blouse and skirt which gleamed in the sunlight. He could smell the freshness of her perfume as she drew nearer.

'Excuse me,' he said. 'I couldn't help noticing where you went. Do you help with the *Compassione* soup kitchen?'

'Not the soup kitchen. I help out in the office. Why?'

Chapman explained who he was and introduced Enzo. The woman recognised his name.

'Enzo Mattei? You wrote that piece in this morning's paper?'

He nodded. 'Could we talk to you about Father Vivaldi? In the office, maybe.'

'It's locked. The police sealed it yesterday. I thought I might be able to get in today but . . .' She gave a slight shrug. 'I don't feel much like working anyway.'

'Can we buy you a drink across the street?'

She hesitated, half glancing over her shoulder as if she feared someone might be watching her.

'All right,' she said. 'A quick one.'

They found a table at the back of the bar where they'd had lunch. It was hidden away in the gloomy recesses, out of direct sunlight but still too hot and airless for comfort. The door to the lavatory was close by and the faint odour of sewage wafted out, less fetid than the stench in the soup kitchen but unpleasant all the same. Italians rarely sat down in bars because it put up the price of drinks. These greasy brown-topped tables and the cheap wooden chairs around them were little used except by the unsuspecting backpackers and student travellers from the cheap *pensioni* in the surrounding streets who came in for *cappuccini* at breakfast and paid for them through the nose.

The woman said her name was Giulietta Ricci. She'd worked for Antonio Vivaldi for the past four years, typing his letters, answering the telephone, arranging meetings, doing the books and the general adminis-tration of his charity.

'His death must have hit you hard,' Chapman said.

Her mouth twitched mournfully. 'It did. I spent most of yesterday in tears. After the police had finished questioning me, I went home and wept all afternoon. He was a wonderful man. The kind of priest who made you believe in goodness. He was overflowing with it.'

Giulietta smiled. 'He had this public image of a turbulent, rebellious cleric, but he wasn't like that at all. He was outspoken, and I think he enjoyed upsetting the Vatican – he regarded it as his duty to shake them out of their complacency, to remind them of the Church's obligation to protect the poor and the defenceless – but he was a different man in his daily life. Gentle, quietly spoken, humorous. Ask anyone who knew him.'

She glanced at them, a little apologetically. 'I'm sorry. I'm being rather gushing about him.'

Chapman studied her casually as she sipped her Campari and ice. She looked as if she was in her late thirties, maybe a bit older, but there was something youthful and almost ingenuous about her. She had one of those open, trusting natures that journalists relished.

'We tried to talk to the nuns in the soup kitchen earlier,' he said. 'They weren't very helpful.'

Giulietta waved a contemptuous hand. 'They're not very friendly. They help out but they're still, you know, nuns. What I mean is, they're part of the organised Church. They didn't work specifically for Father Vivaldi.'

'Which you did?'

'Oh yes. I'm paid a small salary by the charity. The nuns are volunteers. They're good women, but' – this was her real gripe – 'they're very bossy. They think they can tell everyone what to do.'

Enzo sympathised with the comment. 'Yes, we noticed that too,' he said sourly.

'What will happen to *Compassione* now?' Chapman asked.

'I don't know. But Father Vivaldi's work must carry on. The trustees of the charity will have to find someone to take his place.'

'The trustees. Not the Vatican?'

'Oh no, it's nothing to do with them. If they had had their way it would have been closed down long ago.'

'Don't they approve of it? A soup kitchen for the homeless?'

'No, it's not that.' She rolled the ice cubes around in the bottom of her glass. 'It was Father Vivaldi they didn't approve of. They didn't support *Compassione* – I mean financially. They didn't give it any money. But it was the Father they wanted out of the way.' She paused and seemed to reconsider her phrasing. 'You know, out of their hair. He made things difficult for them.'

'He had quite a few disputes with them, didn't he?' Chapman said.

'It was like a running battle. He was there only the day before yesterday, in fact.'

Chapman turned his head to look at Enzo who sat up and started to pay more attention.

'He liked to go there,' Giulietta said. 'To ruffle their feathers and defend himself. I think he found it, well, invigorating.'

Chapman lifted a hand to stop her. 'You say he went to the Vatican the day before yesterday?'

'That's right.'

Enzo leaned closer across the table. 'The day he died?'

'Yes, I suppose it was. In the afternoon.'

'Was that out of the ordinary?'

She nodded. 'It surprised me. He wasn't exactly *persona grata* there.'

'Was he summoned?'

'I can't think why else he would've gone. I don't know much about it, I'm afraid. He went to hospital in the morning . . .'

'Was he ill?' Chapman interrupted.

'Oh no, to visit a patient. He did that all the time. Then, when he came back, he went upstairs to his apartment to do some work. It was after lunch that he came into the office and said he had to go to the Vatican.'

'Did he say why?'

'No. He was in a hurry. He just mentioned it in passing and left. I didn't see him again after that.'

The implications of what she'd said seemed to hit her. She swallowed hard and touched her mouth to stop her lips trembling.

'What's this all about?' she asked nervously. 'You're not going to quote me on any of this, are you?' She seemed to be regretting her openness now.

'It's just background,' Chapman said reassuringly.

'I'm not sure I should have said anything.'

'It was all true, wasn't it?'

'Yes, of course.'

'Then there's nothing to worry about.'

Giulietta pushed back her chair and picked up her handbag. 'I have to be going. You're sure my name won't appear in the paper?'

'Promise,' Enzo said.

They watched her walk across the bar and out on to the street. Then Chapman stretched out his legs and put his hands behind his head.

'Interesting, eh? He goes to the Vatican the day he's killed. Is that just a coincidence?'

Enzo clicked his tongue impatiently. 'In Italy, Andy,' he said slowly, as if he were addressing a simpleton, 'there is no such thing as a coincidence.'

SIX

The papers were arranged in neat piles on the shiny surface of the desk. Archbishop Tomassi fingered them pensively, straightening their sides in a nervous gesture which betrayed the turmoil inside his head. There had been few occasions in his life when the process of making a decision had been so hard. He had always, even as a young priest, had a belief in himself, a certainty of purpose which had marked out the path he should take with a clarity that allowed for no doubts.

It was a characteristic that, allied with a fierce, single-minded ambition, had brought him to the top of the most powerful sacred congregation in the Catholic Church. In the closed world of the Vatican, a spiritual haven riven by temporal in-fighting and rivalry, it made him a feared and formidable operator. It gave him the strength to crush his opponents, to force through his views. But when, infrequent though it was, that strength failed him, he was left feeling impotent and confused, for neither his personality nor his experience had prepared him for uncertainty.

He got up from his chair and walked to the window of his office. He was torn between his duty to himself as an honest man and his duty to the Church as its faithful servant. He had talked to the Cardinal Secretary of State and spent some time in his private chapel, praying for guidance, but was still unsure what to do. Even the Lord, it seemed, had temporarily deserted him.

He looked out of the window. The Palace of the Holy Office was on the south side of St Peter's Square, outside the walls of the Vatican City itself but still part of the Holy See. He had a clear view across to the Apostolic Palace and the windows of the papal apartments where the Holy Father lived and worked. Below, in the piazza, the crowds of tourists were milling around the obelisk of Caligula in the hot afternoon sun. Others were seeking shade beneath the spreading arms of Bernini's colonnade or climbing the steps into the cool opulence of the basilica. He stood here every day yet had never lost the sense of awe he'd felt the first time he'd set eyes on St Peter's, some fifty years earlier when his father had brought him to Rome as a boy. The square, the cupola, the interior of the cathedral still overpowered him with their sheer scale and their beauty. He was not a sentimental man, but he could never gaze on them without feeling moved by the grace of God's creation.

He watched the people, tourists and pilgrims, making their way across the vast piazza, wondering how many of them had never seen St Peter's before, envying them that first wondrous glimpse that would never be his again and remembering the ten-year-old boy who had stood open-mouthed in the nave of the basilica and decided there and then to become a priest.

He turned away, feeling burdened by the weight of his position. It was impossible to work in the Vatican without being aware of its history, without being intimidated by the two thousand years of faith that had passed and the thousands more that were to come. To the true believer, the lifespan of the Church was infinite. It would be here long after Tomassi was gone and it was sometimes difficult for him to come to terms with his own paltry insignificance.

His predecessors had no doubt faced decisions of equal, if not greater, magnitude. The Holy Office went back more than four centuries to the Congregation for the Holy Inquisition of Heretical Error, to the bloodcurdling days of the rack, the *auto-da-fé* and the stake. Rebels and heretics were easier to control then, though none the less numerous despite the Draconian penalties. The human spirit could resist anything for its beliefs. It was what had founded and then sustained the Christian Church over two millennia. Tomassi admired this strength of purpose in dissenters even when their opinions infuriated him, but it caused him heartache to deal with them. Antonio Vivaldi had been a troublesome priest in life, but his legacy was proving to be more dangerous by far.

The archbishop sat down again at his desk and touched the piles of papers once more. For better or worse, he had made his decision.

He picked up the telephone and asked his secretary to get him the Rome public prosecutor's office.

'Dottoressa,' he said when Elena Fiorini came on the line, 'I have reconsidered my position. I would be grateful if you would come to my office. I will send a car for you. Then I will hand over Father Vivaldi's papers to you in person.'

It was like a furnace in the back seat of the Alfa Romeo.

Elena had her window full open but the air blowing in was warm and thick with exhaust fumes. She rested an arm on the window ledge to allow the draught to circulate under her jacket and around her back, but it didn't make much difference. With her handkerchief she discreetly wiped a drop of perspiration from her forehead and pulled her hair back behind her ears.

The archbishop's telephone call had surprised her, as much by its placatory tone as by its content. She had expected him to make things much more difficult for her. She would have preferred to drive herself – sending a car gave Tomassi the initiative, which she didn't like – but it seemed churlish to refuse his offer of a lift. And besides, it was far simpler to cross the frontier into the Vatican City in an official car than have all the fuss of arranging entrance and parking permits for her own vehicle.

They drove south from the Piazzale Clodio, looping round the open end of St Peter's Square and in through the gates to the left of the basilica. The Swiss Guards, resplendent in their blue, orange and red slashed doublets, saluted as the Alfa Romeo passed by and parked in front of the Palace of the Holy Office. The young priest sent to collect her, who'd introduced himself politely as Father Ivan Simčić and said not a word more the whole journey, escorted her into the building and up in a lift to the fourth floor. The palace wasn't air-conditioned, but its thick stone walls and gloomy passages made it pleasantly cool.

Father Simčić opened a pair of double doors and showed Elena into a spacious, marble-floored office. Archbishop Tomassi stood up and came out from behind his desk, one arm extended. He was only of medium height, but the long black cassock he was wearing made him appear taller.

Elena shook his hand. 'Your grace.'

'Dottoressa Fiorini. Thank you for coming. May I offer you some refreshment? Tea, coffee, something cold? Mineral water, fruit juice? We have a refrigerator in the outer office.'

'Mineral water would be nice, thank you.'

The archbishop nodded at his secretary who went out through another door and closed it behind him.

'Please take a seat,' Tomassi said, going back to his own chair. He adjusted the angle of the electric fan on the desk to direct the cool air nearer to Elena.

'Have you been in the Vatican before?'

'Only St Peter's and the museum,' Elena said.

He told her a little about the Palace of the Holy Office and the Congregation, making small talk while they studied and assessed each other.

Elena saw an elderly but energetic man with plump features and sharp eyes behind his horn-rimmed spectacles. He had a touch of colour in his cheeks and the look of someone who enjoyed good food and wine. He didn't resemble at all the image she'd had in her mind of a gaunt, ascetic archbishop.

Tomassi, for his part, saw an attractive dark-haired woman, younger than he'd expected. He was indifferent to women on a sexual level but he could still admire their form and beauty as he might a fine painting. She wasn't exceptionally beautiful, but there was warmth and character in her face and something about her manner that spoke of integrity. There was nothing deferential in her demeanour. She was confident, neither overawed nor intimidated by the Vatican or him. He was unaccustomed to dealing with women who were used to power and who handled it well. He had to remind himself that she was a magistrate with considerable status in Italy. None in the Vatican, of course, but that didn't mean he should be any less wary of her.

'The Congregation for the Doctrine of the Faith deals with all aspects of the teaching of the Catholic faith,' he was saying. 'We have a duty to examine theological texts and other writings to ensure they are consistent with papal policy.'

'And if they are not?' Elena asked.

'Then we must condemn the errors and make sure they are corrected.'

'Do you not believe then in constructive debate?'

Tomassi eyed her narrowly, aware that this was dangerous ground, but confident that he would have the upper hand in any discussion of Church affairs.

'A certain amount of pluralism is inevitable in this world,' he said. 'But that doesn't mean it's not possible to achieve a unity of knowledge and faith.'

'You mean, that everyone will eventually come round to your way of thinking?' Elena said provocatively. 'Is that what you hoped would happen with Father Vivaldi?'

'Father Vivaldi and I had many things in common.'

'But he was a thorn in your flesh.'

'On certain issues. We had our differences, of course. I believe a priest's role is primarily spiritual and pastoral. Father Vivaldi added a political dimension that was unacceptable to the leaders of the Church.'

Elena regarded him drily. 'Come now, your grace, are you saying there is nothing political about the Vatican?'

115

'In our relations with the Italian Republic, no. It is no part of a priest's duties to influence social policy in Italy.'

'Even when he sees injustice and hardship around him?'

The archbishop was saved from answering by the door opening. Father Simčić entered and placed a tray on a table at the side of the office. He poured mineral water into a glass and turned to Elena.

'Lemon and ice, dottoressa?'

'Thank you.'

He brought it over to her. He was about her age, slightly built with a sallow skin and dark, sunken eyes. Elena guessed he was the priest who'd been sent to remove the papers from Antonio Vivaldi's apartment.

Tomassi waited for a cup of tea to be poured and brought to his desk, and for his secretary to leave, before he said: 'Our differences of opinion with Father Vivaldi received a lot of unfortunate publicity, but I admired him in many ways. He was a man of conscience, who practised what he preached. But he was naive in his criticisms of the Church.'

The archbishop removed the wedge of lemon from his tea and deposited it in his saucer. Then he stirred the liquid carefully with a tiny silver spoon.

'He believed the Church could function today the way it did two thousand years ago. One man and a few disciples spreading the word of God, living simply, depending on others for alms. That is not a realistic proposition in the modern world. Whether we like it or not, the Catholic Church is a vast multinational organisation with salaries to pay, buildings to maintain.'

'A bureaucracy to support, Father Vivaldi would have said,' Elena interjected.

The archbishop sniffed impatiently. 'Someone has to run it. Yes, the Curia is a bureaucracy but compared to most governments, most civil servants, we are cheap and efficient. We do not live in the lap of luxury, our salaries are low. We are men without families to support and we dedicate our lives to the service of the Church. Is that such a bad thing?'

Elena sipped her mineral water, wondering when they would get to the real purpose of her visit. The archbishop was hospitable and disarming but she hadn't forgotten what he'd done, nor forgotten his hostility on the telephone.

'Your grace,' she said. 'Father Vivaldi's papers.'

'Ah, yes. They are ready for you, though I doubt you will find much of interest in them.'

'You have vetted them?'

'I wouldn't put it quite like that.'

'How would you put it?'

Tomassi shifted in his seat and fiddled with the gold cross at his breast. 'I'm aware you disapprove of what we did,' he said.

'My approval or disapproval doesn't enter into it,' Elena replied. 'I am a public servant. I act on behalf of the people.'

'*Salus populi suprema est lex.* "The good of the people . . ."'

'"Is the chief law."' Elena finished the quotation for him. 'Yes, I know my Cicero. It's a worthy sentiment, but I think I prefer Juvenal: *Omnia Romae cum pretio.* "Everything in Rome has its price." That seems more accurate in this day and age, don't you agree?'

'We're not in Rome, dottoressa.'

'I know. As you so kindly reminded me on the phone.'

She was being discourteous and knew it. But the archbishop's manner was just a little too conciliatory to be believable.

'It was important for us to look at the papers,' Tomassi said. 'Many of them are confidential. Many relate to Church business. We were worried. Things have a habit of leaking out once the police get their hands on them.'

'I can assure you nothing will leak out from my office,' Elena said.

'I'm sure it won't.'

She drank the last of her water and stood up. 'Perhaps I could take them now.'

'They're rather heavy. My secretary will carry them out to the car for you. Thank you for your time.'

He showed her to the door and shook her hand again. Elena smiled politely, wondering why he was being so cooperative. Over the years in the *pubblico ministero* she'd developed a nose for evasion. She knew when someone, even an archbishop, wasn't telling her the whole truth.

Tomassi gave her time to leave, watching his secretary follow her out of the office with two large cardboard boxes full of papers. Then he closed his door and walked back to his desk. Pulling open the top drawer, he took out a thin sheaf of documents and studied them for perhaps the twentieth time since Simčić had brought them from Vivaldi's apartment. Tomassi could tell from the paper and the writing on them that they were photocopies. What he had to do now was find out where the originals were.

The Piazza dei Cinquecento, in front of Termini, the central railway station, was always teeming with people; passengers streaming out of the huge terminal building, others queuing for taxis or waiting for buses at one of the many ranks drawn up across the square. In daylight, it had a functional seediness. Apart from the scattering of tramps and drunks, nearly everyone had a purpose for being there. They were travellers hurrying for a train, workers heading for the office or home, tourists emerging blinking into the harsh sunlight looking for hotels or the bus to San Pietro. But at night it took on a different aspect altogether.

As dusk fell, and the workers disappeared to the suburbs, the square was taken over by a new, more colourful array of characters: Ethiopians in long robes selling trinkets and wooden carvings; youths clustered in groups eating slices of pizza from the nearby *trattorie*; and crowds of Filipinos, domestic servants in Rome as they were elsewhere, meeting friends and relatives as if the piazza were some kind of open-air salon. Backpackers and foreign students drifted around the edges looking for somewhere cheap to eat or simply soaking up the atmosphere, and under the streetlights, garishly clad and plastered with make-up, transvestite prostitutes touted for trade.

Chapman walked across towards the station, for once looking for vagrants and beggars rather than trying to avoid them. He'd been round the streets next to Termini, been through the courtyards of the buildings near Antonio Vivaldi's apartment and checked every corner of the piazza itself. Now only the railway terminal remained.

In his jacket pockets were a large bottle of strong *grappa* and a supply of cigarettes, already depleted by the packets he'd given away as bribes in his search for the one-eared vagrant named Beppe.

He went through the main doors into the ticket hall of the station, then on into the concourse. Even at this time of night it was crowded with people. The destination boards at the ends of the platforms were mostly blank, but a few announced late departures to places as diverse as Naples, Milan, Venice and Paris. The night train to Zürich was just pulling out, the clatter of its carriages echoing around the lofty vaults of the concourse.

Chapman loved continental railway stations. More than anywhere else in the world they seemed to have retained the true glamour of travel. The bustling excitement, the smells and crowds, the exotic locations that conjured up memories of sleepers to Moscow, the Orient Express, images from films of beautiful blondes and dangerous men crossing platforms shrouded in smoke and mystery. They were places where even the most commonplace journey could be transformed into an adventure by a little imagination and a whiff of nostalgia.

But tonight Termini was just another ugly, soulless building. A place of straggling travellers and itinerants huddled in corners, of bored ticket collectors and porters, of dirty carriages and characterless electric locomotives, and a tired, lone journalist looking for a tramp who seemed to have disappeared off the face of the earth.

Chapman toured the perimeter of the concourse, questioning the down-and-outs who were settling down for the night, overcoming their foul-mouthed hostility with offers of a cigarette and a swig of *grappa*. He asked a cleaner, a ticket inspector and the barman at the station cafe too but, though they knew who Beppe was, none of them had seen him for a couple of days.

He went to the far end and out on to the platform. A couple of trains were waiting on *binari* 10 and 11 in the centre, but the other tracks were deserted. Chapman walked along the platform, keeping to the shadows near the wall. He emerged from under the station roof and kept going. There were lights ahead of him marking the way to the signal box. He went down the ramp at the end of the platform and crunched along the gravel beside the track. Empty coaches were parked in a siding to the right. Chapman clambered on board one and walked down the corridor peering into the compartments. He went through into the next coach, and the next, and found a dosser stretched out across the seats. He was wrapped up in a tatty old blanket and had his head propped up on a bulging canvas sack. The compartment stank of brandy even cheaper than the bottle Chapman had in his pocket.

'You awake?'

The dosser didn't stir. Chapman prodded him with his foot.

'Wake up.'

The man rolled on to his side and grunted. Chapman sat down on the row of seats opposite and pulled out the *grappa*.

'You want a drink?'

121

The man opened his eyes and looked at him. Chapman could see the whites standing out in a face so caked in muck it blended seamlessly into the darkness all around it.

'Uh?'

'A drink.'

Chapman offered him the bottle. The tramp reached out a hand and grabbed the bottle by the neck. He gulped down a large mouthful before Chapman snatched it back.

'Gimme some more,' the tramp said aggressively.

'I'm looking for someone called Beppe. You know him?'

'Give it here.'

'He hangs around the station. Where does he sleep?'

The tramp pushed himself up on an unsteady elbow, breathing noxious fumes across the compartment.

'What?'

'Have you seen him?'

'Who?'

'Beppe. Only one ear.'

The tramp flailed out with a hand, trying to get the bottle, but he was so drunk he misjudged the distance and tumbled off the seat on to the floor. Chapman lifted his feet and put them down on the tramp's back.

'Where can I find him?'

'Uh?'

Chapman tried one last time. 'Beppe. Do you know where he is?'

The tramp waved an arm. 'Don't know. Down there. Under wall. Get off me.'

Chapman lifted his feet and pulled himself up, stepping over the tramp to reach the door.

'Hey, *grappa*,' the tramp mumbled angrily, trying to sit up.

'It's bad for you,' Chapman said and went out.

He climbed down from the train and kept on walking along the side of the tracks. There were fifteen or sixteen lines running parallel to each other here, but as he got further from the station they started to merge together, reducing to only four. Rows of low-rise flats poked their unsightly heads over the wall that formed the boundary of the railway property and in front of the wall, mixed in incongruously with the modern brickwork, were the remains of an ancient Roman aqueduct. It was hard to believe that this whole area, now a barren wilderness criss-crossed with steel rails and a spider's web of overhead electric wires, had once been the gardens and citrus groves of the Villa Massimo Negroni.

Chapman walked on for another half kilometre, scouring the shadows by the wall for any signs of life but, as far as he could see, the area was deserted. He stopped and looked back. The roof of the station was a stark silhouette against the pale Roman skyline. A few hazy lamps glinted in the concourse, providing just enough light to show up the tiny matchstick figures moving around the platforms.

There was no one out here. The tracks stretched endlessly into the distance, the rails silver and shiny like giant slug trails. It was eerily quiet except for the hum of the breeze through the catenary wires and the background throb of the city traffic. There was no point in going any further. It was too bleak, too exposed out here for any vagrant. They would be back closer to civilisation, scavenging around the

123

yards of the restaurants and bars or seeking company for the long hours of darkness.

Chapman retraced his steps and it was only then, approaching from a different direction, that he noticed a faint orange glow low down on a section of wall set back from the rest. From the flickering fingers of light and the wisps of smoke he could tell it was a fire. He cut across the open land next to the track and, behind a stack of concrete railway sleepers, found a slight figure sitting cross-legged by a tiny campfire. The figure glanced up as Chapman loomed over him. He had long, unkempt hair hanging down to his shoulders but in the light from the fire Chapman could see the ugly, swollen scar where his left ear should have been.

'You're Beppe, aren't you?'

Beppe looked back at the fire, not saying anything. Chapman crouched down.

'Mind if I stay a while?'

He took some cigarettes out of his pocket and offered the tramp one. Beppe took it without a word and lit it with a piece of glowing wood from the campfire. His hands were shaking.

'You all on your own out here?'

Beppe sucked in on his cigarette and blew smoke out through nostrils caked in dirt.

'You want those cigarettes?' he said.

Chapman gave him the packet. Then he took the brown paper bag containing the *grappa* out of his jacket and placed it on the ground. Beppe saw the neck of the bottle protruding from the bag.

'Who are you?'

'How about a drink?'

124

'You don't look like one of those *FS* bastards, come to move me on.'

'I just want a chat.'

'You a fucking priest?'

'Do I look like a priest?'

Chapman reached into the bag and brought out the *grappa* while Beppe studied his face and clothes.

'Maybe not. The priests never bring booze. Just a sermon and enough pity to make you puke.'

Chapman gave him the bottle. 'Did Antonio Vivaldi do that?'

Beppe took a long swig and hung on to the bottle. He was little more than a boy. He had a young body and face, but the eyes of someone much older, someone much more cynical than any kid his age deserved to be.

'Vivaldi?' he said. 'You a cop?'

'No. You use the *Compassione* soup kitchen, don't you? You weren't there today.' Chapman looked around. They were in a slight hollow, sheltered from the wind by the stack of sleepers. 'You sleep out here at night?'

'Sometimes.' Beppe took the cigarette out of his mouth and rested his hand on his knee. The cigarette smoke drifted away, blending with the thicker smoke from the wood fire. 'What do you want?'

'To talk about Vivaldi.'

'Vivaldi's dead.'

'Did he come out here ever? To give you a sermon?'

'He was different. He did something useful. He gave people food but didn't think that meant we had to listen to him spouting on about God.'

'How come you weren't there today?'

'I don't go every day.'

'Why not? Free food, someone to talk to, why not today?'

'You're not a cop, you're not a priest or a railway worker. What are you?'

'Journalist.'

Beppe seemed relieved by the answer. Chapman took back the bottle of *grappa* and had a sip himself, just to be sociable. It burnt his throat on the way down.

'How did you find me?' Beppe asked.

'Luck.'

'Anyone tell you where to look?'

'I looked everywhere. The streets, in front of Termini. This was the only place left.'

He'd been fortunate. Beppe had chosen a good spot, hidden on three sides by the brick wall and the sleepers. If he hadn't lit a fire, Chapman would never have found him.

'I thought you slept near the soup kitchen. In the courtyard.'

'Who told you that?'

'A neighbour.'

Beppe reached out for the *grappa* and gulped down a mouthful as if it were water. He was on edge. His bony fingers and gaunt arms – scarred with the marks of the needle – twitched constantly. Chapman had seen his type before; damaged kids whose idea of mortality extended to their next fix and not beyond.

'How did you lose your ear?' he asked.

'Why would you care?'

'I was just interested. Did you like Father Vivaldi?'

'What's it to you?'

Beppe was getting irritated by all the questions. It

126

was what Chapman wanted. A chink in the armour of cool indifference that he could prise open a little.

'Are you glad he's dead?'

'What the fuck is this? Leave me alone.' Beppe had some more *grappa*, then a drag on his cigarette.

'The neighbour thought he might have been killed by one of the street people who used the soup kitchen.'

'What?' Beppe squinted at him through the smoke.

'For the cash in his apartment. Money to buy drugs.'

'It's always us, isn't it?' Beppe said angrily. 'Every fucking thing that happens, we're to blame. No homes, no jobs, no money, we're just idle bums, parasites who live off everyone else. Tramps who make pricks like you feel guilty, maybe a little scared, so you have to turn your anger on us to make yourselves feel better. Why would any of us have wanted to kill Vivaldi? He helped us, for Christ's sake, which is more than the likes of you do.'

'But he was a soft touch, wasn't he? Someone you could take advantage of. It would've been easy to go up to his apartment, get him to let you in, then kill him and take what you could.'

'You're talking through your arse,' Beppe said, leaning aggressively across the fire. 'I can tell you for a fact that none of us had anything to do with it.'

'Oh yeah? How can you be so sure? Was it you? Did you do it?'

'Fuck off.'

Beppe downed another mouthful of *grappa*, the alcohol fuelling his fury. Chapman kept at him.

'Who're you hiding from, Beppe?'

'What?' He looked up sharply.

'Out here. Is it the cops?' Chapman knew this wasn't the tramp's regular pitch. He could tell from the surroundings; the absence of rubbish, of discarded cigarette butts, of any sign that someone had lived here for any period.

'You're scared, aren't you? Scared they'll find you and take you in. Why did you do it? Was it drugs? Why did you batter him to death, Beppe?'

'Listen, shitface, I had nothing to do with it.'

'So why are you scared?'

Chapman clenched a fist and tapped Beppe hard on the chest, antagonising him. The kid pushed his hand roughly aside.

'Of course I'm scared,' he exploded. 'You'd be fucking scared if you'd seen Cesare fucking Scarfone going into the building.'

The instant he said it he seemed to regret it. His mouth clamped shut and he hurled his cigarette away into the darkness, the tip glowing like a firefly.

Chapman said nothing for a time. He was too stunned to speak, but he also wanted to give Beppe the chance to cool down. He needed him calm, more coherent now.

'Cesare Scarfone,' he repeated. 'The politician?'

Beppe was looking the other way. He still had the bottle clutched in his hand. He lifted the neck to his mouth and poured in the brandy so fast it overflowed down his chin and on to his soiled shirt.

'The politician?' Chapman said again.

Beppe rounded on him. 'How many other fucking Cesare Scarfones are there?'

'You sure?'

The kid wiped his mouth on his sleeve and lit up another cigarette with trembling hands.

Chapman softened his tone. 'You've told me this much. You might as well go on.'

Beppe took his time, smoking a quarter of his cigarette before saying finally: 'I'm sure.' The anger had changed to resignation, weariness.

'When did he go in?'

'How should I know? You think I have a watch? Late. Midnight, maybe later.'

'It was dark. Perhaps you were mistaken.'

'I saw his face. I've seen it in the papers.'

'You read the papers?'

'Christ, what d'you think I do all day, go to the office and shag my secretary? I read 'em all. Pick them up off benches, from rubbish bins. I even sleep with the fucking papers.'

He rummaged inside his coat and pulled out a few crumpled copies of *Il Messaggero*.

'Was he alone?' Chapman asked.

Beppe shook his head. 'Two other men with him.'

'Where were you?'

'Kipping down in a corner of the courtyard. Behind the dustbins by the archway.'

'Did you see them come out?'

'No. I must've been asleep.'

'So they didn't see you?'

'I don't think so.'

'But you're not taking any chances. That's why you came out here.'

Beppe hesitated, then nodded. Chapman leaned back on the concrete sleepers. There was a faint rattling sound behind him, growing louder. He twisted his head and saw the headlights of a train piercing the darkness. The locomotive and carriages rattled past and on into the night. He turned back to Beppe.

'You should go to the police.'

Beppe gave a harsh laugh. 'What for?'

'That's important information.'

'You think they'll believe me, even if I wanted to tell them?'

Chapman was silent. He knew the kid was right.

'Look, I could get you a hotel room. Somewhere you can hole up for a while. You might feel safer.'

'I'm safe out here. Where I know everybody, where I know the area. Now leave me alone.'

Chapman took out a business card with his work address and phone number on it.

'If you need any help, you can get in touch with me here.'

Beppe took the card and threw it on to the fire without looking at it. 'I don't know who you are. I've never spoken to you. Say otherwise and I'll deny it.'

Chapman didn't move. Beppe was looking at him coolly.

'Now fuck off.'

Chapman pulled himself to his feet. He picked up the brown paper bag he'd brought the brandy in. 'Keep the *grappa*.'

He walked away from the fire and around the stack of sleepers. When he was fifty metres away, heading back along the tracks towards the station, he opened the paper bag and switched off the tiny portable cassette recorder inside.

*　　*　　*

'Play that bit again,' Enzo said.

Chapman wound back the tape and pressed the 'play' button.

'*Of course I'm scared. You'd be fucking scared if you'd seen Cesare fucking Scarfone going into the building.*'

Chapman let it continue. The sound quality was poor, the voices kept coming and going, broken up in places by a crackling noise. But the key bits were clear enough. Enzo sat forward in his armchair, his elbows resting on his legs. He had a glass of wine in one hand but he hadn't touched it, he was concentrating so hard on the recording. Even when Chapman pressed the button to stop the tape, Enzo remained in exactly the same position for a few seconds. Then he sat back heavily and let out a deep breath.

'*Merda!*'

'What do you think?'

'I don't know, Andy. If it's true . . . You believe him?'

'Yes. I was thinking about it on the way over. He was quite definite about it, and why should he lie?'

'But Cesare Scarfone. I don't like it.'

Enzo got up and took a few paces around the room, walking off some of the tension. Cesare Scarfone was a deputy in Parliament, leader of a breakaway right-wing faction with views so extreme they made Mussolini look like a liberal.

'I can't use it,' Enzo said eventually. 'It's too hot to touch. Are you going to file?'

'I'd like some corroboration first.'

'I know now my editor won't accept it. Scarfone's a *deputato*. Okay, one without much of a reputation. But he'd sue, for certain. Who's going to believe the word

131

of a tramp from Termini who's probably drunk or on drugs?'

'I know, he's not a credible witness.'

Enzo sat down again and drank some of his wine. It was nearly one o'clock in the morning. He was wearing a towelling bathrobe which had fallen open to reveal his hairy chest, flabby stomach and a pair of garish yellow boxer shorts.

'You know what you should do?' he said. 'Get it made official. So it's not us putting the story out but the *pubblico ministero*.'

'You mean give it to the magistrate, Fiorini?'

Enzo nodded. 'Let her deal with the implications. A story that she's investigating allegations against Scarfone – *that* we can run. This we can't.'

'I'm not sure, Enzo. He's a source.'

'Come on, Andy. He's some homeless bum who happened to blurt out a bit of information. You promised him nothing. He told you nothing in confidence. Where's the problem?'

'He's just a kid. A scared kid.'

'All the more reason to tell the prosecutor. If there's any substance to what he's saying – and we don't know yet there is – La Fiorini can protect him better than you. You can't keep this to yourself. This is a murder inquiry. The prosecutor should at least know about it. What she does then is up to her.'

'You think so?'

'Yes. Play her the tape, then let her make the decision.'

132

SEVEN

The phone call had intrigued Elena. Not just for its content – a request for a meeting to discuss some important aspect of the Vivaldi case – but also its source. When Baffi had put through the call to her office it had taken her a moment to remember who Andy Chapman was. But when the realisation came it was accompanied by a sudden twinge, first of irritation and then something else, something harder to identify. A stirring of interest that she puzzled over then instantly suppressed. She listened to what he had to say and was curious enough to find a ten-minute slot for him at the end of the afternoon.

She spent most of the day in court and had just returned to her office when her direct line rang. She picked up the phone automatically, then wished she hadn't.

'Elena? Why haven't you returned my calls?'

It was her husband. Elena sank down into her chair and rubbed her eyes wearily. She could do without this.

'What is it, Franco?'

'I want to talk to you. When can we meet?'

'No.'

'Don't just dismiss it like that. You don't know what I have to say yet.'

Elena sighed. She knew only too well what he had to say.

'I'm not interested in talking,' she said. 'The time for that is passed.'

Franco softened his tone. 'Give me a chance, Elena. Just a drink.'

'We've been over all this. It will serve no purpose.'

'Have you found someone else?'

'That's none of your business.'

'I'm your husband.'

'Not any more, Franco.' Elena looked up. Baffi was standing in the doorway. She put her hand over the receiver.

'The journalist, Chapman, is waiting downstairs at reception,' Baffi said.

'*Dio*, yes, I'd forgotten. Bring him up, will you?' She went back to her husband. 'Franco, I have to go.'

'Hear me out, Elena.' His voice took on an edge of anger. 'You're being so stubborn about this.'

'I have a meeting.'

'You always have a meeting. If you spent less time working, we might still be together.'

His gall took her breath away. 'You know exactly why we split up,' she replied curtly. 'If you have anything else to say, you can do it through my lawyer. Don't call me again.'

She replaced the receiver, then took it off the hook, wondering again how feelings could change so quickly and so irreversibly. How you could love someone enough to marry him, then a few years later feel nothing for him.

She tidied up the mess on her desk and took a moment to compose herself before the journalist was shown in. Baffi brought a chair from the outer office and found a space for it in between the stacks of files. Then he went out leaving them alone.

'Dottoressa, thank you for your time,' Chapman said politely.

His Italian was good, just an occasional hint of an English accent to remind you he was a foreigner. You couldn't tell it from anything else. He had dark hair and a tanned skin that gave him a Mediterranean look and the cut of his clothes – a crisp, short-sleeved white shirt and grey trousers – was undoubtedly Italian.

Elena caught a flash of amusement in his eyes and realised she was staring at him. She glanced down, rearranging the papers in front of her, and said: 'You're taking quite an interest in the death of Antonio Vivaldi.'

'It's a good story.'

'You seem to be particularly well informed. You and Enzo Mattei.' She looked at him coolly and went on: 'You both get to the scene of the crime before I do and seem on close, perhaps too close, terms with the police. Then you both write articles containing confidential details which can only have come from the autopsy report.'

'You read the English papers?'

'They are monitored by the press office. They gave me a cutting this morning, taken from yesterday's edition of your paper. Only you and Mattei had any mention of a neo-Fascist link to the killing.'

'Coincidence.'

'Of course. Which of you got the report, you or him?'

'Report, dottoressa?'

Elena forced a thin smile. 'I've launched an internal investigation to find out who leaked it. And I can assure you, the culprit will be caught.'

'I'm sure they will,' Chapman said, giving her a lopsided, insolent grin she found particularly aggravating. 'But you were going to release the information later, weren't you?'

'Only some of it.'

'So who cares that we got it a little earlier than you wanted us to? That's our job.'

'What was it you wanted to see me about, Signor Chapman?'

He reached into the pocket of the jacket he'd draped over the back of his chair and pulled out a miniature cassette player.

'Did you find out what the official from the Vatican was doing in Vivaldi's apartment before the police?' he asked disarmingly.

'Pardon?' She realised what he'd said and added sharply: 'I hope you haven't come here merely to fish for information I have no intention of giving you. You said on the telephone that you had something important to tell me.'

'I'm getting to that,' Chapman said smoothly. 'I just thought that, as I'm here, I'd ask anyway.'

'I have no comment to make about the Vatican.'

Not that there was anything much to say. Elena had remained in her office until eleven the previous evening, going through the Red Priest's papers which had been returned by Archbishop Tomassi. She could find nothing in them of any relevance to her investigation.

Chapman put the cassette player on the edge of her

desk and explained what he was going to play for her. How he'd obtained it and from whom.

'Before I put it on, I need your assurance that this man will be protected. I'm not being melodramatic. What he has to say is potentially very dangerous.'

'If it's material to the case and puts him at risk, I will arrange for protection,' Elena said.

She listened silently as the tape was played back. She reacted only once, when Scarfone's name was mentioned, but the shock lingered for a while after the cassette recorder was switched off.

'Do you want to hear it again?' Chapman asked.

Elena shook her head, still trying to cope with the implications of what she'd just heard.

'You say you got this from a vagrant?'

Chapman nodded. 'One of the kids Vivaldi helped.'

'Kid? How old is he?'

'It's hard to tell. Nineteen, twenty.'

'Is he on drugs?'

'Probably.'

'So he might have imagined what he saw.'

'I don't think so.'

'Does he drink?'

'Don't we all?'

'It makes a difference to the credibility of what he says.'

'Speak to him yourself. Make your own judgement as to whether you believe him.'

Elena pursed her lips. 'I think I'd better hear it again.'

Chapman rewound the tape and played it back. He studied the magistrate discreetly as she listened. She was attractive. He'd seen prettier women, women with better figures – Rome was full of them, but he'd long outgrown the stage when that was all that mattered to him. He liked her self-assurance, the easy way she handled herself. There was something direct, honest about her. He began to wonder what she was like outside the office.

Midway through the tape the office door opened and Francesca came in. She paused, one hand still on the door handle.

'I'm sorry, am I interrupting?'

'It's okay, Francesca. Come in.'

'I just wanted my briefcase.'

Chapman stopped the tape while Francesca squeezed past him to her desk. She bent over to pick up her brief-case. Elena noticed Chapman watching her colleague, taking in the short skirt tight around her backside, the slim legs. Francesca had that effect on men. Even judges weren't immune from it.

'See you tomorrow.'

Francesca smiled at Elena, nodded briefly at Chapman and went out. Chapman played the rest of the tape, then wound it back and passed it across the desk.

'You can have it.'

Elena left the tape on the surface in front of her, recalling the saying, 'Beware Greeks bringing gifts'. Greeks. And journalists.

'Why are you giving me this?'

'As a record of what he said.'

'I don't mean just the tape. I mean the information.'

'Because it seemed important. I thought you should know about it.'

Elena kept her eyes fixed on his face. He seemed

straightforward enough, but she'd learnt not to trust reporters. All they were interested in was the story.

'I don't think that's the reason, is it? At least, it's not the only reason.'

'Isn't it?' Chapman said innocently.

'There's no way you can use that tape. You need corroboration before you make allegations like that against someone as prominent as Cesare Scarfone. You think I'll get that for you.'

She was astute. Chapman was impressed. There didn't seem much point in denying it.

'Well, the thought had crossed my mind.'

'I don't like being used, Signor Chapman,' Elena said reproachfully. 'I have no choice now but to look into the allegations, but I find your methods leave a lot to be desired.'

'Come on, dottoressa, don't be so self-righteous. So my motives for giving you the tape aren't entirely disinterested. But who cares? You look like an ambitious woman. Do you do everything for the collective good or have you, just occasionally, done something for yourself? If what Beppe has to say is relevant to the murder inquiry, then it's going to help both of us, isn't it?'

Elena was taken aback. She wasn't used to being spoken to quite so directly. People tended to be more circumspect in their dealings with a magistrate. What was particularly galling was that he was right. There was more than a little truth in what he'd said. If she was honest with herself, she had to admit that on hearing the tape her first thought was, my God, this is good stuff, but her second was, this will help my career if

I can crack it. It was hypocritical to pretend that her own self-interest didn't come into it.

'Where do I find this Beppe?'

Chapman gave her a description of the kid and the location of his hiding place by the railway.

Elena made some notes on her pad and looked up.

'Let's get something straight, shall we, Signor Chapman? I don't appreciate outside interference in criminal investigations, particularly from journalists. Your unauthorised presence at the scene of the murder, your use of restricted post-mortem information and now your questioning of what may turn out to be a key witness are all unacceptable to me. I won't tolerate any more of it. I mean that. You interfere with witnesses, or potential witnesses, again and I'll bring charges against you. Do I make myself clear?'

'Perfectly.'

He was leaning back on his chair, his left foot resting casually on his right knee. He wasn't remotely concerned by the reprimand.

'Can I ask a question?' he said.

'Of course.'

'What are you doing for dinner tonight?'

'I can't give you long,' Corona said apologetically, packing files into his scuffed old leather attaché case. 'I have a meeting at the Palace of Justice in half an hour.'

'I think you should hear this,' Elena said.

She inserted the tiny tape into the Dictaphone she'd brought from her office and placed it on the chief's desk. She pressed 'play' but turned the volume down so she could talk over the early part of the recording.

'That voice – that one – is an English journalist named Chapman. The other is some street kid named Beppe. Sleeps rough near Termini. He used the soup kitchen Antonio Vivaldi ran. On the night Vivaldi was killed this Beppe claims he was in the courtyard of the apartment building.'

'Your point, Elena? I'm in rather a hurry.'

'Listen to this bit. It's worth it. Here.'

She turned up the volume. As Scarfone's name was mentioned, Corona went very still, listening intently to the crackly tape. When it had finished he sank slowly down into his chair and ran a hand through his wispy hair. The briefcase lay open and forgotten on his desk.

'Is it genuine?'

'The tape, I think so, yes. The contents, I'm not so sure. It could be the product of a wild imagination, or pure malice. But I don't think we can ignore it.'

'Where did you get it?'

'The journalist gave it to me.'

'The journalist?' Corona pulled a face. 'This has trouble written all over it. A homeless kid, the press. I don't know, Elena. The allegation is pretty unbelievable. The kid probably made it all up to get a bit of attention.'

'He didn't come forward of his own volition. The journalist had to track him down, almost make him talk. You heard the tape. He just blurted it out. It sounded pretty genuine. And he sounded scared.'

'Do you have any other witnesses who saw or heard anything near the apartment?'

'Not one. The police have questioned all the neighbours without turning up anything of significance.'

Corona stared at his desk, massaging his jaw with the ball of his hand.

'I'm going to have to bring Beppe in and question him,' Elena said.

'Do that. I think I'd better sit in on the interview.' He stood up and closed his briefcase, pressing down hard on the lid to engage the catches. 'Hold him overnight. We'll do it tomorrow.'

Elena went with him to the door. As he pulled it open, she caught the sound of movement outside in the secretary's office. But it wasn't Corona's secretary, it was Vespignani, leaning on the corner of the desk leafing through some papers he was clutching in his hand.

'Can I have a minute?' he said to Corona.

'It'll have to wait, Luigi. Unless you walk to the car with me.'

Corona was already striding across the office. Vespignani pushed himself off the desk and hurried out into the corridor after the chief. Elena went back to her office and telephoned Agostini, catching him just as he was leaving for the day.

'I'm sorry, Gianni. This is urgent.'

She told him what she wanted and he agreed to put a couple of officers from the night shift on to it.

'Thanks, Gianni. I'll call you in the morning.'

She clicked the tape out of her Dictaphone and sealed it in a strong brown envelope. Then she wrote what it was on the outside and took it down to the evidence room on the floor below. She entered it into the evidence book and signed her name. The clerk at the desk took the envelope and stapled a serial number on to it before walking away into the stacks of shelves to deposit the item. Elena checked her watch. It was six o'clock. She'd been at work since seven a.m. She considered her options: going home or staying on for a couple more hours. She sighed. It wasn't really a choice.

For just a few seconds after Chapman asked her out for dinner, Elena had been speechless. She thought he was joking, then realised from his expression that he was quite serious. She almost threw him out there and then, but something stopped her. She knew that was what he was expecting and some reckless part of her nature, which she rarely gave free rein, wanted to see his reaction when she said yes. He had some nerve, making a pass at her when she'd just torn him off a strip, but she found that attractive. What was a man good for if he had no balls?

'All right,' she said coolly. 'Where?'

She saw the surprise in his face, the momentary pause for thought. Then he smiled at her. Not smug or sardonic or lecherous. Just a quiet smile that sent a frisson of anticipation through her. He gave her the name and location of a restaurant she'd never heard of and she said she'd meet him there.

He left after that, avoiding any awkward moments, giving her no time to change her mind. It was only when he'd gone that she regretted the perverse impulse that had made her accept his invitation. She knew it had been prompted in part by the phone call from Franco. That she'd said yes as a way of asserting her independence, her determination to break from her failed marriage. She considered phoning Chapman to cry off but didn't have his number and, in any case, she couldn't bring herself to be so pathetically feeble. She was thirty-five years old. She could handle a date with a man by now, for God's sake.

It was a new experience for her, though. She hadn't been out with anyone since she'd separated from Franco nearly eighteen months before. A few of the men in the office had asked her, including Vespignani who – much to her disgust – had invited her out to his weekend villa near Frascati, but she'd turned them all down. She didn't believe in office romances, particularly with the unappealing – and mostly married – prosecutors who seemed to think that because she'd broken up with her husband, she was now sexually available to them. Chapman wasn't a colleague so that made him more acceptable. And he wasn't Italian which gave him a different, foreign feel. Elena was intrigued to find out what he was really like.

She did some paperwork in her office for an hour and a half, then went to the toilets and washed and touched up her make-up. There was a tight knot in her stomach, similar to the nervousness she felt in court, yet somehow different.

She left her car at the *Procura* and took a taxi to the restaurant which was in the city centre where she knew she'd never find anywhere to park. Chapman was waiting outside a tiny *trattoria* in one of the quieter streets near Piazza Navona. He held the taxi door open for her and took her briefcase from her as she climbed out.

'What've you got in here?' he said, caught unawares by the weight. 'Bricks?' He waved her away as she tried to take it back. 'It's okay, I've always wanted a hernia.'

He escorted her into the restaurant, pausing just

inside the door as a small, pot-bellied man hurried forwards between the tables with his arms outstretched.

'Andy, *buona sera*.'

He shook Chapman's hand warmly and stepped
back to look at Elena. 'And the signorina?'

Chapman introduced them, then the little man showed
them to a table for two near the open front window
where the light breeze alleviated the heat inside the
restaurant.

'You obviously come here often,' Elena said, wondering how many other women he'd brought here for
dinner.

'I've been coming for years. Umberto's wife does
the cooking. Nothing too fancy, but I think you'll
like it.'

Elena looked around the room. It was a small, inti-
mate *trattoria*, barely half a dozen tables crammed
into a space not much larger than the average family
dining room. The other tables were all occupied: a few
couples deeply engrossed in conversation over their
food and at the back, near the kitchen, a large, noisy
group of adults and children celebrating a birthday.
Elena felt comfortable in the surroundings, relieved
that it wasn't the kind of place you had to dress
up for. It told her something about Chapman – that
he was at home here too, that he wasn't trying to
impress her.

'You want an aperitif?' he said. 'Or shall we just get
some wine?'

'Wine would be fine.'

Umberto brought them a carafe of the house red and
reeled off a list of the day's specialities.

'Ignore the menu,' Chapman had said when they

were settled in their seats. 'It's a work of fiction on a par with the *Decameron*. Umberto will tell us what's on and, if you're not careful, choose the dishes for you.'

'The *gnocchi* are very good,' Umberto said. '*Alla romana con zafferano*.'

Elena was tempted. It was a while since she'd had the small semolina coins cooked in the oven with butter and Parmesan cheese. But they were desperately fattening and she knew she'd regret it.

'I think perhaps I'll just have a salad,' she said.

'A salad!' Umberto sounded outraged.

'Umberto likes everyone to look like him, don't you?' Chapman said, giving the proprietor's sagging belly a friendly pat.

'And why not? We are not meant to be all skin and bones. I like to see some shape on a man. Even better on a woman, but I'm old-fashioned.' He sighed. 'A salad it is, signorina.'

'But I'll have the *gnocchi*,' Chapman said, 'to make you feel better.'

Elena sipped her wine after they'd ordered, making herself relax. Chapman seemed at ease, not in any hurry to talk.

'Did you come straight from the *Procura*?' he asked in time.

Elena nodded. 'I had some things to finish.'

'On the Vivaldi case?'

'No work talk, please, Signor Chapman.'

'Andy.' He smiled at her. 'We got off to a bad start the other day. Let's pretend it never happened. I promise I won't ask any compromising questions about your job.'

'Good. There's a potential conflict of interest here. I'm not sure I should be having dinner with a journalist.'

'I could put a paper bag over my head, if you like, then no one would know.'

Elena laughed. 'That seems a little extreme.'

'If you're worried, why did you accept my invitation?'

'I don't know. Why did you ask me?'

'I think you can guess that.'

He looked at her directly. She glanced down, wondering if she was flushing.

'A salad for the signorina,' Umberto broke in, putting the dish down in front of her with a flourish. 'And *gnocchi* for you, Andy. *Buon appetito.*'

They ate a little in silence before Chapman said: 'You want to try one of these?'

'No, it's all right.'

'Go on, they're excellent.'

He pushed the hot terracotta dish towards her. Elena hestitated, then spiked one of the *gnocchi* with her fork and popped it into her mouth. She could taste the melted butter and the crisp golden crust of Parmesan.

'Want to change your mind?' he said.

'Don't tempt me,' Elena said with a smile.

She toyed with a piece of lettuce, envying him his freedom to eat whatever he pleased and not have to care about the consequences.

'So whereabouts in England do you come from?'

He told her and asked if she'd been to Britain.

'A school exchange to Cambridge a long time ago,' she said. 'I hated it. Not England, or the English, just being away from home, struggling with the language.

147

I couldn't understand what anyone was saying to me. Where did you learn Italian?'

'I studied it at university, then spent a year teaching English in Milan. You know, to groups of businessmen and executives who wanted to improve their promotion prospects.'

'How did you find the Milanese?'

'Serious.'

'It must have been a shock to come down here to the Third World and mix with the corrupt, decadent Romans.'

'Oh, I don't know. I like a bit of decadence. It all depends on the company really.'

He gave her another look and this time Elena held his gaze.

They ate their main courses: *saltimbocca alla romana* – veal escalope with ham and sage – for Chapman, and *melanzane alla partenopea* – aubergines baked with mozzarella, hard-boiled egg and a tomato sauce – for Elena.

She was enjoying the evening. Chapman was an easy companion. Neither too reserved nor too talkative, he was quietly attentive but didn't push her too far if she didn't want it. She found herself warming to him, talking about herself, confiding things that surprised her. Telling him something of her past, mentioning briefly the separation from her husband though not the reasons for it. He had a way of subtly extracting information from you so that you only became aware of it moments later when you wondered why you'd been so open with him. But Elena didn't care. He was so clearly interested in her it made her feel attractive again. It was a long while since that had happened.

Only when Umberto asked them if they wanted coffee did she glance at her watch and realise how late it was. She let out an exclamation.

'I'm sorry, I have to be going. I've work to do before tomorrow. Could I call a taxi?'

'I'll give you a lift, my car's round the corner,' Chapman said.

'No, I couldn't.'

'Where do you live?'

'Well, Parioli, but . . .'

'It's on my way.'

He asked for the bill and they had a good-humoured dispute about how it should be paid.

'It's on me,' Chapman said. 'If we split it, it might look as if you're trying to bribe me.'

'But this way it looks as if you're bribing *me*,' Elena said.

'Impossible,' Chapman replied. 'Everyone knows magistrates are completely incorruptible.'

'Are you in a fit state to drive?' Elena asked as they got to his car.

'I only had a couple of glasses,' he replied and Elena realised with slight alarm that she must have drunk the rest of the carafe of wine.

They said little on the journey up the Tiber and then around the Villa Borghese to the expensive suburb of Parioli. Elena was tired, the long day and the alcohol making her drowsy.

'Turn right here,' she said when they reached the Piazza Santiago del Cile. 'Just at the end on the left. Here.'

Chapman pulled in and turned off the engine. Elena looked across at him, not sure what to say.

'I had a lovely evening, thank you,' she said eventually.

Chapman smiled at her. 'I'll help you in with your briefcase.'

She knew she should have said no immediately. But what harm was there in accepting? She was in control of the situation. They went up in the lift and when they were in her apartment she suddenly didn't want him to go.

'Would you like some coffee? It'll have to be quick,' she added hurriedly, 'I have work to do.'

He nodded. 'I'll give you a hand.'

He followed her into the kitchen and leaned on the work surface while she put the espresso maker on. She took down some cups and saucers and arranged them on the side, aware that he'd come up behind her. She felt his fingers touch her shoulder lightly and went very still, more nervous than she'd been in years. He pulled her hair to one side and gently kissed her neck. She knew she had to stop him. She turned.

'Andy, look, I don't think . . .'

He pulled her to him and kissed her on the mouth. Her arms went up around his neck. It was so long since she'd been kissed she'd forgotten what it did to her.

She broke away. 'We shouldn't. I have work to do.'

His arms went around her waist and he kissed her again. She put up no resistance. She felt his hand slip under her blouse and caress her skin.

'Andy, no,' she murmured. 'I have . . .'

'I know, you said.'

His fingers were unclipping her bra now. The elastic snapped back, loosening the cups. His hand went underneath, finding the swell of her breast. This shouldn't be happening, she thought. I'm in control. I'm always in control.

'Andy, this isn't . . .'

His lips were all over hers, his hand straying across under her blouse.

'I have . . . files to read.'

'I know.'

'Cases to . . . prepare. Andy.'

He pulled his mouth away, nuzzling the side of her neck, his fingers touching, stroking her. She dug her nails into his back.

'Are we going to do this or not?' he whispered.

'Jesus, yes,' Elena said. 'I'm ready. What about you?' She slipped her hand down between them.

'Silly question.'

It was two in the morning when she awoke and saw him getting dressed on the other side of the bed.

'Are you going?'

'Yes.'

She didn't try to argue with him. She was disappointed, but also a little relieved. She didn't want the neighbours to see him leaving after breakfast.

'You didn't say where you lived.'

'Trastevere.'

She propped herself up on an elbow. 'Trastevere? But that's . . . You said this was on your way.'

She saw him smile in the semi-darkness.

'Anywhere would have been on my way.'

He leaned across the bed and kissed her. 'Can I call you later?'

'After what's just happened, you'd better,' Elena replied.

EIGHT

For the first time in months, Elena didn't see the sun rise. When she opened her eyes, she was aware immediately of the light filtering in through the wooden shutters. She rolled over, suddenly wide awake, and looked at the alarm clock she'd forgotten to set. Seven-thirty-two, it read. *Merda!* She threw back the sheet and scrambled out of bed. A wave of dizziness hit her and she sat back down on the mattress, waiting for it to pass. Relax, she told herself. It's not that late. But she could feel the tension in her muscles, the guilt inside her that made her drive herself so hard. They were difficult to overcome.

She went through naked into the bathroom and stepped into the shower. Only when she was soaping herself under the jet of warm water did she allow herself to remember Chapman. She paused, momentarily reliving the night before, wondering briefly what it would have been like to have him here now in the shower with her.

She had no regrets. At least, not about sleeping with him. It had been fun, tender, confused. A release she'd needed for a long time. But she was annoyed with herself for forgetting the alarm, and for neglecting the work she'd brought home with her. Her briefcase, the symbol of her enslavement, lay unopened in the living room where she'd left it. She couldn't remember the last time that had happened.

She made coffee and, recalling that she'd left her car at the *Procura*, rang for a taxi. She sipped the espresso as she got dressed and put on her make-up, her thoughts straying from her timetable for the day to Andy Chapman. She could still see his face, his body. She could almost feel his touch. Yet she was glad he wasn't there. The morning after was nearly always an anticlimax. The embarrassment, the awkward silences, the weak attempts at conversation, each of you wondering what the other was thinking. She didn't need any of that now.

It was eight-thirty when she walked into her office. Francesca, unusually, was in before her. She was sitting at her desk dictating letters into her Dictaphone. She clicked it off and waited for Elena to squeeze through the chaos to her chair.

'You're late today.'

'Traffic,' Elena said, pulling files out of her briefcase.

'Agostini called.'

'When?'

'About half an hour ago. He wants you to ring back.'

'Thanks.'

Elena picked up the phone and punched in the number of Agostini's direct line.

'Gianni? Elena Fiorini.'

'Dottoressa. This vagrant called Beppe you wanted to see . . .'

'Yes, did you bring him in?'

'We couldn't find him last night. We looked everywhere but he wasn't where you said.'

'Wasn't he? My information seemed reliable.'

'But we've found him now.'

'Where is he?'

'In the morgue.'

'What!' The shock hit her like a punch in the gut, rendering her temporarily speechless.

'His body was found on the railway line early this morning,' Agostini continued. 'He'd been cut in two by a train.'

'Dio. An accident?'

'Looks like it.'

'Who found him?'

'A couple of railway workers walking along the line. He's a real mess.'

Elena felt a moment's queasiness. She knew it wasn't an accident.

'Did anyone see it happen?' she asked.

'It was dark. It was an isolated spot. Our chances of finding a witness are negligible.'

'Gianni.' Elena chose her words carefully. 'Who knew about him?'

'What do you mean?'

'Who else knew I wanted him brought in?'

'The two officers I sent to find him. The night duty inspector. Anyone at the desk could have seen the duty sheet. You're not suggesting that . . .'

'I want to know what happened to him.'

'He was just a bum. He was probably drunk. He steps out in front of a train. There's nothing the driver can do. Bang! It's happened before.'

'I want a scene-of-crime team out there, going over

154

the ground where he was found, and the surrounding area.'

'There'll be nothing there, you know.'

'Do it, please, Gianni. And question anyone who
might have seen it. Other vagrants, railway staff.'

Agostini sighed. 'You think there are are suspicious
circumstances?'

'Until we find otherwise, yes.'

Elena put down the phone and, ignoring Francesca's
inquiring glance, went out of the office and down the
corridor to find Corona. The chief's secretary said he
was tied up most of the morning but could probably
see her after lunch. Elena said she'd come back later
and returned to her office. Baffi put a hand over his
phone as she passed his desk.

'Andy Chapman for you. Shall I put him through?'

Elena hesitated. She would have to tell him. 'Yes,
put him on.'

'*Ciao*, how are you?' Chapman said when she picked
up her receiver.

'I'm fine.'

'You sleep okay?'

'Yes.'

'You sound a bit funny. Are you all right?'

'Yes. No.' She took a deep breath. 'It's that kid
Beppe.'

She told him what had happened. Chapman listened without interrupting and still said nothing at
the end.

'It might have been an accident, or even suicide,'
Elena said without much conviction, filling in the
silence.

'You don't believe that.'

155

'I don't know what to believe.'

'He was just a boy,' Chapman said, with an edge of bitterness. 'You said you'd protect him.'

'I had the police out there yesterday evening, looking for him.'

'Someone else was obviously looking for him too.' The accusation was clear in his voice.

'I did all I could,' Elena said defensively.

'Who did you tell about him?'

'That doesn't need to concern you. It's an internal matter.'

'Don't fob me off with that. I gave him to you on a plate and now he's dead. I'm responsible for that.'

'You didn't kill him.'

'You think he'd be dead if I hadn't come to you?'

'You don't know what might have happened. It's not your fault. We can't be certain why or how he was killed.'

'Let's not fool ourselves. We both know why he was killed. Who betrayed him, the police?'

'I don't know.'

'Are you going to find out?'

'Don't get aggressive with me. I'm doing all I can. If it makes you feel any better, I feel just as responsible for it as you do.'

'Thanks,' he said sarcastically. 'That makes me feel great.'

'Listen,' Elena said sharply, 'he was a tramp. You came to me about him because you thought there was a story there you could exploit. Don't try to pretend you cared about him. Wallow in a bit of guilt by all means, but it changes nothing. He's still dead. And we still don't know the whys and wherefores of it so let's not jump to conclusions. I'm following it up and I can do without you shooting your mouth off at me.'

There was a silence. Then Chapman said, puzzled now: 'You're like two different women, you know. There was one last night, in the restaurant and later. I sort of liked her. Then there's this one now. I'm not sure about her.'

'I'm just trying to do my fucking job, all right?' Elena snapped and slammed down the phone.

Her relationship with Andy Chapman, it appeared, was going to be a one-night stand and nothing more.

Whenever he had a few moments of leisure – a rare occurrence given his demanding workload – or felt the need to reflect on something in peace and tranquillity, Archbishop Tomassi liked to walk in the Vatican gardens. There, wandering along the paths between box hedges and cascading rockeries, pausing in secluded grottoes beneath the shade of palms and cypresses, he could be alone with his thoughts. The gardens were always quiet. There was the soothing plash of the water in the fountains, the click of shears or scrunch of a wheelbarrow on gravel as the unobtrusive gardeners went about their work, but nothing marred the atmosphere that Tomassi found so conducive to meditation.

He stopped by a wall of green laurel and looked back down the hill towards the basilica. From the rear, the cupola could be seen in all its full splendour – a far better view than from the front. Tomassi studied the architecture, the perfect symmetry of the design, then his eyes were drawn to the city beyond the Leonine walls. Across the Tiber to the distant gardens of the

Villa Medici and the *Trinità dei Monti* at the top of the Spanish Steps. He listened. This was one of very few places in the city where you could hear birdsong without the intrusive chorus of the internal combustion engine.

He had grown up in the countryside of Lombardy, on the plains of the Po Valley where the cornfields, dotted with red-roofed farmhouses, stretched for miles. He had long since become an urban creature but a part of him still missed the open spaces of his youth; the vast sky filling the horizon, the woods and the river banks where he and his friends had bathed in the summer heat. Where were those friends now? He hadn't been back to his home village for more than thirty years and he'd lost touch with his boyhood companions even before that. The priesthood set you apart from other men. If you chose to serve the Church, you opened up your life to spiritual fulfilment but inevitably closed out the experiences that formed the core of ordinary men's lives: sexual love, marriage, children, the milestones marking the path towards death that he would never pass.

He had few regrets. He had felt the calling as an adolescent and the vows of a priest had caused him little true hardship. He had never been very interested in women. He didn't dislike them but he found them dull. In a way, they were too balanced, too practical to be particularly stimulating company. Men were much more self-centred. They could find time to indulge their whims and eccentricities, to pursue occupations and passions at the expense of their families.

It was the exclusion of responsibility for wives and children which Tomassi found attractive about the priesthood. The freedom from worldly distraction gave him time for reflection and study, time to concentrate on spiritual matters and the service of God. Any doubts he might once have had about his chosen course had long since been dismissed or sublimated into his work. He was an ambitious man. He knew that, in time, he would wear the red biretta of a cardinal and that the Secretariat of State was a prize he could well attain to crown his career. He had no desire to be Pope. No sensible man did. The loss of freedom would be intolerable to him. But even the biretta would slip from his grasp if he made a mistake over Antonio Vivaldi.

He took one last turn around the gardens then walked briskly down the hill to the complex of buildings which formed the papal palaces and the Vatican museum. Next to the open courtyard known as the *Cortile del Belvedere* were the Vatican Library and the *L'Archivio Segreto Vaticano*, the Vatican Secret Archives, which housed the vast collection of historical treasures of the Catholic Church. Here, in thirty-five kilometres of shelving, were stored the extant parchments and manuscripts, the documents and letters of all the popes and their servants, most of them dating back centuries. And in a massive steel safe were kept the papers of such priceless importance that they could not be risked out in the open: the Dogma of the Immaculate Conception; the last letter of Mary Stuart to the Pope in which she informs him that Queen Elizabeth has instructed her to prepare herself for death; and the petition from the lords of England asking for the annulment of the marriage between King Henry VIII and Catherine of Aragon, a request which, if granted, would have prevented the split from Rome and the foundation of the Anglican Church.

But though the historical treasures were the most valuable part of the Secret Archives, there was another section devoted entirely to the working files of the Curia. This was where you came if you wanted to refer to the routine correspondence, the contemporary files of the Catholic bureaucracy.

Archbishop Tomassi approached the senior archivist, seated at his desk near the entrance to the Archives, and asked to see the records of the Secretariat of State for 1945. The archivist led him into the labyrinth of shelves and pointed out a section in the middle. The files were arranged in a fairly haphazard fashion – to organise and catalogue all the documents in the Archives would have taken centuries – and it took Tomassi close on an hour to find what he was looking for. He carried the cardboard folder out to one of the tables and opened it. He selected a few of the papers from the folder and spread them out in front of him, reading each one carefully.

One was a letter headed *Repubblica Sociale Italiana*, the Republic of Salò which Mussolini had set up as a puppet state of the Nazis in northern Italy after his overthrow. It was dated 25th March 1945, and signed by the Duce himself. The others were copies of letters sent by the Vatican to Mussolini, all signed by the then Under-Secretary of State, Giovanni Montini, and one was an internal Vatican memo marked 'Confidential' and signed by Pope Pius XII himself.

Tomassi stared at them, appalled yet also fascinated by their contents. Here was confirmation, in the clearest possible terms, of his worst fears. He was under no illusions about their importance. They would shake the foundations of the Catholic Church if they ever became public knowledge. He himself, no stranger to cover-ups within the Vatican, was shocked by what they revealed. He knew they should be destroyed. That he should slip them under his cassock now and take them back to his office and burn them. But he couldn't bring himself to do it. There was something sacred about the Secret Archives. They were the written testament of a faith. It would be sacrilege to destroy any part of it.

The papers would be safe here. It was the most secure hiding place on earth. They would lie on the shelf gathering dust for centuries and probably never see the light of day. Tomassi collected them together and put them back in the folder. Then he put the folder back where he'd found it and left the Secret Archives. When he got back to the Palace of the Holy Office, he went into his private chapel, knelt down and prayed.

'So who was the guy in here yesterday?' Francesca said. 'Elena?'

Elena looked up. 'What?'

'The guy yesterday. With the tape recorder.'

'What about him?'

'You're not listening, are you?'

'Sorry. I've things on my mind.'

'Who was he?'

'Oh, no one.'

Elena picked up a sliver of tomato which had escaped from her sandwich and put it in her mouth.

'Come on,' Francesca said coaxingly. 'He wasn't bad-looking. He wasn't a cop, or a lawyer, I could tell. So who was he?'

'No one.'

'Elena.'

'Look, he was a journalist, okay?' Elena said, irritated by the questions.

Francesca gave her a knowing smile and bit into her second slice of pizza, holding the crust in the square of greaseproof paper in which it had been delivered. They'd sent out for lunch, as they did most days they were in the office. There was no time to go out to a restaurant or a bar. Sometimes it was even hard finding a few minutes for a snack at their desks. Elena watched her friend savouring her mushroom and anchovy pizza and wished she had more than a small dried-out ham salad sandwich in front of her. Francesca was one of those annoying women who could eat whatever they liked, in whatever quantity, and not put on weight. They were friends, but if there was one thing Elena hated her for it was her metabolism.

'You fancy him?' Francesca said slyly.

'What?'

'He looked about the right age, attractive, nice clothes. How many guys do you meet like that?'

'It was business.'

'Ask him out.'

'Leave it, Francesca.'

'You know what happens if you sit and wait for them.' Francesca looked at her affectionately. 'It's time you found someone else, Elena. Make the most of your opportunities.'

'If you must know, we went out for dinner last night.'

Francesca's eyes opened wide. 'You kept that quiet,' she said reproachfully.

'It was only last night. When was I supposed to tell you?'

'The minute you came in this morning. I have to know immediately.' Francesca paused, thinking something through. 'That's why you were late, isn't it? You spent the night with him.'

Elena looked down, concentrating on her sandwich.

'You did, didn't you? Elena, talk to me.'

'What if I did?' Elena snapped back.

'Oh, touchy.' Francesca reached out for a piece of paper and pretended to scribble on it. 'I'll just draft a memo for the noticeboard: "Elena Fiorini got laid at last. All staff to be given one day's holiday in celebration."'

Elena couldn't help smiling. 'It's no big deal.'

'No? Why are you being so cagey about it then? What was he like? Well hung?'

'Francesca!'

'I want all the details. You know I won't tell anyone. Well, except my mother. And her friend, Tiziana. And maybe Corona, the Superior Magisterial Council and the entire Court of Cassation. But what's a secret between friends?'

'There's nothing to tell,' Elena said. 'It was a mistake. It's not going to happen again.'

'A mistake?'

'I don't want to talk about it.'

'Yes, you do.' Francesca waited, then said in a quiet, wheedling tone: 'Come on, tell me about him.'

Elena took her time, rounding up a few crumbs from her sandwich and licking them off her fingers first. Francesca knew her well, probably better than anyone. She did want to talk about it, but she never liked to volunteer personal details. She needed to have them drawn out of her.

'He came to me with some information about the Vivaldi case,' she said. 'Something a witness had seen. He had a tape of a conversation with the witness. He played the tape for me. It was unbelievable stuff.'

She told Francesca what was on the tape. And what had happened to Beppe. Francesca stared at her.

'This is getting nasty. You should be careful. Have you spoken to Corona?'

'Not yet. Chapman, the journalist, blames me for what happened to the vagrant. That was him on the phone earlier. You heard what I said to him. I somehow doubt we'll be meeting again.'

'And Scarfone? What are you going to do about him?'

'Without the witness, there's nothing to implicate him.'

'You still have the tape.'

Elena had forgotten about the tape. 'Yes, I still . . .'

She stopped, shivering suddenly with a premonition. She pushed back her chair and walked quickly out of the office. She almost ran down the corridor, her heart pounding with more than just the exertion. She didn't wait for the lift but took the stairs to the floor below, running down three steps at a time and nearly twisting her ankle at the bottom. The clerk at the counter looked up as Elena rushed into the evidence store and asked to see the record book. He pulled a thick, dog-eared ledger out from under the counter and opened it. Elena leafed hurriedly through the pages and found the entry for the envelope she'd brought down the previous evening.

'That one,' she said, her finger marking the place.

The clerk wrote down the serial number on a chit and entered the withdrawal in another ledger. Elena bit her lip, trying to control her impatience.

'I need it now, please.'

'Of course.'

The clerk completed the formalities and strolled at a leisurely pace into the stacks of shelves. Elena counted the seconds, unable to keep still.

'It's not there,' the clerk said, coming back to the counter.

'Let me see.'

Elena practically snatched the chit from his hand and plunged into the storage area, scanning the numbers on the sides of the shelves. The clerk came up to her shoulder and pointed to the space where the envelope should have been. There was nothing there.

'Could it have been misplaced?' Elena said, a sickly, hollow feeling in her stomach.

The clerk shook his head. 'That's where I put it last night. It should be there.'

Elena searched along the surrounding shelves, checking the serial numbers on all the items in case the envelope had somehow strayed. But she knew she was wasting her time.

'Who else has been in this morning?' she asked, already turning and heading back to the counter.

There were numerous entries in the withdrawals ledger; magistrates or their clerks taking out items for the preparation of a case or court hearings. Corona himself had been in. Vespignani and Francesca and Baffi too. Plus half a dozen other prosecutors. Elena checked all the serial numbers next to their names in case her envelope had been withdrawn by mistake. But it wasn't mentioned.

She rounded on the clerk, ready to explode. 'Has this room been left unattended at any time this morning?'

'No.'

'Has anyone been in the stacks?'

The clerk hesitated. 'No.'

Elena knew the security in the evidence room was poor. She'd been into the shelves and taken out items herself in the past.

'Then how do you explain the missing envelope?' she demanded. 'That was important evidence. Where is it?'

The clerk held out his hands defensively. 'I don't know. I don't know what's happened to it.'

'I want the whole store searched. Every shelf, every item examined. If that envelope is in here, I want it found. You understand? And I'll be notifying the chief prosecutor. This isn't going to stop here.'

Elena marched out furiously and went back up the stairs to her office, giving herself time to cool off. Her legs felt heavy, but her brain was distracted, agitated. She wondered which of her colleagues had betrayed her.

NINE

The pictures on the early-evening television news were so explicit, so stomach-churningly gory that it took a real effort of will for Chapman to make himself watch them. There were two bodies lying in an alley off one of the side streets near Termini. They were both Somali immigrants, young men in their twenties, who had been stabbed repeatedly in the chest and stomach. Seventy-three times in total, the reporter's phlegmatic voice-over intoned. Chapman knew the details already – he'd attended a press conference at the *Questura* earlier in the day – but he hadn't seen the bodies until now.

The camera lingered on the bloody torsos, then panned up to the victims' faces. Carved into their foreheads with a knife were the initials SS, the trademark of a shadowy right-wing group who called themselves the *Sansepolcristi*, a name which had unpleasant historical associations in Italy. In 1919, the first meeting of what was to become the Fascist Party had been held in San Sepolcro Square, in Milan. Those who had attended, who had christened themselves the *Sansepolcristi*, had become the elite inner core of Mussolini's dictatorship. Their modern namesakes were also Fascists, engaged in a campaign of terror against Jews, immigrants and communists. The synagogue in Rome had been bombed eight months earlier, killing three Jews and a passer-by, and since then there had been a series of attacks on the immigrant community in the city; attacks notable for the random selection of their targets and their frenzied brutality.

The television pictures cut abruptly from the bodies in the alley to a serious-looking man in a dark suit and sober tie. This was Cesare Scarfone, leader of the *Movimento Patriottico Italiano*, one of the more extreme right-wing political parties with representation in Parliament. He was condemning the attack on the Somalis and denouncing the perpetrators as lawless thugs. But there was something ambivalent about his stance for, almost in the same breath, he was saying it was time to stop immigrants coming into the country in the first place.

Chapman watched him. Scarfone was a slick performer, adept at using the media to his own advantage and displaying a public persona which was misleadingly at odds with his repugnant political philosophy. A young, energetic lawyer from the south, he was one of the prime beneficiaries of the *Tangentopoli* corruption scandals which had destroyed the old political order in Italy.

The Christian Democratic Party, the most powerful force in postwar Italian politics, had disappeared completely. The Socialists had been wiped out, the Communists had changed their name and split into factions. But, significantly, the extreme Right had escaped from the political ghetto and found more respectability – and support – than they'd had for half a century.

The Italian constitution expressly prohibited the refounding of the National Fascist Party, but that hadn't stopped the setting up of neo-Fascist parties with different names but with the same policies and outlook as the Fascists. These parties had always been excluded from government until the chaos of *Tangentopoli* coupled with universal disgust with the old politicians had brought them back into the fold. They had not been tarnished by the corruption scandals, simply because they had no power and so no one had deemed it worthwhile to bribe them, and their views on immigration and tax were becoming more acceptable to the electorate. This changing political climate had brought a new wave of right-wing members into Parliament and prominent among them was Cesare Scarfone.

He'd been elected to the Chamber of Deputies for the *Alleanza Nazionale*, but almost immediately had fallen out with the leadership and formed his own splinter party with policies even further to the right. His racist, rabble-rousing rhetoric and unabashed admiration for Mussolini made many Italians uncomfortable, but had won him a loyal following amongst young working-class men and many middle-class businessmen. In public he came across as a charming, persuasive individual, evincing a mastery of the soundbite without which no modern politician could hope to survive. But Chapman saw through the public-relations gloss to the calculating, ruthless operator underneath. He had no doubt that this was a man who could kill a priest – and a homeless kid.

There'd been no mention of Beppe on the news. The apparently accidental death of a vagrant wasn't worth even a passing mention, but Chapman had been thinking about him all day. Not wallowing in guilt, as Elena Fiorini had put it, but blaming himself, all the same. Who else was there to blame? He'd used the kid for his own purposes, exploited him in pursuit of a story, and the death was on his conscience.

He switched off the television and went into the kitchen to make himself something to eat – spaghetti tossed in melted butter and grated Parmesan. He was in the middle of eating it, thinking now about Elena, wondering if she was as hard as she seemed, when the telephone rang. It was Enzo.

'You busy this evening?' he asked.

'No. Why?'

'I spoke to a contact who moves in neo-Fascist circles. Fellow named Pinocchio.'

'That's an unfortunate name for a source.'

'He knows his stuff. I've used him in the past – he's reliable. I asked him about the Red Priest. He said he'd see what he could find out.'

'And?'

'He wants to meet me tonight. I think you'd better be there too.'

'Where?'

'EUR. Piazza Marconi. You know it?'

'Yes.'

'I'd pick you up but I've something else to do.'

Chapman didn't ask what. He could guess the answer.

'Eleven-thirty, okay?' Enzo said.

'I'll be there.'

Family dinners were something of an ordeal for Elena. Part duty, part pleasure, they aroused mixed feelings inside her. She liked to see her parents and brother, looked forward to their infrequent meetings, yet when they finally took place they were always less enjoyable than she'd anticipated.

She was in the kitchen of her parents' house, watching her mother cook, just as she had watched her when she was a little girl. Sipping a glass of white wine and listening to her mother talk, she was reminded of why she'd spent so long trying to get away from home. You could have too much of your family. She'd grown up here, lived here while she did her law degree at Rome University and remained for a few years after until she could afford a flat of her own. The lack of privacy, the lack of freedom had been unbearable. She had had to account for all her movements; where she'd been, with whom, for how long. It had been hard to bring friends home and there had been nowhere else to go, the reason that – like all her contemporaries – her sexual experiences, from the first fumbled gropings through to losing her virginity and beyond, had taken place in the back seat of a Fiat.

Her mother modelled her conversation on the Spanish Inquisition. Even now, Elena grown up and a magistrate, a casual chat with her mother was more like an interrogation than a discussion between equals. They never would be equal, of course. Her mother was still *mamma*, and Elena was still the small girl hanging on her apron strings. At times it was comforting to know that very little had changed, but there were other moments, as now, when it was intensely annoying. Her mother had finally, and not altogether unexpectedly, got on to the subject of Elena's imminent divorce. It was a sore point and one which Elena had no desire to discuss yet again. But Franco had been on the phone to her mother, asking her to intercede on his behalf, and her mother was determined to make her case.

'Mamma,' Elena said wearily, 'we've been over this time and time again.'

'I know we have. But you're being so pig-headed about it. You should show more understanding. It was only some casual fling.'

'It wasn't casual. It had been going on for months. He moved out to live with her, remember?'

'You threw him out.'

Elena sighed. 'Look, he only wants to come back now she's dumped him for someone else.'

'Yes, all right. He's behaved badly. But that's no reason for you to behave like a fool.'

'A fool? I don't want him back.'

'He's your husband.'

'He's a liar and a cheat.'

Elena moved across the kitchen to look out of the window at the parched garden. Neither of her parents was interested in gardening and the patch of yellowing grass surrounded by woody shrubs and clusters of weeds reflected that indifference. There'd been a swing on the lawn when Elena was small but that had long since disappeared, its place taken by a collection of white plastic chairs on which her parents and friends would sit on warm summer evenings.

'All men have affairs,' her mother said. 'It's stupid to make a fuss about them. It's no grounds for divorce to a sensible woman. There are more important things than a faithful husband.'

She finished peeling the potatoes and began to chop

them into small cubes for frying in olive oil. Elena turned and watched her. Her mother was a pragmatist. Any sense of romance she may once have had had been knocked out of her by the process of bearing and bringing up five children. She'd devoted herself to her family and her home; she wasn't going to let a trivial thing like adultery ruin everything she'd built up. Elena knew she was at fault in her mother's eyes. She'd thrown her husband out. That was a cardinal sin in a marriage.

'Men have always been unfaithful. You modern women are fools to expect otherwise. If he puts food on the table and treats you with respect, you shouldn't ask for more. If he went out and ate dinner somewhere else instead of coming home, you wouldn't kick him out.'

'You think eating out is the same as adultery?' Elena said.

'It is to men. It's not important to them.'

'It is to me.'

'They all do it.'

'Does Papa?'

Her mother looked up angrily. 'How dare you! You have no business asking things like that.'

'You ask me plenty.'

'Your father is a good husband, and a good father.'

Elena wondered. Had her father been unfaithful? He'd certainly had the opportunity. He was almost never home, and when he was, he always seemed to be in his study, working. Was that being a good father?

'Let's drop the subject, shall we?' Elena said, too tired to argue.

But her mother never let matters rest. 'All I'm saying is that you should give him a second chance.'

'I don't love him any more. As far as I'm concerned, the marriage is over.'

'You young people want everything to be easy. If something doesn't work, you give up and look elsewhere. You have to work at marriage.'

'Did Franco work at it?'

Her mother's mouth tightened but, for once, she said nothing. She took some slices of young lamb from the fridge and started rolling them in seasoned flour.

Elena's relationship with her mother had always been fraught with conflict. Elena desperately wanted her approval, for her mother to be proud of her, but her mother withheld it. She wasn't impressed that Elena was a magistrate. If anything, she believed it was her daughter's career that had destroyed her marriage. If Elena had had children and stayed at home, she and Franco would still be together. That was how her mother saw it. She didn't understand, or didn't want to understand, that times had changed. Elena sometimes wondered if her mother was jealous of the choices, of the freedom her daughter's generation had had; if she resented the fact that she had never had those same opportunities and didn't want her daughter to have them either. Her mother was all mixed up. Hard on Elena but always there with a mother's unconditional love. She wanted Elena to be happy yet couldn't stop herself running her down all the time.

A key turned in the front door lock and Elena's younger brother, Ugo, breezed in.

'Where is everyone?'

'In here,' Elena called out.

'*Ciao.*'

Ugo strolled through the doorway in a pair of smart slacks, Gucci loafers and an Armani shirt, open at the neck. He kissed his mother and Elena and plonked the sports bag he was carrying down in a corner. The zip was partially undone and Elena could see a dirty sock poking out. Thirty years old and Ugo still brought his washing home for *mamma* to do. And what's more, she *did* it. Elena found it annoying, knowing what her mother's reaction would be if *she* were to bring her laundry home.

'What's that you're drinking?' Ugo asked.

'Wine,' Elena said.

'I can see that. What sort?'

'I don't know. Just wine.'

Ugo picked up the bottle from the table and studied the label. 'Mmm. Good year. How is it? Light and fruity, a bite of vanilla? That's how I like my whites.'

Ugo had a degree in bullshit, which was perhaps as well, considering he worked in advertising where it was the only language anyone understood. Elena was envious, and just a little resentful, of his easy life. Everything seemed to fall into place for him so effortlessly. Whatever happened he always managed to land on his feet and believed it was due to his abilities rather than luck. He had an unshakeable self-confidence and conviction of his own superiority which had no foundation in reality, but which cushioned his path through the world. Since childhood nothing had been Ugo's fault. Someone – usually his mother – had been there to absolve him from blame and pick up the pieces. She was still doing it long after Elena believed he should have been told to stand on his own two feet. That was really the core of the problem; her mother thought the sun shone out of Ugo's backside. In contrast to her attitude to Elena, she never criticised her son, yet he showed her no gratitude, treating her with disdain and coming to visit only when he wanted something.

He poured himself a glass of wine and slumped down on a chair, stretching out his long legs.

'So, who've you put in the slammer today?' he said facetiously to Elena. He didn't wait for a reply but went on: 'I saw you on the news the other night. You looked really odd in the TV lights. You know, pale and haggard.'

'Thanks.'

'They caught you out with that question, didn't they? You should have seen your faces: mouths hanging open, blank stares. It was quite funny really.'

Elena said nothing. She didn't want to be reminded of the moment.

'What're we eating?' Ugo said.

'Lamb with black olives,' his mother replied.

'I had a big lunch. I probably won't want much.'

Elena saw her mother's face and marvelled at her brother's insensitivity. But he was off, telling them what he'd eaten, who the clients were, what it had cost. Elena switched off and tried not to let him irritate her.

Her father came home shortly afterwards and they settled down to a quiet meal, chatting about what they'd been doing; the news from the three other children who'd moved away from Rome, two of them with families of their own now; all the minutiae of their lives that, though tedious to outsiders, was the mortar that held the family together.

Elena helped her mother with the washing up while Ugo lounged in the sitting room, flipping through the TV channels to see if there was anything to watch. Then she went into her father's study. Eugenio Fiorini was seated behind his antique desk, papers spread out in front of him. He looked up as Elena entered and removed his reading glasses.

'Am I disturbing you, Papa?'

He smiled. 'No. Come in.'

She went round behind the desk and put a hand on her father's shoulder. He touched her fingers with his own hand and spun his chair round to look at her.

'You're working too hard, Papa.'

'I always do.'

'Come and have a liqueur with us.'

'Not tonight. I have some things to finish.'

Eugenio had a thriving law practice, mostly corporate and commercial business. He was sixty-seven years old but showed no signs of letting up. Elena knew he'd never retire. He wouldn't know what to do with his time. Work was his life. Sometimes Elena thought it was his escape too – from his wife, from his children, from domestic responsibilities. He had never come on family holidays when she was growing up. He would drive them to the coast and leave them there, joining them at weekends if he wasn't too busy. Elena saw now how hard it must have been for her mother, coping with five children on her own.

Elena was like him in many ways, and not simply

because she'd chosen a career in the law. They had the same dogged determination, the same dedication to their work. Yet, looking at her father now, virtually chained to his desk, his hair silvering, his body starting to wear out, she wondered if this was what she wanted from her life. No one ever died wishing they'd spent more time in the office.

'How are you, Elena?'

'I'm fine.'

'You look tired.'

'I've been working long hours.'

'You shouldn't overdo it.'

Elena laughed. 'You're one to talk.'

'I'm an old man. You're young. You should get out more – meet people, enjoy yourself.'

'Mamma thinks I should get back with Franco.'

'Ah, she's been talking to you, has she?'

There was a gleam of amusement in his eyes. He hadn't been married for thirty-seven years without learning about his wife's ability to get her teeth into a subject and shake it to death.

'Do you want to be back with Franco?'

'No.'

'Then there's an end to it.' He paused, then said: 'Is there someone else?'

Elena thought fleetingly of Andy Chapman. 'No,' she said.

She stayed a while longer, talking to her father about her case-load. He was the only member of the family who took a genuine interest in what she did. Her mother found it all too tedious and esoteric and Ugo was too wrapped up in himself to care. But Elena's father liked to chat with her about the law. He was proud of her achievements. He knew how difficult it was to do what she had done: completing her law degree in four years, a feat very few managed; passing her magistrate's exams with the sixth highest marks in the country; being appointed to a plum post in the Rome *pubblico ministero*. He knew the application and ability those achievements had taken and admired his daughter for them.

'I'll leave you to your work, Papa,' Elena said in time.

'Come and see us again soon.'

She kissed him on the cheek and went out to say goodbye to her mother. Ugo, watching some puerile comedy film on television, lifted a hand but didn't get up to see her off.

At the door, Elena gave her mother a hug and kissed her on both cheeks.

'Talk to Franco,' her mother said.

Elena walked out without replying.

EUR was one of the most extraordinary places Chapman had ever been. A vast artificial suburb on the southern fringes of the city, it had been created by Mussolini in the 1930s for the *Esposizione Universale di Roma*, a showcase for Fascism and its achievements which never came off because of the intervention of the Second World War. It had since been turned into a satellite city and trading centre, but had never lost the macabre atmosphere of emptiness and cold modernism that made it seem more like a film set than a place where real people lived and worked. The broad streets with bizarre names like Boulevard of Electronics and Social Security Avenue were as unwelcoming as the ugly, solid Fascist buildings along their edges. In daylight, the clinical sterility of the place was alleviated by the hordes of workers streaming in and out of the high-rise office blocks. But at night it felt like a surreal ghost town long deserted by its citizens, as if a plague or some deadly virus had left it poisoned and uninhabitable. The streets and squares, bustling with cars and people just hours earlier, became dark sinister ghettos strafed by biting winds and the echoes of a dead civilisation.

The Piazza Marconi, the geographical heart of EUR, was a huge square cut in two by a wide six-lane highway and surrounded by more gloomy Fascist monuments. It was only when he arrived that Chapman remembered just how big the piazza was and how vague the instructions he'd been given by Enzo. He'd said the square, but given no indication *where* in the square. Chapman parked in the south-west corner and turned off his lights. It was a little before eleven-thirty and he sat in the darkness, watching through the window for Enzo's car.

A few minutes elapsed before he saw headlights coming slowly round the other side of the piazza. A black BMW with three men inside pulled in to the kerb. Chapman felt the hairs on his neck start to prickle. He looked across the square. The three men were still inside the car. Waiting. Chapman was uneasy. He wondered if he was being silly. They could be anyone. One of them might even be Enzo's contact, Pinocchio. But their presence disturbed him nevertheless.

Another car turned into the square. Chapman recognised the streamlined shape of Enzo's Alfa Romeo.

It stopped some fifty metres from the BMW. Chapman climbed out on to the pavement. He started to cross the piazza. The front passenger door of the BMW opened and a man got out. Enzo saw him and clambered out too, raising his arm in a gesture of greeting. Chapman, crossing the grass in the centre of the square, saw a second man emerging from the rear of the BMW. The light from a streetlamp glinted momentarily on something in the man's hand. A fraction too late, Chapman realised what it was. A gun. He shouted a warning to Enzo, running towards him. Enzo turned his head. 'Get back,' Chapman yelled. But the second man was already closing in. Enzo saw him coming and spun round, sprinting back to his car. The first bullet hit him in the back before he'd gone three metres. The second exploded through his head, showering tissue and blood everywhere. Enzo's body crumpled to the ground like a marionette.

The gunman turned sideways. Chapman saw his face briefly in the streetlamp, then ran for his car. The man came after him. Chapman heard car doors slam and an engine start up. The BMW was on the move. He ducked round the back of his car as a bullet shattered one of the side windows. He dropped to a crouch and flung open his door, keys in hand, searching for the ignition. The gunman fired again. The bullet ricocheted off the roof and away into the night. The engine kicked into life and Chapman floored the accelerator, spinning the wheel to come round into the gunman's path. The gunman dived sideways as the car knifed towards him. Chapman saw the BMW in his lights and kept going. At the last moment, when a collision seemed unavoidable, the BMW swerved off on to the pavement, its brakes screaming. Chapman had all the start he needed. He skidded round into a side street, made two right turns, doubling back on himself, and shot through a red light on to the main highway north to the city centre. He could see in his mind Enzo's body shuddering and falling, and burnt into his retinas, clear as a photograph, the face of the man who'd shot him.

TEN

For once, their moods seemed to coincide. Elena felt in need of companionship, of something soft to stroke and cuddle and Livia, often so distant and haughty, was feeling affectionate for a change. The cat came across the hall as Elena entered the flat and rubbed itself against her legs, purring. Elena picked it up and carried it through into the living room, slumping down into an armchair with Livia nestling in her arms. It was late. Elena knew she should go to bed, but the effort was too much. She closed her eyes and rested her head on the back of the chair.

The noise of the telephone woke her with a jolt. She blinked, taking a few moments to realise where she was, what the ringing was. She pulled herself up and stumbled over to the phone, trying to clear her head.

'*Pronto.*'

'Elena? Is that you?' A man's voice, urgent, a little garbled. 'It's Andy Chapman.'

'Chapman? How did you get this number?'

'Enzo's dead. Enzo Mattei. He was shot just now. I saw it. D'you hear me?'

She was awake now. 'Slow down. Where are you?'

'I don't know what to do. Jesus, they killed him. Gunned him down in front of me.'

He was in distress, almost sobbing out the words.

'Andy,' Elena said, forcing herself to stay calm. Her heart was beating like a jackhammer. 'Where was this?'

'EUR. I didn't know who else to call.'

'Have you contacted the police?'

'What?'

'The police.'

'Shit, no. They came after me. Three of them. Black BMW. He went down. Two bullets. Christ, it was awful.'

'Where in EUR?'

'Piazza Marconi. He's there, on the ground, dead.'

'Andy, just shut up. Answer my questions, nothing more. Where are you?'

'A call-box.'

'In EUR?'

'No. Tre Fontane. I pulled off the Cristoforo Columbo. I'm by the *Centro Sportivo*.'

'Stay there. I'll pick you up.'

'The police . . . shall I . . .'

'Leave it with me. I'll be there as soon as I can.'

She put down the phone and called the duty officer at the *Questura*. Then she went out to her car and drove south out of the city. She saw the call-box outside the Tre Fontane sports centre as soon as she turned off the main road. There was a car parked beside it containing a lone man. Elena drove past it to make sure. Chapman turned his head and saw her. She pulled in to the kerb in front and watched in her mirror as Chapman got out of his car and walked up to her window.

'Get in,' Elena said.

He came round to the other side and slid into the passenger seat.

'Thanks for coming,' he said. He was calmer now but still in something of a daze. Elena had seen it before in victims of shock.

'You okay?' she said.

Chapman nodded. 'My car?'

'We'll pick it up later.'

Elena did a U-turn and drove back the way she'd come. The police were already in the Piazza Marconi when they got there. Elena parked behind one of their cars and climbed out. 'Stay here,' she said to Chapman. A uniformed officer waved her back, then stepped aside as she identified herself. Chapman watched her through the windscreen: ducking under the plastic tape which cordoned off the north-west corner of the square, talking to the officer in charge, walking on to look down at something on the ground Chapman couldn't see but which he knew was Enzo's body. He felt cold and numb. The energy seemed to have been drained out of him. He didn't feel like sleep but every movement, every thought was an effort.

An ambulance arrived, followed by more plain-clothes officers and an equipment truck. Two men in overalls began to rig up standing lights to illuminate the scene which, until now, had been floodlit by the headlights of the police cars. Elena was talking to a plain-clothes detective, telling him something. Chapman could see her face in profile, one hand lifted to shield her eyes from the harsh glare of the spotlights. He remembered that first day he'd seen her, in the doorway of the Red Priest's apartment. The air of competence around her; the quiet natural authority she exuded which made even experienced cops defer to her.

She turned and came back towards the car, the plain-clothes detective by her side. She slipped back into the driver's seat while the detective clambered into the rear, pulling out a notebook and pen from his jacket.

'This is Inspector Piccoli,' she said to Chapman. 'You'd better tell him what happened.'

Chapman twisted round so he could see both Elena and the inspector. Piccoli was a short, swarthy fellow with fleshy jowls and a head which seemed to sprout straight from his shoulders without any neck in between.

'Enzo and I were supposed to meet someone here,' Chapman said. 'A contact of his. He was supposed to have information for us about neo-Fascist involvement in the death of Antonio Vivaldi. I got here first. Then Enzo arrived.'

Chapman told them what happened next, going through it all slowly so Piccoli could take notes.

'I lost them on the main road,' he said finally. 'Then I turned off and found a call-box. That's all.'

'Did you get the number of the BMW?' Piccoli asked.

'It was too dark. And by the end I wasn't thinking of things like that. I just wanted to get away from them.'

'Had you seen any of the men before?'

Chapman shook his head.

'Can you describe them?'

'Not very well. The third man never got out of the car. I didn't see anything of him. But the killer, I'd recognise him. I saw his face in the streetlight.'

'Do you have any idea what information he was going to give you?' Elena asked.

'No.'

'Or who the contact was?'

'I know nothing at all about him.'

'I'd like you to come back to the *Questura* and look at some photographs,' Piccoli said. 'To see if you can pick out the gunman.'

'I have to tell Enzo's wife.'

'The police will do that,' Elena said.

'No, it's for me to do.'

Piccoli glanced at Elena. She nodded.

'After that then. As soon as you can,' the inspector said, putting his notebook away.

Elena stepped out and had another brief discussion in the street with Piccoli before getting back in and driving Chapman to his car.

'I appreciate what you did,' Chapman said.

'It's my job.'

'You didn't have to come out yourself.'

'I knew Enzo Mattei.' She paused. 'You didn't listen, did you? I told you not to interfere. You're fishing in dangerous waters. I won't warn you again.'

'You think I'm going to stop now? With Enzo dead.'

'Stubborn, aren't you?'

'Let's not have another argument, Elena.'

She looked out of her window. 'Where did you get my number? I'm ex-directory.'

'It's written on your handset. I copied it down before I left last night. Do you want me to tear it up now?'

Elena turned back to him. 'Not if you don't want to.'

'I don't want to,' Chapman said.

He climbed out and walked to his car. Elena saw him lift a hand in acknowledgement as she turned and drove away.

Chapman didn't start his engine immediately. He sat and thought about Enzo, wondering what he was going to say to Claudia. Wondering what she and Carlo and Paolo would do with Enzo gone. His vision misted over. He rubbed his eyes hard and turned the key in the ignition.

Claudia's voice on the entryphone was sleepy, puzzled.

'Andy? What are you doing here? Do you know what time it is?'

'Let me up, Claudia.'

'What's going on, Andy?' she said when she opened the door to their flat. 'Where's Enzo?'

'Enzo's dead, Claudia.'

He caught her in his arms as she fell.

There was shock, followed by numb disbelief, then the tears which Chapman could do nothing to stop. He didn't try. He sat with Claudia in the darkened living room, holding her close and listening to her sob. Feeling her body shaking. He hoped to God the boys wouldn't wake up. He didn't know how he'd cope with three of them.

When, in time, she stopped crying, he made some coffee and they talked, keeping their voices low like conspirators. Claudia too wanted her sons to stay asleep. They would find out soon enough what had happened.

They went over and over the same things. There was only so much you could say but it seemed important to keep repeating it, for every minute spent talking was one minute less for thinking. And right now Claudia didn't want too much time to think. She would have a lifetime for that.

Chapman stayed until morning. Claudia dozed off on his shoulder and then he too dropped off, waking at first light with a stiff arm and sore eyes. He left before Carlo and Paolo were up. Claudia wanted to be by herself when she told them.

He drove into the city and found a bar on the Via Nazionale where he had a *caffè latte* before going to the *Questura*. Piccoli took him upstairs to his office and had him sign a statement outlining what had happened at EUR. Then the inspector produced a collection of large albums containing photographs of convicted criminals and made Chapman go through them page by page. It was a long, laborious process. They took a break after an hour and Piccoli quizzed him some more about the rendezvous in Piazza Marconi as if he didn't quite believe all he'd been told already. Chapman went over it again patiently, wanting only to go home to bed, then they returned to the albums and the interminable pages of photographs which were all starting to look the same. Chapman knew it was something that had to be done, but still regarded it as a waste of time. 'One more,' Piccoli said, placing the last album on the desk in front of them. Chapman sighed and opened the cover.

Fifteen pages in, they found him. A black and white photo of a man with close-cropped black hair, a squashed nose and flabby mouth twisted into a contemptuous sneer. Chapman knew without a doubt it was the gunman. He would never forget that face.

'You sure?' Piccoli said.

Chapman nodded. 'Who is he?'

'Vincenzo Volpi. I'll have to check his record on the computer, but from what I can recall he's got a few convictions for assault. An unpleasant, violent character but murder's a new departure for him.'

'Are you going to arrest him?'

'If we can find him,' Piccoli said.

Chapman drove home in a semi-trance, automatically going through the motions of steering and changing gear but his mind elsewhere, fixed in a limbo of exhaustion and dull incomprehension. He'd been there, but he still couldn't fully understand that Enzo was dead.

An elderly lady was opening the front door of the apartment building as he arrived. He said good morning to her and exchanged a few idle words. She lived in the flat below him but he knew very little about her except her name, Signora Campanella. It was an Italian name but she wasn't Italian. She spoke the language with a distinct foreign accent. It sounded East European to Chapman, maybe Polish, but he wasn't sure. Their relationship was so polite and superficial he'd never had an opportunity to find out about her background.

She was carrying two large plastic bags of groceries she'd bought at the local market. Chapman helped her carry them up the stairs and waited while she fumbled in her pocket for her keys.

He heard footsteps above him. Someone running heavily down the stairs. He leaned over the rail and caught a glimpse of a hand, the sleeve of a dark jacket. The fuzziness in his head cleared abruptly. He grabbed the keys from Signora Campanella and inserted them into the lock. Then he threw open the door and stepped inside the flat, pushing the door half closed to conceal himself behind it.

The footsteps stopped. A man's voice said, 'Oh.' Chapman peered out through the crack between the door and the frame. He couldn't see the man's face, just the left side of his body, his hand still resting on the stair rail. The man grunted indistinctly and went back up the stairs. Chapman listened hard. He heard another voice faintly, then the click of a door. They were waiting for him inside his flat.

Signora Campanella came through the doorway looking a little bemused. Chapman closed the door behind her.

'Signora,' he said. 'I wonder if I could use your phone.'

It was the second shock of the day for Elena. The first, Chapman's call in the early hours, had stunned, and then distressed her. Enzo Mattei had not been a friend, or even an acquaintance, but she'd met him in the course of her work and had a professional respect for him. His death had touched her, though she felt no real personal loss.

This one was different. It wasn't a death, wasn't on the surface very important at all, but it shook her nonetheless.

'Say that again,' she said to Corona.

'You're under investigation by the *Guardia di Finanza*.'

Elena pulled out the chair in front of the chief prosecutor's desk and sat down with a thud.

'Under investigation?' she said in a whisper.

'Nothing to worry about,' Corona said.

He passed her a letter headed *Guardia di Finanza, Comando Generale*. Elena read through it, surprised to notice that her hand was shaking. Her stomach felt as if it were being crushed in a vice. On the face of it, there was nothing in the letter to concern her unduly. It was couched in polite, diplomatic terms and appeared simply to be a request for information. But Elena knew there was more to it than that.

'It's routine,' Corona reassured her. 'You know they do random checks all the time. On any employee in the country.'

'You believe that?'

'Why shouldn't I? It's just a request for details of your salary and expenses, nothing more.'

'They have those already from my tax return.'

'So they're cross-checking with the employer's records. It's nothing sinister, Elena.'

'I don't like the timing,' Elena said.

Corona peered at her. 'Timing?'

'It's a strange coincidence that just as I'm investigating possible neo-Fascist involvement in three homicides, the Revenue Guards decide to do a routine check on my personal finances.'

'You think the neo-Fascists can influence the *Guardia*?'

'I don't know. I just think it's suspicious.'

'Don't get paranoid, Elena.'

She leaned over the desk. 'They're putting improper pressure on me,' she said earnestly.

'They're acting within their rights.'

Elena looked away. After the death of Beppe and the disappearance of the tape, she was reluctant to confide in Corona, or anyone else in the *Procura*.

'Are you going to comply?' she asked.

'I have no choice. I'm obliged to give them the information. Have you anything to hide?'

'Of course not.'

'Then it's only a formality. It will probably go no further than this.'

But Elena knew she wasn't being paranoid. What counted was the feeling in her gut, the intuition, the ghostly fingers playing chopsticks on her spine that told her she should watch her back.

The telephone rang when she returned to her office. It was Piccoli.

'We've got an ID on the gunman who shot Mattei,' he said.

'Good. Have you managed to locate him?'

'He's waiting in an interview room,' Piccoli said. 'When can you get here?'

Elena peered through the tiny observation hatch in the door of the interview room. There were two men seated next to each other at the table inside. One she recognised, a smooth, greasy-haired lawyer named Francesco Menotti who'd represented a number of right-wing agitators, including four alleged *Sansepolcristi* currently in the Regina Coeli prison awaiting trial for the Rome synagogue bombing. The other man, Vincenzo Volpi, she'd never seen before, but he had certain characteristics she'd encountered in other violent criminals. He was physically unattractive, his coarse peasant's face made uglier by his cropped hair and protruding ears. But it was the look in his eyes she'd seen before. They had the cold dullness of someone who could kill another and feel not just no remorse, but nothing at all.

She snapped shut the hatch and turned to Piccoli. 'Where did you find him?'

'The journalist, Chapman, telephoned. He thought someone was waiting for him in his apartment. We went round. There were a couple of men there but they got away down the fire escape. We searched the surrounding streets and found Volpi in a bar having an espresso.'

'What a coincidence. Does he live around there?'

'No. Centocelle.'

'How did Menotti get here?'

'Showed up out of the blue, demanding to see his client. The other fellow, the one who got away, must have seen us pick up Volpi and called the lawyer for him.'

'Okay, let's see what fairy story he has for us,' Elena said.

They went into the interview room and sat down at the table. Menotti waited for Elena to switch on the tape recorder and complete the interview formalities before he started to protest.

'The treatment of my client is outrageous. Can a citizen not sit and enjoy a quiet coffee without being harassed by the police? Is sitting in a bar an offence now? This is a gross infringement of his civil rights and I urge you to release him immediately.'

'We take note of your complaint, dottore,' Elena said. 'But we'd like to talk to your client about something rather more serious than sitting in a bar. Where were you last night about half past eleven?'

'My client was with some friends, playing poker,' Menotti said.

'I'd like Signor Volpi to answer the questions.'

Elena looked at Volpi. His eyes came to rest on her and she almost shivered. She'd seen both good and evil in the faces of men she'd interviewed but Volpi's contained neither. There was just a cold amorality that acknowledged no concept of right or wrong.

'I was playing poker with some friends,' Volpi said. His voice was low, the words slurred together in a thick Roman accent.

'Where?'

He looked at his lawyer. Menotti nodded his permission and Volpi gave them an address on the Via Nomentana.

'These friends,' Elena said. 'What are their names and addresses?'

Another nod from Menotti. Volpi ran off a list of names and Piccoli wrote them down on a pad of paper.

'You say you were playing poker with them,' Elena continued. 'From what time?'

'I don't know. Maybe nine, ten o'clock.'

'Until when?'

'Two in the morning.'

'Did you leave the house at any time?'

'My client has told you,' Menotti interjected, 'he was playing poker all that time.'

'Answer the question, please,' Elena said to Volpi.

'I never left the house.'

'Were you in EUR last night?'

'Dottoressa,' Menotti said, 'if he was in the Via Nomentana, how could he have been in EUR?'

'Have you heard of a journalist named Enzo Mattei?'

'I don't read the papers.'

'He was shot dead last night in EUR. We have a witness who can identify you as the killer.'

'I'm sorry,' Menotti broke in. 'I cannot allow you to ask my client questions about an event which took place when he was elsewhere. He knows nothing about any shooting in EUR.'

'Did you kill Enzo Mattei?' Elena asked.

Volpi's face was expressionless. 'No.'

'So how do you explain our witness's identification of you?'

'He doesn't have to explain it,' Menotti said tetchily. 'He wasn't there. Your witness has made a mistake. It was night time, he thought he saw someone who looked like my client but it wasn't. There's an end to it. Now, are you going to release Signor Volpi or not?'

Elena ignored the lawyer, her attention focused solely on Volpi.

'Which political party do you support?' she asked.

'Really, this is completely irrelevant.'

'Dottore Menotti,' Elena said icily, 'we could finish this more quickly if you stopped interrupting.'

Menotti threw up his arms in a gesture of helpless despair and shook his head. But he kept his mouth shut.

'Well?' Elena said to Volpi.

Volpi shrugged and straightened the lapels of his creased leather jacket. He was ignorant, uneducated, but there was a streak of cunning in him that in his walk of life counted for more than brains.

'I'm not interested in politics,' he said.

'You have several convictions for violence. One for an unprovoked attack on an African man. You don't like immigrants, do you?'

'Don't answer that,' Menotti said quickly.

Volpi grinned at Elena. A vulpine leer that unsettled

her but also made her angry. She knew she was going to get nothing out of him. But she wanted to cover all her queries, for the record.

'What were you doing in Trastevere this morning?'

'Having a coffee.'

'It's a long way from home.'

'So?'

'Why go there for coffee?'

'Why shouldn't I?'

'Let me put this to you. You were in EUR last night. You shot dead Enzo Mattei and attempted to kill a colleague of his. Then you went to the colleague's apartment and waited for him to come home but the police came instead. You managed to escape and went into a bar hoping to hide. That's why you were having a coffee.'

'I don't know what you're talking about.'

Volpi leaned back casually and curled his lip at Elena. He'd been in custody before. It didn't bother him in any way. Elena switched off the tape recorder and stood up.

'I presume you're going to release my client,' Menotti said. 'You have no grounds for holding him.'

'I'll let you know my decision in due course,' Elena said.

She went out of the interview room and waited for Piccoli to join her.

'We won't get far with that one,' Piccoli said in disgust.

Elena nodded. 'Check his alibi with his friends. They'll all confirm it, no doubt, but we have to make sure.'

'It was all prepared in advance.'

'I know. Menotti made it rather obvious at the beginning when he answered my first question for Volpi. He seemed to know in advance what day and time I was going to ask about.'

'And if the alibi is watertight, what do we do?'

Elena had been giving it some thought. She could have Volpi detained without charge. It was often a useful way to get prisoners to cooperate. But she didn't think it would work with Volpi. He wasn't the type to confess, and he'd been inside before so a prison cell held no fears for him.

'Release him,' she said.

'He did it, you know,' Piccoli said. 'Maybe we should keep him off the streets for as long as we can.'

'He's no use to me locked up. Let him go and put him under surveillance. Have you the manpower for that?'

'I can find it.'

'He's smug, confident. Sooner or later he'll over-reach himself. Someone hired, or ordered, him to kill Mattei. If we're patient, he may lead us to them.'

Elena knew there was something wrong as soon as she opened the door to her apartment. She paused on the threshold, listening. She could hear nothing. She clicked on the hall light. She wasn't nervous. There was no feeling of danger. Just the sense that all wasn't quite right.

She advanced down the hall and switched on the living room light. Nothing was out of place. The room was exactly the way she'd left it that morning. She sniffed. There was an underlying smell of something unpleasant. That wasn't unusual in a Roman summer when the drains and sewers started to sweat. But this smell was different, and more localised.

She put down her briefcase and pushed open the door to the kitchen. The stench almost knocked her out, it was so overpowering. On the floor by the cooker was a shapeless lump of what looked like meat. There was blood smeared on the tiles and splashes of red on the front of the oven. Elena realised what it was and started to retch. She cupped a hand under her mouth and ran for the bathroom, throwing herself to her knees and vomiting into the toilet.

The spasms took a while to subside. Elena stayed where she was on the floor, breathing heavily, perspiration trickling down her nose. Then she made herself stand up and wash her face in the basin. It was while she was drying her face on a towel that the telephone rang.

She hesitated before she answered, fearing who it might be. But when she picked it up it was Chapman.

'Elena? Elena, are you there?'

She cleared her throat. 'They've killed my cat.'

'What?'

'Livia. I've just found her. She's been bludgeoned to death.'

'I'll be there in ten minutes.'

She opened the door for him when he arrived. The nausea had passed but her limbs were still shaking.

'Where is she?' Chapman said.

'In the kitchen.'

She heard him open the kitchen door, his exclamation. Then he came back out.

'You've called the police?'

Elena shook her head. 'I suppose I should. They must have broken in. Oh God, I can't face it.'

The police officers taking over her flat for perhaps several hours, the questions, the intrusion, the forensic team poking around for evidence. And all of it a waste of time for she knew that whoever had done it would have left behind no clues. But she knew she had to do it. She was a magistrate. It had to go on the record.

'I'll call them,' Chapman said.

'Andy, you don't have to.'

'You helped me last night. Now it's my turn to help you.'

It was gone midnight when the police team finally left. They took the remains of the cat with them, but the marks of her slaughter were still present in the kitchen. Chapman found a bucket and cleaning materials and, kneeling down, scrubbed the blood off the tiles and the oven, the strong scent of disinfectant fumigating the room.

When he'd finished, he found Elena lying on her bed with her eyes closed. He could tell she'd been crying.

'Can I get you anything? A drink, something to eat?' he said.

'I don't feel like eating.'

Chapman hesitated, looking down at her. 'My phone call this afternoon . . .' he began.

Elena nodded. 'Yes, I brought it.'

She swung her legs off the bed and stood up. She went into the living room and rummaged in her brief-case, pulling out a transparent plastic bag containing a thick, well-thumbed red book. She weighed it in her hand, aware she was about to do something she would never, in the past, have contemplated. But she was worried. A little scared too. This wasn't like any other investigation she'd handled. The *Guardia di Finanza* check on her finances, now Livia. It was starting to get personal. The disappearance of the tape was at the back of her mind too. She wasn't sure who she could trust. But she had faith in Chapman. His friend had been killed, he'd nearly been killed himself. She knew where he stood, and it was time to trust him some more. She handed him the plastic bag.

'I shouldn't be doing this, it's against all the rules.'

'There aren't any rules,' Chapman said. 'Do you think that would have happened' – he nodded towards the kitchen – 'if there were rules? We have to play this their way.'

Elena gave him a pair of thin white cotton gloves, the kind worn by scene-of-crime officers. Then she crossed the room and opened the window, trying to expel the smell of disinfectant. It had started to rain; great heavy drops which splattered on to the pavement below like globules of spit. There was a sudden flash of lightning on the horizon, a distant growl of thunder. Elena leaned on the windowsill, letting the stormy air clear her lungs.

Chapman slipped on the gloves, removed the book from the evidence bag and examined it. It was Enzo's contacts book which he carried everywhere with him. It had been in his jacket pocket when he was killed. Chapman leafed through the pages to the letter P. It was there, scribbled untidily in the list of names and numbers: Pinocchio. No address, just a phone number. Chapman copied it down on to a piece of paper from his notebook and put the contacts book back in the plastic bag.

Elena had turned and was watching him. 'You're looking for the person who set him up, aren't you?'

'You don't want to know what I'm doing,' Chapman replied. 'Can you check this number for me? Get me the address. I'll understand if you say no.'

'You should leave this to the police.'

'The way I left Beppe, you mean?'

'Enzo Mattei was killed for prying where someone didn't want him to pry.'

'I know the risks. That's why I want to do it, not leave it to you.'

'I don't need protecting,' Elena said.

'You think they're going to stop at your cat if you keep asking questions?'

'There are procedures for this. I'm in a better position to find out what's going on.'

'These guys don't recognise procedures. You're a magistrate, Elena. There are things you can't do. My hands aren't tied in the same way.'

She closed the shutters over the window and came across the room to sit down next to him on the settee.

'Three people are dead already, Andy.'

'I know what I'm doing.'

He pulled her to him. She put her head on his chest and wrapped her arms around him.

'Will you stay tonight?' she said. 'I don't want to be on my own.'

'Yes.'

He stroked her hair, feeling the warmth of her body. They held each other, listening to the rain lashing against the shutters, the storm buckling the sky outside.

PART TWO

ELEVEN

Piedmont, June 1944

Michaela walked up the stony path from the village, fording the stream where it cascaded down a cliff sending sprays of misty water into the air, then climbed up through the trees into the cool heart of the forest. Once out of sight of prying eyes she hitched her skirt up around her waist to make walking easier. She felt the breeze on her bare legs, the brush of the undergrowth on her ankles and calves as she clambered up the rocky slope.

Beyond the woods she emerged into the high summer pastures. The grass was long here. It rippled caressingly against her thighs. Everywhere she looked there were flowers; a tapestry of reds and yellows and violets interwoven with the grass. It was early but already the heat was beginning to smother the hillside, bathing it in hazy light.

He was waiting for her where the ground levelled out, a blanket rolled under one arm. They looked at each other without speaking. Then they started to flatten an area of meadowland, pushing the grass over with their feet and pressing the stalks to the ground. The young man spread the blanket out in the clearing and they lay down next to each other. They were surrounded by a wall of grass that shielded them from view. Michaela could smell the scents of the flowers – the poppies, the celandine, the wild lavender – that had been crushed beneath them.

His hand touched her face. Now she could smell the male odour of his skin. Without a word they kissed. At first gently, then harder. She could feel the roughness of his stubble on her face. Her skirt was still up above her thighs. His hand slipped between her legs, exploring the curves, probing deeper into the moist valley. She tugged at his shirt, undoing the buttons and pulling it down over his shoulders. She touched his chest, running her fingers over the muscles, his body lean and hard from exercise and the privations of war.

They could wait no longer. They tore at one another's clothes, fumbling with buttons, with belts and clasps, stripping each other. They paused, absorbing the other's nakedness. The sleek lines, the hairs, the shadows. Then they kissed again, carried away by a fierce, desperate passion. He grasped her breasts, kneading them roughly like dough and biting the nipples. She reached down to his groin and gripped him, squeezing hard, wanting to hurt him too. But when she threw open her legs and he entered her, she gave a cry not of pain but of release.

Afterwards they lay on their backs on the coarse blanket and stared up at the sky, squinting through the bright sunlight. They still hadn't said a word. High above them a formation of American Flying Fortresses cruised past like a shoal of silvery fish. Their crews, looking down, could have seen the swathes of grass on the hillside but not the naked bodies, not the warm damp slivers of flesh that glowed and opened themselves like two more meadow flowers.

The young man put his hand on Michaela's thigh. Tender, gentle now.

She turned her head to look at him. 'What are you thinking?' she said.

'That when all this is over, I want to marry you.'

She was touched, but she didn't believe him. She was used to men and their carelessness with words. She knew him only as Scuro, the dark one, a *nom de guerre* which concealed both his real name and the other, more important, facets of his identity. How could you really know a man whose name was a mystery to you?

When she didn't respond he rolled over on to his side, facing her, and propped himself up on an elbow.

'I mean it,' he said.

'When all this is over, you will forget me,' Michaela said.

'No. I want you to be my wife.'

'Don't say such things. We may neither of us live to see it.'

'Then it's even more important to say something now. I love you, Michaela. Do you love me?'

'I don't even know who you are. Where you come from, what you did before the war. You are a shadow without substance to me. How can I love a shadow?'

Scuro looked down at her, tracing a line around her face with his fingertip, touching her forehead, her cheeks, her lips.

'My name is Roberto Ferrero. I come from Lombardy, from a village near Bellagio, on Lake Como. Before the war I was, well, I was just a boy, helping my father on the land.'

He picked up his discarded trousers and pulled out a

thin chain from one of the pockets. Suspended from the chain was a light metal disc with numbers and letters stamped on it in relief. It was a Royal Army identity tag. Michaela had seen one before, though not on a partisan. They were not supposed to carry anything that might identify them or their families. Roberto gave it to her. It could be split into two identical halves, one to be kept with the body, the other to be sent to his next of kin. Michaela read the inscription which gave his serial number and name and other details including his home town and parents' names. She knew he'd shown it to her as a gesture of sincerity, to prove he was telling her the truth. It wasn't much, but in the midst of such uncertainty, such chaos, it felt like a pledge of lifelong fidelity.

'I should have thrown it away,' Roberto said. 'But if I'm killed I want my mother and father to know. I don't want them to spend the rest of their lives wondering what became of their son.'

Michaela handed the disc back to him. The sun had risen higher in the sky. She could feel its rays prickling her skin, burning the paler patches across her breasts and belly.

'We should move into the shade,' she said.

They picked up their clothes and the blanket and walked naked through the meadow to the fringes of the wood where they sat down under the trees and ate the bread and goat's cheese Michaela had brought from their farm in the valley. Then they made love again, slowly, savouring each other, not knowing when the next time would be.

'You haven't given me an answer,' Roberto said when they'd dressed and were ready to part.

Michaela put her arms around his waist and rested her head on his heart.

'Yes,' she said.

Roberto lay on his back on the exposed hillside, wondering how he could be bored out of his mind and scared to death at the same time. It was the unresolved dichotomy of a partisan's life: the days and weeks of tedium in the mountains, living with lice and cold and hunger, interspersed with moments of sheer terror.

It had been the same in the army. Roberto remembered his first taste of action with vivid, gut-churning clarity, the way he recalled his first nerve-racking day at school or the first time he made love to a girl. He'd been sick on the ship across the Adriatic to Albania. He'd made out it was the motion of the sea but in reality, for him as for the thousands of other boys in the convoy, it had been fear – of death, of the unknown, of going into battle without knowing what the fuck you were doing.

They should have realised it was going to be a balls-up the moment they arrived at Durazzo and found the harbour choked with merchant ships unloading marble for some Fascist building programme in Albania. It was an ill omen which only hinted at the farce that was to follow – the shortage of transport which meant they went to the front with most of their *matériel* sitting on a quayside; the lack of proper boots and clothing to keep out the cold in the mountains; but, most importantly, their complete ignorance of the Greeks which led them to make the fatal error of underestimating the enemy.

They were supposed to be in Athens in a couple of

weeks. The Greeks, their leaders bribed to surrender, were supposed to throw down their weapons, turn tail and run. But no one seemed to have told the foot soldiers in Macedonia. Just five miles inside the Greek frontier, digging in along the Kalamos River, the Italians met such fierce resistance from the Greek army that they were forced to retreat. And retreat again, and again as the Greeks pursued them into southern Albania with an aggression so relentless the French, reputedly, put up signs in the Alps reading: 'Greeks! Stop here. This is the French frontier.'

Even now, baking in the Italian summer, Roberto could remember the bitter cold in the mountains of Albania. Sitting in a wet dug-out wearing only cardboard boots which fell apart in the rain, shivering in his Lanital overcoat which gave about as much protection from the weather as toilet paper. He'd seen men lose fingers and toes from frostbite, hundreds die from cold and starvation. And this was the Royal Army, the pride of Italy. Brave, bewildered young men who fought with valour but were up against not only the tenacity of the enemy but the incompetence of their own leaders.

It was his memories of royalist officers that led Roberto, fleeing north to avoid deportation to a labour camp in Germany after the Armistice, to join the communist partisans, the red *Garibaldini*, rather than the royalist *Badogliani* partisans. He preferred to be commanded by workers and peasants, his own kind, rather than former army captains whose past records did little to inspire him with confidence in their abilities.

He put his arm over his eyes, shading them from the sun. It was warm on the hillside. At any other time it might have been pleasant to lie there; listening to the flies buzzing, the click of the cicadas in the grass, inhaling the aromas of flowers and pine. He could have fallen asleep and dreamed of Michaela. But not today. He was too tense to sleep.

He turned his head. Ettore was next to him, cradling the Breda machine-gun in his arms. Between them, wrapped in a cloth to keep the dirt off them, were the strips of ammunition and the interchangeable barrels. Roberto had a British Lee Enfield rifle, dropped two days earlier by the RAF. It had been intended for the royalists, but the *Garibaldini* had listened to the coded message from the BBC and copied the layout of the *Badogliani* signal fires to make the pilots drop the supplies in the wrong place. There'd been rifles, ammunition, English cigarettes with cork tips and packets of K-rations which the partisans tasted and immediately threw away, they were so revolting. Even in starvation they couldn't stomach such dreadful food.

But even so they were poorly armed compared to the Germans and the Fascists. It was that knowledge that accounted for the tight knot in Roberto's stomach. That, and the waiting.

Further down the hill the partisan who called himself Jimmy rolled on to his side and urinated. The piss hissed on the chalky ground and trickled away down the slope. Roberto thought of Michaela, of her soft body and warm skin, then shut it out, not because there was anything else to think about but because it seemed bad luck to think of her now.

He sensed Ettore shift next to him and heard the murmured words he'd dreaded all afternoon: 'They're coming.'

Roberto lifted his head and looked across to the spur of rock where the forward guard was keeping watch over the valley. A small hand-mirror was flashing with reflected sunlight, the signal repeated three times before the guard slipped down from the spur to join his comrades. Roberto could hear the engines now, the throaty rumble of lorries coming up the twisting mountain road.

Ettore had the Breda set up on its bipod and was lying behind it, the sights trained on a straight section of road where there were no trees blocking his line of fire. Roberto crouched down next to him, preparing to feed in the ammunition and change the barrels. His mouth was dry, the blood throbbing inside his skull. The other partisans were ready, watching for the signal from the brigade commander. The engine noise got louder. To Roberto, it seemed to echo around the valley sides and focus on a point exactly by his ears, vibrating so loudly it obliterated all thoughts from his head.

The first vehicle came around the corner. It took them all by surprise. It was an *autobilinda*, an armoured car with a heavy machine-gun mounted on the top. Behind it came two trucks of Fascist militiamen. The convoy crept up the incline, partially hidden by tree foliage and the stone walls which flanked the road. The brigade commander waited for the AB to emerge fully into the open before he gave the signal to attack. Ettore let rip with the Breda while the others fired off round after round with their rifles. Bullets tore into the canvas sides of the lorries or bounced off the metalwork like peas. The lorries came to an abrupt halt and the militiamen dived off the backs into the cover of the wall. The machine-gun on the top of the *autobilinda* swung round and fired a long sweeping burst across the hillside. Jimmy was caught as he ran for cover. The bullets hit him in the chest and his white shirt erupted in a fountain of scarlet. He went down and was still.

Ettore was on his feet, the Breda clutched in his arms. He ducked behind a cluster of boulders and set the machine-gun up on the top. Roberto scuttled after him and changed the barrel which was burning hot. A mortar came over from the road and exploded well down the hill. A second got closer, showering them with earth. The mortarman was getting his range. Soon he would blanket the whole slope with a barrage of explosives.

Ettore caught sight of a militiaman poking his head above the wall and fired on him. But the Breda, as it did so often, jammed, the lubricating pump clogging up with grit. 'Fuck!' Ettore spat. He picked up the gun and they ran in a crouch behind the boulders and into the shelter of a gully. More partisans joined them. The AB was firing again, the rattle of its machine-gun broken up by intermittent mortar explosions. The brigade commander staggered into the gully, his arm around the waist of a wounded comrade.

'How many?' he said.

'Jimmy's down,' Roberto said.

'And Biondo,' said another. 'That fucking AB.'

They picked up the wounded partisan and retreated along the gully, the escape route worked out in advance. They never prolonged a skirmish. They attacked, did what damage they could and got out. In guerrilla warfare there were no heroes: only the quick and the dead.

*   *   *

215

The Blackshirts came early in the morning, before the village was awake, before the *contadini* were out in the fields. They kicked in the doors of the houses and dragged the occupants out into the square. Michaela was terrified. She knew what was going to happen.

They were herded into a corner beside the village pump: women, children and old men. There were no young men. They'd all been deported to Germany, conscripted into the militias or had taken to the hills with the partisans. The villagers stood there, shaking in their nightclothes while the Blackshirt officer told them there'd been an attack on a militia convoy the day before. Two soldiers had been killed. For each of those soldiers, ten peasants would be executed as a reprisal – to teach them to collaborate with the partisans.

Armed Blackshirts moved into the crowd of frightened people, taking hold of all the old men and hauling them out into the centre of the square. Michaela's father and grandfather were among them. The officer counted them. There were only nineteen. He gave an order and one of the children, a boy of ten, was dragged from his mother's arms. She clung on to him, screaming at the soldiers, begging them to take her in his place. But a Blackshirt hit her in the stomach with his rifle butt and she fell to the ground in a sobbing heap. The men – some so frail they could barely stand – and the trembling boy were lined up against a wall and shot. Michaela turned away and embraced her mother as the deafening volley shuddered around the square.

The Blackshirts left the bodies where they had fallen. Then they took tins of black paint from their lorries and scrawled 'Long Live the Duce, Long Live Graziani' on the walls of the surrounding buildings as the dawn air filled to saturation with the sound of weeping women and screaming children.

In February of the following year, Michaela gave birth to a son. It had been a hard, icy winter and there was very little fuel to spare so the child was born in the animal shed under the house where the warmth from the cows and the donkey and the insulating bales of hay kept the cold away.

Michaela lay on a straw-filled palliasse through the long, painful hours of labour, her mother by her side to grip her hand as she cried out. Then when it was all over, she put the baby to her breast, holding him inside her clothes to keep him warm. As the child suckled she thought about Roberto. She hadn't seen him for four months. The partisans had been holed up somewhere in the mountains all winter, lying low while the Germans and the Fascists stepped up their campaign to wipe them out. Michaela didn't know where he was, didn't know even if he was alive.

She looked down at the tiny bundle in her arms. His eyes were closed, his cheeks moving in and out contentedly as he gulped down the milk. He was the only creature in the whole village who would be warm and well fed. Michaela held him close, keeping him safe until his father came back.

TWELVE

Rome, present day

Enzo's funeral was intended to be a quiet farewell attended only by his family and a few friends and colleagues. But inevitably, given his prominence in the Rome press corps and the circumstances of his death, it turned into a media occasion with photographers and television crews clambering over each other to record the event.

Chapman shut out their intrusive presence and stood by the graveside, blinking back the tears as the coffin was lowered into the earth. He could hardly bear to look at Claudia or the two boys. They were in a huddle together, arms around each other, weeping softly. And next to them, frail and alone, was Enzo's elderly mother. Her face bleak and full of pain, not yet able to comprehend that her son had gone before her.

It was a clear, hot morning, suffused with a dazzling light that, no matter how brilliant, could not dispel the cloud of gloom that hung over the mourners like a shroud. It was the sort of day that might, in another time, another place, have touched you with the joy of being alive, but now served only to remind you of what Enzo had lost – and what his wife and sons, still early in their grief, would never share with him again.

After the interment they went to a restaurant where food and drink had been provided. Chapman lingered on the fringes, not wanting to be there but feeling the burden of duty. He'd been to funerals where the deceased had been old or in the throes of a painful, terminal illness; where it was possible to feel that death had been a release for both them and their families; and where, amid the grief, there was a flicker of hope for the future. But not this time. Here there was nothing to alleviate the distress, nothing you could say to Claudia or Paolo or Carlo to comfort them. A husband and a father had been taken from them in his prime and words of condolence had no more substance than dust in the wind.

So Chapman embraced them silently, his arms encompassing their bereavement, transmitting his own. And Claudia held his hands and thanked him for coming. Then she asked him to come to the apartment later and he said he would.

It was a relief for him to get away. He went into the city and walked in the parkland of the Villa Borghese, reflecting on death and taking stock of his own life. He went down the hill to the *Giardino Zoologico* where the air was ripe with the smell of animal dung. The road by the zoo was a favourite rendezvous for courting couples and illicit lovers. In the evening there were cars parked all along it; young kids with nowhere else to go, work colleagues having a last, furtive embrace before returning home to their spouses. He'd met Gabriella here once or twice before she moved to Florence with her husband. He was getting too old for that kind of thing. He was pushing forty now, a string of lovers behind him like a *curriculum vitae*

219

advertising his unreliability and failure to commit. The fire had gone out of his relationship with Gabriella. Was it even a relationship any more? It was more of a business arrangement, convenient for both of them but ultimately transient and unsatisfactory. Sex once a week when her job brought her to Rome. It was a straightforward set-up, uncomplicated by anything other than animal desire, but was that all he wanted from a woman? He wondered if he was falling in love with Elena Fiorini.

He walked round past the Temple of Aesculapius, the weathered marble shrine which was perched on a tongue of land protruding into a small lake, and sat down on a wooden bench, watching the ducks paddling across the water. Enzo had been one of his closest friends in Italy. A true friend as well as a colleague for, since they wrote for different markets in different countries, there was no professional rivalry between them. The grief he felt was for the loss of that friend, but also for the loss of a relationship that had given a stability and a continuity to his life in Italy. With Enzo gone it was impossible for Chapman to avoid assessing his future in the country.

He'd been a foreign correspondent in Rome for eight years now. That was a long time for a posting. He'd been offered other countries in the past but always turned them down. There was a letter in his desk from his editor, offering him a job on the foreign desk in London, but he was vacillating about making a decision. He loved Italy and the Italians and had been seduced by their way of life. He was no innocent virgin, forced into doing something against his will. Seduction needed the consent of both parties and he'd succumbed to the *dolce vita* with his eyes wide open. But he was aware that the years were slipping by and he didn't know where they'd gone. Life was too easy, too comfortable. He was in danger of becoming a stateless person, neither English nor Italian, unable to adapt to life back in England yet always a foreigner in Italy.

He stood up and walked away across the park, skirting the horses exercising on the *Galoppatoio* before ascending the hill to the gardens of the Pincio. He paused briefly to lean on the parapet, admiring the view of St Peter's, then went down the Spanish Steps and strolled the last few hundred metres to his desk in the *Stampa Estera*.

He settled into the routine of an ordinary working day, calling London, reading the papers, trying to take his mind off the funeral. But he couldn't concentrate. It was only when the phone rang and he heard Elena's voice that he felt the first slight spark of pleasure he'd had all morning.

'How was it?' she said.

'Not easy. I came back here to get away from it all, but it hasn't worked.'

'That's because it's inside your head. It doesn't matter where you are. Take the day off, go for a walk.'

'I've done that already.'

There was a momentary silence, then Elena said: 'I don't know if this is a good time.'

'For what?'

'I checked out that phone number you gave me. Do you want to talk about it, or leave it for now?'

'Tell me,' Chapman said.

'It's listed under the name Bruno Cavallo. Does that mean anything to you?'

'No. What's the address?'

She gave him the name of a street in Centocelle, one of the rough, crime-ridden suburbs on the eastern side of the city.

'I can have him brought in for questioning,' she said.

'Elena, this isn't a criticism, but how far did you get with Volpi? It'll be the same with this guy. He'll have an alibi for the time of the shooting. He'll deny ever knowing Enzo. You'll get nowhere.'

'Was he there?'

'I think so. I can't be sure without seeing him.'

'I want to come with you. This is my investigation.'

'I have to do this my way.'

'Anything you find out that may be of use to me you have to hand over,' she said.

'I'm not sure that's wise.'

'What do you mean?'

'You know what I mean. You told me yourself. What happened to the tape recording of Beppe? If we make this official, Cavallo may just end up dead too.'

Elena said nothing. He had a point, but she didn't like unorthodox approaches to the investigation of crime. They had a tendency to take you outside the law. And that went against all her instincts as a magistrate.

'Okay then, let's keep it unofficial,' she said eventually.

She knew he was going to go ahead whatever her objections. This was her way of ensuring she had a degree of control over it.

'But I still want to come with you. You owe me that, Andy.'

'We'll go to see him this evening,' Chapman said. 'I'll pick you up at home. Eight o'clock.'

'I'll still be working then,' she said doubtfully.

'Elena, this *is* work.'

Claudia opened the door to him still in the plain black suit she'd worn at the funeral. It seemed to accentuate the paleness of her face. She looked ill, Chapman thought, but then what was grief but a form of illness?

He hugged her tight, holding on to her for a long while. She felt small, insubstantial in his arms and he wondered how she would stand up to the rigours of the days to come. But when she pulled away and looked up at him, he saw a quiet resilience in her eyes. She was tougher than she seemed.

'How are you, Claudia?' he said, knowing it was a foolish question to which they both knew the answer. But he had to say it. He couldn't ignore how she felt, couldn't pretend there was nothing there to discuss.

'A little better now it's all over,' she said.

'And the boys?'

'I sent them out for a walk with my sister. They were just moping around the apartment not knowing what to do with themselves. You want to get back to normal but it seems, well, disrespectful. It doesn't seem right to carry on with routine, everyday things. Cooking, eating, watching television. But what else can we do? What else is there?'

'It's not disrespectful,' Chapman said. 'You'll still be mourning, no matter what you're doing.'

'Would you like a drink? I've a bottle of Frascati in the fridge.'

Chapman nodded. He didn't feel like wine, but it gave them something to do, something to fill in the awkward silences, the lack of words that were a necessary accompaniment to bereavement.

They went into the kitchen and Claudia poured two glasses. She held hers in her hand but didn't touch it. Maybe she didn't feel like it either.

'I'm sorry to ask you round,' she said. 'I know it's the last thing anyone would want, babysitting a widow.'

'Don't be silly. I'm happy to come.'

'I'm not being maudlin. I know how people feel. At times like this you want to get away from it all. You want to forget it's happened and being with the widow just reminds you all over again.'

'Claudia, Enzo was my friend. You're my friend. I'm not going to forget what happened. I'm here for you whenever you need me. You know that.'

She forced a wan smile. 'Thank you, Andy. People are being very kind, but no one knows really what to say to me. I've just got to get on with my life. One day at a time.'

'If there's anything I can do, just say,' Chapman said. 'I mean that. It's not just words.'

Claudia pulled out one of the kitchen chairs and sat down. She put the glass of wine on the table and stroked the stem pensively.

'It's strange how you can think you know someone,' she said. 'Enzo and I were married for fourteen years. I thought I knew all about him. His moods, his character, his weaknesses, even his secrets, the things he tried to conceal from me but which I guessed anyway.' She lifted her eyes to Chapman. 'You have to be very careful, or very devious, to keep secrets from the person you live with and Enzo was neither.

'But now he's gone, I'm not sure I knew him at all. It's only been a few days yet already I'm starting to forget things. Or maybe I'm not forgetting, maybe I never knew them. I'm not expressing myself very well here. Enzo is still clear in my memory. I still don't really believe he's gone for ever. Even the funeral didn't make me believe that. It seemed impossible to me that it was Enzo inside the coffin. But now I'm back home the apartment seems terribly empty. Enzo's personality used to fill it so much. Without him here, without some daily reminder of him, I feel he'll start to fade from my mind. Like a ghost walking through a wall. Bits of him disappearing until finally there's nothing left. That frightens me.'

'He's not going to fade away, Claudia,' Chapman said, touching her hand. 'But he's not going to be here either. The pain is bound to get less in time. If it didn't, we'd spend our whole lives grieving.'

'I wonder if we shouldn't. Doesn't a husband, a father, deserve more than a few weeks, a few months of mourning?'

'What would be the point in being alive then? We're born, we die. We have to do something in between. We're always going to lose people we love. We mourn them and in time we live with their loss and get on with our lives as best we can. Those sound like platitudes now because you can't see a time when you won't mourn. But it will change. Life would be unbearable if it didn't.'

Claudia nodded bleakly. 'Yes, I'm sure you're right. It just doesn't feel that way at the moment.'

Chapman drank some of his wine, easing the dryness in his mouth. He was uncomfortable but trying not to show it.

'Are you going to be all right financially?' he asked, steering the conversation on to more practical matters.

'I think so. I have my job and Enzo was insured. I haven't thought about it much. His paper has said they'll help. He was killed while he was working, after all. I can't concentrate on things like that.' She glanced at him. 'It's good to talk, but that's not why I asked you to come round.'

She stood up and left the kitchen. Chapman saw her go down the hall into the bedroom. When she came out again she was holding a large manilla envelope.

'This came for Enzo the day after he was killed. I only got round to opening it yesterday.'

Chapman opened the flap of the envelope and peered inside. It contained a thin sheaf of papers which he pulled out a few inches. They appeared to be letters, most of them brittle and yellow with age. But the top sheet was newer, a handwritten covering letter dated only a few days earlier. It had a Rome address at the top and said: 'Dear Mr Mattei, I've read your newspaper articles on the murder of Father Vivaldi. I don't know whether these documents are relevant, but I think you should have them.' It was signed 'Maria Casella'.

'Do you know this woman?' Chapman asked Claudia.

'No.'

'What are these papers?'

'I didn't look at them. I just read that letter and

knew I should give them to you. Enzo would have wanted it.'

Chapman leafed carefully through the papers. They were torn and faded, the writing on many of them hard to decipher. At the top of one page he saw some words he didn't understand. It looked like a foreign language but he couldn't place it. He shrugged and slipped the documents back into the envelope.

'I'll study them later. They were delivered here?'

Claudia nodded. 'In the ordinary mail.'

'Was Enzo expecting them?'

'If he was, he didn't say anything to me.'

'I'll see what I can do with them.'

Claudia saw him snatch a look at the clock on the wall. 'Do you have to go?'

'I'm meeting someone. But I don't like leaving you on your own.'

'My sister's staying for a few days. And I have the boys. Don't worry about me.'

'But I *do* worry, Claudia.'

She reached out and took his hand, holding it tight.

'Do something for me, Andy,' she said. 'Find out who killed Enzo. Bring them to justice.'

Since the morning after Enzo's murder, Chapman had been back to his flat only intermittently – to pick up his mail or clean clothes – and only in daylight. The two men lying in wait for him had shaken him quite badly and he'd checked into a hotel immediately afterwards as a precaution. He didn't think the men would come back, not after the police had chased them away, but he wasn't going to take any chances.

The moment of inserting the key and opening the

door to his apartment gave him an attack of nerves, of blind fear even worse than he'd experienced in EUR. Then he'd reacted automatically to the threat to his life. It had been so quick, so instinctive that he hadn't had to think about what he was doing. All he knew was that he had to get away. But now, on the landing outside his apartment, he was well aware of the risks he was taking. His brain told him that, in all probability, there was no one lurking inside, but his senses and his stomach took no notice of logic or odds. They were bombarding him with impulses, leaking chemicals into his system which made his guts churn and his muscles tremble, preparing for flight.

He turned the key in the lock and pushed the door open, stepping back quickly, ready to run down the stairs if anyone came for him. The flat seemed to be empty. Chapman listened from the doorway for a minute or more before he went in and cautiously checked all the rooms. There was no one there. He locked and bolted the front door, then took a shower and changed into fresh clothes.

It was gone half past seven when he'd finished. The envelope Claudia had given him was lying on the bed. There was no time to study the contents thoroughly but he pulled the papers out and glanced through them again, seeing if he could decipher the indistinct text. It was hard going. The letters were not only old – he could just make out the date, 2nd April 1945, at the top of one – but badly stained. It looked as if they'd been splashed with water or grease at some point or kept somewhere damp. There was a greyish mould on the paper and large chunks of type were either obscured or obliterated altogether.

Mixed in with the letters was a dog-eared black and white photograph. It showed Mussolini standing in a group in front of an elegant stone building. Chapman gave it a perfunctory examination, then put it back in the envelope with the other documents. He knew, without being sure exactly why, that the papers were important. His apartment wasn't a safe place to leave them, nor was his car. But where else could he put them?

He threw some clean underwear and shirts into a sports bag and left the flat. On the floor below he knocked on Signora Campanella's door.

'Who is it?' she called out from inside.

'Signor Chapman. From upstairs.'

He waited while she undid the locks and chains and opened the door.

'I'm sorry to disturb you,' Chapman said. 'I wonder if I could ask you a favour. I have to go away for a couple of days. Would you mind keeping this envelope for me? I don't want to leave it in my empty apartment.'

Signora Campanella looked at the envelope and shrugged. 'All right. What is it?'

'Just work papers. Nothing much.'

He gave her the envelope. 'Thank you, signora. I'm very grateful. *Buona sera.*'

Signora Campanella closed her door and locked it. Chapman stayed where he was on the landing until he heard her footsteps recede, then he went downstairs and out into the bustling evening.

They parked on the opposite side of the road from the grim concrete apartment building in which Bruno

PAUL ADAM

Cavallo lived. It was growing dark, but even the Stygian depths of night couldn't conceal the ugly rows of tenements and graffitied walls that formed the decaying heart of Centocelle. Elena looked out through the car windscreen, knowing that this was somewhere she would never come on her own, and wondering what she was doing here now with Chapman.

'What do you intend to do?' she asked as he turned off the engine and slouched lower in his seat.

He shrugged. 'Talk to him, I suppose.'

'About Mattei?'

'About everything. Enzo had used him before. He was a good source.'

'He set him up.'

'I know. But why? Why now?'

'You think he'll give you any answers?'

'I've got a better chance than a cop. Or a magistrate. I want to see him face to face first. Size him up.' Chapman turned his head to her. 'I think I should go in alone.'

'Not a chance.'

'I can look after myself.'

'And who's going to look after me? You think I'm going to sit here in the car while every foul-mouthed yob in the neighbourhood ogles at me through the windows, or worse.'

'You wanted to come, Elena.'

'Come *with* you. And that's what I intend to do. You don't have to tell him who I am.'

'You like to get your own way, don't you?'

She grinned at him. 'I'm a woman.'

'So what else do you know about Cavallo?'

'What do you mean?'

230

'You're not telling me you checked out the telephone number of someone you suspected was involved in a murder and only came up with his address? Come on, Elena. This is virtually a police state. There are files on everything and everybody; tax, employment records, criminal records, all of it on computer. I bet you cross-checked everything.'

'I don't have access to everything. Not without a court order.'

'But you know if he has previous convictions.'

She said nothing.

'I need to know whom I'm dealing with, Elena.'

'Two,' she said. 'One for theft, one for wounding with intent. He was involved in a street brawl and stuck a knife in someone's back. He's a nasty piece of work, Andy. I still think you should leave him to the police.'

'We've been over that. You ready?' Chapman pulled the lever to open his door, and stopped. 'Wait a minute.'

A man with a shaven head was coming out of the main entrance to the apartment block. He paused on the pavement, glancing up and down the street, waiting for someone. Chapman saw his face in profile. In the fading light, and from a distance, he couldn't be absolutely sure this was the man he'd seen get out of the BMW in EUR. But there were similarities. And, more tellingly, the man had a long pointed nose which protruded from his face like a sawn-off cigar. If anyone was going to acquire the nickname Pinocchio, it was this individual.

'That's him,' Chapman said, watching as Pinocchio walked quickly out to a dented Fiat Uno which had

PAUL ADAM

pulled in next to the parked cars. He climbed into the back and the Fiat drove off down the street. Chapman turned on his engine and went after it.

'Are you sure?' Elena said.

Chapman nodded. 'You notice anything odd about him?'

'Not particularly, no.'

'He was wearing an overcoat. Would you wear a coat in this heat?'

'It was only a light mackintosh. Maybe he's expecting rain.'

'Then why not carry it? No, I think he's hiding something underneath it.'

They drove south out of the city, running parallel to the path of the Via Ostiense which in Roman times led to the port of Ostia at the mouth of the Tiber. Ancient Ostia itself was no longer inhabited. Its ruined streets were now the province of archaeologists and tourists, but the road still ran past it; in summer a long traffic jam of sweaty Romans heading to the seaside resort of Lido di Ostia for their weekend grilling on the beach – a hazardous journey, for if a multiple pile-up on the way didn't kill you then the pollution in the sea almost certainly would.

Chapman stayed well back, keeping one or two other cars in between him and the Fiat. They drove steadily for half an hour, the driver of the Fiat maintaining a cautious approach to speed and safety which was strikingly unusual for the Romans, who regarded road traffic regulations as suggestions rather than rules. They reached a turn-off and the Fiat slowed and began to indicate. Chapman followed it down the slip road into the modern town of Ostia. They drove straight through and out on to the dark road which led to the excavations of Ostia Antica.

Chapman knew the area well. He liked to come out here on bright spring days when it was quiet, to wander among the ancient buildings and sit beneath the spreading pines watching lizards sunning themselves on stones which, two thousand years earlier, a Roman mason had hewn by hand. It was a vast site, a whole city reclaimed from the earth. Even in summer there was space enough to get away from the coach parties and their guides, but out of season it had the tranquillity of a secluded garden.

The Fiat slowed as it neared the main entrance to the excavations. The electrically operated steel gates had been left open. The Fiat drove in and parked behind a line of other cars at the edge of the road which led round to the museum. Chapman turned off into the car park outside the gates and extinguished his headlights. More cars came past, heading into the ruined city. Shadowy male figures emerged from the vehicles and disappeared into the darkness.

'It looks like a meeting of some sort,' Chapman said, opening his door. 'Stay here.'

'Oh no, I told you . . .'

'I'll be right back,' he interrupted. 'You're a woman, you're too conspicuous.'

He walked towards the entrance, keeping under the trees which fringed the north side of the car park. He paused and watched the groups of men streaming silently into the excavations. All of them were wearing long coats or leather jackets. Some were carrying bags. Chapman turned and walked back to his car.

'What's happening?' Elena said.

'I don't know. We'll give them a few minutes, then go and see.'

He reached across and unlocked the glove compartment, taking out a 35 mm camera with a telephoto lens attached. He checked the film and kept the camera on his lap, watching the road. No more cars arrived. He waited until there was no sign of movement beyond the gates before he got out again. He slung the camera over his shoulder and headed for the entrance, Elena walking next to him. They didn't talk. Sound would travel a long way out there.

They passed through the gates. There were dozens of cars parked along the grass verge inside. Their occupants had chosen the spot carefully, well away from the main road and any prying eyes in the houses on the outskirts of Ostia.

Chapman and Elena cut across behind the pay kiosk and on to the ancient paved road that led into the excavated city. The slabs of rock were hard and uneven beneath their feet, deep ruts worn into their surface by chariot and wagon wheels. On either side, fragments of walls poked up through the soil like chipped teeth. Pine trees and cedars cast deep shadows across the terrain which was gradually being colonised by weeds and thigh-deep grass and clumps of unruly shrubs.

Up ahead, in the heart of the city, many buildings were still standing, some two storeys high, a few still with their roofs intact. There were baths and temples and dozens of *horreae*, the warehouses used for storing the grain and other commodities that flooded into Ostia for the burgeoning capital of the empire twenty kilometres up the Tiber. These were the warehouses which contained the *Annona*, the handouts of free food to idle Roman citizens, the bread to go with the circuses that prevented unrest among a disgruntled populace.

It was pitch dark on the track, no city lights or moonlight to illuminate their path, but in the near distance, shielded by the buildings, was a faint glow spreading upwards into the sky. Chapman took Elena's hand.

'I know a better way. I think we should keep off the main track.'

He led her down one of the side streets, then through a gap in a wall and across the interior of a ruined house. They skirted a fenced-off area around a precious floor mosaic and passed under an archway into a dark vault. Chapman kept hold of Elena's hand, feeling his way through the blackness.

'Where are we going?' she whispered.

'Just follow me.'

He paused, getting his bearings.

'You've been here before?' Elena said.

'Many times. I love this city. I love the feeling that we're walking through the streets the ancient Romans trod, the buildings they lived in. You know, just over there' – he pointed – 'is the brothel where they specialised in providing sex with male dwarfs.'

'My kind of town,' Elena said drily.

They turned into what seemed to be a tunnel or an arcade, the roof arching over their heads. As they neared the end, they became aware not just of a faint light outside, but also a noise that was both familiar yet hard to place. Elena listened and realised it was the sound of people, of a crowd gathered together, talking, moving around.

They emerged into the fresh air and Chapman stopped

abruptly. He pulled Elena back into the shadows and put a finger on her lips. Standing just a few metres away from them, his back turned to them, was a man. He was wearing high leather boots, breeches and a long-sleeved black shirt, plain except for a white badge on the upper sleeve. The badge caught the reflected light from somewhere in front and Chapman made out the axe and bundle of elm rods embroidered on it: the *fasces* which the ancient Romans had used to symbolise the military and judicial powers of their empire and which Mussolini had later appropriated as the emblem of his political movement and the symbol after which it was named. With the black ceremonial fez with tassel on the man's shaven head, this was the uniform of a Blackshirt, a Fascist soldier.

Chapman retreated back into the tunnel, knowing now for certain what they'd stumbled upon. He led Elena back the way they'd come and took a different turning into a walled courtyard. A flight of stone steps led up on to what remained of the roof. Chapman climbed up them in a crouch and motioned to Elena to keep down. On their hands and knees they crawled across the roof and peered over the low parapet protecting its edges.

Chapman gaped open-mouthed at the scene below them. In the Forum of ancient Ostia, lined up in tight military formation, was a vast crowd of young men, each identically dressed in black shirts with the *fasces* on the sleeves. There must have been four, maybe five hundred of them. At the head of each rank stood a Blackshirt holding a flag like a Roman *vexillum*; a rectangle of black cloth suspended from a horizontal crossbar. Embroidered on each flag were an eagle with spread wings and the name and number of the legion it represented. At the finial of the brass staff was another spread eagle in the centre of a wreath and immediately below that a tablet inscribed with the initials MVSN.

'Jesus Christ,' Elena breathed.

She stared at the crowd for a moment, then slumped back down below the parapet and leaned her shoulders against it. Chapman ducked down next to her and took the lens cap off his camera.

Elena glanced at him uneasily. 'We should get out of here,' she said. 'Immediately. Did you see the flags? Those are MVSN legions. You know what the MVSN was, don't you?'

'*Milizia Volontaria per la Sicurezza Nazionale.* Mussolini's Blackshirt militia.'

'Those aren't neo-Fascists down there. They're the real thing.'

'I'm going to try to get some pictures. I don't know whether there's enough light.'

Elena opened her mouth to object, but the words were drowned out by a massive roar from the Blackshirts. She and Chapman poked their heads above the parapet again. At the far end of the Forum a floodlit wooden platform had been constructed on the steps of the Capitolium. A large banner above the platform read: '*Credire, Ubbidire, Combattere*' – Believe, Obey, Fight – one of Mussolini's much-parroted aphorisms; and standing under the banner acknowledging the adulation of the crowd was a cluster of men in black shirts. At the forefront, the clear leader of the group, was Cesare Scarfone.

Elena took in his upraised arms, his militaristic posturing, not overly surprised to see him at a Fascist

237

rally. But as she ran her eyes over the other men on the platform, she saw someone whose presence made her reel with shock. She took a deep breath, feeling slightly giddy. *Dio*, it couldn't be.

The cheers subsided and, as one, the assembled files of Blackshirts started to sing the Fascist anthem, *Giovinezza*. Elena felt the skin on her neck turn suddenly cold and clammy. The sound, like the chanting of a stadium of football hooligans, filled her with dread.

'Let's go, Andy,' she said.

Chapman had his camera resting on the top of the parapet, the telephoto lens focused on the brightly lit platform. He clicked off several shots then sat down next to her as the singing stopped and Scarfone's voice boomed out through the speakers at either side of the platform.

'My friends, we are gathered here to witness the rebirth of a nation. To begin the fight that will wipe out the traitors who have brought our country to its knees. To build a new, stronger Italy. To bring back the glories of ancient Rome for the youth of the twenty-first century.'

Chapman knelt back up and snapped off half a dozen more shots as Scarfone, shouting above the well-orchestrated responses of the crowd, continued a speech brimming over with nationalism, bigotry and hatred. A speech that could have been made at Nuremberg or from the balcony of the Palazzo Venezia.

Then, for just an instant, the crowd lapsed into silence and the click of the camera shutter seemed as loud and conspicuous as a firecracker. A Blackshirt sentry, standing guard on the perimeter of the Forum, looked up and saw Chapman's face over the parapet. He gave a shout but the warning was drowned out by a sudden cheer from the crowd. Chapman grabbed Elena's hand and they ran for the steps, stumbling down them as fast as they could. They crossed the courtyard at the bottom and emerged through a doorway on to a narrow side street. Chapman looked both ways, trying to guess from which direction the sentry would come. Either way was a gamble. He turned left, picking a path over the uneven surface. There were potholes everywhere, treacherous cracks in the stone paving which it was impossible to see in the dark. He glanced back. The sentry had just come round the corner from the Forum. He couldn't fail to see them.

Chapman turned into a narrow path between two buildings. Elena came behind him, her arms outstretched, touching the walls on either side to keep her balance as she ran. Ahead of them, at the end of the path, a figure flashed by. Another Blackshirt. Chapman didn't think the man had seen them, but he wasn't going to depend on it. The wall on the right had gaps in it where the stonework had crumbled away. Chapman climbed through one into a wide chamber open to the sky. There was a deep trench immediately in front of them and stone benches around the walls with holes cut in the tops.

'Mind your feet,' Chapman whispered. 'You could easily turn an ankle.'

'What is this?'

'The *forica*. The public toilet,' Chapman said. 'It could seat twenty. The rich men of ancient Ostia used to come here for a gossip. They'd send a servant on ahead of them to keep their seat warm for them.'

'You're a mine of fascinating information,' Elena said, 'but I'm not sure this is an appropriate moment to share it with me.'

They picked their way across and out through another hole into a dark corridor. It was tempting to stay where they were rather than venture out again into the open, but Chapman knew there were no safe hiding places in Ostia Antica. The longer they delayed, the more Blackshirts would be drafted in to search for them. They'd get torches and go through every building in the city until they found them.

There was a gap in the wall to the left. Chapman stuck his head through it cautiously. There was a courtyard on the other side. He climbed out into it and reached back to help Elena. As she emerged, there was the sound of running footsteps in the street beyond the courtyard. Chapman put his arms around her and pulled her back into a shadowy alcove. A man stepped through an archway and gave the courtyard a perfunctory examination. Chapman held his breath. Elena was still in his arms. He could feel her trembling slightly. The man retreated through the arch and Chapman relaxed. In the distance they could hear Scarfone's voice over the loudspeakers, the intermittent applause of the crowd. Chapman was relieved. The rally was still in progress. A few sentries they might evade, if they were lucky. Five hundred fired-up Blackshirts was a different matter altogether.

There was a second exit at the side of the courtyard. Chapman and Elena checked the street outside and dashed across it into the shelter of a ruined wall. Elena had lost all sense of direction in the warren of paths and alleys.

'Which way's the car?' she breathed softly.

'Stay with me,' Chapman replied.

He moved out into the open and was caught silhouetted against the skyline as one of the sentries came round the corner of a building. The sentry shouted and came for them. Chapman and Elena sprinted down the street and dived through a doorway into a lofty warehouse. Something exploded against the lintel of the door, sending splinters of stone into the air. Elena became aware a split second later of a bang which could only be the report of a gun.

'Jesus,' she murmured. 'They're shooting at us.'

They were on their knees now, crawling into one of the chambers along the side of the warehouse. They pressed deep into a dark corner and sat motionless, watching the door. Chapman could feel Elena's breath warm on his cheek. His pulse was racing, his guts turning to jelly.

The Blackshirt came through the opening, a pistol raised in his right hand. He came round the edge of the warehouse, keeping close to the wall. Chapman felt around on the ground beside him. His fingers closed around a small stone. He waited. The Blackshirt was getting closer, his head turning from side to side as he tried to see into the recesses of the building. Chapman gripped the stone in his left hand. His right was still clutching the strap of his camera. The Blackshirt was almost in front of them. Chapman threw the stone out into the centre of the warehouse. It clattered across the floor. The Blackshirt spun round towards the sudden noise and at that moment Chapman launched himself at him, his camera coming down in a long vicious arc. The metal case thudded into the side of the Blackshirt's head and he collapsed to the ground, unconscious.

Chapman looked down at him, aware of Elena coming up to his shoulder.

'They'll have heard the shot,' she said.

They went to the doorway and stopped on the threshold. The loudspeakers in the Forum were silent now. There was no more applause, no more adulatory cheers. Either the rally was over, or it had been prematurely halted to enlist the Blackshirts in the hunt for the two interlopers. Chapman prayed it was the former, then realised with a sickening jab of fear that his prayers hadn't been answered. Away down the street, pouring out from the Forum, were dozens of dancing lights – torches, with shadowy Blackshirts moving behind them. They kept on coming, splitting off into groups and disappearing into the labyrinth of ancient avenues.

For an instant, Chapman and Elena were paralysed by fear. Then Chapman tore his eyes away and, grabbing Elena by the hand, began to run towards the perimeter of the city. They kept close to the buildings, to the walls, anything that might give them some cover. The torches behind them moved in and out of side streets and doorways. The Blackshirts were searching methodically through every nook and cranny of the excavations, starting at the Forum and working outwards. But it wouldn't be long before they sent an advance party out to seal the exit and start the search from the other direction.

The ruins began to peter out. The low walls and isolated stubs of pillars and arches remained, but they afforded no real protection from the hunters' eyes.

Chapman bent his knees and back, trying to reduce the possibility of being highlighted against the pale backdrop of the sky.

Elena touched his arm. 'Andy.' She was gasping for breath.

He glanced sideways and saw her pointing away to their left. He dropped immediately to the ground and pulled her down next to him. They lay flat on their bellies watching as a squad of Blackshirts ran along the track that led to the main entrance to the city.

'Shit!' Chapman murmured.

'They're going to trap us in the middle,' Elena whispered. 'We have to get to the fence.'

Chapman knelt up. He could see scattered torch beams back in the excavations and now a new cluster near the main exit. A motor whirred and the heavy steel gates clanged shut across the road.

'Stay as low as you can and follow me,' he said.

They crawled through the maze of ruined buildings, heading for the perimeter fence. The Blackshirts at the exit were fanning out, getting into position for a sweep back across the excavations. Chapman dropped down into a hollow at the edge of a clearing. He peered across towards the fence. There was no way of telling exactly where the Blackshirts were looking, but he knew that any delay could be fatal. They just had to hope the Blackshirts' attention was momentarily focused on the perimeter, and go for it. He rose into a crouch and sprinted across the clearing, throwing himself down on the other side. Elena's body landed heavily next to his. They waited for the shout, a sign that they'd been spotted, but nothing came. Then they snaked away behind a low brick wall and started to head in a diagonal line for the perimeter fence.

The terrain was in their favour. Criss-crossed with ruins, the earth pitted with trenches and ditches overgrown with vegetation. Their hands and knees were torn and bruised but they barely noticed the pain. They were intent only on staying hidden and reaching the fence. Nothing else mattered.

The Blackshirts were fifty metres apart, moving in from the perimeter in a line, their torches scything over the earth. Chapman risked a peek over a wall. The gap between the hunters was wide, too wide to cover adequately with a hand torch. That gave him hope. They had to find the point midway between two of the Blackshirts and rely on the beams being too weak to probe the hidden cavities of the terrain.

Chapman turned directly towards the fence, Elena crawling along in his lee. The Blackshirts were less than thirty metres away, moving in much faster than he'd expected. They had to find somewhere to hide or they'd be caught. A stray torch beam lanced over their heads. Chapman pressed his face into the earth and the light passed by. There were Blackshirts on either flank. There had to be a hole somewhere, a hollow they could crawl into. Then Chapman saw it. A trench just in front of them. He scuttled forwards and rolled down into the trench. Elena slithered after him and he pulled her into the shelter of a slight overhang. They lay there, clinging to each other as the beams of light swept over the ground all around them. Then the torches were gone, the Blackshirts moving on through the excavations.

Chapman and Elena stayed put for a minute or more. Then they crawled out and broke their way through the thick undergrowth to the fence. Chapman gave Elena a leg up and she scrambled over the top on to the road. Chapman climbed over behind her and they ran to the car. He started the engine, knowing the Blackshirts would hear it, but it didn't matter now. He waited until they were a hundred metres down the road before he switched on the headlights, then put his foot down. Elena leaned back on the headrest, getting her breath back.

'You okay?' Chapman said.

She nodded. '*Dio*. I've never been so frightened in my life. My heartbeat was going through the roof back there.'

He put a hand on her knee. 'We're out of it now.'

'Those men on the platform with Scarfone,' Elena said. 'I recognised one of them. At the back, keeping out of the limelight. He had a priest's collar on.'

'There was a priest?' Chapman's head jolted round. 'Are you sure?'

'I've met him. His name is Father Ivan Simčić, Secretary to Archbishop Tomassi. He was the Vatican official who was in Antonio Vivaldi's apartment before the police.'

They found a bar in Ostia where Elena telephoned the headquarters of the *Carabinieri* in Rome. She spoke to the duty officer for some ten minutes, then came back out to the car.

'They're taking care of it,' she said. 'There's nothing more we can do.'

They drove back to Elena's apartment and Chapman came in with her. It wasn't something they'd discussed – they both just assumed he'd be staying. They shared a bottle of beer from the fridge, talking a little about what had happened, getting the tension out of their systems. Then Elena went into the bathroom and turned on the shower. They stripped off their grimy, sweat-soaked clothes and stepped into the cubicle together, soaping each other, holding each other as the jet of water rinsed them off.

They went into the bedroom still naked and damp. Chapman pulled Elena down on to the bed and they kissed for a long time. His hand touched her skin, cupping the soft flesh, arousing her. She pulled him on top, bringing her legs up around him as he came inside. Then the telephone by the bed rang.

'Don't answer it,' Chapman said.

'It might be important. Don't go away.'

She reached out and picked up the receiver, listening for a moment. Chapman propped himself up on his arms, concentrating on her naked body, shutting out the sound of her voice on the telephone. After a few minutes she replaced the receiver.

'That was the *Carabinieri*. They sealed off Ostia Antica and searched the place. There was no one there. They found the platform and lights but the Blackshirts had all disappeared. Their cars too. The officer in charge said they were going to . . .'

'Elena,' Chapman broke in, 'to quote you, you're a mine of fascinating information but I'm not sure this is an appropriate moment to share it with me.'

Elena smiled at him. 'Okay.' She ran her hands down his back and dug her fingers into his buttocks.

'Now, where were we?' she said.

THIRTEEN

Chapman awoke to find himself alone in the double bed. He felt the sheet next to him. It was still warm from Elena's body. He climbed out and slipped on his pants and trousers. The faint murmur of Elena's voice came from the study across the hall as he went through into the kitchen to make coffee.

He had the espresso on the table, cups and a jug of hot milk next to it, by the time Elena came in. She was barefoot, her cotton robe tied loosely at the waist.

'Mmm, I could get used to this,' she said, helping herself to coffee.

'I couldn't find anything to eat,' Chapman said.

'That's because there isn't anything.'

She ran a hand through her tangled hair. She'd hoped to tidy herself up, to wash and put on some make-up before Chapman was awake, but he'd caught her unawares. Not that he looked much better: unshaven, his hair sticking up in tufts, his trousers crumpled and stained with the dirt from Ostia Antica.

'I was talking to the *Carabinieri* duty officer,' she said. 'They didn't manage to pick up a single one of those Blackshirt bastards.'

247

'You think they tried very hard?' Chapman said. The *Carabinieri* were not renowned for their left-wing sympathies.

Elena shrugged. 'Who knows? Five hundred crop-headed thugs are pretty hard to miss, but they had plenty of time to get away. The *Carabinieri* didn't start a search of the surrounding roads and villages until they'd checked the whole of Ostia Antica.'

'So they've got no one at all?'

'One of the custodians is under arrest. He's admitted taking five hundred thousand lire to leave the gates open and make himself scarce for the evening.'

'Five hundred thousand from whom?'

'No one we'll ever identify.' Elena added more milk to her coffee and drank some. 'I'll have to have the film from your camera.'

Chapman eyed her pensively. 'I don't really have a choice, do I?'

'No.' She gave a brief smile. 'It's evidence. I need it to make a case against Scarfone, you know that. It might help us ID some of the others who were there too.'

'There's always Bruno Cavallo,' Chapman said.

'He's gone to ground. I gave his name and address to the *Carabinieri* on the phone last night. They sent a car over but he never came home.'

'And the priest? What was his name again?'

'Ivan Simčić. He'll be safe in the Vatican by now.'

Chapman nodded, swirling the dregs of coffee around in his cup.

'My film,' he said. 'Keep the negatives, but let me have a set of prints.'

'You're doing a story?'

'Not until I've got the whole picture. But I'll need them then.'

Elena gave it a moment's thought. 'Okay. I'll have them sent over to you.' She stood up from the table. 'You want a shower?'

Chapman shook his head. 'I'll have one at my hotel. I have to go there to shave and change my trousers anyway.'

'You're not moving back into your apartment yet?'

'I'll give it another day or so.'

Elena went through into the bathroom. Chapman finished his coffee and got dressed. Elena was just stepping out of the shower, her body glistening with moisture, when he came into the bathroom to say goodbye. He looked at her standing there naked, taking in the smooth contours of her body. She wrapped a towel around herself and tugged a lock of wet hair away from her face.

'The top drawer of the desk in my study,' she said casually, 'there's a spare set of keys for my apartment. Take them if you like.'

His eyes met hers. 'You sure?'

'No,' she said. 'I'm not sure. But what the hell, you're fully house-trained.'

He stepped towards her and put his arms around her, feeling the towel warm and damp against him. She smelt of soap and shampoo. They kissed. Chapman's fingers slipped down her back, lifting the towel, touching her underneath. She pulled his hands away.

'I have to go to work. So do you.'

'It's still early.'

'I've just had a shower.'

'We'll have another together afterwards.'

249

'Andy . . .'

He took her hand and led her through into the bedroom. He kissed her again, his hands sliding under the towel, caressing her. Elena sighed softly.

'You work too hard anyway,' he said.

'God, you're a terrible influence on me.'

She pulled his mouth down on to hers. She fumbled with the buttons on his shirt, ripping it off him. Then her hands dropped to his belt, tugging at it as he tore away her towel. They fell back on to the bed, limbs entwined, reaching for each other with a frenzied passion.

Chapman broke away and leaned across to take the phone off the hook.

'This time, no interruptions,' he said.

Maria Casella lived in the cool labyrinth of streets between the Corso Vittorio Emanuele and the Tiber, a long, triangular sliver of land broken up by cobbled throughfares and stone buildings whose massive walls glowered menacingly over passers-by and the inevitable clusters of parked cars which clung to every nook and cranny of the quarter like sleeping cockroaches.

This had once been the heart of Renaissance Rome, where merchants and artisans – bowmakers, locksmiths, saddlers – plied their trades in the shadow of the great palaces, the Farnese and the Spada; where Benvenuto Cellini drank and brawled and the Borgias went about their sinister intrigues. Its atmosphere was more subdued now: no horses galloping through, no swordplay in the streets or papal processions winding their magnificent path from the Vatican to the Lateran. But in the Campo de' Fiori, with its bustling fruit and vegetable market, the shouts of its roguish traders and pungent aromas, you could still catch a glimpse of what it must once have been like.

Signora Casella's apartment was at the top of an unprepossessing block to the west of the Campo, a solid sixteenth-century edifice with stones the size of suitcases blackened by years of grime and pollution. It was nothing to look at from the outside, but in this prime slice of city centre, mere yards from the fashionable galleries of the Via Giulia and – more importantly – divided up into spacious, rent-controlled flats, it was a residence any Roman would have killed to possess.

Chapman took the stairs up to the fourth floor and rang the doorbell. A lock snapped open and a woman's face peered out above the steel chain.

'Signora Casella?'

'Yes.'

'My name is Chapman. I'm a journalist. A friend of Enzo Mattei's.'

Maria Casella studied him for a moment with nervous, darting eyes.

'I've come about the papers you sent him.'

'Have you any identification?'

Chapman held his press accreditation up to the crack. She examined it carefully then pushed the door to and unlatched the chain to let him in.

'I'm sorry, I'm a little on edge at the moment,' she explained, closing and locking the door behind him. Her hands were trembling.

In contrast to the gloomy exterior of the building, Signora Casella's apartment was light and airy. Chapman had been in these old flats before and had expected acres of dark, heavy furniture, family heir-looms handed down through the generations of occupants who, once they had a hold on the apartment, never relinquished it.

But the sunlight which flooded in through the unshuttered windows illuminated a living room whose modern, minimalist style, though at odds with the fabric of the building, seemed perfectly appropriate to the high, lofty interiors. Sparsely furnished, it had a pine-framed sofa and matching armchair in the centre of the tiled floor, and vivid abstract prints on the plain white walls.

'Can I offer you some coffee?' Signora Casella asked.

'Thank you.'

Chapman watched her go out to the kitchen, then wandered over to the window. They were high enough up to escape the shadows of the surrounding buildings. Looking west, he could see the statue of Garibaldi on the Janiculum Hill and, below it, the botanical gardens which cascaded down the slope towards the river. A corner of the Regina Coeli – Queen of the Heavens – prison, a wonderfully evocative name for such an ugly carbuncle, was visible between the rooftops and, just downstream, a part of the Villa Farnesina where the Renaissance banker, Agostino Chigi, had once hosted extravagant banquets at which his servants would toss the gold and silver plate into the Tiber between courses – an ostentatious display of wealth somewhat undermined by the fact that he'd placed hidden nets in the water beforehand so the valuables could be recovered after his guests had gone.

'How do you like it?'

Chapman turned. 'Black, no sugar.'

She gave him a small china cup and saucer glazed with the same pattern as that on the furniture.

'You know Enzo is dead, don't you?' Chapman said.

'Yes, I saw it in the newspaper.'

'Did you know him?'

'No.'

'But you sent him some papers.'

'I read his reports on Father Vivaldi's death. He seemed the best person to have them.'

She lowered herself on to the edge of the sofa, sitting very upright, tense. The cup of coffee rested on her knees, one of her hands gripping the handle, the other the saucer. From the lines on her face, Chapman guessed she was in her fifties. With her bony legs, arms like brittle twigs and the skin of her neck starting to loosen, she was on the borderline of being scrawny. But she carried herself well, with a studied elegance that made him wonder if she'd been a dancer or a model.

'His widow passed them on to me,' Chapman said. 'They're not very easy to read. Can you tell me what they are?'

Signora Casella shook her head. 'I'm afraid not. I didn't look at them very closely myself.'

'Yet you thought they might be useful to Enzo?'

'It seemed possible.'

'Why?'

She gave a slight shrug. 'I'm not sure. Perhaps because of Antonio's attitude to them.'

'Antonio? You mean Father Vivaldi?'

'That's who gave them to me.'

Chapman came away from the window and sank

down into the armchair. 'Father Vivaldi gave them to you?' he repeated.

'For safekeeping, he said. That's why I knew they were important. He'd never done that before.'

'You were a friend of his?'

There was only a tiny hesitation before she answered, 'Yes, you could say that.'

'But he didn't tell you what they were?'

'He said it was better for me not to know.'

'Why would he have done that?'

'I think he was scared.'

'Scared? Scared of what?'

Signora Casella swallowed some of her coffee. When she put the cup back down she had to grip it hard to stop it rattling on the saucer.

'You said you were on edge, signora,' Chapman said. 'Why is that?'

She glanced up at him. She was still a beautiful woman. The flesh was starting to sag a little, but the bone structure underneath was fundamentally sound. She was one of the lucky ones who would grow old gracefully.

'You are a colleague of Signor Mattei's?' she said.

'Yes.'

'But you're not Italian.'

'We were working together, investigating Father Vivaldi's death. Enzo was my friend. I was there when he was killed. You can trust me, signora, I assure you of that.'

When she didn't reply, he said gently: 'What is it you're afraid of?'

'Antonio is dead. Your friend Enzo Mattei is dead,' she said abruptly. 'Aren't you scared?'

254

'That's different. I'm in the middle of it all, I know the risks. But you're just on the periphery. Why should you be in danger?'

She put her cup and saucer down on the floor and stood up, smoothing her skirt with the palms of her hands. Chapman watched her walk to the window and look out into the street. He didn't press her. When you'd been a reporter for as long as he had, you learned to sense when someone was going to talk to you eventually. You just had to give them the space.

Without turning around she said: 'I was . . . close to Antonio.' She paused to let the words sink in. 'Closer than anyone.'

Her face was hidden, but Chapman could see the tightness in her shoulders as she leaned forwards on the windowsill.

'I'm not sure I understand you, signora.'

She turned her head, then her body. 'The day he died. He came here in the afternoon.'

'The afternoon? I understood he went to the Vatican then?'

Signora Casella was surprised. 'You knew about that? Yes, he was on his way to the Vatican City when he stopped off. He was in a hurry. He had a taxi downstairs waiting. He came in with the papers in an envelope. He told me to put them somewhere safe for him.'

She walked back over from the window, the heels of her shoes tapping lightly on the marble tiles.

'He only stayed a few minutes. I put them away in a drawer and forgot about them. It was only later, after it . . . happened . . . that I thought about them. I took them out and looked at them. I was curious to know what they were. Most of them were impossible to read, but one was clear enough to see the Vatican heading on the notepaper. That's when I sent them to your friend.'

'Why not give them to the police?'

'The police?' Her lips moved contemptuously. 'If Antonio was killed by neo-Fascists, the police are the last people I would ask to investigate it.'

'Do *you* believe it was neo-Fascists?'

'I don't know.'

'Had anyone threatened Father Vivaldi?'

'No.'

'You seem very sure.'

'He would have told me. He told me everything.'

Chapman stared down into his coffee cup while he wondered how to phrase his next question.

'Signora,' he said finally, 'can I ask you something very personal? I hope you won't be offended. When you said you were close to Father Vivaldi, what exactly did you mean?'

He raised his eyes to her face, looking for the signs of anger in her expression. But she seemed almost relieved by the question. She sagged down into the corner of the sofa and slumped back on the cushions, relaxing for the first time since Chapman arrived.

'Antonio and I were lovers,' she said phlegmatically. 'We had been for five years.'

The silence that followed was oppressive, smothering. Chapman resisted the temptation to fill it with chatter. There seemed nothing appropriate to say.

'I see you're shocked,' Signora Casella said.

'No, I'm not shocked. Just surprised, I suppose.'

'Antonio was a priest. But he was also a man. It happens.'

Chapman nodded. He knew it wasn't uncommon in Italy. In religion, as in everything else, the Italians demonstrated a worldly tolerance of human frailties. This was the home of Catholicism yet despite, perhaps because of, that proximity the natives were the least dogmatic about adhering to every last tenet of the faith. Why else did they accept abortion, why else was the Italian birth rate the lowest in Europe, never mind the wider Catholic diaspora, why else did so many, though professing their allegiance to the Church, do so little to follow its more restrictive teachings?

'Antonio was an independent thinker,' Signora Casella said. 'He believed our relationship made him a better priest. He didn't regard it as a sin. He took a vow of celibacy, an undertaking not to marry, not a vow of chastity. It's easy to confuse the two.

'My husband died of cancer ten years ago. Antonio was a friend of the family. He helped me through my husband's final months and afterwards he gave me comfort in my grief. That's the difference between then and now. I've loved two men in my life. When my husband died I could acknowledge that love, and my loss. With Antonio I must bear it all in silence and isolation.'

Chapman understood. It was never easy being a mistress. She would always be in the shadows, even more so in death. But with a priest she was completely invisible.

'When someone is terminally ill over a period of months you have time to prepare for the end,' she continued. 'Time to say things to them that you've never got round to saying before. It focuses your mind. But with Antonio there was time for none of that. We

257

exchanged a few hurried words and that was it. Our last words together were meaningless banalities. I find that hard to come to terms with.'

'He didn't telephone later, or call in?'

'No. We were always discreet. He came round once or twice a week. We had to be careful.'

'Did you ever go to his apartment?'

'Never.'

'Do you know why he was summoned to the Vatican that afternoon?'

'Summoned? He wasn't sent for. He made the appointment himself.'

'Did he? With whom?'

'Archbishop Tomassi.'

'Did he say what the meeting was about?'

'No, he didn't.'

'Did it relate to the papers?'

'Antonio didn't say, but . . .'

'But you think it did?'

'Yes.'

'Thank you, signora. I'm sorry to have troubled you.'

'I'm glad to help in any way I can. Antonio was a remarkable man. I want someone to pay for his death,' Maria Casella replied.

The heat outside hit him in the face like a blast from an oven door. He strolled the short distance to the river and stood in the shade of a plane tree looking down over the stone parapet at the sluggish waters of the Tiber. Behind him the traffic pulsed along Lungotevere, the fumes catching at his throat. Antonio Vivaldi had had many fine qualities as both a man and a priest. But Chapman couldn't help thinking that the most admirable of them was that he'd had the courage to love a woman.

Elena was nervous. She was aware of all the familiar symptoms: the edge of nausea in her stomach, a dampness on the palms of her hands and the back of her neck, a slight breathlessness that made the heat of the day even more unbearable. She was used to the sensation. She felt it every time she stood up to cross-examine in court, or to address one of the more reactionary *Tribunale* judges who disapproved of female prosecutors and saw it as their mission in life to put them in their place.

But there was something different about it this time. It was more than just nerves. The butchering of her cat, the rally at Ostia Antica had, for the first time in her career, given her an uneasy feeling of real personal jeopardy. She felt threatened. She felt as if each step in the investigation she was conducting were taking her deeper and deeper into a dark forest where she could see neither the path nor the enemies lurking in the trees. She had an innate toughness, a natural tenacity which in the past had seen her through most crises in her job and life. But it came as a shock to realise that this time she was not simply unnerved by events, she was genuinely scared by them.

'Signor Guarnieri will be with you shortly.'

Elena turned to look at the languid blonde who was seated behind the long glass-topped reception desk.

'Thank you.'

Elena resumed her casual scrutiny of the paintings on the walls of the room. They were modern oils and acrylics, most little more than indefinable splodges of colour on blank canvas backdrops. There was more skill in the fashioning of the frames that there was in the paintings themselves, but Elena knew they would have cost a small fortune. Fausto Guarnieri had a reputation as a collector; a reputation based rather less on the quality of his taste than the thickness of his wallet.

She was looking at the paintings but barely seeing them. Her mind was too preoccupied with the meeting that was to come. Going over the facts in her head, rehearsing what she was going to say to Cesare Scarfone and his lawyer. She found it impossible to keep still. She wanted to walk out into the street and burn off some of the surplus energy that was throbbing through her body, disperse some of the anxiety that was chewing at her insides.

Scarfone, as she had expected, had proved a difficult man to pin down. Arrogant, evasive, contemptuous of magistrates, he had refused point-blank to come to the *Procura* to be interviewed. Elena, acutely aware of the subtle power games a politician of Scarfone's guile was used to playing, had no intention of meeting him on his territory, either in the Chamber of Deputies or the offices of his political faction, so as a compromise they had agreed to meet in the office of his lawyer near Montecitorio.

She'd been kept waiting for ten minutes already. She had no doubt it was deliberate – a crude show of disrespect intended to humble her, to remind her whom she was dealing with. It made her angry, but she was determined not to show it. This was one interview she was going to keep as cool and unemotional as possible.

'Dottoressa Fiorini, forgive me. Please come through.'

Fausto Guarnieri was standing in the open door of his office. Tall, with sleek, dark hair combed back above a narrow forehead and magnificent beaked nose, he was the epitome of the patrician lawyers who had run Rome since its founding. He stood back to let Elena pass, then closed the door behind her.

The office had the quiet, devout atmosphere of a chapel: soft lighting, thick carpet and double-glazed windows to reduce the noise, a heavy oak desk set in front of the main wall like an altar. Elena half expected to hear a muted chamber organ playing Bach in one of the dark corners. But from Guarnieri's appearance, his expensive suit and silk tie, his polished shoes and manicured hands, she knew this was a temple not to God but to Mammon.

'Please take a seat.'

It was only as Elena lowered her briefcase to sit down that she noticed Cesare Scarfone ensconced in a high leather armchair to one side of the desk. He was wearing a light grey suit and pearl tie which emphasised the deep suntan on his face and hands. He made no attempt to acknowledge her presence, treating her with the disdain he would a servant or a tiresome bluebottle. Elena crossed her legs and forced herself to wait. Let them make the first move.

'Well, dottoressa,' Guarnieri said, taking his seat behind the desk, 'here we are.'

He had a deep, reassuring voice which he used like a stage hypnotist inducing a trance in his audience.

'My client is a busy man,' he added when Elena didn't reply.

She glanced at Scarfone. He was affecting a manner

of extreme boredom, studying his fingernails and rolling his eyes occasionally in one of the over-theatrical gestures he used to such effect on the political podium.

'I'm sure he is,' she said. 'We all are.'

'Then perhaps we could get down to business,' Guarnieri said, a trace of irritation creeping into his tone.

'Whenever Signor Scarfone is ready,' Elena said mildly.

She waited. She had no intention of proceeding until the deputy gave her his full attention.

He looked her in the eye for the first time. 'I'm ready,' he said tersely. 'What's this all about?'

'You attended a political rally in Ostia Antica last night,' Elena said.

'How do you know?'

She ignored the evasion. 'Who organised it?'

'What business is it of yours what I do?'

'You can confirm that you were there?'

'Dottoressa Fiorini,' Guarnieri interjected smoothly, 'my client will be unable to assist you unless you tell him exactly why you're so interested in his activities.'

Elena kept her gaze fixed on Scarfone. 'You're aware it was an illegal gathering?'

'Illegal?' Scarfone raised a mocking eyebrow. 'Since when have political rallies been illegal in Italy?'

'Ostia Antica is a protected archaeological site. You need permission to hold any kind of meeting there. That permission was not obtained.'

Scarfone let out a short burst of incredulous laughter. '*That*'s why you've brought me here this afternoon? To ask me about some trivial little permit. Good grief, hasn't the *pubblico ministero* got anything better to do with its time?'

'Did you organise the meeting?'

'No.'

'But your party did?'

'If you must know, it was organised by some enthusiastic patriots who asked me to speak.'

'Which enthusiastic patriots?'

Scarfone looked appealingly at his lawyer. 'This is ridiculous. Tell her, Fausto.'

Guarnieri frowned disapprovingly at Elena. 'You are wasting our time, dottoressa. When you arranged this meeting you led us to believe that there were matters of great import to discuss. I hardly think a discrepancy over a simple permit falls into that category.'

Elena turned to study him. She rarely encountered lawyers of his pedigree in the normal course of her work. Occasionally she met colleagues and acquaintances of her father's; respected, successful civil lawyers whose private practices thrived on the costly, arcane machinations of the Italian legal system. But Guarnieri was a class apart, one of the privileged elite who moved effortlessly between the political and legal worlds. A man without principles or particular political beliefs, he oiled the wheels of patronage and corruption which still drove the Italian state and was addicted to the power it brought him.

'Unfortunately, it's not just a question of the permit,' Elena said. 'There are other, more serious, matters to consider.'

'Such as?' Scarfone demanded.

Elena picked up her briefcase and clicked it open on her lap. She pulled out a large document-sized

manilla envelope which she put to one side while she
closed her case. She didn't hurry. She was in control of
the interview. The two men, for all their self-assured
arrogance, would have to follow the agenda she set.

She opened the envelope. Inside was a thick wad
of blown-up black and white photographs taken from
the film Chapman had shot at Ostia Antica. She'd
had them developed in the police laboratories first
thing that morning. She held them on her knee, the
picture side facing down. Scarfone leaned forwards in
his armchair, trying to see what they were.

Elena turned to him. 'These enthusiastic patriots you
mentioned; did they tell you what kind of meeting they
wanted you to address?'

'What kind of meeting?' Scarfone repeated, his eyes
flicking across to his lawyer.

'Yes. They must have told you who the audience
was going to be.'

'I'm not sure they did.'

'Come now, *Onorevole*, you're a politician. Do you
ever make a speech without knowing in advance who's
going to be listening to it? I hardly think so.'

'You show your ignorance of politics,' Scarfone replied
impatiently. 'How can I possibly know in advance –
how can anyone possibly know – who might turn up
for a public meeting?'

'You're saying this was a public meeting? At Ostia
Antica, late at night? Where was it publicised? Where
were the posters, the newspaper advertisement announcing it was taking place?'

'Publicising the event was not my responsibility.'

'So who was there?' Elena said. 'You must have seen
them when you were speaking.'

'Where is all this leading?' Guarnieri asked tetchily.

'You must have been aware that you were addressing an illegal private army,' Elena said.

Scarfone sat back heavily in the armchair. 'I don't know what you're talking about,' he said. But there was no conviction in his voice.

A look of alarm passed across Guarnieri's face. Then he leaned his thin elbows on the surface of his desk and glared angrily at Elena.

'That is a serious allegation, dottoressa.'

'I know.'

'Do you have any evidence to support it? Because if you don't, I warn you . . .'

'*Avvocato*,' Elena interrupted, 'save your indignation for those who might be swayed by it. You're wasting your breath on me.'

She spread the photographs out on the top of the lawyer's desk.

'I'd say these were pretty persuasive, wouldn't you?'

She sat back down in her chair and watched Guarnieri's expression change as he studied the prints. The lawyer glanced at Scarfone, his mouth tightening into a slit. He hadn't expected this.

'I think you should look at them too,' Elena said to Scarfone.

'Why? It was no concern of mine who was there. I can't vet every person I speak to.'

'Let me put something to you. You were asked to address a meeting. When you stepped on to the platform you must have seen who the audience was. It's hard to miss: legions of Blackshirts, many of them armed, lined up in rows. You must have known it was an illegal gathering of a private army so why did you make a speech to them? Why didn't you walk out and telephone the police as any law-abiding citizen, never mind a parliamentary deputy, would have felt duty-bound to do?'

'Blackshirts? What Blackshirts?'

Elena picked up one of the photographs and held it out in front of Scarfone's nose.

'That looks like a Blackshirt uniform to me. Doesn't it to you?'

'It was dark,' Scarfone blustered. 'There were bright lights shining on my face. I couldn't see everyone who was out there.'

'You expect me to believe that?'

'Are you calling me a liar?' He was on the defensive now, attempting to cover up his insecurity with aggression.

'I'm saying that any person with normal eyesight could hardly fail to notice the military formations the crowd adopted. Or the flags at the head of each file.'

She held up another photograph. 'It's difficult to miss the flags. Or the images on them – the eagle, the legion numbers and names. You knew exactly whom you were addressing.'

Scarfone leapt forwards out of his chair, his face taut with anger. 'You watch what you say to me.'

'Are you threatening me, Signor Scarfone?'

Guarnieri held up a hand. 'I think we should terminate this discussion now. If you have any further questions, dottoressa, I suggest you submit them to me in writing.'

Scarfone hitched up the sleeves of his jacket as if he were about to start a fight. His sallow skin was shining with a gloss of sweat and he was breathing heavily. He stepped closer to Elena. She could smell the cloying sweetness of his aftershave lotion.

'How dare you come here and attempt to smear me,' he said venomously. 'Let me remind you that I am an elected member of the Chamber of Deputies. You can't touch me. And you know it.'

'Signor Scarfone,' Guarnieri warned sharply, 'I must advise you to remain silent.'

But Scarfone ignored him. He swept the photographs off the desk with his hand, the underlying thug in his nature breaking through the layers of practised sophistication until it came into view in all its primitive ugliness.

'These photographs are meaningless. How do I know they're not fakes made up by my enemies to discredit me? How do I know this isn't just another crude attempt to set me up?'

'I have two witnesses who saw the whole thing,' Elena said. 'And, believe me, they are a hundred per cent reliable.'

Guarnieri was out from behind his desk now, coming between them.

'The meeting is over. We have nothing more to say.'

'Who organised the rally?' Elena said, not taking her eyes off Scarfone. 'Tell me that. Who provided the arms and the uniforms for those Blackshirts? I want some answers.'

'I must ask you to leave, dottoressa,' Guarnieri said, gathering up her photographs from the floor.

Scarfone had composed himself. He adjusted his tie and jacket, transforming himself back into the suave politician.

PAUL ADAM

'I have nothing to add,' he said glibly.

'I want their names,' Elena continued, undeterred. 'You know where to contact me.'

'You'll be waiting a long time,' Scarfone retorted. 'As far as I'm concerned, this matter is at an end.'

'On the contrary,' Elena replied, 'it's only just beginning.'

FOURTEEN

Chapman lingered for a while on the banks of the Tiber near Maria Casella's apartment, then walked back across the city centre, absorbed in thought. When he reached his desk at the *Stampa Estera*, he looked up the number of the *Compassione* office and called Giulietta Ricci. She remembered who he was, though she seemed a little reluctant to talk.

'The office is open again then?' Chapman said, making idle conversation.

'Yes, the police finished here a couple of days ago. Was there something you wanted?'

'That day we spoke – in the cafe across the street. You remember?'

'Yes.' She was wary now. 'I'm sorry, but I can say nothing more about Father Vivaldi. I've told you too much already.'

'You said he went to visit someone in hospital the day he died. In the morning. Do you have the name of the patient?'

'Look, I'm rather busy at the moment.'

'That's all I want to know. I won't trouble you again, signora.'

'It's probably in the diary somewhere. I would've written it down. But I've got other things to do.'

'I'll wait. I'd really appreciate the information now. Then I won't have to call you back.'

He heard her sigh heavily at the other end of the line.

'All right, I'll see if I can find it.'

Chapman waited, doodling idly on the pad of paper in front of him. One of the other foreign correspondents walked past on his way to his desk. Chapman looked up and acknowledged his greeting.

'Yes, it's here . . . hello?'

'Yes, signora.'

'His name was Roberto Ferrero.'

'Which hospital was he in?'

'Santo Stefano.'

'The one out beyond the Villa Ada?'

'Yes.'

'Do you know why Father Vivaldi visited him?'

'No, I don't. Even if I did, that would be confidential. I thought all you wanted was his name?'

'That's right,' Chapman said. 'Had he visited him before?'

'Signor Chapman, I can tell you nothing more. Father Vivaldi made many hospital visits. Some were to parishioners, others were to people he had never set eyes on before. We would get phone calls, people asking to see him. He was probably the best-known priest in Rome. When someone wanted a priest and didn't have one of their own they would often ask for Father Vivaldi. I never knew him to turn down a request. Now I really have to get on with my work. Good day.'

The line went dead. Chapman replaced the receiver and found the number of the Clinico Santo Stefano in the directory. He knew of it by name and reputation but had never been there. It was one of those discreet, expensive private hospitals used by politicians and rich businessmen who, in Italy as in other countries, praised the achievements of the state health system, the dedication and professionalism of its hard-pressed staff, but declined to sample the service firsthand. Not that anyone blamed them; the hazards of the Italian health service were legendary. When Chapman had first arrived in Italy he had been told by one of the old hands in the foreign press corps – and it wasn't a joke – that the best hospital in Rome was Fiumicino Airport. If there was anything the matter with you, you got on a plane and went somewhere – anywhere – else to have it treated.

Roberto Ferrero, whoever he was, obviously had money, for just a few days' stay in the Clinico Santo Stefano was unlikely to leave you with much change from ten million lire, several months' wages for the average manual worker.

Chapman dialled the number of the hospital and was put through to the administrator's office. He explained that he was an old friend of Signor Ferrero's and had only just heard that he'd been taken ill. He was ringing now to find out how he was. There was an embarrassed silence before the administrator, a softly spoken woman with the polite, over-solicitous manner of someone accustomed to dealing with the very rich, broke the bad news.

'Signor Ferrero? I regret to inform you that Signor Ferrero died a week ago.'

'Died?'

'I know it must be something of a shock to you.

271

But his injuries were, unfortunately, quite severe. He passed into a coma and never came out of it. I'm very sorry.'

'What injuries?' Chapman asked, then listened attentively while the administrator explained how Signor Ferrero had been beaten up in his home, sustaining serious injuries to the head.

'He was quite lucid towards the end,' she continued. 'We had hopes that he would make a full recovery, but . . .' She left the sentence hanging in mid-air.

'When was this?' Chapman said.

'Excuse me, I'll have to check the file for the exact date.'

When she came back on the line she told him the assault had taken place on 8th June. Signor Ferrero had been admitted late in the afternoon of the same day and had died four days later, in the evening of 12th June. Chapman scribbled the details down in his notepad. 12th June. That was the day Antonio Vivaldi had also died.

Chapman thanked the administrator for her help and hung up. Then he left his desk and walked the short distance from the *Stampa Estera* to the offices of Enzo's newspaper where he had a regular arrangement to use the cuttings library.

He looked up the name Roberto Ferrero in the files and found a slim cardboard folder containing just two small articles from the paper. One was a short death notice which recorded simply the facts of his passing away: his name, age, the hospital where he died. The other was a longer piece about the initial attack which had caused him to be admitted to Santo Stefano. The identity of his assailant and the circumstances of the attack were unknown. All the police knew for certain was that the eighty-eight-year-old Ferrero had been found unconscious on the floor of his study by his housekeeper, a Signora Potesta. There was blood on his face from a deep wound to the side of the head and, lying nearby, a bloodstained poker which had apparently been used to inflict the injury. There were no signs of a break-in and nothing appeared to have been taken from the house so the motives for the assault were unclear. Signor Ferrero, described as a retired businessman, had lived a quiet, reclusive life. According to the housekeeper he had had almost no visitors and rarely left the confines of his house and garden.

Chapman made a note of the address and went to pick up his car. He drove south-east out of the city into the Alban Hills, the horseshoe-shaped rim of an ancient volcanic crater which was the vineyard of Rome and a cool retreat for those of its citizens wealthy enough to afford a weekend cottage there. Scattered across the wooded slopes of the hills were the Castelli Romani, the ancient towns which two thousand years earlier had been the bulwark of the Latin League and which, though badly bombed during the fight for Rome in 1944, were still attractive destinations for day-trippers seeking to escape the torrid heat of the capital.

Chapman had visited most of them over the years, coming out in summer to sit in the gloom of a wine cellar drinking Frascati, or walk along the shores of one of the steep crater lakes that spotted the area like enormous eye sockets.

Roberto Ferrero's house was on the fringes of Castel

273

Gandolfo, the picturesque, cramped little town where the Pope had his summer palace. It was bigger than Chapman had expected, a large elegant stone villa hidden from the road by a high brick wall. There was a lodge just inside the steel gates and, beyond it, a gravel drive that curved around a lawn as smooth and green as a billiard table to the overhanging porch of the house. Chapman studied the building through the spray of water from the sprinklers which were showering the manicured grass. The shutters on the windows were partially open, the glass panes inside pulled back to allow air into the house. It still looked inhabited though its owner was dead. A flat-backed truck with the name of a contract gardening firm stencilled on the cab was parked by the front door and from somewhere, away behind the clumps of tall shrubs, came the intermittent buzz of a hedge trimmer.

Chapman pressed the bell on the gatepost and waited for the voice on the entryphone grille to ask him what he wanted. But it never came. The lock on the gates simply clicked open and they swung back in an arc to let him enter. He strolled past the lodge and on down the drive. The sun was already hot, searing the exposed skin on his forearms and face. He was tempted to stray across the grass into the cool mist from the sprinklers, but the appearance of a woman on the front steps of the villa deterred him. She watched him approach, a puzzled frown furrowing her brow.

'You're not Signor Locatelli,' she said accusingly as Chapman came to a halt below her.

'No.'

'I was expecting Signor Locatelli. You're from the estate agent's?'

'I'm afraid not.'

He explained who he was. The woman's nose wrinkled and Chapman, from long experience, recognised the first signs of the allergy to journalists that, if he didn't act quickly, would lead to his rapid ejection from the premises.

'You must be Signora Potesta,' he said. She had the sturdy body and formidable air of no nonsense which was the universal hallmark of headmistresses, hospital sisters and housekeepers. Chapman knew she would be impervious to any kind of bribe or inducement, but that didn't mean she didn't have a weak spot that could be exploited to his own ends.

'I read about you in the papers,' he said. 'It must have been a terrible ordeal for you, finding Signor Ferrero's body like that. Terrible. I hope I'm not intruding, but I wondered if you were up to talking about it yet?'

She looked at him suspiciously. 'Talking about it?'

Chapman nodded. 'No one has really had your personal side of the story. Perhaps you would have a few minutes to talk to me now? Just a short chat, perhaps a couple of photographs, if you don't mind.'

'Photographs?'

She adjusted her posture slightly, already slipping into a different pose at the mere mention of the word. One hand went to her hair, patting it into place.

'This is a beautiful house. Did you look after it all by yourself?'

Chapman started up the steps, conversing easily

275

with her, showing an interest in her life. It was a form of flattery which he knew could disarm even the most hostile interviewee.

'The house is on the market, I suppose?' he said, peering in through the open door. 'Is that real marble? That's extraordinary. May I . . . ?'

He walked into the entrance hall and took in the high stairwell, the polished stone floor.

'Would you mind very much showing me around? I won't keep you too long. We can talk as we go.'

The housekeeper thought it over, then shrugged. 'Why not. I'll be showing plenty of others around now.'

'Was it just you and Signor Ferrero who lived here?'

'Well, my quarters are in the lodge,' Signora Potesta said, a little primly.

'Of course.'

'But Signor Ferrero lived alone. He was a widower with no children. His wife died before I came here so I never met her.'

They walked through a doorway into a spacious living room. There were expensive rugs on the marble floor, gilt-framed paintings on the walls and antique furniture which looked as if it had been bought more for investment than comfort. It was too perfect, too uncluttered for Chapman's taste, but the opulence was impressive.

'I understand Signor Ferrero was a retired business-man,' he said. 'What business was he in?'

'I couldn't really tell you,' the housekeeper replied. 'He was a very private man. He never seemed to do much all the time I knew him. I think he must have made his money when he was a young man and retired early. He had a war pension but that obviously wouldn't have paid for all this.'

'A pension? He'd been a soldier?'

Signora Potesta nodded. 'He never talked about it. But his pension came every month up until the time he died. You seem very interested in him.'

'He died in intriguing circumstances. Newspaper readers love mysteries. You didn't see his killer?'

'No. I'd driven into the town to do the shopping. When I came back I found him lying on the floor in a pool of blood.'

'In here?'

'No, in his study.'

'May I see?'

'There's nothing *to* see.'

Chapman pulled open a door which led into what looked like a dining room. There was a long gleaming table in the centre with twelve matching chairs around it. Chapman tried to imagine the elderly Roberto Ferrero taking his meals alone in here.

'You cooked for him?' he asked the housekeeper.

'Yes.'

'Did he ever have company?'

'Never. He kept himself very much to himself. I don't think he had many friends. At his funeral there was only me, the priest and the men from the undertaker's.'

'That's sad.'

'Yes, it is rather.'

'Was Father Antonio Vivaldi not a friend?'

The housekeeper glanced sharply at him. 'Father Vivaldi? Why do you ask about him?'

277

Some of her suspicion had returned. Chapman looked over his shoulder, as if checking they were alone, and lowered his voice.

'Signora, is there somewhere more private we can talk?'

'Private? Well, there's the study. Through here. But why . . .'

Chapman took her firmly by the arm and led her through into the adjoining room. It was smaller than the others and somehow more personal. It looked as if someone might actually have lived in it rather than kept it purely for show.

'Forgive me, signora,' Chapman said, 'but one has to be careful.'

He had her attention now. Her eyes were fixed on his face, glowing with suppressed curiosity. Chapman had learnt long ago that one of the most effective ways of prising information out of someone was to share something confidential with them in return. Especially Italians, for whom conspiracy was like an addictive drug.

'You are aware that Father Vivaldi visited Signor Ferrero in hospital?' he said.

The housekeeper looked disappointed. 'Of course,' she said flatly. 'I was the one who arranged it.'

'You did?'

'Certainly. I was visiting Signor Ferrero myself as usual – I went in twice a day to see how he was – when he asked me to telephone Father Vivaldi and ask him to come to the hospital.'

'When was this?'

'The day before he passed away. I rang the Father's office and told him what had happened to Signor

Ferrero. He agreed to come to the clinic the following day.'

'Did they know each other?'

'I don't think so. Signor Ferrero wasn't a religious man. He never went to church the whole time I worked for him.'

'He didn't say why he wanted Father Vivaldi to come?'

'No.' Signora Potesta paused. 'He didn't say . . . but I got the impression he wanted to talk to a priest. You know, it's something you think of when you're his age and in hospital.'

'You mean for extreme unction?'

'Oh no, not that. He died without making his final confession. He went into a coma so quickly, you see. There wasn't time for the clinic to call a priest.'

'But he wanted to get something off his chest all the same?'

'That was what I thought at the time.'

Chapman drifted away around the study, touching the furniture, feeling the surface of the large leather-topped desk, running his fingers over the back of the chair. Trying to get a sense of the kind of man Roberto Ferrero had been.

Outside the window was a terrace running the full width of the house. Beyond the terrace the ground fell away steeply into a deep volcanic caldera, a precipitous drop that ended some thousand feet lower with the dark, unfathomable waters of Lake Albano. The ancient Romans used to come out here to watch bloody mock sea fights from their lakeside villas. The boats were still there: sleek sailing dinghies moored along the sandy shores; motorboats full of tanned young men and their topless girlfriends, cruising around near the bobbing heads of bathers. But the drama had gone. Albano remained a weekend playground for affluent Romans but the violent tastes of their forebears had been replaced by the more sedate pastimes of sunbathing and drinking Campari on cafe terraces.

'Is this where you found him?'

Signora Potesta nodded. 'On the floor over there. He was unconscious. There was blood everywhere.'

'How do you think his killer got in?'

'I don't know. The police examined the whole house and could find no signs of a break-in.'

'Maybe Signor Ferrero let him in himself?'

'That's possible.'

'The newspaper report said nothing was taken.'

'As far as I could tell, nothing was.'

'Signor Ferrero must have been a rich man, to afford all this. There are a lot of valuable things in the house.'

'Yes, he was well off.'

'He must have given some indication of where it all came from.'

The housekeeper shrugged. 'I think he had investments – shares, that kind of thing. He used to go north once a year. In June. To Milan and Switzerland, I think. But that stopped seven or eight years ago when he started to feel his age. His legs, you know. He found it hard getting around.'

There was a framed photograph of an old man on the wall beside the window.

'Is this him?' Chapman asked.

'Yes. I had it taken for him on his seventy-fifth

birthday. He didn't like being photographed but I persuaded him to have it done. He had no photos of himself in the house, not one. I couldn't understand it. But he wasn't a sentimental man.'

He looked a tough old boy, Chapman thought, peering more closely at the photograph: bony features, a wrinkled forehead giving way to a bald, shiny pate, eyes with a hard edge of ruthlessness to them.

'Were you present when Father Vivaldi visited him at the clinic?' he asked.

'No.'

'So you don't know what they talked about?'

Signora Potesta shook her head. 'I asked the Father later if Signor Ferrero was all right but he wasn't very forthcoming.'

'Later?'

'When he came here.'

Chapman stared at her. 'Father Vivaldi came here, to the house?'

'To collect some papers he said Signor Ferrero wanted him to have.'

'What papers?'

'Just some old letters, I think. Signor Ferrero had them in an ancient leather pouch in the bottom drawer of his desk. I'd never seen it before. That's it there on the side.'

She indicated a battered old document case which was lying on a table against the wall. Chapman picked it up and undid the creased leather straps. There was nothing inside.

'The Father didn't want the pouch, just the contents,' Signora Potesta explained.

The document case was scuffed and soiled, the

leather badly worn. In places it looked as if someone had scrubbed it clean with something abrasive. The surface was rough and striated, the fibres of the hide peeling off to expose the paler, untanned layers below. On the front, a circular emblem of some sort had been embossed on to the leather, but it was so badly scratched and torn it was impossible to make out what it had been.

'Did he have any more papers?' Chapman said.

'Just the usual sort of things – bills, bank statements. I sorted them out and packed them up in bags for his lawyers.'

'And they are where now?'

'In his lawyers' office. They wanted Signor Ferrero's personal effects out of the house before they put it on the market.'

'Tell me, signora,' Chapman said, 'have you told the police about Father Vivaldi coming here?'

'No. I haven't spoken to the police since Signor Ferrero was attacked.'

'They haven't been back since his death?'

'No.' She frowned. 'You think there might be a . . .'

The words were interrupted by a bell ringing somewhere at the front of the house. The housekeeper excused herself and went to answer it, leaving Chapman alone in the study. He pulled open the desk drawers and searched through them quickly. They'd been cleaned out completely.

He looked around the room. There were shelves on one of the walls crammed with tatty old books. Chapman ran his fingers along them, noting a few of the titles in passing. There were books on military history, the Ethiopian and North African campaigns, biographies of Garibaldi and Mussolini, gaudy translations of English and American thrillers. At the end of one of the rows, squeezed in on its side like a thick novel, was a wooden box. Chapman pulled it out. It was about the size of a woman's jewellery case, veneered with a marquetry pattern in yellowing ivory. He tried to open it but it was locked.

He could hear Signora Potesta's footsteps returning through the house. The box was too bulky to conceal on his person but he knew he had to look inside it. He snatched up a metal paper knife from the tray on the desk and inserted the point between the two halves of the box. The wood splintered around the lock as the lid snapped open. Inside were some shiny war medals and something long and thin wrapped in a strip of oilcloth. Chapman slipped them into his trouser pocket and replaced the box on the shelf just as the door swung open and the housekeeper came back in.

'The estate agent is here. You'll have to leave now.'

'Of course. Signora, I wonder if I might borrow the pouch for a couple of days.'

'The pouch?'

'I'll return it. You're not using it, are you?'

'Well, no.' She shrugged. 'I suppose there's no reason why you shouldn't.'

'Thank you, signora. You've been most helpful.'

Chapman drove back along the main road into Castel Gandolfo and parked in one of the quieter side streets, away from the town centre.

He pulled the collection of medals out of his pocket and examined them. They'd been well looked after.

The metal had been polished to prevent tarnishing and the ribbons were crisp and clean. Two in particular caught his attention. Almost identical, except for a slight variation in the blue ribbons, they had the coat of arms of the House of Savoy, the Italian royal family, on the front surrounded by a laurel wreath and the words *Al Valore Militare*. Chapman turned them over. On the back was engraved what seemed to be the name of the recipient. But it didn't say 'Roberto Ferrero' on either medal. It said 'Domenico Salvitti'. On one medal, in addition to the name, were the words *CC.NN Divisione 3 '21 Aprile', Adowa, 1935*, and on the other *CC.NN Divisione 1 '23 Marzo' Libica, Bardia, 1941*.

Chapman checked the other medals. They all had the name 'Domenico Salvitti' on the back. There was something else with them too: a lighter metal disc which wasn't a medal. Split into two identical halves and stamped in relief with tiny rows of words and numbers, it was clearly an army identity tag. The name on this item alone was 'Roberto Ferrero'.

Chapman turned his attention to the long, thin strip of oilcloth, unwrapping it carefully to reveal a slim, polished dagger. It had a plain burnished-metal grip and some words inscribed on the razor-sharp blade: *Ai Moschettieri silenziosi, fedeli* – 'to the silent, faithful Musketeers'. Underneath the inscription, engraved into the steel, was Mussolini's signature.

Chapman wrapped up the knife again and stowed it with the medals in the glove compartment of the car. Then he drove around the town until he found a stationery shop in a narrow street behind a church. He went in and bought a sheet of tracing paper and a soft pencil. Returning to his car, he put the leather document pouch on his lap and covered the faded emblem on the front with the tracing paper. He rubbed the tip of the pencil gently over the surface, letting the graphite gradually pick out the shape of the raised pattern on the leather underneath.

He held the tracing paper up. The image was a little smudged but it was possible to identify what it was. In the middle was the *fasces* of ancient Rome, the bundle of elm rods tied to an axe. And in the circle around this were the words *Repubblica Sociale Italiana*.

Chapman lifted his head and stared straight ahead through the windscreen, chewing the end of the pencil thoughtfully.

Elena worked on late into the evening, writing out a detailed report of the incident at Ostia Antica and her interview with Cesare Scarfone. Scarfone had over-stated his case when he'd said that Elena couldn't touch him. As a deputy he had certain privileges, but he wasn't entirely above the law. The immunity from prosecution which Members of Parliament had enjoyed, and which had made the *Tangentopoli* corruption scandals so difficult for magistrates to investigate, had been abolished. Elena couldn't tap his phone or search his home, but she could order his arrest provided she had the permission of Parliament.

Given Scarfone's uncooperative attitude and the evidence from Ostia Antica of his involvement in illegal activities, Elena was quite prepared to go that far, and she spent some time drafting the official application to the Speaker of the Chamber of Deputies for Scarfone's immunity to be lifted. Although she had the power to make the application on her own, under normal circumstances she would have wanted to clear it with Corona first. But he was away in Milan until the following evening. She filed the papers away in her desk. She'd decide what to do with them in the morning.

She was getting ready to leave the office when the telephone rang. It was Chapman.

'You're working late,' he said.

'I'm nearly finished. Where are you?'

'At your apartment. Do you want to go out for dinner?'

'I'd rather stay in.'

'I'll make us something. How does linguini with porcini and black olives, a green salad and a bottle of Chianti sound?'

'Why didn't I meet you sooner? Do you clean floors and wash up as well?'

'You'd be surprised what I do.'

'I hope so,' Elena said.

She tidied up her desk and walked downstairs to the main exit, enjoying the anticipation of, for once, not returning home to an empty flat. The *Procura* was quiet, the offices closed up for the night, the courtrooms and corridors – a swirling riot of lawyers, defendants and witnesses during the day – dark and deserted. She'd parked her car away from the main building, in one of the side streets near Piazzale Clodio. She walked out and turned left along the side of the *Procura*. The sun had gone down but the air was still warm and sultry. Elena walked quickly, her briefcase banging awkwardly against her leg.

As she turned the next corner, they were waiting for her.

An arm came out from nowhere and grabbed her around the throat. A hand, a strong, calloused hand that reeked of engine oil, clamped itself firmly over her mouth to stifle any screams. More hands grasped her arms and legs. Elena found herself as tightly restrained as if she'd been bound with ropes. She attempted to break loose but she was completely immobilised. There must have been three, maybe four, men holding her. She could smell their presence even though she couldn't turn her head to see them. She took a deep breath and tried to cry out, but the pressure on her windpipe and mouth increased, choking the sound off before it could even begin.

She was dragged back into the shadows. Her limbs were trembling, her stomach seized in the fierce grip of a debilitating nausea. If the men hadn't been holding her up, her legs would have given way and she would have collapsed to the pavement.

A man stepped out in front of her. He was about her height, with broad shoulders and a thick, stubby body. His chest and upper arms, swelling beneath a dirty white T-shirt, were knotted with muscle like the torso of a committed bodybuilder or a manual labourer. Elena couldn't see his face. It was concealed by a black hood with slits for his eyes and mouth.

He looked at her for a long moment as if he were savouring her powerlessness.

'It's time someone taught you a lesson,' he said in a harsh Roman accent.

Elena was transfixed, unable to take her eyes off the black hangman's hood. Her instinct was to try and reason with him, to dissuade him with words. But she couldn't speak, could barely breathe. And besides, she knew words were useless. These were violent, primitive men who had been given a task to carry out and would dispatch it with clinical efficiency.

The man reached out and cupped her breasts with his hands, feeling the flesh under the thin material of her blouse. Through the mouth slit in the hood Elena could see his chipped, uneven teeth and knew he was grinning at her. She struggled to free one of her legs, to kick out at him, but she was pinned back as securely as a butterfly on a specimen tray.

His hands slid down her body, touching her roughly, wanting to hurt her. She felt her skirt being lifted, the hands moving underneath it. Her eyes watered. With pain, with fear and the screaming frustration of being unable to fight back.

She wondered what they were going to do, her mind and body so paralysed by terror that she was no longer thinking of escape. Just getting it over with. Just getting out alive.

The man took something out of his trouser pocket. Something that glinted in the faint light. It was a small glass bottle. He unscrewed the lid and lifted it to Elena's face. She could see the viscous, colourless liquid moving around inside it. The hand covering her mouth was removed and the hooded man jammed the neck of the bottle between her lips, tipping the bottle up to pour the liquid down her throat. She gagged, then choked as the fluid filled her mouth, overflowing down her chin. It tasted disgusting, worse than anything she'd ever experienced. She thought it might be poison then realised, almost with relief, that it was castor oil. The man gripped her jaw hard, holding her mouth open until the bottle was empty.

Elena retched. Her stomach churned, squeezing and twisting itself in uncontrollable convulsions. She felt the nausea rising. The men behind her knew what was coming. They released her arms and legs and stepped back as the vomit exploded from her mouth.

Elena spat it out on to the pavement, half choking on the surge of liquid, the acrid taste that stung the membranes of her throat and lips. She was bent double, trying to ease the cramp in her belly. But through the haze of pain she became aware that the men had moved away from her, that her arms and legs were free. As the nausea began to ease she acted instinctively, lashing out at the man in the hood and running past him into the street. She was a few metres away before they reacted. Elena heard the footsteps behind her. A hand caught hold of her arm. Elena screamed. She dodged between two parked cars, tearing her arm loose. The man caught his leg on the bumper of one of the cars and tumbled to the ground. Elena ran, stumbling in her heeled shoes. She kicked them off and continued barefoot.

Headlights turned into the street ahead of her. The beams flashed across her face. She looked back. The men had stopped. They were staring at the oncoming car, unsure what to do. One of them panicked and broke away, running back the way he'd come. Another followed, then a third. The man in the hood yelled at them furiously but they were already disappearing around a corner. The car came to a halt outside an apartment building. A couple got out. The man in the hood turned to stare up the street at Elena. She'd paused as she reached the lights of the main road and was panting for breath, the spasms of fear and sickness starting to subside. The man stood motionless for a short time, watching her, before he too turned and ran off into the darkness. Elena leaned back on a wall and sobbed, her limbs trembling, her stomach aching, the foul taste of castor oil burning her mouth.

Chapman saw the police car pull up outside from the window of Elena's kitchen. He watched the hunched figure climb unsteadily out of the back and took just a moment to realise who it was. Then he was out of the apartment and scrambling down the stairs, throwing open the front door and helping her in.

'Elena, what happened? Jesus, what was it?'

The uniformed police officer accompanying her gave Elena a quizzical look. She nodded weakly.

'It's okay. Thank you for bringing me home.'

The officer let go of her arm and handed the briefcase he was carrying to Chapman, then he went back out to his car. Elena leaned on Chapman as he pressed the button for the lift. He put an arm around her shoulders. She was shaking.

Upstairs, he guided her into the apartment and eased her down into an armchair.

'Tell me,' he said, studying her anxiously.

'Can I have a drink?'

'What would you like? Water?'

'Some of that Chianti you mentioned.'

She gulped down the wine, erasing the lingering taste of the castor oil, and told him what had happened.

'Have you seen a doctor?' Chapman asked. Her face was pale and drawn. She looked ill.

'At the police station,' she said. 'I'm all right. Just shaken. I think I'll take a bath. I feel so dirty.'

'Did you make a statement?'

She nodded.

'You need proper protection.'

'I don't want to think about it at the moment.'

'I'll run your bath,' Chapman said.

She finished her wine and soaked herself for a long time in the hot soapy water. Then she climbed into bed and Chapman held her until she fell asleep.

FIFTEEN

'The day he died,' Chapman said, pouring thick black espresso into two cups, 'Antonio Vivaldi went to visit a patient in hospital – the Clinico Santo Stefano. The patient was an old man named Roberto Ferrero. He'd been attacked in his home at Castel Gandolfo a few days earlier and had serious head injuries.'

Chapman carried the cups to the table, added hot milk and passed one to Elena who was slumped forwards on her elbows, her chin cradled in her hands. She looked as if she had a hangover.

'Drink some, you'll feel better,' he said.

Elena took a sip and swallowed with difficulty. Her stomach felt hollow and tender. She wondered if she was going to be sick again, but the coffee was warm and soothing and the momentary sensation of nausea passed.

Chapman was watching her, concerned. 'You should take the day off, stay at home and rest.'

Elena shook her head stubbornly. 'I've too much to do.'

'Forget your work. Put yourself first for a change.'

'I keep telling you I'm fine.'

Chapman looked at her over his coffee cup. 'You went through a traumatic experience last night. Whatever you think, it's going to take you a long time to get over it.'

'I'll only dwell on it if I stay at home. I'd rather do something to take my mind off it. Now what's this about Vivaldi?'

Chapman spread butter and apricot jam on a slice of toast and weighed it in his hand. Bread was sold by the kilo in Italy so the bakers made it as heavy as possible. It had the texture and density of a sponge dipped in concrete.

'He saw the old man in hospital,' he continued, 'then went out to his house to pick up some papers Ferrero wanted him to have.'

'Papers?' Elena straightened up, paying attention now.

'He took them away with him. That evening Ferrero went into a coma and died. A few hours later Vivaldi also died.'

'You think they're linked? That the people who killed Vivaldi also beat up this old man?'

Chapman nodded. 'It seems a fair guess.'

'For these papers?'

'That I'm not sure about. The papers were in an unlocked drawer in Ferrero's desk. They wouldn't have taken much finding. Yet whoever beat him up didn't bother searching for them.'

'Do you know what was in the papers?'

'No,' Chapman replied. Strictly speaking, he was being truthful. He didn't tell Elena he had them in his possession. She'd insist he handed them over to her.

'Why are you telling me this?' Elena said.

Chapman gave her a dry look. 'You still don't trust me, do you? I'm trying to help. Don't you think it might be relevant?'

'Maybe.'

'And besides you're in a better position than I am to find out the exact circumstances of the attack on Ferrero.'

'Meaning?'

'All I've seen is a newspaper cutting which told me almost nothing. I'd like to know what the autopsy report said. Whether there were any similarities between the beating Ferrero received and the one Vivaldi was subjected to. Whether there was castor oil in Ferrero's stomach too.'

'Even if I find out, I can't tell you,' Elena said.

'You could whisper it in your sleep.'

'I'm a magistrate, Andy.'

Chapman shrugged and smiled briefly. 'I thought you should know. I won't compromise you by asking you to share the information with me. You have your duty as a prosecutor to think of. You must do whatever you think is right.'

'All right, all right, don't pile it on with a trowel,' Elena said, but she was half smiling. 'I'll see what I can do.'

He touched her hand. 'We have to help each other, Elena. We need each other. After last night you need looking after.'

'I can look after myself,' Elena said.

She stood up and went through into the bathroom. Chapman followed her and sat on the edge of the bath with his coffee while she applied her make-up. He liked the intimacy of mornings with a woman. Waking up with her, sharing breakfast, watching her wash and go through the ritual of painting her face. It was a mundane routine in many ways but he always found it slightly erotic; the privacy of it, the nakedness – not always literal – that exposed a woman in the sleepy disarray that she rarely showed outside her home. It made him feel like a voyeur.

She gave him a quick smile in the mirror as she brushed mascara on her eyelashes.

'I'm fine, honest.'

'I worry about you, Elena. You should have a body-guard.'

'I'll talk to my boss about it.'

'Those men could have killed you.'

Chapman came up behind her and slipped his arms around her waist. She leaned back on him, letting him nuzzle her neck.

'Promise me you'll arrange for protection.'

She twisted her head around and kissed him lightly, trying not to smudge her lipstick.

'I'm a grown woman, stop worrying.'

'Scarfone is a formidable opponent,' Chapman said.

'If they think they can intimidate me, they've picked the wrong person,' Elena said.

She looked back in the mirror, checking her appearance.

'What can you do?' Chapman said. 'A Member of Parliament is pretty near untouchable.'

'There are ways of getting to him,' Elena said.

'Like what?'

'I'll see you tonight. Call me during the day if you get a minute.'

'Elena.'

She touched his lips with her finger. 'No more questions. Can you drop me off at the office?'

She was in a determined mood. The attack had

shaken her badly but she was surprised at how well she was managing to suppress the after-effects of the ordeal. She'd slept reasonably well, considering; only one nightmare, in the middle of which she'd woken in a panic, breathing heavily, her heart pounding. But Chapman had calmed her down, reassured her and she'd drifted back into sleep until first light.

She knew the shock was still there, lurking somewhere under the surface. But she knew also that the way to cope with it was to keep it out of sight, to refuse to let it seep out and infect her mind. She'd been terrified, but if she allowed herself to acknowledge that fear it would paralyse her. Scarfone – and she had no doubts that the hooded man and his companions had been instructed by the deputy – would be relying on that to block or, at the very least, slow down her investigation into his activities. That was all the more reason why she should hit back at him hard, and at once.

As soon as she reached the *Procura*, she took out the application for the lifting of Scarfone's immunity from arrest and made out an *avviso di garanzia*, the official warrant informing him he was under investigation by the judiciary, and gave them both to Baffi to courier over to the Chamber of Deputies. Corona's blessing would have to wait until later. Then she made a series of phone calls.

The first was to the duty inspector at the police station in Castel Gandolfo. The second was to Chapman at the *Stampa Estera*.

'It's me,' she said. 'About Roberto Ferrero. There don't appear to be any similarities between his beating and Vivaldi's. And there was no castor oil in his stomach.'

'Thanks.'

'Do you want an exclusive? I've just made an official application to Parliament to have Scarfone's immunity from arrest lifted.'

'You don't hang about, do you?'

'Give it a couple of hours, then ring the Speaker's office at Montecitorio and put some pressure on them for me. I want a vote as soon as possible and a little media interest won't do any harm.'

'If I'd known you were this good a source, I'd have slept with you sooner,' Chapman said.

Elena laughed and hung up. Then she called Agostini at Judicial Police Headquarters.

'Gianni, this is Elena Fiorini,' she said. 'Can you get me some men and a van? I've got a little job for you.'

'Which way now?' Agostini asked.

Elena looked out of the car window, checking their whereabouts. They were speeding east along the Corso Vittorio Emanuele, approaching Largo Argentina where the Via Arenula branched off south towards the river.

'Right,' she said.

Agostini braked hard and careered across the busy intersection, the flashing lights and siren on the car roof clearing the road of traffic. Behind them, the driver of the dark blue Judicial Police van banged his horn and forced a path through the log-jam of vehicles, sticking close to Agostini's bumper as if joined to it by some invisible umbilical cord. On either side cars screeched to a halt, their drivers shouting and gesturing obscenely as the police convoy hurtled through the square leaving in its wake a trail of stalled engines, scratched wings and frayed tempers.

Agostini glanced across at Elena. 'It would help if we knew where we were going,' he said impatiently.

Elena didn't answer. She knew she'd hurt his feelings by not confiding in him. But it was a price she was happy to pay if it ensured that there were no slip-ups. She trusted the inspector, but she was taking no chances. She wanted no leaks, no quiet tip-offs from police headquarters on this one, and if the only way to guarantee that was a few wounded egos then so be it.

'Turn the lights and siren off please,' she said.

Agostini bit back the terse response that was on his lips and leaned forwards to do as she asked. Taking their cue from the lead car, the lights and siren on the police van behind were abruptly cut off too.

'I'm sorry, Gianni,' Elena said sympathetically. 'But I had my reasons, and they're nothing to do with you.'

'I take it we're nearly there? I think you'd better tell me the target.'

'The MPI offices.'

His head turned sharply towards her. She met his gaze. There was surprise in his face; an expression that quickly changed to one of understanding and respect. Agostini knew what had happened to her the previous night. The report on the attack – like anything else that involved the magistracy – had been automatically copied to him. They hadn't discussed it yet, but he was filled with admiration for her resilience.

'If you don't mind my saying so, dottoressa,' he said, 'you've got some guts. It's time we hit those neo-Fascist bastards where it hurts.'

He turned off before the river, into the side streets

behind the Theatre of Marcellus, driving with one hand while holding the radio and barking instructions to his men in the following van.

As they pulled in outside a tall, anonymous-looking stone building with iron grilles over the ground-floor windows, Elena took out the search warrant and handed it to Agostini.

'I want everything,' she said. 'Every last piece of paper, every computer disk you can find. And any weapons, uniforms, flags or other Fascist paraphernalia.'

The inspector nodded and threw open his door, shouting and gesticulating at the five officers who were jumping down from the Judicial Police van. Two of them ran down a narrow alley towards the rear of the building while Agostini led the others in through the front entrance. Elena waited a few seconds then went after them.

The offices of the *Movimento Patriottico Italiano* were on the first floor, at the top of a wide, brightly lit staircase. A thickly carpeted reception area gave way to a suite of six large rooms, each furnished in some style: expensive desks and swivel chairs, recessed lighting, artwork on the walls and an array of advanced office and computer equipment that would keep even the most demanding techno-nerd happy for months.

Elena stood in the doorway of the main office, taking in the air of no-expense-spared opulence and reflecting on the fact that every political party, whatever their funds or philosophy, seemed to believe in comfort for their leaders and bureaucrats.

Agostini was rounding up the office workers, herding them out into the reception area and instructing them to sit down. A short, balding man was protesting indignantly, but vainly, at their treatment. He picked up the telephone on the receptionist's desk and started to punch in a number. Agostini snatched the receiver away from him and slammed it down on to its rest.

'No phone calls,' he snapped. 'And no one leaves the building.'

'This is outrageous,' the balding man yelled. 'You can't stop us making phone calls.'

'Talk to the magistrate,' Agostini said and walked away to supervise the removal of files from the cabinets in the nearest office.

There was shouting somewhere at the back of the suite, a man's voice raised in anger and getting nearer. The two police officers who'd been assigned to the rear of the building came along a corridor, a scruffy, shaven-headed youth held tightly between them. The youth was spitting and swearing at them, the saliva trickling out of the corners of his mouth.

'We caught him in the back room,' one of the officers explained to Elena, struggling to restrain the youth who was kicking out violently with his steel-capped leather boots. 'He was trying to shred these files.'

The officer handed her a bundle of bright green cardboard folders.

'Put him outside with the others,' Elena ordered. 'If he causes any trouble, handcuff him and put him in the van.'

'What the hell is going on?' the short, balding man demanded aggressively, sticking his face so close to Elena she could feel his breath warm on her cheeks. 'Are you in charge? What is this? I want to call our lawyers. You can't take those files.'

'Read the warrant,' Elena said, moving away.

The man grabbed hold of her sleeve. Elena swung round and glared at him icily.

'Touch me again and I'll have you arrested, you understand? Now sit down and shut up.'

She walked through into one of the offices where files and papers and disks from the computers were being placed carefully in plastic sacks.

'This lot will keep you busy,' Agostini said drily.

'I like a bit of light reading,' Elena replied, glancing around the room. On one of the walls was a large framed photograph of Mussolini standing on the balcony of the Palazzo Venezia. His glazed, maniacal eyes stared out at her unnervingly.

'Imagine having to work with *him* watching you,' she said.

They were there for less than an hour, bagging up documents and carrying them down to the van. They found no arms or Blackshirt apparel. Elena wasn't surprised. Scarfone wasn't stupid enough to keep them in the offices of his political party.

Elena watched the police officers take out the last of the plastic sacks before picking up the receptionist's phone and punching in a number she'd written down and brought with her from the *Procura*.

'Cesare Scarfone,' she said when the call was connected.

She waited a moment until the deputy came on the line.

'This is Elena Fiorini,' she said coolly. Then she handed the receiver to the short, balding man.

'Tell him,' she said and walked out.

* * *

It was the sort of shop that, under normal circumstances, Chapman would have entered only under duress. The grimy window outside was cluttered with a crude display of right-wing war memorabilia: Nazi helmets and uniforms, trays of medals and military insignia, photographs of Fascist leaders, both German and Italian, Swastikas and Third Reich mementoes suspended from strings above rows of service daggers and bandoliers and dented old hand-grenades all caked in a thin film of dust.

Inside, the merchandise on offer was more offensive: shelves of Fascist literature, historical and modern; pictures of Hitler and Mussolini in rabble-rousing poses; anti-Semitic posters in German and Italian. There was a glass-fronted cabinet devoted entirely to instruments of torture used by the Gestapo and a display of photographs taken at Auschwitz and Belsen that were so revolting they turned Chapman's stomach as he walked past them to the counter.

The man behind the till had black cropped hair and rolls of fat like bicycle tyres at the back of his neck. He was wearing khaki army surplus trousers and a matching shirt whose sleeves were pulled up to the elbows to reveal a tattoo of the *fasces* on one pudgy forearm and the SS lightning blazes on the other.

He looked up from the military magazine he was reading and fixed Chapman with mean, iron-hard eyes.

'Are you Luca Bracciolini?' Chapman asked. He'd got the name from the shop front outside.

The man grunted, but didn't elaborate. His eyes remained locked on to Chapman's face.

302

Chapman reached inside his jacket pocket and pulled out the medals he'd found in Roberto Ferrero's house.

'Can I show you these?'

Bracciolini's gaze flicked down momentarily, showing little interest.

Chapman placed the medals on the counter. 'Can you tell me something about them?'

'Like what?' the shopkeeper said rudely.

'Like what they are.'

Bracciolini gestured dismissively at the collection. 'Those two are campaign medals for Ethiopia. They're very common. You only had to be there to get them. I've four or five in my window now. Those are for the North African campaign. Again, there's not much of a market for them.'

'And these two?' Chapman pointed at the medals with the blue moire ribbons.

Bracciolini shrugged and picked them up. 'The Military Valour Medal. They're quite rare. People don't usually want to part with them. You're selling?'

Chapman shook his head. 'I just want some information about them.'

'I run a shop, not an information bureau,' Bracciolini said, tossing the medals back. Chapman noticed that tattooed across the shopkeeper's ten knuckles were the words *Viva Il Duce*.

'Were many of them awarded?' Chapman asked, undeterred.

'Enough.' Bracciolini looked at him suspiciously. 'You're not Italian, are you?'

'No, English. Was it common for someone to be awarded two?'

'It happened. There were many brave soldiers in

the Italian army. Contrary to what the English seem to think.'

Bracciolini turned back to his magazine, attempting to terminate the conversation. But Chapman persisted.

'Domenico Salvitti. Does that name mean anything to you?'

The shopkeeper stiffened. His eyes stayed glued to the magazine on his knee, but Chapman got the impression he wasn't taking in any of the words. Then he lifted his head.

'Domenico what?' he asked casually.

'Salvitti,' Chapman repeated.

'Let me see.'

Bracciolini reached out and took the medals back, turning them over to study the inscription on the reverse side.

'No, I don't know the name,' he said finally. 'Where did you get these?'

Chapman evaded the question with one of his own. 'Those letters and dates, what do they mean?'

'CC.NN. *Camicie Nere*,' Bracciolini said.

'He was a Blackshirt? And the rest of the inscription?'

'*Divisione 3 "21 Aprile"*. The Blackshirt divisions were named after key dates in the Fascist calendar. 21st April was a Fascist holiday, *Natale di Roma*. And this one.' He held out the second medal. '*CC.NN Divisione 1 "23 Marzo", Libica*. Twenty-third March 1919. That was the date of the first meeting of the *Sansepolcristi*, the founders of the Fascist Party. The "*23 Marzo*" was one of the Blackshirt divisions that fought alongside the Royal Army in Libya in 1941.'

'And the place names?'

The shopkeeper sighed impatiently. 'Adowa. That was one of the battles in the Ethiopian campaign. Where we gave the fucking darkies a pasting. Bardia . . .' he pulled a sour face, '. . . you should know. It was where the British wiped out virtually the entire Blackshirt force in North Africa.'

His tone was indifferent, his manner offhand, but he was cupping the medals greedily in his thick sausage fingers.

'Are you sure you don't want to sell? I could give you a good price.'

'They aren't mine,' Chapman replied, pulling Roberto Ferrero's identity disc out of his pocket. Bracciolini's eyes gleamed when he saw it.

'Where did you get that?'

He practically snatched it from Chapman's grasp and examined it avidly.

'Oh.' He was disappointed. He dropped the disc down on to the counter. 'Royal Army ID tags. I've seen plenty of them. They're almost worthless.'

Chapman hesitated, wondering if he should leave now. The shopkeeper was clearly not in the mood for many more questions. But he decided to ask all the same.

'I've something else to show you.'

He took out the strip of oilcloth and laid it down on the counter.

'Don't waste my time,' Bracciolini said surlily.

'You might find this interesting.'

'Look, either you're buying, or you're selling. There's nothing in between. You get me? So why don't you . . .'

He stopped, his eyes bulging with amazement as

Chapman unfolded the oilcloth to reveal the engraved dagger. Bracciolini licked his lips and stared covetously at the knife.

'Where did you get that?' he breathed. 'Let me see.'

He took hold of the dagger, handling it delicately in his fleshy hands as if it were made of porcelain not steel. He touched the blade, ran the tips of his fingers over Mussolini's engraved signature like a blind man reading Braille.

'This I have to have,' he said.

'What is it?'

'A Musketeer's dagger. Only the Duce's personal bodyguards carried them. I've only seen one other before. I'll give you twenty million for it.'

'It's not mine to sell.'

'Forty million.'

'I'm sorry.'

'Who does it belong to? I'll contact them directly.'

Chapman shook his head. 'It's not for sale.'

He tried to take the dagger back but the shopkeeper clung on to it.

'Just let me hold it a moment longer. Fifty million,' he added.

Chapman watched him, fascinated yet also repulsed by the display of naked desire. He wondered what it was about collectors that made them so passionate about their obsessions. What it was about an object that could arouse such a consuming greed, such a need to possess. But he knew the answer in this particular case. There was something about Mussolini, as there was about Hitler, and Napoleon before them, that attracted the fanatic. In death, as in life, they were capable of inspiring an unthinking, absolute loyalty that was chilling and incomprehensible.

Chapman didn't understand it, but he could feel its power in that dark, dingy shop. It was just a simple dagger, an unsophisticated weapon that had been transformed into an object of veneration by the addition of a few words and a signature.

He eased the dagger out of the shopkeeper's hands. He thought Bracciolini might put up some resistance but he let the knife go with only a fond glance of regret.

'If the owner ever decides to sell, you come here first, okay?'

Chapman nodded automatically as he collected up the medals and identity disc and slipped them into his pocket with the wrapped dagger. He was anxious to get away. The shopkeeper, the surroundings with their overwhelming Fascist trappings, made him uncomfortable.

Bracciolini watched him hurry to the door and go out. Then the shopkeeper picked up the telephone and dialled a number.

'It's Bracciolini,' he said softly. 'Someone's just been in, an Englishman. He had Domenico Salvitti's medals and Musketeer's dagger. He had something else too – a Royal Army identity disc.'

SIXTEEN

It was the middle of the morning when Chapman returned to the *Stampa Estera*. He immediately rang the office of the Speaker of the Chamber of Deputies, as Elena had requested, and asked about the judicial investigation into Cesare Scarfone's activities, pressing for information and a timetable for the vote required to lift Scarfone's parliamentary immunity from arrest. The Speaker's staff declined to comment and referred him to the press office who, clearly unbriefed about the whole affair, resorted to their usual line of saying they'd issue a statement later.

Chapman could foresee that a story of this magnitude was never, whatever Elena had said, going to be an exclusive for him. By the afternoon every journalist in Rome would know about it. So he decided to earn himself a few favours by sharing the news with his colleagues in the foreign press corps and the newsdesk of Enzo's paper. That would quickly stir things up, putting even more pressure on the Speaker's office.

After a break for a coffee round the corner in a bar in Piazza San Silvestro, he went back to his desk and telephoned London to let them know what he was doing.

'Andy,' the foreign editor said drily at the end of

their conversation, 'we'd like a decision on the job offer before we all drop dead from old age.'

'I'm still thinking it over,' Chapman said.

'You've had six weeks. We need to know very soon.'

'Give me another fortnight.'

The foreign editor sighed. 'Okay. But no more.'

Chapman was torn. The years he'd spent in Italy had changed his outlook on life. Being a correspondent in Rome was an easy posting. The English weren't very interested in the Italians; at least not on news pages (they preferred them in the more frivolous arena of Travel and Arts, or under the generic heading of Comic Foreigners). Italy wasn't perceived as a serious country, in the way that France or Germany or the USA were, with the result that correspondents there weren't expected to deliver very much. At the beginning, Chapman had found it frustrating, to have story after story he'd worked hard on spiked, either because there was no space, or because they weren't seen as important. Now it was a blessing. It meant he chose carefully what he wrote about and that gave him more time to sit in the sun and absorb the flavour of Italy.

He'd become lazy, but underneath there was still a vestige of his old ambition remaining. The post of deputy foreign editor was a tempting carrot, but he had serious doubts about whether he really wanted to return to a desk job in London, a city he regarded with no affection whatsoever.

He put on his jacket and went out for some fresh air to clear his head. He walked up through the shady side streets to the Piazza Barberini, then hailed a taxi and headed across the city to the National Library near the ugly sprawl of Rome University. He spent most of the rest of the day in the archives, searching for information on Domenico Salvitti. There was no mention of the name in the central computer index, but he found a few brief references in biographies of Mussolini and a larger passage in a book on the history of the MVSN, the Blackshirt militia.

Salvitti was something of a hero in Fascist mythology, although virtually unknown outside those circles. Born in Naples in 1909, he'd been just thirteen years old when Mussolini came to power. Like many of his contemporaries, he'd joined Fascist youth organisations, probably for the companionship, free sporting activities and free meals on a Saturday as much as through any kind of political commitment. After the Balilla Corps – named after an eighteenth-century Genoese street boy who'd hurled stones at occupying Austrian soldiers – he'd graduated to the Balilla Musketeers, the Vanguards and finally the *Giovani Fascisti*. He'd become a part-time soldier in the MVSN in 1930 and a full-time professional in 1935 when he was sent to Ethiopia. By the end of that brief campaign he'd been awarded his first Military Valour Medal for singlehandedly capturing an Ethiopian machine-gun post near Adowa and had been promoted to the Blackshirt rank of *Capo Manipolo*, the army equivalent of a lieutenant.

But it was in North Africa in the Second World War that he really made his reputation. By then a *Centurione*, following the MVSN custom of giving its officers the same ranks as the ancient Roman army, he was assigned to Cyrenaica in northern Libya with the 1st Blackshirt Division, the '23 *Marzo*', fighting alongside the 62nd and 63rd Infantry Divisions of the Royal Army whose regular soldiers despised the Fascist militia. But Salvitti was to prove himself a finer, more courageous fighter than any of them.

In December 1940, dug in at Sidi Barrani in the Western Desert, the Italians came under sustained attack from the British 7th Armoured Division – the soon-to-be-notorious Desert Rats – and were forced to retreat back along the coast. After a futile stand at the Halfaya Ridge, the Italians were finally trapped in Bardia where on 5th January 1941, after a three-day assault by the British, the whole garrison – some 45,000 men – surrendered. Domenico Salvitti was not one of them.

On the night of 4th January, he had led a small group of Blackshirts who had attempted to break out through the encircling British forces. His companions were all either captured or killed in a skirmish just outside the walls of the coastal fortress but Salvitti, determined not to surrender, shot four British soldiers, commandeered their Jeep and headed west towards the remaining Italian forces at Benghazi.

After a drive of three hundred and fifty kilometres, the Jeep broke down and Salvitti completed the last forty kilometres on foot, walking at night through the harsh terrain until, close to death from exhaustion and dehydration, he was picked up by an Italian patrol. He was taken to a field hospital before being flown back to Tripoli and from there to Rome, only days before the rest of the Italian army in Cyrenaica was overrun and captured by the British.

Back in Italy, he was welcomed as a hero and

given his second Military Valour Medal by Mussolini himself. The Duce, anxious to associate himself with a brave soldier, as if some of the glory might rub off on him, made Salvitti a *Seniore*, or major in the *Moschettieri del Duce*, his personal corps of bodyguards, and appointed him as his aide-de-camp, a position he held until the end of the war.

What happened then was something of a mystery. Chapman followed up every reference he could find, but there was no mention of what had become of Salvitti after the Allied liberation of Italy. One book surmised that he may have been executed by partisans along with the Fascist *gerarchi* who had fled from Milan with Mussolini. The better known members of the Duce's entourage – Bombacci, Mezzasoma, Pavolini, Luigi Gatti and several others – were known to have been shot by *Garibaldini* near Lake Como. It was quite possible that Salvitti had been among them but his death had not been recorded. There was such chaos across Italy at the time that thousands of people were unaccounted for.

Chapman took a break from his research and went out to a bar for a sandwich and an iced tea. He had his own suspicions about what had happened to Domenico Salvitti after 1945.

When he returned to the library, he took out the microfilmed newspaper records for January and February 1941, and went through them day by day. It was a slow, tiring exercise, made more difficult by the poor, almost illegible print on many of the pages.

Towards the end of the afternoon, he found what he was looking for. In an edition of *Il Popolo d'Italia*, the paper that Mussolini himself had edited before taking power, was a photograph of Salvitti being presented with his medal by the Duce. The picture was taken in the *Sala del Mappamondo*, Mussolini's vast office in the Palazzo Venezia, which had an ancient fresco of the world on the walls and a mosaic floor on which female visitors were routinely seduced by the priapic dictator.

Salvitti was standing to attention in the dress uniform of the MVSN while Mussolini pinned the medal on to his breast. Chapman studied the microfilm closely, taking in Salvitti's grainy features. He was a young man in his early thirties with a full head of hair and an unlined face. Half a century on it was impossible to be absolutely sure, but Chapman was certain beyond a reasonable doubt that it was the same face he'd seen in the photograph on the wall of Roberto Ferrero's study.

The floor of Elena's office, the adjoining clerk's room and part of the corridor outside were almost completely covered with unstable piles of files and papers. Alberto Baffi and the two secretaries were working their way slowly through them, making an inventory of everything that had been taken from the MPI offices. As each pile was sorted, Elena would remove the documents and stack them on her desk, which had been cleared of its usual debris for the occasion.

There was a daunting number of them. Looking at the sea of brown cardboard folders, Elena wondered, not for the first time in her career, whether she'd bitten off more than she could chew. It would take her days even to skim through them all, never mind study them in detail.

But she had no regrets. She could still taste the castor oil in her mouth, remember the hooded thug's hands probing beneath her skirt. If nothing else, the police raid had reasserted her authority, given her back some of the dignity that had been so brutally taken from her the previous night.

She squeezed in behind her desk and opened the first of the cardboard folders. She knew she had to be selective about what she read or she'd be there till midnight every day for a fortnight. And she didn't have a fortnight. Time was always going to be a problem, but more so since the phone call from the clerk to one of the *Tribunale* examining magistrates. He'd rung almost as soon as Elena returned to her office to inform her that the MPI's lawyers had telephoned demanding the return of their papers. A hearing before the judge had been agreed for the following Wednesday morning. Elena knew that unless she'd found some kind of evidence by then to implicate the MPI in illegal activities, she would be forced to return the documents.

It was halfway through Friday now. That gave her four and a half days. It was going to be a very long weekend.

The first few files made slow, laborious reading. They contained MPI policy documents, page after page of political waffle and meaningless claptrap. But she had to go through them. They were offensive, neo-Fascist tracts, full of bile and right-wing rhetoric but carefully worded to ensure they stayed just the right side of the law. The subtext might have been an incitement to others to beat up immigrants or desecrate Jewish and Muslim temples, but Cesare Scarfone was too clever a lawyer, as well as a politician, to allow anything to go into print that might leave him open to prosecution.

Elena worked through the files methodically, searching for something, anything, that might be construed as a link, however tenuous, to right-wing terrorist groups like the *Sansepolcristi*. She was an experienced sifter of documents, able to spot relevant passages quickly, but even so it took her well into the afternoon to dispense with the first batch of files. Baffi ordered in sandwiches and coffee from a nearby bar and Elena ate a late lunch at her desk, reading MPI correspondence in between mouthfuls of a ham and mozzarella roll.

Shortly afterwards, Vespignani sauntered in and leaned his portly frame on the wall next to the door.

'You look busy,' he said casually, gazing around at the plague of paperwork.

'Did you want something, Luigi?'

The deputy chief prosecutor stroked his beard, smoothing the sleek hairs over his double chin.

'Cesare Scarfone has been on the phone,' he said.

'Oh yes.' Elena didn't look up. She finished the last page of the file she was reading and placed it on the completed pile next to her desk.

'He wasn't a happy man.'

'My heart bleeds for him.'

'I trust you're not letting any personal prejudice influence your work as a prosecutor.'

'And what's that supposed to mean?'

'Nothing, don't take offence.' Vespignani held up a hand to placate her. 'It's just that Corona might not be happy about the *pubblico ministero* becoming too involved in, well, the political arena.'

'Corona is in Milan,' Elena retorted. 'When he returns, I will discuss it with him.'

'Scarfone is not someone you want to cross. He has more influence than you think.'

'Is there a point to this conversation?' Elena said bluntly.

Vespignani hesitated. 'Scarfone says he's received an *avviso di garanzia* from you and notification that you've applied to have his immunity from arrest lifted. Is that true?'

'Yes.'

'You shouldn't have done that without consulting me and the chief.'

'There wasn't time. I had to act quickly,' Elena said.

'You should have waited for our approval.'

'I don't need your approval, Luigi.'

'What evidence do you have against Scarfone?'

'Enough for an *avviso*.'

'I want to see copies of the paperwork you sent to Montecitorio.'

'Not now.'

'Now, Elena.'

Elena lifted her head, her eyes flashing. 'Listen,' she said angrily. 'A few days ago I came home from work to find my cat butchered on my kitchen floor. Then I witnessed a gathering of Blackshirt thugs at Ostia Antica, an illegal rally addressed by Cesare Scarfone, and only narrowly escaped with my life. Then last night I was attacked just yards from the *Procura*. I was sexually assaulted and had castor oil poured down my throat. You think about all that, Luigi. Think how you would like that happening to you and ask yourself why you're standing there harassing me when you should be doing everything you can to back me up.'

'You're claiming Scarfone was behind these attacks?'

'I know he was. And I'm going to nail him for them. Next time he rings for a chat, tell him that from me. Now, if you'll excuse me, I'm very busy.'

Elena turned her attention back to the next card-board folder. Without looking up, she was aware of the deputy chief prosecutor leaving the room and walking out through the clerk's office. She heard his heavy-footed tread on the tiles in the corridor, expect-ing the footsteps to recede into the distance. But there was a sudden silence.

Elena lifted her head. She listened, then stood up, frowning. She took a few paces out through the open door into the clerk's office. Baffi and the secretaries were at one of the desks completing the inventory. Elena stepped sideways, peering out into the corri-dor where the overflow of files was stacked untidily against the wall. Vespignani was bending over one of the stacks, examining the files. He must have sensed Elena's presence for he straightened up and looked round at her. Neither said a word. Vespignani sim-ply turned and hurried away down the corridor, his stubby legs and splayed feet paddling over the stone floor in a gait that reminded Elena of a pregnant penguin.

'It's me, signora. Signor Chapman from upstairs,' Chapman called out loudly.

A key turned in the lock on the other side and the door opened enough for him to see the wrinkled face of the old lady inside.

'I'm sorry to disturb you. I've come for the papers I left with you.'

Signora Campanella unlatched the chain and pulled the door wide open.

'Come in. I'm just making some tea. Would you like some?'

'That's very kind.'

Chapman followed her through into the living room. He didn't really want to stay but it seemed discourteous to refuse her invitation. The shutters were closed, giving the room a gloomy atmosphere that was accentuated by the dark wooden furniture and bottle-green carpet on the floor.

Signora Campanella threw open one of the shutters to let in the early evening light. Outside was the noise of the traffic echoing around the cramped streets, and the clatter of pots and pans as the kitchen staff in the restaurant down below prepared for the first influx of diners.

'Here they are.'

Signora Campanella took the brown manilla envelope out of a drawer in the oak dresser which occupied virtually the whole of one wall and handed it to him.

Chapman thanked her and sank down in a soft armchair. Other than to use the telephone in the hall he'd never been inside the old lady's flat. In five years he'd exchanged barely more than a few good mornings with her. The details of her life: who she was, what she did with her days, were unknown to him.

He looked around. The place had the feel of an old person's apartment: solid, well-crafted furniture that was too big for the space available, as if it had come from a larger home and been crammed in wherever it

happened to fit; too much clutter, mementoes and possessions collected over decades and never discarded;
a faint, distinctive smell of polish and decay that he
always associated with the elderly.

On the mantelpiece and several of the surfaces around
the room were candlesticks and ikons of definite eastern
origin. They reminded Chapman of Orthodox churches
he'd visited in Greece. Perhaps Signora Campanella was
Greek, not Polish as he'd always thought. But on the
wall beside the window was a framed religious print
with writing around the edges that was in the Cyrillic,
not Greek, alphabet.

Chapman pulled back the flap of the envelope and
tipped the contents out on to his lap to study while the
old lady made the tea. He looked at the faded black
and white photograph first. It was clearly taken some
time during the war, though there was nothing on the
back to indicate when or where.

In the centre foreground, surrounded by middle-
aged men in dark suits, was Mussolini. He was glaring
defiantly at the camera, his chest thrust forwards, his
back ramrod straight. It could have been one of the
thousands of propaganda photographs the Duce had
had taken for publication in the Italian newspapers.
It certainly had all the hallmarks: the dictator in full
dress uniform, machine-gun slung over one shoulder,
his tunic dripping with all the medals and ribbons
he'd awarded himself, dominating the men around
him who always looked weak and drab in comparison
to their leader.

But there was something about it that made Chapman feel it wasn't a propaganda picture. For one
thing, though Mussolini was obviously posing for

the camera, the other men in the group were clearly not. They looked embarrassed, sheepish even, as if the photograph were being taken against their will. Chapman had no idea who they were, but assumed they were just some of the fawning acolytes and hangers-on with whom the Duce had surrounded himself.

Behind them, milling around in an ill-disciplined fashion that would never have been tolerated in a true propaganda picture, were German soldiers. Not Wehrmacht, but SS. That was an interesting detail. Chapman was no expert on Italian history, but the presence of SS soldiers, combined with the gaunt, haunted look in Mussolini's face, indicated strongly to him that the photograph was taken at the end of the war when the SS controlled the puppet Republic of Salò and the Duce's health was declining rapidly.

He peered more closely at the background. The group was standing in the courtyard of a building which looked familiar to him. An elegant stone front-age with high arched doorways. He was sure he'd seen it before, but couldn't identify exactly where it was.

He looked up as Signora Campanella came in from the kitchen with a tray of tea things.

'Are you sure you have time?' she said, putting the tray down on the coffee table in front of him.

'Certainly,' Chapman said.

He put the photograph and papers down next to the tray and smiled at the old lady. She must have been in her seventies. The lines were etched deep into her face, across her forehead and around her eyes and mouth. In some old people wrinkles were like exaggerated laughter lines, bringing out the warmth and goodness of their features. But on Signora Campanella they seemed the surface manifestation of a deeper melancholy. Chapman had rarely seen a sadder face on a human being.

'All these years we live in the same building and this is the first time we take tea together,' she said in her accented Italian.

She poured Chapman a cup and passed it across the table.

'I know,' he said. 'It's silly, isn't it?' He paused. 'I'm trying to place your accent, signora. Where do you come from?'

'From Yugoslavia. I am Serb.'

'Ah. So the writing on the print over there?'

'Is Serbo-Croat. Well, Serbian,' she corrected herself. 'The Croats, they use the Roman alphabet. But I have been in Italy fifty years now, since the end of the war. My husband, he was Italian. That's him there.' She pointed at a framed photograph standing on a table in the corner of the room. 'He die fifteen years ago.'

She picked up the teapot to pour her own cup and stretched out a hand to push Chapman's papers away from the tray.

'I move these if you don't mind. You don't want anything to spill on them.'

'Of course.'

Chapman slid the photograph and letters along the table.

There was a sudden, jarring crash. Chapman glanced up. The old lady had dropped the teapot down on to the tray. It had tipped over on its side and tea was flooding from under the lid. Chapman grabbed it by the handle and stood it upright.

'Signora . . .'

The old lady was staring down at the letters on the table, her mouth gaping open, her eyes wide with an expression of horror that made Chapman's skin go cold.

'Signora, what is it?'

The old lady swallowed. She seemed unable to drag her gaze away from the papers. Chapman looked at the yellowing letter on the top of the pile. Across the top it had the printed heading *Nezavisna Država Hrvatska*, and below that the words *Za dom Spremni*.

'Is it these? Signora?'

Chapman felt his mouth go dry. There was something terribly wrong. It was as if the old lady had been temporarily paralysed. Her body was rigid, the muscles frozen like petrified flesh. But it was her face that shook him most. The mixture of shock and horror and what looked like pure terror that was set solid in her features, transforming them into a mask that was cast from pain and the most unimaginable suffering.

'Signora . . .'

Chapman reached out and touched her arm.

'*Ustashe*,' she whispered.

'Pardon?'

'Prebilovci.'

With a fierce effort she pulled her gaze away from the letter. She was trembling now, her mouth and jaw shivering as if she had a fever.

'Can I get you something?' Chapman asked anxiously. 'A drink of water? Some tea?'

Signora Campanella shook her head. 'Go now.'

Chapman held up the letter. 'What is this?'

The old lady recoiled, waving the letter away. 'Go now. I cannot talk about it.'

'Talk about what?'

'Please. Just go. Take them. Take them!'

Chapman gathered up the photograph and papers and slid them back into the envelope.

'I'm sorry,' he said. 'I didn't mean to upset you. Are you sure there's nothing I can do? Shall I call a doctor?'

Signora Campanella gestured towards the door, shaking her head but unable to speak. Chapman watched her, feeling almost sick with concern. But his presence seemed to distress her even more. He took a few paces across the room and glanced back before he left. The old lady was staring at him, staring *through* him as if seeing something that was either far beyond him or deep inside her own mind. On the low table, the spilt tea was overflowing from the tray and dripping slowly down on to the carpet.

Elena's back and shoulders were stiff from sitting hunched in the same position for too long. Her eyes were sore and there was a throbbing pain across the top of her head as if the inside of her cranium were being tapped with drumsticks. She stood up from her desk and stretched her muscles. Then she massaged her temples with her fingers to try to relieve the headache.

She'd been reading solidly without a break for the best part of six hours and wanted only to go home and lie down in a darkened room. Yet she knew she had to persevere. The pile of completed files on the floor by her desk was depressingly small, perhaps a twentieth, maybe less, of the total she had to get through before Wednesday. If she didn't discipline herself to continue, force herself to ignore the fatigue in both her mind and body, she would never complete the task.

It was difficult to maintain concentration, even harder not to feel disheartened by the whole tedious business. She'd read perhaps thirty files but had found nothing that came even close to linking the MPI to anything illegal. No mention of Blackshirts, no membership list with names of known neo-Fascist troublemakers on it, no memos or correspondence about the rally at Ostia Antica. The documents were as dull and innocuous as the minutes of a church council meeting. It was as if anything remotely incriminating had already been removed and shredded.

Elena walked out into the clerk's office, easing the stiffness in her legs and lower back. Baffi and the two secretaries had gone home. So too had most other people in the building. No one worked late on a Friday if they could help it. Elena yawned and listened. The *Procura* was eerily quiet. Normally she liked that, but tonight the silence only seemed to increase her feeling of isolation, the sense that she was frittering away her time on a quest that would prove futile and fruitless.

She turned to go back into her own office. And stopped.

Shredded.

The files were too clean to be believable. The MPI was an extremist political party, and this was Italy, for God's sake. There had to be something in their records that, if not actually illegal, was compromising in other ways – perhaps embarrassing, perhaps sufficient to cause a political scandal or public outrage whilst falling short of outright criminality. But there was nothing.

She remembered the shaven-headed youth who'd been dragged out of one of the MPI offices. He'd been trying to shred documents but had been caught in the middle. The files. The police officer had handed her a bundle of bright green cardboard folders. She'd put them down with all the others but had no idea what had happened to them after that. Presumably they'd been bagged up and brought in the van to the *Procura*.

Elena went back to her desk and leafed through the inventory Baffi had drawn up. It was little more than a brief list of files and their contents, ascertained by a glance at their title pages rather than any detailed study. She'd been through it several times already without seeing anything to arouse her immediate interest. This time was no different. She saw nothing that seemed suspicious or out of the ordinary.

She turned her attention to the mounds of paper in her office, going through each pile and removing all the bright green folders. Then she did the same with the stacks in the clerk's room and out in the corridor. She collected them together and brought them to her desk. There were sixteen of them, all identical on the outside. She sat down and started to skim through them, one by one.

In the seventh folder she found it. It was the sort of document that was easy to overlook – just a few sheets of paper covered in typed figures that looked like petty cash accounts. At least, petty cash accounts until you noticed the amounts involved. Elena read through the document slowly, trying to absorb its significance. It wasn't an MPI document at all. The heading on the first

325

page identified it as a statement from the Union Bank of Switzerland in Zürich. Subsequent pages detailed the transfer of funds from Italy to named accounts in Switzerland over the previous twelve months.

Elena read down the list of names and felt her heart jolt violently, as if she'd been jabbed with an electric cattle prod. Her skin went suddenly clammy and her hands began to tremble. *Dio*. She scanned the list again. Then a third time. There was no mistake. She pushed back her chair and sat motionless for a long while, wondering what to do. Then she reached out for the telephone and dialled a number at the Palace of Justice.

The house was out near the Villa Ada on the northern fringes of the city. In a secluded, exclusive estate that was so small, so secure it was more like the compound of a maximum security prison than a residential development. Except the houses, built amid lush gardens with mature trees and shrubs to protect their occupants' privacy, could never have been mistaken for any part of a penal institution.

They were large, expensive mansions exuding the heady aroma of money from their brightly lit windows and opulent exteriors. But beneath the surface trappings was another scent, a scent encapsulated in the high wire fences surrounding the whole enclave, the closed-circuit television cameras that monitored the fronts and backs of the homes, the constant presence of security guards on the streets and at the checkpoint that protected the one entrance to the estate. It was the scent that everywhere in the world is inseparable from the tang of wealth and privilege: the smell of fear.

The judicial police car in which Elena was travelling was stopped at the barrier blocking the road to the houses. After proving her identity, she was made to wait while the uniformed guard made a telephone call to check that she was expected. There were no unannounced visitors to this particular leafy suburb of the city.

The check completed, she was allowed to proceed down the street. A few hundred metres in, a pair of steel gates on the left swung open and her police driver turned into a drive and stopped by the open front door of a long, two-storey house with stone balconies outside the bedroom windows. There were other cars parked on the forecourt, the dark blue Alfa Romeo saloons used by government ministers and influential public figures. A maid in a white apron was waiting on the threshold to escort her down the hall and into a spacious study lined with leather-bound law reports and legal textbooks.

'Judge Bassano will be with you directly,' the maid said, leaving Elena alone in the room.

Elena stayed exactly where she was. She didn't dare move. There was a ball the size of a melon in her stomach that seemed to be swelling ever larger. She felt like a nervous schoolgirl again, waiting in the Mother Superior's office to be punished for some transgression. She could hear voices and occasional laughter through the open window of the study, the chink of cutlery on china. That made her feel even worse; she was interrupting a dinner party.

'Dottoressa, please be seated.'

Emilio Bassano came into the room and walked round the desk to his chair. He was a broad-shouldered, muscular man in his sixties, with silver hair and thick eyebrows which gave the impression that he was permanently frowning. Elena had seen him before in court and at her parents' house. He'd been a contemporary of her father's in the Rome University Law Department and the two men were still friends. He must have recognised her but he gave no sign of it. This wasn't a social call.

'How can I help you?' he said in a low, gravelly voice.

Elena swallowed, then explained how she'd come across the document she was clutching in her fingers. Judge Bassano watched her face, listening attentively to every word. He had the stillness of power about him, the quiet repose of a man who was accustomed to getting what he wanted without opposition. But then he was the Procurator General of the Court of Cassation, the highest court in the land, and a senior member of the Superior Magisterial Council which regulated every aspect of the Italian judicial system. He was one of the most respected lawyers in the country, a judge who mixed not only with his legal brethren but with senators, cabinet ministers and the President of the Republic himself. Elena found herself wondering who else was at the dinner party she was spoiling.

She passed the sheets of paper across the desk to Bassano.

'I thought I should bring them straight to you,' she said. 'I think there may be a problem with the third name on the list.'

The judge took out a pair of metal-rimmed spectacles and studied the piece of paper for a time.

Then he lifted his head and sighed with a weary resignation.

'Yes, dottoressa, I believe you are right. We do have a problem,' he said.

The third name on the list was Alessandro Corona.

SEVENTEEN

Chapman paused as he opened the door to his apartment, his nostrils dilating as he detected a smell which was familiar yet hard to identify. A sweet, slightly cloying scent that seemed to linger in the heavy evening air. It was only when a woman's voice called out from the living room that he realised what it was.

'Andy, is that you?'

Chapman pushed the door to behind him and leaned on it for a moment, trying to work out what to do.

'Andy?'

He found his voice. 'Yes, it's me.'

He went across the hall and into the living room. Gabriella was stretched out on the settee, drinking a glass of wine and reading a glossy fashion magazine with an anorexic, pouting model on the front cover.

'*Ciao*,' he said casually. He'd forgotten all about her.

'I expected you sooner,' she said chidingly. 'You know I don't like to be kept waiting.'

She swung her legs off the sofa to give him room to sit down. The purple silk robe she was wearing fell open a little. Chapman could see she was naked underneath it. His mouth went suddenly dry. He didn't know how he was going to do this.

'Gabriella . . .'

'Have some wine,' she said.

She poured him a glass of chilled Soave and leaned over to hand it to him, smiling as she saw his eyes drop to the gaping slit in her robe.

'Missed me?' she said.

Chapman drank some of his wine. He hated these moments.

'You should have called,' he said.

'I wanted to surprise you.'

She kissed him on the mouth. He could taste her lipstick, smell her perfume. An erotic charge he was powerless to stop pulsed through his veins. She was undoing his shirt now, slipping her hands through the gap and over the muscles of his chest and shoulders. He knew he had to tell her, it was the only honest, decent thing to do. Tell her now.

'Gabriella . . .'

She lay back on the cushions and threw her robe open wide.

Shit, Chapman thought. Once more, for old times' sake.

For Elena, the evening passed in a blur of intense, but subdued activity, the details of which she could barely recall twelve hours later. She remembered the cathartic sense of relief she'd felt when Emilio Bassano took charge of the case, when he removed the burden of responsibility which had weighed so heavily on her shoulders since she'd first seen Corona's name on the list.

From then on it seemed as if she were only a spectator in the complex legal process the judge set in motion.

She remained in his study, sitting quietly in the chair opposite him while he made a series of telephone calls, listening to his calm, reassuring voice as he arranged for the chief prosecutor to be suspended from his post pending a full investigation into his financial links with the MPI. Then he spoke to the President of the Court of Cassation and the Minister of Grace and Justice himself before calling Bologna to arrange for an independent team from the *pubblico ministero* there to come to Rome to begin the inquiry.

Elena was only vaguely aware of what was going on. Part of her mind seemed to have shut down once Bassano was involved and she was content to sit there in a daze until the judge eventually stood up and came out from behind his desk.

'It is out of your hands now, dottoressa,' he said.

He took her arm and escorted her along the hall to the front door. 'You did the right thing coming to me. You can do nothing more now. Goodnight.'

Elena went down the steps to her car. As the police driver opened the rear door for her, she glanced back at the house. Judge Bassano was silhouetted in the doorway, his face just a shadow. He lifted a hand in a brief farewell then turned and went back to his dinner guests.

Her apartment was in darkness when she got home. She went through the rooms, turning on the lights in an attempt to make them seem more welcoming, less empty. She'd lived alone for a long time and had thought she would never adapt easily to having a man about the house again. But she was disappointed to find Chapman wasn't there. It was foolish, irrational, given the short time they'd known each other, but she'd expected him to be waiting for her.

She made herself some coffee and picked at a chunk of cheese and a few slices of dried-out ham she'd found in the fridge, wondering how she was going to occupy herself for the rest of the evening. She was tired, but she didn't feel like going to bed. She couldn't face the thought of doing any work, there was nothing on television and when she tried reading a book, she couldn't concentrate enough to get beyond the first page.

She wandered restlessly about the apartment thinking, what's the matter with me? Then, finally, she succumbed. She went into her bedroom and picked up the phone.

'Are you going to answer that?' Gabriella said.

'Uh?'

'The phone.'

Chapman opened his eyes, emerging drowsily from a shallow sleep. They were sprawled naked across the bed, relaxed and spent. He dragged himself out from under the crumpled sheet and stumbled into the hall.

'*Pronto.*'

'It's me,' Elena said. 'You went back to your apartment then.'

Chapman's befuddled brain cleared itself abruptly. He glanced towards the open bedroom door and carried the phone into the kitchen.

'Yes,' he said, keeping his voice low. 'I thought it was safe to return.'

'You could come over, if you like.'

'It's a bit late,' Chapman said. He knew it sounded a

lame excuse so he added: 'I'm sorting out a few things here.' There was an awkward silence. 'Why don't I call you tomorrow? We could do something in the evening. Go out for dinner. The cinema maybe.'

'Okay,' Elena said lightly.

She could sense he didn't want to talk. She hung up, wishing she'd never called now. Chapman replaced his receiver and looked up to see Gabriella standing in the kitchen door. She'd put on her silk robe and was gazing at him with an expression he found distinctly unnerving.

'Who was that?' she said.

Chapman hesitated. He thought about lying to her. About spinning some yarn to put off the moment when he would have to tell her. But it would only complicate things more than they were already.

'A friend,' he said, longing for the imprecision of the English language. From the gender in Italian she would know immediately that the 'friend' was female.

'Who is she?' Gabriella said quietly.

'Just someone I met.'

'Met when?'

'Recently.'

'You bastard.'

He knew there was no escape from her anger. Gabriella had a volatile, unpredictable temper. She wouldn't make it easy for him.

'Who is she?' Gabriella repeated.

'You don't need to know that.'

'Don't give me that crap. I have a right to know.'

Chapman held his ground. 'Look, Gabriella, it was always going to happen, wasn't it? Let's not do this acrimoniously.'

'That would suit you, wouldn't it? Are you sleeping with her?'

Chapman looked down. He wasn't much good at this.

'You are, aren't you? You shit, Chapman. You couldn't tell me, could you? You thought you could screw us both.'

'That's not the way it is,' Chapman said feebly.

'You're just like every other man with his brain in his cock. You want to move from woman to woman without any consequences. Well, don't think for a minute that I'm going to be all sweetness and light about it, you despicable fucking rat.'

She continued in the same vein for a while, telling him exactly what she thought of him with a fluency that made Chapman wonder if she'd said it all before to one of his predecessors. He let her go on, knowing her anger would eventually burn itself out.

At the end, he said: 'What did you think was going to happen? That we'd carry on indefinitely?'

'I didn't think it would end like this.'

'You're married, Gabriella.'

'So that makes it all right to dump me, does it? You've been sleeping with this "friend" for months, haven't you? Keeping me as your bit on the side.'

'No, I haven't,' Chapman said. It didn't seem worth pointing out that he'd been her 'bit on the side' for the past year. 'I really did only meet her last week.'

'And it was love at first sight, I suppose?' Gabriella said sarcastically. 'You lying prick, Chapman. What's she like? Younger than me?'

'I don't want to discuss this. Let's just make a clean break. I'm sorry, Gabriella.'

'Sorry? I'm sorry too. Sorry I ever had anything to do with a shit like you. You can go and rot in hell.'

She turned on her heel and marched furiously back into the bedroom. Chapman stayed out of her way. He could hear her getting dressed and packing her overnight case. She was still livid when she reappeared in the kitchen doorway. She was holding her keys to Chapman's apartment.

'You can have these back,' she said. 'Give them to your new girlfriend.'

She hurled the keys at him. He lifted his arms to shield himself but they hit him on the shoulder, the sharp edges gashing the skin.

Gabriella picked up her case and walked out. Chapman could feel the floor vibrate as she slammed the door behind her. He took a deep breath, relieved to have got it over with, glad, in a way, that she'd taken it so badly. If she'd been pleasant and understanding, his feelings of guilt would have been much worse. It was her pride he'd hurt, of course, not her emotions. She wasn't in love with him, he'd always known that. She'd quickly find someone else to satisfy her need for an illicit affair and Chapman, like her previous lovers, would be buried away in some dark corner of her memory and forgotten.

He went through into the bathroom and washed the blood off his shoulder.

Elena made herself get up early next morning. It was Saturday, but she had an enormous mound of files to get through at her office. The suspension of her boss had made no real difference to her objectives. She still wanted to find something to pin directly on to Cesare Scarfone.

She was about to leave her apartment when the buzzer on the main door downstairs sounded. She went to the phone in the hall.

'*Pronto.*'

'Special delivery for Fiorini.'

The motorbike courier brought the package upstairs and Elena signed for it. It was a plain A4 brown envelope about two inches thick. Elena opened it and pulled out a wad of papers. Not more stuff to read, she thought wearily, looking through the sheets for a covering letter of some sort. But there wasn't one. She checked the envelope. It was empty and had nothing on the outside to indicate who had sent it. An anonymous delivery. The warning lights began to click on inside her head. She'd received anonymous packages before, but they'd always come to the office, not her home. To get one at her apartment was worrying, and the timing disturbed her even more.

For a long while she simply looked at the papers without touching them. She contemplated taking them to the *Procura* with her but she didn't know what they were. Finally, she lifted off the top sheet and read it. Then read it again. She couldn't work out what it was. Even reading through the subsequent pages did little to clarify things. They were legal documents, but too complicated for her to understand immediately.

The telephone rang. Elena went out into the hall and picked up the receiver.

'Has it arrived, dottoressa?' a man's voice asked. 'I hope it has.'

'Who is this?' Elena said.

'I don't like what you're doing. I think maybe it's time you reconsidered, don't you?'

It was Scarfone. She recognised his voice now. There was something gloating about his tone.

'What do you want?' she asked.

'You know what I want. Enjoy your reading, dottoressa.'

There was a click as he ended the call. Elena replaced the receiver and went back to look at the documents in the kitchen. She leafed through them, then read one or two more carefully. She had a sudden, heartstopping realisation of what they were. Her legs went weak and she had to sit down for a moment at the table. She was numb with shock. Her senses seemed to have stopped working. The sounds from the street outside were obliterated, all sensation disappeared from her skin so that she could no longer feel the pieces of paper in her hands. Her eyes stared down at the words without taking in what they said. It was as though her mind had been anaesthetised or swathed in a thick layer of cotton wool.

She forced herself to move, going to one of the cupboards and searching through it for an old bottle of *grappa* she knew was there. She poured herself a glass and downed it in one, coughing as the liquid burned her throat. She was too dazed to do anything but stand there looking out of the window with unseeing eyes, wishing Chapman were present to hold her tight and tell her she was wrong. But men were never there when you needed them.

After a long while, she roused herself and went to the telephone. She rang the Regina Coeli prison, identified herself and was put through to the governor.

'I'd like to come in this morning to interview an inmate,' she explained.

'Of course. What is the inmate's name?' the governor asked.

'Geminazza,' Elena said. 'Enrico Geminazza.'

Chapman tried Signora Campanella's apartment first. He rang the doorbell several times and waited outside for a few minutes, calling her name before finally giving up and going downstairs. If the old lady wasn't at home, he had an idea where she might be.

He went round the corner and down an alley into the cramped piazza where, each morning, there was a fruit and vegetable market. He found her selecting a paper bag of plum tomatoes at one of the stalls, her overflowing wicker shopping basket suspended from one bony arm.

Chapman slid the basket off her wrist. 'Let me help you, signora. That looks heavy.'

Signora Campanella glanced up, about to protest, but when she saw who it was she gave a slight nod of acquiescence and let him keep the basket. She handed the bag of tomatoes to the stallholder who weighed them.

'Anything else?' The stallholder said.

The old lady shook her head. '*È basta così.*'

Chapman took the tomatoes and placed them gently next to the lettuce and calabrese and spinach poking out of the top of the basket. Then he walked beside Signora Campanella as she made her way back to her apartment.

'I came to apologise,' he said. 'For upsetting you yesterday. It was completely unintentional.'

'You must forgive my reaction,' she replied. 'It's a long time since I've seen those words. It took me by surprise.'

'The words? The heading on those letters, you mean? What are they?'

The old lady didn't reply. They walked down the alley in silence, Chapman slowing his pace to keep in step with her. She was breathing heavily, though whether from the exertion or some reawakened distress his question had caused, Chapman couldn't tell.

Only when they were outside the apartment building did he press her again.

'Signora, I know this causes you pain, but I have to know. I need your help. What is it about that letter you saw that upsets you so much?'

'*Ustashe*,' Signora Campanella said, her voice cracking a little. 'You know who the *Ustashe* were?'

'Yes.'

'Look up Prebilovci,' she said. The words came out with difficulty and Chapman could see he was distressing her again. But he couldn't let the matter rest. He knew it was important.

'Is that a person, a place?' he asked.

'I was there,' she said quietly. She lifted her head. Her eyes were moist. 'I survived, but I cannot tell you about it.'

She took the shopping basket from Chapman's hand and shuffled into the building without a backward glance.

Chapman was growing accustomed to the distinctive atmosphere inside the National Library: the warm air circulating around the lofty halls, the smell of dust and old leather, the soft-spoken, scholarly readers who padded among the shelves or sat hunched over books at the tables with half-moon glasses perched on the ends of their noses. It seemed atypically Italian to him, so far away from the incessant noise and bustle of the city outside that it might have been a different country. But the Italians, for all their gregarious show, were in many ways a melancholy, reflective race. They liked to make time for thought, to read and study and find solace in the rich annals of their past.

He looked up *Ustashe* in the central index and found several references which he then followed up in books and periodicals. He knew the *Ustashe* were a Fascist militia which had conducted a campaign of terror and genocide in Yugoslavia during the Second World War, but he had to remind himself of the details.

Established in the late 1920s by a lawyer named Ante Pavelić, the *Ustashe* were initially a terrorist organisation which, after being outlawed in Yugoslavia, found a home and considerable military and political support in Mussolini's Italy. When the Nazis conquered Yugoslavia in April 1941, the *Ustashe* returned home and Pavelić was installed as the *Poglavnik*, the *Führer* of the puppet Independent State of Croatia, the *Nezavisna Država Hrvatska*, whose motto was *Za dom Spremni*, 'Ready for the Fatherland'.

Almost immediately, they began a concerted drive to wipe out Jews, Gypsies and the Serbian Orthodox population of Croatia; a campaign of genocide which shocked even the Nazis in its bloody brutality. Fanatical Catholics, in many cases led by Catholic priests or Franciscan friars, the *Ustashe*'s avowed intention was to drive out a third of the Serbs, to convert a third

PAUL ADAM

of them to Catholicism and to kill a third; objectives
which they succeeded in carrying out with a terrifying
ruthlessness.

Chapman was revolted by the facts he found in the
history books. The genocide of the Nazis was well
documented and well known. The Holocaust was in
the conscience and *on* the conscience of the whole
world, but what took place in Croatia between 1941
and 1945 was its equal, if not in scale, then certainly
in horror. The figures were disputed, but in those four
years some half a million people, most of them Serbs,
were liquidated by the *Ustashe*, most by means that
could only be described as butchery. Whole villages
were slaughtered; men, women and children were
hacked to pieces with axes; hundreds were buried
alive or herded into Orthodox churches which were
then set on fire.

Hardly an adult on earth had never heard of Auschwitz
or Belsen or Dachau, but how many knew anything of
Jasenovac, the *Ustashe* concentration camp where tens
of thousands of people were tortured and killed, purely
because of their religion? They were Orthodox Serbs,
yet if they converted to Catholicism many of them were
spared.

It was that which Chapman found the most shocking. The *Ustashe* were rabid Catholic zealots. Catholic
priests were active participants in the slaughter, others
gave tacit support. The priests who were appalled by
the mass murders were not listened to by either Pavelić
or his bloodthirsty militiamen. The Vatican, throughout the period, remained silent – though it knew all too
well what was happening – thus appearing to condone
the atrocities. Indeed, Pope Pius XII received Pavelić

in the Holy See without, it appeared, condemning any of the carnage carried out by the *Poglavnik*'s *Ustashe* butchers, one of the most brutal of whom was the Franciscan Miroslav Filipović, the commandant of the Jasenovac camp, who personally slit the throats of hundreds of its inmates.

Chapman read through the lists of atrocities, wondering how much more of it he could take. Gudovac, Tuke and other villages, two hundred and fifty Serbs bound with wire and buried alive; Glina, hundreds of Serbs herded into the Orthodox church and massacred with axes and knives; Grabovac, a four-day orgy of *Ustashe* killings in which countless Serbs were butchered; Otočac, three hundred Serbs hacked to pieces, including the local Orthodox priest who had his beard and skin torn off and his eyes gouged out before being killed. On and on it went until Chapman felt physically sick.

Then he came to Prebilovci. A village in southern Herzegovina where virtually the whole population had been exterminated by the *Ustashe*. Shot as they tried to flee, disembowelled with bayonets or thrown into pits, family by family. Where infants were swung round in the air and had their heads smashed open on stone walls, where women and young girls were gang-raped and then slaughtered, and others were beaten to death or left to die in crevasses in the ground.

The details were sickening, so numbing in their mindless cruelty that after a while Chapman stopped reading before he became so desensitised by the descriptions that he ceased to remember that these were real people. Real men, women and children who had been massacred in the most sadistic, inhuman manner imaginable.

And Signora Campanella, the old lady who had lived in the apartment below him for years, who went out for her fruit and vegetables each morning like her neighbours and talked about the weather and other trivia as if they really mattered, she had been there. She had survived the slaughter, though Chapman would never know how or why, and would never ask now. He wondered at her resilience, at a human being's ability to endure suffering and come through it with the will to live intact. It was both awesome and humbling.

He cleared the table on which he was working, returned all the books to the shelves or the counter, and took a moment to erase from his mind the disturbing scenes he'd been reading about. To make himself human once again.

Then he took out the envelope of papers he'd left at Signora Campanella's flat and examined them more closely. He started with the letter that had upset the old lady so much. He knew now what the headings meant, but it was the contents that interested him more. It was a short letter, written in Italian and addressed to Mussolini at the villa in Gargnano from where he ostensibly ran the Republic of Salò after his overthrow and the Italian Armistice with the Allies. The text was illegible in places, but from one of the clearer passages the letter appeared to refer to some kind of consignment that was being sent to the Duce. The exact nature of that consignment wasn't specified. The signature at the bottom, confirmed by the typewritten name beneath it, was Ante Pavelić.

Chapman turned to one of the other letters in the envelope. This one was badly damaged by water, or damp, and had several holes in the paper which made it impossible to read. But what was clear was that it came from Mussolini and was sent to the Vatican Secretariat of State in late March 1945, only a few weeks before the Duce was captured and executed by partisans.

A third letter, written on Vatican notepaper and signed by Giovanni Montini, the Vatican Under-Secretary of State, seemed to be a reply to Mussolini's letter. It too was badly damaged, the ink smudged and faded so that it was virtually unreadable. Chapman, after much close scrutiny, could make out the words Red Cross and an indistinct word that looked like *Poglavnik*. Only one short phrase was complete and truly legible. It read: 'We agree to the terms and expect dispatch within a month.'

Chapman fingered the brittle, yellowing papers thoughtfully for a time. He would get nothing more from them without some kind of additional information, something to clarify exactly what the letters referred to. And there was only one place he would find that.

He slipped the papers back into their envelope and went out of the library to find his car.

'Which would you like, red or white?'

'Is the white chilled?' Chapman asked.

'Are you trying to wind me up?' Brian Matheson tugged his sunglasses down his nose and glared at him with mock severity.

'The white it is then.'

Matheson retreated into the house and re-emerged a few minutes later with two glasses and a bottle of white wine in an ice bucket. He pulled the cork and filled the glasses, holding his own up to the sunlight to gauge the colour.

'Not bad,' he said approvingly. 'Orvieto. I had a couple of cases sent down from a vineyard I visited last year. They've made tremendous progress up there. Turned a plonk into a quite passable wine. Try it.'

Chapman took a sip of the wine. 'Seems okay to me.'

'It's ninety per cent Trebbiano grape, ten per cent Grecheto. That's what makes the difference. You taste that nutty flavour, a hint of almond? That's the Grecheto. Gives it a bit more class than the old-style Orvietos.'

'You know, Brian,' Chapman said, 'for a newspaperman, you don't half talk a load of old bollocks.'

Matheson grinned. '*Ex*-newspaperman. You're just jealous because I've got the time to indulge my passions. Cheers.'

They were sitting on the balcony of Matheson's second-storey apartment, looking down at a vista of gardens and tall cypress trees that were so close you could almost reach out and touch their branches. They'd been friends for a long time. Brian Matheson had been a well-established correspondent in Rome when Chapman first arrived in the city and he'd been something of a guide and mentor to the younger man. He'd been retired for three years now but still took an interest in journalistic affairs, particularly gossip from the *Stampa Estera* which Chapman had orders to relay to him at regular intervals.

For a while they talked about common acquaintances and Italian current affairs. They were different generations but there was a bond of affection and respect between them which made the age gap irrelevant.

Finally Matheson said: 'So what brings you out here on a Saturday?'

'I wanted to ask you a favour.'

'Fire away.'

'You always had good contacts in the Vatican. Much better than mine.'

'The religion helps. They feel more comfortable talking to one of their own.'

'Can you get me into the Secret Archives?'

Matheson sipped his wine, then shook his head apologetically.

'Sorry. I couldn't even get myself into them.'

'Is it that hard?'

'They're completely closed to journalists. Only accredited religious scholars are given access.'

'But that's just a formality, isn't it? There must be a way around it. I could say I was a scholar.'

'The security is extremely tight. A layman needs a letter of introduction from a major library or educational institution. A priest must have a letter from his bishop. Everything is checked very thoroughly before a permit is issued giving access to the Archives. And they give out very few a year. The documents are mostly too fragile, and too precious, to stand much handling.'

'This is Italy, Brian. There must be a way of circumventing the bureaucracy,' Chapman said. 'Someone I can cajole or bribe.'

'Don't make the mistake of thinking the Vatican is like Italy just because it's in Rome,' Matheson replied. 'It's a closed world, run by priests whose sense of duty would put most of us to shame. There is no way you could either persuade or corrupt them into letting you into the Secret Archives. They have a strong sense of right and wrong and none of them is interested enough in money to take a backhander. If you want to become rich, you don't choose the priesthood as a career.'

Chapman gave a nod and looked away. Sensing his friend's disappointment, Matheson said: 'I'm sorry I can't help, Andy. Is it important?'

'I think so, yes.'

'What did you want to find?'

'Something from the war.'

'The Second World War?'

Chapman nodded.

'Then getting access to the Archives wouldn't help you. All records after 1922 are closed, even to accredited scholars.'

'Really? Why 1922?'

'You know the answer to that.'

'Yes, of course. I'd forgotten.'

Nineteen twenty-two, the year Mussolini came to power. It was a sensitive topic inside the Vatican. No one behind the Leonine walls wanted anyone taking too close a look at the Catholic Church's relations with the Fascist dictator. There were too many skeletons in too many cupboards.

'They've a hell of a nerve,' Chapman said, a trace of bitterness in his tone. 'Getting into bed with a monster like Mussolini and then preventing anyone from inspecting the dirty laundry.'

Matheson shrugged. 'It's their laundry. Why should they hang it out for the whole world to see?'

'Because the world has a right to know what happened. This is the Catholic Church we're talking about. A faith which preaches honesty and Christian compassion and a respect for others, but thinks it can cover up a whole period in its history because it's terrified of anyone finding out the truth.'

Matheson half smiled at him. 'You're pretty fired up about this, aren't you? It must be a good story.'

'It is.'

Matheson waited. Chapman gave a slight shake of his head.

'You don't want to know, Brian. I'm not exaggerating. It's too dangerous. Enzo Mattei was murdered because he was asking these same questions.'

'You're not suggesting the Vatican played a part in his death?' Matheson said incredulously.

'Not directly. But they're hiding something that has a bearing on his death. I'm sure of that.'

'From the war? It was a long time ago, Andy. Does it matter now?'

'Yes, it matters. It matters to me. It matters to Enzo's widow and sons.'

'So you're on a crusade against the Catholic Church?'

Chapman didn't reply. Matheson swilled the wine around in his glass, watching the sunlight gleaming on the surface of the golden liquid. He took a mouthful and savoured it for a moment before continuing.

'I don't excuse the Church's links with Fascism, but hindsight makes wise men of us all.' He paused, looking out at the swaying cypress trees. 'You have to remember that though the Christian faith was founded by Christ, it has been interpreted and sustained over the centuries by mere men with all the weaknesses and prejudices of men.'

'Religion should be able to transcend the weaknesses of its believers,' Chapman retorted.

'You ask too much. Did you know that Eugenio Pacelli, who became Pope Pius XII in 1939, had a gun put to his head during an abortive Bolshevik uprising when he was Papal Nuncio to Munich after the First World War? It made him virulently anti-communist, so much so that, to him, Fascism was always the lesser of the two evils. Priests are influenced by their experiences just as much as anyone else, and they make their judgements on that basis.'

'I thought they based their judgements on the word of God.'

'Don't be naive, Andy. What is the word of God but a man's opinion, founded on his own beliefs and experiences, as to what God would want in particular circumstances? Even priests don't have a direct line to Heaven.'

Chapman smiled. 'Okay, let's drop it. Discussing politics and religion is a guaranteed way of losing friends.'

'And yet who else can you discuss them with?' Matheson said, reaching out for the bottle of wine. He refilled Chapman's glass and put the bottle back in the ice bucket.

'Drink up. I've got so much wine in the house that Margherita is threatening to divorce me if I don't get rid of some of it.'

'All for research purposes, of course.'

Matheson grinned. 'Naturally.'

Since his retirement, Matheson had been theoretically writing a book on Italian wines but, though plenty of bottles had been drunk, not a word had been written. Chapman reckoned that was getting the balance about right.

Matheson pulled off his sunglasses and rubbed his eyes with the tips of his fingers. He was in good shape for a man of sixty-eight. His face had a dark tan from years of exposure to the Mediterranean sun, but none of the dry leatheriness that usually came with it. He played golf twice a week with some old cronies from the Italian press corps and could still manage three energetic sets of tennis without any adverse effects. Chapman hoped he would be half as fit when he reached the same age.

'You know,' Matheson said, 'I haven't seen you this motivated since, well, since you arrived in Rome. You've seemed pretty jaded for a long time, but you've really got your teeth into this – whatever it is – haven't you?'

'Maybe it's the final dazzling flicker of a candle flame before it goes out.'

Matheson chuckled. 'You're a little too young to retire.'

'I might be going home though.'

Matheson shot him a glance of surprise. 'To England?'

'They've offered me a job in London. Deputy foreign editor.'

'And you're taking it?'

'I don't know. I've been putting off the decision for a few weeks now.'

351

'Well, it's a thought. How long have you been here, six, seven years?'

'Eight.'

'That's a long time.'

'You've been here even longer,' Chapman said.

'That's different. I married an Italian. I have children, grandchildren here. Why would I want to go back to London?'

Why would anyone? Chapman reflected. When you could sit in the sun on a balcony, drinking wine and inhaling the scent of bougainvillaea, why would you want to return to the grey damp of England? Yet . . . yet it wasn't that simple.

Matheson understood the dilemma. He'd faced it himself and could put into words the feelings his friend was struggling to articulate.

'You either have to settle here like I did, become part of the culture, the way of life, or go home. There's nothing in between that will make you happy,' he said. 'At the moment you're just visiting.'

Chapman sighed. 'I know. I should have moved on years ago but I love this country. I love the people. I love the noise, the passion, the infuriating chaos of it all. I'm not sure I can face starting all over again in England.'

Matheson nodded sympathetically. 'The longer you put it off, the harder it will be.'

Chapman drank his wine. He envied Matheson his contentment, the settled tranquillity of his life. He'd adapted well to a foreign country, been so completely assimilated that, though part of him would be forever English, the bits that really mattered – his family, his friends, his daily routines – were essentially Italian and he was happy with it that way. Visiting him, Chapman was always acutely aware of the shortcomings in his own life. The vacuums that had still to be filled.

As if to emphasise that deficit, a woman's voice called out from inside the apartment and Matheson's wife, Margherita, walked out on to the balcony carrying a brace of bulging shopping bags. She greeted Chapman warmly, kissing him on the cheeks and embracing him.

'Look at the time, Brian,' she said, tapping her wrist. 'I thought you'd be ready.'

Matheson rolled his eyes at Chapman. 'See what you're missing.'

'Go on, I'm not taking you out looking like that. We're due at Paola's in ten minutes,' she explained to Chapman as her husband retreated into the house to change his clothes.

She picked up the almost empty bottle of Orvieto. 'You like this?' she asked.

'I'm not much of an expert.'

'Come through here.'

She beckoned Chapman after her, leading the way down the hall and into the spare bedroom. There were cases of wine piled almost to the ceiling.

'Take some,' Margherita said. 'He'll never drink it all. The vineyards keep sending him free samples, hoping he'll give them a favourable mention in his book. Go on, take a few, he won't miss them.'

They went back out into the hall, Chapman struggling with a case of Chianti. Matheson came out of the main bedroom holding a scrap of paper. There was a name and a phone number on it.

'What we were talking about,' he said. 'He may

353

be able to help you. He's been useful to me in the past.'

He slipped the paper into the breast pocket of Chapman's shirt.

'You may not be able to bribe the priests in the Vatican,' he said, 'but there are others who are not so incorruptible.'

It was early evening when Chapman arrived at Elena's apartment. He'd had a lot to do since leaving Brian Matheson's and the signs of fatigue were beginning to show in his face. He opened the door to the flat, looking forward to a lie down and a long cold drink, and was confronted immediately by an angry Elena.

'Where've you been? Where the hell have you been?' she yelled at him.

'What?'

'You said you'd call me.'

He backed away defensively. 'Whoa! What's going on?'

'Why didn't you call?'

'What on earth's the matter? I was working, I didn't have time. Elena, has something happened?'

She was standing in the doorway of the living room, her whole demeanour hostile, almost aggressive. Then suddenly a change came over her. Her shoulders slumped, her face crumpled and she burst into tears. Chapman stared at her in bewilderment.

'Elena . . .'

She turned away and stumbled through into the living room. Chapman went after her. She was sitting on the edge of the settee, leaning forwards resting her elbows on her knees. She was crying her heart out. Chapman sat down next to her and touched her shoulder tentatively.

'I needed you, where were you?' she sobbed.

Chapman didn't answer. She was behaving so irrationally he knew it wasn't the moment for talking. He pulled her to him. She resisted at first, trying to push him away, then relaxed and collapsed into his arms.

He held her while she wept. He'd never seen this facet of her character before. He'd never seen any sign of weakness and it was distressing to watch.

In time, she pulled herself away and wiped away the tears with the back of her hand. There was mascara smudged over her cheeks.

'I'm sorry,' she said, sniffing and suppressing one last sob. 'I'm sorry, I'm being stupid.'

She stood up and went out into the bathroom. Chapman heard her blowing her nose, then the sound of running water. Whatever it was that had upset her, he knew it was nothing to do with his not telephoning.

When she came back in, she'd washed off her make-up and dried her face, but her eyes were red-rimmed.

'I'm sorry,' she said again. 'I don't know what you must think of me.'

'What's happened, Elena?'

She pointed at a pile of papers on the floor by the armchair. 'Take a look at those.'

'What are they?'

'They came this morning by courier.'

Chapman picked up the papers and leafed through them. 'I don't understand. What are they?'

'Scarfone's way of hitting back at me.'

'They're from Scarfone? Elena, you're going to have to explain this to me.'

'He's evil. But very clever. He knows just how to put pressure on people. How to find their weak spots and exploit them.'

She sat down beside Chapman and dabbed at her eyes with a handkerchief. Then she picked out documents from the pile at random.

'These are company formation papers. For a *Società per Azioni*. You know what an SpA is?'

'Yes, it's like a British limited company.'

'And these are copies of documents setting up various offshore companies in the Cayman Islands and the Netherlands Antilles, both of which are classed under Italian law as tax havens. Now look at these.' She pulled more sheets out and placed them on Chapman's lap.

'They mean nothing to me, Elena. I'm not a lawyer.'

'They're records of transfers from the IOR to these companies in the Caymans and the Netherlands Antilles.'

Chapman held up a hand to stop her. 'The IOR? You mean the *Istituto per le Opere di Religione*? The Vatican Bank?'

'Exactly. The money goes to the Caribbean where these companies deposit it in local offshore banks which are beyond the scrutiny of the Italian fiscal authorities. The money is then moved from those banks to the local branches of large international banks. The companies then borrow money from the banks, secured by the deposits, and transfer the funds back to Italy.'

'You've lost me, I'm afraid. You're talking to a man who finds cashing a cheque at the *Credito Italiano* a daunting operation.'

'These companies,' Elena said, 'they're just shells. They don't do anything. They don't manufacture anything or trade legitimately. They're just conduits for money to be taken out of Italy by one route and brought back in by another.'

'Money laundering, you mean?'

She nodded and sagged back in the corner of the settee. Chapman glanced at the papers. For all he understood of them they might have been written in Swahili.

'Money laundering for whom?' he asked. 'The Vatican?'

'The Vatican Bank is just the channel for the cash. An offshore bank within Italy.'

'I thought the IOR had stopped doing all that dodgy sort of stuff?'

'Come on, Andy. If there's money to be made, the Vatican, whatever they claim, isn't going to be averse to sharing in it.'

'So who's it for then?' Chapman said. 'Criminals? The Mafia?'

'It's impossible to tell. They're just cash transfers, figures on bits of paper. And these offshore tax havens are so secretive it's probably impossible to find out who the real beneficiaries are.'

'What makes you so sure they're from Scarfone?'

'He rang to see if I'd received them. He couldn't resist it.'

'I don't get it,' Chapman said, frowning. 'Why would Scarfone send you them?'

'Look at the registers of directors for the companies. You see a name that crops up on almost all of them?'

Chapman scanned the relevant pages and felt his stomach turn to ice.

'Eugenio Fiorini,' he said quietly.

'My father.'

For a long while neither of them spoke. Then Elena ran her hand wearily through her hair and said: 'I've been going round in circles all day. It's been driving me crazy. That's why I yelled at you, I'm sorry. I had no right to take it out on you.'

'I should have called you, as I said I would. I'm sorry too,' Chapman said.

He put the papers back down on the floor, wanting, irrationally, to get rid of them in case they contaminated him.

'What are you going to do?' he said.

'I don't know. They've got me over a barrel. If I do nothing, if I suppress the papers, they've got me in their pockets. They'll control me. They'll always have a hold over me and I might as well abandon my career here and now. But if I take the steps I'm duty-bound as a magistrate to follow, I put my father in the dock.'

Chapman felt the anger welling up inside him, a fierce urge to hit out at something, anything. He realised his fists were clenched and made a conscious effort to relax them.

'Elena, I'm so sorry,' he said gently. 'I don't suppose there's a chance this is all perfectly legitimate?'

'Not a chance in hell. I went to the Regina Coeli this morning. To see a prisoner. One of my cases. A man called Geminazza.'

'Geminazza? Wasn't he a banker, an accountant or something?'

'Accountant,' Elena said. 'He was arrested last year for fraud and embezzlement. Forty billion lire disappeared from three companies he controlled. None of it has been recovered. If anyone knows about offshore accounts it's Geminazza.'

She was lying there in the corner of the settee, utterly drained. Her fury, her frustration had dissipated. She barely had the strength to talk.

'I took these papers with me. I did a deal with him. Agreed not to press a couple of minor charges if he explained what the papers meant. They're dirty all right. More than enough to bring a laundering case against my father.'

'What would happen if he was convicted?' Chapman asked.

'It's a serious offence. He'd almost certainly get a custodial sentence. The appeals process could be dragged out for years so he might not actually end up in prison, but he'd be destroyed just the same. He'd be disgraced. His legal career would be over. I can't do that to him. I can't.'

She lifted her head and looked at Chapman, her eyes filled with a bleak despair.

'It's been tying me in knots since this morning. I can no longer think straight, Andy. What am I going to do? Just tell me, what am I going to do?'

EIGHTEEN

They went round in circles all evening. It was exhausting for both of them. For Elena, who had to deal with the knowledge of her father's corruption, her loyalties torn between her family and her duty as a magistrate. For Chapman, who had to witness her distress and his powerlessness to help her. He could listen as she went over it time and time again, he could do his best to comfort her, but in the end it was her decision, and hers alone.

Chapman longed to escape for just a moment, but he didn't dare. It seemed insensitive to leave her, or to suggest they changed the subject before they both exploded with frustration. When at last, unable to cope with the gnaw of hunger any longer, he proposed that they have something to eat, it seemed a relief to Elena too. They picked at some pasta and a salad in the kitchen then went to bed.

In the morning, Chapman went out to buy the newspapers and some bread and took his time going back to the apartment. He couldn't face any more talking. After breakfast, he ran Elena a deep bath and made her soak in it until she relaxed.

When she came out into the living room, wrapped in a thin cotton robe, she seemed calmer, more at ease with herself. Chapman knew she'd finally decided what to do.

'I'll call him,' she said. 'Arrange to go over this afternoon. I need to speak to him in person.'

Chapman nodded. 'That's a good idea. Maybe there's some simple explanation you haven't thought of.'

He didn't believe it. Neither did Elena, but she nodded in agreement with him all the same.

Only when she was about to get dressed to leave did Chapman tell her he wouldn't be back that night. He'd left it till the last minute because he knew she'd need him later and the thought of a prolonged row was more than he could face right now.

'What do you mean?' she said, irritation already creeping into her voice.

'I won't be back,' he repeated. 'I'm sorry, I know it's a bad time but I fixed it all up yesterday and I might not get another chance.'

'Where are you going?'

'I can't say.'

'Tell me.'

'What I'm doing is not something a public prosecutor should know about. Leave it at that.'

'What is it, something illegal?'

'Elena, for once in your life, don't keep asking questions.'

She frowned at him, pulling the robe tight around her waist and bust in an unconscious gesture of pique. Then she stood up and marched stiffly out of the room.

She left shortly afterwards, still annoyed with him. Chapman breathed a sigh of relief, glad to have the apartment to himself. He made a ham and tomato sandwich for lunch and ate it with a beer while watching television, able to relax without feeling guilt for the first time since he'd come home the previous evening.

Just before two o'clock, he went out to his car and drove to his own flat in Trastevere, stopping off at a cashpoint on the way to withdraw some money from his bank account. Then from a drawer in his desk he took out more cash from his emergency reserve and added it to the pile. He counted it. There was just over a million lire, about three hundred and fifty pounds. He put the wad of notes in an envelope and left his apartment for the short drive up the Tiber to St Peter's.

It was mid-afternoon, but there was still a sizeable queue outside the entrance to the Vatican Museum. The museum, with its seven kilometres of exhibits, was normally closed on Sundays. But this was the last Sunday in the month, when it was not only open, but free and packed with visitors. It was the worst possible time to come if you wanted to look at the treasures on display, but it suited Chapman's purposes to have a lot of people around. He had no interest in art today.

After forty minutes waiting in line he finally passed through the entrance and pushed his way through the sluggish crowd up the stairs to the *Atrio dei Quattro Cancelli* where colour-coded signs defined the various routes you could take around the museum, depending on how much time you had available. The longest would take the best part of a day, there was so much to see, but even the shortest – a sprint down to the Sistine Chapel and back – took ninety minutes.

Chapman knew where he was going. He'd been here many times before, though never with quite such a dangerous objective in mind. He was nervous. If he were caught, the consequences didn't bear thinking about.

He checked his watch. He had plenty of time. He'd arranged to rendezvous with Brian Matheson's contact in the Sistine Chapel at four o'clock, just before the visitors were ushered out for the long walk to the exit in time for the museum to close at a quarter to five.

Nino Casciani was one of the museum custodians. Chapman had telephoned him late the previous afternoon and met him shortly afterwards in a bar by the Piazza del Risorgimento. He was a taciturn man with a wife and six children whom, fortunately for Chapman, he was struggling to support on his meagre salary. The idea of a 'commission' for helping the journalist had been appealing, but nevertheless he'd taken some persuading when Chapman outlined what he wanted to do. He'd agreed only when he was absolutely sure that no blame would fall on him if Chapman were caught. Then it had simply come down to the money. A million lire was a lot of cash, but then Casciani was taking a big risk. Chapman had tried to haggle a little but the custodian wouldn't budge. A million lire, or nothing.

The money was immaterial to Chapman. It was a hefty chunk out of his salary but he knew that, over a time and suitably disguised, he'd be able to claim it back on expenses. The foreign desk in London was notoriously lax about checking expenses claims, probably because they were all fiddling them themselves. Once, on a job in Umbria, Chapman's car had broken down and he'd had to buy a fraying hemp line from a tightfisted farmer to get himself towed to the nearest garage. On his expenses form he'd put: 'Money for old rope, 100,000 lire', and no one had queried it.

He walked at a steady pace through the vaulted galleries which ran for a quarter of a mile to the Sistine Chapel. There were hundreds of people pausing to look at the statues and tapestries, the colourful maps of the ancient world painted on the walls, but Chapman ignored them all. He descended a narrow flight of stairs and emerged suddenly into the chapel.

Each time he walked through the doors and looked up at Michelangelo's ceiling he felt a new, overwhelming sense of awe, a sense almost of reverence for the genius who had painted it. There was nowhere else on earth, created by man alone, where you were literally surrounded by such concentrated evidence of greatness, such beauty and dazzling insight.

But today he had no eyes for the Creation of Man. He was looking only for the short, stocky form of Nino Casciani. The chapel was jammed with people, craning their necks upwards to study the vault or admiring the Last Judgement over the high altar. Chapman squeezed his way through the throng and saw the custodian standing alone against the wall in the far corner. He walked up beside him but didn't look at him.

'You've brought it?' Casciani said.

Chapman took the envelope of cash out of his pocket and held it down by his side. In one slick movement the custodian snatched the envelope away and stowed it securely inside his jacket. Then he glanced around casually.

'You see the door to my left? When I open it, you slip through, okay?'

Chapman nodded. Casciani scanned the chapel. There was another bored-looking custodian on the far side. Casciani waited for a large tour group to pass by, obscuring his colleague's view, then whipped open the door. Chapman darted through the narrow opening. The door closed behind him almost before he was over the threshold. He paused, letting his eyes adjust to the gloom. He was in a cramped antechamber lit only by a couple of dim bulbs on the wall. After the stunning richness of the chapel, it was something of a shock to find himself in such an austere, dilapidated place. You got so used to the opulence of the public rooms in the Vatican that it was easy to forget that the parts you didn't see were as plain and functional as a seminarist's study.

A long corridor opened off the antechamber. Chapman turned right and walked down it quickly, trying to deaden the sound of his footsteps on the worn stone floor. This whole sector was off-limits for visitors. If he were seen by a cleric or a custodian, he would certainly be challenged and summarily ejected from the building.

He was looking for a door on his left. Casciani had said it wasn't very far along the corridor but Chapman could see no sign of it. Behind him, the door to the Sistine Chapel opened suddenly. Chapman glanced over his shoulder. He saw the hem of a priest's robe fluttering in the draught, heard the voices of two men. He ran his eyes over the wall. The door had to be there somewhere. The voices became clearer. A figure in a cassock stepped out into the corridor, pausing to allow his companion through behind him. His back was towards Chapman, but it would only be seconds before he turned and saw him. Chapman reached out, touching the wall, feeling for a handle, a frame, anything. His fingers encountered a thin slit in the wall: the edge of a panel. He fumbled for the handle and wrenched the door open, diving through and pushing it to behind him. He waited, holding his breath. Footsteps and voices passed by on the other side of the panel and faded into the distance.

Chapman relaxed. He was on the landing of a narrow spiral staircase which corkscrewed upwards to the next floor of the museum and down into the basement. He went down. At the bottom was a heavy wooden door which Casciani had said was unlocked in the mornings and closed again at dusk. Chapman passed through it and into another dark corridor lined with shelves of dusty books and bound manuscripts. He was getting closer now. Casciani had said there was access to the Secret Archives from both the ground floor and the basement where many of the older records were stored. The more recent working files of the Curia – and by recent the Vatican meant this century – were all in the main wing of the Archives. To get to them Chapman would have to find his way in undetected and then wait until the archivists left for the night. It was a hazardous operation, but so far Casciani's information had been reliable. Chapman hoped that the rest of the custodian's inside knowledge was as accurate.

Halfway down the corridor, which stretched the full length of the Vatican Museum, a side passage branched off taking Chapman under the main floor of the Archives and the adjacent Vatican Library. At the end of the passage was a pair of high double doors set in a stone archway. They had massive riveted hinges and iron ring handles worn smooth over the years by people's hands. Chapman pressed his ear to the wood and listened. He could hear no sound on the other side. He hesitated. This was by far the most dangerous moment. There was no way of telling for certain if there was anyone in the basement of the Archives. He just had to take a chance and pray.

He took hold of the handle. Casciani had said the door would be unlocked. Chapman turned the handle. The latch clicked open. In the confined space it seemed as noisy as a gunshot. Chapman pushed on the door. It swung back enough for him to peer inside. He saw more stacks of shelves, more ancient tomes gathering dust, but no people. He squeezed through the gap and closed the door behind him, easing the latch back down so it made hardly a sound. Then he moved off cautiously into the stacks, alert to the slightest noise from above. The basement might be deserted, but he knew an archivist could come down the staircase at the far end at any moment. He had to find a hiding place quickly. This was where he was on his own. Casciani knew how to get into the Secret Archives, but his knowledge of the layout thereafter was hazy. It was up to Chapman to ensure he wasn't discovered.

He explored the room methodically, stopping every few paces to listen. It was a vast area, but it quickly became apparent it afforded very few opportunities for concealment. The cupboards were all locked and, though there were plenty of dark corners, they were all too exposed for Chapman to consider as hiding places. He went up and down the different aisles, growing increasingly anxious. He checked his watch. It was gone five o'clock. He had no idea what hours the archivists kept but for all he knew they might be locking up any minute. It was imperative he find somewhere to keep out of sight, and soon.

The double doors loomed up in front of him. He was back where he started. He looked around, determined not to allow himself to be thwarted. There was only one possible location left open to him. He would have to hide amongst the books. He crouched down and examined the shelves. They were solidly constructed to take the weight of the bulky volumes – some of them six inches and more thick – and two feet deep from front to back. They were arranged in rows six or seven shelves high, backing on to one another but with no partition dividing them.

Chapman pulled out some of the books on the bottom shelf and peered in. If he pushed the books to the very front edge, there was a space behind just big enough for a man to lie down. He eased out a whole row and slithered in, replacing the books after him. It was a tight fit. He could stretch out at full length but there was little room for sideways manoeuvre. His arms were constricted, his shoulders squashed tight between the shelves. He could taste the dust that caked everything, smell the musty odour of old manuscript and leather. He closed his eyes and waited.

The smalltalk was driving Elena insane. Having to sit in the living room of her parents' house and listen to her mother wittering on about nothing when all she wanted to do was walk into her father's study and confront him. It took all her self-discipline to make herself sit there drinking coffee while her mother described to her, at tedious length, all the trivial things she'd been doing since Elena last visited.

Finally, her mother turned to the subject that Elena was not prepared to discuss under any circumstances.

'Did you call Franco?'

Elena ignored the question. 'Is Papa going to stay in his study all afternoon?'

'He usually does,' her mother replied dismissively. 'Did you?'

Elena stood up. 'There's something I have to discuss with him. Excuse me a minute.'

She picked up the leather portfolio she'd brought with her and went down the hall to the study. She knocked and went in.

Her father looked up from his desk and removed his reading glasses, smiling at her. Elena closed the door behind her and held his gaze, looking at him in a new light now.

'What is it?' Eugenio Fiorini asked.

'Can I interrupt?'

'Of course.'

He pushed his chair away from the desk and leaned back, his hands crossed in his lap.

'You look very serious, Elena. Is something the matter?'

'I need to talk to you, Papa.'

Elena hesitated. Now the time had come, she wasn't sure she could go through with it. She couldn't bear to see the devastating effect it would have on her father.

'Talk to me about what?'

Elena unzipped the portfolio but didn't take out the papers.

'You know I've been investigating the death of Father Antonio Vivaldi,' she said.

'Yes.'

'Well, in the course of the inquiry I've uncovered evidence that the neo-Fascists played a part in his murder. Evidence that implicates Cesare Scarfone himself.'

Her father's brow knitted. 'Should you be telling me this?'

'He's up to his neck in it, Papa. I just haven't got enough to make a watertight case at the moment. But I will have soon. Scarfone knows that so he's attacking me on the front where I'm most vulnerable. My family.'

'Your family?' Eugenio seemed puzzled, then a ghost of sudden understanding passed across his face and was quickly suppressed.

'I got these yesterday,' Elena said, taking out the wad of documents and placing them on her father's desk.

'What are they?'

'Take a look. Go on, read them.'

Eugenio leaned forwards and slipped his reading glasses on for a moment to glance at the papers. He concealed it well, but Elena noticed the way he stiffened, the way his tongue flicked out to lick dry lips. She'd interviewed enough defendants to recognise guilt when she saw it.

'They came from Scarfone,' she said. 'I don't know where or how he got hold of them, but I know he sent them.'

Her father's face was inscrutable, his eyes hidden behind the lenses of his spectacles.

'You know what they are, don't you, Papa?'

Eugenio remained motionless. The afternoon sun lanced in through the window and bounced off the polished surface of the desk. Somewhere in the distance Elena could hear the muted noise of children playing. But the world outside didn't exist for her.

'Papa, are they genuine?' she asked.

He gave a brief nod. 'I'd lie to you, Elena, but I can't. Yes, they're genuine.'

'Why, Papa?'

'Why?'

'Why did you do it?'

He looked away and shrugged. 'It's my business. I'm a commercial lawyer. I form companies for clients all the time.'

'Do you help launder money for them all the time too?'

'Launder money? You surely don't . . .'

'Papa, don't insult my intelligence,' Elena interrupted.

Eugenio fell silent. He bowed his head. Elena was suddenly aware of how old, how frail he was. It came as a shock that was both painful and disillusioning. Her whole life she'd looked on her father as a figure of strength; as a man of integrity and absolute honesty. Now she saw it for the sham it was. And she saw her own complicity in it. How much of the security she'd taken for granted as she grew up, how many of the material comforts she'd enjoyed, had been founded on corruption?

'Who was your client?' she asked. 'Whose money were all these companies set up to launder?'

'You know I can't tell you that.'

'Was it Scarfone? Was it the neo-Fascists?'

'I have a duty of confidentiality to my clients.'

'Even when what you're doing for them is illegal?'

'What do you want from me, Elena?'

'I want the truth.'

'I can't give you that.'

'You have to, Papa. Can't you see what Scarfone is doing? You're my father. My family means more to me than anything. Yet I have taken an oath of duty to the state. I can't pretend I never saw these papers.'

'I wouldn't expect you to.'

'I would destroy them now if I thought it would put an end to the matter for good. But you know it won't. You know how blackmailers operate. They'll be back for more. When they want something else, they'll be back to bleed us again.'

'I would never want you to compromise yourself, Elena. You must do what you think is right.'

'Oh, Papa. Anyone but you.'

Elena had to fight back the tears. She felt like a small girl again. All she wanted was for her father to come out from behind the desk and hug her. For him to brush away her worries and reassure her that everything would be all right, the way he'd done when she was little. But she was no longer a child.

'I shouldn't have come,' she said. 'I should have handed the papers over to another magistrate immediately. But I felt I owed it to you to give you a chance to make a clean breast of it first.'

'What do you want me to do?' Eugenio's voice was dull, lifeless.

'Go to the police. Tell them everything. Don't wait for them to come to you. It will look better. You might get a deal from them if you cooperate.'

Eugenio nodded. Elena felt a pang of remorse. He looked so weak and pathetic, sitting there ashen-faced and broken. It filled her with guilt to know she was responsible for his pain.

'Will you do that, Papa?'

He didn't reply. Their roles had been reversed now. Elena wanted to go to him and hug him. She wanted to hold him and tell him that, whatever happened, she would look after him. But she didn't dare. She couldn't face the possibility that he might reject her.

'Will you do it?' she said again.

Eugenio lifted his head and forced a smile. There was a sadness in it that Elena found unbearable.

'Yes,' he said, 'I'll do it. Don't worry, I'll do the right thing.'

Chapman was beginning to wish he'd never come anywhere near the Vatican Secret Archives. He'd thought he'd have to stay hidden behind the row of books for just a short time, half an hour, an hour at the most. But he'd been there for nearly three hours already and could see his ordeal being extended further into the night.

He looked at his watch. It was ten minutes to eight. Did the archivists not have anything better to do on a Sunday evening? He knew they were still upstairs. He could hear their feet shuffling around above him and, periodically, one of them would come downstairs to take something off the shelves. They were priests, Chapman thought indignantly. Shouldn't they be in church praying, or reading the Bible in the privacy of their quarters?

He was in agony. His legs were subject to sudden, painful spasms of cramp, he'd lost all sensation in his left hip – on which he was lying – and his shoulders and arms were numb from being squeezed into a space which even a professional contortionist would have found challenging. He closed his eyes, trying to shut out the discomfort and wishing he knew something about transcendental meditation, anything to lift his mind away from the aches in his body.

There were footsteps on the stairs. One of the archivists was coming downstairs into the basement again. Chapman listened. The footsteps drew nearer. Very near. They were coming down the aisle next to him. He lay still, breathing quietly. Over the tops of the books concealing him he saw a black cassock pass by. A key was inserted in the double doors and the lock snapped shut. Thank God, Chapman thought. They're closing up at last.

The archivist retreated back upstairs. Chapman heard the main doors clang shut and stayed where he was for a further fifteen minutes before daring to emerge. He stretched his limbs and walked around for a time to get his muscles working, then crept up the stairs.

At the top he paused to listen again. The lights were switched off but he was leaving nothing to chance. Only when he was satisfied that the Archives were indeed deserted did he venture out from the stairwell.

It was almost dark outside. Enough light penetrated

the windows to show Chapman the ancient wooden tables at which the scholars worked and the stacks of shelves, but not sufficient for him to read by. He pulled a thin pencil torch out of his pocket and, hooding the bulb with his hand to make the beam less conspicuous, started his search.

He didn't know where to begin. In most archives he would have looked for some kind of central index, either on computer or on filing cards. But the Vatican Secret Archives were different from any library or record office he'd ever seen. They were like a relic from some previous age, not just a few years behind the times, but centuries. They had the atmosphere of a medieval monastery: bare floors, plain walls, wooden desks on which huge, cumbersome manuscripts lay open to reveal perfect Latin script and ornate illuminations. He half expected to see cowled monks writing by candlelight with quill pens and ink while the distant sound of plainsong reverberated around the high ceilings.

He explored the area near the main doors first, examining a series of large volumes which looked like indexes. There were several hundred of them; all, as he discovered when he lifted one down and opened it, handwritten in Latin. The handwriting he could cope with, but the Latin was more of a problem. He had no idea what any of it meant. He put the book back and reconsidered his plan of action. If he couldn't make sense of the indexes then there was only one course left open to him: he would have to go directly to the stacks and check the shelves one by one. It was a daunting thought, but he had all night to complete the task. Surely twelve hours would be enough.

The stacks were labelled according to some filing system that was incomprehensible to him so he resorted to wandering up and down the rows picking out items at random to see what they were. After a while he realised there a clear segregation between the books and other bound manuscripts and the working files of the Curia. He concentrated his search on the second area. He could work out what the year 1945 was in Latin numerals and knew from briefings at the Vatican Press Office that the Secretariat of State in Latin was *Secretaria Status Seu Papalis*. All he had to do was combine the two and he'd find the records he was looking for.

That, at any rate, was the theory. In practice it wasn't quite so simple. The Archives were not designed for the convenience of the browser, nor indeed for the outsider. If a scholar or researcher wanted to refer to something, he didn't just go to a shelf and take it out himself, he had to ask an archivist to get it for him. Only the archivists knew where everything was and though their filing system probably made sense to them, it was almost impenetrable to the casual visitor like Chapman.

But he persevered, and a little after midnight found the shelves bearing the Secretariat of State records for March and April 1945. He put the files on the floor by the wall and examined them, shielding the torch with his body to prevent any light reflecting upwards and out through the windows of the Archives.

The letter from Mussolini to the Vatican Under-Secretary of State, the soiled copy of which Chapman had already seen, was there in the file. It had aged a little but the text was clear enough. No water damage or holes in this version. Chapman read it and felt the hairs on the back of his neck stand up. Jesus. He read it again in case he'd misunderstood the Italian. He hadn't.

He browsed through the other papers and found the reply from Giovanni Montini. This too was clean and legible. It shocked him even more than the first letter.

Carefully he checked the rest of the file, pulling out what seemed to be an internal Vatican memo from Pope Pius to Montini. Chapman stared at it, studying each word over and over again, following the lines of the Pope's handwritten signature as if to memorise it.

He clicked off his torch and slumped back against the shelves. He was stunned. His brain felt numb from the shock of what he'd read. If the papers hadn't been here in the Vatican Archives, he would have wondered whether they were clever forgeries. But as he realised the implications of their contents, he felt a pulse of excitement, a buzz that every journalist hopes he'll experience at least once in his career. This was a story that would make headlines not just in Italy or England, but across the world.

Chapman collected the letters and the memo together and slipped them into the pocket of his jacket. Then he replaced the file on the shelf and went back out into the reading area of the Archives.

He knew now why Antonio Vivaldi had been tortured and killed. He knew what Cesare Scarfone had wanted from the priest, knew what it was the neo-Fascists were searching for. Other questions remained unanswered, but slowly the pieces were starting to fall into place.

Chapman sat down on one of the chairs. It was late. He was tired, but too excited to sleep. He stared at the shadows on the walls, engrossed in thought as the heavy, pervasive silence of the Vatican enveloped him.

Eugenio Fiorini rose at dawn as usual and went downstairs to the kitchen in his pyjamas and dressing gown. He made himself a pot of espresso and took it with him to his study. The hazy first light was breaking through the shutters, throwing a silvery cast over the furniture in the room. Eugenio opened the window and stood for a time looking out over the city he loved. He could see the dome of St Peter's, the *Trinità dei Monti* and just a glint of the Tiber as it looped its way past the solid bulk of the Castel Sant'Angelo.

He liked the early morning; the freshness, the breeze rippling the trees in the garden. Some days he would stand there for ten, fifteen minutes, as the sun rose above the hills and embraced the sleeping metropolis. But today there was no time for lingering. He sat down at his desk, took out a pad of notepaper and began to write.

He wrote one letter to his wife – still fast asleep upstairs – and one to Elena, then put them in envelopes. He stood up and opened the safe that was built into the wall behind his desk. Inside were bundles of confidential papers from his law practice, and a loaded Beretta automatic pistol. He removed the pistol and locked the safe, putting the key in the envelope containing the letter to his daughter.

He sealed both envelopes and placed them in the centre of the desk. Then he sat down again. He took one last sip of his coffee and picked up the pistol.

PART THREE

PART THREE

NINETEEN

Lombardy, April 1945

Domenico Salvitti was drenched with sweat, his shirt a soaking wet rag that clung to his shoulders and back, chafing the skin as he dragged the heavy wooden box down the hillside.

He paused to rest. He was breathing heavily, his arms and legs aching from the exertion. Up above him in the cloudless blue sky the sun beat down relentlessly, sapping his body of what little strength remained. He'd been working solidly for three hours now, removing the wooden crates from the back of the lorry and hauling them down the rocky slope to a cave he'd discovered just below the mountain road. He was close to exhaustion, but the iron self-discipline he'd imposed on himself throughout his military career forced him to keep going. Just this one box and he'd be finished.

He bent down and grasped the rope handle, heaving the crate the last few yards to the entrance of the cave. It was a narrow opening, little more than the width of his shoulders. Outside, nestling in a basin in the mountainside, was a small lake of clear, ice-cold water. Salvitti knelt down and bathed his face and neck. Then he cupped his hands and drank deeply, his senses alert to any sign of movement on the valley side below him, any noise of people or vehicles on the road that lay concealed up above the rock escarpment.

He knew he was taking a big risk, wasting valuable time. He should have pressed on towards the Swiss frontier and found a safe place to cross, not lingered on the open road unloading wooden boxes. But if there was one facet of his character that was stronger even than his instinct for self-preservation, it was his greed. He was aware that he was being foolish, but he couldn't help himself. He simply couldn't bear to leave the crates on the lorry and spend the rest of his life wondering what might have happened if he'd taken the time to conceal them.

He dragged the box through the opening, digging the heels of his boots into the ground and leaning backwards, his muscles knotting as he pulled with all his waning strength. The box inched slowly over the stony surface, the edges leaving a deep groove in the soil. A short distance in, the cave opened out into a small chamber about five metres across and just high enough for a man to stand up in. Light filtered down through cracks in the roof, illuminating the pit in the floor of the chamber which Salvitti had dug to take all ten of the crates from the lorry. He slid the final box in next to the others and straightened up, taking a moment to recover his breath.

Then he picked up something from by the wall of the cave where he'd left it. It was the leather document pouch which the Duce had entrusted to him in Milan. Salvitti opened it. Inside was a sheaf of papers; correspondence and documents which Mussolini had decided not to destroy before they left Milan. There was also the roll of film Salvitti had removed from the camera in the lorry and a quantity of foreign currency, Swiss francs and US dollars. Salvitti pulled the notes out and slid them into his trouser pocket, encountering something hard and heavy wrapped up in his handkerchief. He removed the handkerchief and unfolded it to reveal his campaign medals. In the hurry to leave the Palazzo Monforte these were the only personal possessions he'd managed to bring with him. He hated to leave them behind, but it was too dangerous to keep them on his person. If he were caught by partisans or the Allies, he might convince them he was some anonymous footsoldier in the Fascist militias, but not if he was carrying medals that revealed his true identity.

Reluctantly, he wrapped them up again and placed them inside the leather pouch. Then he took his Musketeer's dagger off his belt and put that in on top of the medals. He squeezed the pouch into the gap between two of the wooden crates and, picking up the spade he'd brought down from the lorry, shovelled a layer of earth in on top of them, treading it down firmly before smoothing the surface with the palms of his hands to erase all traces of his boot prints.

He went back out into the sunlight and scrambled up the slope to the road. He was reaching into the cab of the lorry to pull out his jacket when he heard the noise of an engine higher up the road. A black Fiat saloon came round the corner at speed, its wheels throwing up a shower of stones and grey dust. The driver braked when he saw the lorry blocking the path. Salvitti didn't move. He waited, his body partially shielded by the open door of the cab, as two men climbed out of the car. They were thin and unshaven, wearing scruffy shirts and trousers and the red neck-erchiefs of the *Garibaldini*. Both were carrying rifles.

One of them shouted at Salvitti: 'Identify yourself!'

Salvitti held one of his hands up in a gesture of surrender while with his other he grasped hold of the machine-gun that lay on the floor of the cab.

'Stand clear of the lorry!'

Salvitti took a step away from the cab, swinging the machine-gun out and firing off a rapid burst that knocked the first man off his feet, his chest bursting open like a shattered water melon. The second man dived instinctively into the shelter of the Fiat. Salvitti fired another salvo, the bullets ripping into the body-work of the car. The windscreen exploded, sending a spray of glass into the air. The second man scuttled out from behind the Fiat and threw himself off the side of the road, disappearing from sight behind a cluster of rocks. Salvitti ran forwards. The man's rifle lay on the ground where he'd dropped it as he tumbled over the edge. He'd rolled twenty metres down the mountainside and was up on his feet, half running, half slithering down the treacherous slope. Salvitti fired at him. The man fell forwards, rolling over and over down the incline until his body smashed into a boulder and was still.

Salvitti gazed down without emotion at the crumpled figure, then he turned and went back to the first parti-san. He was sprawled on his back beside the Fiat, his shirt saturated with blood. Salvitti studied his face. He was just a boy, a callow youth like most of the others who'd died in the war. Salvitti felt a pang of regret. He'd thought the killing was over now the Allies had conquered the country. But things were never that simple. He could see the bloodshed continuing. The war might be over but there would still be scores to settle. The Italians had been at war with each other as well as the Germans for the past two years. The partisans would take full advantage of their victory. They would not abide by any peace agreement until their thirst for revenge was slaked.

Salvitti bent down and searched through the young man's pockets. He found a few coins, a squashed packet of cigarettes, some matches and, to his surprise, a Royal Army identity disc bearing the name Roberto Ferrero. Salvitti held the disc in his hand, an idea taking shape inside his head. He'd come this far, but he had doubts about going on. A border crossing was hazardous, his reception from the Swiss uncertain to say the least. Perhaps it made more sense to stay in Italy, to go back to one of the cities and blend into the crowds. In the chaos it would be easy to take on a new identity.

Salvitti put the disc and the cigarettes in his pocket and removed the young man's red neckerchief, transferring it to his own neck. He found a scuffed leather jacket in the back of the Fiat and tried it on. To anyone who didn't know him he could pass as a partisan.

He picked up the youth by the arms and heaved him into the front seat of the car. Then he put the gear stick in neutral and pushed the Fiat over the edge of the road. It bounced down the mountainside, faster and faster until it shot out over a precipice and somersaulted down into a deep ravine. Salvitti heard the crash then a sudden muted explosion before a plume of dark smoke drifted up from the valley floor.

The lorry went next. Salvitti simply released the

handbrake and the vehicle rolled back down the hill and over the side on the first bend. He strolled down in time to see it plunge over an escarpment and explode in a searing ball of fire. Then he lit up a cigarette and began the long walk down the mountain.

TWENTY

Rome, present day

Elena became aware of the telephone ringing through the thick fug of sleep which enveloped her. She half opened her eyes, thinking at first that it was the vestige of a dream, or the distant sound of one of the other phones in the building. But when she rolled over on to her back, she realised it was coming from the table beside her bed. She sat up, trying to clear her head, and reached out to pick up the receiver.

'*Pronto.*'

'Elena? Elena? Is that you, Elena?' It was a woman's voice, high-pitched, almost hysterical. It was her mother.

'Mamma, yes it's me. What is it?'

Elena glanced at the alarm clock next to the telephone. It was six-fifteen. Her mother was never up this early. Elena felt a sudden, sickening jolt in her stomach. Something was wrong.

'Mamma, what is it?' she repeated.

Her mother sounded as if she were weeping. Her breaths were coming in great gulps like sobs.

'Mamma, has something happened?'

'Your father. I found him. In his study. I heard the shot, you see, and came down.'

'Shot?' Elena was fully awake now. 'What do you mean?'

'He's there now. I couldn't touch him. I couldn't.'

Her mother was distraught, the words pouring out in a garbled torrent. Elena swung her legs out of bed. Her skin had gone cold.

'Just tell me what happened, Mamma. What shot? What are you talking about?'

'Eugenio. He's shot himself.'

The shock was so great, so numbing, it rendered Elena speechless for a moment.

'Elena, are you there? I don't know what to do. Elena?'

Elena forced herself to say something. 'Have you called an ambulance? The police?'

'No. He's there, slumped over his desk. The blood . . . oh, God.' Her mother started to sob uncontrollably.

'Leave it to me,' Elena said. 'I'll call them. Then I'm coming over. Mamma, did you hear me? I'll be with you as soon as I can. All right?'

Her mother didn't reply. Elena didn't waste time repeating herself. Her mother was too distressed to understand. Elena put down the receiver and dialled 113.

Elena never knew how she drove the short distance to her parents' house. She was in a trance, barely conscious of anything around her. The movements seemed to come automatically. Braking, steering, her awareness of other traffic on the road, they were devolved into some corner of her mind where they needed no overt control. They just happened. Her thoughts, her senses, were completely absorbed by the details of her mother's phone call, the vision of her father lying dead at his desk.

There were no tears, just shock and fear and, underlying everything, the irrational hope that her mother had made a mistake. Elena didn't want to believe it was true. For if it was, she had not only lost her father, but would have to face up to her own part in his death. She knew it wasn't a coincidence. The responsibility, and the burden of guilt, were hers to bear.

An ambulance and two police cars were parked outside the house when she got there. Elena walked into the hall and stopped. Her legs were shaking, her stomach a twisted ball of nerves and nausea. She'd been to many scenes of death before, but this was different. It took all her willpower to make herself walk down the corridor to her father's study. A uniformed police officer came out of the room as she approached. Elena identified herself.

'My mother . . .' she began.

'She's in the kitchen. The ambulance crew are with her.'

'The ambulance crew? So my father . . .'

The police officer shook his head. 'I'm sorry. He was dead when we arrived.'

Elena walked past the open door of the study. She didn't look in. She couldn't bear to see her father's body. Her mother was sitting in a chair at the kitchen table. She was very pale but appeared calm. She was staring listlessly at nothing, her face puffed and swollen from weeping. Elena knelt down beside her and held her, blinking away the tears.

'Are you her daughter?' one of the paramedics asked.

Elena nodded.

'We've given her a sedative. She should rest. Someone will have to stay with her.'

'I'm here now, Mamma,' Elena said softly. 'Everything's going to be all right. Come and lie down.'

She helped her mother to her feet and guided her out of the room, shielding her eyes from the activity in the study as they passed. Upstairs in the bedroom she helped her mother into bed and sat beside her for a time, holding her hand and thinking about the progression everyone made from childhood to adulthood. For most of her life she'd been nurtured, cared for by her parents. Only now was she beginning to realise how things had changed, that there was a point every child passed, perhaps without being aware of it, when they became parent to their own parents. She'd felt it the previous afternoon with her father when she'd wanted to hold him as if he were her son. And she felt it now with her mother, felt a need to protect and comfort her.

Gradually, as the sedative took effect, her mother closed her eyes and fell asleep. Elena went back downstairs. She was tired. She wanted to sit and just do nothing, but she was terrified by the prospect of being alone with her thoughts. She had to shut out the pain with activity.

She made some coffee and drank a little, trying to ignore the sounds of the police officers coming and going from the study. One of the officers came in carrying two plain white envelopes.

'These were on the desk,' he said.

Elena saw her mother's name on one envelope, her own on the other. But she didn't touch them. She just nodded and left them there on the kitchen table. Then she rang Ugo and her three other siblings to tell them what had happened, staying calm, businesslike throughout. Only when she'd finished the calls did she finally break down. She put the envelope addressed to her in her pocket and went out into the garden and sat in one of the plastic chairs, the tears pouring out in a flood that blinded her.

She was still there when Ugo arrived. He came over to her and, without a word, put his arms around her and held her as she sobbed. It was a long while before he released her and gave her his handkerchief to wipe her eyes.

'How's Mamma?' he said.

'She's upstairs in bed. They gave her a sedative. She was hysterical when she rang me.'

'Why did he do it?'

Elena shook her head. She couldn't tell Ugo what she'd done. Not now. Maybe not even later. The guilt was too overwhelming.

'What needs to be done?' Ugo asked.

'I'm not sure. That depends on the police.'

'I'll go and talk to them.'

Ugo went back into the house. Elena stayed in the garden, relieved that her brother was here. She couldn't have coped on her own. She wiped the moisture off her cheeks and brushed away more tears, watching the bees hovering around the bougainvillaea that cascaded over the wall at the far end of the lawn. She knew she ought to go in and help Ugo, but she couldn't summon the energy, nor the willpower. She'd always looked on herself as the strong one in the family, the one who could be relied on in adversity to stay calm and collected. But her self-possession had deserted her. She felt as helpless as a baby.

She was surprised by, and grateful for, her brother's quiet efficiency. He'd never in the past shown signs of leadership qualities, but today he took charge of everything; liaising with the police officers in the house, supervising the removal of the body for the unavoidable autopsy and seeing to the harrowing task of cleaning up the study.

Only when the police had left did Elena go back inside the house. She went into the living room and shut the door, closing out the reminders of what had taken place just down the hall. Then she telephoned Francesca at the *Procura*.

'Where are you?' Francesca wanted to know. 'Baffi's been trying your home number for hours.'

'Why? What's the matter?'

'The matter? You know what's the matter. You started it all. Corona.'

'Oh.' Elena had forgotten all about the chief prosecutor's suspension.

'What have you done to us, Elena? Vespignani's been appointed acting chief and is being even more insufferable than usual. There's a team here from Bologna throwing their weight around and acting as if they think we're all on the take. They've been in here God knows how many times demanding to know your whereabouts. Why aren't you in?'

'I'm over at my parents' house,' Elena said. 'My father's killed himself.'

'*What!*'

Elena gave her the briefest details.

'*Dio*,' Francesca breathed. 'Why didn't you tell me that at the beginning? I feel awful, going on at you like that. Elena, I'm so sorry.'

'I won't be in today. I don't know for sure when I'll be back. Will you ask Alberto to take care of everything for me?'

'Of course. Is there anything I can do?'

'Not just now. But thanks.'

The house was eerily quiet now. Ugo was upstairs with their mother. Elena took the envelope out of her pocket and held it tentatively in her fingers, hardly daring to open it. She stared at her name for a long time, feeling the outline of something small and hard inside the envelope. It seemed to be a key. Finally, she could put it off no longer. She tore open the flap and pulled out the sheet of notepaper. Taking a deep breath, she began to read.

My Dearest Elena,
By the time you read this I will have left you. I know it will cause you great pain and you will despise me for my weakness, but it seemed to me the only honourable way out. I am too old, too tired to see my life – and my family – ruined by disgrace. It is selfish of me, I know, but I have always, to my regret now, put myself first in everything I have done.

I do not blame you for any of this. It is all of my own making. I have done many things of which I am ashamed, associated with many people whose business I should have shunned. But I was in too deep to extricate myself. This seemed the best solution for all concerned.

I have done it for myself. I am too cowardly to face the consequences of my actions. But I hope it may also protect you. They will not be able to reach you through me now. They will not be able to corrupt that integrity which, throughout your life, Elena, you have shown in everything you have done and which I, to my eternal shame, have so conspicuously lacked.

I am proud of you, my child. I only wish I could have given you the same cause to be proud of me. I've been an absent, neglectful father but I have always loved you. And I always will. Look after your mother. Forgive me.

Papa.

Elena gazed down at the letter, her tears dripping on to the paper until the words were just a damp, illegible blur.

Chapman returned home to Elena's apartment in the middle of the morning and went straight to bed. He'd passed an uncomfortable, sleepless night on the floor of the Vatican Secret Archives, followed by an even more unpleasant couple of hours on the bookshelf in the basement, waiting for the Vatican Museum to open so he could slip back into the Sistine Chapel and from there to the exit.

He slept for four hours, then took a shower and

made himself some coffee and toast. He tried Elena's office number and was told she was out all day, her clerk wouldn't say where. Chapman called a colleague at the *Stampa Estera* to bring himself up to date with the day's news before ringing London to say he wouldn't be filing any copy.

He was in the kitchen making more coffee when he heard the front door open. Elena came in slowly looking drawn and weary.

'You're back early,' Chapman said. 'Do you want some coffee?'

Elena shook her head listlessly. 'I'm not staying. I've just come to pick up my nightclothes and wash things.'

'You're going away?'

Elena slumped down on to a chair and put her head in her hands.

'My father's dead,' she said, lifting her eyes momentarily. 'He shot himself this morning.'

Chapman gaped at her. 'Jesus.'

He pulled out another chair and sat down next to her, too stunned to speak. Elena told him what had happened, both that day and the previous afternoon.

'I killed him,' she said. 'My own father.'

'You know that's not true.'

'It is. If I hadn't gone there yesterday, he would be alive now.'

'That doesn't mean you killed him.'

'I asked him to go to the police. I thought he was going to.'

'You did the right thing, Elena. What else could you have done?'

'I could have destroyed the papers, covered them up.'

'We talked about this for hours yesterday,' Chapman said gently. 'You know the arguments backwards. Destroying them would have made no difference. They'd simply have sent more copies to you. Or to another magistrate, or maybe a newspaper.'

'I should have resigned. If I'd known it would end like this, I would have quit immediately. The responsibility is mine. I'm to blame.'

'You feel guilty, but you're not to blame, Elena.'

She turned her eyes to him. Eyes rimmed with red, scarred with a bitter sorrow.

'Aren't I?' she said. 'My family will blame me, just as I blame myself.'

'You weren't to know what would happen.'

'They won't see it that way. Oh, God, how can I tell them?'

'Don't.'

'I'm not sure I can live with it. I'm not that strong.'

Chapman took hold of her hands. 'People are responsible for their own actions. Your father made the choice, not you. You did what your conscience told you had to be done. That's no cause for guilt.'

Elena didn't reply. She pushed herself to her feet and went through into the bedroom. Chapman followed, watching her anxiously as she threw a few clothes into an overnight bag.

'When will you be back?'

'I don't know. My mother's in a bad way. I'll probably stay with her for a few days.'

'I can come with you, if you like.'

Elena touched him on the arm and pressed her head briefly to his chest.

'This is something I have to do on my own,' she said.

TWENTY-ONE

Elena had thought she wouldn't sleep that night, that her conscience wouldn't allow her to escape the waking torment of her guilt. But in the end she dozed off before midnight, too physically and emotionally drained to keep her eyes open.

Ugo stayed over too and, between them, they did all they could to comfort their mother who, once the sedative had worn off, was an inconsolable confusion of grief and uncomprehending bewilderment. Elena said nothing about her conversation with her father on the Sunday afternoon; not because she lacked the courage, but because she couldn't add to her mother's pain, couldn't debase her father's reputation now he was dead. She still had the papers that incriminated him, still had to decide what to do about them. But not for a while.

The new day brought a slight sense of relief to them all. The trauma of Eugenio's death had not lessened, but there were things to occupy them – phone calls, funeral arrangements – so they had less time to dwell on what had happened.

Chapman rang at lunch time and Elena talked to him briefly. She was surprised how much she was missing him, how much she wanted to return to her own apartment and the routine preoccupations of a life unburdened by tragedy. Then Francesca called to ask how she was.

'Coping. That's about all,' Elena said. 'What's happening in the office?'

'You don't want to hear about that at a time like this.'

'Tell me. I need something to take my mind off it all. What's happening with Corona?'

'He's denying any knowledge of a bank account in Switzerland, as you might expect. The Bologna magistrates are questioning him this afternoon.'

'And Vespignani? He'll be enjoying his promotion, no doubt.'

'Enjoying is an understatement,' Francesca said drily. 'He's moved into Corona's office and is already reviewing the allocation of cases. You know, cherry-picking the high-profile ones that will get his name in the papers.'

'Maybe I'll stay away for a while longer.'

'I would.'

There was a pause. Elena sensed something her friend wasn't telling her.

'Have you got something on your mind?'

'No, not really,' Francesca said unconvincingly.

'What is it?'

'It's not a good time to tell you.'

'Tell me what?'

'One of the cases Vespignani is taking over is Antonio Vivaldi.'

'What! He can't do that.'

'He came in this morning and made Baffi give him the file.'

Elena gripped the telephone hard. She'd thought

she was too depressed for any emotion except a sort of listless sorrow, but she was angry now.

'I'd better speak to him. Thanks for letting me know, Francesca.'

She put down the phone and dialled the direct line to the chief prosecutor's office. When Vespignani came on, she wasted no time on small talk.

'Luigi, what's this about you taking over the Vivaldi case?'

'My, news does travel fast,' Vespignani sneered. 'Yes, I'm taking charge of it, seeing that you're not in to handle it yourself.'

'My father is dead, Luigi. That's why I'm not in.'

'I'm aware of that, and of course you have my deepest condolences. But I have a department to run. The Vivaldi case is important to our public profile and as, to date, you've made very little progress in your investigation, I've deemed it appropriate to take it over myself.'

'It's my case,' Elena said fiercely, 'and I resent the implication that I'm handling it badly.'

'Elena, this isn't up for discussion,' Vespignani said sharply. 'I've made the decision. If you don't like it, that's tough. You may have been able to manipulate Corona but you won't do it to me.'

'You shit.'

'Be careful, Elena. You're not in a position to start asserting yourself.'

'And what does that mean?' Elena said, trying to keep her cool.

'It means that I have here on my desk a report from the *Guardia di Finanza* requesting permission – a permission I intend to grant – to interview you about discrepancies in your tax returns.'

Elena's stomach lurched violently downwards. She'd forgotten about the Revenue Guards' investigation. She took a deep breath before she spoke.

'Discrepancies?'

'A sum of ten million lire paid into your bank account that wasn't declared on your income tax return.'

'When was this?'

'I'm sure the *Guardia* will give you all the details when they question you.'

'When, Luigi?'

'A year, eighteen months ago.'

Elena gave a sigh of relief. 'That wasn't income. It was a loan from my parents. To see me through the temporary expenses of separating from my husband. There's nothing in it.'

'Of course,' Vespignani said, his tone leaving her in no doubt that he didn't believe her. 'But, nevertheless, I think you should take some time off until this matter is resolved.'

'Are you suspending me?' Elena said incredulously.

'Not officially. I'm granting you temporary compassionate leave. Corona is more than enough at the moment. We don't want two scandals in the department.'

'I don't accept that. The allegations are baseless.'

'We are public servants,' Vespignani said pompously. 'The impression of impropriety can be as damaging as the real thing. I have a duty to protect the department. You are relieved of your duties until further notice. And, Elena, if you cross me over this, I will make the suspension official and release details of the *Guardia* report to the press. I hope I make myself clear.'

The line went dead. Elena was mute with fury. Her

limbs were trembling and she had a powerful urge to go straight to the *Procura* and punch Vespignani's face in. But she knew her position was difficult. The chief prosecutor had absolute control over all internal affairs in the *pubblico ministero*. There was no one to appeal to over a purely administrative matter like the allocation of cases. And the *Guardia di Finanza* report was worrying. It was nonsense, of course, but it was serious enough to damage her. People remembered allegations being made. They rarely recalled them being rebutted.

She went out into the garden and paced across the lawn, walking off her anger, wondering what, if anything, she could do. Vespignani's attitude had raised her hackles and for a moment she forgot about the loss of her father. But it was only a temporary phenomenon. The memory soon returned in another flood of remorse and she sank down on to one of the chairs, overcome by lethargy. What did any of it matter? Why should she care what Vespignani did, what happened to a particular case? There were more important things to worry about.

Yet she'd never been able to think like that. Part of what made her the woman she was was the fact that she cared about her work. She cared about her cases and, in her idealistic way, she cared about justice. She recalled what her father had written to her in his letter – about her integrity, how proud he was of her. That integrity was now on the line.

She looked up, suddenly remembering the key that had been in the envelope. Her father hadn't put it there by accident, he'd had a reason for giving it to her.

Elena stood up quickly and went into the house.

She got the key from her handbag and examined it. It was the key to her father's safe. Going down the hall, she stopped outside the door to the study. She hadn't been in the room since it had happened. She hesitated, then steeled herself, turned the handle and walked in.

The safe was on the wall behind the desk, concealed by a painting of a Tuscan landscape, all rolling green hills and cypress trees. Elena unlocked it. There were bundles of papers inside. She removed them all and looked around for somewhere to put them. She couldn't bring herself to touch the desk or the chair so she retreated into a corner and sat on the floor reading through the papers. Some were legal documents, others were personal papers concerning her father's pension, investments and financial affairs in general.

One bundle, in particular, caught her eye. It contained correspondence relating to the offshore companies in the Cayman Islands and Netherlands Antilles which her father had been involved in creating. And it contained something else, something that made her heart beat a a little faster: a series of statements headed *Istituto per le Opere di Religione* – the Vatican Bank.

She spread the pages out on the carpet and scrutinised them. From what she could deduce, they were records of cash deposits made at the bank over the past two years. The amounts stunned her. The smallest was two hundred million lire, the largest seven hundred million.

There was a pattern to the deposits. They were made only once a month, on the first Wednesday.

Elena leaned back against the wall. Tomorrow was the first Wednesday of the month. She chewed a fingernail thoughtfully. Then she stood up, went to the desk and telephoned Gianni Agostini.

TWENTY-TWO

Chapman didn't go into the *Stampa Estera* on Wednesday morning. He wanted to keep away from the distractions of the office: the colleagues he would feel obliged to converse with, the newspapers and wire services which needed monitoring, the phone calls from London. He wanted to focus all his attention on the Vivaldi case and nothing else.

For a time, he just sat in an armchair in the living room of his apartment, drinking coffee and going over all the facts in his head; from the death of the Red Priest and the apparent involvement of the neo-Fascists in his killing through to the murders of the vagrant Beppe and Enzo Mattei; the rally at Ostia Antica, the papers Vivaldi had found in Roberto Ferrero's house and his own discovery of who Ferrero really was. It was a complex sequence of related incidents which, in the end, brought him back to the documents he'd taken from the Vatican Secret Archives.

He went through into his study and removed the large manilla envelope from the drawer in the desk where he'd put it for safekeeping. He tipped the contents out on to the desk top and sifted through them. The medals and dagger he pushed to one side; he'd learned all he could about them. The Royal Army identity disc was more intriguing. He wondered who Roberto Ferrero had been. He was presumably dead. Why else would Domenico Salvitti have taken his identity? But how and when had he died? Chapman had an inkling that both those facts were going to be important.

He slipped the disc into his pocket and turned to look at the dog-eared black and white photograph again. Something about it bothered him. He couldn't place exactly what. Was it the men around Mussolini? The building in the background which he'd seen before but still couldn't place?

The doorbell rang. Chapman started. He put the photograph in his pocket and gathered up the papers, returning them to the drawer with the dagger and the medals. He went out into the hall. The doorbell rang again. Chapman hesitated. He wasn't expecting anyone, but the door was locked and bolted. What was there to worry about? He walked cautiously down the hall and checked through the peephole. There was no one there.

'Who is it?' he called.

Something heavy thudded against the outside of the door. The timber shuddered. There was another sudden blow, a faint splintering sound as the screws on the top bolt came loose. Chapman turned and ran back down the hall, heading for the fire escape at the rear of the apartment. Behind him, he heard more juddering blows, then a sharp crack as the lock broke. He raced through the living room and threw open the window. Another man was crouched on the steps of the fire escape outside. He came in quickly, knocking Chapman backwards before he had a chance to register what was happening. He punched Chapman in the guts so hard the air was forced out of him and he fell to the floor doubled up, gasping. There were footsteps in the hall and a second man came into the room. Chapman glanced up, wheezing for breath. It was Vincenzo Volpi, the thug who'd shot Enzo.

'We meet again, you prick,' Volpi said, grinning down at him.

Chapman swallowed, trying to get his breathing back to normal. He was too stunned to think straight. All he was aware of was the pain in his stomach and the two ugly, crop-haired men standing over him. They picked him up and tossed him on to the settee.

'Salvitti's medals, where are they?' Volpi said in his guttural Roman accent.

'Medals?'

Volpi came for him and hammered down with a fist like a piledriver. Chapman's nose burst open, blood splattering out over his mouth and chin.

'We only ask once. Where are they?'

Chapman wiped away the blood with the back of his hand. He could taste it in his mouth, warm and sweet.

'What medals?' he said thickly.

Volpi punched him again, this time on the ear. An excruciating pain shot through Chapman's skull.

'I said we only ask once.'

'We want the papers too,' the other man said.

Chapman blinked at him. His head was throbbing, but through the red haze he was still capable of thinking, of judging how much he could bluff them, how much violence his body could withstand.

'I have the medals,' he mumbled. 'What papers do you mean?'

'We know you've got them, shitface,' Volpi said. 'Vivaldi's papers. You've got Salvitti's medals. The papers go with them. Now where are they?'

'In the study,' Chapman said.

He knew they'd find them eventually. What mattered to him was protecting himself, preserving enough of his strength to give himself a chance against them.

'Show us,' Volpi said, hauling Chapman to his feet and pushing him towards the door.

Chapman stumbled down the hall and into the study. The two men came after him and waited while he went round to the other side of the desk and pulled open the drawer. Chapman grasped hold of the medals and threw them across the desk top. They bounced on the surface and skittered off on to the floor.

Instinctively, the two men bent down to pick them up and in that brief moment, their attention diverted, Chapman lifted the dagger out of the drawer and slipped it into his trouser pocket.

Volpi came round the desk and shoved Chapman out of the way. He seized the papers in the drawer and dropped them on to the desk top.

'Are those the ones?' he asked his companion.

The other man rifled through the sheets and nodded. Volpi took hold of Chapman's shirt collar and dragged him out of the study.

'You miss your friend?' he said, grinning wolfishly. 'I enjoyed it, you know.' He held up his right hand like a gun and pointed it at Chapman's head. 'Pop, pop. Two shots. A clean execution. You see his head explode? Nice, eh?'

Chapman bit back his response. He didn't want to give Volpi the excuse to hit him again.

He knew they were going to kill him. He'd known it from the beginning when they first burst in. They hadn't bothered to conceal their faces because they had no intention of leaving him alive to identify them. The only question was where they were going to do it. Not in the apartment, Chapman guessed. They wouldn't take the risk. They'd go somewhere quieter, more private. Somewhere they, or whoever had sent them, could have a little chat with him before the job was completed.

They took him downstairs, one of them on either side, holding his arms tight. Outside on the street two cars were parked by the kerb: a maroon Fiat and, in front of it, a blue Alfa Romeo saloon. A young man with sallow skin and dark, hooded eyes climbed out of the Alfa Romeo. He was wearing layman's clothes – a black suit and white shirt – but something about the cut of the suit made Chapman certain he was a priest.

The man holding Chapman's right arm released it and stepped forward to hand the priest the papers they'd taken from the apartment. Chapman glanced at Volpi and casually put his hand in his right trouser pocket. He grasped the hilt of the dagger, feeling the metal cool on his fingers.

'In the car,' Volpi said, pushing Chapman towards the Fiat.

Chapman knew he had to act immediately. Once they got him in the car he wouldn't get another chance. He'd never used a knife before, never attacked another man in anger or self-defence. It took a certain kind of personality to inflict violence on another; a personality Chapman didn't have. But he reminded himself

411

what they'd done to Enzo and he didn't hesitate. He whipped the dagger out of his pocket and rammed it hard into the top of Volpi's thigh. Volpi screamed and clutched at his leg as he fell to the ground. The other man spun round. The priest leaped into his car. Chapman turned and sprinted away up the street.

He heard the other man come after him. He looked back. There was less than fifty metres between them. He turned into a small piazza cluttered with parked cars, swerving to avoid the tables and chairs outside a *trattoria*, then ducked into a narrow alley that snaked between two high apartment buildings. Vines cascaded over the sun-faded orange stucco of the walls, writhing across ironwork balconies and wooden shutters, but Chapman had eyes only for the path in front of him. A group of sightseers with cameras and guide books blocked his way for a second. He barged through them and out into a cobbled street, glancing round in the hope that his pursuer might have given up the chase.

There was little sign of that happening. Chapman was running flat out. The man behind was losing ground, but he was fitter than he looked. Though he was struggling to keep going, he had a dogged determination that refused to countenance defeat. He couldn't afford to let Chapman escape.

Chapman turned left, then right, trying to lose his pursuer, trying to get out of sight long enough to find a hiding place. He was feeling the physical strain. His legs were getting heavier, his breathing more laboured. The street started to go uphill, increasing the pressure on his muscles. Chapman veered down another *vicolo*, finding an extra burst of speed. He turned a corner, narrowly missing a motor scooter coming the other way, and burst out into a square. The church of Santa Maria della Scala was directly in front of him. He looked back. The man behind was momentarily lost from view. Chapman staggered up the steps and in through the doors of the church.

He paused at the end of the nave, peering around the gloomy interior. The church was deserted. There were several ornate wooden confession boxes down one side. Chapman pulled open the door of the first and stepped inside. He slumped down on the priest's seat and panted for air, listening hard. There was no sound for a long time. Chapman relaxed. He wiped the sweat off his face and waited.

Then he heard the footsteps. Someone had come into the church. Chapman held his breath. The footsteps came down the side of the nave. Chapman could hear the wheeze of a man's struggling lungs. The noise got nearer, louder. The door to the confessional snapped open suddenly and the man's red face gazed in at him. In his right hand he was holding an automatic pistol.

He gestured at Chapman with the gun. Chapman rose wearily to his feet. He was about to step out of the box when there was a sudden flurry of footsteps and two men in grey suits burst through the church doors. They swung their pistols around.

'*Polizia*,' one of them shouted. 'Gun down. On the floor. Now!'

Archbishop Tomassi stared at the papers his secretary had placed on the desk in front of him. He didn't ask where Father Simčić had obtained them. There were some things it was better not to know. But he was

413

PAUL ADAM

reeling under the shock. The last time he'd seen three of these documents they'd been safely filed away in the Secret Archives. How they'd come to be removed was both a puzzle and a worry to him.

But he contained his curiosity. He knew little about Simčić's private life, the people he mixed with outside his working hours, but he suspected he would not approve of many of them. Tomassi was a practical man. He did not see fit to concern himself with matters that were none of his business, particularly when it was expedient for him to remain in ignorance. All that counted was that the documents had been recovered, and that the papers Antonio Vivaldi had shown him on the day he died were now in his possession. The originals, not photocopies.

Tomassi read the words on the documents again. Then he took a box of matches from his desk. There'd be no mistake this time. The evidence would be destroyed once and for all. The Archbishop struck a match and held the flame to the corner of the first sheet. He watched it burn, then dropped it into the metal waste-paper bin beside him and waited until it was nothing more than charred flakes of paper. He did the same to the others, sifting through the remains with the tip of a pencil to make sure not a single fragment remained unburnt. Then he went through into his private chapel and prayed to the Lord for forgiveness.

Elena was getting bored. This kind of routine surveillance assignment was not something she usually supervised in person. She generally briefed the police and let them get on with it. But this one was different.

414

She had a personal stake in it and it was important for her to be there.

Agostini was sitting next to her in the driver's seat of the unmarked police car. They were parked at the end of a row of cars on the Via di Porta Angelica, about fifty metres from the Porta Santa Anna, the tradesmen's entrance to the Vatican City. They had a clear view of the gates and the checkpoint just inside, manned by Swiss Guards. Beyond the gates, up the Via del Belvedere, were the offices of the *Istituto per le Opere di Religione*, the Vatican Bank. Another unmarked police car was parked further up the Via di Porta Angelica and in a cafe almost opposite the Gates of St Anne were two armed plain-clothes officers.

Agostini looked at his watch and glanced across at Elena.

'I know,' she said. 'Just a while longer.'

They'd been there four hours already and were getting restless. It wasn't so much the tedium of the job – the police were used to that – as the fact that the longer it went on the more doubtful they became about its objectives. Elena was sure a deposit would be made that day. The problem was identifying the courier. She was pretty certain he would come on foot – taking a car into the Vatican was a complicated process – but that didn't narrow the field down much. They'd had two false alarms already; people who'd looked like the target but who, when stopped and questioned, had turned out to have legitimate business in other parts of the Holy See.

Elena kept her nerve. It would have been easier to call off the operation but she was determined to see it through to the end, even if it ultimately proved fruitless. She was worn out. She'd slept badly, still in turmoil over the death of her father. Once or twice she'd almost dozed off in the car, but forced herself to stay awake. It didn't look good if the magistrate in charge fell asleep on the job.

'Dottoressa,' Agostini said suddenly.

His gaze was fixed on a black BMW coming towards them on the other side of the road. It slowed and stopped just short of the Porta Santa Anna. There were two men inside. Elena recognised the driver. It was the foul-mouthed skinhead who'd tried to shred the files during the raid on the MPI offices.

'That's the one,' she said.

Agostini snatched up the radio.

'Target in place. Black BMW. Move in.'

He started the engine. The police car slewed out into the road, forcing the traffic to give way, and shot across to stop, bumper to bumper, in front of the BMW. The second police car came from the other direction, boxing the BMW in. The two men leapt out and tried to run for it. The skinhead dodged through the stream of cars and was almost across the road when the plain-clothes officers in the cafe burst out and wrestled him to the ground. The second man attempted to seek sanctuary in the Vatican but found his path blocked by Swiss Guards. He was cuffed and brought back to the BMW.

Agostini pulled out an attaché case from the rear seat of the car and snapped it open. Inside were neat rows of ten-thousand-lire notes. Agostini lifted out a bundle and flicked through it.

'I think the drinks are on me,' he said.

*   *   *

They questioned the two men in separate rooms at Judicial Police headquarters rather than at the *Procura*. Elena didn't want to go anywhere near her office in case she encountered Vespignani. They started on the skinhead first but got nowhere. He just sat on a chair staring blankly at the wall and refusing to answer anything they put to him. Elena and Agostini, frustrated by the response, moved on to the second man.

He was sitting upright on the hard wooden chair in the interview room, his thick hands resting on the fronts of his thighs. He was powerfully built; the muscles of his arms and shoulders bulged beneath the thin material of his suit.

Elena sat down opposite him and studied his face. His lip curled contemptuously and she saw his chipped, uneven teeth. A tiny spark of recognition flashed through her brain. She'd seen that mouth before somewhere. *Dio.* She suddenly remembered where. Through the slit in a black hangman's hood. He was the leader of the gang of men who'd attacked her on her way home from the *Procura*. She hadn't seen his face but the details of that mouth grinning at her as his hands roved over her body were imprinted indelibly on her mind. She was certain it was him.

For an instant her legs felt weak. She tasted castor oil again. Then the moment passed and she wanted to hit him. She wanted to do to him what he'd done to her. He was grinning at her now, realising she knew who he was. If she'd been a man, Elena would have asked Agostini to leave the room and vented her anger on this animal with a clinical violence. As it was, she bit back her resentment and consoled herself with the thought that, one way or another, she was going to nail the bastard by legitimate means.

Agostini turned on the tape recorder and went through the formalities: the time, the date, the name of the suspect being questioned. They knew from the identity card in his wallet that he was called Fabio Boneschi, though he'd declined to confirm it. They'd done a check to make sure the ID card was genuine and photographed and fingerprinted him as a matter of routine.

Elena asked him a few questions and it became clear immediately that he was going to be no more cooperative than his companion.

'The money in the briefcase you were taking to the Vatican, where did it come from?'

'What money? I wasn't taking any money anywhere.'

'What was it, the proceeds of illegal gambling, extortion, illegal contributions from companies to the neo-Fascists?'

'I'd never seen it before. I don't know how it got in the car. The police must have planted it.'

'Whom do you work for?'

'I'm unemployed. There isn't much work about.'

'Are you a member of the MPI?'

'What's that?'

'Who sent you to the Vatican?'

'I wasn't in the Vatican.'

'You were about to enter through the Porta Santa Anna.'

'Was I?'

Elena persisted, despite his stonewalling. She wasn't in a hurry. She could detain Boneschi indefinitely; time was on her side. But his sneering attitude annoyed her.

After twenty minutes of futile interrogation, Agostini was called out of the room by one of his men. Elena waited until he'd left before turning off the tape recorder.

'We're not getting very far, are we?' she said.

Boneschi leered at her. 'How far do you want to go?'

He glanced at the dormant tape recorder and lowered his voice so the uniformed police officer by the door couldn't hear him.

'You want another feel?' he said lewdly. 'Uh? Get your tits touched up again. You enjoyed it, didn't you? Tight-arsed cow like you, I bet you don't get much. Lock the door, we could do it here on the table. How about it?'

Elena gave him a pitying look. He was tough, but not as tough as he thought. She knew there was very little she could say or do to make him cooperate. He wasn't afraid of her. He wasn't afraid of the police or the judicial system. But she knew there was one thing even men like him were scared of – their own kind.

'Shall I tell you what I'm going to do?' she said.

'No, go on, surprise me,' Boneschi said.

'I'm going to issue a statement to the press saying that you're in custody and are cooperating fully with our investigations into the activities of the neo-Fascists. Then I'm going to have you detained in the Regina Coeli.' She leaned towards him, to emphasise the message. 'And I'll make sure you're put in the same wing of the prison as the *Sansepolcristi* currently awaiting trial for the synagogue bombing and other atrocities.

They'll be delighted to see you. Believe me, Fabio, they'll do a lot more than pour castor oil down your throat.'

She watched Boneschi turn pale. He knew she wasn't bluffing.

'You bitch,' he snarled.

'Maybe,' Elena said. 'But I'm a bitch who's got you by the balls. Think about it.'

She stood up and went out of the room. Agostini was coming along the corridor outside.

'There's been an incident in Trastevere,' he said. 'That English journalist, Chapman.'

Elena stopped dead. Her mouth was suddenly dry. 'What's happened? What's happened to him?'

'He's okay. Beaten up, but not badly injured.'

'Where is he, in hospital?'

'A doctor treated him at the police station. He was lucky. It looks as if a couple of neo-Fascist morons were abducting him. He was close to being shot when the police arrived. Two of Piccoli's men. It seems they were watching one of the morons, fellow named Volpi, Vincenzo Volpi. You knew about that?'

'I asked Piccoli to organise it. Are they in custody?'

'Volpi's in hospital. The journalist stabbed him with a dagger. You'll like this bit. It seems the dagger was some old collector's piece. A Fascist memento with an inscription on it from Mussolini himself. Piccoli's sending the full report to your office.'

'So Chapman's okay, you're sure about that?'

Agostini nodded. Then he gestured towards the interview room. 'How's our friend?'

'Difficult.'

'I have something that might just loosen his tongue. The Red Priest's apartment – you remember there were some fingerprints on the desk we couldn't identify? Guess whose they were?'

Elena smiled at Agostini. 'I'll let you give him the good news.'

They went back into the interview room and switched on the tape recorder. Boneschi looked at them with a hatred that was almost palpable.

'I want a lawyer,' he said.

'And you'll need one,' Agostini replied. 'You haven't got a record, have you? That surprises me, a piece of shit like you. How have you managed to stay out of trouble all this time?'

'I'm a law-abiding citizen,' Boneschi said.

'Sure. A law-abiding citizen carrying around five hundred million lire in used notes in a briefcase.'

'I've already told you. I know nothing about any money.'

'Of course you don't. But that's not what we want to talk to you about. Have you heard of a priest named Antonio Vivaldi?'

'No.'

'Really? He was murdered a couple of weeks ago. It was in all the papers.'

'I don't read the papers.'

'So you don't know him?'

'No.'

'Then how do you explain the fact that your finger-prints were found in his apartment the morning after he was killed?'

Boneschi licked his lips, his eyes opening a little wider. Elena watched him carefully. If they handled it right, Boneschi might just be the conduit that would lead them to Cesare Scarfone himself.

'You realise what we're saying, don't you?' Elena said. 'This isn't some simple money laundering charge, this is murder, and a particularly nasty murder.'

'I had nothing to do with it.'

'But you were there,' Agostini said. 'We have your prints. That alone will be enough to convict you. Unless there was someone else present who did the killing. Was there?'

Boneschi didn't reply. He shifted in his seat, showing the first, faint signs of unease since he'd been arrested. Elena rubbed the point in further.

'Why should you carry the can alone? You'll go down for a long time, you know. Vivaldi was a priest, one of the most respected people in the city. No judge is going to show you any mercy. Public opinion will ensure you never come out. Is that what you want? Do you want to let the others get off scot-free?' She paused. 'Who else was there? Was Cesare Scarfone there?'

Boneschi's hands moved on his thighs. Elena could see the indecision in his eyes. And perhaps a touch of fear.

'Was he?' she repeated.

'You won't touch Scarfone,' Boneschi said. 'He's too clever for you.'

'You're terrified of him, aren't you? He scares the shit out of you. A big guy like you intimidated by a creep like Scarfone. Do you want to spend the rest of your life in prison for a man like him?'

'You offering me a deal?'

'No deals. We don't do deals in the *pubblico ministero*.'

Boneschi laughed in her face. 'Don't you? You're so smug, so pleased with yourself, aren't you, you *puttana*? Coming over all clean and pure when half your colleagues, including your boss, are on the take. That's why you won't get near Scarfone. He knows exactly who to pay off.'

'We know all about that. My boss has been suspended.'

'Yeah?' Boneschi shrugged indifferently. 'Serves him right. People like him make me sick. Spouting morals, making judgements about other people when all the time they're taking bribes. I used to deliver them myself, cash in an envelope. He treated me like dirt. Sitting out there in his fucking villa at Frascati, drinking wine and looking down his nose at me while pocketing ten million lire a month. People like that are worse than the lowest criminal.'

'What did you say?' Elena was frowning at him, her jaw hanging slack.

'People like that are . . .'

'Frascati? Did you say he had a villa at Frascati?'

'Yeah. Flashy place. Paid for with dirty money. If you want to know what . . .'

'Shut up.'

'What?'

Elena stood up from her chair and turned away. Corona didn't have any villa in Frascati. But she knew who did. She ran a hand through her hair, her heart racing, and turned back to Boneschi.

'Who are you talking about? Alessandro Corona?'

'Who? No, short guy with a stupid-looking beard. Vespignani. He's your boss, isn't he? That's what I always thought. Head prosecutor, some shit like that.'

Elena knew what had happened. She'd walked right into it. She'd done the deed for them herself. Given them Corona's head on a plate. They'd made it easy for her. They'd even identified the right files by pretending to shred them at the MPI offices. And she'd taken it all in. There was no account in Switzerland. At least not one that Corona knew anything about. It was just an elaborate set-up to get Vespignani into the chief prosecutor's office.

'These payments,' Elena said. 'Were records kept of them?'

'I don't know. Probably. What use is a bribe if you can't use it to blackmail your victim?'

'Where were they kept?'

'You think they'd tell someone like me that? Scarfone probably has them. Who knows?'

'Was Cesare Scarfone present when Antonio Vivaldi was tortured and killed?' Elena said.

Boneschi looked down. He shook his head, suddenly reluctant to answer. Elena leaned over the table right into his face.

'Was he?'

Boneschi didn't reply. Elena had an overwhelming urge to slap him in the face, but she controlled herself. She wanted everything said in the interview to be admissible in evidence.

'Was he?' she repeated. '*Was he?* I want an answer or you'll be in the Regina Coeli in ten minutes. Was Scarfone there?'

Boneschi hesitated, then raised his head and gave a slight nod.

'Out loud, for the tape,' Elena snapped.

'Yes, Scarfone was there.'

Elena clicked off the recorder and ejected the tape, stowing it safely in her jacket pocket.

'I need to use your phone, Gianni,' she said.

They went upstairs to Agostini's office and Elena called her office.

'Alberto,' she said when Baffi answered. 'It's me. The files we took from the MPI offices. I want you to search through them for something.'

'They're all boxed up and ready to go back,' Alberto said.

'They're *what*?'

'At the hearing this morning, before Judge Vasari, we were ordered to return them.'

'Christ, I'd forgotten about that.'

'Dottore Vespignani handled it. He offered no argument for keeping them.'

'I bet he didn't. Alberto, do something for me. Keep the boxes there. I don't care how you do it, just don't send them back until I get there. Okay?'

Elena put down the phone and turned to Agostini. 'Can you get me a car?'

'I'll drive you myself,' Agostini replied.

They put the lights and siren on and were outside the main entrance of the *Procura* in minutes. Elena and Agostini ran inside and took the lift upstairs. The cardboard boxes with their official seals were stacked in the corridor outside the office. Elena hauled one inside and broke it open, tipping the contents out on to Baffi's desk. Then she brought in a second box and emptied it.

'Search through it. I want anything that looks like a record of payments. Cash books, receipts, anything.'

She went back out into the corridor and carried in

425

more boxes. Agostini helped her. Francesca came out of the inner office and stared at the piles of papers.

'What the hell . . .'

'Don't just stand there,' Elena said. 'Give us a hand.'

She went back into the corridor. Vespignani was coming towards her from his own office. He saw her and broke into a trot. Elena retreated into the clerk's office and took Francesca aside.

'Will you do something for me? Ring Montecitorio and find out when they're taking the vote on whether to lift Scarfone's immunity.'

Francesca stared at her. 'Didn't you know? It was held last night. It was on all the news bulletins. Every newspaper's carrying the story this morning.'

'I've been out of touch.' Elena could feel the tension in her muscles. 'Which way did it go?'

'Your way,' Francesca said.

Vespignani burst in through the doorway, taking in the broken boxes, the mounds of files on the desk and floor.

'What the fuck do you think you're doing?'

Elena ignored him. She drew Francesca away, keeping her voice low. 'Draw up an arrest warrant for me in Scarfone's name. Get the Judicial Police to bring him in immediately. Send them to Montecitorio, his home, the MPI offices. Cover everything.'

'On what charge?'

'The murder of Antonio Vivaldi.'

She could feel the sudden force of Francesca's gaze on her face, but she was already turning away, watching Vespignani picking up the phone and punching in an internal number.

'Security? This is chief prosecutor Vespignani. We

have an incident on the third floor. I want someone up here at once.'

He put down the receiver. 'You're suspended from duty with immediate effect,' he barked at Elena. 'Do you hear me?'

'Go screw yourself,' Elena said.

Vespignani grabbed her by the arm and dragged her out of the office.

'Those are sealed documents you're tampering with. You're in breach of a judicial order,' he shouted.

Elena looked over his shoulder. Two uniformed security guards were running down the corridor. She broke free of Vespignani and went back in to Agostini. She pulled the cassette tape out of her pocket and gave it to him.

'Take this to the Palace of Justice. The Court of Cassation. Judge Bassano.'

Agostini gave a brief nod. They could hear the footsteps of the guards outside.

'What's that you've got there?' Vespignani demanded, seeing Agostini slipping the tape into his tunic pocket.

'Go, Gianni,' Elena murmured.

Agostini pushed Vespignani out of the way and sprinted down the corridor, knocking the two security guards sideways.

'Stop that officer,' Vespignani shouted.

The guards slid to a halt and turned to chase after Agostini. Elena saw the inspector reach the staircase at the far end of the corridor. He turned briefly to look back, then pushed open the doors and disappeared from sight.

Vespignani rounded on Elena, his face contorted with fury.

'As for you, dottoressa,' he yelled. 'Consider yourself under arrest.'

The massive polished oak door was swung open by a clerk and Elena and Vespignani were escorted into the judge's chambers by the two uniformed judicial police officers who had been sent to bring them from the *Procura*.

Emilio Bassano and another man Elena recognised as the President of the Court of Cassation were seated behind the desk. Gianni Agostini was standing to one side, a tape recorder on the surface in front of him.

Vespignani glanced around shiftily. 'Why have we been brought here? I think you should know that Dottoressa Fiorini is suspended from office pending a full inquiry into . . .'

Judge Bassano lifted a hand to silence him. 'All in good time. Please be seated.'

Bassano waited until Vespignani and Elena had sat down, then turned to Agostini.

'Inspector, perhaps you'd be good enough to play us the tape again.'

TWENTY-THREE

There was darkness all around them. Elena glanced at the luminous dial of her watch – it was ten past eight – then across at Agostini who was slouched back in the driver's seat of the unmarked police car, his eyes closed. He looked as if he were asleep, but she knew he wasn't. Periodically, he would lift his head to gaze out of the windows, surveying the surrounding area with a misleadingly casual indifference for he missed nothing. Then, every fifteen minutes, he would pick up the radio handset and talk, in turn, to each of his officers before stretching out his long legs again and settling back to wait. Elena envied him his insouciance, his ability to relax when every muscle of her body was taut with nervous tension.

They were parked up on the Aventine, the most southerly of Rome's original seven hills, a residential area of expensive houses and quiet Renaissance streets and squares. In front of them, over a white stucco wall topped with miniature obelisks, was the church of San Anselmo, its facade partially hidden behind pine trees and spreading palm fronds. On the other side of the square, an equally high wall protected the *Priorato di Malta*, the imposing residence of the Grand Master of the Knights of Malta. In daylight, if you peered through the keyhole in the iron gates to the house, you got a perfect view, down an avenue of trees, of the dome of St Peter's. The more detailed guidebooks mentioned it in passing, but few tourists ventured this far off the beaten track to see it for themselves. The Aventine was, by Roman standards, a secluded backwater, a haven for the decaying nobility, wealthy members of the Establishment and ambitious *arrivistes* like Cesare Scarfone whose elegant, sixteenth-century house was little more than a quarter of a kilometre away.

The deputy had gone to ground, no one knew where. After a morning spent at the Chamber of Deputies, issuing angry denials of involvement in anything illegal and vowing to fight the prosecutors who were unjustly accusing him, he had vanished suddenly from Parliament in mid-afternoon and had not been seen since. Elena had no doubt that his disappearance was due to his finding out that Fabio Boneschi was in custody. The city police, airports and transport police had been informed, but so far there had been no sightings of Scarfone. Some of Agostini's men were keeping watch on the MPI offices and there were two more outside the deputy's house, one concealed at the front and one in the garden at the back. Elena had no business being there. She could have kept in touch with the surveillance operation from police headquarters, but she was too restless to sit in an office. She wanted to be out in the field.

The radio crackled and a low voice said: 'Morelli. Someone's coming over the garden wall.'

Agostini sat up instantly, reaching for the handset. Elena watched him, her pulse suddenly racing.

'Scarfone?' Agostini asked.

'No, it's a kid.'

Elena met Agostini's eye. That was all they needed. Some local delinquent picking tonight to practise his breaking and entering.

'Shall I move in?' Morelli asked.

'Hold back,' Agostini instructed him. 'See what he does.'

'He's got a key to the back door. He's going inside.'

'Leave him to it.'

Agostini started the engine of the car and pulled off slowly, one hand still holding the radio receiver. He left the headlights off. They crept out across the square and past the front of San Anselmo, heading around the southern flank of the hill.

'He's coming out.' Morelli's voice was just a whisper on the radio. 'He's carrying something. A small bag.'

'Let him go,' Agostini said, touching the accelerator lightly to increase their pace.

He turned left and let the car glide to a halt by the kerb, cutting the engine. Elena followed his lead and slumped down low in her seat so that her head, in the darkness, was barely visible through the windscreen. Ahead of them, across another junction, was the back wall of Scarfone's garden. A youth's shaven head appeared over the top, looking carefully from side to side. Then he scrambled over and lowered himself to the pavement. He looked around again and walked quickly away up the street. Agostini let him disappear momentarily from sight before starting the engine and going after him. The youth was nowhere to be seen. For an instant, Elena started to panic, then she saw him hurrying up a road to their left. Agostini saw him too. He braked and turned the wheel. There was a piazza at the top of the hill. The kid went to the side of a bottle-green Mercedes parked in the square and climbed into the passenger seat. There was another man driving. Elena saw him in profile as the car turned across the piazza and sped away down the incline. It was Scarfone.

Agostini accelerated. At the bottom of the hill the Mercedes turned on to the Viale Aventino, heading north-east towards the city centre. Agostini switched on the siren and went after him. Elena saw Scarfone tilt his head back to look in his rear-view mirror, then the Mercedes increased its speed and pulled sharply away from them. Agostini stayed with it, the cars in front pulling over to the side to give him a clear road.

They raced past the side of the United Nations Food and Agriculture Organisation headquarters and entered the Piazza di Porta Capena. On the far side of the square the Mercedes veered suddenly to the left, attempting to cut across the solid line of oncoming traffic and traverse the north side of the Circus Maximus. But Scarfone misjudged the manoeuvre. The first lane of traffic braked in time to avoid a collision but in the second, moving too fast to stop, was a huge articulated lorry which smashed straight into the side of the Mercedes sending the car spinning across the piazza. Agostini slewed to a halt at the side of the road and jumped out. The Mercedes had slithered to a standstill against one of the traffic islands. Its nearside front wing was crumpled like a used tissue. The kid in the passenger seat was slumped forwards, motionless, but Scarfone already had his door open and was pulling himself out. He appeared uninjured. After steadying himself for an instant, he immediately sprinted away through the rows of stationary cars.

Agostini reached the Mercedes and tried to wrench open the passenger door but it was too buckled to dislodge. He looked back at Elena, miming furiously. She nodded and snatched up the radio, calling for an ambulance. In the distance, she saw Scarfone climbing over the fence on to the lower slopes of the Palatine Hill. Agostini was chasing after him, dodging through the tailback of slowing cars on the Via di San Gregorio. He clambered up the fence and heaved himself over, stumbling awkwardly up the steep incline on the other side.

Elena picked up the radio again and spoke to the other Judicial Police team, telling them where Agostini was and instructing them to get round to the other side of the Palatine to cut off Scarfone's escape route. Then she crossed to the wrecked Mercedes and tried to open the passenger door herself, a futile gesture for she was unlikely to succeed where Agostini had failed. But she couldn't wait by the police car and do nothing. The youth inside was hanging forwards in his seat-belt, his face smeared with blood. She didn't know whether he was dead or merely unconscious.

The persistent wail of sirens drew nearer and a police motorbike and then a police car pulled into the piazza. The officers blocked off the area around the Mercedes and started the traffic moving again as an ambulance surged through on the wrong side of

the road. There was nothing more Elena could do. She
retreated to the kerb and peered through the darkness
towards the Palatine. She'd lost sight of both Scarfone
and Agostini. She could wait where she was and leave
Agostini on his own, or she could go after them. She
didn't hesitate.

The traffic was moving at barely more than a crawl.
Elena picked her way across the lanes and ran along
the Via di San Gregorio which skirted the east side
of the Palatine. The fence was too high for her to
climb without difficulty, but she knew that only fifty
metres further on were the pay kiosk and entrance to
the archaeological ruins that covered the whole of the
hill. The fence by the turnstile was easier to clamber
over. She dropped on to the concrete on the other
side and ran up the path that wound its way to the
summit.

It was years since she'd been here, but she remembered the remains of the imperial palaces which littered the site, a palimpsest of crumbling walls and
broken pillars, too overgrown and insubstantial to
give any true idea of how magnificent they had once
been.

She climbed a steep flight of steps and turned right
on to a stony path overshadowed by tall parasol pines.
As she reached the first of the ruins, the sunken stadium of Domitian which lay just below the top of the
hill, she paused, listening hard and looking round.
She'd seen no sign of either Agostini or Scarfone.
Finding them in the dark amongst all the debris of
ancient Rome was going to be nigh on impossible.
If Scarfone chose to hide in any of the thousands of
shadowy corners, the crevasses and holes that pitted

the area, he would not be found until daylight. But Elena guessed he wouldn't want to remain there that long. He would want to get off the hill and back into the crowded streets of the city as soon as he could. And that meant crossing the hill and slipping out on the other side.

She pressed on, ascending more steps and skirting the north end of the stadium. The path here was overhung by trees and bushes which cut out the glow from the streetlights down below. Elena felt her way in the darkness, pausing again as she reached the summit.

On her left were the sprawling remains of Domitian's palace; on her right the path leading down to the Forum. In the distance, illuminated by floodlights, she could see the towering walls of the Colosseum. She scanned the hillside. At the bottom she could just make out the white marble pillars of the Temple of Vesta where the Vestal Virgins had tended the holy fire of Rome, and the formidable arches of the Basilica of Constantine.

Something moved on the Sacra Via, the ancient road that traversed the length of the Forum. The figure of a man. Elena peered into the blackness. The figure was crossing the Forum towards the exit on the north side. The blue flashing lights of a stationary police car danced off the walls of the buildings beside the Via dei Fori Imperiali and then Elena saw torches flickering across the ruins as the police officers entered the Forum. One of the beams lit up the figure of the man. It was Agostini. Elena's eyes moved to and fro over the slope below her. Where was Scarfone? He'd had no time to sneak out of the exit before the police sealed it off so he must still be on the hill. But where?

She felt suddenly exposed on the summit and stepped into the shelter of one of the broken walls that criss-crossed the entire hill. Something moved over on the west side of the slope. A shadow flitting across and into the remains of Domitian's palace. It might simply have been a trick of the light, but it had too defined a shape for that. It was a person.

Elena looked down into the Forum. Agostini and his men had spread out to search the area. By the time they worked their way up the hill Scarfone would have gone. She contemplated shouting to them, but that would alert Scarfone to her presence and lose her the advantage of surprise. She was wasting precious time. All that mattered was following Scarfone, keep-ing track of his whereabouts. She ran along the path and followed the shadow into the ruined palace.

She'd been here before, on school trips and later, but could remember almost nothing about it. In the darkness everything was a confusing jumble of fallen stones and half-demolished rooms whose roofs had long since disappeared. She passed through what was left of the portico and found herself in a stark open courtyard, in the centre of which were the decaying remains of a pool surrounded by a low octagonal brick maze. Elena knew what it was. The boring, long-forgotten facts from one of those distant school excur-sions trickled back into her brain. This was Domitian's great peristyle, the courtyard he had had lined with slabs of highly polished marble to show the reflection of the assassin he expected, almost daily, to creep up on him unawares; a precaution which ultimately proved futile for he was stabbed to death in the portico just a few metres away.

Elena turned round slowly, squinting into the shadowy recesses, listening intently for any sound of movement. Something brushed against her leg and she almost screamed. Looking down, she saw the gleaming eyes of one of the mangy cats that roamed over the Palatine and the Forum. It hissed at her and slunk away into the gloom.

She stopped. She'd lost Scarfone. He could be anywhere in this vast impenetrable labyrinth. She listened again, trusting her ears more than her eyes. But all she heard was the wind blowing through the doorways and passages and the distant throb of the city traffic.

Then she saw him. A shape silhouetted against the skyline for just an instant before it merged once again with the shadows of the earth. He was fifty metres away, maybe less, heading west towards the Farnese Gardens which covered the ancient, partially excavated remains of Tiberius's palace. Elena padded quietly across the courtyard, stepping round the debris on the ground, and out through a gap in the wall. Scarfone was descending a flight of steps just in front of her. She went after him. At the bottom of the steps, stretching further than she could hope to see in the darkness, was a vaulted corridor as black and oppressive as a tunnel.

She hesitated, suddenly on edge. This was the Cryptoporticus, the long passage where Caligula was killed by an assassin's knife. It had an eerie, sinister atmosphere. Elena could feel her heart pounding, a prickle of fear on the back of her neck. She hardly dared enter the passage. It was pitch-dark inside, cool and silent like a mausoleum. She gritted her teeth, trying to shut out the sensations of terror and panic that threatened to overwhelm her. Putting a hand on the wall to steady herself, she stepped into the corridor and began to feel her way along it.

She could see nothing. There were windows high up in the walls on one side of the corridor but the dribbles of light which seeped in were too feeble to illuminate her path. Elena kept her fingers on the wall, feeling its surface pitted by almost two thousand years of decay. One of the bricks was loose. A chunk of it came away and she hung on to it, feeling safer with a weapon in her hand.

Every few feet she paused to listen. But she heard nothing. Scarfone was too far ahead of her. In the enclosed space, the darkness seemed to have a physical presence, as if it were a thick cloak enveloping her, choking the air out of her. She stopped, suddenly short of breath. Nothing had changed outside her. It was all in her mind. But she sensed it. Sensed something close by. Her mouth was like sandpaper, her pulse a throbbing hammer in her chest. Once again she felt the hairs on the back of her neck stand up. It was behind her. She spun round, flailing out with an arm to protect herself. There was nothing there.

She took a deep breath, trying to swallow but her throat was too dry. She turned back.

And walked right into him.

For a second she was paralysed, faint with shock. Then she tried to scream but his hand clamped itself tight over her mouth. He pulled her to him. Something hard and metallic pressed painfully against her temple.

'You're a very persistent woman, dottoressa,' Cesare Scarfone said softly in her ear. 'You know what this is, don't you?' He jabbed the muzzle of the pistol into her skin. 'Don't think I won't use it.'

Elena made a conscious effort to steady herself, to slow her heartbeat, to stop her legs trembling. She felt sick with terror.

'You're tougher than I thought,' Scarfone continued, his breath hissing against her hair. 'I misjudged you when I sent you those papers. I never thought you'd have the guts to confront your father. I underestimated you there. I thought you'd buckle and crack.'

Elena clenched her teeth. Scarfone's fingers were digging into the flesh around her mouth. The pain took her mind off her fear. She balled her fists, feeling the lump of brick in her right hand.

Scarfone leaned over so his lips were right by her ear. She got the impression he was smiling as he whispered: 'Tell me, how does it feel to kill your own father?'

Elena closed her eyes. The fury was so intense, so sudden, she could feel it boiling up from some white-hot core and surging out through her bloodstream. Her hand arched upwards, her biceps knotting as she smashed the brick into Scarfone's face. He screamed, his hand falling away from her mouth, the pistol dropping as he clutched at his shattered nose.

Elena ran. Back the way she'd come. Stumbling over the rough earth, scraping ankles and shins on the protruding stones, nearly falling in her desperate struggle to get away. An archway loomed up on her left. She flung herself through it. At that instant, she heard an explosion, the report of a gun. A sudden, searing pain lanced through her head and everything went black.

She became aware of the voices, the hands grasping her arms and lifting her into a sitting position before she found the strength to open her eyes. She blinked and turned away as the beam of the torch hit her full in the face.

She was too stunned to speak. She looked at the figures above her, only half registering their features. She could feel an intense, burning pain at the front of her head.

'He shot me,' she murmured, surprised to hear her own voice.

Agostini leaned over her. He shook his head. 'You knocked yourself out on the wall. You've got concussion, nothing worse.'

The relief seemed to revive her. She leaned forwards. 'Scarfone . . .'

'I'm sorry,' Agostini said. 'He got away.'

For just a moment after Chapman opened the door of his apartment they stood and gazed at each other.

Then Elena said: 'I don't know which of us looks worse.'

Chapman grinned. 'Or feels worse.'

He stepped back to let her enter. She noticed the broken lock on the door but didn't say anything. The apartment was the way she'd imagined it: light, not much furniture but what there was comfortable and stylish. A cool tiled floor, subtle colours and a clean, masculine feel.

He poured them both a glass of wine and sat down next to her on the settee.

'Your nose looks awful,' Elena said. 'All swollen and bruised. Does it hurt?'

'Not much,' Chapman said. 'The doctor gave me some painkillers.'

She smoothed his hair back from his forehead with her fingertips. He pulled her to him and kissed her. Elena held him. He touched the dressing on her temple.

'And you?'

'I'm okay,' she said. 'They wanted to detain me overnight in the hospital, but I couldn't face it.'

She curled up against him, pressing her face to his chest. She'd told him on the phone what had happened. It all felt a long time ago.

'I didn't know you carried a knife,' she said.

'Fortunately, they didn't either,' Chapman said.

Elena sipped some of her wine. 'Are you going to tell me what it was all about, or do I have to use telepathy?'

He shrugged. 'I had some medals, and a service dagger, belonging to a man called Domenico Salvitti.'

'Who's he?'

'He was Mussolini's aide-de-camp. Something of a hero in Fascist circles, even today.'

'And that's what Volpi was after? Medals?'

Chapman shook his head. 'They wanted some papers Salvitti had kept from the war.'

'Papers?' Elena twisted her head round, looking up

at him narrowly. 'Andy, these wouldn't be the same papers Vivaldi was given by the old man out at Castel Gandolfo, would they?'

The sudden, shrill noise of the telephone spared him from having to reply. He went out into the hall and picked up the receiver.

'For you,' he said, bringing the phone in. 'Inspector Agostini.'

She listened for a time then hung up.

'I gave him your number,' she said. 'You don't mind?'

'No.'

'The kid who was in Scarfone's car recovered consciousness. He's told the police that the bag he brought out of the house contained a gun, two passports and a large quantity of US dollars.'

'*Two* passports?'

Elena nodded. 'One false, of course. He's gone. The bastard has slipped through the net.' She hammered her fist on the arm of the sofa. 'A man of his resources. A private plane from some small airfield; he'll be out of the country by now.' She glanced away. 'People like Cesare Scarfone always win, don't they?'

'Yes,' Chapman agreed. 'And men like Archbishop Tomassi.'

Her eyes swung back to him. 'Tomassi?'

Chapman felt in his pocket and pulled out the creased black and white photograph. 'This is all they left me. Can you make anything of it?'

He handed her the photograph. Elena studied it.

'You know who the men with Mussolini are, where it was taken?' Chapman asked.

Elena pointed with a forefinger. 'That's Alessandro Pavolini, the secretary of the Fascist Party at the end of the war. And that's Nicola Bombacci, one of Mussolini's *gerarchi*. The others I don't know. More *gerarchi*, I suppose.'

'And the building? I think I've been there but I don't remember where it is.'

'I have too,' Elena said. 'I've been there several times. It's the *Prefettura* in Milan. The Palazzo Monforte.'

Chapman sat up abruptly. 'Christ, you're right.' He snatched the photograph back. 'This was taken very near the end. You know what, I think it was taken just before Mussolini fled from Milan to Como. It might even be the last picture that was ever taken of him alive.'

Chapman looked more closely at the photograph. He'd suddenly seen something he hadn't noticed before. He went through into his study and rummaged in his desk, returning with a magnifying glass which he placed over the photograph.

'You see that?'

He indicated one of the windows in the Palazzo Monforte. A man's head was visible through the pane. Elena peered at it.

'He's a priest.'

Chapman shook his head. He recognised the face from his research in the National Library. 'He's wearing a dog collar. But he's not a priest.'

He looked at his watch and stood up.

'Lake Como,' he said. 'We have to end this where it all started. The night train to Milan leaves in half an hour. If we hurry, we'll just catch it.'

*   *   *

They had a four-berth sleeping compartment to themselves. The beds were folded down from the wall and neatly made up but, despite their tiredness, neither Chapman nor Elena felt like sleep. It was stiflingly hot. Elena kicked off her shoes and undid the top buttons of her blouse. She leaned back on the wall at the foot of one of the berths and tucked her legs underneath her. Chapman sat at the opposite end. Outside, the hazy lights of the Roman suburbs flashed past the window as the train headed north.

'It's a myth that at the end of the war thousands of Nazis escaped to South America by U-Boat,' Chapman said. 'How many U-Boats did the Germans have in operation in 1945? Nothing like enough to transport all the war criminals who managed to escape. We've all heard of organisations like Odessa and Die Spinne, but the biggest smuggler of wanted Nazis was the Vatican.

'It's well documented. The Holy See had a comprehensive network of ratlines for spiriting former Nazis out of Europe. They weren't all war criminals, of course, but the Vatican wasn't too choosy about whom they helped. They weren't all Germans either. Some of the most notorious war criminals were from Eastern Europe; Hungarians, Rumanians, Slavs.'

Elena nodded. 'That's been common knowledge in Italy for a long time. I've never understood why they did it though.'

'That's a difficult question to answer. One of the best guesses is fear of Communism. They weren't alone. The British and the Americans were pretty ambivalent about many Nazis. Oh, they rounded up the leaders for the trials at Nuremberg, but they turned a blind eye to some of the smaller fry escaping. They even recruited quite a few of them to send back into Eastern Europe as spies. By 1945 the threat to the West was no longer Hitler, it was Stalin.

'The Catholic Church is terrified of Communism. That's why they helped fleeing Nazis. They could convince themselves they were helping the enemies of Communism. Many of them were brought to Rome and hidden in church properties around the city; some even in the Pope's summer palace at Castel Gandolfo. It's been established for years by some very author-itative research. But real hard facts are difficult to come by. Names to go with the rumours; documentation to back up the allegations. For a time I had proof in my hands, but that's gone now.'

Elena kept her eyes on Chapman's face. 'The man in the photograph, dressed as a priest. Who was he?'

'Ante Pavelić.'

'Jesus Christ!' She was staring at him, aghast. 'The Croatian dictator? You're saying the Vatican helped him escape, a butcher like that?'

'He disappeared from Croatia in April 1945 and later surfaced in Argentina. He survived an assassination attempt in the late fifties, fled to Paraguay and died in Spain in 1959. No one knows exactly how he managed to evade capture and get out of Europe, but the Vatican undoubtedly helped him.'

'That's what the papers were about, isn't it?'

Chapman nodded. 'Pavelić was a devout Catholic, a protected son of the Church. In March 1945, he wrote to Mussolini at Gargnano asking for his assistance in escaping from Croatia. By then, the Nazis and their puppet dictators could see the writing on the wall. They knew they didn't have long before the Allies,

and the Red Army in particular, were knocking on
their doors.

'Mussolini, in turn, wrote to the Vatican to see if
they would help and received a cordial reply from the
Under-Secretary of State, one Giovanni Montini. And
you know who Giovanni Montini became.'

'Pope Paul VI,' Elena said.

'Exactly. This went right to the heart of the Catholic
hierarchy. Pope Pius himself approved the arrangements; I've seen the internal memo. They agreed to
provide Pavelić with a Red Cross passport which, in
postwar Italy, gave the holder the freedom to move
about the country without hindrance. It was, effec-
tively, a clean bill of health.'

'The papers you had,' Elena said, 'they were unequivo-
cal proof of those arrangements?'

'Yes.'

Chapman stood up and went to the window of the
compartment. They'd left the suburbs of the city now
and were out in the open countryside. He let the
slipstream of the train blow through his hair for a
moment, then pulled down the blind and turned back
to Elena. He couldn't keep the anger, the bitterness,
out of his voice.

'I had them in my hand. All the proof I needed. Something the Vatican, for all their deviousness, couldn't
deny.'

His shoulders slumped. The anger subsided, resignation taking its place.

'I was a fool to think I would ever be able to take
them on and win. They've had two thousand years
of practice at concealment and intrigue. Their sordid
secret is dead and buried now.'

'Are you saying the neo-Fascists are in league with the Vatican?' Elena said. 'That they took those papers from you to protect the reputation of the Catholic Church?'

'No. The Vatican wanted the papers. The neo-Fascists wanted something else.'

He sat down on the bed again and stretched out his legs. Elena touched his calf with her fingers in a small gesture of intimacy. Chapman smiled at her. Through the opening in her blouse he could see the white lace trim of her bra.

'Let me tell you what happened the day Antonio Vivaldi died,' he said.

He'd pieced it all together now. Some of it he knew for certain, other parts were based on informed guesswork. But it had a plausibility to it that made him sure he was right.

On that day, 12th June, Vivaldi had gone out to the Clinico Santo Stefano in the morning to visit the badly injured Roberto Ferrero. Ferrero, or Domenico Salvitti to use his real name, was a dying man who, like most people who know the end is near, had a desire to get things off his chest. No one would ever know exactly what passed between them, but Salvitti told Vivaldi of some papers he had in his house and wanted the priest to have. Vivaldi went out to Castel Gandolfo and collected the papers from a leather document pouch embossed with the emblem of Mussolini's Republic of Salò. They were some of the Duce's personal correspondence from the final months of the war and highly embarrassing to the Vatican.

Vivaldi copied the papers and arranged to go to the

Vatican in the afternoon to see Archbishop Tomassi. On the way, he stopped off at his mistress's apartment and left the originals with her for safekeeping.

'His mistress!' Elena exclaimed. 'Vivaldi had a mistress?'

'A male weakness, I'm afraid, even for priests,' Chapman said. 'She kept the documents and later, after Vivaldi died, sent them to Enzo Mattei whose widow passed them on to me. At the Vatican, Vivaldi showed the papers to Tomassi. They were hard to read, but they clearly dealt with some kind of murky deal between the Holy See and Mussolini, something that the Vatican would have been anxious to keep secret. Vivaldi went back to his apartment and later that night a bunch of neo-Fascists came round, tied him up and tortured him so savagely that his heart stopped.'

'They knew he had these papers?' Elena said. 'How?'

'You can work that one out. Ivan Simčić told them. You saw him on the platform at Ostia Antica. He's a neo-Fascist sympathiser; that's not uncommon in the Catholic Church. And, in addition, from his name, I'll wager he's Croatian, like Pavelić and the *Ustashe*.'

'Why would the neo-Fascists want the papers? Just because they belonged to Mussolini?'

Chapman shook his head. 'The papers were irrelevant to them. What they wanted to know was where Vivaldi had obtained them, and from whom. That's why they tortured him. They knew Domenico Salvitti had had them at the end of the war but they didn't know what had become of him after that. And Salvitti was the key to the neo-Fascists' real objective.' Chapman paused. 'You see, the Vatican's decision to help Pavelić escape wasn't a purely ideological one. They had financial reasons for aiding him too. Pavelić was going to pay them.'

'Pay them?'

'In gold. The letter from Mussolini to Montini mentions the amount. Twenty million dollars' worth. At today's prices that would be about a hundred million dollars.'

'*Dio*,' Elena breathed.

'And remember where it came from. It was *Ustashe* gold. Some of it was looted but a lot of it, like the Nazis' gold, came from the victims of their genocide: jewellery, watches, coins, even the fillings from the teeth of murdered Jews, Gypsies and Serbs. You see now why the Vatican is so keen to keep it under wraps.'

'They actually took the gold?' Elena said in disbelief.

'Oh yes. Well, half of it. Mussolini kept the rest. That was the deal.'

'And where's that gold now?'

'That's what the neo-Fascists would dearly like to know.'

TWENTY-FOUR

They slept fitfully together in the same berth, cupped against each other like a pair of spoons. Elena woke early and slipped out from Chapman's arms. She was restless, troubled. She crossed the compartment and sat on one of the other bunks, a blanket wrapped around her bare shoulders. Lifting the corner of the blind, she peered out into the night. The sky was already growing lighter. The horizon was smeared with traces of silvery grey and, on the broad plain that stretched away into the distance beside the railway track, she could see the tiny indistinct outlines of farm buildings dotting the landscape like smudges of charcoal.

Chapman opened his eyes and squinted at her drowsily. 'What are you doing?'

'I couldn't sleep. I've too much on my mind.'

'Come back to bed.'

'I'll only disturb you.'

'What is it? Scarfone? Your father?'

'Everything. I can't relax enough to sleep.'

'Come here.' Chapman stretched out his arms. 'Come on.'

Elena went back to the berth and slid in under the sheet next to him. She felt his body warm against her back. His hands came round and held her breasts. He stroked the skin gently, his lips caressing the nape of her neck. His fingers brushed her nipples. Elena shifted languidly then pressed her buttocks back into his groin. She could feel him returning the pressure.

'I know this is a cliché,' he murmured, 'but you know what you need?'

Elena laughed softly. 'You're just a typical man.'

'I hoped you'd notice.'

He kissed her shoulder, his hands moving down over her stomach. Elena twisted her head round and found his lips. Then she rolled over on to her back.

'I hate to admit it,' she said, 'but I think you might be right.'

'You ever done it on a train?'

'I've led a very sheltered life.'

'It's the only way to travel. What would you like, a single or a return?'

Elena pulled him down. 'Well, as you're asking, I think I might go for a season ticket.'

After coffee and rolls in a cafe near the railway station in Milan, they hired a car and drove north out of the city. They took the road along the eastern shore of Lake Como and climbed up into the hills above Bellagio to a village perched on the side of a steep mountain ravine. There was a cafe in the small village square with tables outside filled with tourists who'd been bussed up to enjoy the view over the water.

Chapman and Elena went inside and asked the proprietor if there was anyone in the area named Ferrero. This was the home village inscribed on the Royal Army identity disc Chapman was carrying in his pocket. The names of Roberto Ferrero's mother and father were also on the disc but they would be long dead now. All he could hope for was that someone remembered them.

The proprietor couldn't help, but he referred them to an elderly lady who was sitting out under the awning, drinking coffee with two friends. She remembered the Ferreros and their son, Roberto.

'But he was killed in the war,' she said. 'They had a daughter too, Manuela. She married a man called Brembilla. Ettore Brembilla. He ran a grocery shop in Bellagio but he retired a few years ago.'

'And Manuela, is she still alive?'

'The last I heard.'

It took Chapman and Elena a while, and several different inquiries, to track down Manuela Brembilla to a small stone house at the top of a steep street on the outskirts of Bellagio. She was hanging out the washing in the garden which climbed up the hillside behind the house in a series of terraces, most of them given over to the cultivation of fruit and vegetables. On the top terrace were the remains of a strange stone construction with small apertures all over the sides. It looked as though it had originally been a short, stubby tower of some sort which had been sliced in half vertically and never rebuilt.

Chapman introduced himself and Elena and explained why they were there. Signora Brembilla looked at them curiously, then shrugged and took them into her kitchen. She must have been in her seventies but she seemed anything but frail; one of those tough peasant women who looked ancient in their fifties but never appeared to age much after that.

Chapman showed her the identity disc and she pulled out a pair of thick reading glasses to study it.

'I found it in a collector's shop,' Chapman explained.

Manuela nodded, accepting the story without question.

'It was never returned to us,' she said. 'We never expected it, of course. Roberto was with the partisans. They didn't carry identification.'

'When was he killed?'

'Right near the end. The war was over really.' She sat down at the table. 'That's the worst of it. For him to survive all that time and then be killed in the last few days. My parents took it very badly. He was their only son.'

'It must have been a blow to you all,' Elena said sympathetically.

'It was. I was fifteen when he was conscripted, nearly twenty when he died. We hardly saw him in all that time. You expected bad news in those days. But when one of his partisan friends arrived to tell us he was dead we didn't believe it. My mother was never the same again.'

'Do you know where and how he was killed?' Chapman asked.

'My husband can tell you that better than I can. He was with Roberto when he died.'

'Your husband?'

Manuela smiled. 'The friend who brought us the news. He stayed for a few days and, well, things happened. He'll be home soon for lunch. He still helps out in the shop, though he's supposed to have handed it over to our son. Men, you know, they find it hard to let things go.'

'Do you mind if we wait for him?'

Manuela shook her head. 'You can sit in the garden.'

She came out with them and pulled up a lettuce and some radishes from the vegetable patch.

Chapman pointed at the ruined tower. 'I'm intrigued by that building, signora. What was it?'

'That? Oh, that was our pigeon loft. We used to breed them to sell in the shop. It fell down back in 1990. An earth tremor, you know. It shook the whole area.'

'Are you going to rebuild it?'

'It's not worth the expense now. Anyway, the birds were a lot of work. And noisy too.'

She moved along the border, lifting carrots and putting them in a woven osier basket she had slung over one sturdy arm.

'Where I come from in England they breed pigeons,' Chapman said. 'Racing pigeons.'

Manuela looked at him, her brow furrowing. 'Racing?' she said, as if she'd misheard. 'Not for eating?'

'No.'

She considered the idea for a moment, then shrugged and shook the soil off another bunch of carrots. She had the countrywoman's practical nature, her dispassionate view of wildlife as either vermin or ingredients for the pot. The concept of breeding racing pigeons was as incomprehensible to her as breeding racing cows or sheep.

There was a slatted wooden bench at one side of the lowest terrace. Chapman and Elena sat on it looking out over the red roofs of Bellagio. A steamer was just arriving at the waterfront pier, disgorging its cargo of tourists and sightseers. It was a cloudless day, clear enough to see far down the lake. Chapman watched the cars winding their way along the road on the western shore, the same road that Mussolini had taken on his last, fateful journey.

It was gone noon when Ettore Brembilla came home. He was a sprightly old boy in a white shirt and wide-brimmed straw hat, his face brown and wrinkled like a well-used boot. He walked into the garden with a spring in his step, barely out of breath from the long pull up the hill. Manuela introduced Elena and Chapman, adding: 'They've been asking about Roberto.'

Ettore looked at them sharply. 'Have they?' He pulled off his hat and fanned himself with it.

'I said you could tell them what happened better than me.'

'Why do you want to know? Roberto died more than fifty years ago.'

'I found this identity disc in a shop in Rome,' Chapman said. 'A war memorabilia shop. I was interested to know more about him, that's all.'

Ettore took the disc from him. 'Come into the house.'

They went into the kitchen and sat down at the table. Ettore examined the identity tag.

'Yes, it's Roberto's,' he said. He lifted his head, his eyes moving shrewdly from Chapman to Elena and back. 'But you didn't find it in a shop, did you?'

Chapman hesitated. 'No,' he admitted.

'Why lie about it?' There was an edge to his voice that hinted at an underlying toughness. Chapman reminded himself that this apparently affable old fellow had once been a partisan, a special breed of man who had seen and survived privations that were beyond Chapman's understanding.

'I'm sorry. I wanted to keep it simple,' Chapman said.

He explained about the death of the old man from Castel Gandolfo. How he'd found the disc in the old man's house. 'He called himself Roberto Ferrero. But I know that wasn't his real name.'

Ettore stood up and went to the sink. He filled himself a glass of water and drank it, staring out of the window into the garden.

'So he took it?' he said without turning round. 'And now he's dead.'

'I don't understand,' Chapman said.

'Roberto carried it with him. I saw it a few times. It was against the rules, but Roberto wasn't much of a one for rules. He had it with him when he died. We never recovered his body. It was in the bottom of a deep ravine, burnt to a cinder.'

'Burnt?'

Ettore nodded and came back to the table. His wife went to the stove and busied herself preparing the pasta for their lunch.

'He was killed on the other side of Lake Como,' Ettore said. 'There's a road above Argegno that goes up into the hills and down into Switzerland. Or it's a road now. Back then it was just a dirt track. Roberto and I had been up at the border, persuading the *Guardia di Finanza* to come over to the partisans. We were on our way back down – Roberto was going home to see his parents – when we encountered a lorry blocking the track.

'There was a man by the cab. He opened fire on us with a machine-gun. Roberto was killed outright. I took off down the mountainside. He tried to kill me too. I fell and knocked myself out on a boulder. When I came round, the man and the lorry had gone. So had our car and Roberto's body. He'd put Roberto inside the car and pushed it over the edge. I climbed down later and got within fifty metres of the wreckage. It was too dangerous to go nearer. The car had exploded. Everything had been incinerated.'

'This man, do you know who he was?'

'A Fascist, that's all I know. The mountains were full of them at that time. Rats deserting a sinking ship. He was probably on the run, trying to cross over to Switzerland. He obviously survived or you wouldn't have found the ID tag,' he added bitterly. 'I suppose I should ask who he was, but I don't really want to know. I'd rather forget all about it.'

'Could you show us on a map where he attacked you?' Chapman said.

'It was a long time ago. There was a small lake just below the track, that's all I remember. I haven't been back since.'

Chapman fingered the disc, feeling the raised letters on it.

'This should be with his family,' he said, offering it to Manuela.

The old woman glanced at her husband. Ettore shook his head.

'We don't want it,' he said. 'Give it to Roberto's son.'

Chapman stared at him. 'He has a son?'

*   *   *

457

The farm was in the lowlands to the west of Como, a patchwork quilt of tiny fields spreading out from a dilapidated stone house. A big man in a soiled cotton vest and stained trousers was in the yard tinkering with the engine of his tractor when Chapman and Elena drove in through the gates. He looked them up and down as they climbed out of the car, taking in their clothes, their soft city appearance.

'Signor Mancini?' Chapman said.

'Yes.'

'Have you a minute? We'd like to talk to you about Roberto Ferrero.'

Mancini started. He stared at them, then his heavy shoulders slumped and he gave a resigned nod. He wiped the oil off his hands with a rag and went into the house. Chapman and Elena followed him into the cool of the large, stone-flagged kitchen. Mancini was washing his hands at the sink.

'I wondered when you'd come,' he said, slumping down on to a chair and passing a hand over his face. 'You're from Rome? Police?'

'*Pubblico ministero*,' Elena said.

Mancini nodded. His powerful frame seemed to have crumpled in the few minutes since Chapman and Elena had arrived.

'It was an accident,' he said. 'I didn't mean to do it.'

Chapman glanced at Elena. She gave a slight shake of the head. They let the farmer continue without interruption.

'He provoked me,' he said. 'Goaded me. I lost control, picked up the poker . . .' His voice petered out. 'I suppose I'll go to jail, won't I?'

'You'd better tell us the whole story,' Elena said. 'We've already spoken to Ettore Brembilla.'

'Yes, I went to see him back in the spring. That was after my mother died. Her name, before she married, was Michaela Rocca. She came from a village in Piedmont, in the mountains. During the war she had an affair with a partisan called Roberto Ferrero. She only told me this at the end. The man she married, Guglielmo Mancini, wasn't my real father. Roberto Ferrero was my father. She'd kept it a secret from me, but she wanted me to know before she died. She said she knew my father had been killed at the end of the war. A friend of his, that was Ettore Brembilla, had told her, but she'd lost touch with him soon after.

'I was curious. All my life I'd thought one man was my father, then I find out he wasn't. Guglielmo Mancini adopted me when he married my mother. Then he inherited this farm from a cousin and we moved away from Piedmont. He was a good man. He treated me like a son. When he died eight years ago I took over the farm.'

Mancini leaned back in his chair, absorbed in his own story. 'My mother's death shattered all my beliefs about who I was. Suddenly I had a father I'd never known. I wanted to find out more about him. Who he was, what he was like. So I went to Como and hired a private investigator to make some inquiries for me. He traced Ettore Brembilla and I went to see him. That seemed to be the end of my quest. My father was long dead. But the private investigator found another Roberto Ferrero in the Ministry of Defence files. A Roberto Ferrero with the same war record as my father who was still alive and drawing a war pension. I went to see this man.'

He lifted his head. 'I wish I hadn't now. He was a vile old man. Rich, arrogant. He took me for a simpleton, an ignorant peasant from the country. I challenged him about his identity, the pension he'd been receiving in my father's name, and he lost his temper. He began shouting at me, insulting me. He boasted about his Fascist past, admitted he'd killed my father and taken his identity disc. He called my father a Communist fool and other things. Terrible things. I lost my temper too and picked up the poker by the fireplace . . . I just wanted to threaten him, to shut him up.'

Mancini put his hands over his face, shaking his head. 'I didn't mean to,' he repeated. 'Sometimes I don't know my own strength.'

He looked at Elena. 'What will happen to me? Are you going to take me into custody?'

Elena shook her head, forgetting for a moment that she was a magistrate. 'This is an unofficial visit. Someone else will be dealing with the case. Nothing will happen for the time being.'

'And then?'

'I don't know. It won't be up to me. If you don't hear from us again, you can assume that no charges will be brought.'

Chapman took the identity disc out of his pocket and handed it to Mancini. 'This was your father's. I think you should have it now.'

Mancini lifted the disc to his face and studied it intently. Then he clasped it tightly in his fingers, the sole, precious legacy of a father he'd never known.

Driving away down the track from the farm, Chapman said to Elena: 'You're not going to press charges against him?'

She shrugged. 'Domenico Salvitti was no loss to the world. He killed that poor man's father. Why should I destroy his life too?'

'I thought you did everything by the book?'

'I'm learning,' Elena said.

They were surrounded by mountains. Not the real high peaks of the Alpine ranges further north, but lower, more rounded hills, their slopes covered with coarse grass and herds of grazing goats. The sun was dipping behind their summits, throwing the west side of the valleys into deep shadow. Chapman and Elena stood on the roadside beside their parked car and looked down the incline at a small, dark blue lake which filled a basin in the hillside.

'That must be the one,' Elena said. 'There are no others marked on the map.'

Chapman did a slow three-hundred-and-sixty-degree turn, surveying the surrounding countryside, trying to imagine what it had been like on that April day more than half a century ago, trying to envisage what had happened: the lorry blocking the dirt track, Roberto Ferrero and his friend Ettore Brembilla coming down the hill from the frontier, Domenico Salvitti waiting for them with a gun. It was so peaceful now, so tame. The occasional vehicle coming past, the distant tinkle of goat bells on the crags. It was hard to believe that a man had died here in one of the final, brief skirmishes of a war which had ravaged a continent.

They scrambled down the steep, rocky slope to the

shore of the lake. It was little more than twenty metres across, deep and impenetrable. Chapman dipped his hand in. It was ice-cold.

Behind the lake was a sheer wall of rock, riven in two by a massive vertical fissure, and to one side were the remains of what looked like a cave. The roof had collapsed, blocking the entrance with fallen boulders.

'What are you looking for?' Elena said.

'A hiding place.'

'You think Salvitti had the gold?'

'I'm certain of it. Mussolini entrusted him with his personal papers. Who better to look after the gold? Salvitti was one of the few people he trusted. Perhaps the only person he trusted. He wasn't a threat to him. He wasn't a rival like all the other Fascist *gerarchi*. If anyone was given the job of transporting the gold, it would have been Salvitti.'

'And you think he hid it here?'

'I'm guessing. Why was he on this road with a truck when Mussolini and the others stayed down by Lake Como? He wouldn't have risked trying to cross into Switzerland with a lorry full of *Ustashe* gold. So what happened to it if Salvitti didn't hide it?'

'Even if he did, surely he would have come back and removed it after the war?' Elena said.

'Oh, he did. What do you think paid for his villa out at Castel Gandolfo? Salvitti was a clever man, but cautious. He would have lain low after the war. He was Mussolini's aide-de-camp, a wanted man living under an assumed identity. He wouldn't have wanted to draw attention to himself by living too ostentatiously. And trying to dispose of that quantity of gold in one go would surely have aroused suspicion.'

'So what did he do?'

'His housekeeper said he came north once a year, to Milan and Switzerland. I reckon he disposed of the gold in stages. Digging it up – it must be buried, it's the safest thing to do – and taking a small quantity of it to Switzerland to sell.'

'It's been fifty years, Andy. There'll be nothing left by now.'

Chapman ran his eyes over the rock wall. 'The housekeeper said he stopped going north about seven or eight years ago. About the time the earth tremor destroyed the Brembillas' pigeon loft. How old do you reckon that fault line is, or the rockfall that blocked that cave?'

Chapman clambered around the edge of the lake, picking his way over the stones and the boulders that littered the shore. When he reached the rock wall the going became more hazardous, but there was a tiny ledge along the base for his feet and enough handholds for him to traverse round to the vertical fissure. He reached back and helped Elena after him.

The fissure had broken the wall in two from top to bottom. It was jammed with fallen boulders and loose rubble. Chapman climbed into the mouth and began to remove the rocks, dragging them out and letting them tumble down into the lake. After twenty minutes' hard, bruising labour, he'd opened up a passage wide enough for them to squeeze through. A few metres in, the crack widened out into a gloomy chamber, lit from the side and above by slivers of sunlight leaking in through gaps in the rock. The floor of the chamber had been split by the same violent earth movement that had caused the fault line in the cliff outside. It fell away into a deep crevasse whose bottom was invisible in the darkness. Chapman pulled Elena back.

'Careful, it might give way.'

He lay down on the ground and eased his way cautiously to the edge of the precipice. Looking down, he could see the splintered end of a wooden box protruding out into space, and below that, on a narrow ledge, a number of objects which glinted dully in the dim light. It took him a few seconds to realise what they were – gold ingots.

'Take a look at this,' he said.

Elena crawled up beside him. He heard the sharp intake of her breath.

'*Dio*, so it's still here.'

'I'm very glad to hear it,' a voice said behind them.

Chapman twisted on to his side and saw Cesare Scarfone coming through the opening in the fissure, a pistol in his hand.

'You seem surprised,' Scarfone said drily.

Chapman and Elena slithered backwards and stood up. Scarfone clambered into the chamber and leaned casually on the rock wall.

'You made the mistake of showing the identity disc to Luca Bracciolini,' he said. 'He has a very good memory.'

'Where did you pick us up? Bellagio?' Chapman said.

Scarfone didn't reply. He moved to the edge of the crevasse and craned his neck over the side.

'So Salvitti had it all along,' he said.

'There's almost none of it left,' Elena said.

'Enough for me.' He looked at Chapman. 'Climb down and bring it up.'

'You can go to hell,' Chapman said.

Scarfone pointed his pistol at Elena. 'I will count to three, and then put a bullet through her head. One, two . . .'

'Okay.' Chapman raised a hand. 'But I'll need a rope.'

'You see one anywhere?'

'That edge could collapse at any time.'

'Then you'll be buried in a golden grave, won't you?' Scarfone said.

Chapman glared at him, knowing he had no choice. Then he took a few paces to the crevasse and lay down on his stomach, lowering himself over the edge. A few crumbs of soil broke away and tumbled down into the void. Chapman felt for a foothold in the wall below him. The first few metres were earth not rock, but that made it all the more precarious. He dug the toe of his shoe in and took his weight on it. The soil collapsed and he slid down a few centimetres, coming to a halt only by digging his fingers in and hugging the wall so the friction between his body and the earth slowed his descent. He twisted his neck upwards to look at Scarfone, his heart thumping.

'It won't hold me,' he said.

'Try.'

'You want the gold, you'll have to lower me down. That's the only way you'll get it.'

Scarfone gestured at Elena to move back into the

depths of the chamber. Then he knelt down by the edge.

'Give me your hand.'

Chapman hesitated.

'Your hand!'

Chapman reached up. Scarfone grasped his hand. For an instant Chapman was suspended in space. Scarfone only had to let go and he would tumble down into the abyss. But the grip held. Scarfone took his weight and leaned out, slowly lowering Chapman down on to the ledge. Chapman tested it beneath his feet. It seemed solid enough. Scarfone let go.

'The gold, pass it up to me,' he said.

Chapman bent down and grasped one of the ingots. He was surprised how heavy it was. He needed two hands to lift it above his head and transfer it to Scarfone who hauled it up over the edge and leaned back on his haunches, gazing down avariciously at the gold.

'I never thought I'd hold one of these in my hands. I wonder if the Duce touched it.' He ran a finger over the surface of the ingot as if he might feel Mussolini's own mark in the metal.

Elena took a step towards him. Scarfone picked up his pistol and waved her back.

'Stay away.'

'Is that why all these people have died?' Elena said. 'For a few measly bars of yellow metal. What use is it to you?'

'You wouldn't understand,' Scarfone sneered. 'It's people like you who've brought this country to its knees. Removed its backbone, filled it with parasites, Jews, Arabs, queers. People have had enough of weak government. They want strong leadership like the Duce gave them.'

'That's what *you* want, you mean. Not the people. The people remember Mussolini. They don't want another, even a pathetic, feeble imitation like you.'

Scarfone stood up and went for her furiously, slapping her with the back of his hand so hard that she fell to the ground.

'You bitch,' he said, looking down at her, panting heavily. His nose and mouth were bruised and swollen from where Elena had hit him on the Palatine.

'The time will come, you'll see. I have more support that you can imagine. Where do you think all that cash came from you found on Boneschi? From companies, from businessmen, individuals who share my vision. Men who are just waiting for the moment when they can come out and openly back me.'

'You're a dreamer, Scarfone. And a wanted fugitive. You're finished in Italy.'

'I can organise it from outside. I have the gold now.'

'That won't get you very far.'

'It's symbolic. That's why it's important. This was the Duce's gold. To my supporters, it's priceless.'

'You're mad.' But as Elena said it she knew she was wrong. What made Scarfone dangerous was the fact that he was all too sane.

Scarfone went back to the edge and looked down at Chapman. 'Now the others.'

Chapman passed up the remaining ingots. There were eight in total.

'Check inside the box,' Scarfone ordered.

Chapman squatted down and peered into the broken

end of the wooden box half buried in the wall of the crevasse. There were four more ingots inside which hadn't spilled out on to the ledge. He handed them up, one after the other.

Elena watched, her heart in her throat, choking with anxiety. She knew that as soon as the gold was all up, Scarfone would kill them. She waited, watching for her moment. Chapman lifted the final ingot. Scarfone leaned down and grasped the end of it in both hands. His pistol was on the ground next to him. As Scarfone took the weight of the gold, Chapman tugged down on the ingot, forcing him off balance. Scarfone swore and tried to steady himself, his attention momentarily diverted. Elena made her move.

She sprang across the chamber. One of her feet kicked out, sending Scarfone's pistol flying into the crevasse. He spun round, attempting to stand up as Elena hurled herself on to him, her fingers gouging at his eyes. He lashed out. They both tumbled sideways and as they landed, the edge gave way. Elena screamed. Scarfone rolled over the lip. His hand clawed at her arm. The sleeve of her blouse tore off and he disappeared over the edge. Elena clung on to the top, feeling the soil moving beneath her. She twisted round and looked down. Scarfone had landed on the ledge next to Chapman. The ledge started to crack, pieces of it breaking away. Scarfone's legs slipped and he jolted downwards.

'My leg. Grab it, Andy,' Elena yelled.

Chapman reached up and took hold of her right leg. Elena dug her left leg and fingers into the earth, feeling his weight dragging her down. He pulled himself up. The ledge below him disintegrated. Elena saw Scarfone's face contort and then he was gone, his final cry of terror echoing around the roof of the chamber.

Chapman found a handhold in the loose soil and let go of Elena's leg. She pulled herself up and over the edge on to the solid floor of the cave, then reached back down to help Chapman. He gripped her hand and slowly climbed the last few feet to the top. They rolled over and lay on their backs, panting for breath. It was a long while before either of them had the strength to move. Then Chapman reached out and pulled Elena to him, holding her tight.

'Thank you,' he said.

They held each other without speaking. The light was fading fast but there was enough for them to see the neat stack of gold ingots on the other side of the chamber.

'What do we do with them?' Chapman said finally. 'There must be a million dollars' worth there. We could keep them. We could hand them in.'

'You know what we have to do,' Elena said.

They helped each other up and went to the stack. Elena bent down and picked up one of the ingots. Chapman lifted another. They looked at each other, then hurled the ingots, one by one, over the edge of the crevasse.

It was almost dark when they squeezed back out of the cave. They squatted down and dipped their hands into the icy waters of the lake as if to wash away the taint of the gold. Then they clambered round along the shore.

Chapman put his arm around Elena, looking out over the valley. She buried her head in his chest and held him. The sky to the west was streaked with slashes of vivid orange. Elena shuddered.

'It's over,' Chapman said.

She tilted her head back to look at him. 'And what now?'

He knew she was talking about them. He thought of everything that had happened. And he thought of the job offer in his desk which he still didn't know whether to accept or decline. All he was aware of was her body pressed against him, the smell of her hair and the wind gusting up the hillside.

'I don't know,' he said. 'You?'

'I don't know either. There are so many things to do, so many loose ends to tie up. Scarfone's death, the Vivaldi case, my father's funeral. I don't even want to begin to think about them all.'

'Let's give it time,' Chapman said. 'See what happens.'

She reached up and kissed him. Then, hand in hand, they scrambled up the track to the road and drove away down the mountain.

Shadow Chasers

ACKNOWLEDGEMENT

I would like to thank the staff of UCLAF for their help in the research for this book.

ONE

Bay of Naples, Italy

The mist hung like drifting smoke over the surface of the water. It was a moonless night, the sky smothered with a dense blanket of low cloud. In the near distance, the lights of Prócida and Ischia burned tiny holes in the darkness and further away, almost due east, a hazy orange glow marked the position of Naples, the aura spreading upwards, dissipating gradually over the shadowy slopes of Mount Vesuvius.

Rob Sullivan stepped out on to the deck of the *Guardia di Finanza* patrol boat. After the warmth of the bridge, the cold sea air momentarily took his breath away. He zipped up his jacket and leant on the port rail next to Stig Enqvist, feeling the hull beneath his feet rocking gently in the swell.

Enqvist shivered and took a drag on his cigarette. 'I didn't think it got this cold down here.'

'Go back inside.'

'It's too stuffy in there. Any sign yet?'

Sullivan shook his head. He peered out into the night, looking for shapes on the water, listening for a sound through the swirling fog though he knew the radar would pick up any movement long before he did.

'You want some *grappa*?'

Enqvist held out a large silver hip flask filled with cheap Italian brandy. Sullivan took a sip and let the liquid slip down slowly, searing his insides. He passed the flask back and Enqvist took a long gulp.

'That volcano gives me the creeps,' Stig said. 'You can feel its presence, can't you? Brooding, menacing. Can you imagine living next to it, wondering when it's going to blow next?'

He swallowed another mouthful of *grappa*.

'Go easy, Stig,' Sullivan said.

'I'm okay,' Enqvist replied, but he slid the flask away into the pocket of his coat.

Sullivan looked at the faint clusters of lights along the curve of the shoreline. The Bay was famous for its beauty, its glorious sunsets, but Enqvist was right, there was something unnerving about it. Not only the threatening bulk of Vesuvius, but the peninsula to the west of the city, the Phlegraean Fields, off which they were anchored, was a throbbing mass of volcanic activity. The whole area was rising and sinking imperceptibly, a fragile crust of rock floating on a subterranean chamber of white hot magma. It was littered with pools of boiling mud and fumaroles belching gas which drifted on the wind to add a hint of sulphur to the salt tang of the ocean.

'You think they're coming?' Enqvist asked.

2

Sullivan shrugged. 'The tip-off was good.'

'How do you know, unless it pays off?'

'Casagrande's sure. He knows what he's doing.'

Sullivan glanced round at the bridge. The *Guardia* major's profile was visible through the side window, the sharp lines of his nose and jaw softened by the reflected glow from the lights on the control panel below him. He looked relaxed, confident, like the rest of the team of Gico commandos who were waiting patiently in the longroom just aft of the bridge. An elite squad from the *Gruppo investigazione sulla criminalità organizzata*, they were slouched on wooden benches in combat fatigues, smoking or talking quietly in the dialects of Lombardy and Piedmont – northerners to the man, chosen specially to be untouched by the slippery tentacles of the Camorra, Mafia or 'Ndrangheta.

The door to the bridge opened and Casagrande leaned out.

'We have something,' he said quietly in English.

Sullivan and Enqvist pushed themselves away from the rail and went back inside. Tendrils of acrid cigarette smoke curled through from the longroom, adding to the close, oppressive atmosphere on the bridge. The captain and first officer were in shirt-sleeves, leaning over the shoulder of a colleague who was seated in front of a luminous green screen dotted with pinpricks of light. They moved aside as Casagrande brought Sullivan and Enqvist forward.

'Just there,' the major said, his fingertip hovering over two pulsing specks.

3

'How do you know it's them?' Sullivan asked.

'The speed. Most of the traffic out there at this time of night is fishing vessels, the occasional cargo ship. Cruising speed maybe twelve, fifteen knots. These two are going closer to forty.'

'How far away?'

'Inside territorial waters. Fifteen minutes and they'll be here.' Casagrande pulled a wry face. 'The waiting is over, *signori*.'

The Gico commandos were crouched in the bottoms of two inflatable rubber dinghies tied to the starboard rail of the patrol boat. The men were silent now, tense and watchful, their sub-machine-guns braced across their chests as the dinghies dipped and rolled with each lap of the waves.

Sullivan could see them through the window of the bridge. Vague outlines in the blackness. Casagrande was sitting in the stern of the leading dinghy, his left hand cupped around the throttle of the idling outboard motor. It was darker now. The deck and cabin lights had been extinguished, leaving only the ghostly green sheen of the radar screen to illuminate the faces of the men gathered around it. The two glowing dots were moving gradually closer.

'They have radar, don't they?' Enqvist asked.

The captain nodded. 'On those boats they have everything.'

'So they can see us too.'

'Not here, anchored among the rocks. We're completely invisible.'

4

'Range, half a mile,' the radar operator said softly.

The first officer clicked on the radio and relayed the information to Casagrande. Enqvist threw an anxious glance at the captain.

'Don't they monitor the radio frequencies?' he said.

'You bet they do. That's why we have a scrambler.' The captain smiled reassuringly. 'Relax, Mr Enqvist. This is one time the bastards aren't going to get away.'

'Quarter of a mile,' the radar operator murmured.

They watched the dots on the screen draw nearer. Sullivan lifted his head and looked out of the window, straining to see. Through the gaps in the rocks he thought he caught a glimpse of two indistinct shapes passing by in the mist, but he couldn't be sure.

The pulsating dots disappeared abruptly from the screen.

'They're in the bay, Major,' the first officer said into the radio as the captain threw open the bridge door and rattled off an order at the two ratings waiting on the starboard deck. The mooring lines were quickly untied and the rubber dinghies surged away towards the headland, their undersides slapping the crests of the waves sending glistening showers of spray into the air.

The captain stepped over to the control panel and fired off more orders, the first officer taking the wheel. The navigation and deck lights snapped back on and there was a muted clanking noise as the anchors were winched in. The patrol boat eased away, manoeuvring carefully through the string of half-submerged rocks, going wide round the jagged tongue of land that protruded into the ocean, its edges concealed beneath a continuous barrage of foaming breakers. The boat had almost reached the shelter of the bay on the other side when there was a distant rattle of tiny explosions that could only be one thing. Gunfire. Sullivan and Enqvist exchanged looks. The first officer opened the throttle and the patrol boat swept round the promontory into the inlet.

Close to the shore, anchored in the shallows, were two sleek, streamlined cabin cruisers. Their decks seemed to be swarming with shadowy figures as the Gico commandos clambered on board from the dinghies. A shot rang out in one of the cabins, answered by a short burst from a machine-gun. Two men threw themselves into the sea and splashed their way towards the shore. One of the dinghies raced after them, scraping to a halt on the shingle beach. Two commandos leapt out and hurled the men brutally to the ground.

Sullivan went out on to the foredeck as the *Guardia* boat moved in closer. The mist was thickening, cloaking the scene with a veil which, coupled with the darkness, was difficult to penetrate. Everything was confused: people yelling, feet thudding on decks, someone screaming in pain, the cacophony all underpinned by the relentless crash of the waves on the beach.

The spotlight on the front of the patrol boat lanced through the fog, illuminating a man struggling out on to the shore. He stumbled on the bank of pebbles and fell headlong. By the time he picked himself up there was a commando standing over him, a sub-machine-gun butt swinging down on to the side of his head. More men went overboard. The sea seemed to be churning with bodies, with flailing limbs. And floating amongst them were several bobbing objects – cardboard boxes which, as the water soaked into them, slowly started to sink.

The commandos dragged the men out of the surf and hauled them up on to the beach, making them lie prone while their hands were cuffed behind their backs. Then the cardboard boxes were salvaged from the sea and others unloaded from the cabin cruisers and stacked above the tide line.

Sullivan and Enqvist were taken ashore in a motor-boat. Casagrande was waiting for them beside the pile of boxes. He bent down and ripped open the tops of several. Inside each were dozens of red and white cartons of Marlboro cigarettes. Casagrande lifted out a carton and opened it, removing a couple of packets. He tossed one to Enqvist.

'Keep it,' he said. 'A souvenir from Naples.'

He offered the second packet to Sullivan.

Sullivan shook his head. 'No thanks, I don't smoke.'

7

Yorkshire, England

'What the hell . . .'

The driver of the prison van rammed his foot down hard on the brake pedal, bracing his arms against the steering wheel as the vehicle skidded to a halt. Slewed across the road in front, almost blocking the narrow country lane, was a maroon Vauxhall Astra, its bonnet crumpled against the stone wall separating the road from the adjoining fields, the glass from its shattered windscreen strewn like diamonds across the asphalt.

A woman with shoulder-length blonde hair was slumped against the side of the car. She turned her head as the van stopped and the driver saw the blood caking her face and neck.

'Jesus!'

He threw open his door. His colleague in the passenger seat climbed out on the other side. The woman staggered towards them, one hand clutching her head. Her eyes were dazed, her mouth contorted in pain and anguish.

'Take it easy, love,' the driver said, catching her in his arms as she fell. 'Better radio for an ambulance, Phil.'

The blonde groaned and pushed herself upright, her hand reaching down into her coat pocket.

'I don't think that will be necessary,' she said coolly, pointing an automatic pistol at the driver's head.

He gaped at her. 'What? Fuck! You bitch!'

The blonde whipped the pistol across his face,

cutting open his cheek. A trickle of blood seeped out from the wound.

'No obscenity, please.'

She swung the pistol between the two guards.

'Face down on the road. Both of you. Now!' she ordered.

The guards looked at each other, but didn't move. A man vaulted over the wall behind them.

'Do as the lady says.'

He was wearing a soiled black balaclava, scuffed leather jacket and old Adidas trainers. But there was nothing used about the gleaming silver Beretta pistol he held in his hand. The two prison guards crouched down and lay flat on the road.

'Give me the keys to the back of the van,' the man in the balaclava said in a lazy drawl.

'We don't have them,' the driver replied, twisting his head so he could see the blonde standing over him. Trying to imprint her bloody features in his memory.

The man in the balaclava stepped over and, without warning, shot the driver in the back of the knee.

'I'll ask you again.'

'You fucking bastard,' the second guard spat. The driver was curled up, holding his shattered knee, screaming in agony.

'The keys.'

The second guard rummaged in his jacket pocket and threw a bunch of keys out on to the road. 'Go fuck yourself.'

The man in the balaclava ignored him. He went

round to the rear of the prison van and unlocked the heavy steel doors, taking a pace back and levelling his pistol at a third uniformed guard who was sitting on the bench inside next to four handcuffed prisoners.

'Maartens, out,' Balaclava said. Then to the guard: 'Unlock his cuffs.'

Frans Maartens was too stunned to move. Short and plump, his red face rimmed with greying hair and a grizzled beard, he simply stared at Balaclava.

'You hear me? Out!'

The prison guard unfastened the handcuffs. His hands were trembling so much he could barely hold the keys. He seized Maartens and pushed him out through the doors.

'Move down the bench to the back,' Balaclava said, standing aside as the blonde forced the other two guards round from the front. The driver was only half conscious, moaning in pain and shock as his colleague lifted him up into the back of the van.

'At least call an ambulance. He needs to get to hospital,' the guard pleaded.

'Get in, or you're next.'

Balaclava swung the doors closed, locked them and threw the keys over the wall. Then he took hold of Maartens by the collar of his jacket and dragged him along the road. A green VW Golf was parked in a copse down a muddy farm track. Balaclava opened the boot and pushed Maartens inside.

'No sound. You understand?'

He slammed the lid shut and ran round to the driver's door, pulling off his balaclava. He clambered in and turned the ignition. The blonde slipped into the seat next to him. She picked up a towel and wiped the fake blood off her face before removing the blonde wig and shaking loose the dark hair underneath. The Golf was moving fast down the bumpy track and out on to the road when she took out a cosmetic bag and mirror and began to touch up her make-up.

They drove east for more than half an hour, across the flat agricultural land north of Hull, sticking to minor roads and deserted country lanes wherever they could. As they neared the coast, the North Sea crept slowly into view, filling the horizon with a wash of still, grey water that was almost indistinguishable from the overcast sky.

The Golf turned down a narrow metalled lane which, after a quarter of a mile, became a rough dirt track, its surface worn into two deep ruts by the heavy wheels of farm vehicles. At the end of the track was a derelict barn. The Golf drove inside and stopped in front of a pile of dirty straw. The roof of the barn had partially fallen in. Panels of rusty corrugated iron dangled from the wooden rafters, held tenuously in place by a few old nails. The lapboard sides had disintegrated leaving gaping holes through which the clifftop could be seen, only yards away.

Balaclava opened the boot of the car. Frans Maartens stared up at him, seeing his face for the first time. He turned pale, a rat's gnaw of fear in his eyes.

'Get out,' Balaclava said.

'Mr Doyle . . .' Maartens stammered in bewilderment. 'What is this?' He spoke English with a marked Dutch accent.

'Get out.'

Maartens clambered awkwardly over the lip of the boot and stood looking at Doyle, licking his fleshy mouth nervously. The woman was over by the door of the barn, gazing out at the patchwork of fields.

Doyle slid a cigarette between his lips and held out the pack. Maartens hesitated, then took one. Doyle lit them both and inhaled deeply, his eyes never leaving Maartens.

'How was your time in prison, Frans?' he said.

'What's going on?' Maartens asked anxiously.

'You had plenty of opportunity for reflection, I hope. To see the error of your ways. You got greedy, Frans. That's not an attractive trait.'

'Greedy?' Maartens attempted a smile, but it came out as more of a grimace. 'Now, I wasn't serious, you know. I didn't mean it. You know how these things are.'

'Of course. You understand our position though, don't you? We didn't want you going through a trial, giving evidence.'

'I wouldn't have said anything. I wouldn't.'

Maartens sucked on his cigarette. His clothes were crumpled, his thinning hair dishevelled. Slightly stooped, cheeks and nose veined with broken blood vessels, he looked much older than his forty-seven years. Doyle smiled icily at him.

'We couldn't afford to take that risk.'

'What am I going to do now?' Maartens said. 'I'm a fugitive, on the run.'

'I expected more gratitude,' Doyle said.

'You should have left me inside. Where am I supposed to go now?'

Doyle threw his cigarette on to the dirt floor and crushed it out with the heel of his shoe.

'You don't need to worry about that, Frans,' he said soothingly. 'We'll take care of you.'

Hendaye, French–Spanish border

The senior customs officer was crowding her, leaning over so close that Claire could smell the residue of the previous night's garlic on his breath.

'How long are you down for?' Bignon said smoothly. 'Perhaps I could show you around. Have you seen the Pyrenees before?'

Claire suppressed a weary sigh and leafed through the documents on the desk in front of her. These Latin men bored her with their predictable chat-up lines, their intrusive hands and tedious insistence on treating her like a little girl in need of a sugar daddy.

Bignon touched her on the shoulder, squeezing her flesh through her jacket and blouse.

'Maybe I could take you out to dinner tonight?' he said.

Claire turned her head to look at him. 'Will your wife be coming too?' she asked.

Bignon took his hand away and smiled thinly. He fingered his pencil-line moustache as if checking it were still there. He wasn't sure quite what to make of this slender young woman whose self-assurance belied her petite, almost fragile, appearance. Claire pulled out a couple of papers from the pile, trying to get back down to business.

'These two interest me. You know the companies?'

The senior customs officer bent over to examine the documents. As he reached out to adjust their position on the desk, his hand brushed against Claire's breast. She gritted her teeth. The first time he'd done that she'd given him the benefit of the doubt, but twice was more than an accident. She pushed back her chair and stood up, digging her heel hard into Bignon's instep. He winced and stifled a cry.

'I'm sorry, was that your foot?' Claire said, picking up the documents and heading for the door.

Outside, the early morning air was thick with diesel fumes from the constant stream of traffic passing over the frontier. To the left, the foothills of the Pyrenees rose in a series of undulating inclines, their grassy slopes dotted with holiday villas; to the right, the sun glinted on the broken waters of the Gulf of Gascony. It was a picturesque setting, but the terrain immediately adjacent to the customs post was depressingly ugly: a vast expanse of grey concrete filled with parked trailers and trucks, a no-man's-land of huge forty-tonne lorries and tired drivers waiting to cross into Spain or France.

Claire absorbed the scene for a moment, watching

a group of earnest young men completing an on-the-spot check of a French lorry laden down with crates of wine. They were plainclothes customs officers but they weren't from Hendaye: this was a team from the central anti-fraud division in Paris.

The group leader, Philippe Allard, strolled across to the customs post. A boyish-faced man in his mid-thirties, he had dark hair cut short in a severe *en brosse* style. Claire gave him a quizzical look and he shook his head.

'Everything in order.'

'You sound disappointed.'

'I know. We couldn't even find some trivial technicality to get him on. What's the world coming to when wine exporters, of all people, are honest?'

'Try this one.' Claire held out one of the papers clasped in her hand. 'It's the blue truck over there. Spanish.'

Allard glanced at the paper. 'Okay. We'll do it next.'

'Do what next?'

Christophe Bignon had come out of the customs post behind them.

'Or aren't you going to tell me?' he added acerbically.

His tone and expression left them in no doubt how he felt about a bunch of smug Parisians coming to throw their weight around in the provinces.

'The Spanish lorry,' Claire said. 'Garcia Saez S.L., San Sebastian.'

'You're wasting your time,' Bignon said contemptuously. 'Those trucks go back and forth every few days. We know all the drivers. We've never had any problems with them.'

'There's a first time for everything,' Claire said.

She walked purposefully across to the blue articulated lorry. It was parked at the front of a line of three commercial vehicles which had been selected for random inspection from the dozens which came over from Irun almost every hour of the day. The driver was standing by his cab, smoking and gossiping with two of his compatriots. Allard asked him to open up the back of his trailer and the driver shot a puzzled look at Bignon.

'Just a formality,' Bignon growled, waving an arm dismissively. 'They're from headquarters.' What else can you expect? was the unspoken sneer in his voice.

The driver walked the length of the vehicle and swung open the rear doors, fastening them back against the sides of the trailer. Inside were rows of shiny metal jerry cans stacked five high on wooden pallets. Allard vaulted agilely inside and pulled down one of the cans, unscrewing the cap and peering at the contents. He lowered his nose and sniffed deeply.

'Seems all right.'

'Extra virgin,' the Spanish driver said in French. 'You won't find any better.'

'You see,' Bignon snorted, turning away with a gesture of impatience.

Allard replaced the can on the pile and squeezed through the narrow gap between the pallets, selecting another container from the back of the consignment.

16

That too seemed in order, as did a third jerry can he lifted down from the top of one of the stacks.

'We'll need a sample, for testing,' Claire said. 'Perhaps Monsieur Bignon would oblige?'

The senior customs officer made no attempt to conceal his irritation.

'Is that really necessary?'

Claire's cool blue eyes settled on his sallow face. She was in charge of the operation but she had no direct authority over Bignon. She wasn't part of Allard's team, wasn't even French despite her fluency in the language. But she wasn't going to allow some petty border official to obstruct her.

'Yes, it's necessary,' she said.

She turned away, not willing to discuss the matter further. She heard Bignon draw in his breath, then his heavy footsteps as he stomped back to the customs post.

'You want to check any more?' Allard inquired.

Claire watched the driver. He was standing to one side, still smoking. He seemed a little on edge but she'd have been surprised if he hadn't been. A random customs search was an unsettling experience, even for those with a clear conscience.

'Maybe one more,' she said.

The driver's shoulders slumped. 'Is all good stuff, you know. I see them press the olives myself. The first oil out, it all go in there.'

'One from the top,' Claire said, pointing.

Allard lifted down the heavy jerry can and placed it on the floor of the trailer by the open doors. Claire

17

took off the cap and studied the viscous golden liquid inside. She inhaled. It was certainly olive oil, but whether it was extra virgin as the transit documents specified was something only the laboratory could determine.

Bignon appeared round the side of the lorry, a sample kit dangling from his hand.

'This one?' he said brusquely.

Claire nodded, moving out of the way to let him ladle a small amount of oil into a plastic container. Bignon sealed the container and filled out the label on the side.

'You finish now?' the driver said in his accented French. 'I'm half an hour late.'

'What do you think?' Claire asked Allard.

'I'm satisfied.'

The driver glanced at Bignon and quickly stepped round to unlatch one of the doors. Something about his manner aroused Claire's attention, she wasn't sure exactly what. The look of relief in his face, the haste with which he started to close up the trailer. He was late and in a hurry, but all the same . . .

'Just a moment,' she said.

Allard caught her eye. He was about to jump down from the trailer but stopped. She nodded discreetly at him.

'I'd like to see one from the bottom.'

'What?' the driver said in exasperation. 'Look, you open four already. How many you want to see?'

'We can open every one if we need to,' Claire said sharply.

She ignored the driver's petulant response, the rolling eyes, the arms thrown wide in disbelief, and indicated a jerry can at the bottom of one of the stacks. Allard removed the top four containers and brought the fifth to the rear of the trailer. Claire was conscious of all three men watching her intently as she unscrewed the cap and lowered her eyes to the opening.

She noticed the difference at once. This liquid was paler, cloudier, and had none of the thick amber lustre of olive oil. She smelt it, then dipped a finger in and tasted it, letting the flavour linger in her mouth.

'So?' Bignon said impatiently. 'Is it good or not?'

'Well,' Claire replied, 'I'm no cook, but I certainly wouldn't put that in my vinaigrette.'

'You know what it is?' Allard said.

'Hazelnut oil.'

He nodded. They both knew what that meant.

'We'll need a lab test to confirm it,' Claire continued, 'but I'm sure.'

She'd encountered it before: it was a common enough fraud. Hazelnut oil was sixty per cent cheaper than olive oil. It had a distinctive flavour on its own, but when mixed with olive oil, to adulterate it, was almost impossible for the human palate to detect provided you kept the proportion below twenty per cent. Which was why the European Union made importers of hazelnut oil pay a substantial security against release for certain authorised uses only.

19

'Where was it going?' she asked.

Allard referred to the transit documents. 'Just up the road. Fonteneau et Delahaye. A bottling plant in Bayonne.'

'Any previous suspicions?'

'We'll have to do a check.' He studied her shrewdly for a moment. 'You knew, didn't you? That's the one you were waiting for.'

Claire walked over to the window of the customs post and looked out. The Spanish lorry had been moved to a secure compound off the main road where Allard's men, watched by Christophe Bignon, were unloading the jerry cans and checking their contents. The driver was being held in an interview room at the back of the customs post, waiting to be questioned.

'This isn't the first time,' Claire said. 'Those lorries have been doing this run for ages. Months, maybe years. Yet they've never been caught.'

'What are you saying?'

Claire took another look outside, then pulled open the door that led to the rest of the customs post. The corridor beyond was deserted. Closing the door again, she walked across to Allard and kept her voice low.

'How many phones are there here?'

Allard frowned. 'Just this one in here, as far as I know. Maybe a couple of extensions, but they're all the same number.'

'Can you get one of your team in here and keep him here on some pretext until we've finished this job?'

'Why?'

20

'I don't want this to leak out.'

Allard eyed her narrowly. 'You don't trust the officers here?'

'Let's not take any chances, Philippe.'

'I can arrange that. And the next move?'

Claire smiled. 'I think it's time we took a closer look at this bottling plant, don't you?'

TWO

'It's not exactly riveting television, is it?' Casagrande said laconically, leaning back in his chair and gazing up at the video screen on the wall.

The grainy black and white picture showed the inside of a Gico interview room – a windowless, white-walled box equipped with a scratched metal table, tape recorder, three steel chairs and all the quaint charm of a run-down public lavatory. In one of the chairs, his clothes still damp from his immersion in the sea, sat a squat middle-aged man with a bruised face and thick matted hair like coconut fibre on his forearms. He was gazing stoically at the two uniformed revenue guards sitting opposite him and grunting occasionally in a guttural language that both Sullivan and Enqvist, watching from the quiet seclusion of Casagrande's office, found incomprehensible.

'What's he saying?' Enqvist asked.

Casagrande shrugged. 'Who knows? I need an interpreter too. They speak Italian, these scum, but they pretend not to. It's tiresome, but we're used to it now. What can you do in a foreign country like this?'

His lip curled sardonically. Casagrande was from Milan, a Lombard who regarded all of Italy south of Rome, maybe even south of Florence, as the sub-Sahara. Temperamentally, and culturally, he had more in common with the Swiss than he did with the Neapolitans.

'One thing you can be absolutely sure of,' he continued, 'he won't tell us a single thing of any interest. We can question him from now until Christmas but he won't say anything. He's too scared of his masters.'

Sullivan studied the image on the screen. The prisoner seemed at ease in the bare, intimidating environment of the interview room. Calm, composed, listening to his interrogators politely, he had more the air of a man being interviewed for a job than a smuggler facing a long term in jail. Arrest was just one of the many hazards of his occupation that he accepted with a quiet resignation.

'He's Camorra, I assume,' Sullivan said.

'Of course,' Casagrande replied with a sigh.

He picked up the remote control from his desk and pressed the mute button, killing the sound on the video monitor.

'Which group?' Sullivan asked.

'It hardly matters, they're all the same. I'd guess the Lucianis. Things are pretty unstable at the moment. People's loyalties are wavering. They're waiting to see who ends up on top.'

'Maybe you should pull out for a time and leave them to sort it out among themselves?'

'I'd love that,' Casagrande said. 'Let the bastards knock each other off, one by one, then move in and pick up the survivors. Unfortunately that's not a solution our political masters find acceptable. The shootings last week have made them nervous. You saw that in Brussels?'

Sullivan nodded. It hadn't made the television news but he'd read about it in the paper. In a bar in one of the northern suburbs of Naples, out near Capodichino airport, four men had been killed in a shoot-out between rival Camorra gangs.

'Who's going to win?' Enqvist asked.

Casagrande gave the facial equivalent of a shrug.

'Do I care? Luciani's on top at the moment, but Dino Falzone controls a lot of territory and is ruthless enough to capture more. The only thing I can be sure of is that whatever happens, nothing will change.'

There was a knock on the door.

'Yes?' the major called out.

The door opened and an orderly came in carrying a tray of coffee and *cornetti*. He placed the tray softly on the desk and went out. Casagrande poured three cups of steaming black espresso and gestured to the others to help themselves to the pastries.

'What was the haul in the end?' Sullivan said, leaning forward in his chair to take a coffee.

'Four hundred cases. They had them stashed every-where, even in the toilets and showers.'

'Four hundred?' Sullivan did the arithmetic in his head. Fifty cartons to a case, ten packets of twenty to a carton, that made a total of four million cigarettes.

24

It was a reasonably impressive catch, but a mere fraction of the vast numbers of contraband cigarettes which flooded into Naples every year and even less significant when compared to the figures for the whole of Italy. None of the three men in the room was under any illusions about the true effectiveness of their night's work.

Casagrande reached out for an electronic calculator and punched in the numbers, talking to himself.

'Two hundred thousand packets. Duty per packet, around eleven hundred lire, that makes . . . *Merda*, there aren't enough digits on the calculator.'

'Two hundred and twenty million lire,' Sullivan said.

Casagrande glanced up at him. 'I'll take your word for that. And in Euros?'

'A lot,' Sullivan said.

'Come on, don't be modest.'

'Nineteen hundred lire to the Euro. Roughly a hundred and fifteen thousand Euros,' Sullivan said.

Casagrande did the sum on his calculator and pulled a face.

'Show-off,' he snarled grudgingly, tossing the calculator away across the desk.

Sullivan grinned at him and took a *cornetto* from the plate. Enqvist was already on his second pastry, the buttery crumbs sticking to his lips and the stubble on his plump chin.

'These are good,' he said thickly, chewing on a mouthful. 'Did they come from the canteen?'

'You must be joking,' Casagrande said. 'I sent out to a *pasticceria* for them. One of the perks of rank.'

Sullivan sipped his espresso, looking around the room. There weren't many other perks of rank on show. Casagrande's office was only marginally better furnished than the interview room they could still see flickering on the screen high up on the side wall. He had a piece of tatty carpet on the floor, a functional desk and a few ugly chairs with central stores reject written all over them, but the budget had obviously run out long before the room could be contaminated with anything approaching comfort. Casagrande wasn't the type to even notice, much less care.

The most disconcerting feature was the metal sheeting over the window, but that had been placed there for security rather than aesthetic reasons. Although Gico was a branch of the *Guardia di Finanza*, its regional headquarters in Naples was housed in a separate compound protected by a high steel fence, razor wire and armed guards. Casagrande, like most of his men, lived in the compound twenty-four hours a day, seven days a week, venturing out only when absolutely necessary. To Sullivan, he seemed remarkably serene for a man who was almost certainly on a Camorra hit list.

'What about the mother vessel?' Sullivan asked.

Casagrande's narrow face brightened momentarily. 'Ah yes, I forgot to say. She's under arrest, currently being escorted into port by a *Guardia* cruiser.'

26

'You got her?' Sullivan found it hard to contain his jubilation. 'What's her name?'

'I know nothing more about her at the moment. As soon as I get any information, I'll let you have it. That's the one thing that cheers me up. Seizing the ship and the cabin cruisers. It should set them back more than confiscating any number of cigarettes. Armando Luciani is going to be shitting himself with fury.'

The major smiled broadly. Then he glanced up at the video monitor and his smile faded. He picked up the remote control and restored the sound to the picture. One of the *Guardia* officers in the interview room was standing up, collecting together his notes, while the other spoke into the tape recorder, terminating the session. The tape was removed, then the two officers walked to the door and knocked on it. It was opened by the guard outside and the two men went out, leaving their interviewee alone in the room.

'It doesn't look as if you got very far,' Sullivan said.

Casagrande pulled a sour face. 'We'll keep at him, make his life difficult at least. He's like all the others. He'll keep his mouth shut, do his time, then come out and start all over again. It's the only way of life they know.'

Up on the video screen, the prisoner turned his head and looked directly at the camera. He appeared tired, but in his eyes was a burning defiance. He shouted something in dialect, then stood up and walked over until he was below the fish-eye lens.

27

He gathered the phlegm in his throat and spat it out and upwards. The image on the video monitor erupted in a shower of frothy saliva.

Casagrande pressed a button and the screen went black.

'Well,' he said dryly. 'He's quite a spitter. All those years of practice, I suppose. They don't learn to read and write, these people, but they could gob for Italy.'

Sullivan and Enqvist laughed. Casagrande spoke English with an accent, but he had an admirable command of the vernacular.

'Sometimes I wonder why we do it,' the major continued, serious now. 'We're just fleas biting on an elephant's backside. I have some sympathy for people like him. He doesn't regard what he does as criminal. After all, cigarettes are a legal product. All he's doing is avoiding excise duty on it. Is that really much different from the wealthy businessmen who pay accountants to fiddle their taxes for them? It's always the same, isn't it? One law for the poor, one for the rich.'

He held out the plate of *cornetti*. 'Come on, finish them off. It was a long, cold night.'

Casagrande poured more espresso into his cup and stirred in some sugar, musing pensively.

'That one in there will go down for a few years. His wife and kids will struggle to survive without him but the *capo* who organised it all, who makes the millions out of it, will carry on as before. Sitting in his villa up in the hills, drinking his expensive wine and planning the next shipment. *He's* the one we'll never catch.'

He was talking more to himself than anyone else. And more in sorrow than anger.

'That doesn't mean we shouldn't try,' Sullivan said.

Casagrande eyed him, the beginnings of a frown wrinkling his forehead.

'Ah, an idealist,' he said. 'But then in Brussels it is possible to have ideals. Here at the sharp end it is not so easy. We were lucky last night. But we shouldn't kid ourselves that we're ever going to do more than scratch the surface, cause some minor inconvenience to these Camorra barons.'

Casagrande lifted his coffee cup and said mockingly: '*Signori*, I give you a toast. To futility.'

He tilted the cup to his lips and downed it in one.

There had always been something fundamentally untrustworthy about Rupert Bird. Looking at him now across the starched linen tablecloth, Hal Montague had a clear, and none too affectionate, recollection of the various indiscretions and betrayals which had marked their joint progression through school and university and which had, in adulthood, made Bird an ideal recruit for the Secret Intelligence Service.

At Harrow, Bird – Bird Minor as he was called, to distinguish him from his older brother, a joke which both masters and boys had persisted in finding funny for about five years longer than its natural lifespan – had been a sneak of the worst kind. Conniving and deceitful, he had been imbued with an instinct for lying and treachery which his fellow pupils had found loathsome but which Her Majesty's Government had regarded as a perfect qualification for a job at the Foreign Office.

Montague had never liked him. They'd never been friends and, after Oxford, where Montague had been at pains to avoid Bird's company, he had broken with him entirely. They'd lost touch for many years, Bird making steady progress through the stuffy ranks of the civil service, Montague making rather more of a mark on the world of business and finance where his talent for taking calculated risks had paid impressive dividends. But a chance encounter at an old boys' fundraising function had renewed their acquaintanceship and led to occasional social contact which had proved mutually beneficial. Montague had a knack of identifying people who could be of use to him and Bird, in the corridors of Whitehall at least, was extremely well-connected.

'Have you chosen yet, Rupert?' Montague asked, aware of the waiter hovering near their table.

'I'm not sure.'

Bird inspected the menu again. Montague contained his impatience, knowing his companion would have the fillet steak as usual. He didn't have the imagination to try anything new.

Montague beckoned the waiter over. 'The rack of lamb for me. And—' He waited.

'The fillet steak, why not?' Bird said.

'New potatoes and vegetables?' the waiter asked.

Montague nodded and ordered a bottle of the

house red. He was rich enough to be a wine snob but he didn't see the point. A 'plain bottle of plonk' – as he was fond of saying, generally in a cod Yorkshire accent – was all he required with his food. That was one of the reasons he liked the Parkside, it had no pretensions. The food was simple and English, well-cooked and plentiful enough to fill his beefy frame. No ridiculous garnishes, no trickles of raspberry sauce with the meat, no main courses balanced in a pile in the middle of the plate so it might as well have been served in a drainpipe.

There were other advantages too, notably the fact that there was an absolute ban on mobile telephones in the dining room. Montague hated mobile phones, regarding them as the status symbol of the office boy, a sign of enslavement rather than liberation. He had one himself, outside in the Bentley, but that was different. He never allowed it to intrude on his life; the whole point of power was to dictate whom you spoke to and when.

But the main advantage of the Parkside was its location: a quiet Kensington backwater, if Kensington really had any backwaters, far enough away from the watering holes of the City and Whitehall for neither of them to be recognised by colleagues or rivals. For what they had to discuss, on the infrequent occasions they met, was always confidential and very often politically and commercially sensitive.

They made idle small-talk while the wine was brought and poured, then Bird leaned forward over the table and said: 'So when exactly are you going?'

'Next week.'

'And your itinerary?'

'Unchanged. Kiev, Odessa, Mariupol.'

Bird nodded. He knew all this already but he liked to check his facts, if only to cover his back with his superiors.

'And you're meeting the Ukrainian trade minister when?'

'Thursday.'

Bird sipped some of his wine. 'How do you rate your prospects?'

'Good. Zuganin is a man of growing influence. He wants to see this project go ahead as much as I do. His political future depends on it.'

Montague didn't add that the minister's bank balance in Zürich also depended on it. Bird didn't need to know the details of the deal.

'Most of the former Soviet republics are teetering on the verge of bankruptcy,' Montague continued. 'They're as desperate for hard currency now as they were in the communist era. The only way they're going to get any kind of political stability is to bring some economic prosperity to their countries. And they're only going to achieve that through Western investment. You know what the average annual earnings in the Ukraine are?'

'No.'

'Forty pounds. That's all they make.'

'No wonder you're so keen to get in there.'

Montague smiled, but his eyes remained cold.

'We'll be using skilled labour,' he said. 'They'll get

32

more than that. But not much more,' he added with a grim chuckle.

Montague liked doing business in Eastern Europe and the old USSR. He had investments in manufacturing in Poland, Russia and the Ukraine, in agriculture in Hungary, and was now spearheading a consortium seeking to explore for petroleum and natural gas near the Sea of Azov. The possibilities for an entrepreneur with guts and guile were limitless. All the people with power in the former communist states were infatuated with capitalism. They wanted to get rich quick and they weren't too scrupulous about how they did it. They'd rejected a system of state control with all its corruption and inefficiencies and replaced it with a culture of uncontrolled laissez-faire gangsterism that, although it didn't work either, had one major advantage over communism: it made the people in charge wealthy enough not to care whether it worked or not. It was little different from the heyday of the robber barons in the United States. Rockefeller and Vanderbilt and Jay Gould would have found a home from home in modern Ukraine, or Russia or Belarus, it didn't matter which. And Montague, who had much in common with those old rogues, was equally comfortable there.

Bird fingered the stem of his wine glass, casting an eye around the restaurant. There were no other diners near enough to overhear what they were saying.

'I've had a word with Our Man in Kiev,' he said pompously.

Montague was amused that people in the FO still

talked like that, as if there were some in-house style book dating back to the Thirties that they were all obliged to use.

'And what did Your Man say?'

'They'd be interested in anything you can pick up. General background information. Economic data, political stuff, you know what I mean. It's all useful.'

'Tittle-tattle, gossip, which minister has a boy-friend, that kind of stuff?' Montague said sarcastically.

Bird forced a weak smile. 'Anything. You can leave it to us to sort the wheat from the chaff.'

'I'm sure I can,' Montague said, though he had his doubts. He regarded the words British Intelligence as something of an oxymoron. Its employees, if Rupert Bird was anything to go by, would probably be hard-pressed to tell the difference between a classified document and a shopping list. But Montague indulged them because it suited his purposes to do so. He'd supplied snippets of information in the past, nothing that would compromise his own self-interest, and was happy to go on doing it. It appealed to the small boy inside him, a childish love of intrigue which he'd never lost. And it created an obligation between him and his old schoolmate, a debt that could be called in whenever he needed it.

A liveried figure appeared at the door of the restaurant: Montague's chauffeur. He walked across the room, manoeuvring his way between the tables.

'I'm sorry to interrupt, sir, but you said I was to let you know immediately. Mr Doyle called.'

'And?' Montague said.

'He said the job had been completed to his satisfaction. He's on his way back to London now.'

'Thank you.'

Bird waited for the chauffeur to leave, then said, as if the interruption hadn't occurred: 'We'd be particularly interested in anything you hear about the hardline Nationalists. They're picking up a lot of support out in the provinces, we gather.'

Montague nodded. 'Hedging your bets?'

'We want to make sure we support the right side.'

'And which is the right side?'

'Whoever wins, of course,' Bird said.

'Rupert, you're beginning to sound like a politician.'

'You'll keep me posted, as usual?'

Montague saw the waiter coming out of the kitchen with their food. He flicked open his napkin and spread it across his lap.

'You know you can rely on me to do my bit for my country,' he said. 'Provided it does its bit for me.'

Simon Doyle switched off his mobile phone and slipped it away into the pocket of his jacket. The balaclava, the leather jacket and trainers had gone – dumped in three separate dustbins in different suburbs of Kingston upon Hull – and he was now dressed in a smart charcoal suit and sober tie, the picture of a junior executive or travelling sales rep. The stolen Golf was a burnt-out skeleton in a wood near Beverley and he was once again sitting behind the wheel of the Ford Mondeo he'd hired the previous day in London. He felt good. His body was pulsing with the kind of fresh vitality he usually associated with a hard work-out in the gym.

He turned his head to look at Serena Montague in the seat next to him. She was flushed, her eyes shining.

'You get a high out of this, don't you?' he said.

She smiled and stretched her long limbs. She reminded Doyle of a resting puma. Sleek, watchful and very dangerous.

'God, if only Hal could see me now,' she said.

'You'd enjoy it if he found out, wouldn't you?'

'I think I might. I do love getting under his skin.'

It was raining outside, the view of wet fields and hedgerows partially obscured by the streaming water on the windscreen. They were parked in a deserted picnic area a few minutes' drive from the westbound M180.

Serena reached across and ran her hand under Doyle's jacket, feeling the muscles of his chest and washboard stomach.

'I think we deserve a little bit of relaxation now,' she said.

Her fingers dropped to his fly. He pushed them away.

'What if someone comes?'

'Who's going to come here on a day like this?'

She started to kiss his neck, watching to see what he did. She liked taking risks. A part of her wanted to get caught.

'We could find a hotel for an hour or two,' he said.

'I don't want to wait.'

'It's either that, or the back seat.'

'What's wrong with that?' Serena said.

Claire looked out of the window of the car as they sped north up the coast road from Hendaye. The waves were rolling in, their crests spewing angry froth, along a huge stretch of beach between the fishing port of St Jean-de-Luz and the more sophisticated haunts of Biarritz. The surf here was renowned as some of the best in Europe. Claire had swum in it, when was it? Eighteen years ago. The realisation numbed her for a second. Where had all the intervening years gone?

She'd been eighteen years old. A group of surfers and their girlfriends had come down from the University of Amsterdam for the long vacation, sleeping rough, living out of camper vans parked near the beach. The girls had lain around on the sand all day while the men surfed. Claire couldn't believe she'd been a surfer's girl, hanging about all summer watching a bunch of brainless boys riding boards. As a joke, the girls had made cardboard stencils of their boyfriends' names and taped them across their stomachs so that the skin didn't tan. For two years after, until it finally faded, she'd had Wim blazoned across her navel. She'd never done anything so silly in her life. Actually, she had. She'd married the guy.

They were on the outskirts of Biarritz now, heading

slightly inland away from the sea. Claire remembered Biarritz as a chic, elegant town, full of fashionable shops and cafes that were too expensive, and too snooty, for penniless students. But none of that was visible from the road which descended to the River Adour and across a bridge into the old port of Bayonne.

Bayonne felt like a real town to Claire, a place where people lived and worked rather than simply idled away their holidays. It had none of the faded charm of its neighbour but it was attractive nonetheless in a plain, stolid sort of way.

The olive oil bottling plant, Fonteneau et Delahaye, was on the northern fringes of the town, in one of the characterless *zones industrielles* with which the French cluttered their sprawling suburbs. A local customs officer was waiting in a car at the entrance to the industrial park with the search warrant he'd obtained on Allard's instructions. There was a brief conference on the verge beside the road, then they drove in convoy to the factory, a large, modern building constructed – like all the others on the site – with great quantities of concrete and steel and very little style.

It was a slick, orderly raid – Allard and his men had carried them out many times before and each member knew exactly what had to be done. Claire kept out of their way, assuming the role of an observer. They went in at the front, asking the receptionist to summon the manager to the foyer, then while Allard and Claire waited for him to emerge from his office, the other customs officers – six in total – went through to the production and storage areas.

The manager, Alain Delahaye, was pushing sixty, a tubby little man with thick black spectacles and wobbly pink jowls like a sow. Allard showed him the warrant and explained what was happening. Delahaye blinked at him, too surprised to speak at first, then he assumed a manner of servile politeness.

'Of course, monsieur. You will have my full co-operation, but I assure you there is nothing here to warrant the attentions of the *Douane*. It's just a simple olive oil bottling plant.'

'You have dealings with a firm in San Sebastian, Garcia Saez?' Allard said.

'Yes. They supply us with much of our oil.'

'Olive oil?'

'Of course.'

'Do you also bottle hazelnut oil?'

Delahaye started, his jowls flapping as his head jolted backwards. Then he recovered himself.

'Hazelnut oil? I'm not sure I understand.'

'Do you bottle it here?'

'Why no.'

'We stopped a lorry at Hendaye earlier this morning,' Allard said. 'It contained a cargo destined for your factory. Concealed among the cans of olive oil were a number filled with what we believe to be hazelnut oil.'

'It wasn't coming here,' Delahaye protested indignantly. 'See for yourself.'

'My men are already doing that,' Allard said. 'Perhaps we should join them.'

The factory floor was a clean, airy space about the size of a football pitch. Rows of fluorescent lights hung on chains from the high vault of the ceiling, illuminating a complex circuit of conveyor belts which looped round and round the floor like a child's train set. Glass bottles rattled along the conveyor, the empty ones passing through a series of machines which filled them with olive oil, then capped and sealed them with a plastic sheath. Labels were stuck on and the bottles removed from the belt to be packed into cardboard boxes. Most of the process was mechanised but there were workers in blue overalls supervising the various stages who turned and stared curiously as Delahaye came out on to the floor.

'Where are the storerooms?' Allard asked.

Delahaye lifted a hand to point but the gesture was unnecessary, for one of Allard's men was already beckoning to them from a doorway on the other side of the production line.

The storeroom had been sealed off and customs officers were sorting through the rows of metal drums and jerry cans inside.

'I think you should see this,' the officer said to Allard.

Stacked at the back of the room were dozens of metal containers identical to the ones on the lorry at Hendaye. The caps of several had been removed. Allard peered into them, then dipped in a finger and tasted the liquid. He turned to Delahaye.

'Do you have a lawyer?' he said.

'Yes.'

'I think you'd better call him.'

The production line had been shut down. Customs officers were inspecting the machinery, taking samples from the tanks of olive oil and from the filled bottles to send away for analysis. The workforce, except those helping on the factory floor, had been asked to wait in the canteen until their turn came to be interviewed.

Allard and Claire were upstairs in Delahaye's office, which had windows on two sides, one set overlooking the production line, the other the yard at the rear of the factory. Claire was leaning on the windowsill while Delahaye's secretary brought in the company's books and other records for Allard to inspect. Delahaye himself was sitting stiffly in a chair, refusing to say anything until his lawyer arrived.

Claire looked down into the yard where an empty lorry was waiting forlornly by the shuttered entrance to the loading bay. She needed a cup of coffee badly but it didn't seem an appropriate moment to ask if there was a machine anywhere. She could always go for a walk, see if she could find one. She pushed herself off the windowsill and stopped dead as she noticed the door next to the loading bay open and a man come out. He was wearing blue overalls like the rest of the workers. Claire frowned. No one was supposed to leave the factory until Allard gave the okay. She watched the man cross the yard and go into a smaller one-storey building on the other side.

Curious, she walked away from the window and, with a nod at Allard, out of the office. There was a corridor outside leading to a flight of stairs which descended to the front foyer. Claire ran down them and paused to take her bearings. She had only a vague idea of the layout of the plant but she knew the loading bay must have access to the storage area where the packaged bottles of olive oil were kept prior to distribution.

She went through the doors on to the factory floor and walked hurriedly around the conveyor belts. Two of Allard's men were still checking through the production storeroom. She could see them as she walked past. Further on was a wide opening which led through into a bay filled with cardboard boxes stacked on pallets. A couple of yellow fork-lift trucks were standing idle against the wall. She pulled open the door beside the high metal loading bay shutters and stepped out into the yard.

Walking across to the other building, she cautiously opened the door. Inside was what looked like another storeroom or perhaps, from the stench of petrol fumes, a garage, with additional access from outside through a pair of double doors. The man in the overalls was loading cardboard boxes into the back of a Renault transit van.

'You need any help?' Claire said.

The man spun round and stared at her.

'Piss off, little girl, this is none of your business,' he snarled angrily.

'You want to show me what you've got in there?'

In reply, the man reached into the van and pulled out a steel tyre wrench. He brandished it in her direction.

'Get out of here. If you've any sense.'

Claire sized him up. He was much bigger than she was but running to fat. He looked strong, certainly, but also out of condition. She could have walked out to get assistance but he might have gone by the time she got back. Besides, she loathed seeming the helpless woman. In many ways it made her more reckless than a man. She took a couple of paces towards him.

'I don't want to hurt you,' he warned. 'But I will if I have to. Now fuck off out of here.'

'Put it down,' Claire said calmly. 'Don't make things worse for yourself.'

He snorted incredulously. 'Worse for me? Don't make me laugh.'

Claire sighed. Basic self-defence techniques had been part of her training, but it seemed a shame to waste her judo skills on a big oaf like this. She took another step towards him, unfastening the buttons on her blouse to expose the flimsy lace cups of her bra.

'Do you want me here, or in the back of the van?' she said.

The man gaped at her. The tyre wrench dropped to his side and his eyes to her cleavage.

'Uh?'

PAUL ADAM

Men, sometimes they were so stupid, Claire thought as she swung back her leg and kicked him hard in the balls. He made a harsh, choking sound and doubled up clutching his groin. Claire gave him a push and he toppled over to the floor. She walked round to the back of the van and ripped open the top of one of the cardboard boxes.

She didn't know what she expected to find, but the contents took her by surprise. She stepped backwards, regaining her composure, then went round all the other boxes, tearing open each one in turn. The man was still moaning in a ball on the floor when Claire walked past him to the door, fastening up the buttons on her blouse.

THREE

It was raining heavily when Sullivan left his apartment for the twenty-minute drive to work across the Forêt de Soignes – or Zoniënwoud, if you preferred the Flemish version. He'd lived in Brussels long enough to get used to the bilingual nature of the city, the double names on all the streets and public buildings. Sometimes it still confused him – he'd hear the Flemish name for something he knew only in French and be perplexed for a time until he realised it was the same thing. It was usually that way round. French was a more familiar language to him and, though he lived in a Flemish-speaking suburb, his command of that language was poor. Like most Englishmen, he was lazy about languages, but the Flemings spoke such good English it seemed unnecessary, perverse even, to converse badly with them in their own tongue. He might have managed it in French but one of the things he'd learnt very quickly about Belgium – a country demarcated along complex linguistic and geographical lines – was that the Flemings spoke French only when it was absolutely unavoidable and the Walloons, well, the Walloons would rather cut out their tongues than utter a single word of Flemish.

The rain had eased a little by the time he emerged from the forest into the built-up area on the south-eastern edge of the city. It was no longer a cold, depressing downpour, merely a cold, depressing drizzle which, he'd come to realise, was an almost permanent meteorological feature of Brussels. It was just his luck that his first, and probably only, job overseas had to be in a country – and there weren't many – where it rained more than it did in England.

The headquarters of UCLAF, the *Unité de Coordination de la Lutte Anti-Fraude* – the European Commission's fraud investigation unit – was in a small part of a vast complex of offices on the Avenue de Beaulieu which also accommodated the directorates for the Environment, Transport, Telecommunications, Personnel and Research and Technology. Constructed on a skeleton of steel girders overlaid with a skin made of huge sheets of glass, the building bore a curious resemblance to an opulent greenhouse, except that the species inside it were anything but tender seedlings in need of protection from the elements. They were hardy perennial bureaucrats and administrators, germinated on the rich manure of tax-free salaries, fed on subsidised food, mulched by first-class travel and special allowances, watered with golden showers of Euros and never ever subject to the painful snip of the pruning shears.

The marble-floored atrium inside was filled with real trees and shrubs bathed in sunlight from the glass roof. Six floors of offices, their windows over-looking the atrium, rose upwards on either side, serviced by banks of glass-walled lifts and open spiral staircases. Sullivan had been told that the complex had originally been designed as a shopping centre but at times, particularly on dank winter days, with its security guards, locked doors, steel gantries and bridges, it had more the feel of a high-tech prison. But it was clean, modern and, above all, light. Sullivan wouldn't have minded the window-cleaning contract for the building, if he weren't almost certain that some *fonctionnaire* had already awarded it to themselves.

The UCLAF offices were on the top three floors at one end of the complex, accessed through doors which could only be opened with a special pass card. Sullivan walked down the corridor to the room he shared with Stig Enqvist and threw himself immediately into the most important business of the day – filling the filter machine with water and coffee and monitoring the liquid carefully for strength and purity as it dripped through. Stig wasn't in yet, but then he rarely was this early in the morning. His timekeeping, never good, had got worse recently, his attendance undermined by a jaded disillusionment which Sullivan found disturbing.

There was a pile of messages waiting for him on the desk, and a further stack of papers which Antonio Casagrande – a man determined to contradict all the common preconceptions about Italian efficiency – had faxed through overnight. Sullivan dealt with the most pressing messages first then turned his attention to the faxes, calling Casagrande on the phone to get an update on the information they contained. He was on his second cup of coffee by the time Enqvist slouched into the office and slumped down in his chair, his overcoat dripping wet from the rain.

'This fucking weather,' the Swede grumbled in his fluent, idiomatic English that Sullivan sometimes thought he'd picked up from some passing unit of linguistically-challenged troopers. 'Every bloody day it's the same. I swear my skin's shrunk since I came here.'

'I've noticed you doing many things,' Sullivan said dryly, 'but shrinking is not one of them.'

Enqvist sniffed and pulled off his coat, draping it over the back of a spare chair to dry. He straightened the jacket of his grey suit and looked down, holding in his stomach. He wasn't fat – not yet anyway – but he was showing noticeable signs of middle-aged spread. Too many waffles and burgers, not enough exercise. He gripped the roll of flesh around his waist and wobbled it up and down.

'Not bad for my age,' he said. 'It just needs a bit of toning.'

'Liposuction more like,' Sullivan said.

'Look, I'll show you.' Enqvist untucked his shirt.

'No thanks,' Sullivan interjected quickly. 'Not this early in the morning. Besides, Carlsen wants to see us in his office.

'About Naples?'

'Casagrande's faxed through the interview tran-
scripts and a few other things. You want to look at
them before we go?'

'Nah, I'll let you do all the talking.'

'Well, that'll make a change.'

They walked down the corridor then took the
stairs to the sixth floor and the office of their section
head, Ole Carlsen – a soft-spoken Dane in his early
fifties with short hair and an iron-grey moustache
which gave him a misleading military air, for he was
actually a career *fonctionnaire* within the Commission
with a distinguished career in the Danish civil service
behind him. He waved them to a couple of chairs and
pushed the file he'd been reading to one side of his
immaculate desk.

'I hear it went well,' he said.

Sullivan glanced at Enqvist. Carlsen had an unnerving habit of being particularly well-informed
about every operation his section undertook, even
when the investigators involved hadn't told him
a thing.

'RAI 1,' Carlsen said by way of explanation, seeing
the puzzled looks on their faces. 'Not the details, but
I got the gist. One dead, that was unfortunate.'

Italian television, of course. Like the BBC, Dutch,
French and German stations, RAI 1 was a standard
part of the cable package provided to virtually every
home in the city. It was one of the reasons the
residents were such phenomenal linguists.

'It sounded an exciting night.'

Sullivan briefed him on the details of the operation.

'Four hundred cases, two speedboats impounded, eight smugglers in custody, that's a good result,' Carlsen said. 'How much excise duty evaded?'

'About a hundred and fifteen thousand Euros.'

'Not bad.'

'A drop in the ocean compared to the total,' Sullivan said.

'But a setback for the Camorra nevertheless.'

'True,' Sullivan conceded. 'But the trail ends there. Eight small fry in jail, no big fish. Gico questioned them all but got nothing.'

'So we don't know where the contraband came from?'

'Oh yes,' Sullivan said casually, saving the best bit till the end. 'A bonded warehouse in Rotterdam. They were supposed to be going to West Africa. At least, that's what the papers on the mother vessel said.'

Carlsen raised an eyebrow. 'They got the mother vessel?'

'Picked her up seventy-five miles off the coast. The master denied any involvement, of course. The usual story. As soon as the *Guardia* cruiser came alongside he contacted Lloyd's for a satellite fix, then started screaming about acts of piracy. They arrested her anyway and brought her into Naples.'

'What nationality is she?'

'Liberian.'

'Now that's a surprise,' Enqvist said ironically.

'The *Maria Vasquez*,' Sullivan said. 'A general cargo freighter, about four thousand tonnes.'

'Can they establish a link?' Carlsen asked.

Although as a general rule it was unlawful to arrest a ship on the high seas, the Geneva and Montego Bay conventions permitted it if you could establish a link between the vessel and the smuggling of contraband.

'Enough,' Sullivan said.

'Aerial surveillance?'

'Only radar. They didn't want to use a plane in case it was spotted and they aborted the drop.'

'But no one actually witnessed the transfer of the cigarettes?'

'No. The circumstantial evidence is pretty damning though. There were thirty thousand master cases on board. Mostly American – Winston, Marlboro, Lucky Strikes.'

'Thirty thousand,' Carlsen said. That was three hundred million cigarettes. 'Going elsewhere?'

'No one knows at the moment. The boys we picked up might have been going back for a few more runs. According to the freight manifest they were all going to Senegal. But it's a funny way to go to Senegal.'

Carlsen nodded in agreement. 'Excellent. I'm very pleased. You did well. That was a damn fine show.'

Carlsen said things like that. He spoke five languages fluently, six if you included the language of bureaucracy which, this being the European Commission, was *de rigueur* in the senior position he occupied. But while Enqvist, for example, spoke the English of the football terraces, Carlsen sometimes appeared to have learnt his during a sojourn at a Home Counties golf club.

'The ship owners are going to court, I assume?' Carlsen continued.

Sullivan nodded. 'I spoke to Casagrande this morning. They've hired a team of heavyweight lawyers, five of them, to fight the seizure.'

'How does Casagrande rate their chances?'

'It's difficult to say. You can never tell with an Italian court. We know it was the *Maria Vasquez*, but there's no absolute conclusive proof that it was her. Not in legal terms.'

'Have Gico sent you any material from the ship?' Carlsen asked.

'I haven't been through it all yet,' Sullivan replied evasively. He knew exactly what was in the faxes, but he guessed what was coming next and didn't want to show his hand.

'Should the courts force the release of the ship,' Carlsen said carefully, 'I want anything you have sent back to Naples immediately. We can't hold material that has resulted from an illegal search.'

Sullivan nodded. Carlsen was a Dane, but he had an almost Germanic obsession with procedure – an essential characteristic given the legal, transnational nature of UCLAF's work, but one that wasn't always shared or appreciated by his staff.

'Okay.'

'Thank you for your time. Keep me informed.'

Carlsen reached over for the file on his desk and opened it again.

'By the way,' he added, 'speak to Claire Colmar. She has something that might interest you.'

Sullivan and Enqvist went out. They were ten metres down the corridor when Sullivan said: 'I'll take Colmar.' Then: 'The pile of faxes on my desk from Casagrande. Why don't you photocopy them and put the copies somewhere safe?'

Enqvist grinned at him. 'Shit, it's uncanny how you can read my mind.'

Claire Colmar was seated at her desk, tapping away at the keyboard of her computer, when Sullivan walked into her office. She finished her sentence and swung round in her chair.

'Hi.'

'Ole says you've got something for us.'

Sullivan pulled up a chair and sat down. Claire crossed her legs and smoothed her skirt over her knees. Sullivan took in her appearance without any conscious scrutiny. She was simply dressed – powder-blue blouse and grey suit – but there was a sort of effortless elegance about her which he'd come to associate with continental professional women. She obviously took care about what she wore, and wasn't averse to spending a lot on her clothes, but there was nothing ornamental about her. Her shoes were flat-heeled and practical, her nails trimmed short and unvarnished, her hair a dark bob that was easy to keep groomed. There was something lithe, athletic about her. Sullivan could see her in a gym or a swimming pool.

'I was down in the Basque country yesterday,' she said. 'With the *Douane*. We raided a factory in

Bayonne. In one of the storerooms we found some cases of cigarettes. I think they're contraband. In fact, I'm sure of it.'

'What makes you so certain?'

'Well, it was an olive oil bottling plant for a start. And I caught one of the employees in the act of moving them. They didn't want us to find them.'

'How many cases?'

'Sixteen.'

'Any indication where they came from?'

'We questioned the factory owner. He said they were for personal consumption.'

'Oh yeah? He's a heavy smoker?'

'So he claimed. But assuming he was on, say, fifty a day, that would give him enough supply for . . .' She paused, hunting around on her desk for her notes.

'About eight and three quarter years,' Sullivan said.

Claire pulled out the sheet of paper on which she'd earlier worked out the numbers with a calculator, just for the hell of it. Eight point seven six seven, she'd scribbled at the bottom. She lifted her head and stared at Sullivan.

'You just figured that out? In your head?' she said.

Sullivan waved a hand as if to dismiss the subject.

'Maybe he likes to buy in bulk. Some people do,' he said. 'You can save a lot of money.'

Claire slid her notes back on to her desk.

'There were no records of purchase,' she said. 'No

receipts, no invoices. You'd expect something for that many cigarettes. The owner says he's lost them but I don't believe it.'

'Did he say where he got them?'

'He can't remember.'

'All that smoking, it must have affected his memory,' Sullivan said.

Claire laughed. 'The *Douane* are still questioning him. I doubt he'll say much, but I have a hunch those sixteen cases were all that's left of a much bigger consignment. Has Bayonne featured in any of your investigations?'

'Not until now. What's the name of the plant?'

'Fonteneau et Delahaye.'

Sullivan shook his head. 'It's new to me. What sort of cigarettes were they?'

'Marlboro.' Claire handed him a piece of paper. 'The serial numbers on the cases. You want me to follow it up?'

'That's okay. We'll look into it. Who's in charge at the French end?'

'Philippe Allard.'

Sullivan folded the sheet of paper and slipped it into his pocket. Then he stood up.

'How's Nicoletti?' Claire asked.

Maurizio Nicoletti was the third member of the Cigarette Task Group, temporarily absent after breaking his right leg in a skiing accident at Cortina d'Ampezzo.

'He's out of hospital,' Sullivan said, 'but still a long way from being fit enough to come back.'

'I'm sorry.'

'He's okay. Thanks for your help.'

'Any time.'

She watched him walk away. He was attractive. A little reserved in that curious way the English had, so that you couldn't be sure whether they were cold or merely shy. But she didn't mind that; it gave you more to discover. She hardly ever spoke to him. He wasn't one of the men in the department – and there were several – who made a point of stopping by her office on the flimsiest pretext and flirting with her. She wondered why not.

She turned back to her computer and finished her mission report on the random customs checks in Hendaye. For once, a tip-off on one of the UCLAF freephone fraud lines had paid off. There was a number in each member state but they all came through to an answering machine at Beaulieu. Claire thought of it as the loony line because most of the calls were from either weirdos or people with gripes: disgruntled employees shopping their boss, business-men stirring up trouble for their rivals, jealous neigh-bours taking revenge by telling malicious lies. Most, particularly the anonymous complaints, could safely be ignored, but just once in a while one turned out to be true, in this case information from an account-ant in San Sebastian who had his suspicions about Garcia Saez.

Claire filed the report, then rang Allard. He was still at the bottling plant in Bayonne, overseeing his team as they questioned the employees and combed through every piece of paper they could lay their hands on.

'We've had the report on the lab samples,' he said.

'And?'

'Seventeen per cent hazelnut oil. In the tanks and the bottles. I doubt this place has ever produced a bottle of pure olive oil.'

'You're having them withdrawn, I take it?'

'We're contacting every wholesaler and retailer on the company books, instructing them to remove any oil from their shelves and return it.'

'And the consumer?'

'There's a press conference this afternoon; newspapers, TV. Same message: return any bottle of oil to the shop where they bought it.'

'You're going to be on television?'

'I'm having my hair done specially,' Allard said. 'You get French TV, don't you? Watch the evening news.'

'I can hardly wait,' Claire said.

It was quite a coup for Allard's team. The publicity would increase their prestige and public awareness of what they did. UCLAF's role in uncovering the fraud would get barely a mention, but Claire didn't resent that. She didn't expect recognition for what she did. That was their job: to remain in the background, an unknown EU support group, while the national agencies took the credit for any successes.

'Philippe, I know you're very busy down there, but

I've been thinking. You remember in Hendaye I said this had been going on for years and I wondered why no one had been caught until now?'

Allard saw where she was heading. 'You think the whole customs post is on the take?'

'I don't know. Maybe some of them.'

'You have anyone in mind?'

'Bignon.'

Claire heard him suck in air through his teeth. Then he said: 'He's a senior, well-respected officer. He's got a good record.'

'Can you check the factory files for when deliveries were made, then crosscheck them against the customs roster? See exactly who was on duty when the Garcia Saez lorries went over.'

There was a silence on the line.

'We're snowed under already, Claire.'

'I know. It's just an idea. It might be important, but it's your decision entirely.'

Allard grunted. 'Jesus, you don't give a guy much chance, do you?'

'That's what they all say,' Claire replied and hung up.

'So you made it back in one piece,' Enqvist jeered as Sullivan came into their office. 'Balls still intact, dick still dangling?'

'I never have any problems with Claire,' Sullivan replied.

'That's because you're the only man in the unit who's never tried it on with her.'

'Have you?' Sullivan was surprised. 'You never said.'

'Before your time. You think I could spend four years here and not have a shot, a woman like that?'

'And she turned you down?'

Enqvist pulled a face but didn't reply.

'I knew she had good taste,' Sullivan continued.

'Piss off.'

'Ah, the wit of the Swedes.'

'So what did she have for us?'

Sullivan told him. Enqvist leaned back in his chair and picked idly at one of his teeth with a fingernail.

'Sixteen cases, that all?' he said. 'It's hardly worth bothering with. American, of course?'

'Marlboros.'

American cigarettes sold well on the European black market. A malicious observer might have added that they were easy for a smuggler to get hold of too, but that would have been to single out the US companies and tar them with a brush that could equally well have been applied to any multi-national cigarette manufacturer. It was true that back in the early Nineties the Italians had accused Philip Morris of dealing with smugglers and temporarily banned the sale of their products in state tobacconists. But there was no absolute proof that they, or any of the other companies, traded with traffickers. Certainly there were vast amounts of contraband cigarettes swilling around the black and grey markets and, equally certain, it was of no concern to the manufacturers whether excise duty was paid on them, but it would have been a gross libel to even suggest that the tobacco barons knew anything about it.

Sullivan sat down at his desk and noticed the wad of papers Enqvist was holding in his hand.

'What's that you've got there?'

'I was looking through the faxes from Casagrande. These are copies of the log from the *Maria Vasquez*. You seen them?'

'I didn't study every page in detail.'

'I noticed something interesting. Two weeks ago the ship was detained by Customs and Excise in Hull. Held for two days. And at the end of those two days the master was replaced.'

'Why?'

'It doesn't say. Suddenly there's a new captain in charge, a Vladimir Strakhov.'

'Russian?' Sullivan said.

'Possibly. These Liberian ships have every nationality in their crews. The previous master was Dutch by the sound of him. Maartens. Frans Maartens.'

Enqvist held out the papers. 'I'll let you take care of it.'

'Why me?'

'Hull, that's in Yorkshire, isn't it? I won't understand a bloody word they say.'

'It's clean,' Doyle said, coming out of the conference room holding a small black box about the size of a brick and an electronic probe which bore a resemblance to a miniature metal detector, only its job was to locate the presence of unauthorised listening devices.

He stowed the equipment in his attaché case and followed Montague back into the room he'd just swept. There was a long polished table in the centre with seating for sixteen around it, although only four of the places were set with the standard appurtenances of a business meeting: notepad and pen, glass for mineral water, a bone china cup and saucer for coffee. It was the middle of the morning, but the blinds over the windows were shut and the fluorescent strips on the ceiling turned on, casting a garish sheen over the mahogany surface below. It seemed a pity because the view from the window, looking out across the Singel canal to the floating flower market, was one of the prettiest in Amsterdam.

Montague went to the chair at the head of the table and tossed down the copy of the *Daily Telegraph* he'd been flicking through outside. A headline near the bottom of the page read: 'Remand prisoner freed in ambush.' Inserted in the text of the story was a police photofit of an unremarkable-looking blonde woman.

'Did you have to shoot the fucking guard?' Montague said acidly, removing his jacket and sitting down.

'We were in a hurry,' Doyle replied. 'He was pissing us around.'

'You know he's likely to lose his left leg below the knee?'

Doyle shrugged. 'So?'

'So was it necessary?'

'You gave me a job to do, Hal. I did it the way I thought best. If you don't like it, do it yourself next time.'

'Let's hope there won't be a next time,' Montague said smoothly, ignoring his assistant's belligerent tone. 'Who was the woman? Some tart of yours?'

'You don't want to know.'

'No, I don't.' Montague glanced at the photofit drawing. 'Can they identify her from that?'

'Not a chance. Doesn't look remotely like her. She was wearing a wig, her face smeared with a bucketload of fake blood. The guards wouldn't recognise her again if they sat next to her on a bus.'

'Is she reliable?'

Doyle's mouth twisted into a sour grin. 'Oh yes, she's reliable.'

He took his place next to Montague as an attractive middle-aged woman entered the room pushing a trolley bearing a large jug of coffee, more cups and two plates of the sweet cinnamon biscuits the Dutch call *spekulaas*.

'Is everything to your satisfaction?' she asked.

'Perfect, as always, Ilse,' Montague said with exaggerated gallantry.

'Your colleagues have just arrived.'

She wheeled the trolley to the side of the room and waited while a group of four other men entered. Only when they were settled into their seats with coffee and biscuits in front of them did she discreetly leave.

Montague looked around the table. The chair next

to Doyle was occupied by Gilles Lafon, a stocky French businessman in his early sixties with leathery skin and tufts of coarse grey hair on the backs of his hands. Strip away his expensive suit and diamond tiepin and he would have looked like an ageing manual labourer, or a trucker, both of which he had been in the early years of his career.

Opposite him was a thick-set tanned man with jet-black hair and a battered face that Montague always likened to a knobbly potato, a simile that would have annoyed Armando Luciani intensely for he prided himself on his rugged good looks. Behind him, seated against the wall, were the two younger men who always accompanied Luciani on his travels. Montague regarded them as a superfluous, and far too conspicuous, entourage but it was none of his business; the Camorra boss probably didn't go to the toilet without a bodyguard to watch his backside.

'Shall we begin?' Montague said, easing effortlessly into the role of chairman of the board. It was such second nature to him that he sometimes had to remind himself that this was no ordinary business meeting despite its formal setting. There was no agenda, no minutes, no voting. The notepads on the table were purely for show: not a single word would ever be written down.

He turned to Luciani and said: 'What happened?'

Luciani grimaced, the expression emphasising the coarseness of his face.

'What happened? I tell you what happened,' he said in English, the language they always used in their meetings. Montague spoke fluent French and passable Italian, acquired from long and regular holidays at his villa in Umbria, but neither Lafon nor Luciani spoke the other's tongue.

'I lost two high-speed motorboats, worth two hundred and fifty thousand dollars each. I lost eight men to the fucking *Guardia* and a whole shipment of cigarettes. That's what happened.'

The anger was still seething beneath the surface, controlled but potentially explosive. Montague chose his next words carefully.

'Are we compromised in any way?'

'What?' Luciani frowned at him.

Montague rephrased the question. 'Are we in danger?'

'You? I'm the one in the fucking shit. What have you lost, eh?'

'I've lost my ship. That's worth a lot more than your speedboats.'

Luciani made a placatory gesture, conceding the point.

'Okay, I'm angry, that's all. When I find the *cazzo* who tipped them off, well, he won't have a fucking *cazzo* for long, that's for sure.'

'You have any indication who it was?'

'No.'

'You'd better find him,' Lafon muttered darkly.

'How do you know it was in Italy?' Luciani demanded. 'It could have been someone in England, someone on the ship.'

'We're all at risk here, Armando,' Montague said

diplomatically. 'We're not apportioning blame. We don't want it happening again.'

'You think *I* do? I've just lost a shipload of fucking cigarettes.'

'So have I,' Lafon said. 'So shut up about what *you've* lost.'

'What?' Luciani glared at the Frenchman. 'What shipload?'

'Not a ship. But I've lost a consignment, part of it.'

Montague turned to Lafon, suddenly disturbed.

'What are you talking about, Gilles?'

The Frenchman dipped a biscuit in his coffee and chewed it. Montague noticed the oil and dirt around his fingertips. Lafon never looked spotlessly clean, but he made such a show of being a horny-handed son of toil that Montague sometimes wondered if the oil weren't applied from a bottle the way a woman put on nail varnish. Surely a man worth five hundred million francs could afford a tub of Swarfega.

'The *Douane*,' Lafon said. 'They raided Fonteneau et Delahaye.'

'They knew the cigarettes were there?' Montague was alarmed now.

'It was pure chance. Fortunately, most of them had already been shipped out.' Lafon picked up another biscuit. 'Maybe we should stop for a time. Things aren't going very well.'

'Stop?' Luciani exploded. 'Listen, if I don't get some more, and soon, Dino Falzone will be all over my territory. I can't afford to be off the streets for even a few days. I have some reserves but I'm going to need a big shipment soon.'

'You'll get it, Armando,' Montague said.

'How? They have your ship.'

'You think I only have one? You'll get your supplies, you can depend on that.'

The girls came in shortly after the meeting was over, opening bottles of champagne and circulating around the room. A tall, slim blonde in a halterneck dress slit to the crotch handed a glass to Montague, then took a Cuban cigar from the humidor on the table, cut off the end and slipped it between his lips. She lit it with a silver lighter adorned with a small sculpture of a couple fornicating and perched herself on the arm of Montague's chair, one hand stroking his hair lightly.

'Christine, my dear, how nice to see you again,' Montague said.

He inhaled on his cigar and let the smoke out slowly, noticing Doyle already leaving the room with a statuesque brunette. Young men, they were always in such a hurry.

'I know those fine gentlemen at the Harvard Business School wouldn't agree with me,' Montague pontificated. 'But there's a hell of a lot to be said for mixing business and pleasure.'

The apartment was in darkness, splashed with icy puddles of light from the streetlamps outside. Sullivan pulled the curtains and switched on a couple of table lamps. It felt warmer then, but no amount of soft lighting could overcome the basic coldness of the flat. Not its temperature – that was kept uncomfortably high by the heating system which served the whole block – but its atmosphere. The floors were bare wood, covered in places by bald rugs, the ceilings high and the walls a plain cream colour that exuded a chilly dampness, as if they'd been painted with melted ice cream.

There was very little furniture. What there was came with the apartment and Sullivan had not chosen to supplement it with any of his own. He didn't see the point. He was only on secondment for three years, four at the most, and buying furniture seemed a waste of money. What did he need it for anyway, except to fill up the sterile emptiness of the flat? It was far too big for one person: three bedrooms, a big gloomy sitting room, a long walled garden outside the French windows. He'd rented it shortly after arriving in Brussels when it had been their intention that his wife and sons would join him, the boys going to the European School in the city. But in the end they'd decided it was better not to interrupt their schooling in England, nor to separate them from their friends. His wife, too, had been reluctant to give up her teaching job and relocate so they'd compromised and he'd kept on the flat so they could all come over and stay in the school holidays.

Sullivan wished it were more welcoming. He was temporary, and felt it, yet three years was still a long time to live out of a suitcase. He liked the comforts of home, missed them, especially on these dark winter nights when he came back to face a long evening alone, but he couldn't be bothered to recreate them for himself. That was something he'd always relied on his wife to do. The decor, the furnishings, the personality, that transformed a four-walled box into a home had always been Kate's. Without her, he didn't feel inclined, or able, to build a second home for himself in Brussels. His home was in England, with her and the boys, and it seemed somehow wrong to create an alternative life without them. So he endured the dismal ambience of the apartment, working long hours to reduce the time spent in it, and consoled himself with the thought of his two weekends a month back in Colchester where he belonged.

Going into the kitchen, he boiled the kettle and made himself a cup of tea. He was too tired to even think about cooking so he worked his way through half a packet of chocolate biscuits then, feeling guilty and not remotely full, wished he'd had something healthier and more substantial. He was losing his discipline. There'd been a time when he would have gone out jogging and then made himself a proper meal, but the willpower was deserting him. The cautionary spectre of Stig Enqvist loomed up before him, a classic example of a man living alone and away from home who was slowly letting his body deteriorate through laziness and indifference. Sullivan didn't want that to happen to him, yet he could see all too clearly how easy it was to let things go and never regain them.

He took his tea through into the sitting room and switched on the television with the sound turned off. He didn't want to watch it; he simply found its colourful glow comforting. Then he picked up the phone and rang home. It was Kate who answered, though he could hear Patrick and James squabbling noisily in the background. Their incessant fighting drove him mad when he was there but now he found himself almost – but not quite – missing the sibling warfare.

'Hi,' he said.

'Hello.'

She sounded tense, under strain. She broke off for a second to tell the boys to shut up, then came back on.

'Sorry.'

'How's things?' Sullivan said.

'Okay.'

'What's the matter?' He could always sense when something wasn't right.

'Nothing.'

'Kate.'

'I'm tired, that's all. It's been a trying couple of days.'

'Why?'

'Oh, nothing in particular. It's all fine now.'

'What's all fine?'

She was being a martyr again. The wife coping on her own, struggling through adversity, not wanting to bother him with what she saw as trivia. But it was the trivia he missed; the boring details of their lives which he wasn't there to share but which, when taken together, gradually built up and solidified to form the bedrock of a happy family.

'It's James,' she said eventually. 'He had an accident last night. He was knocked off his bike.'

'What! Was he hurt?'

'Fortunately not. The car wasn't going very fast. He was lucky, he landed on a grass verge.'

'Was he wearing his helmet?'

'Yes.'

'So there were no injuries at all?'

'A few bruises. He was taken to hospital. We were in Casualty from eight o'clock to gone midnight. The usual waiting around for doctors, X-rays.'

'You should have called me.'

'It was too late by the time we got home.'

'Too late?' Sullivan said in exasperation. 'It's never too late to tell me my son's had an accident. I don't mind what time you call.'

'Yes, okay. Don't get cross about it.'

'I'm *not* cross.'

Silence. Sullivan sighed. It was difficult sustaining a marriage on the end of a phone. They'd had too many of these conversations. They both loathed the instrument. It had the advantage of immediacy, but despite that it didn't seem to bring you closer, only make you more distant.

'Kate?' Sullivan said gently. 'I'm not cross, okay? It's just a shock to find out. I'm worried and I'm too far away to be of any help.'

'I know,' she said. 'But he's fine.'

'And you?'

'I'm fine too.'

'I'm coming home tomorrow,' he said.

'Oh.'

She didn't sound overly excited at the prospect.

'I have to go to Hull. I'll be with you early evening, I hope, depending on the trains.'

'You know we're all tied up on Saturday. I've the school trip and the boys are going up to Norwich with the Mackinnons. I told you weeks ago.'

'Did you?' He didn't remember, but then he wasn't there to be reminded. 'Anyway, it'll be nice to have an extra weekend together.'

'Yes.'

Another silence.

'Do the boys want to say hello?'

'I'll ask them.'

He caught the muffled sounds as she passed on the question to his sons, then heard their blunt, indifferent replies.

'They're a bit tied up at the moment,' Kate said down the phone, softening the blow.

He kept the disappointment out of his voice. 'Okay, I'll see you tomorrow then.'

He replaced the receiver, feeling the silent emptiness of the apartment all around him. Then he picked up his cup of tea and sipped it, his eyes fixed unseeingly on the flickering television.

71

FOUR

If Sullivan had drawn up a list of places he'd like to be on a wet February day, Kingston upon Hull would have come somewhere below Ulan Bator and Vladivostok. It wasn't that he felt any particular antipathy towards the city – it was actually quite an attractive place, certainly more attractive than its reputation suggested – but when the rain beat down in a continuous barrage and the wind swept across from the North Sea, cutting deep into the bones like a blunt saw, he could imagine few locations on earth more miserable.

He'd taken an early morning flight from Zaventem to Leeds – Bradford, then a slow train east across Yorkshire, stopping at Selby, Brough and a half dozen godforsaken outposts in between. He could have carried out his business on the phone, or by fax, but he preferred to visit people in person whenever possible. On the phone he was a faceless Brussels bureaucrat, a distant apparatchik working for an organisation most people in Europe had never heard of. In the flesh, whatever their nationality, they could see him for what he was: an ordinary working man with the same worries and aspirations, the same common decency and basic outlook as they had. And most importantly – particularly in England, given the paranoid suspicions about 'Europe' – they could see he was one of us, not one of them.

From the centre of Hull, he took a taxi out along the Humber to the customs post which served the King George and Queen Elizabeth docks. It was an uninspiring drive: three miles of tatty houses and boarded-up shops interspersed with warehouses and small metal-bashing workshops. He'd been to ports all over the world. Like airports, they were all different yet all essentially the same. The storage sheds, the grain silos and oil tanks, the vast yards full of containers and lorry trailers were identical wherever you went. They were small towns with their own private roads and security guards, strange coastal enclaves where the stench of oil and ship's diesel was always more powerful than the smell of the sea.

Climbing out of the taxi, Sullivan saw the dockside cranes and the superstructure of a roll-on roll-off ferry poking up above the roof of the warehouse across the road. There was a cowl of grey cloud over the estuary and, on the horizon beyond the dipping flocks of gulls, the flat shoreline of Lincolnshire emerged hazily from the mist.

Jeff Goodman, the customs officer he had spoken to on the phone from Brussels, met him at reception and took him through to his office. They had coffee and made small-talk for a while, chatting mostly about the job, the universal gripes of government employees. Sullivan, though he was working for the European Commission, was still a UK customs officer and would return to the service at the end of his secondment. It was a moot point whether he still had the powers of a customs officer or whether they were temporarily held in abeyance, but as far as Goodman was concerned he was an insider and would be given all the assistance he needed.

'You wanted to know about the *Maria Vasquez*,' Goodman said. 'I've got the file here. How can I help you?'

'We've seen a copy of the logbook which indicates the ship was detained here a few weeks ago.'

'That's right,' Goodman said. He was a little younger than Sullivan with curly blond hair and freckles spattering his cheeks and nose. 'January twenty-fourth, that's when she docked.'

'Coming from?' Sullivan asked.

'Rotterdam. Bringing in a mixed cargo of goods: palm oil, nuts, dried fruit, odds and sods. She's one of those freighters that will carry anything, you know the kind. Look at her and you'd think she'd sink before she got a couple of miles down the Humber estuary, but she was built to last. The owners probably picked her up for a song, tarted her up a bit – and I mean a bit – then chartered her out to some bargain basement outfit interested only in doing things on the cheap.'

'She's Liberian, isn't she?'

'Yeah. But the crew were mostly Filipinos. You

74

should have seen the quarters. Jesus, I'd keep pigs in better conditions.'

'You went on board?'

'Searched it from bow to stern.'

'Why?'

'Drugs.'

'You find any?'

Goodman shook his head. 'It was clean.'

'But you thought there were some on board?'

'We knew there were. The master, bloke named Maartens, was bringing the stuff in. Not big quantities, mostly cannabis as far as we can tell. He's Dutch, you can buy it dead easy over there. It's quite a temptation. Pick up a few kilos in Rotterdam, put it in your cabin then sell it once you get to the UK.'

'You caught him at it?'

'Not us. Humberside police. Drugs Squad. They were watching a known dealer in the city. They caught Maartens in the act of handing over four kilos in the toilets of a nightclub. They contacted us and we went on board and took the ship apart. Nothing.'

'You think he'd been bringing it in regularly?'

Goodman shrugged. 'Hard to tell. I met Maartens last year, he was over here every few weeks. He didn't strike me as the criminal mastermind type. He was more your foolhardy chancer. Saw an opportunity to make a bit on the side and couldn't resist it.'

'The police charged him, I assume?'

'Of course. The CPS in Hull have the file. We gave them our report too.'

'I'd be interested in talking to him. About the

movements of the *Maria Vasquez* while he was the master. Who's the CPS lawyer handling the case?'

Goodman checked the file. 'Cosgrove. Kenneth Cosgrove. You may have a long wait.'

Sullivan frowned. 'What?'

'You obviously don't know. Maartens has disappeared. Sprung from the van on his way from the Wolds prison to the remand hearing in court.'

'That was *him*?' Sullivan said. He only occasionally read the English papers, but he vaguely recalled a mention on the BBC news bulletins he received in Belgium.

'Two days ago,' Goodman said. 'He hasn't been seen since. Not as far as I know anyway. You want to call the CPS?'

'Could I?'

Goodman flicked through the pages of the file, then reached out for the phone on his desk and dialled a number.

'I'm afraid we can't help you,' the CPS lawyer said when Sullivan came on the line. 'The case against Maartens is closed.'

'Don't you think he'll turn up somewhere?' Sullivan said.

'Oh he has. He turned up this morning in a derelict barn near the coast. Unfortunately he was dead.'

'Dead?' Sullivan paused, absorbing the information. 'In suspicious circumstances?'

'A bullet through the head. Is that suspicious enough for you?' Cosgrove said.

*   *   *

'Who found him?' Sullivan asked.

Kenneth Cosgrove shifted in his high-backed leather chair and put his hands behind his head, flexing his fingers together. He was a big man with a dark five o'clock shadow across his jawline though it was only just gone noon. It felt insufferably hot in the stuffy warren of offices which the Crown Prosecution Service occupied in the centre of Hull. Already there were damp patches of sweat under the arms of Cosgrove's shirt.

'A farmer. He has a place out near Hornsea. There are some old long abandoned farm buildings on his land. On the clifftop. The farmer uses the barn for storing hay, a few bits of machinery. He doesn't go there all that often, but he did this morning. Maartens was slumped in a corner, a bullet hole in his left temple.'

Sullivan stroked his cheek pensively. 'The same people who ambushed the prison van?'

'Without a doubt. Shows how wrong you can be. When it happened we thought it was friends of his wanting to free him, smuggle him out of the country. It all makes sense now.'

'How do you mean?'

'Maartens was a nobody, a stupid small-time criminal. Okay, he brought in drugs, but it was only cannabis, not the hard stuff. He'd have gone down for a time, a year, maybe two. He had no record, at least not for drugs. Twelve months inside and he'd have been out. So why go to the trouble, and the risk, of springing him from an armoured prison van? We know now.'

'Yet why kill him, if he was such a small fish?'

Cosgrove gave a shrug. 'Your guess is as good as mine. The police are still out there, obviously, picking over the scene. We won't know what they find for a couple of days.'

Sullivan stood up and removed the jacket of his suit, hanging it over the back of his chair.

'You hot?' Cosgrove said. 'Open a window if you like.'

'Do you mind?'

'We get used to the temperature. These new buildings, no proper ventilation. Go ahead.'

Sullivan unlatched one of the windows and swung it open. Down below in Lowgate the rain was spitting on the gleaming pavements, peppering the pedestrians as they hurried about huddled beneath their umbrellas. There was a dazzling gilt statue of William III on an island in the middle of the road, its plinth – in a jarring and somehow disrespectful juxtaposition – immediately above the entrance to an underground public convenience. Sullivan took a breath of the damp sea air. It seemed cold and heavy on his lungs. Then he went back to his chair and sat down.

'Can I ask what the circumstances of his arrest were? Jeff Goodman said it was in a nightclub.'

'That's right. Although I'd use the word nightclub advisedly. It was an old warehouse down by the river. Some wideboy converted it, put in a few bright lights, a bar, a sound system. It's still an old warehouse but the kids who go there are too pissed

78

to notice. I think it's supposed to have atmosphere although what's atmospheric about mouldy walls and the stink of mud at low tide I don't know.'

Sullivan smiled at him. 'You're showing your age.'

'Yeah, I know. Mind, even when I was a teenager you wouldn't have caught me dead in a place like that.' He paused. 'I suppose that's why I became a solicitor.'

'And Maartens?' Sullivan prompted.

'Stuck out like a prick in a convent. He must have been the oldest person there by a long way. Even the undercover cops were only in their twenties. They were watching a guy named Vasili Kravchenko, a known dealer.'

'Kravchenko?'

'You know the name?'

'What nationality is he?'

'Ukrainian originally. Naturalised British. We have quite a problem here with Eastern Europeans: Poles, Ukrainians, Serbs. They're muscling in on every racket you can think of. Drugs, prostitution, contraband cigarettes. But then you probably know all about that already.'

'It occasionally comes to our notice,' Sullivan said dryly.

'Maartens had a holdall with him containing four and a half kilos of weed,' Cosgrove continued. 'The police burst in on them when he was handing it over to Kravchenko.'

'Was he a regular courier?'

'We'll never know now. Maartens was a seedy character. No master with a clean sheet would have touched a tub like the *Maria Vasquez*.'

'He had previous convictions?'

'Not in this country. But the Dutch police knew him. He was linked to a handling case a few years back but there wasn't enough evidence to convict him. There was an attempted extortion too. He demanded money from a married secretary at a shipping agent's in Rotterdam in return for keeping quiet about an affair she was having with her boss. She went to the police but Maartens denied it. It was his word against hers so he was never charged.'

'A pretty unsavoury character,' Sullivan said.

'He was. I reckon he got what was coming to him.'

'Do you mind if I look at the file?'

'Help yourself. You over here for the day?'

'Yes.'

'You want some lunch first? There's a pub down the road serves a nice pint.' Cosgrove smirked. 'On you, of course. This is a deprived area, we need all the help we can get from Brussels.'

Sullivan put on his jacket and raincoat and waited for Cosgrove to get ready. They were downstairs in the foyer, bracing themselves for the penetrating cold outside, when Sullivan said: 'Do the police have any idea who might have killed him?'

Cosgrove pulled open the glass door to the street, letting in a gust of biting wind.

'Some dealer with a grudge, maybe someone scared of what he'd say in court.'

'You think it was a drugs-related murder?'

'What else could it be?' Cosgrove said.

It was nearly eleven o'clock that night when Sullivan arrived home in Colchester. He'd left Hull at four o'clock, relaxed and looking forward to the weekend. By the time the taxi pulled up outside his house he was seething with a frustrated anger that could only be described as 'train rage'.

It was a hundred and twenty miles as the crow flies from Hull to Colchester. It had taken him seven hours, an average speed – as he'd worked out during one of the many longueurs on the journey – of a fraction over seventeen miles an hour, which was probably about the speed at which a crow actually flew.

First of all he'd had to go to York – completely the opposite direction to the one in which he wanted to go – in a clapped-out collection of carriages with a heating system which circulated only marginally more warmth than a pair of bellows and a lighted match. Then in York he'd had to wait close on two hours for the East Coast express which was running late due to some unexplained 'technical problems', a delay which meant he missed his connection at Liverpool Street and had to wait almost another hour for the next train to Colchester.

Kate could tell he was in a foul mood the moment he walked in through the door. She'd got ready for bed earlier and was waiting up in the sitting room in her dressing gown.

'We got anything to eat, I'm starving?' was the first thing he said, coming in and tossing down his overnight bag and briefcase. 'Those bloody trains. No wonder this shitty country is going down the tubes. Seven hours it's taken me, seven bloody hours. It's just up the road, Hull. Stephenson's fucking Rocket could have done it quicker. D'you leave me any dinner?'

'It's nice to see you too, Rob,' Kate said.

But he wasn't listening. He turned and went out. Kate heard him go into the kitchen and open the fridge. She followed and stood in the doorway, leaning on the frame with her arms folded.

'What did you have?' he said, rummaging around the shelves.

'Some pasta. The sauce is in a bowl.'

'You leave me any pasta?'

'I threw it away.'

'Why?'

'You know it's horrible cold. You never eat it.'

'You could've put it in the oven.'

'It's eleven o'clock. I expected you at eight.'

'It's not my fault. I was stuck on a bloody train.'

'God, you're in a mood.'

'What d'you expect? I thought you'd leave me some food. I've been on the go all day.'

'You think I haven't?'

'What did you throw it away for?'

'Don't shout at me.' Kate sighed, trying to cool things down. 'Why don't you have some bread and cheese?'

'Bread and cheese? I want more than bread and sodding cheese. What else have we got?'

He closed the fridge door and circled the kitchen, pulling open the cupboards and slamming them shut.

'There's never anything to eat in this house.'

'I'm going to bed,' Kate said, wanting only to get out of his way.

'What, already?'

'I'm tired. I have to be up early.'

'Why?'

'The school trip. I told you on the phone.'

'Oh.'

She went out before the atmosphere deteriorated any further. It was always the same when he came home. Friday night they always had a row, some trivial but acrimonious exchange which left them both feeling resentful. She knew it was the process of adjusting to the other's presence after a time apart, but knowing the cause of the arguments didn't seem to stop them happening. After nearly two years of seeing Rob only every other weekend, and during the school holidays when she and the boys went and stayed with him in Brussels, she thought she would have got used to it by now. But it seemed to be harder than ever.

At the beginning it had been difficult, but they'd both expected that and made an extra effort to overcome the problems. Now living apart was the norm, the problems were still essentially the same, but neither of them was inclined to try so hard to smooth them out. Kate had got used to the arrangement:

organised her life to cope with her husband not being there most of the time. So when he burst back in twice a month, expecting everything to be dropped for him, expecting their family life to be the same as it had been before he left, it annoyed her. She knew it was tough for him being away from home, but he didn't seem to appreciate how hard it was for her. She was virtually a single mother, holding down a full-time job and bringing up her sons on her own. She would have preferred him to be there to help but she was coping just fine by herself. The last thing she needed were these pointless Friday-night squabbles.

She was drifting off to sleep when Rob finally came upstairs and got into bed. She waited for him to say something, to touch her, put his arms around her and hold her. It had always been an unspoken rule in their marriage, before he went to Brussels, that after a row they would kiss and make up before they went to sleep. But he just lay there and did nothing. She could sense the tension, the contained anger in him, but she was damned if she was going to be the one to make the first move. So they rolled over and ignored each other, two silent, resentful shapes sharing a bed.

By morning they were still a little tentative, unsure what mood the other was in. But Rob came over to her side and slipped his arms around her warm body, gently exploring her contours as if reminding himself what she felt like. Kate rolled over and kissed him.

'Are we friends now?'

'Yes. I'm sorry about last night,' he said sheepishly.

'I just wanted to be here with you, not hanging around some freezing station platform.'

He stroked her softly.

'Don't get any ideas,' Kate said. 'I have to get up.'

'Can't you miss the trip?'

She removed his hands and climbed out of bed, slipping on her dressing gown.

'Why don't you come with us?' she suggested. 'There'll be room on the coach and we could do with another adult.'

Rob pulled a face. Spending the day with a bunch of over-excited nine-year-olds was not his idea of fun.

'You're leaving me on my own,' he said. 'What am I going to do?'

'You could always put up the curtain rail in the kitchen. It's been sitting there for two months.'

'Why is it that whenever I come home, you always have some DIY for me to do?'

Kate smiled. 'Well, you've got to be useful for something.'

She went out of the bedroom. Rob heard her going next door to wake the boys. It was ironic really, he reflected ruefully, that in the early days, when the boys were little and he and Kate desperately needed a lie-in, they never managed one because Patrick and James always came in at the crack of dawn to disturb them. Now things were different and they practically had to drag the boys from their beds, a late rising was a real possibility, yet there was always some pressing reason not to take advantage of it.

Reluctantly, he dragged himself out from the duvet and threw on his clothes. He was in the kitchen, making tea and toast, when his sons came downstairs, a pair of yawning, tousle-haired slobs.

'Morning,' he said.

The boys grunted indistinctly and helped themselves to Weetabix and milk.

'You sleep well?'

They nodded, not looking up from their bowls. He wondered if he should be flattered by their indifference, the way they regarded him as such a fixture in their lives that there was no need to acknowledge his presence. They were beyond the stage of showing how they felt about him, no longer the little boys who got excited when he came home from work, who wanted to be picked up and cuddled. He missed that.

Kate came in and grabbed a slice of toast and a gulp of tea. She'd put on her make-up and her field trip clothes: jeans, woolly jumper, thick socks.

'Come on,' she urged the boys. 'I'll drop you at the Mackinnons on my way.'

'Where exactly are you going?' Rob asked his sons.

'I told you,' Kate said. 'They're going to Norwich. Eric Mackinnon's taking them with David.'

'To do what?'

'It's an Inlines competition.'

'Inlines?' Rob couldn't get used to the new terminology. He still thought of it as Rollerblading. He was perturbed how out of touch he was. He knew the boys had taken up the sport but he didn't realise they were good enough to enter a competition.

'Is James up to it?' he said. 'After his accident.'

'I'm okay,' James protested. 'There's nothing the matter with me.'

'Are you sure?' Rob said, looking at Kate.

She nodded. 'He'll be fine. He wasn't hurt on Wednesday. Go and clean your teeth, boys, we have to leave.'

Rob waited for his sons to go upstairs before saying: 'Is this a good idea?'

'They're resilient things, kids.'

'They're also fragile.'

'Stop worrying. They've been looking forward to this for weeks.'

'Maybe I should go with them.'

'I thought of that, but it's too late. You need a spectator's ticket and I know it was sold out ages ago.'

She kissed him lightly on the lips. 'See you tonight. Enjoy your DIY.'

The house was very quiet after they'd gone. Rob made himself another pot of tea and tried to read the newspaper, but his heart wasn't in it. Did all fathers feel they were losing contact with their children? All parents, maybe. Or just the ones who worked away?

He remembered clearly the day, twelve years ago, when he'd gone to register Patrick's birth. The Registrar, a smiling, chatty woman in her fifties, had said to him, and he could recall her words exactly: 'Make the most of him. It won't be long before you have to give him back.' He knew now what she'd meant, how being a parent was a slow, inexorable process of letting your children go.

It started very early. At playgroup, at school, where your offspring soon created a world of their own from which you were excluded. And later, when they formed friendships and ventured further from the home, asserting their need for independence which, in time, would take them away from you altogether. He knew it was inevitable, wanted, for their sakes, for it to happen because that was what growing up was all about. But he couldn't help feeling a pang of nostalgia for the early days, for the two babies whose entire universe had revolved around their mother and father.

He roused himself and went upstairs to wash and change into his tatty, paint-stained trousers and shirt. Then he returned to the kitchen, took out his toolkit and began the task of putting up the new curtain rail.

There was always the same pattern to his attempts at DIY. He would start off confidently, enthusiastically even, convinced that the job would be a complete doddle. But after half an hour discovering that the walls weren't flat, or vertical, or that the plaster came away like brittle toffee when he touched it and that nothing was ever, ever as simple as the *Reader's Digest* sodding manual said it was, he suddenly remembered how much he loathed the whole business and wished he'd never begun. But he had to carry on; drilling holes that were too big for the

wallplugs, making new ones nearby that were just
as bad, trying to patch things up as best he could
and getting more and more frustrated until he was
in such a state of fury he thought his head would
explode. And what was more, there was no one there
to share, or alleviate, his rabid frenzy. One of the
things he'd noticed over the years was that whenever
he undertook any tasks around the house, the rest of
the family somehow contrived to be elsewhere while
he botched them up.

Two hours later the curtain rail was finished; not
quite straight and slightly wobbly, but he was too
fed up to care. He retired to the local pub for a
pint of bitter and a roast pork sandwich, enduring
an hour of motorcycling – a sport well up there on
the watching-paint-dry scale of fascination – on the
satellite screen before going home to wait for Kate
and the boys to return.

Patrick and James arrived first, tired but elated,
both having done quite well in their respective age
groups. Rob gave them tea and sat with them, listening as they told him about their day. Kate came in
a while later and paused to admire the new curtain
rail – 'I love the way it dips in the middle' – before
going upstairs for a soak in the bath.

They put the boys to bed early and had an Indian
takeaway delivered. Rob had spent a large part of
the day anticipating making love to Kate that night,
but in the end they were both too stuffed with lager,
nan bread, chicken dupiaza and prawn biryani to
even contemplate sex. They sogged on the sofa in

front of the TV then dragged themselves upstairs and curled up together in bed, comfortable, familiar with each other.

The Sunday passed in the quiet family routine of the papers, lunch and a walk in the woods then, just as they were all getting used to each other again, Rob had to pack and prepare himself for the journey back to Brussels. Kate drove him to Colchester station and they sat in the car park, suddenly subdued. They both hated these depressing Sunday nights.

'We'll see you in Brussels next weekend,' Kate said.

Rob nodded. 'It seems a long way off.'

'We'll have a whole week together.'

She reached across and hugged him. They kissed. Gently at first, then more passionately. He slipped his hands under her jumper. She pulled him closer then broke away.

'The timing's never right, is it?' she said disconsolately. 'You'd better go, you'll miss your train.'

He went into London and across to Waterloo on the Underground. The Eurostar departure lounge was full of men just like him, peripatetic fathers returning to exile in Belgium. He wondered if they felt the same way as he did, but from the outside it was impossible to tell.

He got on to the train and stared out of the window as it purred slowly through the suburbs and on into the Kent countryside. Then he pulled some papers from his briefcase, shut down the part of his brain marked 'personal' and immersed himself in the anodyne therapy of work.

FIVE

Stig Enqvist poured himself another cup of coffee, loosened his tie and undid the top button of his shirt, then sat down in his chair and stretched out his arms and legs as if he were sunbathing.

'So what's your theory?' he said.

Sullivan shrugged. 'I don't have one. But I don't think it had anything to do with drugs.'

'Why not? Maybe the CPS guy is right. Someone was scared Maartens would do a deal to get his sentence reduced. Say too much.'

'About what?'

'Where he got the cannabis, who he delivered it to.'

'The police know who he delivered it to. The Ukrainian's in custody. Guy named Vasili Kravchenko. That mean anything to you?'

'No, should it?'

'It sounded familiar so I looked it up on the data base before you came in. You remember last summer, UK Customs raided a clothing warehouse in Nottingham on a tip-off it was being used for storing cigarettes?'

'The abortive one, you mean?'

'Yeah. Place was empty. I called Tony Fitzpatrick who organised the raid. To check on the facts. The manager of the warehouse was called Ivan Kravchenko.'

'Related?'

'Vasili's younger brother.'

'Well, well. So they're into drugs as well as cigarettes. That doesn't surprise me. Maartens brings in cigarettes and does a bit of dope-smuggling on the side. He gets caught so they knock him off. These guys don't take chances. What's one more killing to them?'

Sullivan lifted his leg and placed the sole of his shoe on the edge of his desk, rocking back in his chair.

'I'm not sure it's quite so simple. You find out who owns the *Maria Vasquez* yet?'

'I contacted New York Friday afternoon,' Enqvist said.

For some mysterious reason, probably because no one knew where the hell Monrovia was, the Liberian register of shipping was kept in New York City.

'The answer was waiting for me this morning.' Enqvist picked up a fax from the desk. 'It's owned by a Liberian corporation, of course. Buchanan Investments. But naturally that's just a front. The beneficial owners could be anyone.'

'Dun and Bradstreet?'

'It lists a firm of lawyers in Monrovia as the registered office and a business address in Vaduz.'

'Liechtenstein? Shit, well that's a dead end for a start. We got anything else?'

'There's the stuff from Casagrande, the logbook and so on.'

'We're going to have to go through the log day by day, plot the movements of the *Maria Vasquez*, see exactly where she went and when.'

'Well, as you're volunteering.'

Enqvist pushed the pile of documentation across the desk. Sullivan picked up the logbook and riffled through the photocopied pages without much enthusiasm.

Enqvist sipped his coffee. 'How was your weekend?'

'Okay. Yours?'

'You know, pretty much as usual.'

'You go anywhere?'

'No. Where would I go?'

Enqvist's marriage had broken down three years earlier, before Sullivan was seconded to UCLAF. His wife and daughter were still in Stockholm but Stig rarely visited them. He seemed to spend his weekends either working or talking to strangers in bars. He held his drink well, but Sullivan sometimes worried about him. His eyes were getting increasingly bloodshot and there were moments during the working day when he disappeared to the toilet for ten minutes and came back smelling of mint toothpaste which didn't always disguise the underlying odour of brandy.

Sullivan put down the logbook and glanced at one of the other bits of paper Casagrande had sent from Naples. It was a list of the names of the crew on the

Maria Vasquez. Something about it struck Sullivan as odd. He rummaged in his briefcase and took out a photocopy he'd brought back from Hull.

'What's the matter?' Enqvist asked.

Sullivan compared the two pieces of paper, then searched through the logbook for something that wasn't there.

'This is the crew list from Naples,' he said. 'And this is one I got from the CPS file in Hull. The master is different on each one, we know why. But so is the first officer. When the ship was detained in Hull, and when Customs finally let her sail, he was someone called Joop Broekhuizen. When the *Guardia* arrested the ship the first officer was one Nikolai Tonkov. There's no entry in the log to explain when or why he was replaced.'

'So? Maybe the first guy was tainted by Maartens so the owners got rid of him. Maybe the new master wanted to bring his own first officer with him. There could be any number of reasons why it happened.'

'Yes, perhaps,' Sullivan conceded.

He returned the papers to the collection on the desk and noticed Enqvist holding up another document.

'What's that?'

'Take a look. It's from Dutch Customs. I asked them for it when you were in Hull. It's a copy of the clearance for the cigarettes on the *Maria Vasquez*. They came from a bonded warehouse owned by a Willem Van Vliet.'

Sullivan's brow furrowed as he ran the name through his memory banks.

'I don't recognise it. Any form?'

'Not in our files.'

'Dutch Customs?'

'They're checking, but unlikely. By all accounts it's a reputable, long-established business.'

Sullivan studied the information in the fax.

'You notice the figures?' Enqvist said.

Sullivan didn't reply. He was hunting through the drawers of his desk, taking out wads of paper and flicking through them quickly.

'What are you looking for?' Enqvist asked.

'Got it.'

Sullivan held up a scrap of paper with a few numbers scribbled on it.

'Got what?'

But Sullivan was already on his feet, collecting together the assortment of documents scattered over the surface in front of him.

'We're going to see Carlsen.'

Sullivan spread the papers over the section chief's desk and talked him through them, Stig Enqvist looking on from a chair to one side.

'The *Maria Vasquez* left Rotterdam on February seventh, carrying a cargo of American cigarettes which had been stored in a bonded warehouse belonging to Van Vliet Entrepôt NV. No duty was paid because the cigarettes were being re-exported to Senegal. So far, everything above board.

'Eight days later, on the morning of the fifteenth, the ship is arrested in the Tyrrhenian Sea off the coast of Italy. On board her the *Guardia* find nearly thirty thousand master cases of cigarettes, plus the four hundred cases we recovered from the speedboats. But look at the Rotterdam customs clearances. When she left Holland, the *Maria Vasquez* was loaded with forty-five thousand master cases. Somewhere between Rotterdam and Naples she offloaded a hundred and fifty million cigarettes and you can bet your life it wasn't done legitimately.'

'They made another drop?' Carlsen said, looking up from the documents.

'Offshore,' Sullivan said. 'According to the log, she didn't put in anywhere after she left Rotterdam.'

'That's a lot of coastline. France, Spain, Portugal. Several thousand kilometres.'

'Now look at this,' Sullivan said. 'Claire Colmar gave me the serial numbers of the cases of cigarettes she found in Bayonne. Check them against the Rotterdam customs clearances and the *Guardia di Finanza* seizure list. It was the same consignment.'

Carlsen leaned back, looking directly at Sullivan.

'What do you want me to do?'

'Authorise a raid on the bonded warehouse in Rotterdam. I want to know who ordered the cigarettes, who shipped them and who paid for them.'

'Just us?'

'With Dutch Customs. I think they should be in on it.'

Carlsen gave a nod. That was one of his strengths, the ability to make quick decisions, to trust the professionalism of his investigators.

'I'll talk to Hellendoorn immediately,' he said. 'Have you spoken to Colmar about this?'

'Not yet.'

The section chief mused on something for a time, tugging at the lobe of his left ear with his forefinger and thumb.

'What's the latest on Nicoletti?' he said.

'I spoke to him last week,' Enqvist said. 'Another three weeks, at least. And then he'll probably be on crutches for a time.'

'I'm going to have a word with Pierre Serot,' Carlsen said. 'See if he can spare Colmar for a while. You could use another person on the team. Especially in Rotterdam. She's Dutch, she knows the people there, speaks the language.'

'She might not want to join us,' Sullivan said.

Carlsen smiled knowingly. 'Oh, I think she will.'

Claire Colmar had been with UCLAF for nearly three years, her first twelve months on general agricultural import and export investigations and latterly on the Olive Oil Task Group which, along with the task groups on cigarettes and alcohol, dealt with the high-risk, high-return frauds which were dominated by organised crime gangs. She enjoyed the work, but agriculture had none of the glamour of cigarettes or alcohol. Checking bottles of olive oil was hardly the stuff of dreams and she'd been angling for some time for a transfer to one of the other two task groups. But there'd been no opening until Maurizio Nicoletti slid into a pine tree and snapped his tibia venturing off-piste in the Dolomites. After that she'd approached Carlsen again and made another pitch for a transfer. He'd been cool at first, but Claire had a feeling she'd get her own way eventually. She usually did.

Sullivan and Enqvist were relatively unknown quantities to her. There were almost eighty investigators in the unit and most were so engrossed in their particular specialisations that they had no time to cross over and mix with their colleagues in other sections. Enqvist was probably one of the few who was familiar to everyone in some way. He was coming to the end of his term of secondment so he'd been around for nearly four years, longer than most, and he was a sociable, gregarious individual. Loud would be another, less complimentary way of putting it. He was friendly, talkative – too talkative for some – and always willing to go for a drink after work or to help out a colleague in need. He'd made a pass at Claire once and she'd given him the brush-off, but he didn't seem to resent it and she certainly didn't hold it against him. She was used to working in predominantly male environments and was accustomed to the unwanted attentions that always brought.

Sullivan was harder to categorise. Seemingly distant, contained, he had none of Enqvist's boisterous energy, but he had a quiet, unassuming determination about him, a tough grittiness that was reassuring. Claire sensed almost immediately that, of the two, Sullivan was the one she'd rather have beside her in a tight corner.

But right now they were in a car on the motorway north of Brussels, heading towards Antwerp and then Rotterdam. Enqvist was driving, Sullivan next to him. Claire was in the back listening to the two men talking.

'I like Antwerp,' Enqvist was saying. 'You know why? Because it's a Flemish town. There's something about the Flemings I like. They're friendlier than the Walloons.'

'You mean they drink more,' Sullivan said.

'They're less stand-offish, more parochial in some ways, but that gives the city more character than Brussels, which is too full of foreigners for me.'

'Especially Swedes.'

'You know what I mean. Brussels bores me, particularly stuck there at weekends. You can only wander around the Grand-Place so many times.'

'There's more to see than the Grand-Place, if you want to play tourists.'

'Like what?' Enqvist said. 'The Manneken Pis?'

'There's the Atomium, the Château Royal, the parks, the museums.'

'The museums? I can't think of anything more boring. The only interesting one was the Underpants Museum but that shut a few years ago.'

'There was an Underpants Museum?' Sullivan said incredulously.

'Yeah.'

'You're kidding.'

'No, there was.'

'Containing what?'

'What do you think? Celebrities' underwear.'

'Like whose? Sharon Stone's?'

'Funnily enough, no. That's what made it interesting. It was the only underpants museum in the world not to contain a pair of Sharon Stone's knickers. People flocked there from all over to see why not.'

'Bollocks.'

'It's true,' Enqvist protested.

'Okay, whose underpants were in it?'

'I can't remember exactly. Famous Belgians'.'

'So it was a very small museum?'

'Ho, a cheap jibe.'

'In England, the Belgians are famous for not being famous. I bet you can't name me ten famous Belgians.'

'Easy.' Enqvist paused.

'See,' Sullivan said.

'Wait on, I'm just collecting my thoughts. Okay, Simenon, the writer; César Franck, the composer; Hercule Poirot, the detective.'

'He's not real.'

'He is to me.'

'You might just as well include Tintin, Captain Haddock and Snowy.'

'Hergé, he's another. How many's that?'

'Three.'

'Shit, there must be more than that.'

Claire looked out of the window, marvelling at this stream of drivel, only half listening to these grown men playing the sort of silly game you indulge in when you're drunk, or on surveillance duty to pass the time. They were both former customs officers, maybe that's where they'd acquired the habit.

Claire had once thought that women were better at talking to one another, just chatting easily about whatever happened to occur to them, but men needed a specific subject. Men had to talk *about* a particular topic: about football, or about cars or about women. But over the years, working with men, she'd realised how wrong that was; that men had an innate ability to talk to each other for hours on end about absolutely nothing at all.

'Jean-Claude Van Damme, so-called actor,' Enqvist said. 'The Muscles from Brussels.'

'Is he famous?' Sullivan inquired.

'He thinks he is.'

'That's four.'

They were silent for a long time, Enqvist concentrating on negotiating the ringroad around Antwerp, Sullivan gazing through the windscreen with the kind of fixed focus that implied he wasn't actually looking at the view. Claire put them out of their misery.

'Hieronymus Bosch, Brueghel, Pierre Cuilliford,' she said.

'Who?' Sullivan said.

'The artist. He created the *Schtroumpfs*. Smurfs, you call them in English.'

'Those little blue gits are Belgian? That explains a lot.'

'Rubens, Van Dyck, Magritte.' Claire finished the list. 'I think that's ten.'

That shut them up.

There was a pause, then Enqvist glanced across at Sullivan and said: 'Okay, ten famous Norwegians.'

The grey Renault saloon was two hundred metres from the customs post, anonymous and completely unnoticed amongst the dozens of other vehicles in the car park beside the River Bidassoa. Queyras and Pigout, the two plainclothes customs officers inside the car, had long since run out of things to say to each other. The former was flicking idly through a motoring magazine, looking at the same pictures, the same articles he'd already read at least twice; the latter was listening to Johnny Halliday on his personal stereo and chewing on a slightly stale *pain aux raisins*, his third of the day.

They were old hands at the surveillance game, practised at filling the long hours of tedium it entailed. They had an ability to draw out the simplest activities to an inordinate length: to extend a brief exchange that might normally take five minutes into a half-hour conversation, to stretch a newspaper feature from a two-minute browse to a twenty-minute detailed study, and to break up the numbing boredom of a day's shift with the undercover operative's great solace: food. The inside of the Renault was littered with the debris of their indulgence; crumbs and torn fragments of *baguette*, orange peel, apple cores, discarded pastry bags and innumerable chocolate bar wrappers.

The vacuum flask on the floor had held two

litres of coffee but that had now all been drunk, the evidence clearly visible in the gleaming pools of liquid outside on the asphalt beside the doors. Like professional cyclists who could urinate whilst in the saddle, the two men – not daring, or often finding it impossible, to leave their posts – had perfected the technique of pissing out of the side of a stationary car without drawing attention to themselves.

Queyras checked his watch. 'It's time,' he said, tossing down his magazine.

Pigout switched off his stereo and removed the headphones from his ears. In the distance, three figures came out of the door of the customs post and split up, heading for their cars parked in the lot next to the building. Christophe Bignon climbed into a shiny green Citroën and drove out on to the main road.

'They don't hang around, do they?' Queyras said, starting the engine and spinning the wheel to bring the Renault out on to the highway a hundred metres behind the Citroën. 'The minute the shift finishes, they're off.'

'Can you blame them?' Pigout said.

'It's all right for some.'

'You want to swap with them? Sit around all day in a shitty little backwater like this, counting lorries as they go past?'

Queyras didn't reply. They'd both served their time in the provinces before finally making it to *Douane* headquarters in Paris. Their job had its drawbacks but neither of them wanted to return to the monotonous routine of a frontier posting.

Bignon's car headed north-east up the N10 towards St Jean-de-Luz, but turned off in Urrugne to take a narrow country road which ascended the foot-hills leading to La Rhune, the 900-metre peak which dominated this part of the Basque Coast. A couple of kilometres up the hill he turned into the driveway of a large stone farmhouse commanding a panoramic view of Hendaye, Fuenterrabia and Irun.

Queyras and Pigout drove past the house and found a junction higher up where they turned round and went back down the hill, stopping on the verge next to a stone wall which hid their car from sight of the house. The only problem was that the wall also prevented them seeing the entrance to the driveway. Queyras took out the surveillance log and made a note of the time and Bignon's route home. Then he produced a five franc coin.

'I'll toss you for the first stint.'

Pigout lost. Muttering darkly, he hauled himself out of the car and walked down the hill to a point from which he could see the house without himself being observed. Night had already fallen and there was a cool wind blowing off the black sheet of the ocean far down below him, beyond the scintillating lights of Hendaye Plage. Pigout shivered and but-toned up his coat.

After half an hour, Queyras relieved him and they alternated throughout the evening, freezing their balls off on the roadside before returning to the car to thaw out. Approaching nine o'clock, Bignon came out of the drive in the Citroën and went back down the hill towards the coast. A little more than thirty minutes later he was in the casino at Biarritz.

Queyras and Pigout went in after him and took turns loitering near the roulette table as Bignon played with an intense fervour that marked him out as more than just a casual gambler. He remained there until eleven thirty, then drove home.

Following him in the Renault, Pigout remarked: 'How much do you reckon he just blew?'

'I made it nearly sixty thousand francs.'

'And what does he earn? Thirty thousand a month maximum, even with overtime.'

'So he just lost two months' wages in one evening.'

Pigout nodded. 'And his house, that must be worth, what, two million?'

They held back a little, letting the Citroën get well ahead of them as they went up the hill.

Then Pigout said: 'I think I'd like to have a look at his bank account, wouldn't you?'

'What is the point of these places?' Enqvist demanded rhetorically. 'There are dozens of them all over the world. Not just Andorra. Monaco, San Marino, Liechtenstein, the Channel Islands, every fucking banana republic in the Caribbean. What are they for? We having another bottle of wine, by the way?'

'I'm okay,' Sullivan said.

Claire shook her head, but Enqvist had already made the decision for them. He flagged down a passing waiter and ordered another bottle of Alsace Riesling.

'I'll tell you what they're for,' he said, continuing his train of thought. 'They exist because the rich need them to avoid taxes and if there's one golden rule that applies to every fucking thing in this world, it's that whatever the rich need, they get. The western governments, if they really wanted to, could shut down these ridiculous havens overnight: close their borders, cut off their supplies, invade. You think the French couldn't walk into Monaco and say, 'Okay, guys, the party's over, you're part of France now and we want all the billions you've stashed away.' What are the Monegasques going to do? Send out a bunch of pop stars and playboys in their luxury yachts to stop the French Navy? Wheel out Rainier, Albert, Caroline and all those other royal parasites to lie down in front of the tanks?'

Sullivan caught Claire's eye across the table and smiled.

'Stig is something of a Republican, as you'll notice now you're working with us,' he said.

'I'm just explaining the problems we have to face,' Enqvist said. 'Cigarettes and olive oil are different. Every investigation we undertake sooner or later – and it's usually sooner – we find it somehow involves one of these pisspot little states. Like Andorra, as I said.'

He paused as the waiter brought the second bottle of wine to the table, pulled the cork and let him taste it. Enqvist nodded his approval and waved the waiter away, filling his glass himself.

'Anyone else?'

Sullivan was still on his first glass of the previous bottle and Claire had barely started her second. They both shook their heads.

Enqvist took a gulp of the new wine and said to Claire: 'You ever been to Andorra?'

'No.'

'You should go. Everyone should. I recommend it as a salutary example of what a base, material-istic species we are. It's the most revolting, obscene place I've ever been. Think of all the worst souvenir shops you've seen and put them in the same street and you've got Andorra la Vella, that's the capital. Although capital is a grand word for what is basically the world's largest duty-free shop. That's all there is there. Two long rows of stores selling the same stuff: booze, cigarettes, cameras, perfume. Plus a few bars and some hotels – but not many. No one actually stays in the shitty little hole, they just go there for the day to shop.

'And you know who the Head of State of Andorra is? Well, there are two, it's joint rule. The President of France and, wait for it, the Bishop of Urgel. Isn't that hilarious? A Catholic bishop presiding over the tackiest, most commercialised place on earth.'

Enqvist paused, concentrating on his food. They were in the top floor restaurant of their hotel in Rotterdam, sitting by a window which afforded a view of the modern, high-rise centre of the city and in the distance, beyond the glowing lights of the tower blocks, the Nieuwe Maas waterway which led to the massive Europoort complex, and, ultimately, the North Sea.

Enqvist was filling Claire in on some of the background to the Cigarette Task Group's work, describing how they'd stopped the trafficking from Andorra which had once been a major centre for smugglers.

'We looked at the figures, it was as simple as that,' he said. 'Andorra has a resident population of about sixty-three thousand, plus a few hundred thousand tourists spread out over the year. Yet they import – or at least they did then – several billion cigarettes annually. Not to mention the ones they manufacture under licence within the country. On the figures – and I can't remember them exactly – every man, woman and child in the country must have been smoking something like four hundred cigarettes a day. Now that's what I call a habit.'

Enqvist helped himself to more sauté potatoes from the dish in the middle of the table and used them to mop up the creamy sauce that had come with his veal cutlets.

'What's more,' he continued, 'a large part of the cigarettes imported into Andorra came from the UK, brands that the Andorrans – or for that matter, the Spanish and French – have never traditionally smoked. What was going on?

'Quite simple: the cigarettes were manufactured in Britain, then exported on a T1 to Andorra. Goods in transit across the EU to a non-EU country so no duty payable. The Andorrans then smuggled them over their borders into France and Spain, either across the mountain passes by donkey, or by road declaring them as something else. The cigarettes were then back in the EU and could be moved freely between member states without customs checks. So the smugglers put them on a lorry and took them all the way back to the UK where they sold them on the black market. How much duty evaded? In 1997 alone, about four hundred million ECUs. And that's just one trafficking route. I tell you, the more I do this, the more I realise I'm in the wrong job.'

Claire finished the last morsel of her chicken and sipped her wine, looking across at the two men. Enqvist was shovelling potatoes into his mouth and chewing on them, his cheeks bulging; Sullivan was going slower, eking out his food as if he didn't want to finish first. He hadn't said much during the meal, he'd left all that to Enqvist, but there was nothing intimidating or hostile about his reticence. His manner was warm, welcoming. He seemed glad to have her on the team.

'The Spanish Civil Guard sealed off the entire border,' Enqvist went on. 'Tightened up their frontier controls, stopped and searched as many lorries as they could. The smugglers soon got the message.'

'They stopped doing it, you mean?'

Sullivan shook his head. 'They just moved elsewhere. That's how they work. They go where the smuggling is easiest. If one country gets too hot, they simply find another base. We sorted out Andorra but the truth is we just moved the trafficking into someone else's back yard.'

'Anywhere in particular?'

Sullivan grinned. 'Now if we knew that . . .'

'The bastards are everywhere,' Enqvist said. 'Every mafia-type outfit in the world wants a share of the cake. The Cosa Nostra, Camorra, the Triads, the Turkish Grey Wolves, the Chechens, the Ukrainians, the Colombians, the Serb warlords.'

'The Serbs are into trafficking?' Claire said.

'It's one of the key ways they fund their war machine.'

'But how do all these people get hold of the cigarettes?'

'The manufacturers sell to them. Not directly, of course.' Enqvist's voice took on a tone of heavy sarcasm. 'Cigarette manufacturers are all men of honour, fine law-abiding citizens who would never dream of trading with traffickers. Unfortunately, there are plenty of middle men who have no such scruples. It's hardly the fault of the manufacturers if those middle men sell on what they buy to a bunch of gangsters, now is it?'

'They must know what's going on, surely?' Claire said.

'I'll give you some more statistics, let you draw your own conclusions,' Enqvist said. 'In October 1997 alone, before the clampdown on smugglers by the Civil Guard and the French, the British cigarette firm Gallaher exported a hundred million cigarettes to Andorra. One month later, in November 1997, after the clampdown, they exported precisely zero to Andorra. In October, the other big British manufacturer, Imperial, exported nearly eighty million cigarettes to Andorra. By January 1998, that too was down to zero. The companies say they had no idea where the cigarettes were ultimately going, but who did they think was buying them, the Bishop of fucking Urgel?'

Claire laughed. She had a feeling she was going to enjoy working with these two.

'The middle men are the problem,' Sullivan explained. 'Some of them are traders who deal with legitimate outlets and siphon off a part for sale to traffickers. Others flog on everything they buy to smugglers.'

'You know who they are?'

'Some. A lot of them are Swiss: clever, unscrupulous lawyers and accountants. Rich men in suits who mix with politicians and bankers, sophisticated businessmen who go to black-tie dinners at international finance conferences, who can borrow millions on the shake of a hand. They're crooks, but catching them at it is nigh on impossible. They're always protected by a trail of companies, many of them bogus and all eventually ending up in places like Liechtenstein and the Bahamas and Jersey where their secrets are safe from people like us.'

'Which I think is where we came in,' said Enqvist.

He cleared his plate and poured himself another glass of wine, looking around for a waiter.

'We having dessert?'

He signalled to one of the waiters and asked for the dessert menu. Then Sullivan's mobile phone rang. He answered and had a brief conversation.

'Hellendoorn,' he said, putting the phone back in his jacket pocket.

'Everything fixed?' Stig asked.

'Warrants arranged, his men all ready to go. He'll pick us up from the foyer at seven thirty.'

Enqvist winced. 'So early?'

'He wanted earlier, but I told him you were here so he made a concession. It somehow spoils the impact if one of the team is still wearing his pyjamas.'

'I don't wear pyjamas.'

'Even worse.'

'Are we having dessert or not? Do something useful with your mouth,' Enqvist said, turning his attention to the menu.

Claire could feel the easy rapport between them. They made a good partnership. She'd seen ones like it before in Dutch Customs: men who worked well together, who respected each other but indulged in a smokescreen of casual joshing to disguise the genuine affection they felt for one another.

They went straight to their rooms after they'd finished dinner. They had three next to each other down a long corridor. Enqvist went into his first with a murmured, 'See you in the morning'. Claire unlocked her door as Sullivan walked past her to his room. He paused on the threshold and smiled briefly at her.

'Good night.'

112

'Good night,' she said.

She watched him disappear through the doorway, then pushed open her own door, went inside and locked it behind her.

SIX

Claire had grown up in Haarlem in the province of Noord-Holland, a small parochial town she'd found stiflingly dull as a teenager, and from which she'd taken every possible opportunity to escape. Fortunately, the beach resort of Zandvoort was only a few kilometres away to the west, a refuge during the summer months where she and her friends had spent many a long weekend sunbathing or wandering along the seafront chatting up boys. In winter, and in the evenings, there was Amsterdam, a fifteen-minute train journey away to the east. She'd loved the city back then. It seemed to offer everything Haarlem lacked: bright lights, teeming bars and nightclubs, exotic haunts and the wicked, tantalising flavour of sex, which she was just beginning to try out for herself. Now she was older, Amsterdam was no longer so appealing. The red-light district had lost its fascination and the city was a curious mixture of the tawdry and the picturesque. A centre for tourists that she regarded as Heritage Holland, like windmills and tulip fields and women in clogs and lace shawls.

Rotterdam, in contrast, had almost nothing to offer

the tourist. It had none of the charm of the capital, and the prostitution and drug-dealing were not for sightseers, they were for real. Claire had never really liked the city, but it had an energy and a culture of enterprise that made it an exciting place to live. Virtually destroyed during the war, it had been rebuilt with a fervour and an optimism that had transformed it from the busiest port in Holland into the busiest in the world. Whilst Amsterdam seemed to wallow in its past, Rotterdam, its past bombed to rubble by the *Luftwaffe*, looked only to the future.

No one would have called the vast complex of port facilities that lined the waterway to the North Sea beautiful, but it was impossible not to be impressed, even overawed, by their scale. For thirty kilometres, from Waalhaven docks to the Maasvlakte container terminal opposite the Hook of Holland, the banks of the man-made Nieuwe Waterweg were cluttered with moorings, harbours, refineries, petro-chemical plants, oil and dry bulk storage containers and hundreds of warehouses and 'distriparks' from which goods were distributed across continental Europe.

There was a vibrancy about it that Claire found stimulating. The huge supertankers discharging their crude oil; the container ships – their decks stacked high with multi-coloured boxes which, from a distance, looked like Lego bricks – unloading next to ranks of towering cranes; the incessant activity day and night; the lorries moving in convoy along the perimeter roads and all of it tainted with the windblown taste of the ocean. It was a testament to what man, motivated by the desire to rebuild and reshape his environment, could achieve. And it was a testament to the greed and the ruthlessness which underpinned that desire.

The warehouses of Van Vliet Entrepôt NV were in a distripark adjacent to the Europoort. There were three of them in total, each the size of several supermarkets put together, but only one used for storing bonded goods – cigarettes and alcohol imported duty free and only removed for distribution under the supervision of Customs.

The two navy-blue BMWs drove on to the quayside beside the warehouses and parked near the entrance to the company offices. Claire, Sullivan and Enqvist climbed out of one of the vehicles. With them was Piet Hellendoorn, the anti-fraud liaison officer for the Dutch customs service. Tall and craggy, he had flowing blond hair, ice-blue eyes and – quite apposite considering the task in hand – a nicotine addiction which meant a cigarette was never very far away from his lips. Claire found him passably attractive but he smelt like a four-day-old ash tray.

They went through a pair of glass doors into the foyer and asked to see the owner. Willem Van Vliet was small and wiry with a skein of straw-coloured hair plastered across the top of his head and a blotchy, broken-veined complexion which implied he was no stranger to the bottle, a first impression which was confirmed when he invited them all up to his office and offered them coffee or a shot of *jenever* from the drinks cabinet he kept by his desk. They accepted the coffee but declined the spirit; it was too early, even for Enqvist, to be drinking gin.

The office was spacious but hardly luxurious. To reach it involved a climb up a flight of metal steps and a short walk along an open steel gantry that overlooked the cavernous interior of the bonded warehouse where cases of cigarettes and alcohol were stacked to the roof as far as the eye could see. The desk and chairs were bottom-of-the-range catalogue furniture and the flooring a thin industrial carpeting singed in places by what appeared to be cigarette burns. Van Vliet waved them to the seats and slumped down behind his desk. He was so short that only the upper part of his chest and head were visible.

'This is an unexpected pleasure,' he said in Dutch, smiling to reveal a set of yellowing teeth.

'Perhaps we could speak English,' Hellendoorn said, introducing the others. 'It would be easier for my colleagues from UCLAF.'

'UCLAF?' A flicker of his eyes betrayed Van Vliet's unease. 'So this isn't a routine visit?' he said in English.

'No, I'm afraid not. We'd like to take a look at your records.'

'Which ones?'

'All of them. Is there someone who can show my officers where they are kept, and explain your system to them?'

'Of course. Has there been some irregularity?'

'The records first, Mr Van Vliet.'

Van Vliet shrugged and pushed himself up out of his chair. If it weren't for his aging features, it would have looked as though a schoolboy had sneaked in to take charge of the office. He went through into the adjoining room and barked instructions at the middle-aged woman sitting behind a computer terminal.

'My secretary will take care of everything you need,' he said, returning to his desk.

'Thank you,' Hellendoorn said.

He dispatched his team of investigators. Enqvist went with them, leaving Sullivan and Claire in Van Vliet's office. Hellendoorn deferred to them.

'Miss Colmar and Mr Sullivan are with the Cigarette Task Group. This visit is being carried out at their instigation.'

'For what reason?' Van Vliet enquired politely.

'Are you familiar with a ship named the *Maria Vasquez*?' Sullivan said.

'Yes.'

'She was arrested off the Italian coast last week on suspicion of supplying cigarettes to smugglers. Did you know that?'

'I'd heard something,' Van Vliet replied. 'But I know nothing about any smuggling.'

'We understand the cigarettes she was carrying came from your warehouse.'

'Yes, they did. You want to see the papers?'

'Please.'

'Erik!' Van Vliet called. 'Erik! Excuse me.'

Van Vliet went back out into the adjoining office

just as a shirtsleeved young man came in from the gantry outside. They exchanged a few inaudible words and the young man went to a shelf and took down a box file. Van Vliet tucked it under his arm and returned to his own office. Claire, seated at an oblique angle to the desk, had a clear view of the young man outside reaching for the telephone before Van Vliet closed the door and resumed his seat. Claire stole a furtive glance at her watch. It was 8.25 am.

Van Vliet opened the file and perused its contents.

'She was loaded on the seventh. Forty-five thousand cases. The list of brands is here if you want to see it. Every case was checked out by Customs. They always are. Not a single cigarette leaves this warehouse without customs clearance.'

'She was going to Senegal, according to documents found on board.'

'That's right. Dakar.'

Van Vliet took out a pouch of tobacco and some papers and rolled himself a cigarette, licking the gum and pinching off a few protruding strands of leaf.

'I've run this warehouse for twenty years and I have never had any problems with Customs,' he said, lighting the cigarette and puffing on it. 'What happens to the ships after they leave Rotterdam is not my business. All I do is arrange for the goods to be loaded.'

'You've done business with the *Maria Vasquez* before?' Sullivan said.

'Many times. She's a regular carrier of all sorts of goods.'

'Cigarettes?'

'Yes, but other things too.'

'Do you know who owns the ship?'

'A Liberian corporation, I believe. All Liberian-registered ships have to be owned by a Liberian citizen or corporation. Who owns it is immaterial to me.'

'Who gave you the order for the cigarettes?'

Van Vliet consulted the file. 'A company in London. Cannadine Export Limited. The address is there, if you want it.'

'You've dealt with them in the past?'

'For about six months only. They're a relatively new customer.'

'Who did you deal with there?'

Some ash fell off the tip of Van Vliet's cigarette. He flicked it from his shirtfront with his fingers.

'No one at the company,' he explained. 'My instructions came from their agent, a Herr Walter Busch. He's a lawyer in Vaduz.'

'And payment for the cigarettes?'

'A cheque drawn on a bank in Vaduz.'

Liechtenstein again. Sullivan had never been there but he knew in his gut he wouldn't like it. There were too many lawyers.

'You know Mr Busch?' he said.

'I've never met him. I rarely meet the people I do business with. We communicate by telephone and fax. All I know about him is that he is efficient and pays his bills promptly. Those are great virtues in commerce.'

Van Vliet brushed more ash off his shirt. It was less effort than using an ash tray.

'This company, Cannadine Export Limited,' Sullivan continued. 'Did they only deal in cigarettes?'

'With me, yes.'

'How many shipments in the six months you've been associated with them?'

'Six. One a month.'

'All on the *Maria Vasquez*?'

Van Vliet nodded.

'All bound for Senegal?'

'No. The destinations have all been different. They're here in the file too.'

'Did this company ever use other ships to move cigarettes?'

'I wouldn't know. They never did with me, but there are other bonded warehouses in Rotterdam. You'd have to ask them.'

Sullivan reached out for the file. 'I can take this?'

'It's what you came for, isn't it?' Van Vliet said.

'You never had any suspicions that the *Maria Vasquez* was involved in trafficking?'

'Why would I? I don't check what happens to the cargoes I sell. My only concern is ensuring the legal formalities are observed and that my bills are paid. Believe me, you won't find a single irregularity in that file, or any of the others here. But you're welcome to try.'

*   *   *

121

They found Stig Enqvist downstairs with the other customs officers in a large, airy room which was obviously used for meetings. The long table in the centre was already covered with stacks of files and printouts which the men were sifting through with laborious thoroughness. In theory, the entire operation of the warehouses was done by computer, but in practice, for Van Vliet and every other business Sullivan had ever encountered, the paperless office was a myth. There was always paper. Piles of it. Invoices, receipts, order forms, letters, cargo manifests, customs clearances. Computers had revolutionised the working of commerce, sped up its cogs and wheels so that transactions could be completed in fractions of a second and with an accuracy previous generations could only have dreamt of. But for all their magical efficiency, the machines had been unable to overcome a basic human need to hold something tangible in the hand. People still wanted to see it written on paper and for that small weakness Sullivan would be eternally grateful, because it was in those pieces of paper that a company's secrets were always hidden.

'You finished yet?' Sullivan asked facetiously.

'We were waiting for you,' Enqvist replied. 'What happened to that coffee we were promised?'

Sullivan dropped the file from Van Vliet's office on to the table and sat down.

'The company that owns the *Maria Vasquez*,' he said. 'What was its name? Buchanan Investments?'

'That's right.'

'You said they had a business address in Vaduz.'

'Yeah, a lawyer's office.'

'You remember his name?'

'Busch. Something like that.'

'Walter Busch?'

'Yeah, that's him. Why?'

Sullivan sighed and flipped open the box file. 'It's a very small world,' he said, taking out a thick wad of papers.

He glanced up. On the other side of the room Claire was deep in conversation with Hellendoorn. He caught just a few words of Dutch, picking out a couple he understood but making no sense of them. He turned his attention back to the papers and started to read.

They were there for the rest of the day, going over the company records, examining invoices, payments, every detail of Van Vliet's business. Sullivan found this aspect of his job tedious. He wasn't an accountant and, though he'd done a customs audit many times before, he was only too aware that a clever and careful operator could hide a multitude of sins in the morass of facts and figures. But one of the key guidelines for a fraud investigator was 'follow the paper trail', and this monotonous routine of checking and crosschecking was an essential, and unavoidable, part of the process.

In the middle of the afternoon he left Van Vliet's offices and went across to the nearby customs control post to use the fax machine. When he'd finished he was handed a piece of paper to take back to

Hellendoorn. It was a fax that had arrived earlier, listing a series of telephone numbers and times.

'What's all this, Piet?' he asked when he returned to the bonded warehouse.

'Claire asked for it,' Hellendoorn replied, waving the paper in her direction.

Claire got up from the table and came over. She scanned the list of numbers.

'That one,' she said, underlining it with her pen. 'The Amsterdam number. Can you do the same thing for me again? Get a printout of the calls made from there today?'

Hellendoorn looked at his watch. 'You probably won't get the answer until tomorrow.'

'That's okay.'

'What's going on?' Sullivan asked.

'I'm not sure,' Claire replied. 'But I think it's worth checking.'

By six o'clock Sullivan had had enough. His eyes and neck and shoulders ached and his concentration was so diminished he knew it was silly to continue. It was when you were tired that you made mistakes, started to overlook even the obvious. He approached Claire and perched himself on the edge of the table next to her.

'Are you up to a short trip?' he said.

She pushed back her chair and rubbed her eyes.

'A trip where?'

'Gouda.'

'You want to buy some cheese?'

'To talk to someone. I may need an interpreter.'

'Why not?' she said with a shrug. 'I've had more than I can take of this.'

Enqvist sniffed and made a pretence at appearing wounded when they told him they were going.

'And leaving me here with all this shit?' he said, gesturing at the mounds of files.

Sullivan patted him on the shoulder. 'It's where you're most at home,' he said.

One of Hellendoorn's officers gave them a lift back to their hotel where they picked up their own car and drove the twenty-five kilometres north-east to the small town of Gouda. It was Sullivan's first time there but he knew it was famous for its cheese and its hand-made candles, an appropriate combination consider-ing that, in his opinion, they both tasted of wax.

The address he was looking for, lifted from the CPS file he'd studied in Hull, was near the centre of the town, a first-floor apartment accessed through a door next to a shop whose window was jammed with blue Delft pottery. Claire pressed the bell and had a short exchange in Dutch with a woman on the entryphone. The lock clicked open and they went through and up a steep flight of stairs. A plump woman with a soft face and a cast-iron perm was waiting for them on the landing at the top.

Claire showed her ID card. 'Mrs Maartens?'

'My name is Faassen. Gerda Faassen.'

The woman said something else in Dutch and Claire turned to Sullivan.

'She's Maartens' sister, not his wife. He wasn't married.'

'May we come in?' Claire said.

Mrs Faassen looked puzzled rather than hostile. 'What are you, police?'

'Something like that,' Claire said, which wasn't strictly true. UCLAF had no police powers, but it was sometimes helpful if people believed they did.

Mrs Faassen showed them through into her sitting room. It was small and dim and so crammed with furniture you had to pick your way through an obstacle course to reach a seat. There were ornaments and vases and all manner of bric-a-brac on every surface. A glass-fronted cabinet contained shelves of polished silver and glassware and on the mantelpiece and hanging from brackets on the walls were dozens of china plates, many of them very old. It was like living in an antiques shop where nothing was ever sold.

Claire explained why they were there and – having ascertained that Mrs Faassen spoke little English – translated the conversation for Sullivan's benefit.

Mrs Faassen was quite happy to talk. She'd lived with her brother in the apartment for the previous ten years.

'Since my husband left me,' she explained. 'That's when Frans moved in. To help pay the rent, keep me company. Not that he was here very often. It worked quite well as an arrangement. This place is too small for two people but Frans only came back for a few days every month.'

'How long had he been master of the *Maria Vasquez*?' Claire asked.

'About two years. It wasn't a very good post, he

was worthy of better but . . . well, you take what you can when jobs are scarce. He had a bit of trouble with the police – all nonsense of course – but it puts people off.'

That would have been the attempted blackmail charge, Sullivan reflected as Claire told him what Mrs Faassen had said.

'He loved the sea. We grew up in Rotterdam and as a boy he'd always be down in the harbour watching the ships. He couldn't do anything else. The *Maria Vasquez* was a bit of a comedown for him – he worked on tankers in the Eighties. The pay was dreadful, the hours terrible.' Mrs Faassen glanced apologetically at Sullivan. 'No offence, but the English work their crews like slaves.'

Sullivan frowned as Claire translated the remark.

'It's a Liberian ship,' he said.

Mrs Faassen waved away the objection. 'Yes, yes, but no one really believes that. It was Liberian-registered but owned and run by the English.'

'Are you sure?' Claire said.

'Oh yes. Frans mentioned his boss a few times in passing. He only met him once, I think, but he said he was a typical arrogant Englishman.'

'Did he mention a name?'

'Not that I can remember. To tell you the truth, I wasn't very interested.' She paused. 'Frans and I weren't close. He was my brother but he was always away. He had been since he was eighteen.'

'His death must have shocked you,' Sullivan said.

'Yes, it did.' For a moment she looked away, her

expression hidden in shadow. 'Why would anyone do that? I don't understand it.'

'He was involved in smuggling drugs. That's a murky, violent world.'

'Drugs!' Mrs Faassen exclaimed bitterly. 'It was only a bit of marijuana. The English are so ridiculous about these things. It's much less harmful than cigarettes or alcohol.'

'Did your brother ever talk about the cargoes the *Maria Vasquez* carried, where she went?' Sullivan asked casually.

'No. He went all over. The travelling bored him – it does if you're a sailor, doesn't it? He sent me regular postcards but he never said much in them.'

'From where?'

'Oh.' She stopped to think. 'West Africa, Egypt, Istanbul. I've quite a collection. He'd been almost everywhere over the years. I liked getting his cards. It brought a bit of glamour into the house. I'll miss them.'

She tried a smile which didn't really come off. 'They won't even let me have his body back for burial,' she continued sadly. 'Not until they've finished their investigations.'

She looked at them both, her eyes watering a little. 'Why are you interested in Frans?'

Claire translated the question. 'You want to answer that?' she said in English.

'Ask her if she knows the former first officer, Joop Broekhuizen?'

Claire put the question. Mrs Faassen nodded.

'Joop? Yes, he came here a few times with Frans. A nice enough young man, but a bit wild,' she added unenthusiastically. 'Drank a little too much for my liking. I was very sad to hear about him.'

'Hear what about him?'

'His death. Didn't you know he'd died?'

Claire translated again and Sullivan started with surprise.

'He's dead? When? How?'

Claire conversed with Mrs Faassen for a while. Then she said in English: 'Two weeks ago. He was killed in a hit-and-run accident in northern Holland.'

SEVEN

It was dark outside, but Sullivan was still aware of the monotonous flatness of the terrain as they drove north through Holland. From Gouda to Utrecht and on across the rural plains of Overijssel and Drenthe, the uniform nature of the countryside broken up only by gleaming canals and dykes and isolated patches of forest. This was as far off the beaten track as it was possible to go in Holland, a land of fields and scattered settlements that the urban Dutch, never mind the foreign tourist, rarely had much cause to visit.

Approaching nine o'clock, they stopped at a service station on the A28 and had hamburgers and *vlaamse*, Flemish chips with mayonnaise, for dinner. Rotterdam was a hundred and twenty kilometres behind them, Groningen, their ultimate destination, a further eighty kilometres to the north. They chatted idly for a time, Sullivan telling Claire about his trip to Hull.

'Do you ever talk about anything other than work?' Claire said eventually.

'Sure.' He gave her a clear-eyed look, a smile

grazing the corners of his mouth. 'You have a subject in mind?'

'Not particularly. I'm just tired of all this. It's been a long day.'

'You want to go on tonight, or find somewhere to stay?'

'Let's get there.'

Sullivan dipped a chip into a puddle of creamy mayonnaise. 'I'll drive the next bit. Let you enjoy the view.'

Claire smiled. 'That should keep me awake for all of five minutes.'

'You know this area?'

'Not well.'

'Where's your home?'

'Noord-Holland. The province, that is, not the region. Friesland and Groningen are both further north.'

'Colmar, that's not a very Dutch-sounding name.'

'My father was French.'

'Was?'

'He died a few years ago. And your home?'

'Yorkshire originally. Colchester now. It's a bit like this round there. Flat, agricultural, dull.'

'Do you get home to your wife very often?' Claire said, steering the conversation into an area of greater interest to her.

'How did you know I was married?' Sullivan said.

Men were so naive, or pretended to be. Claire could never be sure which. Did he not realise that the first thing the women in the office did when a

131

new man arrived was ascertain his marital status? Not because they were after husbands, but because it was sensible to know what complications might arise. Nothing made a man hornier than living away from home on a tax-free salary.

'I can tell,' she said.

'I'm not sure that's a compliment. What are the signs?'

She shook her head, not wanting to get too specific. He was warming up. For the first time there was a hint of flirtation in their exchanges. He was looking at her differently too: more like the single guys in the unit.

'What do you do in Brussels when you're not working?' she asked.

'More work. Watch TV. Sometimes I go out with Stig.'

'That must be exhausting.'

'What do you mean?'

'He's hard to keep pace with, isn't he? He's quite a drinker. And a talker.'

'You noticed? I've told him he should form a support group for compulsive talkers. He could call it On and On Anon.'

Claire laughed and he was struck by how easy it was to talk to her. Her understanding of English, even silly jokes, was so effortless that he had to remind himself she was Dutch.

'How about you?' he said. 'Are you attached?'

'Not at the moment.'

'Never married?'

'Once. A long time ago.'

'It didn't work out?'

'Something like that,' Claire said.

She didn't want to tell him too much. In business, knowledge was power. In romance, it was boredom. She was attracted to him. He had a wife but she was used to that. When a woman reached her age all the decent men were married. She'd had affairs with several married men. Too many times. She wondered if that was a coincidence. The relationships were always fundamentally unsatisfactory even though their casual nature appealed to her. There was too much deception involved, too much waiting, having to fit in with his domestic arrangements, and Claire didn't like to wait.

Single men were even worse. She didn't want to get married again, not after her experiences with Wim, and sooner or later a single man's demands always became too much for her. They wanted more of her time, more of her, than she was willing to give and she found herself, sometimes deliberately, sometimes only half consciously, destroying the foundations of the relationship so it couldn't last. She liked the sex, the companionship, when it suited her, but she also liked the freedom to be alone. She'd never subscribed to the extremist view that marriage was a form of legalised prostitution, but it was certainly legal-ised drudgery. She had no intention of ever cooking another meal or washing another pair of sweaty socks for a man again.

Sullivan was watching her, sipping his cup of

coffee slowly. She knew he was curious but he didn't press her. She liked that in a man; the ability to leave things unspoken, undiscovered. She'd dumped her last guy because he dug under her skin too much. That was three months ago. Since then there'd been only a one-night stand with a pilot for Sabena she'd met at a party, and that had been a disaster. She knew the English joked about the initials of the Belgian national airline standing for Such A Bad Experience Never Again. The same could be said of the pilot's performance in bed.

'Shall we go?' Claire said.

They went back out to the car. The wind was blowing from the west, across the reclaimed land on the shores of the Ijsselmeer. With no hills, not even a slight undulation in the ground to block its progress, the gusting air swept over the fields like the backdraft from a jet engine, buffeting the body so it was hard to stay upright. They shut it out with the car doors, listening for a moment to the mournful threnody as the currents wailed and whistled around the contours of the vehicle. Then they started up and continued their journey across the empty darkness of the plain.

Enqvist stayed on late at the warehouse, then left with Hellendoorn and the rest of his team, the files they'd been examining safely locked away under the watchful eyes of a security guard from the customs post in the Europoort. Van Vliet and his staff had made every effort to be as helpful as possible, but no one was going to take the chance that they might stay on into the night with a shredder to hand.

Back at the hotel, Enqvist took a call from Sullivan saying that he and Claire were going north and wouldn't return to Rotterdam until the following day. Enqvist was annoyed. If they'd told him earlier, he could have seen what Hellendoorn was doing for the evening and tagged along. Now he was stuck on his own and he hated that.

He took a shower and changed, then went up to the hotel restaurant and ate dinner alone, looking around for any other single diners – male or female – he could strike up a conversation with. Eating by himself in a strange hotel, surrounded by couples and groups of businessmen, was one of the most depressing activities Stig could think of. He didn't enjoy his own company and was constantly aware of the voices and laughter around him that seemed to increase his feeling of isolation. He ate quickly and left the restaurant as soon as he could.

On the way out he glanced into the bar, but it was deserted except for the barman and a middle-aged couple silently nursing a pair of cocktails at one of the tables. They didn't look much fun and, besides, Enqvist disliked hotel bars. They had no character, no atmosphere. He picked up his coat from his room and got a taxi to the Oudehaven, the old harbour area of the city which had been redeveloped and turned into a lively enclave of restaurants and clubs.

He wandered along the quays for a time then

selected what seemed to be the busiest bar and went inside, forcing his way through the crowds of young people and perching himself on a high stool by the counter. He ordered a shot of *jenever* and peered around in the dim lighting, enjoying the sounds of voices and the underlying throb of the taped music. This was the kind of bar he liked. Where you could forget your own loneliness by sharing vicariously in the friendly conviviality of the groups around you, and where you could get slowly, and anonymously, drunk.

At the other end of the bar, hidden in the shadows and shielded from view by the ranks of boisterous drinkers, a pinch-faced young man was watching Enqvist. He'd spoken to him several times during the day, but he had no interest in socialising with him outside the office. Erik Wissing wasn't there for pleasure, nor was he there by chance. He'd followed Enqvist from his hotel and would stay close to him, unnoticed, until he returned. This was business. Wissing was acting under instructions but he didn't resent the loss of his evening. There were worse ways of earning a bit of overtime.

It was eleven o'clock by the time Sullivan and Claire found a hotel in Groningen and checked in. They went up to their rooms and said good night, two colleagues being polite, friendly, but nothing more. Sullivan washed and cleaned his teeth and was getting undressed when the phone on the bedside table rang. He picked it up.

'Why don't you come next door for a drink?' Claire said.

'I'm not sure that's such a good idea.'

'Come on. I've opened a bottle of wine from the mini-bar. The door's unlocked.'

The line went dead. Sullivan didn't move. He could have rung back and declined, but he didn't. He thought for a time, then put his shoes and shirt back on and went out. He was a grown man, alert and stone-cold sober. He knew exactly what he was doing.

Claire was leaning back on the headboard of the double bed, her legs stretched out on the covers. She still had on her make-up but she'd removed her tights and the jacket of her suit. Sullivan noticed that her toenails were painted with pearl varnish. She was poised, confident and very beautiful.

There were two glasses of wine on the table next to the bed. She handed one to him then took a drag on the cigarette she was holding between her fingers. For the first time, Sullivan noticed the smell in the room: the sweet, distinctive odour of marijuana. She passed him the joint and he sucked in the smoke.

'Have you smoked pot before?' she said.

'Of course.'

'I thought it was illegal in Britain.'

'It is.'

Claire looked at him, this straight Englishman in his button-down shirt and suit trousers.

'Where do you get hold of it?'

'I'm a customs officer,' Sullivan said. 'I confiscate it.'

Claire's eyes widened. 'And use it yourself?'

'You should come to a customs party. The booze, the cigarettes, you think we buy any of it?'

Claire leaned forward and took back the joint.

'I thought you were supposed to burn contraband marijuana?'

'Oh, we do,' Sullivan said. 'We just inhale at the same time.'

He drank some of his wine, wondering if he should leave now. But he'd already made the decision. Claire gave him the joint again. He felt the drug relaxing him as he drew it into his lungs. He closed his eyes.

'Good?' Claire said.

'It makes me want to go to sleep.'

'I'm sure we can think of something to keep you awake,' she said, reaching for him.

Afterwards, lying back on the pillows, naked, smiling at him, Claire said: 'Well, one thing's for sure. You'll never make it as a pilot for Sabena.'

Sullivan said: '*What?*'

There were two empty bottles of vodka on the table and Yevgeny Drozhkin was opening a third and refilling the glasses. Montague didn't touch his, he'd had enough already. He wondered why the Russians seemed able to do business only in a state of semi-intoxication. Actually, Drozhkin was Ukrainian and would have been offended to be mistaken for one of his northern neighbours, but the difference was immaterial to Montague. He thought of all the former Soviets as essentially the same. They were all unpredictable, all coarse and greedy and all endowed with a tolerance to alcohol that was truly terrifying.

Drozhkin was more sophisticated than most. He'd lived in the West and had acquired a patina of cosmopolitan culture to go with his expensive Italian suits, but there was still something of the peasant in his heavy features and pudgy hands. And in his fondness for thirty-per-cent-proof vodka that quite literally took the surface off your throat as you swallowed it.

'Chin-chin,' Drozhkin said in his thick-accented English and raised his glass, draining it in one swift movement.

'You've made the payment?' Montague asked.

'Half has already been transferred to your account in Zürich. The remainder will be paid, as usual, when I've checked the consignment is complete.'

'It's all there,' Montague said. 'You can be sure of that.'

'I'll need more next month.'

'How much?'

'Thirty thousand cases.'

'Business must be booming.'

Drozhkin shrugged non-committally. 'Can you deliver?'

'Oh yes.' Montague paused. 'And the other matters? In Holland?'

'One has been dealt with,' Drozhkin replied.

'And the second?'

'My son is taking care of it.'

Drozhkin nodded at the young man sitting beside him. Mikhail Drozhkin had none of his father's educated veneer. Surly, unshaven, his hair cropped so short you could see every contour of his skull, he looked like a hardened thug or a career soldier, which in the Ukraine were virtually the same thing.

'I want it finished quickly,' Montague said. 'If there's one thing I hate it's blackmailers.'

'We know what we're doing,' Mikhail Drozhkin replied with a dismissive sneer.

'I hope so.'

Yevgeny Drozhkin smiled. It was his teeth that betrayed his nationality. He could buy Western clothes and cars, Rolex watches and French perfumes, but his teeth would always bear the unmistakable stamp of Soviet dentistry.

'Mikhail and his colleagues are good,' he said reassuringly. 'You have nothing to worry about.'

Doyle stood up. 'I'm going to check the containers.'

He went outside on to the quayside. Mikhail Drozhkin came out after him and together they walked across the broad expanse of floodlit concrete towards a shabby freighter that was tied up to the dock. A crane was unloading cardboard boxes, lowering them to the quay where they were transferred by forklift trucks to containers mounted on the backs of articulated lorries.

Doyle pulled up the collar of his coat, hunching his shoulders against the breeze gusting in from the Black Sea. This was his sixth or seventh visit to Odessa, but it didn't get any more attractive. The docks were an ugly sprawl of concrete jetties and decrepit warehouses infested with rats the size of small cats. In winter it was bitingly cold, raked by winds that seemed to come all the way from Central Asia. In summer it stank of fetid water and rotten fish. It amazed him that this was one of the Ukraine's premier holiday resorts. During July and August the beaches outside the city were crammed with fat sweaty tourists, lined up in rows along the sand like sausages on a barbecue. Drozhkin had taken him there one afternoon, but the sight had turned his stomach. Doyle preferred the Ukrainians, even the women – particularly the women – fully clothed.

They watched the ship being unloaded for a time in silence. Then Doyle said: 'Is everything arranged?'

Mikhail Drozhkin nodded. 'They'll be on their way before midnight.'

'And the frontiers?'

'All taken care of.'

Doyle took a wad of dollar bills from his jacket and passed them across to Drozhkin, who counted them carefully.

'It's all there,' Doyle said.

'I like to be sure.'

'Who else knows?'

'Just you, me and my father.'

'Let's keep it that way,' Doyle said.

EIGHT

Sullivan was very quiet at breakfast, but maybe that was the way he always was. The hotel had laid on a full Dutch *ontbijt*: cheese, ham, hard-boiled eggs. Sullivan only had a cup of coffee and a roll. Claire wondered if he was feeling guilty.

In the car later, driving out of the city, he was still subdued, wrapped up in himself. Claire left him alone. They both needed time to reflect on what had happened. The sun was low in the sky. The pale rays glistened on the fields which were dusted with a coating of frost like icing sugar. It was very still. The reeds in the marshes, frozen and brittle, barely moved, and in the distance, by one of the canals, stood a tall windmill, its sails motionless against the blue-grey backdrop of the horizon.

This was how Sullivan had pictured rural Holland. How he'd imagined it from illustrations in children's books, from paintings of ice-skaters and dykes and plump, rosy-cheeked infants wrapped up against the cold. He'd thought they were glamorised, chocolate-box images of the countryside and was captivated to find that they really existed.

A few kilometres south of Groningen, they turned off into a small hamlet and found the address Frans Maartens' sister had given them. It was on the edge of the village, a tiny cottage with two bedroom windows peeping out from the slope of the thatched roof. Behind it, across an expanse of meadowland, was a lake, its surface a mottled sheet of ice.

Sullivan and Claire walked through the garden to the front door, the grass cracking like porcelain beneath their feet. Their breath steamed in billowing clouds that rose and melted away into the thin air.

Joop Broekhuizen's widow was in her early thirties, her face pale and hollow-eyed. Claire explained why they'd come and the woman just turned on her heel and walked back into the house leaving the door open. Two blonde little girls, not yet at school, peeked out curiously from the kitchen and were hastily pulled back as an older woman, presumably Broekhuizen's mother-in-law, came to the front of the house to speak to Claire.

'She doesn't want to talk about it,' the older woman said brusquely. 'It's too upsetting. You can get all the information you need from the police.'

'In Groningen?'

'Across the way.' She gestured with a hand. 'There's a substation in the village. Ask them.'

She retreated into the house and closed the door behind her.

The police station wasn't difficult to find. In the centre of the village, next to a bakery from which the aroma of fresh bread wafted on the breeze, it had a patrol car parked outside and a uniformed constable sitting at a desk just inside the door. Save for his presence and the trappings of a law and order establishment – the sign above the entrance, the official posters on the walls – it could have been any kind of small-town office.

The constable himself was in his forties, a solid but unambitious officer who would no doubt remain at the same lowly rank until he retired and be content with it. He had fat red cheeks, a bushy blond moustache and a beer gut so pronounced he probably had to take his annual fitness test in his patrol car.

'You're investigating Broekhuizen?' he said. 'Well, it's not the first time he's been in trouble.'

'He had a criminal record?' Claire said.

'Nothing serious. Stupid kid's things. He was quite a tearaway when he was a teenager. Going to sea sorted him out, gave him some discipline.'

'You knew him well?'

'Everyone knew Joop round here. He was a bit of a lad, you know. Came home on leave and drank too much, got in a few fights. But he wasn't a bad sort really. He wasn't malicious like some of the kids. Getting married calmed him down a bit. Women do that, don't they?'

The constable guffawed and swivelled round in his chair to open a filing cabinet behind him. He seemed to have organised his office so that once he was settled in his chair he never had to get up for anything. He pulled out a file and swung back to open it on his desk.

'You'll want the details of how he was killed, I suppose.'

Claire nodded. 'We understand it was a hit-and-run.'

'That's right. One of those senseless accidents. I've seen a few in my time. All stupid, all avoidable. Driver was probably drunk. Here we are. It was the third of this month. Joop was walking home along the road down by the lake. He'd been to a bar with a friend. It was dark, the road was icy. The road's quite narrow there, a ditch on either side, so you have to walk along the carriageway. The car hit him from behind on a bend, killed him outright.'

'Was the friend with him?'

The constable nodded. 'That's how we know what happened. He was lucky. He turned and saw the car coming. Threw himself into the ditch just in time.'

'Do you have his name?'

'Kuypers. Jan Kuypers. His address is there if you want it.'

'What about the driver?' Claire asked.

'Never traced. Kuypers gave us a description of the car but no licence plates.'

'You're still looking for him?'

'Groningen took over the case, but they haven't made any progress. Won't either now. Cases like that, the more time goes by the harder it is to solve them.' The constable shook his head. 'It's a sad business. He had two little daughters, lovely girls. His wife's all torn up about it. You're not going to bother her with this, are you?'

PAUL ADAM

Claire glanced at Sullivan and translated what the constable had said. Sullivan shook his head.

'That won't be necessary,' Claire said. 'We don't know for certain he was involved in anything. Can I take his friend's address?'

The constable turned the file round so she could write down the details.

Then she said: 'He was replaced as first officer on his ship a few weeks ago. You wouldn't have any idea why, would you?'

'Sorry,' the constable said. 'It's not the kind of thing I'd know. But he chopped and changed quite a bit. He wasn't the type to hold down a job for too long.'

'First officer is a responsible post.'

'It was only some cheap freighter, wasn't it? I don't know who gave him the job, but I can't see any reputable shipping line making Joop Broekhuizen a first officer. I wouldn't have put him in charge of a rowing boat.'

'The *Maria Vasquez* sounds a fun ship to have been on,' Sullivan said as they drove away from the police station. 'A drug-smuggling master with a handling and extortion record. A first officer with a drink problem.'

'And both of them dead now,' Claire said.

They headed back north, crossing over the motorway and taking a country road which ran along the edge of Groningen airport.

'Do you believe the hit-and-run was an accident?' Claire asked.

146

'Let's see what Kuypers says.'

The house was almost within spitting distance of the airport, a dilapidated wooden bungalow with flaking white paint on the exterior walls and rusty metal window frames; a prefabricated building which looked as if it had been erected after the war as a temporary home and been kept habitable – although only just – ever since. It was in a row of similar houses in varying states of repair, an isolated little estate with fields at the back and the perimeter fence and runway of the airport across the road at the front. In the distance could be seen a couple of hangars, the small terminal building and an assortment of aeroplanes, mostly weekend fliers, but also a large commercial cargo plane.

There was no answer when they rang the bell at the front. Sullivan went round to the back and peered in through the windows. The curtains were open but there was no sign of anyone. The house had a closed-up look to it, like a rented holiday cottage out of season.

He returned to the front and saw Claire talking to an old woman on the step of the house next door. They disappeared inside and Claire emerged a few moments later, the old lady right behind her. Sullivan walked across in time to catch Claire handing one of her business cards to the old lady and saying: 'When he comes back, could you ask him to call me on this number?'

'He's a pilot,' Claire explained to Sullivan, walking back to the car. 'Goes away a lot.'

'Pilot for whom?'

'Some freight company. Flies from the airport. Mostly internal stuff.'

'You get a name?'

Claire held up a scrap of paper. 'And the number. From her phone directory. Paterswolde Air Transport.'

They sat in the car, Sullivan watching a small single-engined aircraft take off while Claire phoned the freight company on his mobile. He was only half listening, and the Dutch was too fast and fluent for him to follow, but he heard in her voice that something was wrong. He turned to look at her, trying to guess what she was saying from her intonation.

She ended the call and handed him back his telephone.

'Kuypers has gone missing,' she said. 'He hasn't shown up for work for two weeks. No one has any idea where he is.'

The cafe was in the centre of Bayonne, in one of the narrow crowded shopping streets near the cathedral. Bignon went in and sat down at a table towards the back from where he had a clear view of the door. It was raining outside. Through the window he could see the pavements wet and glistening like a fishmonger's slab.

Pigout strolled in a few minutes later and found a table up against the side wall. He ordered a coffee and a *pain au chocolat* and began reading a copy of *L'Équipe* he'd picked up at the newsagent's across

the street. Five minutes or more had elapsed when
a hefty, unshaven man in a black leather jacket came
in and walked across to Bignon's table. The two
men nodded at each other. Leather Jacket sat down
opposite Bignon and lit up a cigarette, his eyes wandering casually around the interior of the cafe. Pigout
took a bite of his *pain au chocolat* and concentrated on
his newspaper. He'd done this so many times before
that it was almost second nature to him: watching
out of the corner of his eye, then sensing instinctively
the exact moment to glance across without being
observed.

Leather Jacket was an amateur, Pigout could tell
immediately. His caution was tainted with complacency and, though his movements were slick
enough, they weren't sufficiently discreet to prevent
Pigout seeing the thick brown envelope that he passed
under the table to Bignon.

Almost immediately, Leather Jacket stood up and
left the cafe. Pigout stayed where he was and gave
a slight nod through the window. On the other side
of the street, browsing through a rack of magazines,
Queyras acknowledged the signal with a subtle inclination of his head, then set off in pursuit.

Pigout finished his coffee and remained in his seat
reading the paper even when Bignon got up and
left. The Hendaye customs officer was a secondary
concern now. It was Leather Jacket who mattered.

Paying for his drink and buying another *pain au
chocolat* to take out, Pigout drifted back through the
streets to their car. He'd eaten the pastry and was

listening to the cassette player, his lap sprinkled with greasy crumbs, when his partner climbed in next to him.

'He had a car. Var licence plates,' Queyras said.

'He's a long way from home.'

'How much d'you want to bet he's got a record?' Queyras said, leaning forward to pick up the radio handset.

'I hope you enjoyed yourselves,' Stig Enqvist said sourly as Claire and Sullivan walked into the conference room at Van Vliet's bonded warehouse.

'Very much,' Claire said, smiling enigmatically.

'And you?' Sullivan said.

'Me?' Enqvist waved a hand around the table. 'I've been wading through this crap all day.'

'You find anything of interest?'

Enqvist picked up a thin sheaf of papers. 'Those faxes you sent yesterday. We've had the replies.' He thumbed out the sheets one at a time. 'Dakar, Freetown, Abidjan, Accra, Lagos. All saying the same thing.' He paused for effect.

'You know, Stig,' Sullivan said. 'When you joined the *Tullverk*, the Swedish theatre lost a great ham. What do they say?'

'Guess.'

Sullivan picked up the faxes and skimmed through their contents. When he looked up, Enqvist was smirking at him.

'Better than sex, isn't it, this job?'

'What are you talking about?' Claire said.

'The *Maria Vasquez*,' Sullivan replied. 'She carried five cargoes of cigarettes from here before the last one we intercepted. All for this British company, Cannadine Export Limited. They were all declared as going to five different West African countries, yet according to Customs in those countries, she never went to any of them.'

'A hundred and fifty thousand master cases,' Enqvist said. 'That's one and a half billion cigarettes. All smuggled back into the EU. Duty evaded?' He glanced at Sullivan.

'Depends on which country they ended up in,' Sullivan said. 'But a conservative estimate, about a hundred and thirty million Euros.'

'Jesus!' Claire breathed.

'And that's just one ship, just five cargoes. You see the scale of the problem,' Enqvist said.

'You're checking other vessels?' Sullivan asked.

Enqvist gestured unenthusiastically at the files. 'Going through every export Van Vliet has made for the last two years. You know how many records that entails? I'll be here for fucking days.'

Piet Hellendoorn came into the room, bringing with him the smell of the Dunhills he'd gone outside to smoke. He gave Claire a phone company printout.

'Is that what you wanted?'

'Thanks, Piet.'

'I made a few enquiries for you. The Amsterdam number is a brothel on the Singel Canal.'

'A brothel?'

'It calls itself a hotel – the Golden Valley Inn. Very exclusive, very expensive. You can't just walk in off the street and ask for a room. It's very selective about its clients, caters for wealthy businessmen and celebrities.'

'People with things to hide.'

'Exactly.'

Sullivan looked over Claire's shoulder as she examined the printout.

'Why are you so interested in an Amsterdam brothel?'

'Yeah,' Enqvist said. 'And can we have the number too?'

'Just before we interviewed Van Vliet,' Claire said, 'he said something to his assistant. What's his name?'

'Erik Wissing,' Hellendoorn said.

'I saw Wissing pick up the outer office phone as Van Vliet shut his door. He phoned this brothel, hotel, whatever you want to call it. That was at twenty-five past eight. Immediately after that three consecutive calls were made from the brothel; at eight thirty, eight thirty-four and eight thirty-seven. All international calls. You recognise the codes?'

She held out the paper. 'The first one is a French prefix. Paris. The second?'

'London,' Hellendoorn said.

'And the third. Three nine zero. That's Italy. I don't know the other numbers. Eighty-one. What city is that?'

'It's the code for Naples,' Sullivan said.

*   *   *

Willem Van Vliet rocked back and forth in his high office chair, his mouth puckered into a pout as he looked pensively across the desk at his assistant.

'You think he's vulnerable?'

Wissing nodded. 'I watched him carefully. He's the right type. Away from home, lonely, drinks too much. You know the symptoms.'

'He didn't see you?'

'It was very crowded. He never even glanced my way.'

'What kind of bar was it? Gay?'

'No, he's straight. He tried to chat up a couple of women but they weren't interested.'

Van Vliet let his chair spring upright, then rested his forearms on the top of the desk.

'Thank you, Erik. That was a job well done.'

'You have something in mind for him?'

'Oh yes,' Van Vliet replied. 'I have something in mind for him.'

NINE

'We've been ordered to release the *Maria Vasquez*,' Casagrande said.

The telephone line was clear enough but, nevertheless, Sullivan thought he must have misheard.

'Did you say release?' he asked incredulously.

'The court hearing was yesterday,' Casagrande continued. 'I tried to reach you in the evening but you weren't there.'

'I was in Rotterdam. I got back very late.'

'The *Tribunale* magistrate ruled the seizure was unlawful.'

'What the hell is he talking about? Unlawful?'

'No direct link between the ship and the traffickers.'

Sullivan swore out loud. 'No direct link? Where else did the fucking cigarettes come from?'

'It's politics, Rob,' Casagrande said in a tone of weary resignation. 'In Italy, everything is politics.'

'Are you saying the judge was nobbled by Rome?'

'Nobbled?' Casagrande said, puzzled.

'Influenced.'

'Who knows? The Liberian government has been

making a big noise ever since we arrested her. For all I know the magistrate is in the pocket of the Camorra. He wouldn't be the first Neapolitan judge.'

'You're appealing, I hope?'

'You bet we are. The hearing's next week.'

'The *Maria Vasquez* stays impounded until then?'

'Yes. But if we lose the appeal we'll have to release her immediately.'

'Shit! They don't have a case, do they?'

'They have five very good, very well-connected lawyers acting for them. There were twenty ships out in the Tyrrhenian Sea that night. They're saying the cigarettes could have been offloaded from any one of them.'

'And how do they explain what the *Maria Vasquez* was doing off Italy when she was supposedly going to Senegal?'

'She diverted to pick up an additional cargo from Naples. They have all the paperwork. Forged, of course, but we'll have a hard time proving it. These people are good, Rob. We had no aerial surveillance, no photographs or eyewitness evidence to show the cigarettes being offloaded on to the cabin cruisers. The appeal could go either way without something stronger to link the *Maria Vasquez* with trafficking.'

'How about a pattern of fraudulent shipments? Five cargoes that disappeared en route to West Africa.'

'You have proof?' Casagrande said, his voice rising a couple of tones.

'The paperwork's in Rotterdam. Stig's still up there. I'll get him to send you everything he has.'

'That would be a big help.'

'And can you do something for me, Antonio?'

'Name it.'

'Check a phone number in Naples.'

'Easy.'

Sullivan gave him the number, then hung up and called Enqvist, who had remained behind to complete the inspection of Van Vliet's records.

'No problem,' Stig said. 'I'll fax him this morning. You looked into Cannadine Export yet?'

'Just about to,' Sullivan replied.

He replaced the receiver and called a contact in the Metropolitan Police Fraud Squad. He gave him the address of Cannadine Export Limited in Streatham and asked if he could have someone check it out. Finally, he rang the London number Piet Hellendoorn had given Claire, rehearsing in his head the lines he was going to deliver. He needed some information but he didn't want to arouse their suspicions.

'Corvex Limited,' a woman's voice said.

'I'm sorry, what did you say?' Sullivan asked.

'Corvex Limited,' the woman repeated.

'I think I've got the wrong number. Are you a car spares company?'

'We're shipping agents.'

'I have got the wrong number. I'm sorry to have troubled you.'

He hung up and pulled out the keyboard of his computer. He typed in some commands and waited as the computer accessed the Companies House Direct database which listed records of every company registered in the United Kingdom. He tapped in the name Corvex Limited and the company information appeared on his screen: the names and addresses of its directors and secretary, a list of documents filed, the dates of accounts and annual returns made, and details of disqualified directors. The company secretary was named as Michael Bruton and only one director was listed, a Simon Doyle. Sullivan came out of the database and punched into UCLAF's own records. He ran the names of both men through the system but there was no mention of either. He went back into Companies House Direct and searched under the men's names, looking for any other appointments they had. Bruton was secretary and director of two more companies, Doyle of four more. Sullivan called up each of these additional six companies in turn and made a note of all their directors. In total, excluding Bruton and Doyle, there were twenty-six names. Sullivan checked each one through the UCLAF database.

It was a time-consuming, laborious task but he knew it was essential. Organised criminals were adept at covering their tracks through numerous bogus companies and false names, but most of them, at some point, needed a legal front to assist their activities, if only to launder the proceeds of their fraudulent operations. Finding that one legitimate company, that one director who turned out to be genuine, not some man of straw, was often the key that could unlock the doors leading to the real brains behind a fraud.

All twenty-six names were clean. Sullivan went back to Companies House Direct and searched for any other directorships the men had. He came up with the names of another thirty-two British companies. 'Shit,' he breathed. This was going to take him hours.

He ran all thirty-two names through the UCLAF database. Thirty-one of them turned out to be negative, but one came up positive, a company called Horningtoft Limited with a registered address of Horningtoft Priory, Norfolk. There was no UCLAF file on the company itself but it was listed in a cross-reference to a TF7 report on fraud in the European wheat industry. Sullivan made a note of the serial number of the file and logged off. TF7 was the UCLAF department covering the agricultural sector of the European Union – Claire Colmar's old department. Sullivan got up from his desk. It was about time he saw her again.

Claire's phone rang as she was refilling her coffee cup from the filter machine on the windowsill of her office. It was Philippe Allard.

'I was just about to call you,' she said in French, sitting down behind her desk and crossing her legs.

'That sounds ominous,' Allard replied with a dry chuckle.

'Write this down.'

She read out the Paris number which had been

called from the brothel in Amsterdam and asked Allard if he could get her the name and address of the subscriber.

'I'll put someone on to it,' he said. 'Is it urgent?'

'Any time in the next ten minutes will be fine,' Claire said. 'Now what can I do for you?'

'Christophe Bignon. You guessed right. Every time a Garcia Saez lorry came over through Hendaye, Bignon was in charge of the customs shift. He's living well beyond his official income. Expensive lifestyle, a gambling problem.'

'Did you check his bank account?'

'Nothing suspicious about it. No unexplained or regular deposits apart from his salary. We kept an eye on him and got lucky yesterday. Watched him meet a go-between who slipped him an envelope almost certainly full of cash.'

'Go-between for whom?' Claire asked.

'We can't be certain, but the go-between was an old lag named Thierry Lannay. Done time for assault and theft. Lannay is an associate of a businessman called Gilles Lafon who operates a haulage business out of Paris and Toulon. A big operation, several hundred trucks.'

'You think Lafon is the paymaster?'

'That would be my guess. He's a rich man, but not what you'd call respectable. No convictions but a lot of underworld connections, particularly in Marseille.'

'Is he linked to Fonteneau et Delahaye or Garcia Saez?'

'We're looking into it. I'll let you know what we find.'

'Thanks, Philippe.'

Claire hung up and sipped her coffee. A haulage business, shady friends in Marseille, the organised crime capital of France. She rather liked the sound of Gilles Lafon.

Sullivan had been married for fifteen years, but that night in Groningen was the first time he'd been unfaithful to his wife. Put starkly like that it didn't seem such a terrible transgression – one night in several thousand – but he knew the quantity didn't really count. Once was all it took to break that bond of trust he had with Kate. Yet it disturbed him how easy it had been, how little guilt he felt afterwards. He wasn't sure why he'd succumbed. He'd never felt the inclination before, at least not strongly enough to do anything about it. He was happily married, still passionate about his wife. If Claire hadn't taken the initiative, he certainly wouldn't have attempted to seduce her. That wasn't to put all the responsibility on Claire – he'd been a more than willing partner in the encounter – but it had tipped the balance, making his own complicity easier to reconcile with his conscience.

That wasn't an excuse for his behaviour, it was a rationalisation. Adultery, as some ancient sage had once remarked, was like burglary: ten per cent motivation, ninety per cent opportunity. Sullivan was lazy about sex. Unless they were inveterate womanisers, in which case the chase was as important as the conquest, most men were. Which was why marriage was such a splendid institution – it saved you no end of time and effort and included all sorts of fringe benefits which would have cost a fortune to get someone other than a wife to provide.

Claire had made it easy for him. She'd missed out all the awkward, tentative foreplay and cut straight to the sweaty climax, simultaneously removing the need for much work on his part whilst giving his common sense no chance to override the immediate imperatives of his groin. Strangely, Sullivan hadn't enjoyed it as much as he'd expected. Nothing to do with Claire, more the fact that he wasn't as relaxed as he was with his wife. He'd felt a pressure to perform, sensed she was trying him out in some way. It was better with Kate. They were so easy with each other, so uninhibited together that over the years making love had become more erotic, more satisfying than ever. But Kate – and this was the real, fundamental reason – was in England and he saw her only twice a month. Claire was on the doorstep, available and willing. Those were powerful temptations for a lonely man, living by himself in a foreign city.

Sullivan went upstairs and along the corridor to Claire's office. He had no intention of having an affair with her. He'd had one moment of weakness but there'd be no more. He regarded middle-aged men who cheated on their wives as pathetic. That night in Groningen would be quietly forgotten. Claire was a colleague – she probably regretted it herself – and working together was only going to be possible if they re-established a formal, professional relationship.

She looked up and smiled as he came in. He felt an instinctive warmth towards her that he made himself suppress.

'Hi,' he said.

'You want some coffee?'

'Sure.'

She filled a cup for him and sat back down, cool, not overly familiar. He sensed that, like him, she was taking a step backwards, reassessing what had happened and resolving not to let it happen again. He was relieved but also, perversely, if he was honest, a little disappointed.

They discussed what they'd been doing for a time, exchanging information. Claire told him about Allard's call and Sullivan briefed her on the *Maria Vasquez*. Then he gave her the reference number of the file he was looking for.

'Fraud in the wheat industry?' Claire said. 'That's a bit remote from cigarette-trafficking.'

'You know how it is. Every possible lead, no matter how tenuous, is worth examining.'

'It's outside my area, but I can check it out. What was the name again?'

'Horningtoft Limited.'

Claire scribbled it down. 'If I find anything, I'll bring it to your office.'

'Thanks for the coffee.'

He went back downstairs and almost immediately the telephone rang. It was Mick Linstead, his contact in the Met Fraud Squad.

'Cannadine Exports,' Linstead said. 'I had one of my boys go round. It was just an empty office above a hairdresser's shop. A desk and a phone line. The hairdresser says she sub-let it to the company six months ago.'

'Any names?' Sullivan said.

'She only ever dealt with one man, bloke named Wilson. He paid the rent, monthly in cash, and came round to collect the mail every few days. Then last week he gave notice, paid what he owed her and cleared the place out. No forwarding address. You want me to take it any further?'

'No. Thanks for your help, Mick. I owe you one.'

Sullivan had absolutely no doubt what it was. It bore all the classic hallmarks: an office in some cheap, run-down part of London, no staff, no files, rent paid in cash and no one there when the police came knocking on the door. He'd have to check the names and addresses of the directors but he knew they'd be false, they always were. Setting up a limited company was ridiculously easy. A couple of forms, some Table A Memorandum and Articles of Association you could pick up in a legal stationer's for a fiver, a twenty-pound registration fee and you were in business. No one ever checked whether the directors existed until something went wrong, and by then it was too late.

He pulled out his contacts book and rang the UK

Customs and Excise payments centre in Southend-on-Sea. This was where every VAT-registered business in the country sent their quarterly returns. He was put through to one of the records clerks and asked him if they had a listing for Cannadine Exports. The clerk tapped into the computer system.

'Registered August of last year. Import–export business,' he said.

'How many returns filed?' Sullivan asked.

'Two.'

'Let me guess, each one with a higher input than output tax.'

'Yes, how did you know?'

'How much has been reimbursed to them?'

'In total, nearly eighty thousand pounds.'

Sullivan sighed, thanked the clerk and rang off. These guys had every trick covered. Still, if you were going to be hung, why bother with lambs when there was a whole flock of sheep out there for the taking? It was a simple scam, but relatively risk-free. You set up a company and registered it for VAT. You then charged tax on goods you sold but pocketed it instead of passing it on to the Excise; or you claimed reimbursement of VAT supposedly paid on fictitious goods you'd never actually bought in the first place. Either way the VAT man was cheated and, as your chances of undergoing a random inspection were almost negligible, you got away with it if you didn't push your luck and do it for too long. Then you just disappeared and set up a new company at a new address and started all over again. You could make a tidy living and the only work involved was filling in a form every three months and pushing a wheelbarrow down to the bank to withdraw the proceeds.

Claire walked into his office shortly afterwards, carrying a file under her arm.

'The report you asked for,' she said, dropping the cardboard folder on to his desk with a thud.

Sullivan eyed it apprehensively.

'It looks very thick.'

'It does, doesn't it? I'm glad I'm not the one having to read it.'

'Maybe you should. You know more about agriculture than I do.'

'Nice try, Rob, but do I look like an idiot?'

'It's your area.'

'Wheat? I was in olive oil.'

'It's almost the same thing.'

'Enjoy yourself,' she said, turning to leave. 'Oh, by the way, Philippe Allard just rang back. That Paris number he was checking for me. It was a freight depot near Orly. And you know who it belongs to?'

Sullivan grinned at her. 'Gilles Lafon gets more interesting by the minute.'

'I'll see what else I can dig up.'

She looked directly at him. 'You want to go for a drink later?'

Sullivan met her eyes, remembering his resolution, his loyalty to his wife, his determination not to be another libidinous fool.

'I'll give you a call when I'm finished,' he said.

*　　　*　　　*

There was a word for it in Swedish: *höst depression*, autumn depression, a phenomenon so common it had earned not only its own terminology but recognised medical symptoms to go with it. Other Europeans, even North Europeans like the Germans and the British whose climates were far from perfect, had no idea what a Scandinavian winter was like. They couldn't comprehend just what the prospect of those long bitter nights and all too brief days did to the human spirit; what misery it was to say goodbye to the three short months of summer and contemplate a horizon of unremitting gloom and rain and bone-numbing cold.

Stig Enqvist, like most of his compatriots, had suffered from *höst depression* to varying degrees so he knew what it felt like. And he knew that what he was feeling now was very similar, although he was depressed not at the impending arrival of winter, but the impending end to his attachment to UCLAF.

His four years were nearly up. In six weeks' time he would be gone, his place taken by some other investigator, and he would never come back. One secondment was all you were allowed. It wasn't the thought of returning to Stockholm, or his job at the *Tullverk* that made him despondent. It was more the thought of picking up the pieces of his old life, facing up to the problems which he'd managed to put on hold during his time in Brussels. Living abroad had enabled him to, if not forget, then certainly relegate to an isolated corner of his

166

brain his ex-wife and daughter. He'd helped them financially since the divorce but done little else to form any kind of relationship with the little girl who was now – he had to think about it – nearly five years old. The thought of seeing her again, of coping with the guilt he felt at abandoning her, frightened him. He would have to face up to all that emotional turmoil now. And face up to his remaining years back in his homeland, middle-aged, unattached and lonely.

He helped himself to a miniature whisky from the mini-bar in his hotel room and flicked through the channels on the television set. He'd had enough of Rotterdam, enough of Van Vliet Entrepôt. He wanted to get back to Brussels and . . . and what? What did he have in Brussels that was so special? He downed the whisky angrily and threw on his coat. He was damned if he was going to sit on his bed watching television all evening. He went downstairs and ordered a taxi at reception, then went outside on to the steps to wait.

The taxi arrived a few minutes later. Enqvist watched it pull in and started down the steps, aware of a figure emerging from the hotel and hurrying down next to him. He glanced sideways. It was a woman with long blonde hair cascading over the collar of her black overcoat. She got to the taxi first and pulled open the door.

'I think this is for me,' Enqvist said in English.

The woman turned to look at him. She was strikingly beautiful. She answered in the same language.

'I'm sorry. I ordered one too, I thought this was mine.'

She stepped away from the door. 'Please.'

'No, you take it,' Enqvist said. 'I can wait.'

'Where are you going?'

'I'm not sure. The Oudehaven maybe. I don't care, I'm just going out.'

'You can share it with me,' she said.

'Are you sure?' Enqvist said.

She shrugged. 'I'm going that way.'

He held the door open for her and climbed in after her. She gave the driver instructions in Dutch and settled back in the far corner of the seat. The streetlights touched her hair with a halo of silver, throwing shadows over the curve of her cheeks and the pale outline of her neck.

'Are you staying in the hotel?' Enqvist said.

'Yes. You're English?'

'Swedish,' Enqvist replied.

'From where? Stockholm?'

'You know it?'

'I've been there. I love the old town, what's it called? Gamla . . .'

'Gamla Stan,' Enqvist said.

They chatted intermittently throughout the short journey to the Oudehaven. The taxi pulled in outside a restaurant and the woman got out. Enqvist followed her.

'This will do me too,' he said, paying the driver.

'Here.' She offered him half the fare. 'No, I insist,' she said when he tried to refuse.

She looked at the gold watch on her wrist.

'I'm meeting some friends for dinner. I'm a little early.'

She bit her lip and glanced awkwardly at him. 'I hate sitting on my own in restaurants. You wouldn't have a drink with me, would you? Just until they get here.'

Enqvist pretended to give it some thought, resisting the urge to race into the restaurant and order a couple of aperitifs.

'Sure,' he said as coolly as he could. 'I've nothing planned.'

They sat on a sofa in the bar area, surrounded by diners perusing menus, waiting to be seated. She was easy company: warm, relaxed, with a girlish, slightly giggly personality which took the edge off her intimidating good looks. After ten minutes the head waiter approached her and asked hesitantly: 'Miss Rietveld?'

'Yes.'

'A Miss Noorlander telephoned. She sent her apologies but she and her partner are unable to come. Their baby-sitter hasn't shown up.'

'Ah, thank you.'

Enqvist saw the look on her face though he hadn't been able to follow the Dutch.

'Is something the matter?'

'My friends have cancelled.'

'Do you want a table for two instead?' the head waiter said, speaking in English now.

She was embarrassed. 'Well . . .'

'It would be my pleasure,' Stig said. 'Will you have dinner with me?'

Her name was Juliana Rietveld. She was from Amsterdam, but down in Rotterdam on a two-day modelling assignment.

'Nothing very exciting,' she said. 'Just a clothing catalogue for a mail-order company.'

Enqvist nodded. He'd never been much of a fan of mail-order catalogues, but if the models in them all looked like this girl he'd take out a life subscription immediately.

'It's mostly very boring studio work,' she continued. 'A bit of outdoor shooting but that's even worse. It's summer clothes we're modelling. You've no idea how cold it gets. Your skin goes blue all over.'

Enqvist drank some of his wine and tried not to think about it. He couldn't quite believe he was sitting there having dinner with this young woman who must have been – he guessed – in her late twenties. Old enough for the age gap between them to be not altogether ridiculous. He didn't want to be mistaken for either her father or a cradle snatcher.

He'd never been out with a model before, never actually met one, in fact – Swedish customs officers were not renowned for moving in fashion circles. Juliana was dauntingly pretty, but seemed to be completely unaware of it and the effect it had on men. Enqvist knew it had to be partly a pose, an artifice to prevent accusations of vanity or narcissism, but she carried it off well. After the first few moments at their table, when they were both on edge, the evening progressed with a disarming ease. Enqvist was an entertaining companion when he chose to be and Juliana was a good listener, which certainly helped. By the time they went back to the hotel there was a comfortable rapport between them, almost an intimacy.

They went up in the lift and stopped on the fourth floor – Enqvist's floor. He pressed the button to hold the doors open.

'I enjoyed tonight,' he said.

'So did I.'

Enqvist hesitated. Juliana gave him his cue.

'I go to Brussels quite often on assignments.'

'Really? Look me up, if you like.'

He took out his wallet and gave her one of his business cards.

'Maybe I will,' she said.

'Do you want another drink? In my room?'

She shook her head. 'No thanks. Good night.'

He stepped out of the lift.

'Stig.'

He turned.

'Perhaps I will have that drink.'

They walked down the corridor to his room, not saying anything. He opened the door and as he fumbled for the light switch, he brushed against her, inhaling the smell of her perfume. He didn't know which of them made the move first, whether she came to him or he pulled her, but her body was

171

suddenly pressed hard against him and they were kissing with a ferocious abandon.

They edged their way to the bed, still kissing, discarding clothes as they went. Juliana tugged off his shirt and tie and pushed him down on to the covers. Then her fingers unfastened the zip at the back of her dress and she stepped out of it. Enqvist lay back on the pillow and gazed at her. Rotterdam was the last place on earth he would have thought of as Heaven, but he knew he'd died and gone somewhere.

There was a jaundiced view of male sexuality – often attributed to embittered feminists – that held that a man would shag a revolving door if it had big enough tits. Sullivan didn't subscribe to the theory, regarding it as an offensive slur, but nevertheless he couldn't help wondering what he was doing in Claire Colmar's apartment at eleven o'clock at night.

They'd been for a drink after work, driving into the centre of the city because the residential suburbs around Beaulieu were noticeably devoid of bars. It had seemed natural then to move on to a restaurant and have dinner together. They were in Ixelles, not far from Claire's flat, and when she'd suggested he came back with her for coffee he'd said yes without stopping to think what that signalled. Or rather, he *had* stopped to think, but deluded himself that coffee didn't necessarily entail anything more.

He was a fool, and knew it. There'd been no pressure, Claire had been careful about that. He could have made a clean break and walked away with no feelings hurt, but he'd chosen not to. He knew what he was doing, although he wasn't prepared to admit it to himself: he was allowing himself to be carried along, hoping that he would get to the point where it was too late to pull out and that would justify his actions. It would make him feel that, if he slept with Claire again, it hadn't been a conscious decision on his part, it had just happened. Events had taken over and simply swept them both away.

It was a feeble rationale, but who really concerned themselves with reason when the loins were hot with lust? Claire was attractive, desirable. Being with her gave him a sense of exhilaration, of heightened arousal. He was forty-two years old and a part of him – an immature part, it was true, but that didn't lessen its influence – wondered if he was missing out on some marvellous sexual experience that would never come his way again. Mid-life crisis, the urge to regain lost youth were trite concepts that he didn't really believe in. But he wished he'd slept with more women over the years. That was what it was: he wanted the novelty and the excitement of an affair.

The apartment was on the second floor of a converted house near the Avenue Louise. It had two bedrooms and a big living room with a dining table at one end and French windows leading out on to a small balcony at the other.

They sat on the sofa, beneath a framed Magritte print of a giant apple filling a room, and drank their coffee, lost for words for the first time that evening. Neither of them wanted the drink, it was just a pretext, a formality which had to be observed. Claire waited for him. She appeared composed but Sullivan could sense she was nervous. Tonight it was his turn.

He put his arm along the back of the sofa. She half turned towards him. He stroked her hair gently, feeling the thick dark strands. Then he leaned across and kissed her. Her arms came up around his neck, pulling him to her.

When they broke apart, breathless, Claire said: 'Was it a mistake the other night?'

'Probably.'

'You regret it?'

'No, I don't think I do. You?'

'No,' she said. 'The bedroom's through there.'

He took her hand and pulled her to her feet. It was another mistake. But right now he didn't care.

TEN

Sullivan spent most of the following morning going through the TF7 file on fraud in the European wheat industry, not reading it in detail but scanning the pages for any mention of Horningtoft Limited. He couldn't find a single reference so he rang Claire on the internal line.

'Why would it be mentioned on the database but not in the report?' he asked her.

'I don't know. Maybe it wasn't important enough to include. Have you checked the appendices?'

'Yes, there's nothing.'

'I'll look through the supporting materials on which the report was based. They often log things on the database which don't then find their way into the finished report. You could always try the Intervention Board. They might have something.'

'Anyone in particular?'

'Ask for Chris Carmichael. He's helped me in the past.'

Sullivan rang the Reading headquarters of the Intervention Board, the government agency which distributed EU subsidies to United Kingdom farmers.

Chris Carmichael had a chirpy Cockney voice which made him sound like a dodgy East End barrow boy, but he was helpful enough. He made a note of the name and called back ten minutes later.

'Yeah, we've got a listing for Horningtoft Limited. Can't fink why you've got it though, there's no mention of any irregularity.'

'Do you know anything about it?' Sullivan said.

'Only what I've got here on the screen. It's a big client.'

'What does it do?'

'Manages farms. A few dozen, all over East Anglia mostly.'

'Manages them? For the farmers?'

'Absentee landlords. It's a growing business. The landowner pisses off to the Bahamas, Sarf of France, wherever, leaves the management company to run his farm in return for an agreed share of the profits. A right old bleedin' doss if you ask me.'

'How much EU support does it get?'

'A lot. It's a big operation, manages a ton of land, all prime arable. Cereals – mainly wheat – sugar beet, oilseed rape, milk and dairy as well.'

'Why would we have a reference to it when you have no record of any irregularity?' Sullivan said.

'Can't fink,' Carmichael said. 'Either the reference never came from us or, if there was an allegation, we investigated it and found it to be baseless.'

'Wouldn't that be in your records?'

'Depends how long ago it was. What year we talking abaht?'

'Four years ago.'

'It would be here if we had anything. Can't help you, mate, sorry. As far as we're concerned it's clean. Not a stain on its character.'

'Okay, thanks anyway.'

'Any time.'

Sullivan rang off and stared out of the window. He was overlooking something obvious here. If Horningtoft Limited, a British company receiving EU support payments in the UK, had been suspected of any irregularity, the case would have been dealt with solely by the Intervention Board which had its own investigation department. UCLAF would only have been notified if a second member state were involved, if the irregularity had somehow become a transnational case. Sullivan called Claire.

'The Intervention Board have no record of any suspected fraud,' he said. 'There must have been another country in the frame. Who compiled the report?'

'Mercier and Feenstra, both long gone. There's no one left in TF7 who would remember the details of any investigation. The file is all we've got.'

'There must be a document somewhere. Someone had a reason for putting the company on the database.'

'I'll see what I can do.'

Sullivan was on the phone, talking to Casagrande in Naples, when Claire walked into his office. She sat down in Enqvist's chair and waited for him to finish. Sullivan eyed her slim legs, the dark skirt slipping up above the knee. Then he looked up to see her watching him with detached amusement. He smiled at her and came off the line.

'That Naples number,' he said. 'It was just a bar down near the docks.'

'Camorra?'

'Probably. We'll never know what the message was and for whom. What's that you've got there?'

'It was in the supporting materials for France, not the UK.'

She passed the piece of paper across the desk. It was a letter addressed to UCLAF from the Crown Prosecution Service office in Norwich. Sullivan read through it. The CPS lawyer who'd sent it, a Jim Bristow, was outlining the general nature of an Intervention Board investigation into financial irregularities at Horningtoft Limited, a file which had been passed on to the CPS for legal proceedings to begin. Bristow was asking if UCLAF had any information on the activities of the company in France where they also managed farms and where they were also claiming, and receiving, EU agricultural subsidies.

Sullivan read the letter again, frowning.

'This doesn't make sense. Have you read this? There was clearly an Intervention Board inquiry into Horningtoft, so why isn't it mentioned in the Intervention Board records? And it wasn't just some insignificant irregularity if it had already been passed on to the Crown Prosecution Service. The CPS was ready to prosecute Horningtoft. Can you do something for me, Claire? Check with the French, see what they've got on this.'

'Sure.' She stood up. 'You going for lunch later?'

Sullivan nodded. 'With Stig. He's on his way back this morning. Why don't you join us?'

'A *ménage à trois*? How could I refuse?' Claire said, walking out.

Sullivan watched her go, listening to the sound of her heels receding down the corridor, thinking about the previous night. Wondering what it had meant to him. And to her. Then he focused back on his work and telephoned the CPS in Norwich. He asked to speak to Jim Bristow.

'Who?' the girl on the switchboard said.

'Jim Bristow,' Sullivan repeated.

'We don't have anyone of that name here.'

'He's a lawyer.'

'I'm sorry. Are you sure you've got the right office?'

'I have a letter from him here, dated May 1996.'

'That was before my time. He's not here now.'

'I have a query about one of his cases. Is there anyone else who can help me?'

'I'll put you through to Mr Newman, he's the Area Chief Crown Prosecutor.'

Newman was terse, in a hurry. 'Who's this?' he said curtly.

Sullivan told him who he was and why he was calling.

'1996?' Newman said. 'That's four years ago. My God, you people are even slower than we are. But then you're Brussels,' he added with a sarcastic sneer. 'You have a reputation to keep up.'

Sullivan didn't bother explaining the circumstances. Newman was clearly one of those people – and Sullivan came across a lot – who regarded anyone employed by the European Union as a high-living, contemptible parasite.

'Perhaps you could look up the case for me?' Sullivan said politely.

'I could,' Newman said. 'If I had nothing better to do.'

'It would be very helpful. I gather Jim Bristow is no longer there.'

'He retired a few years ago.'

'Is he still in Norwich?'

'How the hell would I know that? I never knew the fellow.'

'I'd appreciate any information you have on the case,' Sullivan said diplomatically.

He had no power to make the CPS cooperate. He had to depend entirely on their good will, which in Newman's case appeared to be in singularly short supply.

Newman made an impatient clicking noise with his tongue. Sullivan pictured some ferret-faced provincial solicitor, sitting in a high leather chair acting the autocrat in his dismal little empire.

'What was the name of the company again?'

'Horningtoft Limited,' Sullivan said.

'I'll put someone on to it.'

Sullivan gave him his telephone number. 'Will I hear today?'

'You'll hear when we're ready,' Newman said

rudely. 'You've waited four years. What's the big hurry now?'

'Thank you for your help,' Sullivan said.

He released the phone from his clenched fist and replaced it carefully, taking a couple of deep breaths to control his temper.

'And screw you too,' he said with a quiet ferocity.

'What kind of a welcome is that?' Stig Enqvist said from the door.

He came in, pulling off his wet overcoat.

'I leave in a rainstorm, return in one. It's good to know nothing changes,' he said acidly.

He brushed the droplets off his hair, wiping his fingers on the back of his trousers.

'You ready to eat? I'm dying for a drink.'

'So where do we stand?' Sullivan said.

Enqvist took a long pull on his Rodenbach beer and helped himself to a chunk of bread from the basket in the middle of the table.

'Van Vliet is a crook,' he said. 'I'm certain of that. He knows full well that he's dealing with traffickers. Not just Cannadine Export but I found a number of other recent shipments, some by rail, some by sea, that looked suspicious. Several were ordered and paid for by Steinhammer Weiss in Zürich.'

'You're kidding?' Sullivan said. 'I thought Wolf had retired.'

'Apparently not.'

'Who's Wolf?' Claire said.

'Julius Wolf, Swiss lawyer and businessman,'

Sullivan said. 'We have a file on him about this thick. He's getting on a bit now but in his day he was one of the largest cigarette traders in Europe. One of those middle men we told you about who buy from the manufacturers and sell on to traffickers. Steinhammer Weiss is one of his front companies.'

'It would seem he's back in the game,' Enqvist said. 'Unless someone else has taken over his business.'

'Any indication from Van Vliet's records?'

Enqvist shook his head. 'Van Vliet is a very careful man. He makes damn sure every legal nicety is observed, every regulation followed to the letter. His books are clean. He trades in cigarettes quite legitimately. Everything he sells is cleared with Customs. If it's distributed within the EU the duty is paid on the nail. If it's in transit the T1s are perfect. You can't flaw his business methods.'

'But?' Sullivan said.

'But what?'

'Are you saying he's untouchable? You've gone through his records and found no irregularities at all?'

Enqvist shrugged. 'Nothing worth pursuing.'

'Come on, Stig, there must be something. What was the point of raiding the place if we come away with nothing?'

'There's no evidence to implicate Van Vliet in trafficking.'

'But he might just be our conduit to the smugglers.'

Enqvist chewed on his crust of bread, sitting back

to allow the waitress to place a pot of steaming beef carbonnade on the table. The vegetables came next; sliced potatoes garnished with chopped parsley, pickled red cabbage and asparagus tips dripping with melted butter.

He waited until they each had their plates full before he said wearily: 'We all know the obstacles we're up against. Clever, well-organised smugglers with access to virtually unlimited supplies of cigarettes; a huge black market it's impossible to even identify much less stamp out; a shortage of law enforcement resources to adequately police the frontiers of the EU. We're on a hiding to nothing. We confiscate millions of contraband cigarettes each year but billions more slip through the net. We spend our time locking the stable door after the horse has bolted.'

'So isn't it time we caught the nag before she gets out?' Sullivan said.

'We've tried that before. Unless we get a tip-off, like we did in Naples, we have no idea when or where the smugglers are going to strike next.'

'That's still true,' Sullivan said. 'But we have the advantage of more information now. We know that a large number of contraband cigarettes originate from Van Vliet's warehouse.'

'But the smugglers know we have that information,' Claire interjected. 'They'll simply find their supply elsewhere, won't they?'

Sullivan shook his head. 'Finding a new supplier isn't that straightforward. The cigarette companies only deal with a limited number of bonded ware-houses. And besides, these guys are arrogant. They think – no, they *know* – they can outsmart us because they've been doing it successfully for years. They're going to rely on the fact that although we may suspect Van Vliet of supplying them, we still don't know which shipments are legitimate and which aren't. And we certainly don't know how they're going to smuggle the cigarettes back into the EU. The odds are huge and in their favour. The EU has – what? – something like forty thousand kilometres of external frontier. All the smugglers need is a strip fifty metres wide and they can walk in with impunity.'

Sullivan ate some of his stew. He speared a chunk of beef with his fork and loaded it into his mouth, savouring the beer-flavoured sauce.

Le Chasseur Georges – a reference to the proprietor who was a renowned local hunter and celebrated cook of the game he shot for the pot – was one of their favourite restaurants. Just outside Brussels, a short drive across the Forêt de Soignes in Jezus-Eik, it was an unpretentious, noisy place with good plain food and a rustic ambience which – unlike many country restaurants outside the city – owed more to its local clientèle and ancient decor than an interior designer's concept.

'What are you suggesting?' Claire said.

She was sitting next to Sullivan on a narrow bench. She could feel the warmth of his leg pressing against hers.

'You made notes of all those recent shipments from

Van Vliet's warehouse, I assume,' Sullivan asked Enqvist.

'Of course. But they're long gone.'

'And we can find out from Dutch Customs when any new consignments leave. Some of them are going to be legitimate cargoes, some are going to be smuggled back into the EU. The trick is identifying which is which.'

'And how do we do that?' Claire said.

'Well, these guys are big-time. This is organised trafficking on a vast scale. However they smuggle the cigarettes, they'll probably have done a similar, if not identical run before. The infrastructure will be in place, the black marketeers will be expecting a regular supply along certain routes. You don't smuggle a hundred and fifty million cigarettes at a time with a suitcase and a couple of couriers.

'Now, some of the cigarettes are going out by road and rail and will be offloaded illegally in transit across the EU. But the big cargoes will go by sea, we know that from past experience. It's the best way of moving large quantities and the hardest for us to keep tabs on. The *Maria Vasquez* wasn't their only ship, there'll be others. I think we can identify which they are.'

Enqvist drank some of his beer to wash down a mouthful of potatoes.

'That's not going to be easy,' he said gloomily.

'But it's possible. We go through the previous shipments and check every component: the ships, the quantity ordered, the declared destination, the company paying for them. We've got the log of the *Maria Vasquez*. We know where she went and when. We compare her movements with those of the other ships and see if anything is similar, see if there's a pattern of cargoes and destinations. We check with Customs and see if the ships actually went where they were supposed to.'

Sullivan looked at Claire and Enqvist in turn, a raw determination in his eyes and the set of his jaw.

'You've got six weeks left, Stig,' he said. 'Wouldn't you like to go out in a blaze of glory?'

In the middle of the afternoon, Sullivan received a call from the Crown Prosecution Service in Norwich.

'My name's Russell,' the voice on the line said, a hint of a Norfolk burr in his words. 'John Newman asked me to give you a bell.'

'I appreciate it,' Sullivan replied. 'Mr Newman didn't seem exactly keen on helping me.'

Russell gave an abrupt snort of laughter, like a sneeze.

'Take no notice of him. It's just his manner. You wanted to know about Horningtoft Limited.'

'Yes. One of your former colleagues, Jim Bristow, was handling a case against them.'

'Jim? Was he, when?'

'Four years ago.'

'He retired about four years ago. Are you sure?'

'We have a letter from him on file.'

'That's more than we have,' Russell said. 'We have nothing at all. No file, no computer record.'

'That can't be possible. According to Bristow's letter he was about to initiate proceedings against the company. You must have something.'

'I'm afraid not. I've looked everywhere. We have no record of a case against Horningtoft Limited. Are you sure that was the name?' He spelt it out.

'That's the one,' Sullivan said. 'Are you absolutely certain? Could it have been misplaced?'

'It's possible. It was a while ago. All I know is I can't find any trace of it.'

Sullivan screwed up his forehead, staring intensely at the stark walls of his office.

'Are you still there?' Russell said.

'What? Oh, yes, I'm sorry. Tell me, have you seen Jim Bristow since he retired?'

'No, I haven't. I'm not sure anyone in the office has. He moved away from Norwich.'

'Do you know where?'

'I don't have an address, but I believe it was somewhere up near the coast. Wells, Burnham Market, around there.'

Sullivan thanked him for his help and hung up. Stig Enqvist looked at him across the cluttered surfaces of their desks.

'Something the matter?'

'I don't know. Yes, I think something is the matter.'

Sullivan picked up the phone and rang UK Directory Enquiries. Bristow wasn't a particularly common name and there were only three listed for the Wells area of north Norfolk. Sullivan tried each one. The

first didn't answer, the second was a Bed and Breakfast in Little Walsingham and the third a mother with
two young children – he could hear them screaming
in the background – in Brancaster Staithe.

'I'm trying to get in touch with a Jim Bristow who
used to work for the Crown Prosecution Service in
Norwich,' Sullivan explained.

'That's my father-in-law.'

'It is? You couldn't give me his number, could
you?'

It was the first number he'd tried.

'He'll be out in the marshes,' the woman said.
'He's there most afternoons. Try him again around
tea-time.'

Sullivan rang at intervals over the next few hours.
It was six thirty Brussels time, five thirty in the UK,
when he finally got an answer. Bristow's voice was
deep, peremptory, a little intimidating.

'How did you get this number?' he asked before
he would even confirm his identity.

Sullivan told him.

'And you're from UCLAF?' Bristow said, checking
his facts like a good lawyer.

'That's right. I've been reading a letter you wrote
to us about a company called Horningtoft Limited.'

'Horningtoft?' Bristow exclaimed, his tone harsh,
cynical. 'Ah well, better late than never.'

'What do you mean?'

'What do you want, Mr . . .'

'Sullivan. Rob Sullivan. To talk to you about it.'

'I'm retired. I'm not sure I can help you.'

'No one else seems to be able to either. I'd like to know why neither the CPS nor the Intervention Board have any record of an investigation into the company.'

'It's no longer my business, Mr Sullivan,' Bristow said firmly.

'You're the only lead I have. This is important.'

'Not to me.'

'Don't shut me out, please. You pursued this case once. I don't know what happened to it, but I think you do. I need your help, Mr Bristow.'

There was a long silence. Sullivan controlled the urge to say more. Bristow's conscience, his sense of duty would have to do the rest.

'Not on the phone,' Bristow said finally. 'You'll have to come and see me.'

'That's not a problem. What's your address?'

Bristow gave him the name of a house and a street in Burnham Overy Staithe.

'You know this area?' he added.

'I've been there on holiday,' Sullivan said. 'I'll come tomorrow.'

'Mr Sullivan,' Bristow said. Then he paused. 'This sounds rather silly, but don't tell anyone you're coming. I mean that, no one at all.'

ELEVEN

Claire was nervous. She wasn't sure exactly why, but she could feel it in the tightness of her stomach, the insistent thud of her heartbeat. It was a sensation she'd experienced only once before in the course of her work. She and a colleague had been in Italy, in the depths of the rural south, checking stocks of olive oil which the EU had bought into intervention to maintain the price level in the market. There was a suspicion that the olive oil in many of the huge tanks was either Tunisian, smuggled in to fraudulently claim European support payments, or adulterated with hazelnut oil and therefore not eligible for any subsidy. They'd toured the area taking samples for analysis, accompanied by an official from AIMA, the Italian intervention board who, it rapidly became apparent, was in the pocket of the local mafia. In one warehouse Claire had caught the AIMA man in the process of substituting the UCLAF sample bottles for identical ones he'd filled earlier. Then unidentified men in dark glasses had started following them around, tailing their car through the remote villages of Campania.

One night, Claire and her colleague had checked into a hotel and left the olive oil samples locked in their car in the hotel's car park. Within minutes of their leaving the vehicle, its alarm had gone off as someone tried to force the boot. Two men were caught running away by the hotel staff and Claire recognised one of them as the chairman of the agricultural cooperative they'd visited earlier in the day. Fearing a second attempt to tamper with the samples, Claire and her colleague had moved them into their hotel rooms – about 2,000 small plastic bottles in total. Claire had vivid memories of that night, trying to sleep in a room which reeked of olive oil.

The next day the unidentified men in dark glasses had been behind them again, keeping twenty metres away, going everywhere Claire and her colleague went. Claire had been terrified, genuinely scared for her life. They'd abandoned the mission, driven straight to Naples airport and left the country. When they went back, several months later, they had to be escorted by a team of armed officers from the *Guardia di Finanza*. And this wasn't alcohol or cigarettes they were investigating, it was olive oil.

Claire was frightened now. Or rather, on edge. No one was following her, there was no logical reason for her to be worried, but she was. She was driving along a narrow country lane to the west of Bruges, heading towards the Belgian coast which was only a few kilometres away. It was pitch dark outside. Her headlights cut a bright tunnel through the surrounding blackness, glancing off the surface of the road and the patchy hedgerows along the edges of the adjoining fields. It was very quiet. Claire felt as if she were sealed inside the car, moving in a capsule through the flat countryside whose empty spaces and lowering sky seemed to threaten her.

She braked for a junction, peering out to decipher the names on the road sign, then turned right, following the instructions she'd been given. She had no clear idea where she was going, this whole area was unfamiliar to her. Not for the first time she wondered what she was doing, driving alone at night for a rendezvous with a man she'd never met.

He'd called as she was about to leave the office to go home.

'You left your card with a neighbour of mine,' he'd said in Dutch and she'd realised it was Jan Kuypers, the missing pilot from Groningen.

He'd refused to say any more on the telephone, simply told her she'd have to come to him if she wanted to talk. He was at a friend's house near De Haan on the North Sea coast. For one night only, he was leaving in the morning. Claire didn't feel she had a choice.

Outside, the fields were giving way to sparse woodland, stunted poplars and low shrubs which had been planted as windbreaks and to stabilise the sandy dunes that ran in a broad strip along this whole stretch of coast. Claire wound down her window a little. She could smell the sea on the breeze gusting in through the gap, catching at her hair.

Beside the road a weathered wooden sign appeared

in the beam of her headlights. Claire slowed. The wording on the sign was too faded to read but she knew this must be the place. She turned off left down an unmetalled track, feeling the bumps and jolts of the water-filled potholes under the wheels of the car. The thin woodland on either side became gradually denser, the broadleaf deciduous trees being assimilated into a thicker swathe of dark pines. They closed in around the car, coming right down to the edge of the track, shutting out the sky with a canopy of spiky fronds. Claire twisted her hand around to depress the button below the window, centrally locking all the doors. She didn't know why she did it, it just came instinctively. As instinctively as the knot of nervous tension that was tightening around her stomach.

After two hundred metres the track came to an end in a cramped turning circle. Claire swung her car round to face back the way she'd come and switched off the engine. The silence was smothering. Claire resisted an impulse to twist the key in the ignition, to restore the reassuring noise and vibration of the motor. The headlights were still on. It took real willpower to make herself extinguish them. She sat in the darkness listening to the sound of her heart, tempted to drive away immediately. But what was the point of coming all this way if she was going to lose her nerve at the last minute?

She let her eyes adjust to the night, then climbed out, scanning the ranks of pine trees all around. She wished she'd brought a torch. She hadn't expected the house to be quite so isolated. Nothing moved.

There was no sound except the faint rustle of the wind in the branches and a distant, almost inaudible murmur that she realised was the sea breaking along the beach.

Kuypers had said there was a path through the forest from the end of the track, but she couldn't see it. She scoured the perimeter of the turning circle and noticed a break in the undergrowth and a patch of earth beyond it where the soil had been trodden down hard. She took a deep breath, trying to relax, and plunged into the trees.

It was too dark to follow a path, too dark to even see if there was one. She just had to feel her way blind, sensing where a path might have been, and hope for the best. The ground started to go uphill. She could feel the pine needles crunching beneath her shoes, the loose soil crumbling as she dug in her toes. On the brow of the hill she saw ahead of her the lights of a house glowing orange and flickering like candle flames as the branches of the trees danced in front of the windows. She increased her pace, knowing where she was going now, anxious to escape the claustrophobic clutches of the forest.

The house was on the edge of the dunes, separated from the trees by a grassy clearing. It was a small, two-storey wooden cottage with smoke trickling from its chimney and its ground-floor windows ablaze with light, their curtains pulled open to reveal the interiors of the rooms.

Claire walked across the clearing. On the other side of the cottage the hillocks of sand rolled in swollen waves down to the beach. The sea was grey and choppy, the breakers crashing and fizzing along the shoreline.

Claire knocked on the door of the cottage. There was no answer. She tried the handle. The door swung open. She hesitated.

'Kuypers?' she called.

The atmosphere inside the house seemed to seep out and envelop her in a chilling embrace. She realised her legs were trembling.

'Kuypers?' she called again, not because she expected a response but because she wanted to delay going inside.

She looked down across the dunes. Maybe he'd gone for a walk. But there was no sign of any movement on the sand. She couldn't put it off any longer. She stepped over the threshold into the tiny hall of the cottage. Coats and waterproofs were hanging on pegs on the wall and the door leading to the living room beyond was ajar. Claire pushed it with her foot. The sudden creak of the hinges made her start. She got a grip on herself, controlling her breathing, making herself relax. The living room was deserted. The furniture was old and shabby: a couple of armchairs, a sofa draped with a moth-eaten throw. The floor was varnished wood, thick with dust. In the hearth a wood fire burned, the logs charred on the outside but still solid underneath. It had been stoked not all that long ago.

Claire moved cautiously across the room. She felt frighteningly exposed in the glare of the overhead light. She couldn't see out through the windows though she knew she would be clearly visible to anyone outside. She wanted to close the curtains but didn't. She couldn't bring herself to step in front of the glass. There was another door on the far side of the room. She took a couple of quick paces and pressed herself against the wall beside the door. She was aware of the throbbing pulse inside her head, the chemicals flooding her bloodstream with the overwhelming urge to flee. But she had to go on.

She took hold of the door handle and jerked it down, pulling the door open in one swift movement. There was a small vestibule on the other side from which a darkened flight of stairs ascended to the floor above. Another open door gave access to the brightly lit kitchen. Claire glanced up the stairs and moved quickly across into the kitchen. There was no one there. Her eyes flickered around the room, taking in the chipped stone sink, the bottled gas stove, the back door with clear glass panes through which she could see the brick walls of an outhouse. She pulled open the drawers below the worktops, looking for something. In the fourth drawer, by the sink, she found it, a plastic tray full of cutlery. She rummaged through it and pulled out a wooden-handled chopping knife. She grasped it tight, wondering if she was overreacting. But she felt better with it in her hand.

She went back out into the vestibule. The stairwell was a dark cavity above her. She was reluctant to go up, but she had to make sure. She felt around on the wall and clicked on the light. Slowly, she went up the stairs. The first room at the top was a bathroom. She pushed open the door and turned on the light. Again, it was empty. There was one other door off the landing, presumably leading to the bedroom. Claire pushed it open with her left hand, her right holding the chopping knife at the ready. The room beyond was in darkness, but there was enough light on the landing for her to see a double bed and wardrobe. She reached in, her fingers fumbling then finding the switch. The bedroom light snapped on. There was a blue and white striped duvet on the bed, a couple of thin rugs on the floor. The wardrobe, a big heavy piece with brass handles, and a low chest of drawers were the only other items of furniture. Claire leaned back on the wall and took a deep breath, her relief at concluding her search tempered by a nagging worry that kept her on edge. What the hell had happened to Kuypers?

Leaving the lights on, she went back downstairs and checked the kitchen and living room, looking to see if he'd left her a note or a message of any kind. There was nothing.

She thought about waiting, but there didn't seem much point. She had the impression he'd left in a hurry and not too long before she'd arrived. The signs were there: the fire still burning strongly in the grate, the lights on, the house unlocked. But where had he gone? She wondered if he'd had a car. The cottage was in the middle of nowhere; getting to and from it without transport wouldn't have been easy. Maybe he'd driven off somewhere, to buy food, drink, cigarettes. The options were too complicated to consider. But she didn't feel like hanging around for him, not in the house at least. Something about it unnerved her.

She went back outside and gazed down over the dunes again. It was too dark, and there were too many dips and valleys in the sand, for her to be absolutely sure there was no one lurking out there. She gave him one last chance.

'Kuypers!' she called.

Nothing. She waited a few moments, then turned and went back across the clearing to the forest. It was only as she entered the trees that she realised she was still holding the chopping knife. She shrugged. No one would miss it.

The path was just as hard to see this time, but she moved quicker, knowing where she was going. She dropped over the brow of the hill, slithering down the muddy slope on the other side. It was darker here, out of the reach of the light from the cottage. She lost her footing momentarily and overbalanced, tumbling to the ground and rolling a few metres to the bottom of the incline. Winded but unhurt, she knelt up and paused to recover her breath. Then she clambered to her feet and pressed on, no longer on the path but trusting to her sense of direction to bring her out by her car.

She stumbled against something on the ground and almost fell over again, steadying herself with a hand on a nearby tree trunk. She peered down, trying to make out what was blocking her path. It was about

six feet long, with dark limbs outstretched on the
earth. A body. Claire reached down and touched it
tentatively. Jesus, what was the matter with her? She
felt damp bark and moss and a couple of snapped-off
branches. It was just a fallen log. Straightening up,
she took a few deep breaths, forcing the tension out
of her muscles. She wasn't normally this jumpy. In
the distance she could see a smear of sky where there
was a break in the forest. She headed towards it and
broke out through the undergrowth into the turning
circle where she'd parked. She froze.

There was someone in her car.

Someone sitting in the driver's seat.

Claire was behind and a little to the side of the
vehicle so she couldn't make out the features, but
she could see the outline of the shoulders and head
and knew it was a man. She approached the car in
a wide loop, circling round to the driver's door but
stopping dead before she reached it. The man was
slumped in the seat, his head lolling back against the
headrest. There was enough light for her to see his
eyes and mouth gaping like wounds, but the real,
sickening injury was lower down – a livid, blood-
seeping laceration across the full width of his neck.

Claire stared at him, oblivious for a second to
anything except that terrible frozen face, those empty
lifeless eyes gazing back at her while the dark, sticky
gore below glistened and coagulated on his shirt.
Then she became aware of her surroundings again
and spun round, suddenly terrified. The parking
space was deserted. She strained to see into the

forest, to see if she was being watched, but the files of trees were as blank and solid as a wall.

Her instincts were to get out immediately. To jump in her car and drive down the track to the road and keep going, it didn't matter where. But two things stopped her. To use her car would entail moving Kuypers' body – she knew for certain it was him – from the driver's seat and she couldn't bring herself to touch that bloody corpse. And the police would want her to leave everything exactly the way she'd found it. There would be forensic evidence that might be important in identifying the killer. Claire was a law enforcement officer herself, she knew what was required, and her sense of responsibility forbade her to disturb the scene.

She went round to the rear of the car and opened the boot, reaching inside and lifting out the tyre iron from the toolkit. There was no avoiding it: she had to go back to the cottage – there'd been a telephone on the dresser in the living room – and call the police.

She never knew how she made it back through the forest. Her nerves were strung so tight, her guts so twisted with nausea that only a fierce willpower stopped her from throwing up. She ran. Chopping knife in one hand, tyre iron in the other. Ran almost blind, thrusting branches out of the way, tearing at the undergrowth, not caring how much noise she made until she burst out into the clearing on the other side and the reassuring glare of the cottage's lights. She went inside the house and across to the dresser. She picked up the phone. There was no dialling tone. She depressed the button a few times. The line was dead.

'Shit!' she breathed.

She looked around, considering what to do next.

Then the lights went out.

Claire was too shocked to move. She stood there in the darkness, watching the wood embers glowing in the fireplace, then she crouched down automatically, making herself less obtrusive. She was too stunned to be frightened. But she knew that fear preyed on the mind, feeding off insecurity and helplessness. Doing nothing was the surest way of surrendering to it.

She dropped to her belly and snaked across the room. When she reached the corner she twisted round and squatted with her back to the walls. She was thinking quite clearly. Outside in the forest she'd been scared of the unknown, of hidden eyes watching her. Now she was almost relieved. She knew there really was someone there and could work out what to do about it. Imaginary fears were suddenly tangible but that made them easier to deal with. They'd emerged from the dark corners of her mind and taken on human form.

She slowed her breathing, feeling the comforting bulk of the walls behind her, thinking through the alternatives. She could go back outside and hope to run for it, but that would make her an easy target. There was the forest on one side of the cottage, the exposed dunes and beach on the other. Where would she run? Or she could hide somewhere in the house. That seemed equally hazardous, even assuming she could find a suitable place. Claire didn't like the idea of sitting waiting, it wasn't in her nature to be passive, and besides, she had an idea that whoever was out there liked playing games with their victims. Kuypers' body dumped in her car, the electricity supply being cut. Those were the actions of a man showing his power, toying with her before he finished her off. The thought chilled her, but she shut it out, concentrating on her next move.

She had to take the fight to him. He'd expect her to be terrified. She was a woman, vulnerable. He would be sure of himself, perhaps over-confident. He wouldn't expect her to make the first move. She guessed he was somewhere out at the back. He must have cut off the electricity at the fuse box, but where was that? She hadn't seen it in the kitchen. It was probably in the outhouse by the back door. She listened hard. She could hear nothing except her own pulse drumming in her ears.

The embers in the hearth made a faint crackling noise. A glowing sliver of wood burst suddenly into flame for a moment. Claire stared at it, then stood up quickly. She hadn't heard anything, but the fire was more sensitive than her ears. Something had created a draught. Something like the back door opening. Claire crept quietly along the side of the room and stopped by the door to the stairwell. She had the knife in her left hand, the tyre iron raised in her right, ready to strike. She held her breath, listening.

Whoever it was, he was light on his feet. She heard nothing until the door next to her slowly started to open. Claire waited, the tyre iron weighing heavily on her arm. The door swung wider. She expected a figure to appear and prepared herself to strike. But no one came in.

She looked across the room, noticing for the first time in the firelight a faint silvery sheen on the far wall. A sheen dulled in places by distinct shadows. She recognised the shape of one of the shadows and realised too late what it was: her own reflection in a mirror. She started to move, but the man outside was quicker. The door slammed back hard into her body. It would have knocked her off her feet if the wall behind hadn't been there to hold her up. She felt a shudder of pain as her spine crashed against the brickwork. Then a hand grabbed hold of her wrist and tossed her across the room. She landed on her side and slithered along the wood floor. The tyre iron and knife went flying. Claire heard them clatter against the wall, but it was too dark to see where. The impact had knocked the breath out of her. Her right shoulder and hip were throbbing. She rolled over and saw the man towering above her, his face burnished with light from the fire. His hair was cropped short in military fashion, accentuating the hard leanness of his features, his mouth twisted into a curve that might have been either a grin or a snarl. He crouched down, reaching out for her. Claire kicked him. Her foot smashed into his torso but he barely flinched. The vibrations shuddered up her leg, jolting her backwards. She twisted her head, looking around for a weapon, her fingers groping across the floor, trying to find something – anything – to use against him.

One of his hands tore at her jacket, ripping it open. He fumbled for the waistband of her jeans. Claire felt a surge of hope. He was a powerful man. He could have killed her instantly, snapped her neck like balsa wood, but he wanted to draw it out. He wanted to see her frightened, to hurt her first. That was a mistake she could turn to her advantage.

His fingers were hooked under the top of her jeans, tugging them down. Claire stopped struggling suddenly, letting her body go limp. The man paused, glancing up at her face. He had cruel, icy eyes. A sadist's eyes. Claire waited for him to drop his guard. She saw his lips move in a smile of triumph, his gaze drop to her crotch. Then, simultaneously, she clawed at his face with her fingers and brought her right knee up hard into his groin. The man grunted and clutched himself. Claire's fingernails dug into his eye sockets, gouging at the delicate membranes. The man flailed out, trying to grasp her arms, but Claire was already rolling over, twisting sideways and squirming out from under him.

He spat out an exclamation in a language she didn't understand and went for her angrily. Claire kicked out desperately, sliding backwards across the floor. She knew she had to get to her feet to give herself any chance of survival. To run for it, escape the house and seek refuge in the forest. His fingers closed around her right ankle. Claire kicked him in the face with her other foot and wriggled free. She got to her knees and was almost upright when he threw himself at her, his weight crushing her to the floor. He slapped her face, shouting something in his own language. Claire's head snapped round, her eyes watering with pain. She blinked, feeling his hands on her breasts, between her legs.

Then she saw it.

A length of steel glinting at the base of the wall. The tyre iron. Her hand stretched out. Just a bit further. Just a few more centimetres. She could almost touch it. She summoned all her strength, twisting round to give herself that extra bit of reach. Her fingers closed around the metal. She brought the tyre iron up in an arc and smashed it hard into the side of the man's head. He slumped over, moaning in agony, his hands trying to stanch the blood. Claire hit him again. His eyes went suddenly blank. He rolled on to the floor and was still.

Claire slithered away and stood up. She gazed down at him, panting for breath. It was a while before she could bring herself to touch him. Her fingers felt for the pulse on the side of his neck. It was there, faint but detectable. He was still alive. She left him lying on the floor and went out of the cottage, running hard through the forest, down the muddy track on to the main road and back towards a farmhouse whose lights glimmered dimly on the horizon.

Claire let the police go in before her. One of the officers found the fuse box in the outhouse and restored the electricity supply. The cottage lights blazed back on, blinding them all for an instant. Claire let her eyes adjust, then stared around the living room. There was a puddle of blood on the wooden floor and more red smears by the door. But the wounded man had gone.

TWELVE

Hal Montague liked a full house for the weekend. He was a gregarious man who was fond of company and took genuine pleasure in seeing others enjoying themselves, but what he liked most – and he was honest enough to admit it – was showing off. And he had plenty to show off. His country house in Norfolk was a handsome red-brick mansion, parts of which dated back to the sixteenth century, with six hundred acres of parkland and woods and some of the finest shooting in East Anglia. Though small by stately-home standards, it was grand enough to impress almost anyone except the landed aristocracy and royalty – two categories of people with whom he never had the slightest inclination to mix. They were too inbred, too stupid and too terminally dull for his tastes. Yet even they would have been hard-pressed not to admire the opulence of the house, the rich furnishings and antiques that filled it, the stable of twenty horses and the extravagant quantities of food and drink lavished on the guests. Montague might not have had much of a pedigree, but what he lacked in lineage he more than made up for in hard cash.

It was his custom, whenever he was in the UK for a weekend, to invite a group of friends and acquaintances to stay. Or rather, to get his wife to invite them for him. Serena was good at organising house parties. She had a knack of selecting exactly the right combination of guests, choosing people who would gel well together but who were sufficiently different to ensure that the weekend stayed lively without becoming acrimonious. She was also skilled at inviting individuals who might be of assistance to her husband – he was often astonished at just how astute some of her choices turned out to be.

Montague watched her now, sitting at the opposite end of the table orchestrating the lunchtime conversation to make sure everyone was included. She was a very beautiful woman. A cynic – and plenty of people were cynical about Hal Montague – would have called her a trophy wife. There was some truth in the accusation, even Montague acknowledged that. She was twenty years younger than he was, a second wife acquired after a bitter divorce, and she fitted many of the other stereotypes of the breed: she was attractive, well-dressed, nubile. But she was no one's trophy. Serena Montague would never be dressing for any man's table or bed, nor a bimbo to hang off his arm or an exhibit to bolster his ego – and anyone foolhardy enough to suggest it to her face would have rapidly found themselves in need of the nearest Casualty Department.

Montague caught her eye and smiled. She'd selected an interesting collection of guests this weekend.

Simon Doyle and another business colleague; a pony-tailed artist whose work Serena liked buying though Montague would have baulked at even hanging his canvases in the stable block for fear of frightening the horses; a showbiz couple who thought they were rather more fascinating than anyone else did; and a pompous but insecure junior minister at the Department of Trade and Industry and his wife who seemed overawed by the whole occasion.

Montague disliked politicians as a species. He regarded them as vain, avaricious, essentially talent-less individuals, elevated to a station well above their abilities and fit only for the House of Commons, which he saw as an anachronistic club for syco-phants and ambitious no-hopers. He despised them, but recognised they were influential people worth cultivating. He had several backbenchers on his books as paid consultants – tame poodles who could be relied on to put the interests of their wallets before the interests of the country – and there were many more who'd enjoyed, and been subtly corrupted by, his hospitality. Politicians couldn't resist the high life. They were starstruck by successful businessmen, in thrall to them. They thought businessmen could do anything, run anything, even though the only thing businessmen really knew how to do was make money. Montague was adept at exploiting that delusion. A weekend in the country, a few days on his yacht in the Med, and it was amazing how receptive politicians became not just to his particular brand of free-market ideology – of which he had practical experience – but to his opinions on a dozen or more other subjects about which he knew absolutely nothing.

The dining-room door opened and the housekeeper came in. She went straight to Simon Doyle and whispered in his ear. Doyle got up from his chair and headed for the door, glancing across at Montague who raised an enquiring eyebrow at him. Doyle shook his head and left the room.

Montague topped up his wine glass with Puligny-Montrachet and passed the bottle to the elderly man sitting on his right hand. Dr Julius Wolf was a regular visitor to the house but he was hardly the life and soul of the party. He spent most of his time in his room, watching a catholic selection of pornographic movies which Montague always provided for his amusement. Montague didn't know why he watched them – nostalgia perhaps – for the old duffer was almost certainly impotent, age and the three bottles of wine he consumed daily would have seen to that. Montague invited him out of pity and a sense of obligation for it was Wolf who had introduced him to the lucrative possibilities of cigarette-trafficking and who, though now a sleeping partner in the enterprise – sometimes literally – was still a valuable source of advice.

Montague liked doing business with Swiss traders like Wolf. You knew where you stood with them. Unlike the Latin races, or even the north Europeans, the Swiss never did anything for sentimental or altruistic reasons. The bottom line was the only thing that concerned them. They were crooks, of course, but Montague understood that. He was one himself. But the key thing about Switzerland – that perfectly placed Fifth Column, at the very heart of Europe, yet outside the EU and so ideal for trafficking and money-laundering – was that because of its commercial secrecy laws no one could ever find out exactly how crooked you were.

Doyle came back into the room and crossed immediately to Montague, bending down and saying quietly: 'I think you'd better come. Frank Barron's on the phone.'

'What does he want?' Montague said after they'd left the dining room and were walking down the hall towards the study. Frank Barron was a senior civil servant in the Ministry of Agriculture, Fisheries and Food.

'Someone has been asking questions about the Intervention Board investigation into Horningtoft.'

Montague jolted to a halt. 'What? Who?'

'UCLAF.'

'Shit!'

Montague went into the study and picked up the phone as Doyle shut the door behind them.

'What the fuck's going on, Frank? I thought you'd buried that investigation.'

Barron let out a feeble sigh. 'So did I, Hal, believe me.'

'So how did UCLAF get on to it?'

'I don't know. As far as MAFF is concerned it's dead in the water. The file has been destroyed, all

211

mention of it deleted from the computer records. I have no control over UCLAF but there's nothing for them to find.'

'There'd better not be,' Montague said menacingly. 'Not if you think you're retiring from Whitehall and slipping into some nice cushy non-executive directorships with my companies.'

'Relax, Hal, there's nothing to worry about. Everything remotely incriminating has been destroyed. I'm just letting you know, that's all.'

'I expect to be protected on this one, Frank, you understand me? It's your neck on the block as well as mine. If I go down I'll make sure a lot of others go with me.'

Barron swallowed. 'There's no need to get so angry about it.'

'There's every fucking need. You were supposed to have taken care of all this. Why do you think I paid you all that money?'

'Hal, I assure you . . .'

'Yes, yes,' Montague interrupted. 'I want no excuses. What's the name of the UCLAF investigator?'

'Sullivan. Rob Sullivan.'

'British?'

'Yes.'

'Good. You keep your eye on this one, Frank. I want this investigation blocked.'

'I'll do my best, but it may not be easy. Brussels is outside my jurisdiction.'

'Don't give me that shit,' Montague spat down the phone. 'You're a civil servant. Stalling, delaying, sitting on your hands, it's what you're fucking trained to do. And I expect you to do it for me.'

Montague slammed the receiver down hard and stood up, pacing agitatedly around the study.

'Those UCLAF bastards are sticking their noses into my affairs,' he said furiously, clenching his teeth and fists.

'Why would they be interested in some four-year-old investigation that went nowhere?' Doyle said calmly.

'They're not, you know that as well as I do. They're on our fucking tails. Or they think they are.'

Doyle rested his backside on the edge of the desk, watching his employer roaming restlessly across the room. It wasn't often that he saw Montague this rattled.

'Maybe we should be careful, lie low for a while.'

'No way,' Montague said irascibly. 'Those Brussels wankers don't scare me. Bunch of narrow-minded bureaucrats who couldn't investigate their way out of a paper bag.'

'Van Vliet's worried about them.'

'No wonder, they've been taking his warehouse apart. But nothing can be traced directly back to us. The important thing is not to panic, to carry on exactly as normal. But just as a precaution I want you to make sure everyone involved knows to keep their mouths shut. If anyone comes asking questions, they say nothing and let me know immediately.'

Doyle nodded. 'You trust Barron?'

'He'll do his best, but that's not really good enough. As with everything else, if you want something doing properly, do it yourself. Get me Rupert Bird.'

Doyle pushed himself off the desk, looked up a number in his contacts book and dialled it. He handed the receiver to Montague.

'Go and see to the guests. I'll be in shortly,' Montague said.

A voice came on the line.

'Hello?'

'Rupert? Hal Montague.'

Serena was upstairs in her bedroom, changing into her riding clothes, when Doyle walked in. He closed the door and leaned back on it, watching her doing up the buttons on her white, high-necked blouse. She looked good in jodhpurs and boots. They showed off her legs, her tight buttocks. She turned away from the mirror and smiled at him.

'Lock the door, Simon.'

'What?'

'Do you want Hal to walk in on us?'

She took hold of her dark hair and twisted it up on to the back of her head, fastening it in place with a metal clip. Doyle locked the door and came across the room to her.

'How are the guests?' she said.

'Whitton is fixing the ladies up with hard hats and boots. Hal's showing the men the billiards room and then they're going out shooting. Well, all except Wolf. He's gone to his room with a bottle of port.'

'He give me the creeps, that man. I wish Hal wouldn't invite him.'

'Be nice to him, Serena. We may need him. He's an old drunk but he still has a lot of influence.'

Serena adjusted her cravat and slipped on her riding jacket.

'He's a pervert. Every time he looks at me I get the feeling he wants to strip me naked and do God knows what to me.'

Doyle's mouth curled. 'I thought you liked that.'

She glanced at him over her shoulder. 'It depends who's doing the stripping.'

She buttoned up her jacket and turned to face him. 'Well?'

Doyle studied her dispassionately, trying to suppress the stirrings she always aroused in him. They were playing a dangerous game. He knew that was part of the appeal for Serena. In everything she did, riding, skiing, sex, it was the element of risk she liked. The greater the danger, the greater her enjoyment. But he was more careful. Risk for him was something you calculated and eliminated. It was a means, not an end.

'Very nice,' he said coolly.

'Is that all?' she said, feigning disappointment.

'You look good in riding clothes.'

'But better without them, eh?'

She picked up her riding crop from the bed and ran the tip of it up the inside of his leg. He took hold of the crop and pulled her to him, kissing her roughly.

Serena pushed him away, her objective fulfilled.

'That's better,' she said. 'I hate your self-control.'

She turned to look at herself in the floor-length mirror again.

'What was the phone call?' she asked. 'Hal looked absolutely livid when he came back in.'

'His lapdog at MAFF.'

'Trouble?'

Doyle shook his head. 'Nothing we can't handle.'

'Are you sure?'

'Trust me, Serena.'

She glanced at her watch and pouted.

'I suppose I ought to join the ladies. What are you going to do, go shooting?'

Doyle sneered. 'What, potting a few bloody rabbits with the green-wellie brigade? You must be joking.'

'Poor Simon,' Serena said, stroking his face sympathetically. 'We'll have to find something to amuse you later.'

The tide had gone out, leaving the boats stranded on the mud flats, some tilted over sideways on their hulls, others with their keels half buried in the sticky brown ooze. Mooring ropes hung loose from the harbour wall, straddling the channel which the sea and river had cut deep into the salt marshes. Only a narrow ribbon of dirty water meandered its way out to the ocean, navigable in a rowing boat or canoe but nothing bigger. It was a bright, clear day. A stiff breeze was blowing in over the land, tugging at the metal halyards on the yachts so they tinkled against the masts like tin cans on a string.

'There you are,' Jim Bristow said, pointing across the flats at a bird with black and white plumage and a deep orange-red bill. 'Oystercatcher. You see it?'

He handed Sullivan his binoculars and Sullivan felt obliged to look though he had no interest whatsoever in birds.

'Beautiful, isn't she?'

'Mmm,' Sullivan murmured.

'They're here all winter. Oystercatchers, grey plovers, curlews, dunlins, all manner of shore waders. People say it's a dull time of year, February, before the spring migrants arrive, but I find plenty to look at.'

Sullivan gave him back his binoculars and buried his hands in his pockets. He wasn't dressed for a walk along the Norfolk coast in mid-winter, but Bristow had insisted they went out, whether because he wanted the fresh air or because he felt more comfortable talking in the open Sullivan wasn't sure. There was something cautious about him: the way he'd refused to say much on the telephone, his reluctance to discuss anything inside his house. Paranoid was too strong a word, but Bristow was certainly taking no chances that anyone might eavesdrop on their conversation.

'Horningtoft,' Sullivan prompted him.

Bristow took a last look at the oystercatcher and walked on along the path which followed the top of a raised dyke between the mud flats and the Overy marshes.

'I took early retirement,' he said. 'I'd had enough of

217

all the crap you get in the CPS. The bureaucracy, the constant reorganisation, patronising magistrates who know damn-all about the law, whingeing coppers who moan on and on about guilty criminals who're never brought to trial but who don't give you the evidence to make a case in the first place.

'I couldn't wait to get out. My son and his family had settled up here so I moved from Norwich to be near them. I do a bit of painting, watercolours mostly – this coast is beautiful for painting, you should see the light on an autumn evening. And I've always liked birds. I've been here nearly four years now. I'm reasonably contented. Why should I dig up old memories of some trivial legal case I'd rather forget all about?'

'Would you?' Sullivan said. 'Then why did you invite me here?'

'You won't manage to revive it, you know.'

'That's not what I want.'

Bristow turned his head to look at him. He had a walker's build, tall and rangy with long legs and a measured gait that gave the impression he could keep going all day without feeling fatigue.

'What *do* you want, Mr Sullivan?' he said.

'I'm not sure at the moment. If you tell me about Horningtoft, I might have a clearer idea.'

Bristow was silent for a time, collecting his thoughts.

Then he said: 'Have you heard of a man called Henry Montague?'

'No.'

'He's a businessman. Calls himself Hal, like Henry

the Fifth – an absurd affectation, but he's rich enough to afford a little vanity. He has a big estate not far from here, Horningtoft Priory, hence the name of his company. *One* of his companies, I should say. He has dozens, maybe hundreds. He's that kind of businessman. Everything concealed behind a web of impenetrable corporations.'

'What's his principal business, agriculture?' Sullivan said.

'Hardly. Montague is a hobby farmer. That's not to say he doesn't take it seriously – he takes everything he does very seriously – but he doesn't devote much time to it. He comes into the country at weekends, talks to his estate manager, strolls around in wellies and pokes the occasional pig. But he doesn't know the first thing about farming. His main interests are in the City.'

'Doing what?'

Bristow smiled sardonically. 'What does anyone in the City do? He's what you might call a 'player'. Buys and sells companies, invests in speculative ventures, moves bits of paper around – well, it's all done electronically now, you don't even need to lift any paper, just press a few buttons and the computer does the rest for you. Nice work if you can get it. If you're part of the coterie of old school and university chums who pass jobs around between themselves, charging vast commissions, scratching each other's back with large wads of cash.'

'You've met him?'

Bristow shook his head. 'But I made a few enquiries

after the Intervention Board report landed on my desk. Got him worried enough to reveal his true nature. He made it his business to threaten me.'

'He *threatened* you?' Sullivan said.

'Why do you think I wasn't anxious to talk about him on the phone? He's a dangerous man with powerful connections.'

'What did he do?'

'Oh, nothing overt, nothing you could ever prove against him, but it was a threat nonetheless. He didn't do it himself, of course. He got his assistant to do it for him. A nasty piece of work named Simon Doyle.'

'Doyle?'

'You know him?'

'Just the name. He's a director of another company I've been looking into.'

'Oh yes, he's on the board of quite a few of Montague's companies. Men like Hal Montague always need a Simon Doyle, a reliable sidekick who doesn't mind getting his hands dirty, a lackey – well-paid, but still a lackey – who's always there to wipe his arse for him.'

'I see you're a fan of Montague's.'

'He has the arrogance of a certain class of Englishman who thinks he can do anything, get away with anything. He was outraged that anyone – particularly a provincial prosecutor like me – could be so presumptuous as to question his probity.'

'He's a criminal?' Sullivan said.

'I doubt he'd use the word. He'd be affronted. To Montague, criminals are working-class people who mug old ladies in the street or break into houses and steal your video recorder. Montague is a businessman, an entrepreneur who plays the system. A system which glorifies people like him.'

Bristow sighed. 'Maybe it's my age, maybe I'm old-fashioned, but I don't understand this modern cult of the businessman. We're supposed to admire them for their energy, their daring, but what are they except well-dressed wideboys flogging dodgy goods off the back of a lorry? The only difference between Hal Montague and some East End gangland thug is that Montague knows the words to the Eton Boating Song.'

'He went to Eton?'

'Harrow, actually, but you get my point. Harrow's on a hill, isn't it? Maybe they have a Mountaineering Song.'

Sullivan smiled. At his Leeds comprehensive they hadn't concerned themselves much with vocal tradition.

'So what did the Horningtoft report say?' he asked.

Bristow lifted his binoculars and trained them on a bird far out on the rippled surface of the mud flats.

'Curlew,' he said. 'You want a look?'

'No thanks,' Sullivan said.

'You know, what I like most about birds is that you can see them. They don't hide in burrows or only come out at night. They're there every day, all around you. On the ground, in the air, I never tire of watching them.'

They were nearing the sea now, the salt marshes petering out against the base of the dunes that formed a long ridge behind the beach. The sky, veined with torn strands of cloud, filled the horizon. Sullivan could almost feel its weight pressing down on the thin sliver of earth around him. He looked across to the mouth of the estuary where a strip of sand was bathed in sunshine. It was so quiet he could hear the rushes swaying in the breeze. Then the shrill cry of birds broke the silence. A distant flock of gulls rose into the air like flecks of dirt, curling around and swooping away towards the sea.

'You work for the European Commission,' Bristow said. 'You must know better than anyone what a target the EU is for criminals. There's a lot of money swilling around over there in Brussels. It's a gravy train that everyone wants to jump on to, but not everyone wants to pay for their ticket. The farmers around here have benefited enormously from the CAP. Sometimes I wonder how anything got grown before we joined the Common Market. There's a culture of subsidy in the agricultural industry. Farmers can't even fart without being given a methane support grant from Brussels. But they've become so dependent on handouts they've become greedy. And a lot take advantage of the system.'

'Did Montague?'

'Of course. Horningtoft is a farm management company. You knew that, I assume. There are economies of scale in running several farms together, even the ones round here which are some of the largest in Europe. The EU support payments can be huge – up to half a million pounds for a single farm. Horningtoft were suspected of breaking their milk quota, producing more than their allocation and selling it on the black market. It's quite a temptation to a farmer. If he produces too much milk, he has to pour it down the drain. He's not allowed to sell it. And yet we import milk from other EU countries to meet our needs. It's crazy.'

Sullivan nodded. It was one of the many absurdities of the Common Agricultural Policy. The UK could have been self-sufficient in milk production, but because of its quota allocation was forced to buy in part of its requirements from overseas. Many dairies and cheese manufacturers, starved of home-produced milk and so obliged to pay more for imports, were not averse to buying a little extra non-quota milk from their local farmers at a knockdown price.

'There were also irregularities in applications for crop subsidy and set-aside,' Bristow continued. 'Discrepancies in the tonnage of wheat eligible for price support, and doubts over the growing of wheat for industrial use on set-aside land. A very grey area, as you know.'

Sullivan shook his head. 'I'm not an agricultural specialist. What do you mean?'

'A farmer can claim payment for setting aside land, but that doesn't mean he has to leave it fallow. He's allowed to grow crops on it provided they're not for human consumption. So he can grow wheat for industrial purposes – fuel for example – and sell it without losing his set-aside allowance. You can see the problem. Do you know anyone who can tell the difference between wheat grown for human consumption and wheat grown for some other purpose? The whole thing's a farce.'

'Irregularities, you said?'

'Administrative errors was what Montague called them.'

'How much was involved?'

'Over a period of several years, about five and a half million ECUs.'

Sullivan paused for a second, astonished, then he walked on.

'That's some administrative error.'

'Montague claimed one of his managers was responsible and sacked him. Paid him off to keep his mouth shut was the rumour I heard. It was clearly fraud.'

'Yet he wasn't prosecuted.'

'No, he wasn't.'

'Why not?'

'That's a good question. I wish I knew the answer.'

They walked up a slight incline on to the top of the dunes. The whole sweep of Holkham Bay, a vast expanse of gleaming wet sand, was before them. Apart from a woman walking her dog, the shoreline was deserted.

'The case was taken out of my hands by my superior,' Bristow continued.

'Newman?'

'His predecessor, a man named Charmbury. But

it's no use asking him. He retired shortly after I did and was dead two years later – liver cancer. No further action was taken. Charmbury said there wasn't enough evidence to prosecute.'

'Was there?'

'In my opinion, yes.'

'You couldn't persuade Charmbury to proceed?'

'I tried.' Bristow hesitated. 'I was told in no uncertain terms to leave it well alone. I think it was one of the reasons they offered me early retirement. I've no real proof of this, but I got the feeling that someone further up the line had made the decision not to prosecute.'

'What do you mean, "further up the line"?'

'In London.'

Sullivan stared at him. 'You mean the DPP's office?'

Bristow nodded.

'Why?' Sullivan said.

'Montague is an influential man. He has a lot of friends.'

'Enough to influence the DPP?'

Bristow laughed cynically. 'Who can tell? I know one thing though, I worked for the CPS long enough to realise that decisions whether to prosecute are not always taken for legal reasons.'

'You're saying someone's protecting him?'

'What do you think? Who destroyed the CPS and Intervention Board records of the case?'

They walked on along the dunes. The sand was soft and fine as dust, held in place by clumps of tall marram grass whose stalks were bent almost to the ground by the wind. Down on the beach the dog was splashing in and out of the water, retrieving a ball thrown by its owner. An occasional bark ripped through the cold afternoon air.

Then Bristow said: 'If you're not an agricultural specialist, Mr Sullivan, why are you interested in Horningtoft?'

Sullivan took a moment to reply. 'I'm fishing, I suppose. Looking for possible links with another case I'm working on.'

'Some other kind of fraud?'

'Something like that,' Sullivan replied evasively.

'Don't insult me. You came here asking for confidential information. Do me the courtesy of telling me why.'

'I'm sorry,' Sullivan said. 'Yes, you're entitled to know. Cigarette-trafficking.'

Bristow turned his head. He had a thin, bony face and bushy salt-and-pepper eyebrows. Wisps of untidy light hair protruded from beneath the sides of his pork-pie hat.

'You suspect Montague of cigarette-trafficking?' he said, disbelief in his voice.

'You think it unlikely?'

'No, I don't. It just took me by surprise. I wouldn't put anything past a man like Montague. But I'd be careful, Mr Sullivan. He may be too big to get caught.'

'His friends, you mean?'

'There's an old adage in business,' Bristow said.

'If you borrow ten thousand pounds from the bank, you're at their mercy. If you borrow ten million, they're at *your* mercy. It's the same everywhere. Fiddle a hundred pounds on your tax bill and the Inland Revenue will spend thousands chasing you to get it back. Fiddle millions and you get a knighthood for services to industry. It never pays to be a small fish in the sea. You get eaten too easily.'

'I don't follow you.'

'Prosecuting someone like Montague would be an embarrassment to the government. The amounts involved are too great. They'd prefer to sweep it all under the carpet and pretend it never happened. Besides, do you really want to be the Eliot Ness of Eurofraud?'

'Pardon?'

'Don't waste your bullets. You'll only get one shot at a man like Hal Montague. Remember Al Capone. A bootlegger, murderer, one of the worst gangsters in history and yet all Ness managed to pin on him was a charge of tax evasion. If Montague's trafficking in cigarettes, cheating the EU of millions, you don't want to prosecute him for fiddling his milk quotas, do you?'

Bristow turned away, raising his binoculars and focusing them on a tiny bird of prey hovering over the marshes.

'Merlin,' he murmured softly.

Sullivan lifted his head and watched as the merlin plummeted into a steep dive, sleek and streamlined, its wings swept back. It raced towards the ground then pulled up suddenly into a perfect glide, swooping low over the salt grass to take its unseen, unsuspecting prey.

THIRTEEN

When Sullivan first joined UCLAF, he'd been taken for lunch in the Beaulieu canteen by a colleague, a garrulous Welshman named Barry Morgan who worked in TF4, the unit responsible for fighting fraud against the structural funds of the EU.

Morgan had told him a story about a poor village in southern Spain which was twinned with an equally poor village in Greece. One summer, the mayor of the Greek village visited his counterpart in the Spanish village and was taken aback by his host's opulent house – a large, porticoed villa with lush gardens and its own swimming pool.

'How on earth can you afford a place like this?' the Greek asked in astonishment. 'You're only a struggling farmer like me.'

The Spanish mayor took his visitor out into his garden and pointed down into the valley.

'You see that bridge across the ravine? We got funds from Brussels to build a four-lane highway across it, but we made it one lane instead and put traffic lights at each end. *That's* what paid for this house.'

A few years later the Greek mayor returned the favour and invited the Spaniard to his village in southern Greece. The Spanish mayor walked into the Greek's house, his jaw dropping at the marble floors, the paintings on the walls, the patio and large swimming pool he could see outside in the garden.

'What the hell were you going on about *my* house for?' he said. 'Look at this place. How does a poor farmer like you afford a home like this?'

'Ah,' said the Greek, leading his visitor outside into the landscaped gardens. 'You see that bridge down there in the valley?'

The Spaniard squinted into the distance. 'No, I don't see any bridge.'

'That's what paid for this house,' said the Greek.

It was a joke, but only just, as Sullivan discovered when Morgan took him back to his office and pulled out a pile of files which detailed the misappropriation of EU structural funds.

'It's all in there,' Morgan said. 'The projects which never happened: bridges which were never built, roads which go nowhere, community sports centres which turned out to be a pool and tennis court in the mayor's back garden. We have the names, the towns, the amounts involved. Millions and millions embezzled. All of it true.'

'Jesus,' Sullivan said, flicking through the documents. 'Have you recovered any of it?'

'Almost none. We prepare reports and send them to the public prosecutors in the responsible member states, but most of them do sod-all about it. No legal proceedings, no money repaid, not a single penny. It happens all the time. That's the depressing thing. We have no powers to prosecute ourselves, we depend on the member states to do it. If they choose not to, we can do nothing to make them.'

Morgan grinned. 'Welcome to UCLAF, boyo. I'm telling you, by the time you finish your attachment you'll have a big bruise right here in the middle of your forehead from banging your head against a brick wall.'

So far, Sullivan had escaped the bruise, but he'd had quite a few headaches. The system was a mess, a fraudster's dream. A budget of eighty billion Euros distributed around fifteen different countries by twenty-plus directorates within the Commission, none of whom had the slightest idea what the others were doing, and all of it monitored, in theory, by a tiny unit of eighty investigators with no police or prosecuting powers.

There was a lot of truth in what Bristow had said about Montague being too big and influential to prosecute. It was common knowledge that EU governments didn't report a large proportion of the frauds they detected in their own countries. It made them look bad if their citizens were seen to be dishonest and there was a real possibility that money lost to fraud would have to be repaid to the Commission, something no government was keen to do. Sullivan had no illusions about his fellow countrymen, but it had still surprised him that no action had been taken against Hal Montague and Horningtoft.

It was late afternoon when he left Burnham Overy Staithe, still frozen from the walk along the coast despite the tea and toast Bristow had given him afterwards at his house. The village of Horningtoft was only a couple of miles off his route to Colchester and, on impulse, he made a detour to take a look at it.

It was a tiny place, more a hamlet than a village. The Priory, being the only building of any size, was easy to find. Sullivan stopped outside the open gates and looked down the drive at the imposing brick mansion silhouetted against the dusk sky. It was partially hidden behind the skeletal outlines of a copse of leafless trees so Sullivan got out of his car and walked down the drive to get a better look. The house had four storeys, a separate stable block at one end and at the other, incorporated into the fabric of the building, a chapel with ornate Gothic windows which Sullivan guessed had been part of the original priory.

The ground-floor windows were illuminated, throwing pools of misty light out on to the gravel forecourt. One of the first-floor windows was also lit up. A figure appeared behind the glass. An elderly man, a little bowed at the shoulders with black-framed spectacles and a shock of silver-grey hair. It was a striking face. Not a face you could easily mistake for any other. Sullivan stared up at it, absorbing the features, trying to recall where he'd seen it before. When it came to him, it was with a sudden jar that momentarily nonplussed him. Surely not. He studied the face again. There was no doubt about it.

'You know you're trespassing, don't you?' a harsh voice said behind him.

Sullivan turned and saw a large hefty man in a Barbour jacket, wellies and flat cap. Tucked under his right arm was a Purdey shotgun.

'Pardon?'

'This is private property,' Montague said. 'I suggest you leave before I call the police.'

Sullivan studied him intently, guessing who he was. He was bigger, fleshier than he'd imagined, his face getting puffy around the cheeks and jowls, his double chin sagging above the neck.

'I was just going. I only wanted to look at the house,' Sullivan said.

'When we want tourists and day-trippers rubber-necking around the place, we'll put a sign up by the gates,' Montague replied with a sneer. 'Robinson, see this man off the estate.'

Five other men had come across the lawns behind Montague, all carrying shotguns. One of them, a gamekeeper by the look of him, stepped forward out of the group and waited for Sullivan to walk away up the drive. He followed him to the gates and watched as Sullivan climbed into his car and drove away. Then he took a pen out of his inside coat pocket and scribbled the number of the car on the palm of his hand.

The road took a loop around the side of the Priory, heading away from the village. Looking across through the gloom, Sullivan could vaguely make out the shapes of figures going up the steps into the

house. He turned off right, negotiating his way back
to the main road through the twilit countryside. The
horizon was a vista of dark clouds slashed with pale
streaks of light which glanced off the bare fields,
tinting the furrows of frozen earth with a sheen
of platinum. Sullivan barely noticed. He had other
things on his mind.

The first thing that struck him when he got home was
the noise level. Living on his own for most of the time
he got used to silence, and the return to family life
was always a rude awakening.

Patrick and James were playing some indefinable
game which, like most of their games, seemed to
involve charging around the house at high speed,
shouting and yelling and hitting each other with
whatever came to hand. Sullivan and Kate retreated
to the kitchen and sat at the table drinking tea,
talking about what had happened since they last
spoke on the telephone. It was an unsatisfactory way
of keeping in touch, these catch-up conversations
which could never hope to recapture the immediacy
and spontaneity of actually living the experiences
together. But it was a method they'd evolved over
the previous two years to keep each other informed
about the separate strands of their lives.

Sometimes Sullivan got the impression that it was
becoming an effort for Kate to recount to him what
had occurred during his absence. Every time he came
home she seemed more tired, more rundown than
before. It was particularly bad this time, but then

she'd just come to the end of the first half of the spring term – the most depressing of the school year with its dark, cold days – and was in need of a break.

'Would you mind if we didn't come back with you tomorrow?' she said, broaching something which had obviously been troubling her.

'Why? What's happened?' Sullivan said sharply.

Kate and the boys always came over to Brussels for the half-term holiday. His wife had given no hint on the telephone that she wanted to change the arrangement.

'I thought we might make our own way over later. Maybe Tuesday. I'm tired, so are the boys. And I've got a lot of stuff to prepare for school. I need a couple of days here.'

Kate listened to the appeasing tone in her voice and wondered why she had to justify herself. She knew he didn't understand what hard work it was uprooting every holiday to stay with him. He just carried on as normal, taking the occasional day off to do something with them, but for her and the boys it was disruptive and exhausting. They had to pack, arrange their travel, endure the journey, adapt to the apartment in Tervuren where none of them felt at home. The whole thing was a chore and the boys were starting to resent it. They had friends in England they wanted to see in the holidays and Brussels bored them. Kate put up with all the hassle – and most of it fell on her – because she believed it was important to keep the family together.

But even she was beginning to wonder if it was worth it.

'Oh,' was all Sullivan said.

'We'll still have most of the week with you,' Kate continued, trying to sound upbeat.

'Fine, that's okay.'

'You don't mind?'

'No, why should I?'

Kate was a little taken aback. She'd thought he would be more difficult. School holidays in Brussels had hitherto been a sacrosanct part of their family life, something that was fixed and untouchable. She knew that Rob, for all his veneer of modern enlightenment – his approval of women having careers, of equal rights and the rest of it – still deep down believed a wife's place was with her husband. She'd expected much more hostility to a change in their routine.

'Are you sure?' she said.

'Yes. Come over whenever you're ready.'

He smiled at her. He was thinking of Claire Colmar, remembering the night in her apartment and anticipating, with a mixture of exhilaration and guilt, another clandestine encounter.

The Eurostar terminal at Waterloo had been deliberately – and expensively – designed to look nothing like a traditional British railway station. There were carpets on the floor of the departure lounge, soft lighting and overpriced souvenir and gift shops. The toilets had fake marble washbasins and individual hand-dryers next to each one, and the coffee shop served espresso and cappuccino and six different types of tea. It was all very comfortable and pleasant yet somehow bland and characterless, just like the airport terminals it had been built to resemble – as if airport architecture were something worth emulating.

Sullivan arrived early for his train back to Brussels. He slid his ticket into the automatic check-in machine and passed through the barrier into the terminal. In a glass-walled booth to one side, a Eurostar employee and a tall, cadaverous man in a dark mackintosh were scrutinising the passengers as they went through passport control. Sullivan glanced at them casually and made his way out into the crowded departure lounge.

Queuing up at the coffee shop, he bought a cup of Earl Grey and a Danish pastry which, from the price, must have been flown in specially from Copenhagen. Then he found an empty table and sat down, feeling almost nostalgic for the days of British Rail: the draughty platforms; the waiting rooms which were stuffy in summer, freezing in winter; the stewed tea strong enough to remove the enamel from your teeth and the appalling standard of service which – like the Blitz – gave the British a feeling of solidarity, of common purpose and, above all, a universal, enduring subject to moan about.

The Eurostar terminal was too artificial, too regulated an environment to create any kind of rapport between the diverse passengers scattered around the departure lounge. Sullivan had waited there on

countless occasions but not once had any other traveller attempted to converse with him. Which was why
he was so surprised when the cadaverous man he'd
seen in passport control came up to him and said
curtly: 'Mr Sullivan?'

'Yes.'

'I wonder if I might have a word with you?'

'What about?' Sullivan said, thinking it was probably some customer service or marketing survey.
He'd been cornered before and persuaded to answer a
few harmless questions, killing time while he waited
for his train. But the questioners had always been
attractive young women in Eurostar uniforms, not
middle-aged men with red noses, and none of them
had ever known his name.

The man glanced around and gestured towards the
side of the lounge.

'Perhaps we could talk somewhere a little more
private?' he said nasally, exuding a faint aroma of
menthol cough sweets.

Sullivan was intrigued enough to pick up his bags
and follow the man over to the seating area by the
windows which was almost empty.

'How did you know my name?' he asked.

Rupert Bird ignored the question. It was hardly
worth an answer. The registration number of the car
at Horningtoft – easily traceable to a hire company
at Waterloo – a description from Montague plus the
Eurostar passenger reservations list made the identification elementary even for a desk man like him.

'I work for the government,' he began. 'The British

government,' he added in case there was any doubt.

'Oh yes. Which bit?'

'The Foreign Office,' Bird said reluctantly, gauging how much he should reveal. 'We understand you've been asking questions about Henry Montague.'

Sullivan kept his face expressionless, wondering who had told them. Not Bristow, surely. He was a cynic, an outsider, whilst this man with his chalk-striped suit and his plummy public-school drawl had Establishment stamped all over him.

'How do you know that?'

Bird gave a dismissive shrug. 'That doesn't need to concern you.'

He took a soggy handkerchief out of his coat pocket and blew his nose, wiping his nostrils carefully.

'And what if I say it does concern me?' Sullivan asked.

Bird put his handkerchief away and said thickly: 'Would you mind telling me why you're interested in him?'

'Yes, I would mind,' Sullivan replied. The man's manner, patronising, arrogant, annoyed him.

'Ah,' Bird said. 'I was hoping you would be a little more cooperative.'

'I'll cooperate if you tell me who you are and why you want to know. Show me some ID.'

'This is an unofficial approach, Mr Sullivan. All off the record.'

'What's your name?'

'You don't need to know that.'

'Tell me,' Sullivan said acidly. 'Can you give me

any good reason why I should talk about my work to a complete stranger who approaches me at a railway station and won't tell me who he is? If not, I suggest you piss off before I call the police.'

'That wouldn't be a good idea.'

'You could be anyone. How do I know you work for the government?'

'You'll have to take my word for that.'

Sullivan gave a snort of disbelief. 'You're going to have to do better than that.'

Rupert Bird cleared his throat. Damn Hal Montague for making him come back into London on a wet Sunday night when he should have been home in bed with a couple of aspirin and a bucket of hot toddy.

'I'm sure you're a loyal British citizen, Mr Sullivan,' he said. 'Even though you do work in Brussels.'

'The two aren't mutually exclusive, you know,' Sullivan replied.

'Aren't they? What if there's a conflict of interest? Which side would you take then?'

'Conflict of interest?'

'Yes. Which would you put first, your duty to Europe or your duty to your country?'

'I'm not aware of any conflict of interest,' Sullivan said. 'What do you mean?'

'You can't serve two masters, can you? There's your country of birth, where you grew up, where your family lives, where you acquired your cultural and historical identity. Then there's the European Commission, an unelected quango of bureaucrats

240

serving fifteen different countries. When push comes to shove, who do you put first?'

Sullivan was amused by the phrasing, the blatant manifestation of the Europhobia which infected the corridors of power in London.

'Do I have to choose between the two?' he said.

'Don't be naive,' Bird said, turning his head away to sneeze. He blew his nose again on his sopping hanky. The skin around his nostrils was raw and tender. Sullivan drew back as far as his seat allowed, trying to keep away from the germs. 'Do you really think the interests of the UK and Europe are the same?'

'Politicians are always telling us they are,' Sullivan said provocatively.

Bird grunted contemptuously. 'What politicians say and what politicians mean are not always the same thing.'

'But you're a Foreign Office civil servant, aren't you?' Sullivan said. 'Don't you write their speeches for them? Or is that a different bit of the FO?'

Bird didn't reply. Sullivan probed him some more, to see the reaction rather than because he expected an answer.

'Which bit of the Foreign Office are you in, Mr . . . ? And what has Henry Montague, or my work, got to do with you?'

'I believe I asked first,' Bird said, as if they were two kids arguing in the playground. 'What is your interest in Montague?'

Sullivan weighed up his answer. He was inclined

to believe the man really did work for the FO. He had all the marks of a particular kind of civil servant: the voice, the clothes, the class traits of condescension and impatience which an impostor could never have mastered this well. But Sullivan's investigation was still none of his business.

'I'm not prepared to tell you that,' he said.

Bird's mouth tightened angrily. He rubbed the edge of his forefinger across the base of his nose, trying to suppress a sneeze which came anyway. The shower of mucus sprayed out on to his coat and he rummaged desperately for his handkerchief to wipe it away. Sullivan watched him, reflecting how the common cold could reduce all men to the same level of spluttering indignity.

'I'm appealing to you as a British citizen,' Bird said eventually. 'Henry Montague does valuable work for this country. We don't want him to be compromised by some misguided investigation into his business affairs.'

'What are you talking about, "valuable work"?'

'You would hardly expect me to tell you that.'

Sullivan realised suddenly, belatedly, which bit of the FO the man worked for.

'You think I'm compromising him?' he said. 'Have you ever thought he might be compromising you?'

Bird brushed aside the question. 'There is nothing for you to find. It might be better if you called off your investigation.'

'Let me get this straight,' Sullivan said. 'You're telling me, an employee of the European Commission, to stop an investigation because it might embarrass the British government?'

'I'm not telling you. I'm merely making a suggestion.'

'And if I say no?'

'That would be unfortunate,' Bird said. 'Let's not be hasty. I hope you give it your full and ample consideration.'

'And if I still refuse?'

'That is your decision entirely.'

'I sense a proviso here,' Sullivan said.

Bird attempted a smile but it twisted mid-way into a sneer. He leaned closer and said menacingly: 'You're not really an employee of the European Commission, are you? You still work for UK Customs and Excise, and when you've finished your junket in Brussels, you'll have to come back to this country. When you do, don't think we won't remember which side you chose.'

Sullivan stared at him. 'You're threatening me?'

'I'm sure you're fully aware of the situation. You're an intelligent man. You can work it out for yourself. Give it some thought, eh?'

'I don't need to think about it,' Sullivan replied, controlling his anger. 'I know exactly where my duty lies. You can take your "suggestion", wrap it up in that snotty handkerchief of yours and shove it so far up your arse you can wipe your nose from the inside.'

He stood up. 'Excuse me, I have a train to catch.'

* * *

Montague sometimes wondered what defect in his character had made him deviate from the path of lawful commerce, what fundamental flaw in his make-up had led him to become a trafficker in cigarettes. A fortuitous encounter with Julius Wolf, when the Swiss lawyer was brokering a legitimate business deal for him, had opened up the doors of the smuggling world, but nothing had forced Montague to walk through them, or to seize the opportunity with quite such determined relish. It was easy money, it was true, but money had never been the most important thing in his business life, and besides, he'd made more than he could spend through his legitimate enterprises. He had absolutely no need to turn to crime for the money alone.

So what was it? He knew psychologists recognised that certain types of people required an abnormal level of danger and risk in their lives to keep them happy. Bungee jumpers, powerboat racers, mountaineers, obsessives who parachuted off skyscrapers or slid down Everest on kitchen trays. They were people who were constantly finding some new challenge to stimulate themselves and stave off boredom, even though they knew it might kill them. Montague shared something in common with these individuals – most of whom he regarded as certifiably insane. He'd never felt an overwhelming need for physical danger in his life but he needed risk as surely as he needed air and water. He'd succeeded in business because he lacked the sense of caution most people possessed and, once he'd achieved a certain level of wealth and satisfaction, had turned to trafficking to provide the new challenge his personality and intellect demanded.

He had an immense belief in himself. He'd failed at very few things in his life and though, like any businessman, he'd experienced setbacks, he had always recovered and returned to the fray with renewed vigour. But he was too intelligent not to be aware that self-confidence could easily slip over into hubris. For that reason he'd spent most of Sunday reconsidering his strategy in the light of what Frank Barron had told him the previous day. If he was now under scrutiny by the fraud investigators of the European Commission, it made sense to draw up contingency plans to protect his interests.

He was still in his study, drinking Chablis and talking to Doyle, when Rupert Bird rang him.

'Where are you, Rupert?' he asked.

'On my mobile outside Waterloo Station,' Bird replied, breaking off momentarily to sneeze.

'You located him?'

'Yes.'

'And?'

'No deal, I'm afraid.'

Montague gritted his teeth and rolled his eyes at Doyle.

'What do you mean? You turned the screws, I hope?'

'I appealed to his sense of patriotism,' Bird said.

'You did *what*?' Montague said incredulously. 'What did you do, stand up and sing Land of Hope and Fucking Glory?'

'There's no call for that, Hal. I've come all the way into town for you, and with a streaming cold. You might be a little more grateful.'

'You poor thing,' Montague said sarcastically. 'What did you tell him?'

'I did everything I could. He wouldn't be persuaded.'

'Everyone's persuadable. You just need to know their weaknesses.'

'There are limits to how far I can go,' Bird said stiffly. 'I had to keep it unofficial, you understand that.'

'That should have made it easier. You can say what you like, make threats without any comeback.'

'He refused to cooperate. I spelt out the consequences to him, but it made no difference. What did you expect me to do, knock him over the head and bundle him into a waiting car? This is the real world, not some trashy film.'

'You know, Rupert,' Montague said with a sigh, 'you always were a useless prick.'

He put down the phone and turned to Doyle.

'I've taken a dislike to those UCLAF bastards. I think it's time we clipped their wings.'

It was a dark rainy night, a pungent fog hanging low over the city, swirling in eddies across the surface of the sea. The navy-blue Fiat van slowed and pulled in by the kerb at the edge of the harbour road. The driver waited for a couple of cars to go past, then reversed out along a small concrete jetty which protruded into the bay. He climbed out and opened the rear doors of the van. A second man jumped down and together they lifted out a long, streamlined object which resembled a small bobsleigh but without the runners. It had two handles at the back and a propeller protected by a mesh guard. The men peered around through the fog to ensure no one was watching and lowered the object – an underwater sledge – into the sea.

A third man emerged from the rear of the van. He was dressed in diving gear: wet suit, flippers, mask, a compressed air tank strapped to his back. He moved swiftly to the edge of the jetty, shielded by the bulk of the van, and dropped over the side with barely a splash. The two other men passed down to him four heavy metal discs which he stowed in a well in the centre of the sledge. The diver switched on the electric motor, then adjusted the buoyancy of the sledge, flooding the tanks along its sides to make it sink. As the sledge slowly disappeared under the water, the diver grasped the handles at the back and twisted the throttle. The sledge surged away into the inky depths, towing the diver behind. The whole operation had taken less than five minutes.

Twenty minutes later, he was in the main harbour, coming up beneath the rusty hull of a freighter. He clamped the four magnetic discs to the bow plates of the ship and set the timers. Then he grabbed hold of the sledge and turned back the way he'd come.

The navy-blue van with its three occupants was on the A3 south of Vesuvius, near Torre Annunziata, when the charges detonated, blowing four large holes in the hull of the ship. The holds flooded with water and very slowly the *Maria Vasquez* keeled over and sank.

FOURTEEN

'Take a seat. Help yourselves to coffee.'

Ole Carlsen was standing up behind his desk, drifting about aimlessly, fidgeting with the buttons on his jacket as if he didn't know what to do with his hands. Claire had never seen him so tense.

Carlsen waited for the three of them to settle in their chairs, cups and saucers on their laps, before he sat down.

'I think it's time we reviewed this operation,' he said. 'Claire, tell them what happened on Friday night.'

Slowly, calmly, Claire described her ordeal at the cottage on the coast. She'd had the weekend to recover but was still surprised that she could recount the details without feeling unduly distressed. It had happened, it was over now, that was all she felt.

No one spoke for a time after she'd finished. Then Sullivan said: 'Jesus! Are you okay?'

Claire nodded. 'A few bruises, that's all.'

'And mentally?'

'I'm fine.'

Sullivan glanced at Carlsen, the concern apparent in his expression.

'I've suggested Claire takes a few days off,' Carlsen said, answering Sullivan's unspoken question. 'But she'd rather continue working. That is her decision.'

'Are you sure?' Sullivan said.

'Yes,' Claire replied brusquely.

Men always reacted in the same way to any kind of threat to a woman. Shock, then anxiety giving way to an over-protectiveness she found patronising. They would never have condescended in the same way to a male colleague.

'Do we know who your attacker was?' Sullivan asked.

'No. I've given a description to the police. He was young, fit, tough, with cropped hair like a soldier.'

'A soldier? What nationality?'

'I don't know. He said a few words in a language I didn't understand. It sounded Eastern European, Slavic.'

'Can you remember any of the words?'

'Just one. *Sooka*, something like that.'

'*Sooka*?' Stig Enqvist said.

'You know it?' Sullivan asked.

'*Cyka*, it's Russian for bitch.'

'I didn't know you spoke Russian.'

Enqvist smirked, easing the tense atmosphere. 'Only the rude words.'

'Why the hell would a Russian want to kill you?' Sullivan said to Claire.

'I don't think he knew who I was. I just happened to be there at the wrong time. It was Kuypers they wanted.'

'Why?'

'If I'd got there earlier, he might have told me.'

'And your attacker's body?'

'He had an accomplice, it's the only possible explanation. There was no way he was going to walk out of that house in the state I left him. The police found fresh tyre marks on a track through the forest to the east of the cottage. They had a car waiting.'

'Is there any trace of them?'

Claire shook her head. 'The police alerted all the hospitals in the area, set up roadblocks, but there's been no sign of them. He was badly injured, in need of urgent medical treatment. He must have gone somewhere.'

'From now on,' Carlsen said gravely, looking at each of them in turn, 'you must exercise the greatest caution in everything you do. I don't like the way this investigation is going. You do nothing without telling me first, and you go nowhere without the appropriate police or customs support. These are clearly violent people we are dealing with and I'm concerned about some of the military elements that seem to be creeping into the situation.'

'What military elements?' Sullivan said. 'The fact that Claire's attacker looked like a soldier?'

'Not just that,' Carlsen said. 'Did you see the breakfast news at all?'

'No.'

'It was on RAI. The *Maria Vasquez* was blown up in Naples harbour last night.'

'It was *what*? Shit!' Sullivan said. 'How? Who by?'

'I suggest you call Casagrande for the details. But it was done from under the water. The ship was moored in the Italian navy docks, with guards on the quayside. No one went on board her.'

'A diver?' Claire said.

'And underwater charges, probably mines of some sort. Who would have the expertise, the trained personnel and access to explosives like that except the military? You see why I'm concerned.'

'Which military?'

'I don't think we'll gain anything by speculating. We must leave it to the Italians,' Carlsen said. 'Now where are we going next? Rob?'

'I have a lead which is interesting. A British businessman named Henry Montague who's linked in a complicated chain of companies and directorships to Corvex Limited, a British firm we believe has some kind of connection with Van Vliet in Rotterdam.'

'How firm a lead?' Carlsen said.

'Well, out of curiosity, I went to look at his country house in Norfolk over the weekend and saw someone in the window I recognised. Dr Julius Wolf.'

Carlsen sat back abruptly in his chair. He stared at Sullivan.

'Are you certain?'

'No doubt about it. And Wolf's been trading again. Or at least, Steinhammer Weiss has.'

'You think he has a new partner?'

'Maybe not so new,' Sullivan said.

'What do you know about this man Montague?' Carlsen said.

'Not much at the moment. I have to find out more, but that may not be easy.'

'You have the usual sources, don't you? Police, SFO, Customs?'

'In theory, yes,' Sullivan said. 'The problem is, he has influential friends in the British government.'

'Meaning?'

'Well, it would seem he has links with the intelligence services.'

Carlsen blinked at him in disbelief. 'How can you possibly know that?'

Sullivan told them about his encounter at Waterloo Station.

'This man didn't actually say Montague worked for them?' Carlsen said.

'It was the impression I was intended to get. Either way, Montague has powerful friends protecting him. I can check him out, but the confidential stuff may be difficult to obtain.'

'And the way this Foreign Office man threatened you? Do you want to make a formal complaint? I'm prepared to go to the Commissioner.'

Sullivan shook his head. He'd cooled down since the previous evening. 'They'd only deny it and we'd end up looking foolish.'

Carlsen stroked his moustache pensively. 'It has to go on the record. They're attempting to influence our investigation. That's a serious matter. And they're putting pressure on one of my investigators, jeopardising your career. I can't allow that. We have to make this official, and at the highest level of the

Commission. I want a written report of exactly what happened, what was said. Now, while it's fresh in your mind.'

'Okay,' Sullivan said wearily. 'I'll do it this morning.'

'Good man.'

Carlsen turned to Enqvist. 'What about you, Stig?'

Enqvist was gazing distractedly at the wall, as if he hadn't been listening.

'Did you say Kuypers?' he asked Claire suddenly, going off at a tangent. His forehead was ridged with a frown of puzzlement.

'Yes, Jan Kuypers,' Claire replied. 'Why?'

'Wait here a minute.'

Enqvist went out of the office and walked away down the corridor. The others sat in silence, drinking their coffee, until he returned carrying a thick file under his arm. He slumped down and opened the file on his knees.

'I thought it was familiar,' he said. 'Vitoria. The Ilyushin-76 the Spanish seized. It came from Ostend originally, remember?'

'So?' Sullivan said.

'But the cigarettes started off in Holland. The pilot who flew them to Ostend was called Jan Kuypers.'

'I don't remember that.'

Enqvist twisted the file round and showed it to him.

'He was a minor player. He was questioned by the delinquents, but never charged with anything.'

The 'delinquents' was the Cigarette Task Group's

affectionate nickname for the OCRDEFO, the *Office Central pour la Répression de la Délinquance Économique et Financière Organisée*, the Belgian organised crime investigation unit.

'Would someone mind telling me what you're talking about?' Claire said.

'A smuggling operation we broke last year,' Sullivan said. 'A Ukrainian Ilyushin-76 cargo plane took a consignment of cigarettes from Ostend airport to Belgrade. It stopped to refuel in Greece and the cargo manifests were changed. The plane then flew to Vitoria in northern Spain and declared the freight as electrical spare parts. We were there on the runway waiting for them with the *Guardia Civil*. We found seventeen hundred cases of contraband cigarettes on board.'

'They'd been doing it for months,' Enqvist added. 'Nearly eighteen thousand cases had already been flown in. That's about fifteen million Euros in lost customs duties.'

'And Kuypers was involved in it?'

'Not directly. He was part of the supply chain but he did nothing illegal. All he did was fly the cigarettes from a bonded warehouse in Rotterdam to Ostend.'

'Not Van Vliet's warehouse?' Claire said.

Enqvist shook his head. 'Snoeck and Verheggen, another warehouse company. But this is the best bit: the Spanish impounded the Ilyushin but had to give it back because it turned out it belonged to the Ukrainian government, and the crew were all former Soviet airforce personnel. And what's more, the Ukrainian government, despite the protocols on mutual assistance with the EU, refused to give us any help at all in our investigation.'

Enqvist leaned forward, his eyes gleaming.

'You know what,' he said. 'I'm willing to bet a large chunk of my salary that the Russian and Ukrainian words for bitch are the same.'

It was early afternoon when Casagrande called back.

'I'm sorry about the delay,' he said apologetically. 'I've been busy.'

That was something of an understatement. Sullivan knew from the Gico duty officer in Naples that Casagrande had been up most of the previous night.

'I appreciate your time, Antonio. What happened?'

'Someone swam into the harbour under cover of darkness and stuck magnetic mines to the bottom of the ship. We've had divers down there but it's hard to tell exactly how many charges. Three, maybe four. Enough to take away half the bow plates.'

'Is she salvageable?'

'That depends what you mean. We're certainly going to get her out of the water. She's blocking off a large part of the Navy docks. But she'll never sail again. It wouldn't be worth patching her up, not a rusty old boat like that.'

'One less ship for our smuggling friends.'

'That's true. We're not crying about it here.'

'Antonio,' Sullivan said. 'It wasn't you, was it?'

Casagrande chuckled. 'If it were, I would hardly tell you, would I? I wish it had been actually. It would save me a hell of a lot of time tracking down the culprits.'

'You have anything?'

'Someone saw a blue Fiat van parked on a fishing jetty down towards Pórtici, but we haven't managed to trace it.'

'Who would have done it? Rival *camorristi*?'

'It's possible. Falzone's boys wouldn't have the skill to do a job like that themselves, but they've got the money to hire someone to do it for them. There are plenty of mercenaries around if you know where to look. Listen, I have to go, Rob. The pricks in Rome are shitting themselves over this. The ship was in a military zone. It could have been a Navy cruiser that went up. The Minister of Defence is flying down later to look at the wreck for himself and shout at the easiest person to blame.'

'You?'

'Probably.'

'Can I leave something with you? Not for now. Maybe for one of your men when this is all out of the way. Two names. Henry Montague and Simon Doyle.'

'Who are they?'

'I have a hunch, and that's all it is at the moment, that behind all the Liberian bullshit Montague is the real owner of the *Maria Vasquez*.'

'I'll see if we've got anything,' Casagrande said.

'Give my regards to the Minister of Defence.'

Casagrande laughed cynically and hung up.

Sullivan pushed back his chair and got to his

feet, walking to the window to look down into the shrub-filled atrium of the building. He thought about Claire, wondering whether he should go and see her. In Carlsen's office he'd felt a powerful urge to touch her, a palpable ache of sexual desire that was with him still.

'Something on your mind?' Enqvist asked.

Sullivan turned and shrugged, focusing his mind on less personal matters.

'The bodies are piling up, aren't they?'

'Smuggling's a dangerous game.'

'It's never been like this before. Maartens, Broek-huizen, now Kuypers. Why?'

'To punish them, to silence them,' Enqvist said. 'Maybe both.'

'The Ukrainians?'

'Kuypers, certainly. The others, who knows?'

'The hit-and-run near Groningen. What if they were after Kuypers, not Broekhuizen?'

'What difference does it make? They're both dead now.'

Sullivan looked back out of the window, reverting to his earlier thoughts.

'Have you ever committed adultery?' he asked casually.

'What?'

'Were you ever unfaithful to Anna?'

'Not when I was sober,' Enqvist said.

'I'm serious. Were you?'

Stig put down his pen and pushed himself away from the desk.

'You having problems with Kate?'

'No, I'm just interested. You can tell me it's none of my business.'

'Once,' Stig said. 'With a girl at the *Tullverk*. After a party.'

'Why did you do it?'

'Because she was there, I suppose.'

'Did you feel guilty?'

'I can't remember. Probably. Everyone does, don't they?'

'Did you tell Anna?'

'God, no. Never tell them. Not if you want to keep them.'

Enqvist broke off to answer the telephone on his desk.

'UCLAF, Enqvist.'

'This is Juliana. You remember me?'

Stig's mouth went dry. He licked his lips and said coolly: 'Sure. How are you?'

'I'm in Brussels. How are you fixed for dinner tonight?'

'I think I'm free. I'll just check my diary . . .'

Sullivan turned away, shutting out Stig's voice on the telephone. Was that why he'd slept with Claire? Was that why he'd cheated on his wife? Because she was there? It seemed a tawdry reason, but then affairs *were* tawdry, weren't they?

Enqvist put down the phone and gave Sullivan a shrewd look.

'You been playing around, or are you just thinking about it?'

'I was simply wondering,' Sullivan said. 'In an abstract sort of way.'

'Adultery is never abstract,' Enqvist said.

Claire was sitting at her desk, writing on a large pad of lined paper. Sullivan stood in the doorway and watched her for a moment. Her face was hidden. All he could see was the dark bob of shiny hair, the glint of a silver ring in one of her ears. Sensing his presence, she looked up. She smiled uncertainly.

'I came to see how you were,' Sullivan said.

'I'm fine.'

'You sure? Can I do anything?'

'I'm not a little girl,' Claire said with a note of irritation.

'I noticed.'

They looked at each other. Sullivan wanted to go to her and hold her, but he couldn't tell how she'd react. How she felt. It was strange how you could sleep with someone and yet not be close to them.

'Okay, I just thought I'd check.'

He turned to go.

'Rob.'

Claire came out from behind her desk and walked over to him. She pushed the door to.

'Stay for a bit, if you like.'

She was only a couple of feet away. Small, slender, desirable. Sullivan reached out and took her hand. She didn't stop him. He pulled her closer, slipping his arms around her waist. Claire stretched upwards and kissed him. He felt her lips soft and yielding, her hands on his neck, his hair. She broke away and pressed herself against him. Sullivan held her, stroking her back. His fingers slid down over the curve of her buttocks. Claire pulled them away.

'Not here.'

She walked back to her desk and took out a small mirror and make-up holder from her shoulderbag. She studied her face in the mirror and wiped away the smeared lipstick with a tissue before applying a fresh layer. Sullivan wondered how many times she'd done this with other men, other colleagues. It didn't make him want her less.

'Can I see you tonight?' he said.

She put the mirror and cosmetics away in her bag.

'I'd like to, but I'm busy. A long-standing appointment with an old friend. A woman,' she added, knowing how men's minds worked.

'Oh.'

'Maybe later in the week.'

Sullivan shrugged non-committally. Kate and the boys would be with him then, but he banished the thought from his head. It weighed too heavily on his conscience.

After he'd gone, Claire couldn't concentrate on her work. Why did relationships never get any easier? She'd been cooler with Sullivan than she'd intended. It was a form of protection that was second nature to her. He was married and she'd learnt that married men, whatever they said, had ties with their wives that were hard to sever. Ties of shared experience, of familiarity, of children that were bonded together and reinforced with a steel core of responsibility and loyalty. She knew never to underestimate the power of male guilt.

She wondered what she was doing, getting involved with yet another attached man. Hadn't she had enough of all that? She was thirty-six years old and was getting tired of the emotional stress an affair put her through. Yet she seemed addicted to it. She seemed unable to make things easy for herself; there always had to be complications.

She'd always been attracted to unsuitable men, it was one of her failings. Since her divorce from Wim, there'd been a series of partners, some more serious than others but none she regarded as long-term prospects. And now there was Rob Sullivan. If he'd been single . . . She didn't concern herself with hypothetical questions. If he'd been single, she probably wouldn't have been attracted to him.

She abandoned what she was doing and went to the window to look out at the darkening sky.

'Shit!' she said to herself, wondering why she'd told him she was busy that evening. It was true, she did have an appointment with an old friend, but she would much rather have cancelled and spent the time with him. So why hadn't she? She wanted him, yet instinctively she shied away from getting too emotionally involved with him.

She went to the telephone and dialled an internal number.

'Rob.' She paused. 'Why don't you come round later? I'll be home after eleven.'

*   *   *

She was even more beautiful than he remembered. Enqvist found himself looking away deliberately during dinner because to gaze at that perfect face for too long was more than he could take. She was utterly breathtaking – so flawless she left him struggling for air, his heart beating as if he'd just run up four flights of stairs. It had never happened to him before, even when he first met Anna, who was a very attractive woman. But Anna had been real, with the defects and imperfections of a real woman. Juliana Rietveld seemed unreal, her beauty like a hallucinatory vision or a mirage that would disappear if you dared to reach out and touch it. Yet Stig *had* touched it that night in Rotterdam, and the possibility, the hope, that he might do so again afflicted him with a nervous tension that was akin to a fever. His hands were clammy, his mouth like sandpaper, his stomach a tight ball of writhing eels. For probably the first time in his life he was tongue-tied until a couple of dry martinis began to relax him.

They were in a restaurant in the centre of Brussels, a quiet, exclusive cordon bleu cathedral where the *maître d'* was the archbishop, the waiters priests ministering to their congregation, the chef God and the bill large enough to re-roof the nave and still leave enough change for a trip to Lourdes. Enqvist didn't take much notice of the food, or the prices, he was too preoccupied with entertaining his guest and wondering what on earth she was doing there with him. He was forty-five years old, an obscure customs officer from Stockholm with a spare tyre

263

and thinning hair, a modest amount of charisma and a salary which, though comfortable enough, was hardly much to get excited about. What did she see in him? he thought periodically during the meal, dismissing such negative reflections immediately with the reassuring riposte, who cares? She was there opposite him, chatting easily, laughing at his jokes and the focus of so much drooling attention the waiters' tongues were practically scraping the carpet. Stig intended to make the most of it.

Dinner over, they went for a walk around the Grand-Place. Stig sucked in a few deep breaths of the damp night air. His head felt thick, his legs a little unsteady. How much had he drunk? Two martinis, a bottle and a half of wine, a liqueur. No more than he was used to, but he could feel the effects nevertheless.

Juliana held his arm, pressing close to him as they strolled the short distance to her hotel. They went up to her room and she opened a couple of miniature brandies from the mini-bar. Stig sipped his slowly, wishing he'd said no. His head was starting to swim, the dizziness turning to nausea.

They sat in armchairs talking in the desultory fashion of two people who know that conversation is not the main reason for their being together. Stig waited for her to make the first move. She'd invited him back to her room, but he was taking nothing for granted.

Finally, she stood up and came across to him. She'd kicked off her shoes and removed her silk jacket. Underneath she was wearing a tight black dress which clung to her figure like a second skin, revealing only her slim arms and a curve of tanned flesh between her neck and breasts. She knelt down beside his chair and kissed him with a lingering sensuousness. Stig ran his hands through her soft blonde hair and then down over her shoulders and back.

They moved to the bed, pulling off each other's clothes, slipping naked beneath the sheet. They kissed again. Juliana touched him. Stig was aware immediately that something was wrong. The desire was there, emerging even through the haze of drunkenness, but it made no difference. He tried to focus his thoughts, to concentrate. Juliana stroked him, kissing him hard. Stig broke away, overcome with embarrassment.

'I'm sorry,' he said.

'That's okay.'

'I really am.'

'It happens, don't worry about it.'

'I've drunk too much.'

'It doesn't matter, Stig.'

He sat up. The dizziness was getting worse. The room was starting to spin. He swung his legs off the bed and staggered into the bathroom, closing the door behind him. A hot and cold wave of nausea overwhelmed him. He threw himself to his knees and was sick in the toilet.

He crouched there on the floor, holding the sides of the bowl until the retching stopped. Even then he waited a while, too faint to stand up.

'Are you all right, Stig?' Juliana called.

'Yes,' he mumbled.

He flushed the toilet and pulled himself to his feet, leaning on the washbasin. He was ashamed to go back out into the bedroom.

'Stig?'

He rinsed his face with cold water and rubbed it dry on a towel. Then he steadied himself and pulled open the door. Juliana was outside. He expected to see disgust in her expression but she seemed more concerned than repulsed.

'I'm sorry,' he said. 'I'm so sorry.'

He stumbled over to the bed, searching for his clothes.

'I'd better go.'

'Don't be silly. You're in no state to go anywhere.'

'I'm sure you want me to leave. I'm sorry.'

'Stop saying sorry. Lie down.'

'Juliana . . .'

She pushed him gently down on to the pillow.

'Lie down.'

She slid in beside him.

'Don't you want me to go?' he said.

'I want you to stay.'

She curled up against him, her head on his shoulder. She was warm, comforting. Stig stared at the ceiling, trying to blot out his thoughts, until his eyes grew heavy and he drifted off into a leaden sleep.

Dr Julius Wolf poured himself another three fingers of cognac and took a long gulp, washing away the feelings of self-revulsion in a torrent of alcohol. A decade ago he would have paid the night porter to find him a companion; there were always call girls on hand for appetites which the official hotel room service was unable to satisfy. But he'd long passed the point where they could do anything for him. He was seventy-five years old, a frail man living on memories, taking his bitter vicarious pleasure by watching others enjoying what he had lost and blotting out the present and the future with the numbing anaesthetic of booze.

The bottle of Courvoisier on the table beside him was three quarters empty, the smoked salmon and avocado sandwich next to the bottle barely touched. On the television screen at the foot of the bed a repetitive, obscene hard-core porn movie was flickering. His watery eyes blinking behind his thick spectacles, Wolf watched the images of young bodies writhing and coupling. He'd seen it all before, loathed himself for his addiction, but had nothing else to give him solace in his declining years. He was a childless widower, his wife taken by cancer twelve years earlier, and what few friends he had were far away in Zürich. He had money enough to afford a luxury suite in the best hotel in Antwerp but not enough – or too much – to buy someone to share it with him.

He refilled his glass with cognac and drank it, feeling his vision blurring. The pictures on the television screen started to shake and Wolf closed his eyes momentarily, trying to clear the fug in his head.

Slowly, he became aware of a knocking noise which he thought at first was on the movie. But when he opened his eyes he realised it was coming from the door to his room. He ignored it but it continued, low and insistent.

Wolf swung his legs off the bed and pushed himself unsteadily to his feet. He staggered awkwardly across the room, supporting himself on the edge of the bed and then the wall.

'Who is it?'

'Me,' a voice said softly through the panel.

Wolf snapped back the lock and opened the door. Simon Doyle stepped inside and pushed the door to. Wolf was already stumbling back towards the bed. As he neared the footboard, his legs gave way and he tumbled over sideways, hitting the floor with a shuddering thud. Doyle walked across to him and knelt down, checking Wolf's pulse. Then he glanced around, taking in the almost empty bottle of brandy and the naked bodies on the television. He watched the movie for a few moments before switching it off.

Leaving Wolf where he'd fallen, Doyle went into the bathroom and ran a bath. He still had on his winter coat and black leather gloves. He added some of the hotel's complimentary foambath to the water and let it rise hot and steaming to a good depth. Then he went back out and stripped Wolf of his clothes, tossing the garments on to the bottom of the bed. He lifted the old man up by his arms and dragged him through into the bathroom.

Wolf's body was pale and emaciated, the skin loose and blotchy. Doyle picked him up easily and lowered him into the bath. The feel of the water, the sudden change in temperature, something, brought the old man round. His eyes fluttered open and he stared up at Doyle.

'What . . .' he murmured feebly, barely emerging from his alcoholic stupor.

'Relax, Julius,' Doyle said emolliently. 'Go back to sleep.'

Wolf reached out for the edges of the bath, fumbling for a handhold to stop himself slipping lower into the water.

'Why are you here?' he mumbled, slurring his words so they were almost indistinct.

Doyle gripped Wolf's hair in one hand, his shoulder in the other and pushed him under the surface. The old man struggled, flailing out with his bony arms, the air bubbling up from his mouth and mingling with the perfumed froth of the foambath. Even when sober he would have been no match for Doyle. His body saturated with brandy, he had no hope of escape.

Doyle held him under implacably, showing no emotion. Wolf, finding some final, desperate reserves of strength, fought to free himself. The water splashed out over the sides, soaking the floor and bathmat. But Doyle held on, pushing the old man's head to the bottom, pressing down until the convulsions stopped and Wolf lay still.

Doyle straightened up and rubbed the moisture off his clothes with a towel, then wiped the tiles on the floor, soaking up the overspill from the bath. He hung the towel on a radiator to dry and took a last look at Wolf's lifeless face staring up grotesquely from beneath the water.

'I'm sorry, Julius,' he said. 'We all have to make sacrifices.'

They started kissing the moment he walked through the door. No attempt at conversation, no drinks, no pretence. Just a basic animal desire that overwhelmed them both.

They went through into the bedroom and tore off their clothes. Claire's body was warm and soft. Sullivan touched her, stroked her. She kissed him hard, her hands roving over his skin. He thought fleetingly of his wife before a wave of intense physical pleasure swept over him, drowning out all feelings of guilt and doubt.

Enqvist awoke as Juliana extricated herself from his arms and climbed out of the bed. He blinked. His head ached as if someone had buried a tomahawk in his skull and was joggling it to and fro. He watched her walk naked into the bathroom, the shafts of sunlight breaking through the curtains touching her buttocks and legs with a warm glow. The memories of the previous evening flooded back and he winced with renewed shame and embarrassment. Juliana had been very understanding about the whole sorry episode. Perhaps too understanding.

Stig sat up, wondering about that, asking himself

again what she saw in him. He was as vain as most men, but he tried not to let his vanity interfere with his intellect. And he tried not to let it make a fool of him.

Throwing aside the sheet, he slipped out of bed and stood up, pausing to let his head settle. Juliana's handbag was on the top of the desk. Enqvist padded across and looked down at it. She'd have her Dutch identity card inside, perhaps a passport. All he had to do was open the bag. He hesitated. He couldn't bring himself to do it. It seemed underhand, treacherous. Maybe he didn't want to know. He heard the bathroom door click open and went quickly back to the bed.

'How're you feeling?' Juliana asked, walking over and sitting down next to him.

'Not too bad. Look . . .'

She stopped him. 'It's all forgotten. Okay?'

Stig nodded. Juliana smiled and reached out, running her fingers over his bare chest.

'How are you fixed for time?' she said.

'I'm in no hurry. Why?'

'We've some unfinished business from last night.'

FIFTEEN

The two desks were almost hidden beneath a stack of thick reference books and a large spread-out map of Europe, North Africa and the Middle East. Stig Enqvist was sitting in his chair, leafing carelessly through the photocopied logbook of the *Maria Vasquez* while Sullivan and Claire pored over the map.

'What if they were unloaded somewhere along the Basque Coast?' Sullivan said.

'Spain or France?' Claire asked.

'Spain. Maybe somewhere here between San Sebastian and Bilbao.' He followed the indented coastline with his finger.

'I'm not sure,' Claire said doubtfully. 'That's a well-populated stretch, a major port at either end. Too much customs, coastguard activity.'

'Where would you go?'

Claire pointed to the west coast of France. 'Here. The Landes. It's perfect. From Arcachon to Biarritz there's no coastal town of any size. Just a hundred kilometres of deserted beach backed by pine forest. I've been there. There are dozens of places you could bring cigarettes in by speedboat. You have lorries waiting and an hour later you're unloading in the warehouse at Bayonne. That's what I would do if I were a smuggler.'

'It's persuasive,' Sullivan admitted. 'You could use all these minor roads. Who would notice you?'

He reached out to indicate the possible routes the lorries could take and accidentally touched Claire's hand. The contact sent a shiver up his arm and he had to stop himself from taking hold of her fingers and squeezing. He glanced across at Enqvist but his colleague hadn't noticed, he was too engrossed in the logbook. Sullivan looked at Claire, acutely conscious of how close she was. Her perfume was in his nostrils, her hair near enough to touch. She smiled, as if she knew what he was thinking, and leaned sideways, brushing his body with her shoulder for an instant before bending over the map again.

'The cigarettes are left at Fonteneau et Delahaye,' she said phlegmatically. 'Then distributed across France. The Spanish consignments are taken across the border in the Garcia Saez olive oil lorries which are returning empty to San Sebastian, crossing at Hendaye where one of the senior customs officers is in their pocket. They've thought through every aspect. It all fits together.'

'Let's check the figures. Give us the times, Stig. Stig?'

Enqvist looked up. 'Uh?'

'You okay?' Sullivan said.

'Yeah. What is it?'

273

'Give me the time the *Maria Vasquez* left Rotterdam and the time she arrived in the Bay of Naples.'

Enqvist consulted the logbook.

'February seventh, leaves Rotterdam at nine am. February fifteenth, two am, stopped and boarded by the *Guardia di Finanza*.'

'That's, what, seven and a bit days. I make that a hundred and eighty-five hours,' Sullivan said, picking up the Lloyd's Register of Shipping and Reed's Marine Distance Tables from the one corner of the desk not covered by the map. He handed the register to Claire.

'Give me her speed.'

He opened the marine tables and calculated the distance between Rotterdam and Naples.

'Two thousand three hundred and fifty nautical miles.'

'Normal service speed thirteen knots,' Claire said.

She tapped the figures into her electronic calculator.

'A hundred and eighty hours,' Sullivan said.

Claire pulled a face.

'I wish you'd stop doing that.'

'Five hours less than she actually took,' Sullivan said. 'Even allowing for bad weather and reduced sailing speed that's more than enough time to stop in the Bay of Biscay and unload a few thousand cases.'

'She did the same run last November as well,' Enqvist said, leafing back through the logbook.

He frowned. 'There's something funny about this log.'

'How do you mean?' Sullivan said.

'I don't know. I can't put my finger on it.'

Enqvist flicked back through the pages. He wasn't in the mood for work. The pain in his head had eased but his eyes felt tired and sore. He wanted to rest his head on the desk and go back to sleep.

The telephone beside him rang. He picked up the receiver and listened lethargically, then suddenly came awake.

'*Merde!*' he said under his breath, continuing in French. 'Yes, I'll come straight away.'

He hung up and tossed the logbook across the desk.

'You two take care of it. See what you can find.'

'Why, what are you doing?' Sullivan asked suspiciously.

Enqvist went to the door and lifted down his overcoat from the peg, glad of an excuse to get out of the office.

'Stig,' Sullivan said. 'Who was on the phone?'

'Only Janvier.'

Richard Janvier was one of the 'delinquents', a senior official in the OCRDEFO.

'What did he want?'

'One of us. Don't worry, I'll take care of it.'

'Take care of what?'

Enqvist slipped on his coat and fastened up the buttons.

'Julius Wolf was found dead in an Antwerp hotel room this morning. Perhaps there is a God after all.'

* * *

Janvier met him in the foyer of the Hotel Rubens and escorted him upstairs in the lift. The Rubens was an old, long-established hotel, built in the nineteenth century for the wealthy merchants who came to Antwerp to trade in diamonds. It had been renovated and refurbished several times since, but still retained an old-fashioned ambience despite the air conditioning, double glazing and electronic work stations in the conference centre behind reception.

Julius Wolf's room was a large suite on the fourth floor facing west towards the River Schelde. It had been carefully furnished by an interior designer with a fondness for thick embossed wallpaper and polished mahogany, but it still looked like an ordinary hotel room: expensive, yet somehow dreary and unwelcoming. Its functional atmosphere wasn't helped that afternoon by the fingerprint dust sprinkled liberally over every surface and the quiet men in overalls and white gloves who were slowly and methodically inspecting every square centimetre of the place.

Enqvist took a look around from the doorway before following Janvier inside.

'He was in his bath,' Janvier said in French. 'The housemaid found him.'

Enqvist glanced automatically through the open door into the bathroom though there was nothing to see: the body had been taken away hours ago.

'Cause of death?' he asked.

'It looked like drowning. We won't know for certain, of course, until after the autopsy. There was

276

an almost empty bottle of cognac beside the bed, brought up by room service yesterday evening.'

'He drank it all?'

Janvier shrugged. 'We're waiting for the blood analysis results. On first impressions, yes. There was only one glass.'

Enqvist nodded, watching the scene-of-crime team going about their painstaking work.

'I assume from all this that you don't think it was an accident, or natural causes?'

'Come downstairs,' Janvier said. 'I've something to show you.'

They went down to the ground floor and through to one of the rooms in the conference centre which the police were using as their incident station. A coffee machine, the first priority after a few desks and telephones, had been installed in one corner. Janvier filled a couple of polystyrene cups and they sat down at an empty desk. The room was deserted except for a pretty uniformed policewoman who'd been dumped with the tedious task of manning the phone lines and taking messages.

'He checked in yesterday about four pm,' Janvier said. 'Went out for a couple of hours then came back, went up to his room and ordered the bottle of brandy and a sandwich. About nine o'clock he called reception to access the video channel on his television. They're centrally controlled. Choose your film from a list and the charge is added to your bill.'

'What did he watch?'

'California Cocksuckers.'

'Ah, a Disney fan,' Enqvist said.

'It's a Danish film, despite the title.'

'I didn't know Wolf spoke Danish.'

'I don't think he was watching it for the dialogue.'

Janvier drank some of his coffee. He was a short man in his forties with grey wiry hair and a slow, almost lugubrious way of talking that had fooled a lot of people over the years into thinking he wasn't very bright. Enqvist liked him. He had a relaxed, informal approach to his job which made him easy to deal with. He wasn't a believer in 'official channels', which did nothing except create delays and bureaucracy. If he wanted something from UCLAF or any other agency, he called them direct, circumventing both his superiors and the Ministry of Justice who, theoretically, were supposed to be notified of any transnational enquiries.

'What time did he die?' Enqvist asked.

'The doctor couldn't be specific. Not on medical grounds. But other evidence points to around eleven, eleven thirty.'

'What other evidence?'

'A woman in the room across the corridor. Says she heard someone knocking on Wolf's door about then. She couldn't be absolutely sure, she had her television on, but it looks as if Wolf had a visitor.'

'Any indication who?'

'No. The fingerprints are a mess, as you'd expect in a hotel room with people coming and going all the time. Reception didn't notice anyone coming in downstairs – certainly no one asked for Wolf's room number – but anyone could have walked in without attracting attention.'

'And the visitor killed him?'

'It's a theory,' Janvier said.

'You have any others?'

'No.'

'What makes you think it wasn't natural causes? A heart attack in the bath. He was an old man, after all.'

'The doctor examined the body before it was taken to the morgue. There were marks on Wolf's left shoulder. The kind of bruises you'd expect if he'd been held under the water. And a chunk of his hair had been half pulled out of his scalp.'

Enqvist looked across at the policewoman. She was speaking in Flemish into the telephone and scribbling notes on a pad of paper.

'Why?' he said.

Janvier swallowed some coffee and grimaced. He put the cup down on the desk and pushed it away.

'That's the worst thing about these incident rooms,' he said. 'The coffee. And these crappy polystyrene cups. Why?' he repeated Enqvist's question. 'You know why. A man like Julius Wolf. He had so many enemies they were probably queuing up to kill him.'

'Why *now*?' Enqvist qualified the enquiry.

Janvier gave a shrug. 'Maybe time just ran out for him. He was lucky, doing what he did for so many years without anybody catching up with him.'

'What was he doing here? Buying?'

Antwerp was the largest cigarette *entrepôt* in Europe.

A huge proportion of the imports from the UK and America were held in bonded warehouses in the city. Both Enqvist and Janvier knew that Wolf had been a regular, if undesirable, visitor to the port.

Janvier unlocked the bottom drawer of the desk and pulled out an expensive-looking black attaché case which he placed on the top of the desk. The combination locks on the case had been forced open.

'Did you do that?' Enqvist asked.

Janvier nodded. 'It was in the hotel safe. It was the first thing I asked about when I got here. The local plods weren't too happy about my having it, but, you know, we're all on the same side, aren't we?'

There was a subtle undertone of irony in his voice. Janvier was a Walloon and, worse, a Walloon from the central authorities in Brussels. Antwerp was the capital of Flanders and the city's police officers would have welcomed his arrival with about as much enthusiasm as they would a dose of the clap.

Janvier opened the lid of the case and lifted out some papers.

'Wolf left it at reception,' he said. 'They make interesting reading.'

'Can I take them away?' Enqvist asked.

Janvier shook his head. 'Evidence in a murder investigation. Sorry. But you can have a look at them.'

Enqvist read through some of the documents. There were letters, invoices, order forms, lists of phone numbers and addresses. There were names of companies, some of which Enqvist recognised, some of which he didn't. And there was a business diary full of times and appointments. It was all too complicated to remember or to make notes of.

'I need more time to study these, Richard,' Enqvist said.

Janvier glanced at the Flemish policewoman but she was showing no interest in their conversation.

'I'm going to find a toilet,' he said. 'There's a photocopier behind reception, but I didn't tell you it was there.'

Enqvist grinned at him. 'Make it a long piss,' he said.

Even in summer the apartment in Tervuren was gloomy and cheerless. But in winter, arriving there on a dank February day, it had a cold, forbidding oppressiveness about it that Kate found intensely depressing. She'd never liked it. The rooms were too big and bare, there was a smell of damp that persisted throughout the year no matter how warm the weather, and whatever she did it never seemed remotely like a permanent home.

It was only mid-afternoon when they drove down the narrow street and pulled in outside the ancient apartment building, but already it was dark enough to feel like dusk. There were horse chestnut trees on the pavements on either side of the road which, though they were leafless, formed a canopy of interlocking twigs, blocking out the light even more than the grey clouds smeared across the sun. Climbing out, Kate felt the raindrops dripping down from the branches, pitter-pattering on the bonnet of the car and splashing her hair with icy pearls that trickled in rivulets down the back of her neck.

The boys loved those trees, particularly in autumn when the ground beneath them was scattered with shiny brown horse chestnuts that were left there to rot or to be carried away by the neighbourhood squirrels. The strange English custom of conkers was unknown in Belgium, the idea that small boys might devote hours of their time to throwing sticks into trees, collecting the fallen fruit to soak in vinegar and thread on to strings for fights in the playground somehow beyond the grasp of continental children who had more serious pastimes with which to amuse themselves. But that ignorance was Patrick and James's gain for the two of them went back to England after each autumn half term with so many conkers in their suitcases there was barely room for their clothes.

There were few other advantages to living in Tervuren as far as Kate was concerned. It was a pretty enough Flemish town, nestling in the Forêt de Soignes some thirteen kilometres east of Brussels. It had a sizeable expat British community, partly because the British School of Brussels was there, but that wasn't much of a plus: Kate had always found the British abroad worse than the British at home. It seemed to her an alien place, far away from the culture and language with which she was familiar, yet not sufficiently different or exotic to arouse her curiosity. It was wet and drab and boring and made her wonder why she'd driven three hundred miles when she could have stayed in Colchester, which was equally wet and drab and boring but at least had the boys' schoolfriends nearby.

Keeping Patrick and James happy and entertained for the holiday was her most daunting challenge. They had the attention spans of hyperactive infants but much more energy, coupled with a surly awkwardness that drove her to distraction. They moaned constantly, bickered as if their lives depended on it and seemed incapable of enjoying any activity which wasn't dirty, dangerous or illegal. The journey had been bad enough, listening to them squabbling, but now they'd arrived and were unpacking the car, complaining about the weather and the apartment and God knows what, Kate was ready to scream.

'If I hear one more word, I'm leaving you here and going straight back to England. Do you hear?' she shouted at them in exasperation. 'Now get your bags inside.'

They went upstairs to the first floor and unlocked the apartment. It smelt musty inside, as if it hadn't been occupied for months, and Kate could see the dust on the polished wooden floor. She didn't believe Rob ever cleaned the place in between their visits; it certainly never looked as if he did. Her first day there was always spent vacuuming and dusting, hating herself for saving her husband the effort, but she just couldn't live in the squalor he seemed not to notice.

The boys went through into their bedroom with instructions to unpack their clothes and put them away in the chest of drawers and wardrobe. Kate, relieved to get them out of sight and hearing for a few minutes, sought refuge in the kitchen and made herself a pot of tea. There was milk in the fridge but that was about all. She swore under her breath. Did Rob not eat anything in the apartment when he was here alone? It annoyed her that, once again, she'd driven all the way from England to find that he hadn't bothered to stock up with any provisions for them.

'Mum, can we watch television?'

Patrick and James were standing in the doorway.

'Have you unpacked?'

'Sort of.'

'What do you mean, sort of?'

'We can do it later.'

'You can do it now,' Kate said, wishing that motherhood didn't have to turn you into a bad-tempered shrew.

'Aw, Mum.'

'Go on. No television until you've unpacked everything. I know you, you'll spend the whole week living out of suitcases.'

The boys groaned in the exaggerated theatrical fashion perfected by adolescents of all generations, but they went back into their room. Kate finished her tea and walked through into the master bedroom. The double bed was a crumpled mess. She pulled up the duvet and plumped up the pillows, then went to the window to close the curtains. The bedroom was at the front of the apartment, overlooking the street. Kate glanced out of the window. It was almost dark outside. The streetlights were on, the pavements glistening wet. She reached out for the curtains.

It was then that she noticed the car parked in the street below.

A dark Peugeot saloon with two men sitting inside.

Enqvist was excited. It had been obvious the moment he walked back into the office and dropped the sheaf of photocopied papers on to his desk.

'We've struck gold,' he announced with a flourish. 'Pure fucking gold. Take a look at that lot. Wolf's personal papers, even his diary showing who he met and when.'

Sullivan felt the contagious enthusiasm in his colleague's voice and manner but resisted it, suspicious of anything that hadn't been checked and cross-checked a dozen times.

'Oh yes?' he said cautiously.

'Don't be so fucking English,' Enqvist said. 'Look at them. You too, Claire.'

Sullivan left the papers on the desk. Claire made no move to pick them up either.

'Where did you get them?' Sullivan said.

'Janvier gave them to me. Wolf left them in the hotel safe. They're bloody complicated, but if we pick our way through them I reckon there must be a goldmine of information in them. Think about it. Julius Wolf, one of Europe's biggest cigarette dealers, a guy we've had our eye on for years without once catching him doing anything illegal. We've got letters, order sheets, times, dates, everything we need to piece together the secrets of his business. Whom he dealt with, when, where, how much he bought, whom he sold to.'

Enqvist threw off his coat and sat down, flicking eagerly through the papers. Sullivan and Claire watched him.

'How did he die?' Claire asked.

Enqvist repeated what Janvier had told him.

'He'll let us know the results of the autopsy when he gets them, but they're working on the assumption it was murder. The old bastard led a charmed life but it couldn't last forever.'

Enqvist collected together a pile of pages and passed them across to Sullivan.

'You take the diary, see what you can make of it.'

'And me?' Claire said.

'How far have you got with the log of the *Maria Vasquez*?'

She made a face. 'I get all the interesting jobs, I see,' she said dryly, flashing him a half smile to show there was no real resentment.

'Teamwork,' said Enqvist, 'is everyone else doing what I say.'

'Who do I have to sleep with to get a transfer back to olive oil?' Claire retorted, studiously avoiding Sullivan's gaze.

The sharp ring of the telephone interrupted them. Sullivan answered it in a businesslike voice, then shifted his tone to something softer, more affectionate. Claire knew he was talking to his wife.

'How was the journey?' he said.

Claire sat down at Nicoletti's desk, trying not to listen to Sullivan as he chatted, a little self-consciously, on the phone.

'Yeah, I shouldn't be late. How are the boys? I'm sorry, I meant to. I'll stop at the supermarket on my way home. Yeah, okay.'

There was a silence, then he said: 'What is it?' with a note of such concern that both Claire and Enqvist glanced up at him.

'It's probably nothing,' Kate said. 'You'll think I'm being silly.'

'No I won't. What's the matter?'

'You know I don't like this place on my own. It's creepy in the dark.'

'Kate, just tell me.'

'There's a car out at the front. There are two men inside it.'

Sullivan felt his stomach knot. It was pure instinct, there was no rational explanation for it. But Kate was obviously worried and her anxiety was rubbing off on him.

'So what?' he said, trying to sound reassuring. 'They're probably waiting for someone.'

'Yes, I suppose so. It just struck me as funny. You know how quiet it is here. When have you ever seen two young men sitting in a car outside the building?'

'Are they still there?' Sullivan said.

'I'll check.'

Kate put down the phone and went through into

the bedroom. She pulled back the edge of the curtain and peeped out. The Peugeot saloon was in the same place. She could see the shadowy faces of the two men through the windscreen. She went back to the phone.

'Yes.'

'I wouldn't worry,' Sullivan said. 'I'm sure it's nothing.' As an afterthought, he added: 'What do they look like?'

'Late twenties,' Kate said. 'Casual clothes, short-cropped hair. It's hard to see the details in the dark. One of them seems to have a bandage around his head.'

Sullivan became aware of a pain in his ear and realised he was pressing the receiver hard into the side of his head.

'A bandage?' he said calmly.

'Yes.'

'Look, I think I'll come home now.'

'Why?' Kate said quickly. 'Who are they?'

'Relax, I don't like you worried. Just to be on the safe side I'll come home and check. Are the boys inside?'

'Watching television.'

'Lock and bolt the doors.'

'Rob, what's going on?'

'I'm on my way, okay?'

Sullivan walked quickly down the corridor and out through the security door to the lift. He pressed the button and waited impatiently for the lift to arrive. He wondered if he was overreacting, but he remembered what had happened to Claire. This was his wife and kids; it wasn't possible to overreact where their safety was concerned.

He stayed calm as the lift took him down into the basement car park. But when the doors opened, he burst out through the gap and sprinted for his car.

Kate went to the front door and locked it with the keys before pushing the bolts into place at the top and bottom and attaching the safety chain. Her hands were trembling a little and she felt queasy, a reaction not just to the men waiting outside at the front but to Rob's response when she'd told him. She knew he was keeping something from her and that only added to her anxiety.

Going back into the bedroom, she peeked out of the window again. The men were still there. One of them looked up and saw her. He said something to his companion who lifted his eyes and fixed them on Kate. She suppressed a shiver. In the harsh light of the streetlamps their heads resembled faceless skulls: bony, hollow-eyed, devoid of skin or hair.

The two men opened the car doors and climbed out. One reached back inside and lifted out a sports bag.

Then they walked across the pavement and into the entrance to the apartment building.

*   *   *

Heading east away from Brussels on the Tervurses-teenweg, Sullivan drove one-handed whilst punching in his home number on his mobile phone. He let it ring a dozen times.

There was no answer.

He pressed redial and let it ring again.

Still no answer.

He called the office. Enqvist answered.

'Stig, do something for me,' Sullivan said abruptly. 'Look up the number of the Tervuren police. Something's wrong. Tell them to get over to my apartment immediately.'

'What's going on?'

'Just do it, Stig. Now.'

Kate had frozen. This was way outside her experience. She didn't know what to do. The telephone rang but she ignored it. Maybe she was wrong. Maybe she was being stupid. She stood in the hall, staring at the locks on the door, the solid wooden panels, wondering if they would hold. She heard footsteps on the stairs outside. They jolted her into action. She picked up the boys' coats and went through into the living room. She switched off the television, slipping on her own coat. She turned to the boys, trying to keep her voice calm. She didn't want them to panic.

'Put your coats on. Do exactly as I say.'

Enqvist riffled through the Brussels area telephone directory, tearing at the pages in his haste. He found the number and dialled it.

It was engaged.

'What is it?' Claire said. 'Has something happened?'

Enqvist tried again.

Still engaged.

'Shit!'

He paused to think. Then he punched in a number he knew by heart.

'Get me Richard Janvier,' he said in French. 'Then *interrupt* him. This is Stig Enqvist, UCLAF. Tell him it's urgent.'

The first shuddering bang came as Kate and the boys stepped out on to the narrow balcony outside the living room French windows. Patrick and James turned their heads, startled by the noise.

'Mum.'

Kate didn't give them time to think, much less to speak.

'Over the rail. Quickly,' she said.

There was another blow from the front door. Kate urged the boys over the metal railing around the balcony. She knew they could do it: one of their favourite ways of riling her was to drop off the balcony into the garden instead of going downstairs to use the door. The question was whether *she* could do it.

Patrick went first, lowering himself from the top rail down to the concrete edge of the balcony floor, then letting himself go until he landed on the soft lawn below. James went after him with all the supple agility of a young boy.

'Get out through the gate,' Kate shouted to them.

They didn't move.

'Go!'

'Not without you, Mum.'

Kate scrambled over the railings, copying what her sons had done. Why didn't they run, the stupid children? she screamed inside her head. Don't worry about me. Just get out!

'We'll catch you, Mum. Come on.'

They held out their arms, standing underneath her on the grass. Kate heard another juddering bang followed by the crash of the door. They were inside the apartment. She looked down and let go. She felt the boys' arms support her as she hit the ground and stumbled.

'You okay?' Patrick said.

Kate nodded. 'The gate.'

They ran across the wet soggy lawn. There was a wooden gate in the brick wall that surrounded the garden.

It was locked.

Kate looked back. The key was on a hook just inside the rear door of the building, but there was no time to go and get it.

'Over the wall,' she said.

She gave Patrick a leg-up. He pulled himself on to the top and straddled it. Kate lifted James around the waist. Patrick grabbed his brother's hand and heaved him up beside him.

There was a shout from the apartment. A figure appeared in silhouette on the balcony. He started to climb over the railings. Kate bent her knees and leapt upwards, getting a hand on the top of the wall. Patrick and James caught her other arm and pulled her up. Her legs scraped against the rough brickwork but she managed to hook one foot over the top and lever herself into a sitting position. One of the men – with the bandaged head – was already running towards them across the lawn. The second was clambering down from the balcony.

Patrick and James didn't need to be told what to do. They swung their legs over and jumped down on the other side of the wall. Kate delayed a second too long, wanting to see them safe before she followed. The first man came up below her and grasped her left leg. Kate clung on to the top of the wall as he attempted to drag her off it. She felt her grip loosening, her fingers rubbing raw on the uneven bricks. She took a deep breath and, with a viciousness she didn't know she had in her, kicked down hard with her foot. The heel of her shoe slammed into the man's nose. He let go of her leg and clutched at his bloody face. Kate twisted round and almost threw herself over the wall. The boys were waiting below on the muddy path that ran through the woods to a lake. People jogged or walked their dogs here in daylight, but it was deserted now darkness had fallen.

'This way, Mum.'

Patrick and James took her hands, dragging her along the path. No questions, no wasted words, they knew the urgency of the situation. Kate had been along here a few times, but the boys knew every inch of the network of tracks that criss-crossed the woods. They'd spent hours exploring them.

They came to a fork in the path and went right, running as fast as they could in the thick darkness. The trees were like pillars lining the path, the undergrowth a dense wall which spread out before them, threatening to trip them up. Kate stumbled several times on the muddy, pot-holed ground but the boys held her up. They were children still but Kate felt them grow into men, protecting her as much as she was protecting them.

She glanced back. The two men couldn't be far behind. They would be faster than them, stronger. She thought she saw a shadow flitting along the path but couldn't be sure. She listened. The rasping sound of her own breath drowned out any other sound. She knew running wasn't the answer. The men would catch up with them before they'd gone any distance. They had to hide, seek sanctuary in the blackness of the forest.

Patrick and James seemed to sense it too. They veered off the path, pushing through the shrubs, taking her along with them. The ground started to dip down into a hollow. There was a fallen tree at the bottom, its roots torn out of the ground to leave behind a shallow hole. Patrick and James slid down into the hole. Kate followed. They lay on the ground, catching their breath, trying to deaden the noise as they gasped for air. Around them, the trees were dark sentinels, the undergrowth a bastion. They waited, praying silently that the night would shield them from their pursuers.

Sullivan pulled in outside the apartment building and leapt out of his car. Kate's black Fiesta was parked just in front of him, a Peugeot saloon a few yards further up the street. Sullivan ran into the entrance to the building and saw that the lock on the main door was broken. He pushed it open and sprinted up the stairs. On the first-floor landing he stopped.

The door to the apartment was wide open. One edge of it was chipped and splintered with the marks of some heavy implement. The locks and bolts had been torn off, the safety chain dangled loose from its slot.

Sullivan walked in, knowing he was too late.

'Kate!'

He ran from room to room, calling his wife's name. Then he saw the French windows swinging open in the breeze. He walked on to the balcony and stared out into the night, looking beyond the wall at the black, impenetrable woodland.

'Kate!' he yelled.

He listened for a response, for any slight sound. Nothing. He turned to go.

Wait a minute.

He swung back. Crossing the lawn, bruising the surface of the long wet grass, was a series of tracks. Tracks which stopped at the wall at the bottom of the garden.

Sullivan spun round and ran out of the apartment. Downstairs on the ground floor, he snatched the key off the hook on the wall and threw open the door to the garden. He reached the perimeter wall and fumbled for the keyhole in the wooden gate. He turned the lock, whipped open the gate and ran out into the woods.

Kate could feel the two boys next to her, pressing in close. She had an arm around each of them, holding them tight. She knew they must be as scared as she was, but they were hiding it well.

'Who are they, Mum?' James whispered tremulously. 'What do they want?'

'I don't know,' Kate said, squeezing his shoulders.

'Where's Dad?'

'He's on his way. We'll be okay.'

'Sssh,' Patrick hissed.

Kate peered out over the lip of the hole. A tall figure was moving along the path about fifty metres away. He stopped. It was too dark to see his face, or where he was looking. Kate pressed her head to the ground, pulling the boys in against her, trying to reassure them. She could feel their slight, wiry bodies trembling.

The man glided away, running through the trees towards the lake. Kate twisted round but lost sight of him. Where was the second man? Kate didn't dare move until she knew. She wanted to get out of the woods and back to the houses, to streetlights, cars and people. They were vulnerable staying put, even under cover of darkness, but more at risk trying to move until they were sure they wouldn't be observed.

'Are they going to kill us?' James breathed in her ear.

Kate hugged him. 'We'll be fine, you see,' she said, submerging her own fears beneath the need to be strong for the boys' sake.

The undergrowth rustled suddenly behind them. Kate glanced over her shoulder, then sat up quickly. The man with the bandaged head was standing on the rim of the hole, looking down at them. The blood was smeared across his nose and cheeks. He shouted something, calling to his companion. Then he smiled wolfishly and slid down the muddy incline.

Sullivan heard the shout and stopped dead, trying to pinpoint exactly where it had come from. Somewhere to his right, and not too far away. He turned off the path and took the shortest course, running in a straight line through the trees.

Kate scrambled to her feet, pulling the boys up after her and backing away slowly. The sides of the hole rose steeply behind them. Their feet slipped on the damp earth. Kate kept her eyes fixed on the man while she pushed Patrick and James away.

'Run,' she said quietly.

The boys stayed where they were.

'Go on,' she urged them.

The man took a step towards them. Then lunged

suddenly for Kate. She attempted to dodge his out-stretched arms and lost her footing, toppling to the ground. The man loomed over her. Kate's fingers dug into the soft earth. She hurled a fistful of soil up into his face and, while he was temporarily blinded, scuttled sideways and clambered to her feet. She looked around for a weapon: a rock, a branch. There was nothing to hand. She grabbed more earth, flinging it at the man's head. He lashed out with an arm and sent her flying.

Kate rolled over on the ground and saw Patrick and James going for the man, trying to push him, to hit him with their tiny fists. He knocked them both over like skittles. A fury, a maternal protectiveness overwhelmed Kate and she threw herself on to the man's back, clawing at his face with her nails, kicking his legs as hard as she could. His body was solid and muscled. He wrenched her hands off and tossed her to the ground. Then swung down with a clenched fist that never connected for, at that moment, another figure burst out through the undergrowth, a heavy branch raised in his hands which he brought down in a savage arc, smashing so hard into the man's back the timber broke in two.

It was Rob. Kate picked herself up and backed away, her immediate relief rapidly giving way to fear for her husband's safety. But he seemed to know what he was doing. The other man was younger, probably in better shape, but Rob had more to lose. Kate had never seen him so aggressive, so furiously violent. His foot sank into the man's belly, doubling him up, then he pummelled him with his fists, punching him to the ground where he rained more heavy blows down on him. Kate pulled the boys up the slope out of the way, averting their eyes from the bare brutality of male anger.

Then the odds changed. The second man appeared in the clearing. He took in the scene and raced to the assistance of his companion.

'Rob!' Kate screamed a warning.

Rob turned, but too late. The man dived on top of him, knocking him over. They struggled and writhed, punching and kneeing each other in a rabid frenzy. Kate couldn't stand by and watch. She picked up a length of fallen branch and hurled herself back down into the hole, clubbing the man about the head and shoulders. He lifted his hands to protect himself and Rob rolled out from under him.

The two assailants staggered to their feet, bruised and bloody. In the distance, the sudden strident noise of police sirens ripped through the night. The men glanced at each other, then turned and sprinted away through the woods.

Rob let them go, too dazed and hurting to prolong the confrontation. He bent over, hands on knees, struggling to breathe.

'Rob, are you okay?'

He straightened up, nodding wearily. He held out his arms. Kate and the boys came to him and they held each other in a fierce, tearful embrace.

SIXTEEN

There were people everywhere. The apartment was
crawling with them: uniformed police officers,
plainclothes detectives, forensic specialists from the
scene-of-crime team, a photographer and his assistant. A joiner and a locksmith were lounging in a
couple of chairs, waiting for the fingerprint officers
to finish with the front door and, in the bedroom, a
police doctor was examining Kate and the boys.

Sullivan was in the kitchen with Stig and Claire
and Richard Janvier who had taken charge of the
operation.

'You'll get an armed police guard twenty-four
hours a day,' Janvier said. 'Three shifts. I'll need
some official paperwork from the Commission but
I can make the arrangements without it.'

'I'll call Carlsen,' Enqvist said. 'He'll take care of
it.'

Janvier gave a nod and looked at Sullivan. 'We'll
need statements from your wife and children when
they're up to answering questions. From you too.'

'I'll do it now.'

'Has the doctor seen you yet?'

'No. Kate and the boys are in a worse state than I am.'

Janvier grunted sceptically, studying Sullivan's face which had a livid bruise on one cheek, a cut and swollen mouth and dried blood matted into his hair from a gash above his ear.

'You look awful.'

'You should see the other two guys.' Sullivan tried a smile but abandoned it midway, it hurt his mouth too much.

'I hope so,' Janvier said. 'We've closed down the whole of Tervuren. If they're still here we'll find them.'

'What about their car?'

'Stolen earlier this afternoon from a car park near Zaventem.'

'You think they flew in today?' Sullivan said.

'We're checking the airline passenger lists. We'll have a photofit from your description we can show to cabin crews, see if anyone recognises them.'

'It's a long shot.'

Janvier shrugged. 'We don't have much else to go on.'

The police doctor walked in from the hall, his black bag dangling from his hand.

'How are they?' Sullivan asked anxiously.

'Physically, relatively unscathed,' the doctor replied. 'Some cuts, grazes, nothing serious. But mentally . . . well, you can imagine. They seem to be coping well. The boys seem resilient but don't let that fool you. Once they have time to reflect they may suffer considerable stress: nightmares, palpitations, that kind of thing.'

'And my wife?'

'She's worried about the boys. In some ways that makes it easier for her. She's suppressing her own emotions and concentrating on them. But it adds to the strain she's under. She's going to have a tough few days. I've given her some tranquillisers. Don't be afraid to use them.'

The doctor placed his bag on the kitchen table and snapped it open.

'Now you,' he said, pulling out a chair for Sullivan to sit down.

Claire went out into the hall. The joiner was patching up the front door, replacing the sections of timber which had been damaged. She pushed open the door to the main bedroom and went in. Kate was sitting on the bed, her arms wrapped around Patrick and James. All three were pale and drawn. They looked up at her with tired eyes.

'Is there anything I can get you?' Claire said. 'Something to drink perhaps.'

Kate shook her head listlessly. 'Where's my husband?'

'In the kitchen. The doctor's seeing to his cuts and bruises.'

'The men . . .' Kate's voice trailed away. She seemed too drained to talk.

'They haven't been found yet. The police are still searching the woods and the streets.'

'And all the people? Out there?'

'They'll soon be finished. Are you sure I can't get you anything?'

'Yes, I'm sure.'

Claire found herself assessing Kate, trying to work out what kind of a woman she was. She was a few years older than Claire, her figure heavier through age and the inevitable side effects of having children. But she was still attractive, even now after the trauma she'd just been through. She looked intelligent, able, determined. Not all that different from me, Claire thought.

Kate was looking at her curiously, frowning a little. 'Are you with the police?'

'I'm a colleague of your husband's.'

'Are you?'

'Claire Colmar.' Claire smiled. 'Not the best time to be introduced, I know. I came with Stig. I'll see what's happening for you.'

She went out of the room and closed the door to shut out the noise and the constant comings and goings. She had an idea what Kate was going through. It must have been similar to what she herself had felt after her ordeal at the cottage on the coast. Similar, but probably worse. Kate had children to fear for, and she was a spouse on the periphery of everything, which must have left her feeling impotent and bewildered. Claire, at least, was an active participant. She'd faced risks before and was better equipped to deal with them. But an investigator's wife and children, they were supposed to be sacrosanct.

She returned to the kitchen. The doctor was still

attending to Sullivan's face. Claire walked to the far end of the room with Enqvist.

'Why?' she said in a low voice she knew Sullivan couldn't hear. 'Why go after a woman and two young boys? What did they intend to do, kidnap them, kill them?'

'Neither makes much sense,' Enqvist said. 'A hit team wouldn't sit outside in a car in full view for all that time. They'd come straight in, probably the back way, do the job and leave.'

'So what were they doing?'

'Scaring them. Warning us off. That would be my guess. They must be worried, whoever they are, to do something so extreme.'

'Worried?' Claire said.

'We're getting close to something big, I can feel it here.' Enqvist touched his belly, then glanced at his watch. 'You busy tonight?'

'No.'

'Good. We've got a lot of work to do.'

They waited until everyone was gone and the boys were in bed before they sat down together to talk. After the chaos of the previous few hours it was a relief to be alone. Rob put his arms around his wife and they held each other for a long time. He felt her tremble and start to shake, then the tears came in cathartic sobs. He let her cry, not saying anything. It was the best thing she could do.

'I'm sorry,' she said eventually, wiping her eyes. 'This isn't going to help.'

'It is. Let it all out.'

'I was so scared. The boys were incredible. They wouldn't leave me. I told them to but they wouldn't. They stayed with me even though they must have been terrified. I don't know what would have happened if you hadn't come just then.'

She blew her nose and sniffed away more tears. 'Do you think they'll be all right?'

'They'll come through it,' Rob said.

'How can you be sure? What if they're permanently damaged?'

'We can help them. With our support they'll be okay.' He brushed away a stray tear from her cheek. 'It's all my fault. The moment you phoned, I should have called the police.'

'You weren't to know what would happen.'

'I shouldn't have taken the chance.'

'It won't happen again, will it?'

'No,' Rob said, wanting to reassure her.

But he was worried. The two men hadn't been caught, though the police had been scouring the neighbourhood for several hours. It was a difficult task in the dark. The men might have holed up somewhere, but it was more than possible they'd got out of Tervuren before the orchestrated search began.

'I want to go home,' Kate said.

'You're safer here. With me.'

'We'll be safe at home.'

'Things are simpler here,' Rob said gently. 'Brussels is a Commission town. The Commission wields a lot of power. The police understand that. They're used to dealing with diplomats, with international residents. I'm a Commission employee in Brussels and the Commission will make sure you're properly protected. If you go back to England, what do the British police care? To them you're a suburban schoolteacher and I'm a customs officer who just happens to be working abroad. The European Commission means nothing to them. It has absolutely no clout in Colchester.

'Besides,' he added. 'I want you here with me. You're going to need me. And I need you.'

He pulled her close to him, trying not to dwell on what had happened, feeling guilty because it was his job that had put them in danger.

'I think you'd better tell me everything,' Kate said. 'What's changed? Why did those men come after us?'

'That I don't know,' Sullivan said. 'But from the moment we seized the *Maria Vasquez* things have been different. It's not been like other investigations. Too many people have died.'

'I'm frightened for you, Rob. It's never been like this before.'

'I'm quite safe,' he said soothingly. 'So are you and the boys now.'

'You don't know that.'

'They won't get near you again. You're too well-protected.'

'And your investigation?'

'Carries on as before. They're not going to stop us. Whoever sent those two men, I'm going to nail the bastards.'

Kate rested her head on his shoulder. Then she said: 'Who's Claire Colmar?'

'Claire?' He was taken by surprise. 'She's standing in for Maurizio.'

'She's attractive.'

Rob didn't acknowledge the remark.

'You haven't mentioned her before.'

'She's only just transferred.'

'She seems nice.'

'She is.' He changed the subject. 'Why don't we go to bed? You must be shattered.'

He stood up and offered Kate his hand, pulling her to her feet. They looked in on the boys before they went into their own bedroom. Both Patrick and James were sleeping soundly, physically and emotionally exhausted. Rob put his arm around Kate as they watched the unconscious figures in the beds, listening to their soft breathing. He felt a surge of protectiveness, of love for them all; a moment of bonding and gratitude to his wife, the mother of his children, which overpowered him with its intensity. He drew Kate into his arms and held her close in a pledge of commitment and fidelity.

Stig Enqvist rubbed his eyes and got up from his desk, stretching his arms above his head to ease the stiffness in his back. It was approaching eleven o'clock. He and Claire had been sifting through Wolf's papers for nearly five hours and the strain was beginning to show. Claire was on the telephone, talking in English and making notes on a pad.

Enqvist walked around the office and waited for her to finish.

'The number in the diary is a cargo warehouse at East Midlands Airport,' she said. 'A company called Freightstorage Services Limited.'

'Clean?'

'As far as UK Customs are aware, yes.'

'Why would Wolf have their number?'

'Maybe he's used them for legitimate cargoes.'

'Hmm.' Enqvist went back to his desk and sat down. 'Let's see if we've got anything on them.'

He logged on to his computer and accessed the UCLAF database. There was no listing for Freightstorage Services. He checked Companies House Direct. The company's registered office was an address in Nottingham. There were only two directors: Clyde Barrow and Kyril Shafranov. Enqvist read the names out to Claire.

'Shafranov. What nationality do you reckon that is?'

'Sounds Russian,' Claire said. She paused. 'Or maybe Ukrainian.'

Sullivan woke early next morning and slipped quietly out of bed, leaving Kate sleeping peacefully under the duvet. He pulled aside the curtain and looked briefly out of the window. The unmarked police car was down below in the street, two plainclothes officers sitting in the front. Reassured, Sullivan went out to the kitchen and made some coffee.

The night had been easier than he'd expected. The

boys hadn't woken at all and Kate only once that he was aware of – a short natural interruption after which she'd quickly gone back to sleep. He was relieved, but suspected future nights might not be so tranquil. The after-effects of an ordeal like the one they'd endured were not easy to predict.

Breakfast was a subdued affair. Patrick and James were never at their best first thing in the morning, but today they seemed to be even less communicative than usual. Sullivan left them alone for a while, then probed them gently.

'Don't bottle anything up,' he said. 'If you want to talk about it, we're here to listen.'

The boys nodded silently.

'Everything's going to be okay. You're bound to be affected by what happened. Just say if you need to talk.'

'We don't need to talk,' Patrick said stoically. 'We're all right.'

'Well, you know we're here,' Sullivan said, not wanting to push them.

He wondered if they blamed him the way he blamed himself. Children, even your own, were hard to read.

During the morning Carlsen telephoned, as he had the previous evening, to ask how they were and reaffirm that Sullivan didn't need to come into work. Then Janvier called, checking that the protection officers were in place and confessing apologetically that, despite the overnight police search, the two men had not been caught.

'They've gone, haven't they?' Rob said.

'I fear so,' Janvier replied. 'They've slipped the net.'

Sullivan took a shower and went into the bedroom with the phone. The sombre, but understandable, atmosphere in the apartment, such a contrast to the previous times when the family had stayed, was getting to him. It was dispiriting and he felt powerless to help.

He rang Stig Enqvist and they talked for a while about how they were coping.

'What's happening?' Rob asked finally.

'You don't want to worry about that,' Enqvist replied.

'I do. I want to know. I *need* to know.'

Enqvist said nothing.

'Stig,' Rob said, sensing something even at the other end of a phone line. 'What's happening?'

Enqvist sighed. 'You really want to know? Claire and I worked late last night. Checking through the papers we found in Wolf's attaché case, making a few phone calls. When he arrived in Antwerp, he went out and had a meeting at Laterveer Voorden.'

'Oh yes.' Laterveer Voorden was a bonded warehouse company down by the docks.

'He ordered two thousand cases of cigarettes, Marlboros, and arranged for them to be transported to Kiev. They were flown out yesterday morning from Antwerp airport.'

'Even though Wolf was dead by then?'

'The freight company didn't know that. Anyway, it

wouldn't have made any difference. Wolf placed the order on behalf of Steinhammer Weiss with payment from his bank in Zürich. We checked with Customs at Antwerp and . . .'

Rob could tell by the way Enqvist paused that something important was coming next.

'And?' he prompted.

'And discovered that the plane used to transport the cigarettes was an Ilyushin-76.'

'Shit!' Rob said. 'Registration mark?'

'You can guess.'

'You sure it's the same?'

'No doubt. A different charter company but it's the same plane all right.'

'There's more, isn't there?' Rob said.

'Claire found it. There were other papers in the attaché case. I won't bore you with the details, but we found a telephone number scribbled on one of them, a number that was repeated on a page of Wolf's diary.'

'Which page?'

'The day before he died. It was a UK number. We checked it out. It's a cargo warehouse at East Midlands Airport owned by a company called Freightstorage Services. One of the directors is a Kyril Shafranov who turns out to be of Ukrainian origin.'

'Go on.'

'And Shafranov's son-in-law is Ivan Kravchenko, manager of the clothing warehouse in Nottingham raided by UK Customs last summer.'

'And brother of Vasili, Frans Maartens' drug-dealing

friend in Hull. This gets better and better,' Sullivan said. 'You reckon they're flying cigarettes in, storing them at the airport and using a network of Ukrainians to distribute them?'

'I can think of worse guesses. Claire called Customs at East Midlands and what do you know, they're expecting a cargo flight from Kiev via Athens this evening. A shipment of Ukrainian pottery.'

'*Pottery?*' Sullivan said.

'Yeah, interesting, isn't it? I know you're not exactly well-informed on these matters, but would you say Ukrainian pottery was all the rage in England right now?'

Sullivan was silent for a moment, thinking through everything he'd been told.

'The Ilyushin again?'

'Uncle Romeo 79705. It's them, no question about it.'

'You're going over?'

'This afternoon.'

Sullivan hesitated. 'I ought to come too.'

'That's not necessary, you know that.'

'I should be there.'

'Claire and I can handle it,' Enqvist said. 'Take some time off, your family needs you.'

'When's your flight?'

'Rob, how many times? You don't need to come.'

'Yes, okay. Let me know how it goes.'

Sullivan hung up. The apartment was very quiet. He went out of the bedroom and found Kate in the kitchen, scrubbing the draining board beside the sink as if housework were some kind of therapy.

'Don't you ever clean this?' she said, throwing the remark at him over her shoulder.

Sullivan didn't respond immediately, sensing the opening line of an argument they'd had many times before.

'You don't need to do that,' he said, sitting down at the table.

'Well, as you never do,' Kate said. 'This place is absolutely filthy.'

She scrubbed vigorously at the stainless steel with a scouring pad. She was angry, but Rob knew the state of the apartment had nothing to do with it.

'Come and sit down,' he said gently.

'I'm fine here.'

'Kate.'

He stood up and took the scouring pad from her hand, then led her to a chair. She offered no resistance.

'I have to do something,' she said. 'Cooped up here all day.'

'I know it's not going to be easy for you,' he said. 'But it will get better. Things will get back to normal.'

'Oh yeah? When?'

'It's been less than twenty-four hours. Try and forget about it.'

'You know I can't forget it. Nor can the boys.'

'I'll make us some coffee.'

Sullivan filled the kettle and switched it on.

'They haven't caught them, have they?' Kate said.

'No.'

'Great. So they're out there somewhere just waiting to do it again.'

'They're not out there. I doubt they're even in the country by now. And you have two armed policemen sitting outside. They have instructions to check you're all right every hour, and there's a panic button in the hall you can press if you need them in between. You couldn't be safer.'

Sullivan spooned coffee grounds into the cafetière and filled it with boiling water.

'Who was that on the phone?' Kate said.

'Only Stig.'

He took two mugs out of a cupboard and put them down on the table. Kate was watching him.

'You want to go back to work, don't you?' she said.

'No,' he said quickly.

'Jesus, Rob, do you think I can't tell? You hate this, playing nursemaid to your family.'

'I don't. I'm concerned about you.'

'I know you're concerned, of course you are. But you're prowling about the place like a caged animal. What did Stig say?'

'A consignment's on the move. The Ilyushin we caught at Vitoria but had to hand back to the Ukrainians is taking a cargo from Kiev to East Midlands tonight.'

Kate kept her eyes on his face. 'And you want to be there to meet it.'

'It's our operation.'

'Why can't UK Customs handle it?'

'We're supplying the information. It's our responsibility.'

'Stig's going, I suppose?'

'Yes.'

'And Claire?'

'She's going too.'

Kate sighed. She depressed the plunger on the
cafetière and filled the mugs with coffee.

'You can't bear to be left out, can you?'

'It's not that.'

'Isn't it? Come on, Rob, you always like to be in on
the kill. It's what you enjoy.'

'Okay,' he admitted. 'But there are other reasons
in this case.'

'Oh yes?' She waited.

'The men who attacked you may have been
Ukrainians. One of them looked very similar to
a thug who nearly killed Claire at a beach house
near De Haan. She fought him off with a tyre iron,
wounded him badly in the head, but he got away.'

'A tyre iron? That pretty, petite girl?'

'She's not a girl.'

'Christ, I hope you never borrow her pencils without asking.'

Sullivan ignored the remark. 'The crew of the
Ilyushin are going to be Ukrainian, I'm sure of that.
I want to be there when they're caught red-handed
with a planeload of contraband cigarettes. If we can
crack them, we may find out who attacked Claire and
who attacked you. That's what I want above all.'

'You never told me before she'd been attacked. Why not?'

'I didn't want to worry you. Besides, you didn't know who she was until yesterday.'

Kate drank her coffee, wondering why Rob's colleagues had never interested her greatly until now. She resisted the temptation to probe further.

'Have you told Stig you're going?'

'No. I'm not, if you don't want me to.'

'You're asking me to make the decision?'

'I'm saying, if you want me here, then I'll stay.'

'Don't *you* want to be here?' Kate said.

'Yes, of course. You always come first.'

'But?'

'No buts.'

Kate shook her head. 'I don't believe this. One minute you're telling me we can't go home to England because we'll be safer here with you to look after us, the next you're pissing off to England on business leaving us here on our own.'

'You won't be on your own. There are . . .'

'Yes, I know. The US fucking cavalry are waiting outside the front door.'

'It's my *job*, Kate.'

'And we're your family.'

'Look, let's not argue about it. I understand how you feel. I'm not going.'

He got up from the table. Kate reached out and took his hand.

'You're right, it's not worth an argument.'

She thought of the old joke about give and take in

a marriage, wondering why it was always the wife who had to do the giving. Perhaps that was the only way the institution survived.

'Go,' she said. 'We'll be all right.'

'No, I'm staying.'

'Go on, before I change my mind.'

There was a crackle of interference on the radio, then a faint, garbled voice relaying some information that Enqvist, Claire and Sullivan, standing ten yards away, didn't quite catch. Tony Fitzpatrick, from UK Customs, acknowledged the message and nodded across at them.

'This is the one,' he said.

They stepped out of the shelter of the hangar doors, exposing themselves to the piercing wind gusting across the airfield, and looked up at the clear night sky. A couple of lights glowed brightly on the horizon to the east, one of them flashing intermittently as the plane made its final approach. The lights came gradually lower, descending in a shallow curve over the hidden carriageways of the M1, and across the perimeter fence of the airport. The harsh roar of the engines became audible, throbbing over the flat terrain. The wheels touched down and the bulky snub-nosed silhouette raced along the runway in front of them.

Enqvist watched the Ilyushin slow and turn off, taxiing across the apron towards the cargo hangar. It was months since he'd had such a feeling of excitement, such a sense of purpose and anticipation. There were three dark blue transit vans parked on the concrete just outside the hangar doors. As the plane came to a standstill and cut its engines, two of the vans sped out and slewed to a halt beside it. Officers from the Nottinghamshire Constabulary Armed Response Team jumped out and took up positions around the Ilyushin. Steps were manoeuvred into position and the door on the side of the plane swung outwards. Two officers wearing helmets and Kevlar jackets sprinted up the steps into the cockpit, their sub-machine-guns gripped in their hands. More officers followed.

Moments later, the rear door of the third transit van, the ART communications unit, opened and a uniformed inspector climbed out.

'The target has been secured,' he announced laconically, pulling on his leather gloves and strolling across the apron.

The crew of the Ilyushin were being herded down the steps and into a cluster by one of the vans. They were protesting angrily in accented English.

Enqvist, Claire and Sullivan walked out with Fitzpatrick and waited for the rear loading ramp of the Ilyushin to be lowered, revealing the vast cargo hold inside the bowels of the plane. Thousands of cardboard boxes, stacked inside wheeled mesh cages, were lined up down the length of the fuselage. A cargo service truck was brought in to tow the first of the cages down the ramp on to the apron. Fitzpatrick glanced at the UCLAF contingent.

'Your honour, I think,' he said, holding out a pocket knife.

Enqvist took the knife, aware that everyone beside the plane – crew, police and customs officers – was watching him. He lifted down one of the boxes and slit open the top, Sullivan and Claire standing next to him. He cut open a second box, then a third, working his way through the whole stack.

He rummaged through the contents of each box and straightened up, unable to meet the eyes of his colleagues. He took a deep gulp of the chill night air and looked away, across the airfield to the string of runway lights which sparkled in the darkness like fallen stars.

SEVENTEEN

'CRACKPOTS!'

The headline was splashed across the front page of the newspaper in huge screaming type. Every other British tabloid had something similar. Even the broadsheets had given it prominence, though in less hysterical fashion.

Carlsen tossed the pile across his desk for them to see, giving them time to absorb the embarrassing details, to squirm uncomfortably in their seats.

'So what happened?' he said.

He was a man of great self-control, who took care to suppress his emotions, both good and bad, but this morning there was no doubting he was angry. Livid. And Ole Carlsen was not angry very often.

The others didn't say anything. Sullivan was staring down at the carpet and Claire had her eyes fixed on the wall next to the window. Enqvist was slumped in his chair, subdued, completely chastened by their experience. They'd got it wrong, but none of them had expected their mistake to be blazoned across every newspaper in Britain and quite a few of the continental ones too.

Carlsen picked up a couple of tabloids from the pile and selected a few choice quotes at random from the text, rubbing salt in their wounds with uncharacteristic callousness.

'"Europe's so-called elite team of fraudbusters staged an armed ambush on British soil last night and netted – fifteen hundred boxes of crockery."

'"What is UCLAF, this cowboy outfit of gung-ho foreigners who think they can come over here and throw their weight around? We say *they* are the Eurofrauds, wasting taxpayers' money on foolish antics like this."

'"Britain's Boys in Blue were put on full alert, at vast cost, to help these Brussels Buffoons intercept a cargo of cups and saucers."'

Carlsen paused. 'You want me to go on?'

Sullivan looked up. 'We made a mistake. No excuses, but these things happen. You know they do.'

'Is that all you can say? Is that what you want me to tell the Director when I see him in half an hour? Is that what you want the Commission to put in the press statement, these things happen? The British papers will have even more of a field day.'

'They're blowing it up out of all proportion,' Enqvist said feebly.

'Are they?' Carlsen retorted. 'Let's look at the facts. You organise the search of a cargo plane belonging to a foreign government. You call in UK Customs and the local police armed response unit. You surround the plane with gun-toting cops, arrest the crew and find nothing on board except Ukrainian pottery, exactly as stated in the cargo manifest. That's pretty blown up already, don't you think?'

He looked at each of them in turn and his anger seemed to wane, its place taken by disappointment.

'The papers are right,' he continued sombrely. 'It makes us look like buffoons. We were humiliated last night, made to look like a bunch of amateurish clowns. And it wasn't just UCLAF that looked foolish, it was the entire Commission. You've given every Europhobe in Britain an excuse to mock us, to lambast us as incompetent idiots. And they will grab that excuse with both hands. Do you think it will end here? There will be questions in the British parliament, I can guarantee that. In Strasbourg too. The British press will keep hammering away at the incident because it fits in perfectly with their Eurosceptic agenda. This isn't going to go away.'

Enqvist held up his hands. 'It was all my fault,' he said resolutely.

'No way,' Sullivan demurred.

'We were all responsible,' Claire added. 'But we acted in good faith.'

'I was reckless,' Enqvist insisted. 'I should have checked everything more carefully.'

'Stig,' Sullivan said. 'You didn't have time. We had to move quickly.' He glanced at Carlsen. 'Besides, we all know that if you check every last detail, word gets back to the traffickers and they abort the run. Christ, this isn't all *that* unusual. Customs officers all over Europe, all over the world, stop and search regularly without finding anything of consequence.'

'Unfortunately for us, they don't all have such a high profile as this case,' Carlsen said. 'The scale and nature of the operation makes our failure all the more visible. And all the more embarrassing. Did you really need armed police? Especially in the UK where they're so sensitive about things like that.'

'You know who we were dealing with. You know what happened at Vitoria, how we had to block the runway with fire tenders to stop them escaping,' Sullivan said. 'We had every reason to think they'd try to get away again this time.'

'Only if they'd been smuggling in cigarettes.'

'Hindsight, Ole,' Sullivan said. 'We thought they were. How do you think we'd have looked last night if they *had* been smuggling cigarettes and the Ilyushin had taken off leaving us standing on the airport waving goodbye? We took all the right precautions. We just got the wrong cargo.'

'And that's all anyone is going to remember,' Carlsen fired back. 'I know it's unfair, but no one out there either knows or cares about our successes. It's our failures they will use against us.'

He sighed, running his fingers through his coarse grey hair. 'I'm not blaming any of you. I understand the difficulties under which you are forced to operate, but I'm warning you that we will have questions to answer about everything we did. There will have to be an inquiry. There may be calls for resignations. I will do my utmost to make sure those calls are not heeded, but they may become too strong for the Director to resist. Now take me through every single detail of the operation, from start to finish.'

'We were set up,' Enqvist said bitterly. 'We were fucking set up.'

He kicked the metal wastepaper bin by the side of his desk and watched it skitter across the carpet and bang against the base of the office wall.

'The papers, the diary, they were all planted for us to find. How could we have been so stupid?'

'Because Wolf was dead,' Sullivan said calmly.

Enqvist turned to look at him, then nodded, acknowledging the truth of the remark. That was the crux of the matter. If they'd come across the papers in any other circumstances, they would have gone through them in minute detail, checking the authenticity of every reference: noting the times and dates of Wolf's movements, of the cargoes he'd ordered and where they'd gone. They'd have crosschecked every single bloody item to build up a complete picture of how he operated.

But the Swiss had been dead. It was that which had lulled them into abandoning their usual caution. Wolf himself had placed the documents in the hotel safe, their provenance was impeccable and his subsequent murder seemed only to give the papers more credence. There was no reason to suspect they were fakes. Even now, the debacle at East Midlands Airport fresh in their minds, it was hard to accept the implications of what had happened.

Claire put into words the key concern that was troubling all three of them.

'Are we saying Wolf was killed just to discredit us? I find that difficult to believe. What if there was no connection between his murder and the forging of the papers?'

'They have to be connected,' Sullivan said. 'Someone went to a lot of trouble to mislead us with the documents. Wolf's death was no coincidence or accident.'

'You'd have to be pretty ruthless to think of a plan like that,' Claire said.

Sullivan nodded. 'They *are* ruthless.'

'But Wolf must have been in on it.'

'He was.'

'And they sacrificed him to make us look stupid?'

'Not just for that. They must have wanted him out of the picture for other reasons too.'

'Such as?'

Sullivan shrugged. 'Wolf was a frail old man, but he was still working. Maybe someone wanted to take over his territory.'

'Montague?' Enqvist said.

Sullivan walked to the window of the office. It was raining again outside – he could see the droplets above him on the glass roof – but none of it penetrated through to the atrium whose plants and shrubs had to be artificially fed and watered. The Beaulieu complex was a strange sealed environment, protected from the vagaries of the weather by glass and concrete walls. It seemed to Sullivan like a metaphor for the entire European Commission, a bureaucracy of self-absorbed careerists and time-servers who lived in isolation from the real world. Most of them led lives of dull, sheltered tranquillity. They had no idea, and no interest, in the corrupt, disturbing currents that shaped and distorted the existence of those outside.

But UCLAF was different. It was the only part of the whole organisation whose *raison d'être* was crime, whose staff were steeped – albeit at one sanitised remove – in the murky sediment of human greed and savagery. Sullivan knew how much money was at stake. To an ambitious criminal the murder of an old man was a small price to pay for a larger share of the booty.

'Everything points to him,' he said. 'Wolf was at his house for the few days before his death. That has to be when the papers were prepared.'

'It was a big job,' Claire said sceptically. 'They must have been forging them for weeks.'

'I don't think so,' Sullivan said. 'I think most of those documents are genuine. That's what's clever about it. Even if we *had* checked them more thoroughly we'd have found they added up. All Montague did was slip in a couple of telephone numbers, an order form from Laterveer Voorden and let us do the rest for him.'

'And we walked straight into it,' Enqvist said through gritted teeth. 'If the Director wants a head for this cock-up, it has to be mine, okay? I'm nearly at the end of my time anyway.'

'If you go, Stig, we all go,' Sullivan said. He glanced at Claire and she nodded in agreement. 'We ride out the storm,' he continued. 'And we make sure that next time – and there will be a next time – we get him.'

No one asked the obvious question, how? But Claire was already thinking through the possibilities.

'If most of the papers are genuine,' she said, 'we still have a briefcase full of dynamite. Don't we?'

'They're genuine,' Sullivan replied. 'But useless. Montague will have made sure of that. They'll either be stuff we already know, or false trails leading us into some unsolvable maze of companies. We might manage to implicate Wolf in something, but why waste our time? Wolf is dead.'

'So where do we go from here?' Enqvist said. 'We have no hard evidence against Montague at all.'

'Then we have to find some. My guess is he's going to make his next move soon, while we're still in disarray. He thinks he's got us on the ropes, that we'll be too frightened of getting it wrong again to take any risks. That makes it the perfect time to hit back.'

'Carlsen won't like it,' Enqvist said. 'He's going to want us to lie low for a while until this blows over.'

'We don't tell Carlsen. Not until we've got something positive for him. Something we're absolutely sure of.'

Enqvist stared at him pensively, chewing his lower lip. Sullivan met Claire's eyes, keeping all emotion, all memories of shared intimacy out of his expression. They had to make this decision independently of each other. All three of them. But Sullivan had no compunction about influencing their choice.

'There's a Ukrainian connection,' he said. 'The Ilyushin last night proves that. This is bigger than just Montague. A Ukrainian attacked Claire and Ukrainians threatened my family, I'm sure of that. We can't afford to sit back and do nothing while Carlsen organises an inquiry to placate a few shit-stirrers in the British press.'

Sullivan turned away to let them think about it. He wondered what Kate and the boys were doing, wondered whether his common sense was being submerged by some inflamed, irrational desire for revenge for what had happened to them. He didn't think so. This was business, pure and simple.

'You have something in mind?' Claire said, and Sullivan knew she'd made her decision.

He walked back to his desk and sat down.

'Stig?'

Enqvist sighed and gave a reluctant nod. 'Okay.'

'There are several strands here which we have to link together somehow,' Sullivan said, counting them off on his fingers. 'Montague, Van Vliet, Gilles Lafon, the *Maria Vasquez*, the Camorra, the Ukrainians. Claire, can you call Hellendoorn and ask him if he can put the Golden Valley Inn under surveillance? So far, that brothel's the only link we have between the key players in this. I'll ask UK Customs if they can keep an eye on Montague.'

'What else?' Enqvist said.

'As I said when we went for lunch in Jezus-Eik,' Sullivan replied. 'You don't smuggle cigarettes with a suitcase and a couple of couriers. You don't do it even with an Ilyushin-76 which can carry only a couple of thousand cases at one time and has to land at official airstrips. You do it by sea. You take advantage of miles of unguarded coastline to make your drops. The *Maria Vasquez* is out of the picture, but Montague will have another ship somewhere. We have to identify it.'

Enqvist pulled a face. 'That could take us weeks.'

'We haven't got weeks,' Sullivan said. 'If I'm right, we have just a few days at the most to identify it, and find it.'

The paper was piling up on the desks. Sullivan looked at the growing mound with a sinking heart. Enqvist was right, this could take weeks. And there was no guarantee of success even then.

They'd done their best to narrow down the search, concentrating on shipments from Rotterdam and Antwerp, the two largest cigarette ports in Europe. There were bonded warehouses elsewhere on the continent, but they were too small to supply the quantities a large-scale, serious trafficker would have required. And Sullivan was sure of one thing: Hal Montague, though he'd evaded identification until now, was a big-time smuggler.

They had faxes from Customs in both ports detailing all consignments of cigarettes due to sail in the next seven days. It was a daunting list, comprising some fifty-four ships of varying nationalities.

'It's too many,' Enqvist said.

'Then cut it down,' Sullivan said. 'Let's take out the flags of convenience and concentrate on those.'

They consulted the Lloyd's Register of Shipping and went through the list, ticking off the ships which were registered in the classic flags-of-convenience countries: Liberia, Costa Rica, Panama, Honduras, the Bahamas and Vanuatu.

'How many have we got?' Claire said.

Enqvist counted them. 'Thirty-six.'

'Let's start with the ones taking consignments from Van Vliet's warehouse,' Sullivan said. 'Mark the stated destination of the cargoes, then check with Customs in those countries to see if the ships have been there before and when.'

Enqvist picked up the log of the *Maria Vasquez* and looked at the map of the world they'd taped to the wall. There were sheets of coloured stickers on the desk.

'Red triangles are the *Maria Vasquez*,' he said, peeling off the stickers.

He studied the log and put a red triangle beside each port the ship had visited over the previous two months: Rotterdam, Hull, Algeciras, Istanbul, Odessa, Massawa, Limassol, Bilbao.

Then Sullivan handed him a list of ships to check. He gave Claire another and kept the last few for himself. He reached out for the phone but it rang before he got there. He picked it up.

'UCLAF, Sullivan.'

'This is Janvier,' a voice said in French.

'Richard,' Sullivan said. 'What's new? Any sign of the two men?'

'I'm afraid not,' Janvier replied. 'But we have an ID on one of them. We showed the photofit to airline personnel at Zaventem and got a positive. He came in on an Aeroflot flight from Moscow on Tuesday morning.'

'Moscow?'

'His name's Drozhkin. Mikhail Drozhkin. You were right, he's a Ukrainian.'

'Any form?'

'No, but here's something interesting. His father is Yevgeny Drozhkin. We have a file on him.'

'Should I know the name?' Sullivan said.

'Before the collapse of the Soviet Union, Yevgeny Drozhkin was the GRU Resident in Brussels.'

'Jesus!'

'When the Ukraine became an independent state he went back to Kiev and set up a private security business hiring out bodyguards, providing protection, confidential vetting, you know what I mean. Half the senior officers of the GRU went into the same lucrative line of work. By the looks of it, his son did too. If I get anything more I'll let you know.'

Sullivan hung up. Enqvist and Claire were looking at him expectantly. Sullivan repeated what Janvier had told him.

'The GRU?' Claire said in disbelief. 'Soviet Military Intelligence?'

Sullivan nodded.

'Great,' said Enqvist. 'That's all we fucking need.'

It was late afternoon, the winter darkness closing in around the office, when Sullivan finally remembered to ring Kate. She didn't sound happy.

'You said you'd call this morning,' she said tersely.

'It slipped my mind, I'm sorry.'

'The least you could do was ring. How long does a phone call take?'

'I'm sorry, okay?' Sullivan said, trying not to get irritated by her combative tone.

'We're stuck here in this bloody flat going spare with boredom and you can't even be bothered to see how we are.'

'You're not stuck,' Sullivan said, knowing he was inviting a prolonged argument. 'You can go out.'

'Oh sure, wonderful,' Kate retorted. 'Go out where?'

'Anywhere you like.'

'What, with a couple of plainclothes cops following us?'

'They're there for your protection.'

'We're virtually prisoners here. That's not why we came. The idea was that you would be able to spend more time with your family, take a few days off work. Remember?'

Sullivan controlled his rising feeling of resentment. She had a point, but he didn't want to be reminded of it.

'We've a lot on here,' he said. 'Things we have to clear up.'

'Can't Stig and Claire handle it?'

'It's not that simple.'

'What things?'

'It's too complicated to explain. You wouldn't understand.'

'Oh, pardon me for being so dense.'

'Kate, this isn't helping me.'

'You think going back to work is helping *us*? Have you considered that?'

'We ballsed things up in a big way last night. The British papers are crucifying us. It's important we recover some of our credibility. That's why I'm here, not with you.'

'Credibility? How much credibility do you think you have with the boys now?'

'Don't bring them into it.'

'They're in it already, or hadn't you noticed?'

Sullivan snorted with annoyance, frustrated at the way the conversation was degenerating into an all-out row.

'Look,' he said firmly, 'I wouldn't be here without a damn good reason. If we don't sort this out now, I might be out of a job by the weekend.'

'You know, that might not be such a bad thing for all of us,' Kate said and hung up.

The map of the world was gradually filling up with small coloured stickers: squares, diamonds, circles, stars, some with numbers written on them, each denoting a different ship. Sullivan added another beside the port of Mombasa and turned as Enqvist walked back in carrying a couple of faxes. Sullivan gave him an enquiring glance. Enqvist shook his head.

'*Santa Maria IV* and the *Donna Elvira* both look clean,' he said. 'The *Santa Maria* was in Lagos last month with a mixed cargo including twelve thousand master cases of cigarettes. The *Elvira* took fifteen thousand cases to Haifa five weeks ago. Nothing unloaded en route.'

Sullivan consulted the key beside the map and placed the appropriate stickers next to the ports. Claire came off the phone and scribbled a note on her pad.

'The *Sheerness* looks clean too,' she said. 'Ten thousand master cases to Dakar a month ago. Every case arrived and was checked through Senegalese Customs.'

Enqvist swore in Swedish and sat down at his desk.

'We're wasting our time. All these ships are in the clear.'

'That doesn't mean they're not involved in trafficking,' Claire said. 'If you're a smart smuggler, you'll mix legitimate cigarette shipments in with the contraband shipments to muddy the waters.'

Enqvist sighed. 'I know. But we've got to narrow the field down somehow.'

'None of them are in the clear until we know every single shipment they've made and checked it with the ports concerned.'

'We don't have access to that information,' Enqvist

said. 'Not without their logbooks or the owners' records, and we can't get hold of either of those.'

Sullivan was studying the map on the wall. 'We're doing this the wrong way round,' he said.

'What?'

'We should be starting with the ports, not the ships. We have the log of the *Maria Vasquez*. That's the one ship whose movements we know exactly. What we should do is contact each port the *Maria Vasquez* visited with a list of the thirty-six ships we're checking and see if any of them went there too. See if there's a pattern common to more than one of them.' He tapped the map. 'Particularly ones that also called at Odessa.'

'Odessa?' Enqvist said. 'Shit, yes, I should have spotted that immediately.'

They photocopied the list and Enqvist went down the corridor to fax it to every port mentioned in the *Maria Vasquez*'s log. Claire looked across at Sullivan, but before he could say anything his telephone rang. He picked up the receiver.

'UCLAF, Sullivan.'

'You were lucky last time,' a voice said softly. A man's voice, educated, definitely English.

'Pardon?' Sullivan said.

'We gave you a sporting chance. Let your wife see us first. You won't be so lucky next time.'

Sullivan jolted forwards in his seat. A sudden spasm of nausea shuddered through his stomach.

'Who is this?' he demanded.

'Think about it,' the voice said. 'A woman, two

young boys. Think how vulnerable they are, how easy it is to get to them.'

'Who the hell are you?' Sullivan was almost shouting into the phone.

'Does it matter?'

'What do you want?'

'You know what we want. Back off, Sullivan. Find someone else to pick on. We don't like it.'

'Tough shit.'

'I'm serious. Think about your wife and kids. Why take the risk?'

The line went dead. Sullivan replaced the receiver and swallowed hard, taking deep breaths to ease the sickness in his belly. Claire was watching him.

'Them?' she asked.

Sullivan nodded. He stood up and grabbed his coat.

'I'm going home.'

'They'll be safe, Rob. The police are there.'

'I know. I should be too.'

Claire came round from her desk and pushed the door shut.

'Claire, look . . .'

She stopped him with a shake of her head. 'Let's not talk. It won't help.'

She reached up and kissed him on the mouth. He returned the pressure of her lips, feeling her arms around his neck, her body soft against him. With an effort he broke away.

'I'd better go.'

He pulled open the door and walked out.

*   *   *

Kate was watching television in the living room. She glanced up at him as he came in and turned her head back to the screen. Sullivan sat down in an armchair. His wife exuded a perceptible air of hostility.

'The boys in bed?' he said.

'It's nine o'clock.'

'How are they?'

Without looking at him, she said coldly: 'If you'd come home, you could have asked them yourself.'

The tone was set. Sullivan decided to get it over with now. It would be much worse if he left it until they were in bed together.

'I'm sorry,' he said contritely. 'We had a lot on.'

'Oh yes?' Kate tilted back her head and sniffed a few times.

'I can smell perfume.'

'It's probably Claire's.'

'Ah.' There was a whole wealth of meaning in that short exclamation.

'She wears it,' Sullivan said.

'Did she give you a dab to try too?'

Sullivan gestured in exasperation. 'Come on, Kate, this is silly.'

'It's very strong.'

'It's like cigarette smoke. The smell gets everywhere.'

She was looking at him pensively. For a moment Sullivan thought she was going to come out and ask him directly. But to his relief she changed the subject.

'We're going back to England tomorrow.'

'You're . . . ?' He stared at her. 'That's not a good idea.'

'It's bad enough here at the best of times. I can't take any more of it.'

'You have to stay. For your own safety.'

'The boys want to go home too.'

Sullivan leaned forwards, alarmed. 'You can't. I told you, you'll be better protected here.'

'How long is this going to go on? The boys have to be back at school on Monday. So do I.'

'That's not important right now. You can take a few days off until this all settles down.'

'Like you did, you mean?' she said acidly.

'For Christ's sake,' Sullivan exploded. 'This is their safety we're talking about. Have you thought of that?'

'I've thought about nothing else for the past two days. Which is more than you have.'

'That's not fair.'

'It's true. We've seen what your priorities are. Well my priorities are to get home and back to a normal life for the boys as soon as possible.'

'Give it more time,' Sullivan said.

'For what? You said yourself those men are probably out of the country by now. What real danger are we in?'

Sullivan hesitated. He'd hoped he wouldn't have to tell her about the phone call. He didn't want to worry her any more than necessary. But he had no choice now.

'They called me at the office before I left,' he said.

'Not the men themselves, but someone speaking for them. Maybe the man who sent them. He made threats.'

'Against us?'

'Yes. You have to stay, Kate.'

'What did he say?'

'Not much.'

'What did he say?' Kate repeated.

'Just how you were vulnerable.'

'Was he serious?'

'Yes.'

'And are we vulnerable?'

'You might be.'

'Are you saying that because you believe it, or because you want us to stay here?'

'I'll feel happier with you here.'

'Oh, *you'll* feel happier. Sitting in your office carrying on as normal while we're stuck out here.'

'Kate, let's discuss this rationally. You might still be in danger.'

'Are you going to be with us?'

Sullivan was silent. Then he said lamely: 'That's not the point.'

'No, it's not, is it? Not to you. If you're so concerned, then you'd better arrange for someone to keep an eye on us in Colchester, because that's where we'll be.'

Kate stood up and switched off the television.

'I think we should give this more thought,' Sullivan said.

'I've done all the thinking I need.' She headed for the bedroom.

'Don't you care what my views are?'

Kate stopped. 'Right now, Rob, I don't give a toss what your views are.'

She went into the bedroom and closed the door firmly behind her.

EIGHTEEN

Montague stood by the window, looking out through a narrow gap in the blinds, while Doyle went through his customary routine of checking the room for bugs. The Singel canal outside was a murky brown colour, its surface smeared with the rainbow traces of oil from the passing boats. To his right the floating flower market was an inferno of colour. The wooden platforms were smothered with carnations and chrysanthemums, lilies, roses, irises and a hundred other species. Montague watched the bustle of the market, listening to the cries of the stallholders, the lap of the water against the sides of the pontoons. There was a subdued normality about it all he found soothing.

Behind him, Doyle was packing away his electronic equipment. Montague turned and waited for him to finish.

'It's clean,' Doyle said.

Montague gave a nod. The trolley of coffee and biscuits had already been wheeled in. He poured himself a cup and wandered to the head of the table to sit down. Lafon and Luciani were always late. They had a Mediterranean indifference to punctuality which Montague had learnt to accept though it irritated him immensely. They were the buyers and, as in any other trade, they were always right.

Ten minutes elapsed before the Frenchman and the Neapolitan arrived. Montague always thought of Luciani as Neapolitan, not Italian. There was something coarse, primitive about him. He had a crude vitality and a streak of ruthless cruelty which Montague associated with the *Mezzogiorno*, the southern half of the Italian peninsula where feudal tradition still held sway and where men like Armando Luciani ruled over their cowed subjects like medieval warlords.

The two men sat down and waited in silence for coffee to be brought to them in their seats. Montague made no attempt at small-talk. They were none of them friends. Outside their shared business interests they had absolutely nothing to converse about.

Luciani waved away his bodyguards and fixed his dark, hooded eyes on Montague.

'When do I get my shipment?' he said, getting straight to the point of the meeting.

'The ship leaves Antwerp on Monday morning,' Montague replied. 'She'll be in the Bay of Biscay three days later, the usual location. . .' He looked at Lafon and the Frenchman nodded. '. . . then off the coast of southern Italy in the middle of the following week.'

Luciani scowled. 'No earlier?'

'It's as soon as I can manage. We're having to be very careful this time.'

'How many cases?'

'Twenty-five thousand each. Payment on the usual terms. The master of the ship will contact you when he's nearing the rendezvous positions. I trust that's acceptable to you both.'

Lafon gestured his assent. Luciani grunted, then gave a grudging nod. Even he couldn't complain about twenty-five thousand cases – that was two hundred and fifty million cigarettes with a street value in Naples of approaching twenty million US dollars, more than enough to keep his *camorristi* busy for a few weeks.

'The ship,' Luciani said. 'How safe is she?'

'As safe as I can make her. She's never been stopped or searched. Everything about her is above board and there is no way – absolutely no way – she can ever be traced back to us.'

'What's her name?'

'The *Reunion Star*,' Montague said.

It was a relief to Montague when the meeting was over and Ilse Ameling came in with the girls. Luciani and Lafon seemed to relax immediately and Montague escaped from their surly company to find solace with the house madam. He'd known Ilse for more than fifteen years, since the time she'd been a call girl for one of the high-class, discreet escort agencies in Amsterdam – less obvious than the sordid prostitution available in the city's red-light district and more suitable for Montague's business partners, who would never have dreamt of trawling the streets for their pleasure. She'd set up the Golden Valley Inn at his instigation, tapping into the rich market of peripatetic businessmen who lived their lives away from home and were prepared to pay a premium for the comforts of a five-star hotel with a few extras thrown in which the Hiltons, Sheratons and Dorchesters didn't provide. Montague used her for a lot of his clients. Money oiled the wheels of business but he found that sex was just as good a lubricant, sometimes better.

They drank champagne and chatted casually for a while, then Montague noticed Christine talking to Doyle on the other side of the room. He caught her eye and beckoned her over. He offered her a glass of champagne and lit up a cigar the size of a *baguette*.

'How are you today, my dear?' he asked formally.

Christine smiled archly. 'Don't you want to find out?'

Montague chuckled. 'All in good time.' He puffed contentedly on his cigar then removed it from his mouth and tapped the ash off into a small silver tray. 'How is your assignment going?' he asked.

'I don't want to rush it,' Christine replied. 'But I'm making good progress.'

Montague nodded. 'I trust I'm going to see a return on my investment soon.'

'Oh, you will,' Christine said with conviction. 'Believe me, you will.'

The nondescript white Ford transit van was parked

on the other side of the Singel canal, its curtained rear window facing the entrance to the Golden Valley Inn. Inside, sitting on collapsible camping chairs, were two bored-looking men in crumpled suits. One of the men was peering out cautiously through a slit in the curtain.

'Here we go again,' he said, pulling the slit wider.

His partner lifted his camera to the glass and focused the 400mm lens, clicking off a number of shots in quick succession while the first man spoke quietly into his radio. Five minutes later and, again, a further ten minutes after that, they repeated the exercise. Then they removed the film from the camera, clambered into the front seats of the van and drove away.

Claire was holding the fax sheets in her hand, reading through them one by one, trying to make sense of the information they contained.

'It's hard to know where to start,' she said.

Neither Enqvist nor Sullivan replied. Enqvist was drinking yet another cup of coffee and rubbing his bloodshot eyes. Sullivan was gazing distractedly out of the window, his mind elsewhere. Claire guessed he was thinking about his family.

'Hey, guys,' she said. 'Are we going to do this or not?'

Enqvist nodded unenthusiastically. Claire wondered if it was her imagination or if she could really smell alcohol in the office. Maybe it seeped out of the pores of the skin like sweat.

PAUL ADAM

'Rob?'

Sullivan turned. 'Uh?'

'Come on, we've got all this to sort out. I'm not doing it on my own.'

'Sorry.'

Sullivan drifted back to his desk and got his brain in gear for the job in hand.

'Okay, what do the faxes say?'

Claire read out the names of the ships and the ports. Sullivan scribbled numbers on coloured stickers and handed them to Enqvist who placed them on the map on the wall. There were so many it looked as if a multi-coloured rash had swept across the world.

'What now?' Enqvist said.

Claire looked at Sullivan. 'We match the movements with the route of the *Maria Vasquez*, I suppose. See if any ship followed exactly the same course.'

Sullivan nodded and picked up the log of the *Maria Vasquez*. 'Let's start with Rotterdam.'

He read out each port in order while Enqvist and Claire checked the map and fax sheets. No other ship had called at all the ports. Twenty-six had been to Rotterdam at some point, not surprising given its importance in the world shipping business. Eight had been to Hull, fifteen to Algeciras, ten to Istanbul, eight to Odessa, one to Massawa, seven to Limassol and thirteen to Bilbao.

'Let's take Odessa,' Sullivan said. 'Give me the names of the eight ships which have been there, and the dates.'

Claire read out the names and Sullivan wrote them down on a pad of paper.

'*Sierra Blanca, Allport Castle, Reunion Star, Simonetta, Catriona, Charlotte Anne, Navarino Princess, Nancy Dawson.*'

'The *Charlotte Anne* is in the clear already,' Enqvist said. 'I checked her out yesterday with the Van Vliet shipments.'

'That leaves seven,' Sullivan said. 'Stig, you take the first three on the list, Claire the second two. The remaining two I'll handle.'

They picked up the telephones and the directory of customs posts around the world and started to dial.

By mid-afternoon the information was beginning to trickle back from the ports. Sullivan called out the names of the seven ships in turn.

'*Sierra Blanca*?'

'Clear,' Enqvist said. 'She took fifteen thousand cases to Istanbul on her last trip. All accounted for according to Turkish Customs.'

'*Allport Castle*?'

'Clear.'

'*Reunion Star*?'

'Ditto.'

'*Simonetta*?'

'I'm still waiting for a reply,' Claire said. 'The same with the *Catriona*. Freetown Customs are calling me back when they've located the documentation.'

'The *Navarino Princess* looks to be in the clear,'

Sullivan said. 'No word on the *Nancy Dawson* yet.'

He reviewed the list.

'*Simonetta*, *Catriona* or *Nancy Dawson*. It's one of those three.'

It was growing dark outside. Sullivan could see the distant flicker of car headlights on the roads, the dull glow of the streetlamps. He thought about Kate and the boys yet again. They would be almost home in Colchester by now. He considered ringing but decided not to, unsure of the reception he'd receive. He and Kate had parted under a cloud of frosty politeness, still smarting from the previous night's row. He'd made another attempt to persuade her to stay on in Brussels but she'd refused. They were both stubborn, unwilling to give ground. There'd been other moments like this in their marriage, but they'd always come through them. Maybe they would this time too. Sullivan wasn't sure.

Enqvist came in with two more faxes. He shook his head.

'*Simonetta* and *Nancy Dawson* look to be clear,' he said.

That left the *Catriona*. Claire was on the phone to Customs in Freetown. Sullivan and Enqvist waited for her to finish.

'The *Catriona* took seventeen thousand cases to Sierra Leone in January. Every one arrived,' she said. 'She seems to be in the clear too.'

'Fuck!' said Enqvist.

* * *

'Maybe it's not a flag-of-convenience ship,' Claire speculated.

'It has to be,' Sullivan said. 'Doing offshore drops, they need a compliant Third World crew. Guys who don't care what the ship does provided they get a pay packet at the end of the trip.'

'So maybe we're making a mistake concentrating on Odessa.'

'Maybe.' Sullivan wasn't convinced. He was sure the Ukrainian connection was important.

'We've ruled out Van Vliet and Odessa,' Enqvist said. 'Where do we go from here?'

'We check the remaining ships,' Claire said.

Enqvist grimaced. 'We'll be here all night.'

'Probably longer.'

They were getting nowhere slowly. Twenty-four of the thirty-six ships had been eliminated from the list, but that still left a further twelve to consider. Phone calls had been made, faxes sent. No replies had yet been received. They were starting to get tired, hungry.

'We need a break,' Enqvist said wearily. He was listless, jaded by their lack of progress.

Sullivan was studying the map on the wall, his eyes roving across the names of the ports, the clusters of coloured stickers.

'Somewhere we're missing something,' he said.

Enqvist walked over and stood next to him, looking at the map too.

'I don't know what it is,' Sullivan continued, 'but I know we've overlooked it.'

Behind them the telephone rang. Claire answered and spoke in Dutch for a time.

'Hellendoorn,' she said, coming off the line. 'The surveillance operation on the Golden Valley Inn. There was a meeting there this morning. Three visitors identified as Hal Montague, Gilles Lafon and Armando Luciani. He's faxing through the photos for us now.'

'The vultures are gathering,' Enqvist said. 'Let's go and eat.'

Sullivan stayed behind for a few minutes to call Kate.

'When did you get back?' he said.

'A couple of hours ago.' Her voice was flat, tired.

'You should have called me.'

'Why? You didn't call us.'

'Are you still cross with me?'

'Does it show?'

He tried again.

'Have the police been in touch?'

He'd asked Janvier to arrange for a watch to be kept on them by the Essex police.

'A patrol car came round. They checked the doors and windows, gave me a bleeper to use if anything happened.'

'You should be here.'

'Are we starting all that again?'

Sullivan sighed. 'What about the boys?'

'They're in bed.'

'I'll ring tomorrow. Speak to them then.'

Silence.

'Anything else?' Kate enquired sourly.

He couldn't swallow his anger. 'What do you mean, anything else? I'm your husband, not some bloody nuisance caller.'

'Don't swear at me.'

'How long are you going to keep this up?'

'I'm tired. I'm going to bed now. Good night.'

He couldn't believe she'd hung up on him. He dialled the number again. It rang but there was no reply. He knew it was the line ringing, not the phone. She'd unplugged it from the socket.

He slammed down the receiver and sat motionless for a time, trying to contain his fury. He realised his hands were clenched into tight balls and forced himself to relax before he stood up and went out after Claire and Stig.

The surveillance photographs from Amsterdam, grainy long-distance snaps showing various individuals coming and going from the Golden Valley Inn, were in the fax tray in the secretaries' office down the corridor. Sullivan paused to flick through the pile, wanting to take a good look at the opposition. Montague he recognised from their encounter at Horningtoft. The others, Lafon, Luciani and a third man identified as Simon Doyle, were all new to him. He studied their features, committing them to memory, then tossed the photos back into the tray and went down in the lift.

Sullivan studied the map of the world again when

they came back from dinner. It was getting late but none of them wanted to call it a night just yet. Then he opened the log of the *Maria Vasquez* and read through the pages carefully. He noted the dates and times and did some arithmetic in his head. He returned to the map and peered at it intently.

'What're you doing?' Enqvist asked.

'Pass me the Reed's tables.'

Sullivan checked some of the distances, then did a few more mental calculations.

'I knew something didn't add up. The *Maria Vasquez* was in Massawa, Eritrea, on December fifteenth last year. The next port of call, according to her log, was Limassol, Cyprus, on December twenty-second. It's thirteen hundred nautical miles from Massawa to Limassol. At the *Maria Vasquez*'s normal service speed of thirteen knots it should have taken her four days, say five to allow for delays in the Suez Canal. Yet it took her seven.'

'So she took her time.' Enqvist said.

'Not these ships. They cram in as many cargoes, as much mileage as they can. It's the only way they pay.'

'You think she went somewhere else on the way?' Claire said.

Sullivan nodded. 'And didn't record it in the log.'

Enqvist stared at the map. 'Like where?'

Sullivan turned to Claire.

'Can you ring Dutch Directory Enquiries and get a number for Gerda Faassen?'

'Frans Maartens' sister?' Claire said in surprise.

'It's a long shot, but worth a try.'

Claire replaced the receiver and eyed Sullivan narrowly.

'What on earth made you think of her?'

'I remembered she said she collected them.'

'Her brother sent her a postcard from Port Said, in Egypt, dated December twentieth.'

They checked with Customs in Port Said, then called Massawa and Bilbao, the *Maria Vasquez's* next port of call after Limassol. Sullivan assimilated the notes he'd made and smiled ruefully.

'These guys are good,' he said. 'Very good. You have to admire them. The *Maria Vasquez* loaded ten thousand litres of palm oil in Massawa, Eritrea. At Port Said she took on thirty thousand litres of hazelnut oil. The documentation was changed in transit so that by the time she reached Bilbao she was offloading forty thousand litres of palm oil from Eritrea. No mention of the stop in Port Said or the hazelnut oil.'

'Which went to Garcia Saez in San Sebastian and from there to Bayonne,' Claire said, working it out for herself. 'No security paid and Fonteneau et Delahaye got their regular supply to adulterate their olive oil.'

'But this is the bit I like,' Sullivan said. 'Eritrea is a Lomé Convention country entitled to preferential import tariffs. Egypt isn't. So they pass the hazelnut oil off as Eritrean palm oil and pay no customs duty

353

on it either. It's brilliant. These guys are ripping off the EU in every direction.'

He turned to Stig. 'There was one other ship on our list which called at Massawa. Which one was it?'

Enqvist rummaged through the messy pile of papers on the desk and extracted a single sheet. He ran his finger down the names.

'The *Reunion Star*,' he said.

'That's our baby.'

They double-checked with Bilbao to make absolutely sure. The *Reunion Star* had been there two weeks earlier and unloaded a cargo of palm oil from Eritrea.

'The same run, the same scam,' Sullivan said. '*And* she went to Odessa en route to Massawa. There's no question, she's the target.'

Claire consulted the information they'd received from Customs in Rotterdam and Antwerp.

'She's taking fifty thousand master cases from Laterveer Voorden in Antwerp to Accra.'

'When does she sail?'

'First thing Monday.'

Sullivan glanced at his watch. It was two fifteen in the morning.

'Who wants the pleasure of waking up Carlsen?' he said.

NINETEEN

The aeroplane started to bank as it made its approach
into Capodichino and Doyle caught a glimpse through
the window of the barren summit of Vesuvius and then
the waters of the bay shimmering in the morning sunshine. He pinched his nostrils and blew out through
his nose to ease the pressure on his eardrums. He
felt them pop and leaned his head back, closing his
eyes. He enjoyed flying, but the descents played hell
with his ears. For up to an hour after they'd landed
he knew he'd be partially deaf. The thought didn't
disturb him unduly. This was Naples, after all: partial
deafness was probably a blessing.

Outside the airport terminal he took a taxi into
the centre of the city, asking the driver to drop
him in front of the central station. A scruffy kid
who looked as if he should be in school was on
the forecourt selling black-market cigarettes from
the bonnet of a parked car. There were children
like him on practically every street corner in the
city. Doyle watched him for a moment, wondering
which Camorra gang he was working for, then went
through into the station concourse.

He paused briefly for an espresso at one of the bars before slipping out of a side entrance and hailing another cab to take him to the Castel Nuovo. At the castle, he walked across the piazza, down the street past the Teatro San Carlo and into the Galleria Umberto I. When he emerged from the Galleria, he flagged down a third taxi and gave the driver directions to a bar in a side street near the Piazza Dante. They were elaborate precautions, and probably unnecessary, but Doyle was a careful operator. These were dangerous men he was dealing with.

He was met in the bar, as he always was, by a stocky bull of a man in a sharp grey suit who spoke English like an extra in *The Godfather* but looked like a navvy on his way to church. A dented lump of rusty scrap metal masquerading as a Fiat Punto was parked in a yard behind the bar. Doyle had come to realise in the time he'd been visiting Naples that though the Camorra *capi* had a fondness for vulgar ostentation, their foot soldiers were expected not to draw attention to themselves.

A twenty-minute drive through the belching Naples traffic took them up into the hills behind the city and in through the gates of a magnificent castellated villa which was protected like a fortress. The windows in the house were glazed with bulletproof glass, the sleek gardens patrolled by discreetly armed guards and the reinforced front door looked strong enough to stop a tank. Very little made Simon Doyle nervous, but coming here did.

He was searched once at the main gates, then again

when he entered the villa. Yevgeny Drozhkin and Dino Falzone – tanned, svelte, Armani-clad – were waiting for him in the large sitting room at the back of the house. They shook hands and Falzone offered him coffee and *strúffoli*, small balls of dough dipped in honey and fried, which Doyle declined. They exchanged a few courtesies in English, a language Falzone spoke fluently though with a strong American accent, then the Camorra boss smiled, showing his gold fillings, and shot Doyle a glance of icy penetration.

'Shall we get down to business?' he said.

Ole Carlsen lived in Overijse, one of the Flemish-speaking communes which, like Tervuren, was out beyond the Forêt de Soignes on the south-eastern side of Brussels. His house – two-storey, detached with gardens all around – overlooked the local golf club where he was a keen eight-handicap member and had a regular Saturday morning four-ball which, much to his annoyance, he was having to forego.

Claire arrived first, then Sullivan, who sat down at the opposite end of the living room. Neither said much. Sullivan seemed preoccupied, far away. Claire tried to read his body language, the tone of his voice, but it was impossible to tell what he was really thinking.

Finally, Enqvist turned up half an hour late. Carlsen brought in coffee on a tray and distributed the cups, making sure there were coasters under each one to prevent them marking the polished surfaces of the occasional tables placed around the living room. In his private life Carlsen exhibited the same fastidious neatness he applied to his work. The room was spotlessly clean and so tidily arranged it seemed unnatural. Every ornament had its own allotted position – Carlsen even paused to adjust one which had strayed a couple of millimetres out of line as he circled the room with the coffees – and there was an air of perfection which Sullivan, for one, found intimidating.

Carlsen remained standing by the window. He was dressed in his casual weekend attire of pressed grey trousers and V-necked pullover, under which he wore a plain white shirt and navy-blue tie. Sullivan had never seen him without a tie. Sometimes he wondered if he slept in one. The section chief was clear-eyed and alert. He showed no sign that his rest had been disturbed by a phone call at 2.30 am.

'Let's recap what you told me last night – early this morning,' he corrected himself, looking at Sullivan. 'Just to ensure we have all the facts right.'

Sullivan outlined again how they'd pinpointed the *Reunion Star*. Carlsen listened carefully, taking small sips of coffee from his cup.

'We're guessing she'll make a drop off the coast of France,' Sullivan said. 'Somewhere in the Bay of Biscay beyond the territorial limit. The Gascony coast is perfect for a clandestine landing. Then another drop off the Italian coast. We don't know where. The Bay of Naples is getting too hot for them so I'd guess they'll try somewhere further south.'

'Where?' Carlsen said. 'Calabria?'

'Not Calabria,' Enqvist replied. 'The 'Ndrangheta control too much territory down there. Maybe Puglia or Basilicata. There are plenty of isolated bays they can use.'

'You have some intelligence to back up this guess-work?'

'We know the *Maria Vasquez* made a drop in the Bay of Biscay,' Sullivan said.

'Know?' Carlsen said.

'Well, we're pretty certain. Cigarettes from the ship ended up in a warehouse in Bayonne. The Bay of Biscay seems the most logical place they were offloaded. And we know Hal Montague is supplying both the French and Italian black markets.'

'Do you?'

Sullivan told him about the customs surveillance of the Golden Valley Inn. Carlsen stroked his moustache with the side of his forefinger, something he did when he was thinking, and when he was nervous.

'You *have* been busy,' he said. 'It might have been better if you'd informed me about this earlier.' He gave them a glance of mild reproof.

'We had to move fast,' Sullivan said.

'Hmm.' Carlsen didn't press the point.

'Montague, Luciani, Lafon, a triumvirate who between them control a sizeable part of the European contraband business,' Sullivan continued. 'And the *Reunion Star* is their ship.'

'More guesswork?'

'To some extent,' Sullivan admitted. 'We don't

PAUL ADAM

know much about her. Five-thousand-tonne general
cargo ship, registered in Vanuatu so the true owner-
ship will be hard to verify. The Vanuatu registry of
shipping in New York is closed over the weekend so
we won't be able to find out any more about her till
Monday, late afternoon Brussels time.'

'And she sails?'

'Nine am, from Antwerp.'

Carlsen turned away to look out of the window.
Across the road outside, on the other side of a low
wooden fence, was the Overijse golf course. Two men
in caps and showerproof jackets were about to tee off
on one of the holes. Carlsen watched the first man
drive, following the ball as it soared away through the
air and landed on the mowed stripes of the fairway.

'What are you proposing?' he asked without looking round.

'Twenty-four-hour surveillance from the moment
the *Reunion Star* leaves Antwerp.'

Carlsen turned back. He finished his coffee and
placed the empty cup carefully on the tray before
he spoke.

'On the high seas?'

'And along the French coast,' Sullivan said.

'That will mean satellite surveillance. That's not
easy, and it's very expensive. And the coast, what are
you suggesting? That the whole west coast of France
is watched? Have you spoken to the *Douane*?'

'Not yet,' Claire said. 'I was going to call Allard
after this meeting. Assuming you gave us the go-
ahead, of course,' she added tactfully.

Carlsen acknowledged the remark with a terse snort. He fixed Claire with a look that was almost a glare.

'And what do you think Allard will say?'

Claire shifted uncomfortably in her seat. 'I don't know.'

'I'll tell you what he'll say. He'll say he doesn't have the manpower to mount an effective surveillance of that length of coastline.'

'It won't be the whole coast,' Claire retorted. 'We can narrow it down. Once the *Reunion Star* heaves to and starts to offload, we'll know roughly where the boats intend to come ashore. If we move fast, we can be there waiting for them.'

Carlsen pursed his lips doubtfully and wandered back to the window. Enqvist pressed their case.

'We know these are big-time smugglers, Ole. Now's our chance to get them.'

'Like you did on Wednesday night?' Carlsen said. Then he sighed. 'I'm sorry, that was unfair. But you see my point? You were certain then and look what happened. We're working on supposition, not hard evidence.'

'It's not supposition,' Enqvist said. 'We know the *Reunion Star* has been involved in smuggling.'

'Hazelnut oil, not cigarettes. There's a difference,' Carlsen said.

'The *Maria Vasquez* also smuggled hazelnut oil. The pattern is the same.'

'But we know almost nothing about this ship,' Carlsen said. 'You want me to authorise a massive surveillance operation on little more than guess-work. Even if the *Reunion Star has* shipped contra-band cigarettes in the past, it doesn't necessarily mean she will this trip. What if we mobilise French Customs and the *Reunion Star* sails straight past France and on to West Africa? How will we look then? We can't afford another fiasco like East Mid-lands.'

'There's always an element of risk. Nothing is foolproof,' Sullivan interjected.

'I know what you're saying. But the Director is taking a lot of political criticism after what happened on Wednesday night. It's a bad time to attempt something with this degree of risk attached to it.'

'That's exactly what the smugglers want,' Sullivan responded heatedly. 'They want to tie our hands. That was what East Midlands was all about. If we do nothing they've beaten us. For God's sake, Ole, we're an operational unit. We're not a bunch of pen-pushing bureaucrats waiting for our pensions like everyone else in the Commission. We're here to take action, to *do* something about trafficking. So sometimes we make mistakes. The only people who never make mistakes are people who do nothing all day. If we play this the way the smugglers want it, we might as well give up and go home now.'

Carlsen gazed out of the window again. From his silence, Sullivan knew that his argument was having some effect. But Carlsen wasn't going to be steamrollered.

'I still don't like it,' he said. 'It's too hurried.

Something like this has to be carefully planned and executed.'

'We don't have time,' Sullivan said. 'They're making their move. We have to counter it. They only met yesterday, but I'm certain their next shipment leaves on Monday. We know Montague is connected to Julius Wolf. He may well have been trafficking for years using Wolf as a cover. Gilles Lafon is linked to Montague and implicated in the payment of bribes to at least one senior French customs officer. Armando Luciani is one of the two most powerful Camorra bosses in Naples. And the *Reunion Star* has smuggling written all over her. How much more evidence do you need?'

Out on the golf course a thin stick of a man in a garish yellow sweater was teeing off, hooking his ball far into a patch of long rough. He snatched up his tee angrily and stomped off down the fairway with his partner. Carlsen watched him, then turned and walked to the tray. He poured himself some more coffee, buying a little extra time to think.

Finally he looked up and sighed. 'You'd better be right about this.'

'You're giving us the okay?' Sullivan said.

'Yes, I'm giving you the okay.'

'*Ciao*, Antonio. How's the *Maria Vasquez* investigation going?' Sullivan said.

'Don't ask,' Casagrande replied curtly. 'It's a sore point.'

'Did you find the blue Fiat van?'

'Yes, abandoned in Bari docks.'

'Bari? They went across to Yugoslavia?'

'We don't know where they went. The trail's gone cold. What are you doing anyway, ringing on a Saturday? Haven't you got anything better to do?'

'Things have been happening.' Sullivan explained what they'd agreed with Carlsen.

'I'll see if I can increase the surveillance on Luciani,' Casagrande said.

'It'll only be for a short time. Something's going to happen in the next couple of days, I'm sure of that.'

'I'll put some men on to it. I was intending to ring you in any case.'

'Oh yes?'

'Those names you gave me last week: Montague and Doyle. I had someone keep a lookout on the incoming airline passenger lists. Simon Doyle flew in on Alitalia this morning. A team covered his arrival. He knows his stuff. We lost him for a couple of hours around lunchtime but we were right behind him the rest of the time.'

'What was he doing? Visiting Luciani?'

'Strangely no. He went to see Dino Falzone.'

Sullivan frowned. 'The other Camorra boss. Why?'

'Ah, if only we could eavesdrop on Falzone's meetings. We don't know. Doyle was with him for half an hour. Perhaps they've fallen out with Luciani and are changing sides.'

'Or perhaps they're selling cigarettes to both of them.'

'Now that,' Casagrande said, 'would be a very dangerous game to play.'

They were alone in the office. Enqvist had just left for some unspecified evening appointment. Claire walked over and perched herself on the corner of Sullivan's desk.

'You want to go for dinner?' she said.

Sullivan looked at her. She was very beautiful. He felt the same physical attraction, the same stirrings of desire, but something inside him had changed since Tuesday night. Since Kate and the boys had been attacked. Things were no longer so simple, and it wasn't merely guilt overriding his libido. The attack had jolted him. It had made him reconsider his priorities, reassess his loyalties and what really mattered to him. He wondered what he was going to do.

'Maybe not tonight,' he said.

'What's the matter?'

'I don't know. I'm sorry. I've things on my mind. Worries.'

'Your family?'

Sullivan nodded. 'It's a bad time. I'm sure you understand.'

Claire pursed her lips, giving him a long searching glance.

'Yes, I understand,' she said.

Lying back on the shiny leather sofa in the study of his town house, Montague stared at Doyle with a mixture of puzzlement and surprise.

'He wants to do *what*?' he said.

'Make the payment in person.'

Montague sat up and swung his legs on to the floor.

'What the fuck's he playing at?'

Doyle gave a shrug. 'He wants to see the merchandise for himself before he pays. He says he doesn't see why he should take all the risk.'

'He doesn't trust us?'

'Not after last time. His view is that he paid in advance and ended up with nothing. He thinks we should share the loss if the cigarettes are seized.'

'Does he now?' Montague clenched a fist in anger. 'And where does he think he's going to get his supplies from if we call off the deal? The market's sewn up tighter than a camel's arse in a sandstorm. Does he think the multi-nationals will deal directly with a known racketeer like him?'

'I don't know what he thinks,' Doyle said mildly. 'I'm just telling you what he said. He'll pay for the cigarettes when he sees them for himself.'

'Cash? Does he know what fifteen million dollars looks like? What's he bringing, a removal van?'

'He'll pay in bearer bonds.'

Montague scowled at the wall for a time. Then he said: 'What's he doing? This doesn't make sense.'

'I'll handle it,' Doyle said. 'Leave it to me.'

Montague turned his head to look at him. His lip twisted into a cynical smile.

'Leave you with fifteen million in bearer bonds?'

'I'll look after them.'

'Not without me you won't.'

There was a knock on the door. Serena walked in.

'Hal . . .'

'Yes, yes, I'm coming,' Montague said tetchily. 'We're just finishing.'

'If you don't change now, we'll be late for the show.'

'I'm coming.'

'What are you going to see?' Doyle said.

'Some shitty musical,' Montague said. 'What is it, *Camelot*?'

'It's *Carmen*, the opera,' Serena explained patiently.

'They're all the same to me.'

Montague heaved his large frame up from the sofa and went out of the study. Serena listened for his footsteps on the stairs before gently closing the door.

'Well?'

Doyle nodded. 'It's all fixed.'

'Falzone too?'

'Exactly as we discussed.'

Serena smiled archly. 'What a good boy you are, Simon. And good boys deserve a reward.'

'Give it a rest, Serena.'

'Spoilsport,' she said, stepping nearer and kissing him playfully.

She unzipped his fly. Doyle pushed her hand away.

'Are you mad?'

'Don't you like it? The possibility of getting caught *in flagrante*. Doesn't it turn you on?'

'Not now. Soon we'll have all the time in the world.'

PAUL ADAM

'But I don't want to wait,' Serena said petulantly.
She slipped her hand inside his trousers.

'Christ, Serena, at least lock the bloody door.'

It had been a long time since Enqvist had felt this
way about a woman. Since he'd experienced the
nervous sickness, the sleepless nights and obsessive
thoughts that were the hallmark of sexual infatuation.
He thought he'd long passed the stage when a woman
could arouse such powerful emotions in him. He was
troubled. Unreasoned passion in adolescence was
understandable, a necessary stage in the process of
growing up. But in a middle-aged man it seemed
grotesque, somehow indecent.

He'd dated a few women in the three years since
he'd split up with his wife, slept with some of them.
But none of them had afflicted him with the fierce
irrational desire he felt for Juliana Rietveld. She was
in his thoughts most of his waking hours, a distant,
tantalising dream that distracted and unsettled him.
He wanted her, but he knew there was something
rash about his ardour. He was being a fool, yet
the sensation was so intense and pleasurable he
didn't want to lose it by letting his head overrule
his lust.

Even now, sitting together in a *trattoria* enjoying
pepperoni pizza and a cheap Chianti, he could feel
the raw sexual power of her presence. Juliana was
across the table from him, her lovely features touched
by the flickering candlelight. Stig watched her sur-
reptitiously as she ate. He had no idea how she felt

about him, she'd never opened out in that way, but she seemed to want to be with him and that was more than enough for the time being.

'When do you have to go back to Amsterdam?' he said.

'Tomorrow evening. I have a fitting first thing on Monday morning. But I'm free tomorrow afternoon. The photo shoot should be finished by two at the latest. You could show me some of Brussels.'

'I'd like that,' Stig said. 'But I have to work tomorrow.'

'On Sunday?'

Stig made a face and nodded.

'I thought you Eurocrats only worked Monday to Friday.'

'Something urgent's come up. I can't cancel it, I'm afraid.'

'What time will you finish?' Juliana said. 'Maybe we could have dinner before I catch my train.'

'I may not be in Brussels.'

'Oh. Never mind.'

The disappointment was transparent in her face. Stig took her hand and squeezed it.

'I don't know what I'm doing yet, it hasn't been decided. I might have to leave town at short notice.'

'Somewhere exotic, I hope.'

Stig laughed. 'I'd hardly call Antwerp or Bordeaux exotic.'

'Bring me back a present.'

'I will.'

They went to his apartment after they'd eaten. It

was a cramped one-bedroom flat on the second floor of an old converted house. Enqvist hadn't chosen it for its ambience, nor its location, on the seedier fringes of Schaerbeek. He gave so much of his salary to his ex-wife and daughter – by guilt-ridden choice, not compulsion – that it was all he could sensibly afford. But he'd cleaned and aired it and tidied away the clutter – a rare occurrence – in the hope that Juliana would accompany him home. He had a bottle of champagne in the fridge and Godiva chocolates to go with it. And for once he had a clear head, having made sure he'd drunk only a couple of glasses of wine.

He went into the kitchen and poured the champagne. When he returned to the living room, Juliana was standing by his desk, leafing through an old pile of European Commission periodicals he'd never got round to throwing away.

'This lot looks boring,' she said.

'I wouldn't know. I never read them,' Stig replied. 'Like everyone else in the Commission.'

He handed her a glass and held out the box of chocolates. Juliana shook her head.

'I shouldn't.'

'Go on. Just one.'

Juliana took a sip of her champagne.

'Why don't we take them to bed with us?' she said.

Stig was lying on his back, snoring gently, when Juliana pulled aside the duvet and slipped out of bed. She waited a few seconds. Stig didn't stir. She crept softly to the door and went out. The living room was in darkness, but she knew exactly where she'd left her handbag. She rummaged inside it and took out a cellular phone. She listened again, then went into the bathroom, shutting the door carefully behind her. She sat on the lid of the toilet, the phone in her hand, and tapped in a number.

It was two o'clock in the morning when the sudden, jarring noise of the phone woke him. Montague reached out from the warmth of his bed and fumbled for the receiver.

'Yes?'

It was Ilse Ameling.

Montague sat up and switched on the bedside lamp. He listened for a few minutes, interjecting questions as Ilse spoke. Then he hung up and punched in a number.

'Simon, it's me. Get over here now. I don't care what fucking time it is. Now. There's been a change of plan.'

TWENTY

Sullivan rose early, woken by the dawn chorus of birds in the horse chestnut trees outside the bedroom window. He took a shower and was dressed and finishing breakfast by eight o'clock. He thought about ringing Kate – the bitter rancour of their last exchange still weighed heavily on his conscience – but it was only seven am in England, an ungodly hour to attempt a reconciliation, so he telephoned Stig instead. A prearranged alarm call. They had a lot to get through during the day and Enqvist could never drag himself out of bed on weekdays let alone a Sunday.

There was no reply. Maybe he wasn't home, maybe he'd left for the office already, maybe he was sleeping off a Saturday night on the town. Sullivan knew which option was most likely. He gave him half an hour then called again. Still there was no answer. Sullivan threw on his coat and went out to his car.

The Tervurenlaan through the Forêt de Soignes felt almost deserted the traffic was so thin compared to the weekday rush hour. Sullivan drove at a steady pace and was in Schaerbeek in twenty minutes. He parked up the street and walked the last hundred metres to Stig's apartment building. The front door was swinging open as if someone had just come in or gone out and forgotten to close it properly behind them. Sullivan went upstairs. Approaching the second floor he heard a door click shut and the sound of a woman's high heels on the wooden floorboards. A tall blonde in a black overcoat with a velvet collar was coming away from Enqvist's door. She glanced at Sullivan as she passed him and he turned his head to watch her go down the stairs. There was something familiar about her face. He stood there on the landing for a time, trying unsuccessfully to remember where he'd seen her before. He shrugged and headed for Stig's door. He was about to ring the bell when it came to him.

Dear God, no. It couldn't be.

Perhaps he was mistaken. He'd caught only a brief glimpse of her. Maybe it was simply a likeness he'd detected, some faint similarity that was leading his memory astray. But he had to make sure. He went back out to his car and drove to Beaulieu.

The surveillance photographs from Amsterdam were in the secretaries' office where he'd left them on Friday night. He went through them quickly and found the one he was looking for. He'd hoped he was wrong, but there was no mistake. With dread in his heart, he slid the print into his pocket, returned to his car and drove back to Stig's apartment.

He rang the bell and knocked on the door for almost half a minute before Stig finally answered. He was unshaven, bleary-eyed and barefoot. The navy-blue dressing gown he was wearing was open at the top. Curls of fine blond hair poked out through the gap.

'Did I wake you?' Sullivan said.

'What time is it?'

Sullivan walked into the living room. He pulled open the curtains. Enqvist winced and held up a hand to shield his eyes as the sunlight flooded in. The apartment was tidier than Sullivan had ever seen it. The clothes, the junk, the takeaway food containers and empty beer cans which normally featured prominently were nowhere to be seen. Sullivan could smell traces of a woman's perfume in the air.

'You never told me you had a new girlfriend,' he said.

'Uh?'

Enqvist blinked at him, still half asleep.

'I saw her leave,' Sullivan said.

'That was ages ago. Have you been outside all this time?'

'I went to the office to get something. Have you known her long?'

'A couple of weeks. Why?'

'Nice-looking. Very tasty. Where did you meet her?'

'What is this?' Enqvist said.

'What's her name?'

'What business is it of yours?'

'Her name, Stig. Tell me her name.'

'Juliana Rietveld.'

'Dutch?'

Enqvist stared at him. He was fully awake now.

'What's your problem? Why are you being so aggressive?'

'Where did you meet her?' Sullivan repeated.

'In Rotterdam. She's a model. What the hell is this, an interrogation?'

Sullivan pulled out the photograph and gave it to him.

'That's her, isn't it?'

Enqvist studied the print. 'It looks like her. Where did you get this?'

'It's one of the surveillance pictures from the Golden Valley Inn.'

Enqvist's mouth fell open. He swallowed.

'So?' he said hoarsely.

'You can do better than that. She was photographed coming out of a brothel. What do you think she is, a stunning beauty like her, the cleaning lady?'

'I'm sure there's another explanation,' Enqvist said defensively.

'She's a whore, Stig. Hellendoorn identified her as one. And her name's not Juliana Rietveld, it's Christine Stokkel.'

Enqvist slumped down into an armchair, still holding the photograph. He passed a hand over his face, rubbing his bloodshot eyes and the stubble on his jaw.

'How did you meet her?' Sullivan said.

Enqvist didn't reply. He seemed too numb to speak.

His eyes were fixed on the photograph. On the grainy close-up of a woman emerging from a door, the wind catching at her blonde hair, throwing a few strands across her cheeks.

'Stig?'

'Outside the hotel,' Enqvist replied in a whisper. 'We went for dinner.'

'How many times have you seen her?'

'Just three.'

'Didn't you suspect?'

'Why should I have suspected?'

Enqvist lifted his head and gazed bleakly at Sullivan. Sullivan turned away, unable to look at him. There was no easy, no kind way of doing this.

'Look at her. Then look at yourself.'

It was cruel. But he had to do it.

'I'm not that bad-looking,' Enqvist said plaintively. 'Women fall for uglier men than me.'

'Rich men, famous men, charismatic men. Why would she go for someone like you?'

'Thanks.'

Sullivan sighed. 'Jesus, Stig, wake up. They set you up with a prostitute. What did you tell her?'

'Nothing.'

'You'd better come clean on this. What did you tell her about your work?'

'Nothing. I'm always careful about things like that.'

Sullivan studied him clinically, trying to forget for a moment that Enqvist was his friend.

'You knew, didn't you?'

'No,' Enqvist replied vehemently.

'Or guessed.'

That was closer to the mark. Enqvist heaved himself out of his chair and went to the drinks table against the wall. He poured himself a shot of brandy and gulped down a mouthful. Sullivan didn't try to stop him. One more wouldn't make any difference.

Enqvist returned to the armchair and sat down heavily, the glass clutched between his hands.

'It's all right for you,' he said. 'You have a wife, kids, some kind of life outside the office. What do I have? Nothing. She's a beautiful woman. I fell in love with her.'

'She's a prostitute,' Sullivan said harshly. 'And you got the hots for her.'

Enqvist gave no sign that he'd heard for he went on: 'She's the best thing that has happened to me in years. It's the male business traveller's fantasy, isn't it? Get picked up by a gorgeous woman and screw away the boredom of the Karlsruhe Holiday Inn, or wherever. But it never happened to me. Until Rotterdam.'

He drank some more brandy and stared down at the floor.

'Why should I have guessed? Am I really that unattractive? I was lonely. I thought she genuinely liked me. What was wrong with that?'

His voice cracked. Sullivan hoped he wasn't going to break down on him. He didn't think he could cope with that.

'Did you take money from her?'

'No, never,' Enqvist said fiercely. 'I swear. We just had dinner a few times.'

'Just dinner? You were set up, Stig. Someone paid her to lay you.'

Enqvist was silent. He looked at the photograph again.

'I know,' he said quietly. 'But she was one illusion I could have lived with for longer.'

Sullivan sat down opposite him on the sofa.

'What did you tell her about your work?' he asked again.

'Not much. Nothing of any importance.'

'Think, Stig. Have you mentioned anything about Montague, or Lafon or Luciani?'

'No.'

'Or the *Reunion Star*?'

'No. I told her I had to work tomorrow, but that's hardly classified.'

'Is that all? I need to know, Stig.'

Enqvist drained his glass. He glanced up, then away across the room. Sullivan saw the momentary flicker of guilt in his eyes.

'What else?' he said.

Stig went to refill his glass. Sullivan stood up and snatched the bottle from him.

'What else?'

The reply was a long time coming.

'I mentioned I might have to go to Antwerp or Bordeaux,' Enqvist said eventually, adding hurriedly: 'But that wouldn't mean anything to her.'

'It would mean something to Montague.' Sullivan

was angry now. 'You arsehole, Stig. You think they can't interpret a piece of information like that and work out exactly what we're doing?'

'They'd need more than that.'

'You think they'll take the chance? They know we're on to the *Reunion Star* as sure as if you'd told them so in writing. Christ, Stig, what the fuck were you doing?'

Sullivan walked across the room to the telephone.

'What are you going to do?' Enqvist said.

'What choice do I have?' Sullivan replied. 'You've blown the whole bloody operation.'

'Rob, give me a chance.'

Sullivan paused, his hand hovering over the telephone. Enqvist was gazing at him like a remorseful child, his eyes frightened, despairing.

'You make that call and I'm finished,' he said despondently. 'Not just my career but my life. If this comes out I'll never work again. The *Tullverk* won't take me back and who else would employ me? I know it's what I deserve and I can understand why you're angry.'

'I'm not angry,' Sullivan said. 'Disappointed, sad, but not angry. It was so stupid, so unnecessary.'

'Help me, Rob. I swear that's all I told her. I never took any bribes. I'm not corrupt, just foolish. Give me a chance to redeem myself.'

Sullivan studied him compassionately, remembering the two years they'd worked together and feeling acutely the bonds and responsibilities of friendship. He moved away from the phone and sat down again.

'Redeem yourself how?'

'I don't know. We can work something out. We can sort out the mess without anyone else knowing. I know we can.' He saw the doubts in Sullivan's face and continued: 'I won't jeopardise your future, I promise. If anything happens, I'll say you never knew.'

Sullivan let out a long, weary sigh. 'We'll have to tell Claire.'

'Will we?'

'She's part of the team. She has to be on board. That's the only way it will work.'

'Okay.'

'Get dressed. We'll discuss it on the way to the office.'

Claire sat by her desk in stunned silence, listening to the two men talking, sharing out the explanation between them. Then she turned to Sullivan and said: 'I need to talk to you in private.'

They went down the corridor to the secretaries' office. No one else was in. The building was eerily quiet, all the other doors shut and locked. Claire pushed the door to and looked at Sullivan, her face tight with anger.

'You expect me to go along with this?' she demanded.

'No, I don't expect it. You have to make the decision yourself.'

'And if I say I'm calling Carlsen now?'

'That's your choice.'

'Jesus, Rob, what are you doing?'

'He's my friend. He's made a mistake, but he deserves a chance.'

'A mistake? Is that what you call it?'

'He's not corrupt. He's taken no pay-offs, sold no information.'

'He's blown a major operation. He's slept with a prostitute hired by organised criminals. Don't you think that's serious?'

'Claire, calm down.'

'Don't tell me to calm down.'

Claire took a deep breath. Her eyes were on fire. Sullivan moved towards her and tried to put his hand on her arm. She backed away.

'Don't try that, Rob. This isn't the time. This is business, a question of professional ethics.'

'He made one slip, that's all. As far as Stig was concerned it was an innocent relationship. Have you never told a boyfriend a few details of your job?'

'I've never compromised an important trafficking investigation.'

'Don't be so hard on him.' Sullivan paused. She was hostile, unreceptive, but he was sure he could persuade her. 'Look, you said it's a question of professional ethics. Do you think it's ethical to ruin him because he fell in love with a woman? Is that such a crime?'

'You stick together don't you, you men? It's something you can all see yourselves doing, making fools of yourselves over a whore.'

She turned away, shaking her head. 'You're asking me to cover it up.'

'I'm not. If what we're suggesting works, it won't matter any more.'

Claire looked back at him. 'You think so?'

'Montague knows we're on to the *Reunion Star*, so he'll find another way of getting cigarettes through to his customers. By road or rail. He'll try to do it quickly. He has a distribution network to feed. This is a regular business, he does it all the time. My guess is he'll want to do it today before we find out the *Reunion Star* isn't going to offload. Because while we're concentrating on the ship we won't be watching other routes.'

'You don't know that.'

'I know. It's a risk. But I think it's worth taking.'

Claire didn't respond. She didn't like it. Her head told her to wash her hands of the affair and look out for herself. But there was something selfish, even disloyal about doing that. She was part of a team, and a team could only function on the basis of absolute solidarity between its members. You stuck together or you were nothing.

'Just one day,' Sullivan said. 'Stig deserves that, at least.'

'And if you're wrong?'

'If I'm wrong, we're all in the shit.'

The waiting was beginning to get to them. Sitting in the office, drinking coffee and staring at the walls. Waiting for something to happen.

With each hour that passed Claire began to wonder

again whether they were doing the right thing. No one talked much. Once or twice she caught Sullivan's eye and he looked away, distancing himself from her. She could sense he was cooling towards her. It made her angry. She didn't like being used.

Enqvist walked over to the filter machine and refilled his cup, glancing enquiringly at the other two. They shook their heads. Sullivan felt sick. He was tired but his system was so saturated with caffeine he couldn't relax.

The phone rang, breaking the silence like an alarm. Claire snatched up the receiver.

'Yes?' She listened. 'When?'

She scribbled down a few notes. Then her face fell.

'Yes, thanks anyway.'

She hung up.

'Antwerp,' she said. 'Laterveer Voorden have asked Customs for clearance to release fifteen thousand cases for shipment by rail to Munich.'

'Munich?' Enqvist looked away, disappointed.

They could rule out consignments within the EU, when duty would have to be paid before the cigarettes left the bonded warehouse. They were looking for a destination outside the Fifteen, for cigarettes in transit duty free.

'It's not going to be today,' Claire said pessimistically.

It wasn't what the others wanted to hear.

'Give it a few more hours,' Enqvist said.

* * *

Mid-afternoon there were two phone calls in quick succession.

The first, from UK Customs. Montague and Doyle had taken a British Airways flight from Heathrow to Charles de Gaulle, Paris.

The second, from Casagrande. Armando Luciani had flown Alitalia from Naples to Turin.

Enqvist permitted himself a small smile.

'What did I say? More coffee anyone?'

Half an hour later, the phone rang again. Claire answered.

'It's your wife,' she said to Sullivan.

He took the receiver, turning away and saying quietly: 'Hi. Are you at home? I'll call you back immediately.'

He hung up, sensing Claire watching him, and went out. Down the corridor in the secretaries' office, he clicked the door shut behind him and rang Colchester.

'Sorry, I didn't want Stig and Claire listening in,' he explained. 'How are things?'

'Okay. Very quiet,' Kate said.

'The boys?'

'They're fine. They're out in the garden playing football.'

'And you?'

'I'm fine too.'

Sullivan listened, gauging her mood from the tone of her voice, from the silences between the words. There was no hostility, but he could sense a tension in her; something she wanted to say.

'Rob,' she said and paused. 'I'm sorry about the other day. I was angry. I shouldn't have upped and left like that.'

'I don't blame you,' Sullivan said. 'I was in the wrong. I should have been with you. You needed me.'

'Well, anyway, I behaved badly. I'm sorry.'

'I'm sorry too. It was my fault.'

'Okay, it was your fault,' Kate said.

Sullivan laughed. They'd been together for a long time. They understood each other. There were bonds between them which no row could threaten. Which no casual infidelity could sever. Sullivan felt the permanence of those ties with a profound sense of relief and certainty.

'I wish you were here,' he said. He wanted to hold her, to give her some physical confirmation of his loyalty.

'Me too,' Kate replied. 'We're not meant to be apart. It's not right, we're a family.'

'I'll take some time off when this is out of the way. Come home for more than a weekend.'

'I'd like that. We need it, Rob. Nothing's changed, has it?' Her voice was soft, a little tentative.

'No, I'm still the same. We can make this work. Two more years and I'll be home permanently.'

'I want it to work, don't you?' Kate said.

He didn't hesitate. 'Yes, I want it to work.'

Queyras and Pigout were waiting for Montague and Doyle outside the arrivals terminal at Charles de

Gaulle. They followed the Englishmen's taxi into Paris, crossing the *périphérique* at the Porte de la Chapelle and continuing on towards the city centre. Approaching the Gare du Nord, the taxi turned off west towards Montmartre, finally coming to a halt outside a restaurant near the Place Pigalle. Montague and Doyle paid off the driver and, carrying their small overnight bags, went into the restaurant. Queyras and Pigout watched from their parking space fifty metres up the street.

'Something's not right,' Queyras said, looking out of his window at the seedy shopfronts, the litter-strewn pavements. 'A couple of guys like that, an area like this.'

'Relax,' Pigout said. 'They're crooks. They're at home here.'

'We needed more than one car to do this properly.'

'On Sunday afternoon overtime? Think of the budget,' Pigout said with heavy sarcasm.

Queyras fidgeted restlessly in his seat, tapping his fingers on his outstretched legs. Finally he pushed open his door and got out.

'I'm going to take a look round the back.'

The package was inside the cistern in the men's toilet at the rear of the restaurant, tightly wrapped in oilskin and plastic. Doyle lifted it out and tore off the protective layers. Inside, clean and dry, was a loaded SIG-Sauer automatic pistol and spare clip. Doyle slipped them into his pocket and went back out into the dining area.

The place was almost empty. A few stragglers left over from lunchtime were drinking coffee at their tables but the evening rush was a few hours away yet. Montague was at the bar, sipping an Armagnac while the barman kept out of his way washing glasses at the sink. At the other end of the counter a pug-nosed man in a tan leather jacket was nursing a bottle of beer and a Gauloise. He glanced round as Doyle walked up to the counter and nodded at him, then stubbed out his cigarette and stood up. Doyle and Montague followed him out through the kitchens to the waiting BMW.

Coming round the corner into the backstreet, Queyras was just in time to see the three men climbing into the car and driving off.

Hellendoorn rang from Amsterdam at five thirty in the afternoon. Claire took the call, speaking in Dutch, then relayed the message in English to Sullivan and Enqvist.

'He's just had a fax from Customs in Rotterdam. They've cleared a consignment of twenty thousand master cases for shipment by rail to Belgrade. A last-minute order.'

'Which warehouse?' Sullivan said.

'Van Vliet.'

'And the route?'

'Paris, Lyon, Turin, Trieste, Zagreb.'

Sullivan glanced at Enqvist, feeling a pulse of excitement which he refrained from showing. The ingredients looked right but he'd learnt not to jump to conclusions without a lot more information.

'When does it leave?'

'He's finding out and will call back.'

'Do we know the name of the shipper or the consignee?'

'The shipper is an agent in Rotterdam,' Claire said. 'The consignee, a company in Yugoslavia, Zoric Repajic.'

'Spell that,' Enqvist said, switching on his computer terminal and logging on.

He ran the name through both the UCLAF database and Dun and Bradstreet. The company wasn't listed in either.

'Dead end.'

'I have an idea,' Claire said.

She made a short phone call, speaking in Dutch. Sullivan looked over her shoulder and saw her writing down a number which she then dialled. She had a longer conversation, again in Dutch, taking notes, and hung up.

'That was the agent's office,' she said. 'I said I was ringing from Van Vliet's warehouse, checking the method of payment for the consignment. They gave me a number to call in Liechtenstein. Someone called Baumann.'

'Try it,' Sullivan said.

Claire dialled the number and waited. She let it ring for a long time. There was no reply.

'Another dead end,' Enqvist said.

Sullivan was looking down at Claire's notes.

'Two three seven Konstanzerstrasse, Vaduz? Is that an address for Baumann?'

'Yes. Why?'

Sullivan had his desk drawer open and was sifting though a file. He pulled out a piece of paper.

'Two three seven Konstanzerstrasse is also the address of Herr Walter Busch, the man who paid for the cigarettes on the *Maria Vasquez*. Now is that a coincidence?'

Twenty minutes later Claire took the call from Hellendoorn. She listened, then said something in Dutch which could only have been an expletive.

'The application for customs clearance was made at three o'clock this morning,' she repeated to Sullivan and Enqvist. 'The night shift handled it. The freight arrangements were made shortly afterwards with *Nederlandse Spoorwegen* and the SNCF.'

'And the train? When does it leave Rotterdam?' Sullivan said.

'There was a mix-up at Customs. The information got left in an out-tray and was only noticed at shift change at four o'clock this afternoon. The train left Rotterdam three hours ago.'

They drove flat out to Lille, covering the hundred kilometres in a little under an hour. Philippe Allard had hastily arranged for a helicopter to be waiting there to fly them to Paris. He met them at the heliport at Orly and they transferred to a Customs plane for the flight to Lyon.

Allard had a map of Europe which he spread out over the table inside the plane.

'The train has by-passed Paris and should be somewhere around here by now.' He pointed to a spot about fifty kilometres south of the capital. 'It's scheduled to reach Lyon at half past ten this evening. That's the first stop it makes according to the SNCF freight timetable. It waits there for an hour and a half to unload some wagons and take on more freight, then leaves at midnight for Italy. If they're going to offload the cigarettes within France, Lyon is where they'll do it.'

'There's no possibility of an unscheduled stop before then?' Sullivan said.

Allard shook his head. 'You don't just stop a freight train in the middle of nowhere and unload a few containers. It's not possible, even if you bribed the driver. The SNCF know exactly where all their trains are at a given moment. Lyon is the only place they can do it.'

'And Montague?'

Allard winced. 'We lost him in Paris. He could be anywhere.'

'Shit!'

'Worse. Luciani has disappeared too.'

The freight-marshalling yard was spread out beneath them like a huge steel-ribbed fan, hundreds of wagons lining the silvery tracks.

Allard was by the window of the darkened office, looking out through a pair of night glasses.

'Over there in the middle,' he said. 'Next to the oil tankers. The light grey containers with the black vertical stripes. You see them? That's her.'

Sullivan followed Allard's outstretched arm. There was a line of containers immediately behind the SNCF locomotive. He counted them. Twenty. A thousand master cases to each container, five hundred packets to each case. That was a total of two hundred million cigarettes.

The yard was illuminated by high floodlights placed at intervals across the sidings but much of it, particularly in between the rows of wagons, was in shadow. There was a lot of activity, despite the late hour. Freight cars were being unloaded, their cargoes transferred to waiting lorries, the huge overhead gantry crane was removing containers from flat-backed wagons and a couple of stubby diesel locomotives were shunting rolling stock up and down the tracks. It would have been a relatively simple, inconspicuous operation to unload twenty containers of cigarettes, but there was no sign it was going to happen. In fact, as they watched, more freight cars were being coupled to the rear of the train, making it impossible to detach the cigarette wagons.

They waited ten minutes, then fifteen. Sullivan glanced at his watch. It was nearing eleven o'clock. The fist around his stomach was tightening its grip. No one spoke, the tension in the office had stifled all desire for conversation. They stood by the windows in silence, watching for someone to make a move.

Another ten minutes passed. Then Allard lifted his night glasses and trained them on the wagons.

'Here we are,' he said softly. He picked up his radio and spoke into it.

The others peered out through the glass. The wagons were two hundred metres away but they could just make out the shadowy figure of a man walking down the length of the train and stopping by the cigarette containers.

Allard's radio crackled and a faint voice said something garbled in French. Allard responded with a curt *'Non'*.

He watched the figure through the glasses. The man lit a cigarette, the sudden flare of the match highlighting his face and peaked cap, then he walked on past the wagons.

'SNCF security,' Allard explained. 'Or looks like it.'

'Can we get him out of there?' Sullivan said.

Allard called to one of his colleagues. 'Alain, find out who he is.' Then to Sullivan: 'He might be one of theirs. You can be sure they'll be watching, looking for signs of surveillance. We don't want to show ourselves too soon.'

The man strolled on, seemingly in no hurry to finish his inspection of the train.

'What's he doing?' Enqvist said. 'They're not going to unload with him standing there.'

Allard turned to his colleague who was on the telephone. Alain held up a finger, listening, and came off.

'He's legitimate.'

Allard barked an order into his radio. In the distance, two customs officers jumped down from a wagon parked on the adjacent siding and ran up to the security guard. Words were exchanged and the guard was unceremoniously bundled away.

'Hold him until we've finished,' Allard said into the radio.

Sullivan consulted his watch again. He noticed Allard and then Claire doing the same. Something wasn't right.

'They're not coming,' he said. 'There's no time to unload now.'

'Give it a while longer,' Allard said.

Sullivan shook his head. 'The train leaves in thirty-five minutes. Unless they uncouple the wagons and leave them behind, they're not going to be able to do it.'

'Maybe they're offloading them all in Turin,' Allard said. 'That's the next stop and that's where Luciani disappeared.'

'Maybe,' Sullivan said doubtfully.

They gave it another twenty-five minutes. A final group of wagons was coupled to the back of the cigarette train. Allard checked the cargo manifest they'd obtained from the SNCF.

'That's the lot,' he said. 'It's ready to go now.'

He looked at Sullivan, Claire and Enqvist. 'Perhaps we got the wrong train.'

'No way,' Enqvist said vehemently. 'This is the one. They're going to offload in transit, I'm sure of it.'

Allard shrugged. 'But obviously not here.'

'I want to look inside it,' Sullivan said suddenly.

'What?'

PAUL ADAM

'Just a gut feeling I have. I want to look inside the containers.'

Allard shook his head. 'That's not a good idea. They're sealed.'

'Then we'll unseal them.'

Sullivan headed for the door.

'Rob, don't be hasty,' Enqvist cautioned. 'It might be Turin. We don't want to tamper with the containers if it is.'

'And if it isn't? That train leaves in ten minutes. We need to know now.'

Sullivan broke the customs seal on the first container and swung open the heavy side doors. Crammed tightly inside were brown cardboard boxes marked with serial numbers and the words 'Philip Morris Products Inc, Richmond, VA, USA.' He reached up and dragged one of them out, putting it down on the hard core beside the track and ripping open the top. He shone his torch down. There were red and white cartons of Marlboro cigarettes inside. Sullivan checked a couple, then tipped the box upside down. The cartons tumbled out on to the ground.

'What're you doing?' Allard said, starting to get angry.

Sullivan pulled out another box. Allard grabbed his arm to stop him tearing the top off.

'You can see what's inside. Why open more? You could jeopardise the whole operation.'

Sullivan looked at the faces encircling him: Allard, Claire, Enqvist, a couple of French customs officers.

394

He could see the doubt in their expressions and wondered for an instant whether he was wrong.

'One more,' he said, shaking off Allard's hand.

He ripped open the box and stared down at the cartons inside.

'You see,' Allard said furiously. 'What did you expect to find?'

Embarrassed, Sullivan lifted up the box to replace it in the container. He hesitated. The box didn't feel right. It was too light. He put it back down on the ground.

'What're you doing now?' Allard demanded.

Sullivan lifted out the top layer of cartons. Underneath them was nothing but packing: newspapers and straw and ballast to fill the empty space.

'Merde!' Allard said.

Sullivan walked to the second container and broke open the seals. He swung back the doors. The container was completely empty.

He went down the line, checking the other containers. They were all empty, but in the final one was a single cardboard box. Sullivan carried it back up the track and opened it in front of his colleagues. There was only packing inside. He dug down with his fingers and encountered something hard – a china cup glazed with a dull blue and red pattern. He shone his torch beam on the bottom of the cup and held it up so the others could read the words 'Made in Ukraine'.

'I think they're rubbing it in,' he said.

'How did they *know*?' Stig Enqvist said in disbelief.

'They didn't,' Sullivan replied. 'But Montague's a careful man. That's one of the reasons it's taken us this long to identify him. He couldn't know, but it was worth taking the precaution, running a decoy shipment to keep us busy. What did he have to lose?'

'So where does that leave his trafficking? Where does that leave us?' Enqvist said.

They were back in the office block overlooking the marshalling yard, only this time in a conference room with the lights switched on and the blinds pulled shut. Allard and his team were on one side of the long table, the UCLAF contingent on the other.

'We're missing something,' Claire said. 'Montague's over here, maybe Luciani too. Why, if there's no shipment? What are they doing in France?'

'There is a shipment,' Sullivan said.

'We've checked all the customs clearances,' Enqvist said. 'That train was the only possible target crossing France today.'

'We're overlooking the obvious,' Sullivan said.

Claire sat up abruptly and swore. 'Jesus, of course.'

Enqvist rubbed his eyes. His body was drooping with fatigue.

'Go on,' he said. 'Make me feel stupid.'

'Rotterdam Customs cleared twenty thousand cases for shipment to Yugoslavia by rail,' Claire said. 'If they weren't on the train, and we know now only a few full cases were loaded for show, then where are all the others?' She answered the question herself. 'They're going by road.'

Enqvist blinked. 'How are we going to find twenty-plus lorries in a country the size of France?'

Claire came off the phone to Rotterdam, her face stony.

'The lorries left the warehouse at two o'clock this afternoon, heading for the *Nederlandse Spoorwegen* freight depot in the Europoort,' she said grimly. 'But they never got there, of course. Or at least not those particular lorries. Montague sent substitutes while the real cargo was heading south for France.'

'Two o'clock,' Sullivan said. 'That's ten hours ago. An average speed of, what? Eighty kilometres an hour? Let's say ninety to be safe. They'll have covered nearly a thousand kilometres by now.

They leaned over the map of Europe on the conference table. Allard measured off a length of string according to the mileage table and, putting one end on Rotterdam, drew a pencil arc across France with the other. It formed a curved line starting at the Bay of Biscay just north of Bordeaux, continuing across through the Dordogne, Tarn and mid-Provence and ending at the Italian frontier near Briançon.

'They could have offloaded every single case already,' Claire said. 'And we'll never know where.'

'I think some are going to Italy,' Sullivan replied. 'That's why Luciani's involved.'

Allard glanced at the pencil arc and cursed. 'They could be over the frontier by now,' he said.

He snatched up the telephone, punched in a number and had a short urgent conversation. In mid-flow he broke off and said to Claire: 'Do we know what the lorries look like? Any names, markings?'

Claire shook her head. 'We know nothing about them.'

Allard went back to the phone and resumed his conversation, speaking rapidly, giving instructions.

'We're in luck somewhere at least,' he said, hanging up. 'There's been heavy snow in the Alps. All the northern passes and the Mont Blanc and Frejus tunnels have been closed to traffic since ten o'clock. They'll have to come south, right to the Riviera, to get across into Italy, and every frontier post will be watching for them. They won't get out of France.'

'I wonder if they may be going elsewhere too,' Claire said thoughtfully, looking down at the map.

'What?'

'Some will be offloaded in France, some will be going to Italy, but some may be heading for Spain.' She turned to Allard. 'Can you find out if Bignon is on the night shift at Hendaye?'

Allard gave a nod and picked up the phone. Claire watched him as he spoke, following every word. She knew the answer before he put down the receiver.

'How did you guess?' he said.

'Can you get a team there?'

'You bet I can. The plane is on standby at Lyon airport. I'll make the arrangements now.'

Claire stood up and walked over to the window. She opened a gap in the blinds with her fingers and peered out into the night.

'Something else on your mind?' Sullivan asked. He was standing by her shoulder.

'Montague will expect the frontier customs to be extra vigilant,' she said. 'Land borders are risky. Lorries are too easy to stop and search. What if they're not crossing by road into Italy?'

'How else will they get there?'

'By sea. Lafon runs his business from Toulon. What better way than to transfer the contraband to fast boats and take them along the coast?'

'It's possible,' Sullivan said. 'Perhaps more than possible.'

'What do you say?'

Sullivan reflected for a moment, then nodded. 'Let's go for it.'

Claire looked round at Allard on the phone.

'You'd better make that *two* planes,' she said.

TWENTY-ONE

The atmosphere inside the house was strained. Gilles Lafon, for all his wealth, was an awkward host. He seemed ill at ease in the plush surroundings of his own home, and his obvious discomfort was unsettling for his guests. He'd ordered in drinks and watched them being served by his maid, but his idea of hospitality seemed to go no further. He made no attempt at conversation and constantly drifted in and out of the living room as if he didn't know what to do with himself. Luciani too was on edge, a brooding silent presence who sat in a corner with his two bodyguards, sipping Scotch and glaring at the furniture. Only Montague seemed relaxed. He made a few abortive attempts to break the ice, then gave up when his urbane charm made no inroads into the hostile atmosphere. Losing patience, he escaped on to the terrace at the back of the house with Simon Doyle.

'It's like a fucking funeral in there,' Montague complained irascibly. 'What's the matter with them?'

'They're nervous,' Doyle replied. 'They've never been at the sharp end before. They usually leave all the messy stuff to their subordinates.'

'Nobody made Luciani come, it was his choice,' Montague said. 'Besides, nothing's going to go wrong. I don't know what they're worried about.'

He pulled a cigar from his pocket and lit it, blowing smoke out over the stone parapet. Below them the garden of Lafon's house fell away in a series of steep terraces, each one carefully landscaped with rockeries and shrubs and winding gravel paths. A low brick wall marked the boundary of the property and beyond that was nothing – literally nothing, for the ground ended abruptly in a precipitous cliff which plummeted a hundred feet or more to the rocky shore of the Mediterranean.

Doyle shivered and buttoned up his jacket. The weather was closing in. When they'd first arrived, half an hour earlier, it had been possible to see the glow of lights in the sky above Toulon. Now the skeins of mist had obliterated everything outside a radius of two hundred metres. And the visibility was getting worse. The mist was becoming thicker, the ghost trails merging into a dense sheet of fog which twisted and swirled in the gusting breeze, wrapping ever tighter around the exposed peninsula.

Doyle felt the damp air soak into his flesh, chilling him to the bone. His ears were still aching from the private jet flight that had brought them from Paris to the south coast. The cool wind made them hurt more and he wanted only to go back inside to the warmth of the living room. But Montague was in the mood for talking.

'I don't expect my business dealings to be a party,'

he said, 'but those two, Christ, they're like a couple of corpses. Lafon's a miserable sod, isn't he? All that money and, you know, I think he'd be happier if he were still driving a truck. And Luciani, well, he's just an uncouth thug. Has he got the bearer bonds?'

'In his briefcase, I reckon. He hasn't let it out of his sight.'

Montague sucked on his cigar and exhaled. The smoke drifted out across the garden and was lost in the eddies of mist.

'I don't trust the little shit. What's this all about, bringing me down here to do the deal? Is he plotting something with Lafon?'

Doyle shrugged. 'What would they have to gain? They need you more than you need them.'

'You think so.'

'With Wolf out of the way you control a considerable chunk of the European cigarette market. They can't afford to cross you.'

'Hmm.'

Montague didn't sound convinced. He watched the fog settling over the garden, coiling around the trees and shrubs, insinuating itself into every hidden corner. Beneath the groan of the wind was the distant roar of the waves breaking over the rocks at the base of the cliff.

'Where's your gun?' Montague said quietly.

'Under my jacket.'

Montague nodded. 'Keep it handy.'

The door swung open and four men walked into

the customs post. The sudden draught caught at the papers on the desk, blowing them on to the floor.

'Who the devil are you?' Bignon snarled, bending down to retrieve the documents.

Stig Enqvist pulled out his identity card and held it in front of Bignon's nose.

'We're taking over this post for the night.'

'You're *what*? On whose authority?'

'How many men are on this shift?'

'I don't see what . . .'

'How *many*?'

'Three, including me. What's going on?'

'You'll soon find out.'

Montague looked up at the sky, aware suddenly of a milky luminosity which hadn't been there before. Turning his head, he saw the lance of headlights piercing the mist, the hazy outlines of the lorries behind as they came up the drive from the road.

'About bloody time,' he said, tossing his cigar away.

The haulage depot was on the western fringes of Toulon, an ugly collection of metal-roofed warehouses clustered around a yard filled with trailers and trucks bearing the legend 'G Lafon – haulier'. Allard was searching the inside of the main warehouse with his team of customs officers and a squad from the tactical support unit of the local *gendarmerie*. Sullivan and Claire were checking the yard, examining the containers stacked three high in rows next to the chainlink perimeter fence. The depot had been closed up tight for the night when they'd arrived, a nightwatchman and a security guard the only people on the premises. There was no sign that any lorries had either recently unloaded or were expected.

Claire came out from behind a container and shrugged at Sullivan.

'I can't see anything suspicious. Can you?'

'Is this his only depot?'

'As far as we know.'

'What about the docks? Maybe the lorries are unloading down there.'

Claire shook her head. 'Customs have been on the alert since we left Lyon. There's no way any cigarettes could have been offloaded on to boats without their noticing.'

She stared around the yard. The low mist, tainted a garish yellow by the streetlights, looked like some noxious gas seeping from the earth.

'I'm still sure we're right,' she said. 'Where the hell are they?'

She took a step forward, about to walk out across the yard. Suddenly, Sullivan grabbed her arm and hauled her roughly back into the shelter of the container.

'What the . . .'

'Sssh.'

He gestured at her to be silent then jabbed a finger towards the main warehouse. They peered out carefully, hidden by the bulk of the container.

A door down the side of the building had opened and a figure was waiting in the shadows. It was the security guard. He turned his head, scanning the yard and the road at the front of the depot. Then he sprinted for a gate in the perimeter fence and was momentarily lost from sight. Claire and Sullivan ducked out. The guard was climbing into a Citroën saloon parked in the side street next to the depot. The engine turned over and the headlights blazed out through the darkness. Sullivan and Claire ran to the front of the warehouse. Claire tore open the door of the car they'd arrived in.

'Allard?' Sullivan said.

'No time.'

She was already in the driver's seat, turning the key in the ignition. Sullivan jumped in beside her, pulling his door shut as the car slewed round across the yard and out on to the road. Claire turned down the side street, accelerating hard then jamming on the brakes as they reached a T-junction.

'You see it?' she said.

'No.'

'Shit!'

'Yes, there. Left.'

Claire spun the wheel. The Citroën was a hundred metres in front, turning left on to the main road out of Toulon. Claire sped after it and settled in behind, letting two other cars come in between them. They took the road around the west side of the bay, passing through La Seyne-sur-Mer before climbing the hill towards Cap Sicié. There was less traffic on the road now. Claire let the Citroën pull away a little, following the dull red glow of its rear fog lamps as they twisted their way around the headland. Sullivan suddenly remembered Allard. He pulled out his mobile phone and punched in his number.

'Philippe? Philippe, can you hear me?'

The interference was a harsh, intermittent crackle in his ear. He tried again.

'Philippe, it's Sullivan. We're on Cap Sicié, heading south-west after the security guard. Did you hear me? Fuck!'

The signal broke up altogether, disintegrating into a continuous roar.

'Did he get the message?' Claire said.

'I don't know.'

Enqvist stepped out into the road, swinging his flashlight in an arc. The lorry slowed a little, the brakes hissing, the engine growling as the driver changed gear. Enqvist saw the driver's face in the glare of the frontier floodlights and something about it, the eyes, the expression, made him sure this was the one. He lifted a hand, signalling it to stop.

Then the engine noise changed. Enqvist took a moment to register the difference, to realise the lorry was not slowing now, but accelerating. He flung himself sideways, feeling the current of air tugging at his coat as the lorry raced past. Rolling over on the damp asphalt, he twisted his head round and was just in time to see the chain of steel spikes springing up across the road.

The lorry's front tyres punctured immediately. The cab veered across the carriageway, the tyres shredding, the trailer swinging dangerously out of control behind. The driver braked, fighting to keep the vehicle on the road. The front wheels locked and the cab slewed round. But the articulated trailer kept going, jack-knifing into an unstoppable skid. It swayed violently, its nearside wheels lifting off the road. For a moment it seemed as if it might stay upright, but then, almost in slow motion, it began to keel over. The side of the container hit the ground and with a scream of tortured metal, sparks flying, the trailer slid fifty metres along the road and came to a stop blocking both carriageways.

Enqvist picked himself up, the noise of the crash still ringing in his ears. Two of the customs officers he'd brought with him from Lyon were already at the lorry, clambering on to the side of the cab to get the driver out. The other officers were flagging down traffic, stopping another four identical trucks which were following the first.

Enqvist walked to the overturned lorry. Using a crowbar, he broke open the rear doors of the container. A stack of cardboard boxes tumbled out on to the road. Enqvist ripped one open. A violent spasm of relief and elation surged through him as he looked down at the red and white cartons of cigarettes.

Ten lorries were parked in the wide open courtyard to the side of Lafon's house and on the grass beside the drive. Floodlights on the walls of the buildings around the courtyard illuminated the open doors of one of the containers. Luciani's two bodyguards were hauling out cases of cigarettes and cutting open their tops to check their contents while the Camorra boss watched impassively from the steps leading up to the house.

'It's all in order,' Montague said, unable to conceal his irritation. 'Why would I try to cheat you when I know you're going to open every single case at the other end?'

Luciani said nothing. He waited for his bodyguards to open five or six more boxes and inspect the cartons of cigarettes inside.

'We're wasting time,' Lafon snapped. 'Let's get them out.'

He signalled to a group of thick-set unshaven men standing in front of the servants' quarters. They came across the courtyard, pushing Luciani's bodyguards out of the way, and formed a line from the lorry to the rear of the house where a long flight of steps disappeared over the edge of the cliff. Above the steps, slung between metal pylons, was a thick steel cable which descended in a parabola to the rocky cove below. A metal cage was suspended from a pulley on the cable. The first cases of cigarettes, passed along the line of men, were loaded into the cage and dispatched over the cliff. It was a slick operation, one which the men had obviously carried out many times before.

Montague watched for a moment then went back

into the house with Doyle. They waited for Luciani and his bodyguards to join them in the living room.

'Satisfied?' Montague said.

Luciani sat down and slipped his leather briefcase along the side of the armchair.

'Are you going to give me the money now?' Montague demanded.

The Italian's eyes rolled up slowly from below their heavy lids.

'We have things to talk about first.'

The fog started to thicken as the car sped up the winding coast road, the headlights dancing over the hillside, tracing patterns in the shifting curtain of mist. Sullivan risked a look out of his window as Claire threw the vehicle into another bend and wished he hadn't. The drop to the sea was almost vertical, a sheer wall of rock disappearing into a dark, swirling abyss.

Up ahead, the security guard's Citroën was swinging back and forth across the road, going way too fast for the treacherous conditions. Claire kept pace with him, her mouth clenched tight in concentration. Sullivan hung on to his seat and closed his eyes in silent prayer.

At the brow of the hill, the road straightened out, still running close to the clifftop, then turned inland up a gentler incline. There was forest on one side, rough meadowland on the other – coarse grass and the occasional tree clinging precariously to the slope before it plunged over the edge. In the distance, on a

PAUL ADAM

slight promontory, a house was just visible through the ebb and flow of the mist. Its forecourt was a harsh puddle of light, a bright hole cut out of the surrounding blackness. Figures could be seen moving around in the centre, and on the periphery, little more than hazy shadows, was a cluster of lorries.

The security guard turned off the road into a long driveway leading to the house. Claire braked and pulled over on to the verge, extinguishing the headlights. Sullivan punched in Allard's number on his mobile again. The interference was still there, so loud he had to hold the phone away from his ear. He switched it off and tossed it angrily on to the dashboard.

'We're on our own,' he said.

'What are you talking about?'

Montague maintained his air of pained bemusement, but beneath the frown his mind was racing, calculating the odds, assessing his chances of emerging unscathed from this confrontation.

'You know what I'm talking about,' Luciani said.

'I assure you I don't.'

'Don't fuck with me. I *know* you've been supplying Falzone.'

'Armando, I don't know who told you that, but . . .'

'I *know*,' Luciani broke in fiercely. 'You and the fucking Ukrainians.'

Montague gave an involuntary start. He was alarmed now, his legendary self-assurance starting to slip. Luciani almost smiled.

'I know it all, you *cazzo*. You deal behind my back with my greatest enemy and think I won't find out.'

'I have never dealt with Falzone,' Montague said emphatically.

'No? But you trade with the Ukrainians knowing they're shipping the stuff over from Montenegro into my back yard. Competing directly with me in my own territory. You expect me to sit and take that?'

'You're wrong.'

'Don't tell me I'm wrong.'

Luciani thrust himself up out of his chair to within spitting distance of Montague. Doyle stepped between them, fending Luciani off.

'Calm down,' Doyle said, his hands raised, palms outwards in a gesture of peace.

Luciani glared at Montague and turned away towards his bodyguards who were hovering uncertainly on the edges of the dispute.

Montague recovered his composure but his legs were trembling. He wasn't a physical man; violence scared him.

'I don't know which Ukrainians you mean,' he said. 'I'm sure there's been a misunderstanding.'

Luciani snorted. 'I'll tell you which Ukrainians I mean. I mean the Ukrainians who came to Naples and blew up the *Maria Vasquez*. *Those* Ukrainians.'

'What?'

Montague gaped at him, genuinely stunned.

Luciani grinned. 'You didn't know that, did you? You made a big mistake dealing with *them*. They have

411

no honour, no sense of loyalty. They trade with you then betray you behind your back.'

'They sank her,' Montague whispered. 'Why?'

'Because you're a fool. Work it out. Because the *Maria Vasquez* was supplying me, and they were supplying Falzone. They cut me out of the market there's all the more for them.'

Luciani wiped the spittle off his lips with the back of his hand.

'But we've talked enough.'

He signalled to his bodyguards. They stepped forward, hands reaching inside their jackets. Montague felt his legs give way. His bowels turned to water.

Then suddenly the door banged open and Lafon burst in, his face twisted with panic.

'The *Douane*, they know,' he shouted almost incoherently. 'We have to get out.'

Lying flat in the long wet grass just inside the gates, Claire looked across towards the house. It was half a kilometre away, but the courtyard was so brightly lit it was possible, even in the mist, to see the vertical wall of the cliffs plunging away behind the outbuildings.

'They must have a harbour, a jetty at the very least, down at the bottom,' she said.

Sullivan nodded. 'We have to block their escape routes. Contain them until we can get some back-up.'

'You check the cliff, I'll deal with the drive,' Claire said.

She pulled herself to her feet and took off in a low crouch towards the line of parked lorries.

Lafon was in a state of extreme agitation, babbling uncontrollably, saying the same things over and over.

'They'll come here next, I'm sure of it. After they've finished at the warehouse they'll come here. They know. They *know*, you understand me?'

'Shut up,' Doyle said curtly, stepping in to take charge. He could see from the faces around him that he was the only one calm enough to think clearly.

'They're searching my depot, did you hear me?' Lafon yelled. 'We have to get out.'

'I said shut up. How much time have we got?'

'How should I know? Ten minutes, half an hour.'

'How many lorries have still to be unloaded?'

'What?'

'Get them up to the house now. The cigarettes are what count. We get as many on to the boats as possible and burn the rest.'

'Burn?' Lafon frowned at him.

'Without the cigarettes they have nothing on us. Move yourself, Gilles. Now!'

Lafon stared at him for a second, then spun round and ran out of the living room. Doyle walked over to the window and pulled back the curtain. He could see the lorries lined up down the drive and the curve of the road beyond, but nothing else. No vehicles approaching, no lights, no people. He turned back to the others. The Italians were flustered, thrown by Lafon's interruption. But Luciani was regaining

his composure, remembering what he'd been saying.
Doyle slipped the SIG-Sauer from the waistband of
his trousers. Very coolly, he stepped up behind the
two bodyguards and shot them in the back of the
head. Luciani whipped round, his mouth hanging
open in stunned horror. Doyle shot him between
the eyes.

'Jesus!'

Montague, licking dry lips, was gaping at his aide.
Then his eyes dropped to the three crumpled bodies
on the floor, the blood seeping from their heads and
soaking into the carpet.

Doyle tucked the pistol away under his jacket and
picked up Luciani's briefcase. He snapped it open
and looked inside, going very still. He turned the case
round to show Montague. It was completely empty.

Claire was climbing up into the cab of the nearest
articulated lorry when she heard shouting from the
house and saw men running out from the courtyard
and down the drive. She clicked the door shut behind
her and cast an eye over the controls. No keys in the
ignition. Crouching down, she risked a look out over
the dashboard. The men were splitting up, taking a
lorry each. A short man in a quilted jacket was heading straight for hers, the last in the line. Claire ducked
down and rummaged under the seats. Her fingers
encountered a lumpy plastic satchel – a toolkit. She
felt inside and pulled out a heavy spanner. Holding
her breath, she listened to the footsteps of the driver
as he ran up beside the truck.

He threw open the door and clambered up the steps. As his head came into view, Claire lunged forward, the spanner thudding down on to the top of his skull. The man emitted a low moan and fell backwards off the cab. Claire jumped out. The man was unconscious on the drive, the keys to the lorry next to his outstretched arm. Claire snatched them up, climbed back into the cab and started the engine. She had no licence but she'd been in enough freight depots and stopped enough HGVs to know how to drive one. She engaged reverse gear, removed the handbrake and backed the lorry down the slope, turning the wheel so the trailer swung across in front of the gates, blocking the exit. She leaped down from the cab and hurled the keys away into the night.

Sullivan peered cautiously over the edge of the cliff. Down below was a small semi-circular cove hemmed in by steep rock walls. The sea, confined by jagged outcrops on either side of the cove, raced in through the open mouth in turbulent waves, crashing furiously on to the small shingle beach.

At the far side of the bay, at the bottom of the steps from the house, was a tiny harbour – horseshoe-shaped with a quayside and two concrete jetties protruding into the sea. Three boats were moored inside the shelter of the harbour: two cabin cruisers, the sort of expensive leisure boats that would arouse no suspicion along the Côte d'Azur, and a larger, sleeker craft that most certainly would – a former

East German torpedo boat, the cigarette trafficker's favourite vessel, capable of carrying two thousand cases and, with a top speed in excess of fifty knots, of outrunning every coastguard ship in the Mediterranean.

There were four or five men on the quayside, hurriedly unloading cardboard boxes from the metal cage at the foot of the cable run and carrying them to the torpedo boat. One of them pressed a button on a control panel next to the bottom pylon, activating an electric motor. Swaying violently in the wind, the empty cage started to ascend back up the cliff.

Sullivan scanned the wall below him. It was nothing like as sheer as it first appeared, and it wasn't all rock. In places there were ledges of coarse grass and bare earth cutting across the face. He looked up towards the house. To reach the steps to the cove entailed getting across the brightly lit courtyard in full view of half a dozen people. He had no choice. He lowered his legs over the edge and began to climb down.

'Something's wrong.'

Doyle was standing in the courtyard, staring across the grounds at the HGV blocking the gates.

'Why hasn't that lorry been moved? Where's the driver? What the hell is . . .'

He broke off abruptly. He'd seen something else, an outline on the drive too far away to identify clearly.

'Stay here,' he ordered Montague.

He sprinted across the lawn and down the winding drive. Within fifty metres he knew what the shape on the ground was. He pulled the SIG-Sauer from his jacket and dropped instinctively into a simian crouch as he approached the body. He felt the driver's pulse, saw the sticky coagulated blood on the top of his head. Squatting down, he peered around intently, his spine tingling. He could see nothing suspicious.

He straightened up and ran to the lorry, climbing up into the cab and checking the dashboard. There were no keys in the ignition. He dropped down to the ground again and raced back up the drive.

'Can you move it?' Montague asked anxiously.

'No.'

'*What*? That's the only exit. How do we get the car out? How do we . . .'

'Shut up!' Doyle snarled, his eyes roaming over the grounds, the courtyard, the clifftop. 'Stay close to me and do exactly as I say.'

The fog was getting worse, drifting down into the cove in pea-soup waves. It gusted along the cliffs in patches, one moment revealing the drop to the rocks, the next concealing it. Sullivan was ten metres down, traversing across towards the centre of the bay where the edge had given way to form a spur that dropped in a steep, but not vertical, line to the shore.

He felt his way across, choosing his foot- and hand-holds carefully. The vegetation was wet and slippery. He dug into the thin layer of underlying soil with his fingers and inched cautiously down, his body pressed hard against the edge.

He reached an outcrop of solid rock, its surface

pitted with holes and cracks. This was the first really dangerous moment. There was nothing below the outcrop but a thirty-metre drop to the beach. And no alternative but to cross it.

Sullivan studied the rock face, looking for the darker shadows, the changes in texture which indicated possible ledges or crevasses. Then he stretched out and ran his fingers over the greasy surface, searching for a handhold. His fingers slipped into a narrow gap. He tested it. It was strong enough to hold him. He found a cleft for his toes and pulled himself out on to the outcrop. Very slowly, he manoeuvred his way along it, testing every handhold before he risked his weight on it. The blood was throbbing in his head and he was aware of the sweat beading his forehead. He reached a narrow ledge and paused. He was halfway across the outcrop. Ten more feet and he'd be at the spur.

He went on. He found another crevice for his feet and handholds higher up, spread-eagling himself over the rock. He pulled himself along, feeling with his toes, hanging on tight with his fingers. The spur was almost within reach when he put his left foot on to a tiny ledge and searched for a hold with his left hand. He jammed it into a fissure above his head and swung his right foot across.

Suddenly, the ledge gave way. The rock snapped off with a splintering crack. Sullivan's left foot jolted down and his body dangled loose in space, the weight tearing at his shoulders and arms. He hung on, ignoring the pain in his tendons, feeling desperately for purchase with his feet. His right hand started to slip. He clung on with his fingers till he could feel the jagged rock breaking his skin. His shoes scuffed the cliff below him, searching for something, for anything that would hold. His right foot located a cleft. Sullivan forced his toe in and tested the rock. It held. He eased the pressure on his arms and straightened up, taking his weight on his right leg. Then he slid his left foot into another crack and rested his face on the damp rock, breathing heavily, sick with terror.

He pressed on quickly before he lost his nerve. He concentrated solely on the few feet of rock immediately in front of him, taking each bit as it came. The rest of the outcrop, the drop to the shore didn't exist.

The side of the spur came into view. Sullivan heaved himself up on to it and drew breath.

The ground sloped away beneath him, its surface a mixture of soil and boulders and loose scree. Below, on the quayside, he caught fleeting glimpses of the men loading cases of cigarettes on to the torpedo boat. The fog was so dense now he knew he couldn't be seen on the spur, even if the men looked his way. He scrambled down as quietly as he could, climbing some of it, sliding the rest until he dropped the last few feet to the shore. The concrete harbour wall was to his right, a couple of metres above the level of the beach. He clambered on to a group of large fallen rocks and peered over the top of the wall.

Just in front of him was a brick boathouse. Sullivan

heaved himself over the wall and scuttled into the lee of the building, crouching down to poke his head round the corner. The men were further along the quayside, still carrying cases to the torpedo boat. Sullivan ruled out any hope of disabling the vessel. But the two cabin cruisers, moored on either side of the harbour, were a different matter. They had yet to be loaded and neither appeared to have anyone on board. Sullivan waited for his moment. The men all had their backs to him, faint figures moving around in the black fog. He shot out along the concrete jetty towards the nearer of the cabin cruisers, dropping swiftly over the edge on to the aft deck of the boat.

Claire pressed close to the wall of the house and waited. She'd circled round to approach from the far side, away from all the activity in the courtyard. She listened, trying to ignore the thud of her own heartbeat. It seemed safe. Softly, she crept through the gateway into the back garden. There was no one about. She passed the French windows fronting the terrace and glanced inside, stopping abruptly when she saw the three bodies on the floor. There was no doubt they were dead, she could see the blood spattered across the carpet. The sight unnerved her momentarily. She fought back the rising nausea and hurried past the windows, leaning back on the brickwork to ease the feeling of sickness. Where was Sullivan? She'd been to the clifftop but had seen no sign of him. She wondered if somehow he had got inside the house, if something had happened to him.

The sound of footsteps startled her. She stayed exactly where she was and turned her head a little. Two men had come round the corner of the house from the courtyard and were pausing at the top of the steps to the cove. Claire saw enough of their faces to recognise them from the surveillance photographs. Montague and Doyle. They exchanged a few words in muffled voices, then headed down the steps.

Claire darted across the terrace and dropped to the ground by the low garden wall. The two men were following the steps across the face of the cliff, the flights descending to the shore in a long winding zig-zag. In the other direction, at the rear of the courtyard, Lafon's men were finishing loading the cage with more cases of cigarettes. The electric motor whirred and the cage swung out over the edge. Claire watched it drop. It was gliding only a matter of feet above the shallow incline at the top of the cliff.

She acted almost without thinking. Vaulted over the wall and across the steps. Slithered down the slope a few feet then dived forwards. Her fingers hooked around the mesh on the underside of the cage. It lurched violently and sagged under her weight but continued its descent. Claire hung on tight. Her feet lifted off the ground. Below her she could see the cliff falling suddenly away into a sheer drop. The cage slid out into space. There was nothing underneath now but fog and thin air. Claire gritted her teeth. The mesh cut into her fingers like cheese wire, her shoulders felt as if they were being prised from their sockets. But she barely noticed the agony. She was too concerned with just hanging on.

She counted the seconds. One, two . . . A pylon loomed up out of the mist. Was that halfway or were there more to come? Six, seven . . . Christ, how much longer? She looked to her right. She could see the steps but not Montague and Doyle. Were they behind or in front of her? Eleven, twelve . . . I'm going to let go. I can't take this, it's too much. Fourteen, fifteen . . . Just a while longer. You can do it. You can *do* it.

She saw the ground below sweeping up towards her. There were figures on the quayside. Figures standing still, then suddenly running. Through the throbbing haze of pain she became aware of a noise outside and beyond her body. Sirens. The loud, unmistakable shriek of police sirens.

The cage started to slow. The smooth concrete surface of the quay emerged through the fog. Claire let go, dropping heavily to the ground and rolling over to break her fall. The sirens were louder now, getting nearer. Claire looked around for the men. They'd abandoned the remaining cases of cigarettes and were clambering on board the torpedo boat. The boat surged away from the harbour and out of the cove, heading straight out to sea where it was quickly lost from sight in the mist.

Claire sensed a movement along the cliff. Montague and Doyle ran down the last few steps and stopped on the quayside. Claire ducked swifly behind the boathouse before they saw her.

'What kept you?' a whispered voice asked in her ear.

Claire spun round, stifling a cry of shock. Sullivan was leaning on the wall in the shadows.

'Jesus,' Claire breathed. 'What the hell are you doing?'

The sound of automatic gunfire from the top of the cliff stopped him replying. The noise seemed to paralyse them both for a few seconds. Only when it ceased did Claire nod urgently towards the steps and say: 'Montague and Doyle.'

She peered out along the quayside. The two men were still at the base of the steps, apparently listening as there was more sporadic gunfire from above. Then they ran for the first of the two cabin cruisers.

'Fuck,' Sullivan murmured. 'That's the one I haven't disabled yet.'

Montague and Doyle were out on the jetty. They disappeared behind the superstructure of the boat.

'Now!' Claire said.

She sprinted across the quay and in one seamless movement dropped over the edge into the water. Sullivan followed without hesitation. It was only about twenty metres to the cabin cruiser. The mist was drifting low over the harbour but through the cloudy veil they could see Montague on the deck by the controls. Doyle was still on the jetty untying the ropes. Claire and Sullivan filled their lungs and plunged under, swimming hard through the inky water.

They surfaced under the hull and, unseen, worked

their way round to the bow. Sullivan reached up and grabbed the forerail. He pulled himself up out of the water and checked the aft deck. Doyle was jumping on board, saying something to Montague. Neither man was looking towards the bow. Sullivan swung his legs up and slithered under the rail. He unclipped the hatch cover on the foredeck and pulled it open as Claire came up behind him. They snaked down through the opening and pulled the hatch shut on top of them.

Montague depressed the starter button. The engine turned over and kicked into life. Doyle leaned over the gunnel and pushed the boat away from the jetty, then threw himself abruptly to the deck as a shower of bullets peppered the water beside them. The gendarmes were halfway down the cliff steps. They fired another warning burst but Montague was already opening up the throttle, sending the cabin cruiser foaming out across the cove. He accelerated. The hull slapped against the waves, dipping and rolling in the swell. Once out on the open sea, Montague turned the wheel to starboard, heading west around the headland.

'There must be a chart somewhere,' he said. 'Look around for it.'

'We don't need a chart,' Doyle replied, hanging on to the taffrail as the boat suddenly pitched forwards. 'The first suitable bay we find, we go ashore. We're not staying out here any longer than absolutely necessary.'

'How long have we got?'

Doyle shrugged. 'The weather's on our side. They can't get a chopper up, but there's half the fucking French Navy in Toulon. If they put out a couple of boats, with radar they'll spot us in minutes.'

Montague throttled back a little in the turbulent sea. He stayed as close to the shore as he dared, keeping clear of the submerged rocks but not losing sight of the land. The fog was so thick now that, at times, the headland was almost invisible.

'What the hell was all that about Falzone and the Ukrainians?' he said. 'What's going on?'

Doyle didn't reply. Montague turned his head to look at him. Doyle had the SIG-Sauer out, swinging loose by his side.

'You knew, didn't you?' Montague said shrewdly.

'Of course. I arranged it,' Doyle said. 'And tipped off Luciani. I needed him here. That was part of the deal with Falzone.'

Montague stared at him.

'What are you talking about?'

'Dead men's shoes, Hal.'

'What?'

Doyle raised the pistol, his finger tightening on the trigger. Montague pulled down hard on the wheel, sending the boat lurching to port. Doyle fell over sideways. The bullet shot up through the awning above the deck. Montague hurled himself down the steps into the main cabin and lumbered clumsily towards the bow.

* * *

Crouching dripping wet in the forecabin, Sullivan and Claire were thrown against the bunk as the boat veered violently to the left. The report of the gunshot reverberated through the walls.

'Was that . . .' Claire said, the question tailing off into nothing.

Sullivan nodded. He lifted the lid of a wooden locker next to the bunk and rummaged urgently through it. There were ropes and life jackets and floats inside and at the bottom, underneath all the sailing paraphernalia, two curious metal objects which looked like oversized handguns with swollen barrels. Sullivan examined one of them.

'Flareguns,' he said. 'Loaded. It's the best we can do.'

He handed one to Claire.

'I'll take the deck,' she said.

She stood on the bunk and reached up, unfastening the hatch and pulling herself out through the narrow opening. Sullivan swung back the cabin door and looked out. Montague was scrambling towards him down the central passageway, his face twisted into a paroxysm of fear. Their eyes met and Montague stopped for an instant, stunned surprise then a flicker of hope transforming his fleshy features.

'He's going to kill me. Do something,' he gasped. 'Please.'

He pushed past Sullivan into the cabin and looked around desperately.

'He's going to kill me,' he repeated. 'You have to stop him.'

He noticed the open hatch in the cabin roof and stretched up, trying to haul his heavy frame through the gap. Sullivan saw Doyle come down the steps at the far end of the passageway, a pistol in his hand. He slammed the door shut and locked it automatically though he knew it afforded little protection. Montague was halfway out through the hatch. Sullivan grabbed his legs and pushed him the rest of the way. The door handle rattled. Sullivan grasped the edge of the hatch opening and heaved himself up. The door cracked, then splintered as something heavy smashed into it. It burst open and Doyle stepped into the cabin, his pistol searching for a target. Sullivan propelled himself up through the hatch, whipping his legs out and rolling away across the deck as a bullet sizzled out from below.

Sullivan knelt up, trying to keep his balance with the cabin cruiser corkscrewing out to sea. Montague was crouching on the foredeck, watching him hawkishly. Sullivan's eyes swept around the boat. There was nowhere to hide. Where was Claire? Where was Doyle for that matter? Sullivan pointed the flaregun at the hatch, his hands shaking. He waited, but Doyle didn't appear.

Montague edged round behind him. Sullivan sensed the movement. He glanced over his shoulder, but a moment too late. Montague's fist caught him full on the temple. Sullivan keeled over, his head spinning. Montague made a grab for the flaregun, attempting to wrench it from Sullivan's hands. Sullivan, half dazed, lashed out with his arm. His elbow sank

427

hard into Montague's belly. Montague grunted and fell backwards, still clutching at Sullivan's hand. The flaregun skittered away across the deck, coming to rest against one of the bow cleats only inches from the side. Montague crawled towards it. Sullivan dived on top of him and they rolled over, punching, kneeing, jabbing at each other. Sullivan's fist hammered into Montague's face. Montague lifted his hands instinctively to shield himself and Sullivan broke away.

The boat dipped forwards suddenly. The flaregun started to slide towards the edge. Sullivan hurled himself across the deck, one arm outstretched, and caught it as it went over the side. Hooking his arm around the bowrail, he pulled himself to his knees. Montague was still lying on the deck, his face smeared with blood.

'You keep back, you understand?' Sullivan gasped.

'He's going to kill me.'

'You think I give a shit?'

Sullivan dropped to his stomach and slithered away along the starboard gangway. He paused, listening, watching for Doyle. Then he snaked towards the stern, the flaregun in his right hand, his left gripping the bottom of the deck rail to stop himself rolling overboard in the violent churning of the hull. He could see the waves curling and foaming below him.

The boat plunged abruptly to starboard and the sea smashed over Sullivan's head. His body thudded against the rail and for an instant his legs swung out over the side. He clung to the stanchion, the water pouring off the deck, almost dragging him with it, then the boat dipped to port and he was hurled the other way against the raised side of the main cabin. He coughed, spitting out the foul salty water, and lifted his head to peer around. Montague was right behind him, close enough to touch. He was hanging awkwardly on to the rail, endeavouring to pull himself upright. The cabin cruiser listed heavily to starboard again. Montague was thrown over the rail, but somehow managed to hold on to the top bar. He screamed.

'Help me!'

Sullivan turned to look.

'For God's sake, help me!'

Sullivan reached back and grasped Montague's wrist with his left hand, wrapping his right arm around the metal upright to hold himself fast to the deck. Another wave surged over them. Sullivan shuddered under the impact but kept his grip on Montague, trying in vain to pull him back on board.

Montague's face, streaming with water, was screwed up in agony as he struggled to hold on. His legs were trailing in the water, the forward motion of the boat dragging him backwards. He turned his head. Something in his eyes made Sullivan twist round. Doyle was on the starboard side of the aft deck, only a few metres away. He brought up his pistol and fired twice. Montague jolted back, flailing out over the water into the fierce, enveloping waves.

Doyle swung the pistol round. Sullivan fumbled with his flaregun, his fingers slipping on the wet surface. Then a figure moved on the port side. Claire came forward out of the shadows. Her flaregun blazed. The missile exploded across the aft deck, shooting out over the ocean mere inches from Doyle's head. Doyle wheeled round and fired once, the pistol bucking in his fist. The bullet hit Claire in the shoulder and she staggered backwards, a rose of blood sprouting from her jacket. Sullivan squeezed the trigger of his flaregun. The flare smashed into Doyle's torso, the explosion lifting him into the air and back on to the deck.

Sullivan turned in time to see Claire toppling over the port rail into the sea. He didn't hesitate. He ran to the side and dived over after her.

The water was ice-cold, frothing in the wind. Sullivan swallowed a mouthful and coughed it out, treading water and straining to see in the darkness. There was no sign of Claire. He swam back the way they'd come, fighting against the rolling waves. He tried to guess exactly where she'd gone over, calculating how far the cabin cruiser had travelled before he dived in. It had to be somewhere about here. He stared around desperately. The waves were so high he could see only a few metres. Maybe it was further. He swam on, keeping his head high, snatching quick breaths before the next wave crashed over him.

The visibility was deteriorating. There was no moon, not even a glimmer of light in the sky, and the fog was trailing low, almost kissing the tops of the waves. He took a few more strokes and paused again. He'd caught a glimpse of something pale up ahead: a hand, a face, he might have imagined it. He splashed towards it and saw a tiny sliver of whitish flesh, a cloudy opalescence sinking slowly beneath the surface. He ducked under and swam down, kicking so hard that he almost collided with the body. Her eyes were closed, her hair floating loose. He grasped her under the arms and dragged her back up to the surface.

She was unconscious but he could feel a pulse. He held her against him, protecting her face from the buffeting of the waves. *Hold on, Claire. Just hold on.* He turned on to his back, gripping her under her arms, and struck out for the shore.

He had no idea how far it was. He felt drained of energy. His clothes, sodden with water, weighed him down, making every stroke an effort. But from somewhere he found the strength to stay afloat.

Twisting round, he could see nothing but a wall of water behind him. A surge of spume hit him full in the face. He choked and trod water, trying furiously to clear his lungs. Claire's body began to sink. He held her up, whooping for air. Then another wave hit him. He lost his grip on Claire, felt himself start to founder. His body was leaden, growing heavier. The water was lapping around his chin. He threw back his head and gulped in more air. He pulled Claire to him and held her in his arms, pressing her face to his own, feeling her skin cold and clammy. He was too exhausted to go on.

Then suddenly a beam of light pierced the fog,

glancing off a nearby wave. Sullivan turned his head and saw a coastguard patrol boat looming up through the darkness. He lifted an arm and waved frantically as the spotlight swung round and settled on his face.

Sullivan had lost track of how long he'd been waiting. There was no clock in the tiny refreshment area next to the surgical wing of the hospital, and his own watch had stopped working after its immersion in the sea. But he knew it was several hours because of the way the sky outside the window had grown gradually lighter and from the mounting stack of empty plastic cups on the floor by his chair. One of the night nurses had brought coffee out to him at regular intervals, to warm him up after his ordeal, and to give him something to do. It was the only sign of activity he'd seen since they'd brought Claire in.

The naval hospital was eerily quiet, the long echoing corridors devoid of people. Occasionally he heard footsteps in the distance, the faint sound of voices, but they didn't come nearer. He was alone. Sitting on a cheap plastic chair in the ill-fitting clothes lent to him by one of the coastguard officers. Alone, unable to think of anything except Claire in the operating theatre a hundred metres down the corridor.

He stood up and walked around a little, too tense to stay in the same position for long. Through the glass panes in the door he saw Philippe Allard coming towards him from the main reception.

'We recovered the boat,' Allard said, pushing open the doors. 'One body on board.'

Sullivan nodded blankly. He knew he'd killed Doyle. At that range an explosive flare was as lethal as a bullet.

'Lafon's dead too,' Allard continued. 'Killed in the shootout at his house. We're still looking for Montague's body.'

Sullivan didn't say anything. He wasn't interested. He sat down and stared at the wall. The silence was too much for Allard.

'We got most of the cigarettes. The *Guardia di Finanza* are on the lookout for the torpedo boat. They should pick it up very soon.' He paused. 'Are they looking after you? Do you need anything?'

Sullivan shook his head. Allard watched him awkwardly, then turned away.

It might have been half an hour later, an hour maybe, that they heard the surgeon coming down the corridor from the theatre. He was still in his operating gown, his rubber boots padding over the linoleum floor tiles.

'Your colleague was seriously injured,' he said phlegmatically. 'She'd lost a lot of blood. We've done all we can, but she remains in a critical condition.'

'Will she live?' Sullivan said.

'It's too early to say. I'm sorry.'

Sullivan turned away and walked through the swing doors. Down the long corridors, through door after door, not knowing, or caring, where he was going. He emerged through an exit and found himself on the quayside, looking out over Toulon harbour. The ships of the French Mediterranean fleet were moored in front of him. He walked along the quay past them. The mist was lifting, the first glimmers of a new dawn breaking through from the east.

Sullivan walked on, oblivious to everything around him. There was an emptiness inside his head, like a bleak wasteland, riven by the scream of seagulls and the howl of the wind.

EPILOGUE

Six weeks later

Sullivan got to his feet and walked to the window. It was wet and grey outside, a steady drizzle spattering on the glass roof of the atrium. It was spring in Brussels, but how did anyone tell?

He gazed into the distance, reflecting how things changed yet everything remained the same. Behind him, Maurizio Nicoletti was back at his desk, talking on the telephone in Italian to Casagrande. Enqvist's replacement, a grim, humourless German named Erwin Halsch, on secondment from the *Zollkriminalamt* in Cologne, was leafing through the files, acquainting himself with past cases. Sullivan's own in-tray was brimming over with papers, information that would have to be digested, collated, disseminated to the appropriate parts of the EU. It was all so relentless, so ultimately futile, but someone had to do it.

'You want to go to Naples with me at the weekend?' Nicoletti said, coming off the phone.

Sullivan turned. 'Me?'

'Casagrande's had word of a shipment coming over from Montenegro.'

The thought of two days in the sun was appealing, but Sullivan didn't succumb. He shook his head.

'Take Erwin, throw him in at the deep end.'

Halsch looked up, frowning earnestly. 'I would like that. It will be good for me,' he said. 'I've never been to Naples before.'

'It's an experience,' Sullivan said.

'You don't fancy a trip?' Nicoletti asked Sullivan.

'I'm going home for the weekend. See Kate and the boys.'

'You went home last weekend.'

'I know. And every one from now on. It's the only . . .'

He broke off, staring across the office. Claire was standing in the doorway. Her left arm was in a sling, her jacket draped casually across her shoulders.

'Hello,' she said.

'Claire,' Sullivan said. 'Hi.'

He paused, thinking what to say. 'It's good to see you back. How are you?'

'I'm fine.'

She looked at him. His manner was cool, professional, nothing more. He made no move to come to her. Even to shake hands.

'We didn't expect you back so soon,' he said.

'I was getting bored at home. My shoulder's almost healed now.'

'Good.'

'Who's this?' Claire asked, glancing at Halsch.

Sullivan introduced them. Halsch stood up and offered his hand formally.

436

'I hope you enjoy your time here,' Claire said.

'Thank you.'

There didn't seem to be much else to say. Claire felt awkward, exposed, standing there in the doorway.

'Ah well, back to counting olive oil bottles,' she said, unable to keep the bitterness from her voice. 'I'll see you around.'

'Yes,' Sullivan said. 'See you around.'

She forced a smile that went nowhere near her eyes and walked away down the corridor.

Sullivan drifted back towards his desk, feeling hollow, suddenly low. The telephone rang and Halsch picked it up.

'It's for you,' he said to Sullivan.

'Who is it?'

'He didn't say.'

Sullivan took the receiver. 'Yes?'

A familiar voice said: 'Okay, ten famous Hungarians.'

Serena vaulted the last hedge and urged her horse into a gallop, leaning forwards over the stallion's neck, enjoying the raw power of the animal, the feel of the breeze in her face. They raced across the field adjoining the house and round the front into the stable block where she dismounted and handed the reins to the stable hand. She was flushed, sweating from the exercise. Removing her riding hat, she shook loose her dark hair and walked across the yard into the house.

She showered and changed into a short black skirt and jacket, then went to the window of her bedroom.

A dark grey Mercedes was pulling in on the gravel forecourt below. Serena waited a few minutes before going downstairs. The housemaid had shown the visitors into the dining room. Serena checked her appearance in the hall mirror, smoothing back a stray hair, and made her entrance.

Yevgeny Drozhkin and Dino Falzone were standing by the long rosewood table. Serena smiled and shook hands with them, conscious of their cold eyes on her face, her figure, her clothes – assessing her not just as a woman, but as a partner.

'Please sit down,' she said. 'I've ordered coffee.'

The two men pulled out chairs and waited politely for Serena to take her place at the table before they joined her.

'I was very sorry to hear about your husband,' Falzone said. 'It was a tragic business.'

'Yes, it was. But we must put all that behind us. It's what Hal would have wanted.'

She looked at each man in turn, appraising them now. They would be unsure of her, perhaps wary. She had to reassure them that she was someone they could deal with safely, professionally.

'As you know,' she said smoothly, 'my husband left me everything in his will. His property, his land, his stocks and shares, including a controlling interest in all his companies. I intend to honour all outstanding supply arrangements with you.'

Drozhkin sniffed and glanced at Falzone. 'But can you deliver?'

'Of course. The cigarette manufacturers traded

438

with my husband's companies, not with him personally. Those contracts are still in place and will be fulfilled.'

'On the same terms, in the same way?'

Serena smiled, knowing she could handle them.

'Gentlemen, as far as I'm concerned, it's business as usual.'